10/06 5131

D0406969

DEATH BEFORE DISHONOUR

Also by Barnaby Williams

REVOLUTION
ANNO DOMINI
CRUSADERS

DEATH BEFORE DISHONOUR

Barnaby Williams

SIMON & SCHUSTER
A VIACOM COMPANY

First published by Simon & Schuster, 1997
An imprint of Simon & Schuster Ltd
A Viacom Company

Simon & Schuster
West Garden Place
Kendal Street
London W2 2AQ

Simon & Schuster of Australia
Sydney

A CIP catalogue record for this book is available
from the British Library.

ISBN 0–684–81636–9

This book is a work of fiction. Names, characters, places
and incidents either are products of the author's imagination or are
used fictitiously.

Typeset by Palimpsest Book Production Limited,
Polmont, Stirlingshire
Printed and bound in Great Britain by
Butler & Tanner Ltd, Frome and London

For Anne, Abbey and Philippa,
who mean everything to me.

Acknowledgements. With thanks:

To my publisher, Nick
To my hard-working and talented editor, Jacquie
To my splendid agent, Anne
To my mother, for her support
To my lawyer, Simon Wakefield
for invaluable help and advice
To Jon Blake for marvellous covers

Author's Note

William I's victory over Harold at Hastings in 1066 created a new English aristocracy from the knights and barons who fought there for him, men who became, once the land was pacified, lords of all they surveyed. However, only a few of the great names were destined to remain in being throughout the centuries ahead. Too many dangers awaited them. The Crusades, the Wars of the Roses, the judicial murders of the middle ages, the Civil War. A failure to beget male heirs, unsuccessful litigation, the manoeuvrings and actions of ambitious upstarts and regal favourites, all could and did unseat these English samurai.

To survive as a great noble house required ruthlessness and cunning, intelligence, courage and more than a little luck – all allied with honour, without which the system would fail. Only a few, like the fictional de Clares of this story, managed to emerge into the twentieth century with their names and power intact.

In 1914, the aristocrats still ruled, still held their enormous wealth, land and power. The century was to prove a most unfriendly one for the *ancien regime*, however, and it all began with the Great War, the war of 1914–18, the First World War.

The war was a disaster for everyone concerned. The outpouring of blood and treasure benefited no one. At its end, great ancient royal houses and empires lay shattered and overthrown throughout Europe. After a last 100 days of fighting in which the British Imperial Armies won victories over the Germans in the field to rival those of Marlborough two centuries earlier, the peace was botched. For those with vision, it was clear that at some stage the contest would be resumed, and indeed it was, as the Second World War.

For the English aristocracy, the war and its aftermath were terrible. True to their code of honour, the sons of the nobility were at the forefront of the fighting and suffered commensurately. Afterwards, weakened, they faced the attacks of Lloyd George upon their land

and wealth. Fish out of water, they had to exist in a democratic age to which they were not suited.

The consequences of the First World War were almost wholly evil. From the ruins it created came the horrors of Stalin's Russia and Hitler's Germany. For the British, the victors, it meant a huge diminution in their wealth and power, and a weakening of their Empire, one of the great institutions of history. Their society was damaged. Influential figures espoused communist and pseudo-communist ideas while Stalin's Terror was at its height. The Church of England, one of its great pillars, had had a bad war, and afterwards increasingly turned towards progressive politics as a pleasing substitute for a dogmatic belief in God, and thus began its long decline.

The war drew Britain back into the European orbit, which was ultimately fatal. The rise of Great Britain to its position of unrivalled power and influence had begun with the severing of the nation from the continent by the Tudors. To return was probably the greatest mistake the British ever made – not only for them but for the nations they ruled in their Empire.

The final consequence of the war was the worst – total war created the total state. Until August 1914 'a sensible, law-abiding Englishman could pass through life and hardly notice the existence of the state, beyond the post office and the policeman. He could live where he liked and as he liked. He had no official number or identity card. The Englishman paid taxes on a modest scale . . . rather less than eight per cent of the national income. Broadly speaking, the state acted only to help those who could not help themselves. It left the adult citizen alone.'[1]

It was never to be the same again.

[1] A. J. P. Taylor. English History 1914–1945.

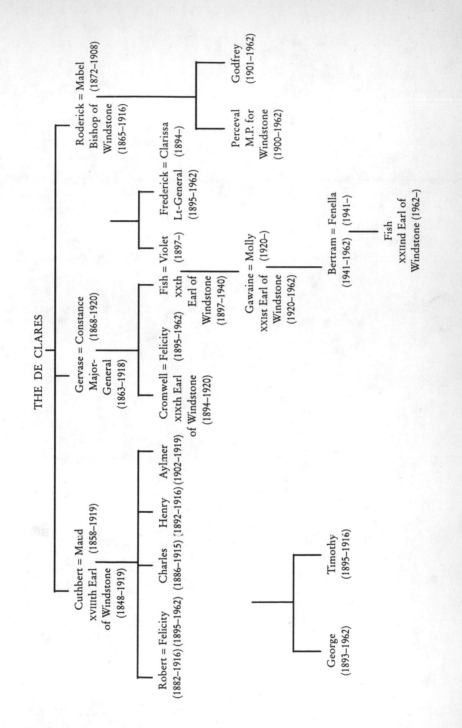

THE DE CLARES

1

All be Over by Christmas

Windstone Castle, Windshire, November 1914

'Clare Rules, young Fish,' Robert called, as Fish emerged through the early morning mist.

The heir to the castle smiled at his cousin and straightened up from where he had been poking at the ground of his inheritance with his hazel stick. He pointed to the lichened stonework darkening the mist.

'Six if you hit the ramparts, and a dozen if you can give it such a whack you get it into the moat.'

'A d-d-dozen!' Fish laughed. He was a boy of about seventeen who had grown tall suddenly, and was thin as though he had been squeezed briskly to produce the growth.

'Clare Rules, I told you.' Robert turned and pointed away from the medieval ramparts to the castle itself, on whose tall, broad windows the rising sun was beginning to glint.

'Six runs in the flowerbeds,' said Robert, eldest son and heir of the eighteenth Earl, 'and a dozen if you break a window.'

'Uncle w-w-will be jolly cross,' Fish suggested judiciously.

Robert surveyed the distance between them and the massive bulk of the castle and its towers. 'I think you'd need to hit like the Doctor to manage it,' he admitted. 'Still, something to aim for.'

Fish peered down at the tussocky grass. 'And the pitch will need mowing.'

'I'm having Crowbotham dig up the entire square. This Windstone marl's got no bounce. Doesn't take spin. I want it ready for the season. We've plenty of matches to play. I've organised the calendar to get as much in as possible. I've worked out I can get the late train down from the House each Friday.'

'I got that. The exp-p-p . . .'

Robert waited courteously for his young cousin to excavate the word he wanted from his vocabulary.

'The exp-*express*. They stopped it for me last night at the Halt.'

'Couldn't wait to get here?' Robert asked, affectionately.

'Couldn't wait. I love it here.' Fish said simply. 'Even my st-stammer goes away here.'

'School all right?'

'Oh, yes. I say, Robert, there's a chance I may play in the Eton–Harrow next year!'

'Good chap! Listen, we're having a scratch match in the great hall tonight, after dinner. You can be on my team.'

'Super. Who else is here? I got in so late I just raided the kitchens and went to bed.'

'Oh, we're all *in situ*. The usual de Clare mob, you know. Henry sent his man down in his new Napier, but he isn't here yet. Hodgkiss says he's coming down today, in time for the shoot. Freddie's here, somewhere.' Robert paused, glancing sympathetically at his cousin. 'I'm afraid your father the Brigadier is here.'

'F-F-Father?' Fish said, looking up in alarm. 'I th-th-thought he was at the w-w-war!'

'Well, he was. He's got some French *generalissimo* with him. A fat chap with soup stains down his front. Also his own general, Sir Hubert Mordaunt. Also a fat chap, but takes more care when lowering the soup. Come for the shooting, I think. I've told Simkins in the stables to get a shire ready in case he wants to go on the hunt tomorrow.'

'What about Mother?'

'Aunt Connie? No, she's not here.'

'Oh, well. P-p-perhaps he'll be called away to watch manoeuvres or s-s-s-something.'

'You never know,' Viscount Clare said optimistically. The sun was beginning to chase away the mist, and the last of the russet leaves were now showing on the trees, spiky and bare in their winter bones. Through the gap where the rampart had fallen away into a heap of ancient rubble, the great mound, site of the original fort, was beginning to glow. From it, on a clear day, it was possible to see three counties and the sea, glinting to the south. In the years following the Battle of Hastings Baron Bohamond de Clare of Normandy had ruled all this land, and his death slab now lay in the stone chapel built by the sixth Earl, along with all his successors. Their bones lay in the crypt, and the battle flags of the de Clares still hung from standards above. God was a warrior and, the de Clares were absolutely certain, a distant relation as well.

Somebody was coming through the rising mist, a tall young man, dressed as they were, in tweed shooting-jacket and trousers ending in thick woollen socks. He was carrying a strange globular construction in one hand.

'H-Hallo, Freddie! When d-did you get in? And why are you c-carrying a lampshade?'

'Managed to do a bunk before chapel yesterday,' the young man said. 'Got down on the afternoon train. And it's a *Montgolfiere*.'

He held it up so that they could see it.

'So it is,' said Robert. 'Silk, what?'

'That's it. I've stiffened it with dope. Look, it's really light.' He tossed the yellow silk balloon up in the air.

'How do you fill it with hot air?'

'Candle. I melted down wax and made a flat one with several wicks. Pushes out the heat. Want to see it go?'

'Oh, y-yes.'

'Any news from Charlie?' Freddie asked, bending down to place the ballooon on the turf.

'Yes! Got a letter from him last week. He's somewhere near Auchy. Flanders,' Robert replied.

'Is he seeing much fighting?' Fish asked eagerly.

'They seem to have come to a bit of a stop. The Germans one way and us the other. Everybody will probably go into winter quarters until the spring.'

'Do let me have his address. I w-want to write and hear how exciting it is.'

'I don't think it's very exciting at the moment,' Robert said thoughtfully. 'Charlie asked Father to send over a load of picks and shovels, because the army doesn't have enough.'

'Shovels? What for?' asked Freddie.

'To dig. Breastworks and trenches,' Robert explained. 'The two sides are peering at each other over an expanse of mud. Something like an East Anglian beach at low tide, Charlie says. So they need to throw up earthworks to avoid getting shot at. Father sent five hundred shovels and picks out in a motor lorry. Fusgott drove it in his chauffeur's uniform. He got it all muddy! That and tins of dubbin. Charlie says his boots are getting soggy.'

'It rains a lot in Belgium,' Fish said knowledgeably. 'Charlie will be much happier when spring comes and they can get on with pushing the Germans back to Berlin.'

'Anyway, you should be able to talk to him yourself. He's got a bit of leave. We should see him soon.'

'Bring your gun?' Robert enquired.

'I keep it in the g-gun room,' Fish explained. 'Uncle said I could.

They don't like us having our guns with us at school, Lord Cherwell used to fire at masters he didn't like, about a hundred years ago. Bagged the dean and two classics scholars, they say. Warmed their backsides from fifty paces, m-moving fast.'

Robert looked up at the sky, turning a milky blue. 'It's going to be clear, at any rate. Hopcroft was worried they wouldn't get up into the mist.'

Freddie produced a box of Swan matches. 'Ready?' he enquired. He bent down, lit the match and ran its sizzling flame over the wicks beneath the neck of the balloon, like lighting birthday-cake candles.

'There,' he said, standing up. They all stood round, looking down. The inside of the balloon glowed bright yellow. It trembled, began to lift, brushed a tussock of grass, then climbed slowly, swaying slightly, past their heads. Fish smelled hot candle wax. The balloon began to drift on the breeze, heading towards the house, and they followed it.

'Think it'll clear the roof?'

'Should do.'

As the breeze took hold, the balloon narrowly avoided a massive chimney stack, wide as an ocean liner's funnel, swayed in the turbulence, and climbed away over the stretches of the Windstone Water. Freddie waved to it as it ascended, shining in the sun.

They reached the sweeping stone steps that led up to the house and began to ascend. From the top they could see the great drive cast down like a sword before them, lined with elm as tall and straight as guardsmen. The Water glinted in the gathering sun, and mist still hung in the woods of the deer park, behind its old curving stone walls.

'Y-Your sister here?'

'Vi?' said Freddie de Clare. 'Yes, somewhere. She was asking about you too, for some reason.'

'I l-like Vi. She's g-good fun.'

'You wouldn't say that if she was your sister.'

They went through the huge oak double doors, under the great coat of arms of the de Clares, carved into the Windstone rock of the arch in chisel strokes four inches deep. As it had for centuries, a passant dragon crushed the head of a gryphon with one powerful, taloned foot, as the rampant lion supporters of the shield looked on. Below was the motto, *Death Before Dishonour.*

'I'm going to get some breakfast before we go out,' said Freddie.

Robert and Fish headed down one of the many marble-flagged corridors. The great house was alive with the sound of people. Girls' voices came laughing from the long breakfast room, there was the light clatter of shoes coming down the grand stair, then, after a moment's silence, a rising screech of joy and a large thump.

'Cousin Violet,' said Robert. 'If I am not mistaken. She is unable to see a banister without sliding down it.'

The portrait-lined corridor gave way to wood panelling and the smell of linseed and gun oil, mixed with that of wet mackintoshes. In a long room with walls decorated with stuffed fish of varying sizes and the heads of animals, all baring their teeth, a middle-aged gentleman in stout brogues surmounted by thick woollen socks and knee breeches was peering through the barrels of a twelve-bore. It was the eighteenth Earl of Windstone, Cuthbert, Lord de Clare.

'Ah, you're here, young Fish,' he said affably. 'Good journey, what?'

'I c-came down last n-night, sir,' Fish explained. 'The exp-express stopped at the Halt for me and I walked up.'

'Good show. Dashed useful having the Halt in the grounds. Come for your gun have you?'

Robert had gone on, and Fish was rummaging in the lines of carefully-stacked weapons that filled the length of the room.

'Get out Henry's rifle while you're over there will you? His man says he's coming down this morning. He'd better get a move on, I want to be knocking down our first birds at half past. So how's Eton, eh?'

'Very good, sir,' said Fish, bringing out a slim-barrelled rifle, checking it for ammunition and laying it on the table that ran along the middle of the room. He found his own twelve-bore next to the immense black-powder elephant-gun of the seventeenth Earl, and ran his hands over it affectionately, feeling the smooth wood, the precise fit of barrels and stock, the click of the hammers. Earl Cuthbert had put down his gun and had turned to a large leather-bound book that was also lying on the table.

'Very good, y'say? Couldn't be worse than in my day, young Fish. I was a King's Scholar, lived in Long Chamber. Law of the jungle then, boy. Survival of the fittest, yes. Bullied frightfully I was by Linky Mumford, me and quite a few others. But we got fed up with it in the end and suspended old Linky upside down from a window. We left him there all night and he was a changed chap in the morning. Now then, where was I . . .' He turned the pages of the book. 'Not a bad bag last year . . . Hopcroft tells me they're flying well, so we may . . . ah yes, you seen this, young Fish? Teach you the importance of keeping good records.'

Fish came over and stood next to his uncle, peering down at the book. In it, neat columns totalled up the game shot on any particular day on the estate, under the headings of 'Partridges', 'Pheasants', 'Hares', 'Rabbits', 'Woodcock', 'Snipe' and so on.

'Now this is something you won't see too often, Fish,' he said, pointing to the column marked 'Various'. In it, in a neat hand, was written '1 viscount'. 'My Great-uncle Bumpy,' he explained. 'His wife went off with Fruity Cookshotte and it made him down in the mouth. Decided to end it all, did himself in over in the corner there, poor chap. You can still see the marks in the ceiling. Waste of shot, young Fish! She was a bad lot and so was he. Welshed on a gambling debt two years later and got cut by the entire county. Died miserably of Java belly in Cawnpore or some such hole. Don't you ever do anything so stupid. Blowing his head off over a woman indeed . . .'

'No, sir,' Fish agreed politely.

The Earl rested his clean gun in the rack and went to the window, looking out at the retreating mist with some satisfaction, as though having put it to rout personally. In the great window was a small one, a casement, and he twisted the fastening with his thumb, allowing it to spring open and catch on its hasp. He stood, inhaling the morning air as he looked out over the land, then turned his head to glance sympathetically at his nephew.

'He was a bully, y'know. Fruity. Just like Linky. All you've to do with a bully, m'boy, is to stand up to them. We stood up to Linky and he was a changed man, let me tell you. Y'can't always suspend bullies out of windows but you can stand up to them. Understand me?'

'Y-Yes, sir.'

'Good. No names, no pack drill, but no time like the present, eh what?'

'No, sir.'

Fish soaked up the atmosphere of the room like a peregrinating bird that has arrived back at its home. He was always happy here. The gun-room was a microcosm of all of the family history that filled the castle. The young boy felt it all about him, with every visit he imbibed more, collecting the lore that had been passed down through generations.

The Earl was staring with his usual dislike at the great elm boulevard. 'Blast Clarence,' he said, cursing the thirteenth Earl as though he were in the next room instead of in the crypt of the chapel, as he had been for nigh on two hundred years. 'What the hell did he mean, putting in that monstrosity straight through English countryside?' he demanded.

'He was a Whig, sir,' Fish said, with a straight face, knowing what was coming.

'Of course he was a Whig!' the older man bellowed irascibly. 'They were all at it then, cutting blasted great roads through fine woods, just in order to stand at one end and see a church tower at the other, or a pillar or suchlike. Clarence cut a damned great lane through an excellent oak wood simply in order to see that foul temple he had put up at the other end. There it is, polluting the landscape outside the walls. The English landscape wants no gardening, young Fish! It cannot bear gardening, it needs no gardening. Walk through it! Nothing is left unclothed, not even an old wall. Nature is the best gardener, and she abhors straight lines. Look at the deer park. There's a proper road, a highway, going round between tree and hedgerow, field and meadow. On it, you catch a glimpse of Furncott Steeple here, old Waltbrook village there. No blasted straight vista, no wretched Greek temple. Rot old Clarence, I'm glad he died before he could disfigure any more. Folly, pure folly.'

There was a clatter of riding boots on the flags outside and a man in the uniform of a brigadier came in. He had a neatly trimmed moustache, and it bristled upwards as he saw Fish.

'So you're here, are you?' he said without pleasure.

'Good m-morning, sir,' Fish said to his father.

'Damn you, Gervase,' the Earl snapped, 'must you wear that blasted rig out here. This is the country.'

'There's a war going on,' his younger brother said dismissively. 'As you and a lot of other people will soon be finding out.'

'All be over by Christmas,' muttered Lord de Clare. 'Then perhaps you'll have the decency to dress like a gentleman when you come here.'

'I hope you've got a good show for us,' Brigadier de Clare said thrustingly. 'I have Generals Legrand and Mordaunt with me. I trust we can show them some decent shooting.'

'If you want a blasted *battue* you had better beat a path to Walsingham's place. You know perfectly well we raise no artificial birds here.' Cuthbert turned a couple of pages of the big book. 'The old place has never let us down yet, though,' he said, softening a little. 'I think you can tell your fat Froggie friend there will be ample for him to aim at.' He peered at his brother's chest. 'Got a medal already? Some foreign bit of gaud by the look of it,' he said offensively.

'French. They are our allies, y'know.'

'They damned well shouldn't be,' Lord de Clare muttered, having turned back to the window, where he was peering out once again. 'Nothing but trouble, the damned Frogs. What do we think we're doing getting together with them when we've done nothing but fight them for centuries?'

'Do you want the Kaiser to win?'

'What do you think the Navy's for? A-hah!' Moving with the speed of long practice he reached out for the long brass field-glass brought back by some member of the clan from the seige of Seringapatam. From constant use, there was a shiny rim in the faint discolouration of its oxidation, and Lord de Clare was able to draw it out to its correct focus in a second.

'A-hah!' he said again. 'I knew it. Rooks are leaving the elm. They know, do the rooks, they know when the tree's dying. Fish! Run down and tell Mr Crowbotham I'll have a word with him down by the elms before the first drive.'

'Yes, sir,' Fish said, moving quickly out of the room.

His father's voice followed him as he rattled down the corridor: 'Good of you to put him up. Though I don't know how you stomach it. All that blasted stammering. And he's a cripple.'

'I like the boy,' Lord de Clare said sharply, 'and he's left-handed, that's all.'

'He's a bloody cripple. Born that way, like some sickly calf. Should've been put down at birth. The ancient Greeks had the right idea. Expose 'em on the hillside, let the foxes do the job.' In the corridor, flying under the rows of portraits, Fish felt his cheeks burn.

'What-ho, Fish!' a voice cried cheerfully, and he skidded to a halt by a bust of Clarence, once and briefly the chief of the King's ministers, and creator of the sword-straight blot of elms on the English landscape outside.

'Hallo, Violet!' he said, spying his cousin emerging in heather-mixture tweed from the breakfast room.

'Where are you off to, red in the face?' she demanded, falling in with him.

'Crowbotham, if he's in the garden. Uncle has discovered one of the elms is dying. He's pleased as punch.'

They scurried across the grand hall with its sweeping staircase, heading for the door that lead out to the formal and kitchen gardens behind the ground of the bailey, where Robert was preparing his cricket pitch. They went by the big fire in the hall fragrant with the scent of the apple logs burning in the grate, a yard at a time. There was a large supply of the wood in a dry barn on the estate, Lord de Clare having replanted the cider orchard some years before. The new orchard was now in full flow, the brewhouse producing jugs of light, dry, golden scrumpy on demand, and the old trees had been cut up for firewood.

Violet paused, peering at his mouth. 'What have you done to your lip, Fish?' she demanded.

'Oh. Got bashed in the Wall Game. Chipped a bit off my tooth, actually.'

'So you have. You look like the leader of the "Desperate Nine" Here, race you to Crowbotham.' She darted forward, making for the door. 'Last one there's a squashed tomato!' she cried happily, having jumped the start, and Fish clattered after her.

They found the head gardener supervising the putting into clamps of various root vegetables for winter storage in the walled kitchen garden, where greenhouses of vines and peach trees lined the western boundary.

'Crowbotham!' Violet called out cheerfully. 'His Lordship says the elms are blighted.'

'He wants to see you there before the first drive,' Fish confirmed, and the head-gardener, in his round-brimmed felt hat, went off towards the great lane of trees.

'I see you're ready,' Violet said, somewhat resentfully, looking at Fish in his shooting clothes. 'I declare it is quite unfair.'

'Unfair on whom? The pheasants?'

'Unfair on *me*!' the young woman said indignantly. 'Why shouldn't I shoot too?'

'Tradition,' Fish suggested, as they meandered out and found their way along the edge of the Windstone Water under the old ramparts.

'Tradition, poppycock! It's just an excuse by men to hog all the fun.'

'How is your aunt?' Fish asked, knowing full well that Violet hadn't arrived at this opinion independently.

'Aunt Hermione? She's here, they let her out of jail last month. I suppose she's fattening up in case she needs to go on hunger strike again.'

'Think it's worth it?' Fish asked mischievously.

'Of course! We women have had enough of servitude, young Fish. This is the twentieth century, not the eighteenth. You see what we'll do.'

'You're riding in the hunt tomorrow, aren't you?'

'Try to keep me away,' the young woman said confidently. As they emerged around the Old Ruin where Godfrey de Montfort's miners had succeeded in collapsing part of the old curtain wall, they crossed the Red Ground where his knights had been slaughtered by trebuchet and quarrel-fire from the twin towers behind. The grass always grew thick and green there, and it's lushness was said to date from that day.

They encountered a tall young man, about five years older than them, coming from the direction of the chapel. The circular, white collar of his calling gleamed about his neck in the sunshine.

'Hallo, George!' they cried together.

'Hallo, Violet, Fish,' he beamed.

'I th-thought you were in the East E-End,' said Fish. 'Doing good works.'

'I was, under the bishop's direction,' George de Clare agreed.

'What's it like there?' Violet demanded. 'Is it very terrible?'

'There is considerable want.'

'Do they have houses, then?'

'Not perhaps as you might understand them. Slums.'

'So what are you doing here instead of ladling out the soup to these thirsty bimbos?'

'The war,' George said simply. 'The men are going to the war. I feel my place is to be with them, bringing the presence of God to them in their times of hardship and danger. I must receive the permission of Bishop Roderick first.'

'Where is Uncle R-Roderick anyway?'

'Not here. In London at the moment.'

'Perceval and Godfrey?'

'Still at that ghastly school of theirs.'

'I don't know why he doesn't send them to Eton like the rest of us.'

'Bishop Roderick is somewhat parsimonious,' George observed. 'The school offers the sons of the clergy a substantial reduction in fees.'

They had come up to the end of the elm row, where Fish's father stood. He overheard the conversation.

'Waste of blasted time in my case,' said Brigadier de Clare, having seen Fish approaching. Walking up with her arm linked through his, Violet felt Fish stiffen. 'Don't,' she murmured, 'it isn't worth it.'

'Oh, y-yes,' Fish muttered, 'it b-bally well is.'

She turned to look him in the eyes. 'Take him on, then,' she urged.

'I th-think that's what Uncle was telling me,' Fish said.

'I think I'll walk up with you this morning,' she said thoughtfully. Then the air was rent by a roar from the trees.

'A-HAH!' Cuthbert bellowed triumphantly, thrusting the spear of his shooting stick into the base of the offending elm. With an expert twist of his wrist, he ripped away a section of spongy wood. 'Y'see?' he demanded of all. 'Bad stock, bad stock. Typical of Clarence, blast him. Couldn't even plant a row of trees that would stand up for more than a season.'

'Two hundred years,' Gervase de Clare demurred.

The Earl pointed his stick at the dark fastnesses of the deer park behind their retaining wall. 'Oaks in there that were standing when our ancestor Godfroy came to these parts with Duke William!' he said derisively. 'Two hundred years? Pah!' He swept aside a rim of grass and exposed a sinister crenellation of brown toadstools sprouting from the bark for all to witness. 'Rooks know, y'see,' he said triumphantly. 'Crowbotham? *Crowbotham!*'

'Here, my lord,' said the head gardener, straightening up from the tree's neighbour.

'The entire row is a menace,' the Earl pronounced, with a certain, deep satisfaction. 'Make plans to remove it.'

'Not now Cuthbert,' said a woman approaching from the house. She was dressed in a tweed skirt and jacket, her hair tied up in a bun and pinned with a gold brooch. She was Lady Maud, Countess of Windstone, the Earl's wife. 'You have a shoot to go to,' she said firmly. Glancing up from his proposed work of destruction, or restoration, depending upon point of view, he could see that it was so. The keepers and beaters were assembling under the direction of Hopcroft, the head keeper, whose weather-polished face matched his boots.

Brigadier de Clare's gaze swept over the keepers and beaters as he waited for Generals Legrand and Mordaunt to finish breakfast and join them. He stiffened, like a pointer sensing game. 'You there!' he barked. 'You . . . Furzegrove, isn't it?'

A man dressed in strong serge trousers and a shapeless jacket of brown and grey, the colours of the wood, came over, moving smartly. He was in his twenties.

'Yes, my lord?' he asked.

'Cuthbert! What's this fella doing here?'

'Furzegrove knows the woods,' Lord de Clare said mildly.

'I'll say he does! I gave him two guineas without the option eighteen months ago. You're a poacher, sir!'

'Furzegrove, where's the stag?' the Earl asked.

'Find 'im over by Holpit Wood, my lord, in the valley. Have to put hounds over the Rimford water else they'll not get scent of 'im.'

'Thank you, Furzegrove. Let's hope we have a good day's sport today, what?'

'They'll be flying well today, my lord.'

'That's good to hear.'

He looked at his brother as the beater and poacher went back to join the others. 'Furzegrove knows the woods,' he said, with the satisfaction of a man who has just squashed his younger brother. 'Hopcroft!' he called, and the keeper came smartly over, a man with keen eyes and a weathered face, dressed in the rainproof velveteen of his calling.

'Yes, m'lord?'

'How shall we arrange our affairs this morning?' he asked, deferring to his keeper's wisdom.

'Wind's from the north, m'lord. Be best to beat the Farnton Wood first, I'd say, for the pheasants. Be some ground game come through, too. Then we can move over to the two root fields on Farnton Top. With the weather the way it's been I think we should find good partridges in among the roots there, and have two or even three drives. That'll take us up to the barn for lunch m'lord, and we can decide on the afternoon's programme then. Ground's warming up nicely, got some moisture in it, be good scent for the dogs. We might try the twenty-acre wood and the big arable. Perhaps we can go through the Battle Pasture on the way home.'

'Think you can manage 'em along the top, man?' asked Brigadier de Clare. 'Not an easy line that.'

'With the wind from the north quarter, m'lord, they must come across the top for they roots. It's their line, and with the wind, where else can they go?'

'Quite right. Very good, Hopcroft,' the Earl agreed.

Hopcroft blew his short horn, the command of the head keeper for the guns to assemble for the first drive, and they moved away from the castle into the surrounding land. The golden stubble of harvest crunched pleasingly under their feet, the flocks of finches, redwings and fieldfares busy scouring the cornfield for what the horse-drawn combine had left, fluttered briefly into the air out of their way before settling back to their task. The sun had burned away the last of the mist, and shone now out of a polished-blue sky. In the distance white smoke drifted from the chimneys of the farms and cottages; in the hedgerow that marked the boundary, elder and hawthorn, dogwood and sloe berries hung red and purple. Their feet kicked up the drifts of red and gold leaves as they moved on towards the wood, sending delicious autumn scents into the air.

In the tribe of tweeded men making their way up, Fish suddenly noticed a newcomer. He smiled, and put on speed.

'Hullo, Cromwell, I didn't know you were coming.'

His older brother smiled back in greeting. 'I came up yesterday,' he explained.

Under the command of Hopcroft, the beaters were making their way to the far side of the wood, and the guns assembled on the other. Earl Cuthbert found his brother in the throng.

'So, tell me about this damned war,' he demanded. 'Last after Christmas, y'say?'

'Certain of it. Probably well into next year.'

'Don't like it. Don't like it at all. We have no business involving ourselves. Don't need to be there.'

'Are we simply to let the Germans conquer the French?'

'Why not?' the Earl demanded irascibly. 'We conquered them a hundred years ago. Why not let the Germans have their turn? The Germans are no threat to us.'

'It isn't that simple.'

'Oh, yes it is!' his brother said hotly. 'We fought the Russians at Crimea, we've always fought the French, and quite right too. The Russkis and the Frogs, all they ever want is to go out conquering people. Now they're our *allies*?' The Earl's eyebrows rose in astonishment. 'This is madness, Gervase. What quarrel do we have with the Germans? None. We should pack up and come home.'

'Too late for that. Well, here we are, Cuthbert. How do you want us to line up?'

'You think on what I say,' the Earl finished, fumbling in his capacious pocket and drawing out a silver cylinder. Removing its top, he exposed the slender ivory fingers inside. 'Gather round,' he called. 'We'll draw for stands.'

The guns arrayed themselves along the wide ridge that formed the edge of the wood. Glumly, Fish found himself on the right-hand side of his father. Violet took up station behind him. To Fish's right was the great bulk of General Legrand. The stands were marked by hazel wands, each marked by a numbered card impaled in a cleft, forty yards apart.

The Earl blew his silver whistle twice, and heard Hopcroft reply. Fish took two scarlet cartridges from the soft leather bag over his shoulder and slipped them into his gun. The round brass bases gleamed briefly at him, their copper centres like eyes, as he swung the breech shut with the pleasing soft click of perfectly fitting parts. With his left thumb he brought back the twin hammers, and waited in anticipation, his left thumb on the safety, left forefinger alongside the trigger guard. Wet earth, fresh autumn leaves, old leaf mould and pools of still water scented the autumn air. He breathed it in like perfume, suddenly feeling happy. Just then he heard his father's voice grating on the breeze, just loud enough for him alone to hear.

'I shall appreciate it if you don't let me down by behaving like a blasted escapee from the deformed ward, Fish.'

Fish hesitated, about to reverse his gun to hold it with his right hand at the safety and trigger, ready to bring up to his right shoulder. He knew it would feel very uncomfortable after holding it left-handed.

Then a clear, young voice spoke from behind: 'Did you know that Lord Forbes shoots left-handed like you, Fish?' Violet said cheerfully. 'He's the best shot in the Home Counties, they say. You're in good company.'

Brigadier de Clare snapped a glance across from his butt. 'I'll mind you to mind your own affairs, young lady,' he said viciously.

'Fish's my cousin,' she said. 'I mind for him.'

'He's *my* son,' Gervase de Clare grated. 'He does what I say.'

'He's a man,' Violet retorted. 'He does what he thinks fit.'

Fish retained his gun under his left arm. 'L-Lord Forbes, you say, Vi?'

'The very one,' she said.

The brigadier stared angrily at them, and then turned to face the oncoming game. For a little while there was silence, only the sound of the beaters calling to one another to keep the line, and the hollow knock of their sticks on the trees. The wood in front of them was marked by red dogwood, a valance of russet twigs glowing like smoky fires, tumbling out of the tree line into the long grass with its polished-gold seed heads.

There. A hare, cantering quietly out from the cover. She put on a burst of speed, espying the line of men.

'*A vous mon General*!' Robert called.

She was jinking at full speed, her great legs leaping her yards through the air at a time. General Legrand moved with a fluidity that belied his bulk, the gun as familiar in his hands as a walking stick. There was a sudden report, and the bounding animal tumbled into the grass.

'*Vive la France!*'

Then rabbits appeared, never pausing but coming out at full speed, only intermittently visible as they scuttled through the grass, and the line echoed with shot, the air puffed here and there with fragrant smoke, blue in the sunshine. Another hare came out of the wood in front of Brigadier de Clare, and darted to her left.

'*Yours, Fish.*'

He swung smoothly, taking the bead through the head, and squeezed. The hare tumbled, and was still.

'In the air, gentlemen.'

From the woods the first loud 'whirr-r-r' was heard, followed by the 'cock, cock, cock-cockle' of the cock pheasant; suddenly the air was filled with golden shells, one after the other, and the line echoed with shot.

The guns slapped in Fish's ears; he gritted his teeth to track the sudden gold bundles catapulting from the trees, and fired. A cock came out over him, high and fast; he forced himself to take his time, lifted, swung, fired, and saw the head fall and the wings fold. It thudded at the feet of his father and he felt a peculiar, sudden rage. Strangely pleasant, it burned away inside him, as hot as the barrels of the gun in his hands. Now the birds were coming over in twos and threes, cocks and hens, guns were slamming along the line, an irregular crackling of burning brushwood.

A hen bird came from the trees as though hurled by rubber. Reverend George swung and fired: a profusion of tail feathers exploding in the air announced a lack of lead and the bird flustered its way down to a landing, then increased speed on the ground.

'Pedestrian!'

The pheasant made for cover like a greyhound, and Cromwell despatched it with one clean shot.

The beaters' cries and the rattling of their sticks was growing louder, a warning note coming into their voices. Fish saw two birds, cocks, high and fast, tail feathers streaming like pennants, he could do it, he lifted and swung, taking the first with the choke barrel. As it tumbled down towards him he hit the second in a burst of golden feathers. The bird towered, struggling straight up on failing wings. Then they folded, the cock plummetting in a long, lazy curve to earth and once again a bird thudded in front of his father. The same burning in his throat.

Figures showed briefly at the edge of the wood. A solitary cock showed himself in the dogwood, and went running down the line like a Harlequin's winger, watched with amusement by the guns, who appreciated the cunning of the old stager. Hopcroft blew his whistle sharply, and the drive was over.

Fish opened his gun and walked forward to gather up the limp birds in front of his stand. To his surprise he found two and a half brace. Walking to the dogwood he picked up the hare. Salmon-pink blood flecked its long ears. He dropped the game in front of his wand

and walked over to his father, retrieving the two cock birds he had dropped there.

'M-m-mine, I th-think,' he said, and to his great joy, his father said nothing, but turned away to talk to the French general who was waddling up. He suddenly realised that with the brace in his hand he had shot more than his father.

'Well done, Fish,' Violet said, an intense glee in her voice.

As the pickers-up roved in the rear, calling to their dogs, searching for kills, hunting for runners, the guns gathered, lighting cigarettes and pipes. Everybody seemed in a capital humour, it was a fine start to the day.

'I say, Fish!' Robert called warmly. 'Damned fine left and right there. Don't think I'd have managed that myself.'

Fish felt his face flush with pleasure. 'Thank you,' he said.

A strange noise was on the air. A sound like a sustained exhalation of wind. It was coming from the sky.

'What the deuce is that?' Cuthbert demanded.

A small gleaming speck appeared in the distance; Fish was the first to see it. 'It's H-H-Henry!' he said. 'In his aero-p-plane!'

Soon the machine was clearly visible to all. Painted white, it shone in the sun as it descended, circling around them as they stood in the ride, the occupant clearly visible, waving down, white scarf streaming in the breeze.

'Good man,' Brigadier de Clare grunted approvingly.

'What's that y'say?' his brother demanded.

'He's in uniform. Can spot it. Must have joined up.'

The biplane, as white as a swan, levelled out and performed a square descent about the field of golden stubble, losing altitude all the time. It turned into the wind, cleared the far hedge by a few feet and touched down with a rumble from its thin tyres. The engine coughed and spluttered, the propeller kicked to a stop. A grinning figure climbed out, discarding helmet, scarf and gauntlets. The Earl broke into a trot and was the first to shake hands with his son, and squeeze him by the shoulder.

Henry reached inside the cockpit, securing the control column with his wide leather seat belt. Brigadier de Clare stood watching him curiously. 'What regiment's this?' he demanded.

'RFC, uncle! Royal Flying Corps.'

'Cavalry,' he decided. 'Hussars, what?'

'Yes, sir.'

'Hrrumph . . .' called the Earl. 'If we're all ready, gentlemen . . . Hopcroft?'

'Yes, m'lord. Shall be make our way up to Farnton Top? I'd like plenty o'quiet now, they partridges be feeding in the arable and we can drive them nicely, but only if they still be there for us.' Walking into the wind, guns and beaters began making their way up from the cornfield to the ridgeline in the distance, where the big fields of turnip, kale and cabbage lay.

Lunch was in an old stone barn seated on straw bales, eating Windstone eggs – brown and white and blue from the ducks – Windstone ham and beef, thick slices of white bread, still warm from the oven, and yellow butter and cheese, all washed down with Windstone ale. Afterwards they took King Richard's lane up to Battle Top, their feet padding softly on the carpet of damp yellow and russet leaves. The lane was quiet, the banks drifting with leaf mould. They moved on up into the sunshine again, and Fish found himself walking by Henry. 'Think you'll see much of the w-war, Henry?'

'See is about it. We go up and look down on the enemy below. See what he's up to. Take photographs, tell the artillery if they're shooting straight. We don't actually fight.'

'Be a bit difficult, I suppose.'

'Perhaps we ought to attach lances to our aeroplanes! Jousting at five thousand feet . . .' They came to the hedge where the hazel wands had been set up. 'I suppose one could take one's twelve-bore up there,' Henry said, quite thoughtfully, 'and blaze away if you saw a Hun.'

They were quiet as they took up position, some ten yards behind the hedge. When everyone was ready Earl de Clare blew his whistle once, sharply, and they knew that the beaters were beginning to move. At first, there was just the sound of the breeze going across the hedge and rustling of the brown and red leaves not yet fallen. Fish stood with his right shoulder and foot forward, the gun cradled in his hands, listening for the sudden whirr of a rising covey. Partridges were fast, much faster than pheasants.

Whi-r-r-r, kuk-kuk, kuk-kuk. Through the thinned twigs of the hedge Fish saw the covey rise, about eight birds, skimming over the arable.

There! Hup! The outside bird breasted the hedge and saw him waiting. It rose for a second, half-turning away; he tracked through it, everything moving very slowly, the partridge's wings beating, it seemed to him, just like a butterfly's. He squeezed the trigger and felt the tap against his shoulder, saw the fleck of black skimming straight as a ruler against the blue sky, the puff of feathers floating in the air, the bird folding, and his finger squeezed again as the last one came at him, right overhead, and he felt the same feeling of slowness, the same little knock in the shoulder, and a double thud on the ground behind him, one after the other, as the birds came down.

He was somehow aware that as he had been shooting, two other birds had gone down, to Cromwell and Henry, and four survivors had skimmed away over the arable. He didn't manage that again, but he did hit three more before the drive was over, and afterwards his cousins clustered round, and clapped him on the shoulder. He stood with the gun under his left arm as his father came by with the General, but he had no words for his son.

Earl Cuthbert looked out over his lands, bathed in the late autumn sunshine. 'Dashed good day,' he pronounced. 'What do y'say we give the beggars a rest until next time? Hopcroft! Hopcroft, we'll let them off the last drive.'

In the distance the white Avro biplane shone against the golden stubble of the field. 'I must move her,' said Henry. 'Father, may I fly her over to the long barn to put her under cover?'

'Eh? Yes, yes. Go on, boy. We'll watch you take the air, eh what?'

Henry turned to Fish. 'Like a spin?' he said casually.

Fish swallowed, momentarily silent. 'Y-yes, please,' he said.

They crossed the Battle Water by the natural stepping stones where Goderick of Poitiers had slipped and fallen in his flight, losing both his life, and his claim to the Clare lands – the Earl was walking with General Legrand, giving him a history lesson as they went along.

'*Ici?*'

'Between those two rocks,' said Earl Clare, as though it were yesterday. 'Teach the beggar a lesson. The Poitiers were always a grasping lot. Tried to change sides at Bosworth Field and were slaughtered to a man, I'm glad to say. Serve 'em right, a man's only as good as his word, they should have stuck to King Richard.'

'My memory is as you say, fogged. King Richard?'

'He was killed, of course. Bleating for a horse, they say, though I don't know that for sure.'

Legrand frowned. 'I do not understand. They should have stayed with him?'

'They died without honour!' de Clare barked. 'Thrown into some commoners' gravepit, their name sullied for ever. Where are the Poitiers now, may I ask? Do you know? No, I'm damned sure I don't. We are the de Clares, and we hold what we own, because we live with honour.' They made their way up to the field in

the glorious November sunset that painted the corn stubble gold-
en.

'Which side were you on when these Poitiers were killed?'

'We were with Henry Tudor, who became King Henry. King
Richard was a bad sort and a poor politician to boot. King Henry
was smarter than he was. When you give your word General, you
had better be very careful to whom you give it.'

Legrand smiled, cynically. 'Yais, I can understand that.'

They arrived at the Avro. Henry visited the three corners of the
aircraft, undoing the ropes that had held it against a sudden rise in
the wind. 'They fly very easily,' he explained to Fish, who followed
him round. 'There's a lot of lift in the wings. If the wind gets up
she'll blow away like a kite that's broken its string.'

The aeroplane sat on a pair of wheels like a large perambulator's;
as Henry undid the ropes it rocked gently. 'Hop in,' he said to
Fish, indicating the forward of the two cockpits, directly under the
centre of the top wing. 'Buckle up,' he said, and Fish strapped the
wide leather belt that was lying on the seat about his waist. In the
cockpit about him were various levers, plungers and controls. As
Henry hung over his own cockpit these began to move into various
positions with satisfying yet mysterious clicks and whirrs, as if of
their own accord.

'What are you doing?'

'I'll explain another time,' Henry called. 'We'd better get into the
air while there's still light to land by. Flying's a sort of mixture of
playing the harmonium, working the village pump and sculling a boat.
There. That should do it.'

Looking over his shoulder, Fish saw Henry running his eyes over
whatever settings he had made before dropping down to the ground.

'It's lovely, though,' he said quietly, almost to himself. He went
round to the front of the aeroplane. 'This bit's the part that can hurt
you,' he called to the rest of the shooting party, standing agog on the
stubble. 'It's about the size and shape of a sword and the engine whirls
it about just like our ancestors did, so don't go near the front, I beg
you. Also if you walk into it you will break it and they cost about
seven guineas to replace.'

So saying, he gave the propeller a practised heave, stepping smartly
backwards out of the way as it turned. As Fish watched, the varnished
wood of the propeller vanished into a blur, and a strangely scented,
warmish wind blew over his face. The leather-covered coaming where
he rested his hands trembled with life. He pulled the goggles Henry
had given him over his eyes.

The aeroplane rocked as Henry climbed in. There was a sudden roar from the engine, and they began to move over the stubble, the wings rocking. The pedals by his feet and the stick in front of Fish moved by themselves and he watched them, fascinated. Looking behind him he could see the shooting party running all over the field, trying to catch their hats which had blown away in the sudden gale. He laughed, and Henry grinned at him. 'There's no wind, so we'll take off downhill,' he shouted, and as he twisted the aeroplane around, the orange ball of the sun setting to the west of the wood swung through the spars and rigging. A lever to Fish's left moved forward, and the roar became a tornado. They rolled and bumped forward, the tail behind them came up, a bump, a hop, and . . .

'We're flying!' Fish shouted.

The golden field fell away, the trees of the long hedge vanished under the wings, and as Fish looked about him in wonder he saw down on the ground a small black aeroplane chasing them across the land, their shadow in the setting sun. They climbed up into the sky, completely alone in the cool, smooth air.

They seemed to level out. Controls moved and twisted, the noise of the engine settled into a sweet humming sound. They were a fine sailing dinghy running under a steady breeze, its sheets and tiller set. Below the Windstone Water gleamed golden, the land was filled with tiny wriggling, glinting streams. The castle stood strong, yellow and grey and green, holding the land about it. They flew over it, and people waved at them.

'There's Violet!' shouted Fish. He waved vigorously over the side.

The woods were pools of darkness. In the distance, the sea gleamed, a steamer left a vanishing trail of smoke over the water. The city was a smudge inland, the express going down to Cornwall carved a line of smoke across the fields, slowly drifting away, breaking up into tiny clouds. Windows in the carriages glinted as they hurtled over the steel rails, as bright as swords.

'You try it!' Henry called. Fish twisted round and saw to his horror that Henry was sitting back in his cockpit, grinning at him, his hands behind his head. 'Go on!'

Gingerly, he took the stick in front of him. He pressed it a little to the left, and it was springy, responsive, the aeroplane's wings tilted over, and they turned to the left. He pressed it back to the right, and the wings reversed themselves. It seemed to him as though he and the aeroplane were still and the sky was moving about him. He put the stick forward and the ground tilted alarmingly, spreading itself out in front of him, and getting larger. The noise of the engine and the whirling propeller blew into a terrifying roar. He pulled back on the stick in alarm and the ground whipped away from sight. Now he was looking at the sky. The noise of the engine and the propeller began to die away, the stick began to become slack in his hand.

He felt sudden, confident movements going through the controls. The earth reappeared in its rightful place, the engine hummed. He twisted round, and saw Henry laughing at him. 'Take us home, Henry!' he called.

Fish looked about him. The earth was a bewildering combination of sun streaks on the fields and long marching shadows of hedgerows and woods. He had no idea where he was. Then the noise of the engine died away, and the nose tilted down. Silently and gloriously, they glided out of the sky. There. There was the castle. Now he knew where he was. The water was burnished, it flashed in his eyes. They came over the trees and he could smell the fresh leaf mould, damp on the air.

There was a rumble from the wheels beneath them, a sudden brief roar from the engine, a blast of scented warm air over his face. The long barn blocked out the sun, Henry cut the throttle and they rolled to a stop.

Fish sat in the sudden silence, his ears singing, his skin tight and cold on his face. His heart was racing, the scent of the machine was in his nostrils. He undid his seat belt with fingers that trembled, and climbed out with feet that seemed not to recognise the unyielding ground.

Henry was standing there already, he looked at his face with knowing eyes. 'Sorry,' he said, and he laughed. 'I've given you something. You'll not be the same, now.'

'That was wonderful,' Fish said sincerely, and did not stutter at all.

The castle corridors were labyrinthine, almost matching the great maze of King Henry in the Tudor garden, in which, legend had it, entire skeletons could be found. They were filled with dark shadows, black as pitch – nooks and corners in which a man might hide, and never be seen, certainly not once Foskett had turned the lights out.

Bridadier de Clare padded soft-foot along the corridor in his dressing gown, navigating the right-angles and junctions with an expertise born of his childhood in the castle. He left a pleasing smell of cologne in his wake, and of Trumper's hair-tonic. He paused by a section of cream-painted doorways, unerringly picking the one he wanted in the gloom. He tapped lightly, a little message in Morse, and a second later the door opened. There was a feminine laugh, very low and quiet, and de Clare's deeper chuckle, and then the door closed again with him inside it. No light showed.

Fish emerged from the shadows, and padded back along the corridor in the direction from whence his father had come. In the dark, his nose wrinkled with distaste as he smelled the perfumes. He stopped at a doorway, and silently twisted the handle, without knocking. The door opened and he slipped inside. A few moments later he re-emerged, carrying a bundle over his arm. He closed the door once more, and slipped silently along the corridor. At a junction he paused, hiding in the deep shadow of a doorway, as he checked for people.

In the dark the door opened, and a hand grabbed him, yanking him inside the room. The door closed.

'Wh-wh-what—'

'Fish, it's me.'

The hand gently twisted the wheel of an oil lamp and a golden glow suffused the room. It was Violet, in a white cotton nightshirt, embroidered with lace. Fish was fully dressed, in jodhpurs and a jersey, soft boots on his feet.

'I'm terribly nosy,' Violet said. 'There's always a terrific traffic along this corridor when there's a house party and I like to see who's with who. Lo and behold, Fish, first I see your father hot foot to . . .'

'M-M-Mrs Berthold,' Fish stuttered softly. 'H-H-He always does.'

'But then,' Violet said, looking at him wide-eyed, 'what do I see but Fish, going the other way.'

'V-V-Violet!'

'And then, back you come with . . .' Violet peered at the bundle Fish was carrying. 'With . . . somebody's washing?'

A slow smile spread all over Fish's face. 'They're Father's trousers,' he said proudly, 'His riding breeches.'

'Where are you taking them?'

'I'm going to hang them from Gaston's Gibbet.'

'Where they used to hang them in chains, on the old watchtower?'

'Yes.'

'Isn't it ruined?'

'You can just get up there. I did it the other day.'

Violet stood looking at him. 'I'm so jolly proud of you, Fish,' she said quietly. 'I thought you were scared of your father.'

'I a-a-am. B-B-But he's only a rotten bully. If you s-s-stand up to b-b-bullies they go away and p-p-pick on somebody else. Uncle was telling me that. And you encouraged me shooting today. So I'm going to hang his bags on the gibbet. He'll be ever so cross. He hasn't got any others and he's v-v-vain about the way he dresses.'

Violet scampered over to a wardrobe and yanked a pair of jodhpurs out of it. She pulled them on and Fish had an involuntary glimpse of long, slender legs. He looked away, blushing slightly. She pulled on elastic-sided riding boots and a jersey. 'Come on, then.'

'You?'

'Fish, if you can climb up there it must be like walking up the grand staircase. Come on.'

The two slipped out into the darkness. Soon they were outside in the castle grounds. 'Stick to the shadows,' Fish whispered, and they flitted along the walls towards the tower. Inside, it was very dark. A pit, as black as coal, led down into the bowels of the earth, to Bohamond's *oubliette*, a dreadful place where men had once been put and left, forgotten, to die. Ancient, lichened steps led upwards in a ruined stair to a platform from which condemned men had been hung in chains, suspended one hundred feet above the earth to perish, as a terrible warning to others.

The two cousins picked their way up very carefully, using the light of the moon. Clouds were coming over, and the light brightened and faded as they did so. 'This is the tricky bit,' Fish whispered. The wall had fallen away, taking the stair with it. Only the sockets of the missing stone treads remained, black in the ancient masonry. Fish had fixed the breeches about his neck, hanging them over his back by the braces. Very carefully, he clambered out over the abyss clinging to the wall like a spider. Violet watched, her heart beating fast as he climbed up and round. He pulled himself up on to the remaining section of stair, and waited for her.

She had noted the sockets he had used; she gripped the jutting pieces of masonry, and fitted her feet into the holes. Little by little, she went round.

'Just above there,' Fish urged. 'Feel for the notch in the wall. That's it . . .' There was the last pull up to the stair. Fish reached out and they gripped each other's wrist. With a co-ordinated heave, she was up. The rest of the climb was easy, and in a few moments they were out on the flat platform, the gibbet above them.

'That was fun,' she said.

'Isn't it. Hold on to me, now.' Fish swung the trousers out like a man casting a line, and the braces hooked over the old wrought ironwork of the gibbet. He let them go, and they twisted and turned in the breeze. Sitting down on the flat platform, they swung their legs over the sheer drop beneath.

'Gosh, must've been horrid, being hanged up here.'

'The last one was Grimond, Uncle told me. He was a notorious highwayman in these parts. The Earl hunted him down with staghounds. Got 'im after a six-mile chase across good country. His head's somewhere, the Earl had it preserved and mounted. They hung what was left from the gibbet.'

'He was dead?'

'Oh, yes.'

'Bite 'im and eat 'im?' Violet asked, using the hunting call.

'Bit 'im and ate 'im all right. Then they left the bones up here for the crows to pick.'

'Better than being hanged up here alive, all clanking in chains.'

'Yes. Pretty quick, being munched up by staghounds.' Fish looked at the great hook that had held the suit of chains. 'Anything'd be better than that,' he said thoughtfully. 'I've always been afraid of being closed up somewhere, not able to get out . . . Horrid.'

'Not nice,' Violet agreed. 'Are you staying long at the castle?'

'Half term. My last year at Eton. What about you?'

'I'm going to stay on a bit.'

'Lucky you. I love it here.'

'Me, too. What are you doing when you leave?'

'Don't know. If the war's still on I'll go and do my bit. Then I think I'll be a country gentleman. Hunt and shoot. Perhaps Uncle will let me stay here for a bit. What about you?'

'Going to Cambridge. Girton College,' she said proudly.

'Oh, I say . . . you're so brainy, Vi.'

'We women are going to take over the world,' she said. 'Look, if we're to go hunting tomorrow we'd better get some sleep.'

'Oh, yes. I can't wait to see Father's face tomorrow.'

She giggled. 'Me, too.'

The climb down seemed quite easy. They slipped in through the window they had left ajar, and made their way back to Violet's room. 'Night, Vi,' Fish whispered.

'Night, Fish.'

'Vi?'

'Yes?'

'I th-th-think you l-l-look jolly nice.'

'I like you too, Fish. Night.'

'Night.'

2

There's Nobody to Pick Them up and Put Them in Rows

Lord de Clare came into the gun room in full hunting fig. His mahogany-topped boots shone below white buckskin breeches, his swallow-tailed jacket glowed brighter than a cherry, his face glowered. He stamped to the window, and looked out, as though what he saw there might have changed since he viewed it from higher up in the castle.

The drizzle continued to fall from the grey November sky.

He turned to the barometer on the wall and tapped it in interrogation. The long finger pointed to 'Set Fair'. De Clare's mouth tightened. He tapped it again, and it obstinately refused to move. Seizing the barometer from the wall, he marched to the window and he threw it open. 'See for y'self, you blasted fool!' he shouted, and flung the barometer outside. It landed askew in a bush below.

He turned to find his brother Gervase staring at him, red in the face. He too was fully dressed as a huntsman except that he was carrying his highly polished boots in his hand and his legs were clad in woollen long johns.

'Dash it, Gervase,' said the Earl disapprovingly, 'you cannot go hunting like that. Not even a Conservative would dress like that.'

'I do not want to dress like this!' the Brigadier roared in fury. 'Some benighted bounder has stolen my breeches!'

'Oh. Well, you'll have to borrow a pair of mine. Go and ask Foskett.'

'They won't fit,' his brother said sulkily, 'you eat too much.'

'It's either that or hang about the castle looking foolish,' de Clare said, dismissively. His brother went off, shouting for the butler, and de Clare picked up his top hat. Polishing it on his sleeve, he went along the corridor to the hall. Outside, the hunt was gathering, a swirling medley of scarlet and black coats, check tweed jackets, indigo habits, velvet caps and bowlers, silk top hats. Horses, black and bronze and white, ponies, brown and piebald, hounds with keen eyes and shining white teeth clustered under the vigilant eyes of the 'whippers-in', clad in the scarlet-collared royal blue of the Windstone Hunt, sitting on their horses as if carved in stone.

The Earl's groom was holding his horse. Sweeping the rug over his rump, Lord de Clare walked round him, testing girth and curb-chain, smoothing the shining bronze hide, and then swung himself up into the saddle. The gelding humped his back and skittered sideways a few paces. De Clare gathered in reins and whip, and patted the great strong, arching neck. 'Fine job, Purkiss,' he said, and the groom touched his eyebrow with a bent forefinger as his master rode out into his hunt.

'Morning, Mother,' he said to the dowager Countess de Clare, clad in indigo, tied side-saddle to her mount, her personal groom riding beside her. It had been some years since she had been able to see the jumps in time, but she considered this to be no reason to stop her pleasure.

'Ah, Furzegrove,' said the Earl, spotting the beater of yesterday, mounted on a sturdy piebald cob, 'pity about this blasted weather. I think the Almighty does it to try me.'

Furzegrove shook his head. 'Came over before dawn, m'lord. Passing fancy, I declare. Be fine soon.'

Earl de Clare glanced up. Indeed, the drizzle appeared to be lessening, the sky brightening towards the West. 'Think you're right,' he said, his mood improving with the weather. 'Morning, Cromwell, Robert. Should be clearing up soon, what? Morning, Violet, Fish.'

'There's your father,' said Violet. 'He's not best pleased.' She giggled, behind a gloved hand. Brigadier de Clare swung himself up into the saddle, a belt holding his baggy breeches up, his face like thunder.

The Master of the Hunt looked at his fob and signalled to the huntsman. Hounds and hunt servants moved off, out of the castle grounds, the field following after, an iridescent, talking, chattering cavalcade, their shoulders rising and falling in the rhythm of the trot. As they rounded the bailey, Fish saw one or two arms raised, pointing up at the old tower, heard people guffaw. Behind him, his father saw them too, saw his son trying not to snigger, looking guilty, felt a flush of intense anger. He had never asked for the boy to be born, he thought bitterly, but his training had instilled into him the necessity of never losing one's temper in the heat of battle, and he forced his fury down.

They jogged out into the countryside, the loping black and white pack of bitches in the lead. By now pale sun had appeared in the washed sky, and the hunt, over a hundred strong, was heading out into full country. The ground showed like a map in front of them; a grid of hedges outlining the pastures. There was no wire in the Windstone Hunt, the Earl would not permit it. Water gleamed where the land dipped, the woods poked bare fingers up into the sky. Where the plough had been, the land was masked in sepia. The hunt streamed across the land and Fish felt his heart rise with joy.

They went down into the valley, where the Rimford Water ran deep and fast, carrying the flow from the high hills to the sea. There was only one crossing there, Oliver's bridge, where Cromwell had caught the cavalry of Prince Rupert at the crucial moment of the battle. For over two hundred and fifty years, men casting for fish in those parts had weighted their lines with lead melted from the pistol balls that littered the battlefield. The hunt streamed across the narrow, arched bridge and gathered in the meadow beyond, the dark Holpit Wood ahead of them. The lean Windstone bitches swirled in a great Harlequin pack, their eyes shining, smelling the air, wanting their prey.

Now people weren't talking. Whips were galloping to strategic points, the pack of hounds were about the huntsmen like a great speckled rug; riders shifted forward in their saddles.

'Leu in!' they heard the Master cry, saw his directing scarlet arm. 'Leu in thar!'

The hounds seethed at the edge of the wood, and they seemed to vanish into it like mist blown by the wind. Riders edged forward in anticipation and the pasture around became enveloped in a thin mist, the breath of readied men and their mounts. Horses fretted, sidling and bucking, plunging at their bits.

A hound whimpered, somewhere in the covert, then howled, was answered, and then cried once more. The chorus was taken up by the pack like a choir of voices.

'Hold hard!' the Master of the Hunt commanded, his arm high in the air. 'Give'm a start, gentlemen!'

There.

Far down the hillside, a dark phantom raced. And then, behind him, a crashing waterfall of hounds, music in their throats. A horn sounded, a quick, triple rise in the autumn air. The Master's arm dropped, they clapped in spurs, took off like a squadron of dragoons.

'See you at the finish, Fish!' Violet called mischievously. The hounds were streaming across the field half a mile ahead. Violet had Lady May, her bay, short by the head; she put her at a newly-trimmed hedge, and went hell-for-leather down the slope the other side, Fish at her heels. They took a thick, impenetrable blackthorn together, cat-jumped a low drystone wall and let their horses stretch into full gallop across the pasture. Four fields ahead the hounds raced, a sprinkling of scarlet and black coated thrusters at their tails, and ahead, out-distancing them all, the magnificent dark stag.

Another obstacle: a bank topped by a timber rail. Fish steadied his black gelding, Mikado, collected him between bit and spur, allowed him his moment. His broad black forehead lifted, his quarters slammed like a cannon firing, together, man and beast, they soared out through the air, landing a full yard past the stagnant ditch the obstacle had concealed. He was up on Violet's shoulder and reached down and patted his horse, filled with exaltation. Violet looked over at him, her face flushed with excitement, her teeth and eyes shining. 'There's dowager Gwendolyn!' she called.

On the flank the eighty-year-old raced over the pasture, her groom in attendance. With the wind snoring past their ears from their speed, the two young riders watched her. There was a music in the air, and they realised that she was singing aloud as she galloped. The pasture was marked at its boundary by a strong Quickthorn fence. The old lady and her groom hurtled towards it like cannon shells. The groom prepared himself, shifting in the saddle.

'Ready now, m'lady!' he warned. The fine chestnut beneath her could see the coming fence, her mistress could not. '*Jump*, m'lady!'

Hands still skilled with the reins gave the aids, shoulders square, hands low, and horse and rider rose into the air as one being, landing effortlessly the other side. Across the field came a trilling, the dowager Gwendolyn singing some show-stopping song of the '50s, when she had been a young woman.

Fences, brooks, ditches and streams; low walls, five-barred gates, banks and hedges; fields, avenues, rides and pastures – the great hunting field spread out over a third of a county. They flew past farmhouses and cottages streaming smoke from chimneys, waving children and dairymaids, shepherds and labourers with pitchforks, pausing to savour the sight of the hunt going by. An explosion of hens, a covey of partridges, a hare, leaping along for a few seconds in unison with the horses before diving away into the security of the long grass. Then on to high ground, the earth hard under the horses' feet, sprinkled with a dusting of snow from the clouds that had drizzled lower down. And at last the long dark line of the ancient Windstone Forest, that had once held wolves and elk, where the Earl and his retainers had hunted wild boar with lances. The hounds lapped against its edges like disconsolate foam, scarlet-collared blue jackets looked this way and that.

'Lost his scent, by golly!' Fish cried. They pulled up short of the oaks and elm and beech, chests heaving, man and beast, steam rising from the horses.

The Earl came thumping up, his topper askew, face crimson and perspiring. He pulled out his fob. 'Capital, capital!' he called. 'Eight miles in . . . forty-three minutes. Cracking run, what! Lorst 'im, have they?'

Riders were coming up all the time, all panting and grinning, their eyes shining. Furzegrove was there on his piebald cob, taking off his flat cap and wiping his forehead. 'Cold ground, m'lord,' he called. 'Won't carry a scent. He knows that, does the maister in there, that's why he come up high. He's in there now, m'lord.' Furzegrove looked expertly at the forest.

'Burtlesham torrent sets stream in the forest,' Earl de Clare said, who knew every part of his lands. 'Passes through here on its way to the Windstone Water itself.'

'That's it, m'lord. He's taken to the water, that's why the hounds've lost 'im. He be hiding quiet in some boggy part, awaiting for us to go.' He trotted his cob over to Violet and Fish, sliding off and letting the animal pick at the grass. 'Here, Miss, and young Master Fish, if you will look after old Pebble for me, I'll just go in there a moment . . .' They saw him go over to the huntsman. 'Bring your best bitch,' he said. The huntsman also dismounted, and the two men went into the forest with the hound.

'Here! Here Ramble. Seek 'im.'

Furzegrove stood for a few moments, almost sniffing the air like the hound. 'Now if I was the maister . . .'

It was quiet in the forest, they made not a sound on the centuries of leaf mould under the great trees. 'Yers, look here, Mr Thorpe . . .' Clefts in the soft covering, slotted feet.

'He went this way, Mr Furzegrove,' the huntsman agreed. 'Ramble, Ramble, here girl.'

They pushed on into the forest. Ahead a jay rattled harshly, and the undergrowth thickened. Furzegrove inserted himself into the thicket; the branches parted easily, and the ground became soft underfoot. There was a gurgling of a stream. In the gloom, something great and dark steamed. There was a glint of an eye, a movement as though of massive branches. The bitch Ramble suddenly cried out, and Furzegrove and the huntsman were running back along the path as the pack streamed in. Behind them there was a tremendous crashing, and the huntsman blew his horn.

Violet and Fish were waiting; Fish passed Furzegrove the reins as the hunt poured into the forest.

'Not that way, Miss Violet!' he called, as they were about to give chase. 'The maister, he'll be coming out this way.' He put spur to his cob and they galloped along the side of the forest. They came towards its tip, rounding it in time to see the massive stag leap from the covert in a great bound, racing down the hill with the pack in full cry at his heels. In the valley below the Windstone Water shone in the sunlight like beaten silver, a full quarter of a mile wide before it narrowed at the weirs.

'He be going for the water!' Furzegrove cried. Glancing over his shoulder Fish saw the field pouring out of the forest in their wake as they shot down the slope like thunderbolts.

The stag leaped a blackthorn as big as a National fence. The hounds streamed through crannies and holes like drops of quicksilver, Violet let Lady May drop her bit and they rocketed upwards. Behind her, Fish gave Mikado the office and they soared over. Then it was a straight run down the meadow to the shining water. The stag stumbled, and for a second Fish thought the hounds had him. They thought so too, and their voices were raised in triumph, but he recovered, pecking from tiredness before regaining his huge stride, his heels leaping tantalising feet ahead of the lead bitches and their shining white teeth.

The stag hit the water at full tilt in a vast explosion of foam, and the hounds crashed all about him like shrapnel. As the spray cleared, as they reined in at the water's edge, they saw him swimming strongly, the current taking him further and further away, as the hounds turned disconsolately back, clambering out to shake themselves in a welter of spray.

'Look at him go!' Lord de Clare cried in admiration, as he thundered up. He rested in his saddle after the long chase, looking out over the water where the stag swam strongly for the opposite shore. 'Look at him go . . .' he breathed.

A quarter of a mile away the huge beast came out of the water in a flurry of foam, and looped away up the hill. The huntsman blew, and a tribute echoed across the water.

Lord and Lady de Clare waited to say goodbye to their guests. General Legrand appeared, still shiny from his breakfast, a footman in his wake, carrying his bags to the car.

'Ah, *mon General*, have you everything you require?'

'*Merci, milord*,' said General Legrand, waddling up. 'Lady Clare has been kind enough to supply me with one of your smoked salmons, that are so tasty.'

'Catch'm in the Water out there,' said de Clare. 'Smoke 'em ourselves. Glad you like 'em.'

'These have been *jours d'ore*,' Legrand said effusively. 'Golden days. Now I must be off. *La guerre* is calling me.'

'Make sure we win. Give Fritz a good thrashing.'

'*Bien sur. L'attaque, l'attaque, toujours l'attaque. Et, après – la victoire!*'

'Jolly good. Ah, Gervase. You off too?'

'Yes,' said Brigadier de Clare. 'Where's Fish? Fish, blast you, come here!'

A head poked itself out of a window. 'You w-want me, sir?'

'I'm not yelling your name to exercise my lungs. I want you here.'

Fish's head vanished and in a few moments he appeared. 'Yes, sir?'

'Let me see your teeth. I'm told you've knocked a bit off your tooth. Yes, so you have. Damned stupid of you.'

'It w-was an a-accident.'

'You were an accident, Fish. You'll have to get it seen to, it'll rot in your head and fall out, otherwise. You'll look like a blasted toothless Balkan peasant, and I am damned if you are going to walk about wearing my name looking like that.'

'I'll g-get it s-seen to, sir.'

'Damned right you will, I'm taking you down to the village. Keggs the farrier does work on teeth.'

'*H-Horses'* teeth.'

'Same thing. He does people too. Didn't that kitchen-maid of yours have her teeth pulled by him as a wedding present, Cuthbert?'

'That's so. Frightful nuisance, teeth.'

'Get in the car then. I've got a train to catch.'

With luck, Fish thought, Kegg will be out curing laminitis, or diagnosing the botts.

He wasn't. He was in his room filled with tack and the tools of his calling.

'Kegg,' de Clare said, stumping in. 'Got a tooth for you to look at. Fish, show him your tooth.'

The farrier was a big man with large, capable red hands. 'Ah, yes, m'lord. I see it. Chipped clean across the corner.'

'Plug it, man.'

Kegg showed Fish a strong wooden armed chair. 'Sit there, master Fish. That's where I do my work on teeth.'

Fish sat down. The leather and wood bore nameless stains and as it took his weight an unpleasant, musty smell rose up about him. He gripped the arms with hands that were suddenly slippery. Kegg opened a drawer. 'Been looking for a chance to try out these. Gold, they are, m'lord.'

'Gold good enough for you, Fish?'

'Y-yes sir.'

'I 'ave to make the tooth the right shape to put it in, it needs drilling.'

'Get on with it, I've got a train to catch.'

'I c-could c-come back another d-day.'

'Don't snivel, Fish. If you hang people's bags up on a gibbet then you must learn to take your medicine.'

Kegg rummaged in another drawer, pulling out pronged instruments, knives and files. At Fish's side was a drill, with a string running over pulleys to whirl a metal bit at its tip. Kegg settled himself and began to push a pedal back and forth with his foot. The string whizzed over the pulleys with a whirring sound, and the triangular-headed bit buzzed into life.

'May hurt a little, master Fish,' he said. 'I do hear they 'ave some kind of stuff that makes the flesh dead, so to speak, but I don't 'ave any of it.'

'God's breath!' expostulated de Clare, pausing in the act of lighting a cigarette. 'He's not a blasted woman. Get drilling.'

Kegg pushed with his foot as though pumping life into the church organ, and applied the drill to Fish's tooth. Instantly, agonising pain lanced up into Fish's head. He gripped the arms of the chair as hard as he could, and closed his eyes.

A smell of burning, acrid and pungent, filled his nostrils. As Kegg's leg became tired, the slowing drill caught on an edge, and fresh pain jarred through his jaw. His mouth was filling with saliva, he swallowed, and the sharp filings in his mouth were like sand down his throat.

Kegg put the drill down and took a small file from his collection, and scraped. 'Now let me see, 'ere.'

Something cold and foreign fitted into the tooth. Kegg took it out, smeared something on it, pushed it back. He took a small tack hammer and smacked at it, Fish's head banging like a drum. A revolting taste filled his mouth.

'That be the glue, master Fish,' said Kegg.

'Done?' demanded de Clare.

'That be it, sir.'

'Send me the bill.' De Clare inspected Fish critically as they came out into the open air. 'You're sweating like old pork, Fish,' he said disapprovingly. 'You've a long way to go before they make a man of you.' He climbed into the waiting Daimler. 'You can walk back,' he said. 'It'll do you good.'

Fish watched the Daimler roll away. Outside the village he stopped at a stream and rinsed his mouth until the taste of the glue was gone. He scooped up water in his hands and sluiced his face. He dried himself on his handkerchief and began to walk back up to the castle.

By a small copse Violet suddenly jumped out at him. 'Boo!' she cried cheerfully. 'Fish, what have you done, you're shining like a harvest moon.'

'Kegg put a gold bit in my tooth,' he explained. 'Father took me down there on his way to the station.'

'Kegg?' she said in horror. 'Kegg does horses. I go to Mr Browne in Kensington. Did it hurt?'

'Did a bit.'

She pulled him over to the copse. 'Let me have a look. You know, I think it quite suits you, Fish. It gives you a kind of buccaneerish air.' She slid her arms around his waist. 'Shall I make it better?' she enquired, and kissed him. 'I haven't had much practice at this,' she said, slightly anxiously, breaking off for a moment. 'Am I doing this right?'

'Yes,' Fish mumbled. 'Very right.'

'Goody. Shall we do it again?'

'Yes, please.'

From the copse came an aggrieved voice. 'Oh, I say, you two. How are the damned pigeons to roost with you carrying on like this?' From a hiding place inside the wood, under the red stems of a dogwood, Freddie came out, a gun under his arm.

'Freddie!' Violet said sharply. 'Oh, trust you to get in the way.'

'I was here first. I took a lot of trouble, to get hidden like that.'

From over in the pasture, by the barn, there came a melodious humming. As they watched, the shining white shape of the Avro appeared, lifting up from the ground like a great swan. The biplane climbed into the sky, turning slowly round as it made in the direction of the castle.

'Off to the war.'

'I wish you'd go off to the war, Freddie, instead of ambushing innocent people.'

Fish glanced down the long road that led to the Halt. 'Wait a m-minute!' he cried. 'Look!' A figure in olive uniform was walking towards them. 'It's Charlie!'

They went running down to meet their cousin, passing the wagon of hung game from the shoot as they did so, on its way to the station, and the hotels and butchers' shops of London.

Lieutenant Charles de Clare stopped as he saw them coming, reaching inside his uniform jacket to retrieve a cigarette from his case. 'Hallo, you lot!' he called.

'You missed the shoot!'

'And the hunt!'

'I don't mind,' he said. 'It's nice to be home. For a few days, at any rate.'

'How's the war?' Freddie asked eagerly.

'Oh, the war is the war,' Charlie said, smiling. 'Very muddy, and very cold.'

The wagon came by, with the hare and pheasant and partridges all neatly lined up in rows, line upon line. Charlie de Clare looked at the dead game with an odd expression.

'Have you seen lots of dead Germans?' said Freddie, following his gaze. 'Oh yes,' he said. 'They hang on the wire.' The wagon clopped on its way. 'There's nobody to pick them up and put them in rows,' he said, as though in explanation.

3

Aerial Ballet

Flanders, June 1915

Henry de Clare was hot. It was summer, and he was wearing thigh-length sheepskin boots, a leather jacket with a fleecy collar, a silk scarf, two jerseys, a pair of long-johns he had acquired when skiing in Switzerland before the war, and two sets of gloves, a thin silk pair and a pair of gauntlets. Sweating profusely, he strapped on a webbing harness holding two loaded Webley .44 revolvers, and picked up a sack of Mills bombs, which he carried out to his waiting Bristol Scout – a small, rather pretty biplane, its tailfin and rudder painted red, white, and blue, with similarly marked vivid roundels on its planes.

His fitter was waiting there for him. 'I've put the shell in the holder for you, Mr Henry,' he said.

'Thank you, Hodge. Going to be a scorcher, what? I shall be glad to get to altitude.'

'Nice and cool up there, I'd imagine, sir.'

'It is, Hodge, it is.'

He climbed in, and did up his wide leather seat-belt. He attached his bag of grenades to their hook. By his side an eight-inch artillery shell reposed in a specially made bracket. It shone like gold. He set and adjusted his controls, like a man preparing to play Beethoven on a church organ, and Hodge waited patiently by the propeller. 'Ready, Hodge.'

'Very good, sir.'

The fitter gave a practised whirl of the beautiful laminated-walnut propeller and with a pleasing blur of sound, the eighty horsepower Gnome rotary engine burst into life. Henry opened the throttle, and taxied out. The airfield was a large pasture – one end was decorated with large Bessoneaux canvas and wood hangars for the mixture of aircraft, and various huts and tents were scattered about. A windsock stood on its pole near the hedge, hanging limp, so Henry could simply open up as he chose.

Air swirled about the small aero screen in front of him, the little scout lifted its tail, bouncing on its baby-carriage wheels, once, twice, and then he was airborne, the little whirling rotary engine in front of him humming sweetly. Ahead were green and yellow fields of ripening crops, silver streams glittering in the sunlight, and the darker pools of the woods.

Five thousand feet up, Henry flew over the lines and on to the other side, where once again the countryside was verdant. He identified the small village – its crossroads and the bridge over the river – from his map, somewhat to his relief. The shelling had, in parts of the area, altered the landscape so greatly that the pre-war maps were no longer meaningful – whole woods and villages had become swallowed up in a sea of mud, fed on what had once been sparkling streams.

He found the German artillery battery, indicated by intermittent puffs of dust and smoke from the little forts about each gun. Their observers had seen him, and suddenly puffs of dirty black smoke started appearing in the sky nearby. He smelled it, a nasty, acrid, toxic smell, it made him angry, he liked his air clean.

The eight-inch-high explosive shell was fitted with a wire handle to enable him to draw it from its holster. He pulled it out, and cradled it in his lap with one hand. Then putting the nose down, he dived on the guns.

When he could hear the rattle of machine guns he levelled out, pulling the nose up, tilting his little scout over onto one wing. Right below was the snout of an artillery piece poking from its lair. He tossed out the shell and put his nose down, racing away from the scene.

Squinting over his shoulder he saw a satisfying plume of dirt and smoke rising up behind him. He knew the soldiers in the line hated the artillery, so it seemed only fair to him that those handing it out should have to endure a bit of frightfulness too.

With this done, he climbed back up to altitude, setting a course back to his own side of the lines. He could see where the German shells were falling – puffs of mingled explosive and debris blossoming and drifting away on the wind. Flying a holding pattern above, he craned his neck, searching the sky for the inevitable accompaniment to the shelling – an observation aeroplane, the eyes of the guns.

There it was.

He caught a glint of sunshine off a wing, and applying full throttle, climbed towards it. It was a German Taube, a two-seater monoplane, its striking, dove-shaped wings painted bright green. He fumbled in the bag of grenades, and was soon gripping two in his teeth by their pin-rings. He could see the German observer talking into his bulky radio set as the pilot flew steadily over the shelled trenches below.

Henry swept above them, dragged the grenades from their pins, and threw them one after the other into the path of the Taube, whose pilot banked steeply as he saw the English biplane; Henry noted the puffs of smoke from his grenades bursting a hundred feet away, damaging nothing but the air. Next pursuing the Taube, Henry blazed away at it with his revolver. The enemy pilot seemed to be enjoying the game, he fired back with his own pistol, and the observer blazed away with a shotgun.

Nobody hit anything.

When Henry was out of ammunition for both his pistols, he calmed his flight, and for a few moments the two aircraft flew alongside each other. The German pilot was grinning, Henry waved at him. They both waved back.

By now, he was high over his own lines. He turned away, cutting his engine, and the little scout glided gently down, with just the singing of the air over the wings, whistling in the wires. He knew this area well, and as he glided over the church, his shadow sent the cows running in the pasture. He came over the hedge and touched down, rolling to a stop near the Bessoneau. Hodge was waiting for him.

'Good 'untin', sir?'

'Rotten. Though I tickled up some gun battery with the shell. We ought to hang a couple underneath, have some way of dropping them with a lever. No, Hodge, I found a Taube and we did our usual aerial ballet to the accompaniment of much gunfire, all of it totally ineffective. Might as well have been firing unshotted charge for all the good it did. The Taube told the German battery where their shells were landing and they are, no doubt, pounding the poor bloody infantry with even more vigour as we speak.'

Henry heaved off his boots and his leather jacket, and donned the suede shoes his fitter had brought him. Rules about uniform were very loose. 'That's better. Who's that?'

A Morane monoplane flew over the field. They could see the pilot peering down from his cockpit. 'Not one of ours,' said Henry.

'Perhaps 'e's lorst, sir.'

The Morane was lining up to land, the wings wobbling as the pilot attempted to bring it into line with the field.

'I think,' Henry said, 'that it is being flown by a blind man under instruction from his dog.'

The little craft lurched violently as it encountered the turbulent air rolling from the breeze passing through the hangars, and began to descend rapidly.

'Sinking air, out there,' Henry observed, as the Morane vanished behind the line of Bessoneaux. 'Be prepared to take evasive action, Hodge.'

There was a muffled roar as the pilot applied full power. The Morane shot over their heads in a shower of dirt and wood fragments. The hangar shuddered. The Morane flew on, its tailskid dangling. They could see the pilot frantically craning his neck to see where the ground was, flat and without shadow in the bright sunshine. He sailed past, ten feet up, pawing for the earth with jerks of the stick.

'It would be best if he went around,' Henry observed.

As the ground was not coming to him, the pilot decided that he must go to the ground. He thrust for it, and it hurled him back up into the air with a twang of breaking piano wire. Henry took a bicycle from the wall of the Bessoneau and mounted it.

Close to the edge of the field the Morane sank back to earth. There was another squeal of breaking wires, and the wheels folded up under it as it tripped and skidded along. The engine screamed as the propeller shattered into matchwood, and there was an explosion of black smoke as the pistons parted company with the connecting rods. The aeroplane vanished into the field of corn, still moving fast.

Henry pushed on the pedals, and began to ride across the field, breaking into song: 'We plough the fields and scatter, the good seed on the land . . .'

At the edge of the field he encountered the pilot, stumbling back along the path he had mown through the corn. Incongruously, he was carrying a long parcel under one arm. He pushed up his goggles and smiled in a dazed way at Henry. 'Good morning, sir. You wouldn't happen to be Henry de Clare?'

'In the flesh, old chap.'

'I was told at the depot to give you this,' the young pilot said, holding out the parcel. 'I'm Pemberton-Smythe, the replacement pilot.'

Henry took the parcel and they began to walk back towards the hangars. A gang of fitters was hurrying towards the wreck.

'How many hours do you have, Pemberton?'

'Twelve and a half,' he replied proudly.

'I say,' Henry murmured gently, 'a veteran already. Perhaps you and I can go up later and practice a little.' He held up the long parcel. 'Is this what I think it is?'

'Yes, they said your pa had it brought over for you.'

'Jolly good.'

By the Bristol Scout Henry stripped away the wrapping, and undid
the leather case inside. 'Hodge!' he called. 'The rifle's here.'

'You're hunting game, sir?' Pemberton hazarded.

'Sort of.'

Henry cradled the long-barrelled rifle in his hands. He flicked the
bolt open to check if it was loaded, and put it to his shoulder, tracking
a circling kite. 'Martini-Henry 0.45 inch,' he murmured. 'Ah, thank
you, Hodge.'

Henry took the box his fitter was carrying, and opened it. Inside
were snug rows of gleaming, brass-cased cartridges, necked-down like
small artillery shells. 'You could kill an elephant with this,' he said.
He slipped one into the breech.

'What is it?'

'Incendiary filled, partly jacketed, soft-nose lead. Very unsporting
to use on an elephant.'

'What are you going to shoot with it?'

'A man, I'm afraid. If I can,' said Henry. 'All right, Hodge, get that
bracket fitted up and we'll see.'

The fitter had a light welded structure with him, and he set about
bolting it to the fuselage on the right of Henry's cockpit.

'We have the devil's own problem stopping Fritz sending up his
two-seaters to fly over our trenches and tell his artillery where their
shells are dropping,' Henry explained. 'It's all frightfully unpleasant
for the chaps crouching down there, in their nasty muddy dug-outs.
They want the nuisance to cease. Anti-aircraft fire isn't very effective;
the best way would be to send another aeroplane up there – a
single-seater – to try to damage it, or the pilot. The problem is how
to do it.'

Henry made his hands appear as two aeroplanes: 'There you are,
both of you whizzing about at a hundred miles an hour. You can
chuck a grenade and it bursts miles away. Same with a revolver or a
shotgun. You are firing *at* a moving target *from* a moving platform,
which you happen to be trying to control at the same time. The
combination of all three variables means it's absolutely impossible
to hit anything.'

'They said, sir, that you were a bit of a crack shot.'

'Yes,' Henry said, without any false modesty, 'if I can't do it,
nobody can. However, I think I *do* know how it can be managed:
what you need to do is to make the aircraft like a shotgun, or a rifle
– to attach the gun to the aircraft. Then you aim the aircraft, just as
though you were swinging from the shoulder. Deflection shooting,
just like going for pheasant or partridge.'

He pointed to the cowling in front of his cockpit. 'Ideally, you'd have the gun here, so that you just aim straight ahead. The problem is that the prop's in the way, and you stand a good chance of blowing it off. I've heard that someone's trying to make some sort of interrupting gear that means you can't fire if the prop's in the way. Then you could strap on a bloody great machine gun. But for now, a rifle.'

'Ready, sir,' called Hodge. Henry carefully fitted the Martini-Henry into the bracket. He secured the catches then attached the firing mechanism to the trigger. The long barrel pointed out at a slight angle, clearing the prop. He dropped the box of shells onto his seat.

'Right,' he said quietly. 'Now we'll see.'

It was still cool, at altitude. The heat of the ground below had caused cumulus clouds to form; the little Bristol rocked in the updraughts as it climbed, as though travelling along a bumpy road. Nearly six thousand feet showed on the altimeter before he levelled off just under the cloud layer. Any observation aeroplane the Germans had sent up could fly no higher. Below, the lines crawled in each direction, a suppurating scar on the land.

Henry flew steadily, back and forth over the sector he had chosen. Below, there seemed little activity. Occasionally a plume of dirty dust floating in the breeze signalled a small outburst of hate from one or other side. After an hour he was bored. On an impulse, he opened the throttle and climbed up into the cool canyons of the cumulus clouds. First he clipped the edges and white fog sent cool, damp tendrils rushing through the cockpit; then he pulled the nose up into the whiteness, breathing it in as if it were the fresh morning mist that drifts off the Windstone Water. Then he was bursting back out into the golden sunshine.

The great cloud seemed to boil in the sky, sending up towers to the heavens, creating shimmering white ramparts, outlying forts, lanes and valleys of mist. Henry sent the little scout sliding round and round down the outside of a column of cloud, the wingtip of his plane just cutting its very edge, riding on a helter-skelter of air, pulling out at the bottom to skim along a pure white fairway, chasing his shadow.

Two shadows.

Adrenalin suddenly stabbed his stomach, he twisted in his seat, looking round. A Taube. A Taube with bright, shiny-green wings – the Taube from that morning. The pilot and his observer were laughing at him. They waved.

The Taube barrel-rolled over the top of him; he could see the pilot grinning madly as he demonstrated his expertise. He was a young man, he wore a new moustache.

He pulled level and immediately dived for a tunnel of mist. Henry followed. They swooped under the cloud and then rocketed upwards in a blaze of shimmering wings. The Taube was vertical against the snowy cloud, until the pilot kicked in rudder and the nose fell down in a *chandelle*, zooming away down the slopes of mist like a bird. Henry followed, whipping over the moghuls of cloud, his wings dipping first this way and then that, the two planes tumbling and rising like a great roller-coaster. They played on the white and gold hillsides until they had had enough.

The Taube turned for home, descending from their playground in the heavens. Below the lines crawled, dirty and violent. The pilot and observer looked at the Bristol, flying just a little behind and to their left. They waved happily.

Henry squeezed the trigger. There was a crack, the pilot of the Taube jerked in his seat, his head snapping backwards. A spray of blood from his propwash flicked over Henry's goggles. The nose of the Taube dropped and it plunged downwards.

The observer was alive. Henry followed the falling, stricken craft. The observer was screaming something at him, he pulled out a revolver and blazed at him.

A tongue of flame licked along the Taube's fuselage, a trail of smoke stained the air behind them. The German plane started to gyrate as it fell. Fire played about the observer's cockpit, he beat at it with his hands. The wind whipped it up into an inferno, he clawed at his seat belt as he burned. For one second, standing up in his wrecked machine, he stared at the man who had murdered him, terrible accusation in his eyes, and then he was gone, tumbling to earth in the wake of the blazing aeroplane, his clothes on fire, burning all the way down, leaving a thin trail of smoke in the air.

Henry saw the Taube hit the ground, smashing into a heap of blazing rubbish. The observer vanished into a copse of trees. His hands were shaking uncontrollably, he could barely fly. He set a rough course for his field. He felt an overwhelming need to get ginned.

4

They're All In France

Windstone Castle, September 1915

'Clare rules,' Fish said to Violet, who had just come into the marquee. 'Robert has to wh-whack it into the air. If he can hit the roof he gets a six. We have to catch the ball in our h-hats.'

In a smart yellow dress and a straw hat liberally decorated with silk flowers, Violet observed Robert wearing a black morning coat and striped trousers, standing on one end of a long table holding a small cricket bat in one hand while Freddie prepared to bowl at him with a tennis ball from the other. Various de Clares, similarly clad, were scattered about the table as fielders.

'His bat's been in the wash,' she said. 'It's shrunk.'

'He's had some small ones made from the bat orchard, so we can take them with us,' Fish explained.

Freddie bowled, the tennis ball bounced high off the polished wood and Robert smote it at the ceiling. Baying like hounds, the de Clares ran about, black silk top hats and the ladies' equivalent in their hands. The ball hit the mast and rebounded. With a shriek, Violet tore her hat off and thrust it out as though receiving alms. With a plop it dropped in, swirling round like a ball in a roulette wheel, and she danced about trying to hold it in.

'*How's that?*' she shouted.

Grinning, Robert dropped down, and passed the little bat to Cromwell. 'Well caught, young Vi,' he said.

'Shouldn't you be getting ready to walk solemnly down the aisle?' she demanded.

'I'm terrified just thinking about it,' he confessed. 'That's why I'm playing cricket. Cricket can soothe just about anything.'

'Why scared?'

'I can't imagine why someone as lovely as Felicity said "yes" in the first place. I keep thinking she'll wake up and realise she's made a dreadful mistake.'

'Fish!' somebody yelled, and the ball came screaming across the marquee. Fish swept at it with his hat as though catching a butterfly. There was a sound like a fly being swatted with a newspaper, and the ball tumbled in the air. Dropping his hat, Freddie caught it.

'Out,' he said firmly.

'Your hat's out, Fish,' said Violet.

Picking it up, Fish saw that it resembled a half-opened tin of beans. 'Oh, dear,' he said. 'I'd b-better g-get some glue.'

'I'll come with you.'

'Don't let him get lost,' Robert called, taking up the bowling. 'He's got the ring. He's keeping it for Charlie.'

'Is he here?'

'Supposed to be, he's got some leave. Henry can't make it.'

'I read about him. He shoots down German aeroplanes.'

'Yes, he's what the French call an "ace". Our side doesn't, we're too stuffy.'

As they left, Freddie and Violet saw Aylmer, the youngest of Earl de Clare's sons, coming the other way in his page's outfit of white silk knickerbockers and a matching velvet surcoat. His expression was sombre. 'I feel a complete fool,' he complained. 'I only hope my chums at school don't get to hear about this.'

'Aylmer, wasn't Henry in your *Boy's Own Paper*?'

'Oh, yes! They had a terrific story about how he took on three Huns at once, and shot down two of them. Look, I must go. Perceval and Godfrey are supposed to be pages too, and I've lost them.'

'Apparently Freddie said Henry didn't recognise himself' Violet commented. 'They made him sound like General Gordon. What rank are you, Fish?'

'Subaltern. Freddie and and I are subalterns, and Robert's a captain. Very grand, but of course he was in the Territorials before. And he's an MP. George is with us, of course. He's the chaplain.'

Early autumn sunshine bathed the castle. In the distance on the pasture were rows of military tents and huts. Various flags were flying.

'I've seen lots of people I know. How did you get them all here?'

'Oh, that was me. Uncle sent me out,' replied Aylmer. 'I had great fun. He let me drive his Benz, I practised a bit on the roads on the estate first and when I'd got the hang of it I drove all over the place. After a bit, of course, word got around that we were recruiting and good chaps just showed up of their own accord.'

'But what about you? N-Nursing. I got your letter. D-Did you get mine? Guy's, isn't it? I thought you were going to Cambridge.'

'I'll go when the war stops,' Violet said quietly. 'We all thought it would be over by now, but it isn't, so I'd better do my bit too. I can't go off and fight like you can, so being a nurse seems to be the only option.' She giggled, suddenly. 'I *could* have a baby out of wedlock. The government doesn't seem to disapprove of it now. The poor girls are "producing the warriors of tomorrow!"'

'Waste of t-time,' said Fish. 'This is the war to end war. Th-There won't b-be another, after this.'

'Let's hope.'

'We're w-winning. You've only g-got to r-read the papers.'

'Do you read the casualty lists?'

'No,' Fish said shortly.

'An awful lot of boys are getting killed.'

'B-But that's what *we're* for! The "New Armies"! Don't you know how many of us there are? W-We're going to march to Berlin. What do y-you want in Berlin, Vi? Shall I bring you back a c-cuckoo clock?'

'That's Switzerland.'

'Bet they've g-got cuckoo clocks too.'

'When do you think you'll all be going out?'

'The battalion? We've got to go to Aldershot before we can qualify for service overseas. Three months' training at company, battalion, brigade and divisional level.'

'You sound just like a veteran,' she said, mocking him gently.

'Well, I *am* a soldier.'

'I know. It seems only yesterday you were a schoolboy, making advances to me outside the copse.'

'Here, I say . . .'

'I know,' Violet smiled. 'It's probably in the blood. I had a great aunt who was exiled as a kind of remittance-lady in Cawnpore. She set herself up as a religious prophetess in an ancient temple out there. The main rites seemed to be making love to her in a variety of exotic ways, the governor made quite a stink about it.'

'My gosh. What happened to her?'

'Died during some particularly exciting ritual. They embalmed her and she's still out there, looking down on it all. She was from the Lewisforth side of the family, of course, and they've always been a bit strange.'

'Ah. And you have Lewisforth blood, do you, Vi?'

'Of course.'

'I wonder if Aunt Hermione has. She's here with that young woman of hers, Miss Proctor. You don't think they . . .'

'Oh, I think so,' Violet said. 'When are you off to Aldershot?'

'Ten days. Robert's just got time to go on honeymoon. He and Felicity are going to sail his cutter down in Devon.'

'What's she like? I don't know her.'

'Very pretty, like a sort of elf. A water sprite. Robert met her when he was sailing down at Exmouth. She was catching lobsters in pots! Her father's Bishop down there.'

'I think I know the one. He wants stipends withdrawn from all incumbents intent on flouting the approved rituals of the 1662 Prayer Book – Popery by the back door, as he sees it. That fat fool Temple asked him if he intended that these clergy should then starve and he replied: yes. Is this Felicity like him?'

'I think so. She's very determined, I think she proposed to Robert rather than the other way round!'

'I *shall* like her. Sensible girl, Robert takes for ever to decide anything. Except when it comes to his beloved cricket.'

'Oh, thanks for reminding me. I've got to get the bats. They're coming out of the chapel to an arch of cricket bats!'

'I wish you didn't have to go so soon. I won't see you.'

'We'll write.'

'Oh, yes.'

Violet studied her nails nonchalantly. 'I'm in the Crecy room,' she said, 'you know the one. Down the Chevaliers corridor. Third on the left.'

'I know the one. Great Aunt J-Jemimah used to live in it, you could hear her singing hymns in the bath. "Abide With Me" and "Greenland's Icy Mountains".'

'I'll be in the bath,' Violet said, looking Fish straight in the eyes. 'At about eleven o'clock tonight.'

'G-Great Aunt J-Jemimah had a w-word for g-girls like you. Sh-She called them h-h-h—'

'Hussies,' Violet finished. 'That's me, a brazen hussy. Blame the war, Fish. The long littleness of life suddenly seems short.'

'The long littleness of life . . . that's jolly good.'

'I've been reading Brooke.'

Below them, a black limousine was sweeping along the great drive. It stopped at the grand steps, and a trim military figure got out.

'Oh, no,' Fish said in disgust. 'Father. What's he doing here? Come on, Vi. Let's get some glue for my hat. Eleven o'clock, you say?'

'I do.'

Brigadier de Clare stared in horror at the uniform on its hanger in the Earl's dressing room. His brother was adjusting a silver tie about his neck. 'What's that?' he gargled.

'My uniform,' Lord de Clare said.

'But it's a major-general's uniform!' he protested.

'That's right. Been trainin' up the battalion.'

'What do you know about it?'

'I was in military intelligence in the Boer War, I would remind you,' Lord de Clare said, with some dignity.

'But, but . . . that means you outrank me.'

Lord de Clare secured his tie with a pearl pin and put on his morning coat. A gleaming black top hat and a pair of yellow chamois gloves lay waiting on his dressing table. 'Of course I outrank you. I am the Earl. You are not.'

Brigadier de Clare ground his teeth at the latest manifestation of an unfeeling fate.

'Glad y'could come, anyway,' Lord de Clare said magnanimously. 'Thought the war might keep you. Your fat French friend with you this time?'

'Legrand? No, he's been degummed.'

'De-what?'

'Degummed. Removed from his command. Sent to Limoge.'

'Oh, ah. I see, Stellenbosched, what?'

'Exactly. Limoge is the French equivalent of Stellenbosch. Where they exile the incompetents, those without proper grit.'

'He seemed bloodthirsty enough, the fat one.'

'Wouldn't press home an attack. His men were stopped short of Hill 432.'

'Hill 432? What's that?'

'It's on the map. Four hundred and thirty-two feet above sea level. Or was. We shelled it a lot in the battle, it's Hill 405 now.'

'Do we need this wretched piece of bombed mud that badly?'

'We cannot afford to give the Boche one inch of territory, Cuthbert. If he takes it, we get it back, whatever the cost.'

'What was the cost?' the Earl asked curiously.

'Legrand lost his officers, I believe. NCOs couldn't keep the troops moving forward. Frogs. Rabble, y'see. Limoged him.'

'Lost his officers . . . all of them? Dear God, this is a nasty war.'

'It is,' his brother agreed. 'Modern weapons, y'see. Legrand's men lost their morale under fire, that's why they didn't take the hill.'

'Legrand's men lost all their officers!'

'High losses are to be expected. Matter of fact, we look for high losses. A commander who doesn't have high losses doesn't have the right stuff. Gets degummed. High losses mean high morale. The Japanese defeated the Russians in Manchuria by taking high losses. They defeated them through offensive spirit, high morale and cold steel. Once you can get the men across the fire zone and into the enemy trenches the battle's won. He doesn't like the bayonet, does Hermann Hun. But it takes high morale to get the men there. Offensive spirit, that's the secret.'

'I see ... that's something I wanted to ask you about, Gervase. The battalion's up to strength. They've trained hard, they know the ropes. Country fellows to a man. All know how to shoot. Good on the march. Patriotic chaps, all ready to do their bit ...'

'Good show,' his brother said approvingly. 'That's what we need for the big push next year.'

'Nothing like a bit of experience to give the men confidence though. To have a few veterans among them, chaps who've been through a battle or two, had their baptism of fire, so to speak. I'd like you to transfer a few regular army NCOs to us. Say a sergeant-major or two, a few sergeants. Could do with one or two officers as well, you know the sort. Pre-war regular army, the old school.'

The soldier pursed his lips, blew on his moustache.

'You know the sort I need,' the Earl urged. 'Regulars. The ones who went out with the BEF last August.'

The other shook his head. 'No, no. Sorry. Can't spare any. You'll have to make do.'

'Blast you!' the Earl exploded. 'Do I have to put on my uniform and *order* you to give me some men?'

'Won't do you any good if you do,' Gervase de Clare said, sulkily.

'And why not, may I ask?'

'Haven't got any.'

'What do you mean, you haven't got any?'

'They're all in France.'

'I know they're all in France. That's why I want you to send some home so I can use them.'

There was silence in the room for a few moments. Through the open window they could hear the high-spirited sounds of the young de Clares playing their impromptu game of cricket.

'They are in France,' Clare repeated heavily. 'Literally. *In* France. They're dead, Cuthbert.'

'Dead? What do y'mean, dead?' the Earl said in bewilderment. 'How can they all be dead?'

His brother shrugged. 'The Marne, Aisne, Ypres, Neuve Chappelle, now Loos. We've used them up, Cuthbert. There aren't any left. Not so you'd notice. Anyhow, listen, I must get on.'

As the Brigadier left, the elderly butler came in bearing a small buff envelope on a silver tray. 'A telegram, my lord.'

'Eh? Oh, thank you, Foskett.'

When he was alone, the Earl opened the telegram. For some time he stood staring at the strips of black type. Then he stuffed it in his pocket and went over to the window. He saw Fish and Violet passing below, he leaned out. 'Fish! Fish, m'boy.'

'Yes, sir?' Fish said, looking up.

'Charlie can't make it. Just got a telegram.'

'Oh, I'm sorry to hear that.'

'Stand in for him, there's a good fella.'

As the Brigadier came down the grand stairs a tall woman, suitably dressed for the wedding of an heir to an earldom, approached decisively from a corner of the huge hall, where ostensibly she had been admiring a portrait of the fourteenth Earl. 'Ah, Gervase,' she said, with a slight Boston accent that twenty years of exposure to the English ruling class had failed to eradicate, 'I heard that you were to be here.'

'Ah, Connie,' de Clare replied, eyeing his wife warily. Having not seen each other for months they embraced each other's elbows and aimed a kiss at the air near each other's cheek. 'Walk me round in the fresh air,' she commanded. 'Are you a general yet? I can never decipher these badges of rank.'

'Not yet,' de Clare said grimly. 'I am taking up an appointment with XII Corps shortly – getting back to field command – so my overdue promotion should not be long delayed.'

They went out into the sunshine. In the bailey the marquee stood like a moored galleon, all sails set. They began to walk round the gardens.

'The beds are rather untidy this year,' Lady Constance observed.

'Crowbotham and the others have joined the Yeomanry,' de Clare explained. 'Cuthbert is making do with older men.'

'This Yeomanry seems to be absorbing a large number of the people who live here.'

'Local "pals" battalion.' All volunteers. Best sort. Tenant farmers, peasants, people from the land. None of your poor blood town-bred rubbish.'

'The servants, too.'

'Oh, yes. Cuthbert called them all together and said he wouldn't

stand in the way of anyone who wanted to join. The castle itself is
sending a fine contingent. Gamekeepers, footmen, butler, gardeners,
huntsmen, grooms. Very fine.'

'You had better win this war soon, else English country life will
come to a complete standstill.'

'We shall win, have no fear of that. Our morale, our sense of
Christian purpose is greater than the Hun.'

'Is it his weaker morale and Christian purpose that is causing these
fearful casualty lists?'

'Don't be so damned stupid, Connie,' de Clare snapped. 'What do
you know of soldiering? And the Hun isn't a Christian, anyway.'

'I can read,' she said flatly. 'I read rousing tales of heroism in the
papers, tales – no doubt true – of men fighting with great courage for
King and country. And a few pages on, list upon list of the dead.'

'We are a great empire, Connie. Millions of men have flocked
to the flag to fight, as you say, for King and country. Millions
of men, because we rule hundreds of millions. Modern war is a
fearful thing, but our men are equal to it. We shall overcome for
God, King and country just as our forefathers did at Malplaquet, at
Trafalgar, at Waterloo. We are the British Empire, we became great
by winning wars.'

'I don't doubt you will win this one. But it seems to be taking a
lot of lives.'

'The offensive does. It succeeds by weight of attack – by men of
high morale, of course, as I have said – but sufficient weight of men
will go through anything. Once through the fireswept zone, the moral
force of battle asserts itself, the *sentiment du fer*, as the French say.
Moral force, as Napoleon knew, predominates over the physical at a
ratio of three to one. Once our trained men are into the Hun trenches
it's all over for him.'

'At what cost though? Take this battalion of Windstone Yeomanry,
all these brave volunteers from the castle and its lands. How many
do you think will be killed?'

'That doesn't even occur to them! They just want to get out to
France and get stuck into the Hun!'

'I know,' she said patiently. 'I asked how many would die.'

'I'm not God. I don't know how long the war will last.'

'It was supposed to be over by Christmas last. Shall we say that it
might take as long to be won?'

'Hm. Very well. Let us say Christmas 1916.'

'You senior officers must make predictions as to casualty rates in
order to have fresh units trained to replace them.'

'We do.'

'So how many left, by Christmas 1916?'

'Half?'

'Half alive,' Constance said steadily.

'Half alive, half dead. Yes.'

'And wounded. I saw some boys in Piccadilly the other day, their faces fearfully mutilated.'

'Shrapnel. Yes. Nasty.'

Lady de Clare stopped in her perambulation about the garden in which weeds and seed-blown flowers mingled with fresh blooms.

'My son Cromwell is training with this battalion of soldiers,' she said clearly.

'Cromwell? Yes, yes, I know.'

'I will not have my son sent into battle to be slaughtered or maimed.'

'He must take his chance like the others,' de Clare said, sounding puzzled. 'He's raring to go, I know that. Wrote to me.'

His wife had a face in which young plastic good looks had somehow metamorphosed into rigid determination, like setting concrete. Her expression now was one on which one might sharpen a blade.

'He shall not go,' she said slowly, one word at a time. 'Do you hear me? Cromwell is not going to the front.'

'He has to. He is an officer of the King, he must do as he is ordered. And the Windstone Yeomanry is, I assure you, headed for the front.'

'He will not be with it.'

'Constance, we are at war. A man of his breeding cannot evade it. Should he attempt to do so by staying out of uniform he will be cut by society, his name a hissing and a byword for cowardice. He will never live it down. If he attempts to evade combat whilst in uniform – as he is today – then he will be court-martialled. Found guilty, he will be shot. It is as simple as that.'

'I understand that. It is a question, therefore, of keeping him away from the fighting.'

A faint frown had appeared between the Brigadier's eyebrows. 'Before we go on – if we must – I would point out to you that you have two sons, both of whom are in the Yeomanry, both destined for the front.'

'I am not talking of Fish,' she said in a low voice. 'Fish was an accident. An accident that should not have happened. Let Fish go for both of them. You have always wanted him dead anyhow. Just give me Cromwell.'

De Clare opened his mouth to speak, and his wife forestalled him. 'Don't tell me it cannot be done,' she said quickly. 'Did you not assist the Prince to go on to the staff of Sir John French? Yes, you did. Now tell me, will he ever get close to the fighting?'

'No. The King has forbidden it.'

'Then get Cromwell on to the staff. He is intelligent, certainly more educated than the Prince, I am sure he can aid the war effort just as much as though he were to get massacred in one of your offensives.' She paused, picking her words. 'We don't love each other, you and I. You married me for my money, I you for position. We have both had plenty of time to consider whether we received a bargain in so doing. I think we did. I have helped your career. It cannot have done you any harm to be able to lend many thousands of pounds – my pounds – to your senior officer to pay off his gambling debts and thus stave off bankruptcy and ruin. Promotion in your army is a personal thing, is it not? It cannot have been any coincidence that you rose in rank to colonel shortly afterwards. As for me, yes. I am happy with my bargain. I have Cromwell. With me at his side he can scale the heights of society. He shall never lack.

'I am willing to continue funding your career, but only on the condition that my Cromwell is safe. Not one hair on his head must be harmed. See to it.'

A muffled bang rattled the windows nearby. Looking up they saw a cloud of purple smoke rising up from a distant copse.

'What . . .'

They could see Fish standing on the steps with Violet. They were laughing about something.

'Fish!' de Clare roared. 'What the hell is that?'

Fish came down. 'It's Freddie and Tim,' he said. 'They've been preparing a surprise for Robert and Felicity, when they drive off for their honeymoon. It's just a bit of fun. They learned how to do it all when they went off for their bombing course. They're our bombing officers.'

'What is a bombing officer, Fish?' Constance de Clare asked.

Fish looked at his mother in surprise.

'No, really, I want to know.'

'Well, you see, Mother, we don't have enough proper grenades – the only ones available are from the Crimean War – so Freddie and Tim have been taught how to make them. You take an army jam tin and put some TNT inside. You fill the tin with sharp stones or bits of flint, then you put a detonator with fuse attached into the gun cotton. When you're ready, you light the fuse.'

'Ready for what?'

'Germans. You do it when you have a trench full of Germans. You light the fuse and chuck the bomb at them. Freddie's shown me how to do it. We practised on a dead sheep we found, just to see.'

'And what did you see?'

'Oh, it's the works. Rips it to bits. Bits of sheep everywhere. Look, I must go, Charlie can't make it after all. I'm best man. The guests are arriving.'

They watched Fish run off to join Violet, and both headed purposefully towards the chapel.

'Charlie can't make it? Did you hear that Gervase? Maud will be quite undone. You'll do as I ask.'

The castle was shrouded in dusk. From windows great and arrow-slits narrow, white orange and golden light glowed. Robert had changed into his uniform, Felicity into a yellow silk frock. Standing on the front sheps, the heir to Windstone had to be seen to wear uniform. Beautiful and radiant, Felicity threw her posy of flowers into the waiting crowd of people about the steps, laughing as she did so.

Unaware, Hermione felt something land on her head, and caught it as it fell.

'There you are, Hermione!' the dowager Gwendolyn roared. 'You're to be made a woman at last!'

'Oh, dear!' she said, realising what she had caught. 'I don't think so, dear. Here, Violet, you have it.'

The couple descended the steps to the waiting Napier. In the darkness, one either side of the long elm drive, Freddie and Tim waited, both mounted on bicycles, both armed with ready-lit slow matches. A burst of cheering announced the departure of the couple.

'Now, Tim!' Freddie called. Both lit the first fuse, and then pedalled madly down towards the Bosworth Gates. Every fifty yards they stopped, lighting another. As the Napier swept into the drive, there was a cannonade each side. Gold, scarlet and green rain blossomed in the sky, painting the castle like a rainbow. One after the other, great roman candles and rocketry drew pictures in the air. The Napier turned out of the gates with Freddie and Tim waving and panting and grinning, and iridescent jewels showered down from above on the golden pair.

The Chevaliers corridor was dark, illuminated only by the moonlight on the lake of the Abbey, coming through the great casement at the end. The bones of the sunken monastery still poked up through the water, ruined choirs and fallen roofs now home to the cormorant and the shag. The de Clares had discovered the benefits of the Anglican faith at around the same time as Henry VIII.

Fish padded silently along. The third door on the left opened without a sound, he slipped inside. The darkness smelled of warm perfume, tinged with a faint golden aura from the bathroom. He went towards it and tripped over a chair.

'Sorry, Fish,' Violet called, from the golden glow. 'I put my clothes on that. You all right?'

'Stubbed a toe, that's all.'

He put his head round the door. Violet was lying full length in the bath, her hair tied up with a yellow silk ribbon. Only her head was visible above a sheet of scented white bubbles.

'I was going to just lie here naked,' she said, 'but then I got shy. So you've got me and bubbles.'

'Y-You look t-terrific to me, Vi.'

'Thank you, Fish,' she said gravely. 'You look pretty good too. Come and join me.' Fish took off his dressing gown and put it over a chair. 'Naughty boy, Fish. You've nothing on underneath.'

'This is my c-costume for wh-when I'm invited to b-bathing parties by young w-women,' he said, slipping into the warm water. Violet sat up to give him room, and scented foam slid slowly down her body.

'I s-say, you're jolly p-pretty, Vi.'

'I know. It's nice, isn't it?'

'What are you doing with your foot?'

'What are you doing with yours? I say, Fish, it's moving.'

'Yes, it does.'

'I know, it's just the first time I've had the use of one. My gosh, Fish. This is better than opening parcels at Christmas.'

They leaned forward to each other, kneeling in the water, kissing and embracing each other, their hands running over their slippery bodies, young and strong.

'I say, Fish,' Violet said in a shaky voice. 'I think we'd better go and lie down on the bed. One of us is going to get drowned if we stay here.'

There was a huge towel lying ready at the side, they jumped out, dripping and giggling, and wrapped it about the pair of them. They shuffled through to the bedroom, and clambered in a heap on the bed. The towel heaved and shook like a collapsed tent full of boy scouts.

One of Violet's feet stuck out from under it, she pushed it up against one of the posts.

'I do love you, Fish,' she gasped.

'I love you. Oh, I do.'

The Earl stood alone in his room, still in his finery. The mask he had worn all day finally gave way, and his face became suffused with a terrible grief. He pulled out the telegram, and read it one last time, before he went to his wife.

> Deeply regret to inform you your son Captain Charles de Clare killed in action.

Holding it in his hand, he went out, and down the corridor to Maud's rooms.

The Stuart wing was empty, the floor creaked as Hermione stepped inside. The de Clares had performed the unusual feat of helping to make a king shorter by a head, and afterwards bringing his son back to reign from exile. The de Clares believed in liberty, which they had found under neither Cromwell nor King Charles' brother James, which was why they had helped remove him too, bringing in William of Orange in his place. The de Clares, like the country, had done well out of the great war that followed. The de Clares had been on the high tightrope for a very long time – little ever affected their fortunes except for the better.

Hermione went down the corridor, the white moonlight flooding through the windows. King Charles II had enjoyed staying with the de Clares, as had King William. But royalty came and went, the de Clares were there for ever.

Hermione's thin form was covered in the uniform of a Grenadier. It had belonged to one of the de Clares at Waterloo and had hung in one of the great storerooms of clothes for decades. She had found it, taken it from its cover and put it on. She moved stealthily down the corridor. A door to her left was ajar. She thrust it open, but only the bare bones of a bed and swept boards were inside. As she went out the ceiling creaked.

'I know you're there!' she called and above, something moved. Increasing her pace, she went to the foot of the stair. Looking up, she saw somewthing white slipping away through the banisters. A dress.

A riding crop was in her hand, she slapped it suddenly against the wall, and echoes ricocheted through the silent rooms. 'I'm coming to get you!'

She ran up the stairs in a thunder of noise, stood at the head, looking this way and that along the empty moonlit corridors. Intently, she began to walk down, the way she had seen the dress go, her booted feet marking her progress.

A door, ajar. She pushed it open; in the moonlight a small tableau of Sheraton furniture stood ready for drinks, but nobody was imbibing.

A little further. A blank wall, one final door. 'I know you're there . . .'

The door moved silently, inside it was dark, the moonlight lining the edges of the drawn curtains. She went inside, striking air with her whip.

Was that a pale shadow against the wall?

She struck out again, found something soft, the rasp of silk under the crop. A female voice squealed.

'Got you!' Hermione jumped forward, dropping the whip, seizing her, feeling her body jump with anticipation and released tension. The two struggled across the room in a tangle of uniform and dress, tripped and fell onto the bed. Hermione reached out and yanked back the curtain. The moonlight splashed onto the form of her lover on the bed. The soldier towered over her for a second, then fell upon her, tearing off her clothing until it lay pooled like cream all about her, her ceremonial uniform also crumpled up in a heap.

They lay in a tangle of limbs, Hermione extracted herself from between the girl's thighs, her heart pounding, her breath as though she had been running the mile. She reached out and found the uniform, took out a packet of Red Hussars, and lit two – the wheel of her lighter rasped against the flint, and the room was briefly illuminated with yellow flame. Hermione smoked working-men's tobacco. They lay contentedly puffing, tobacco smoke slowly filling the room. In the silence, they became aware of a faint sound coming through the half-open window.

'What's that?' said Proctor. 'It sounds like someone crying.'

Hermione listened. 'Oh, God. It's Maud,' she said softly. She sat up, began to tug her clothes on. 'Somebody's dead,' she said abruptly, with a sudden prescience.

'It's Charlie. It must be Charlie.'

5

Deo Gratias

St Goderick's College

It was said that the cold, ugly, dark and draughty brick barn had been designed by the same architect that had built the prison at the other end of the town. The one was for locking up criminals, the other for incarcerating boys.

In the line that stood shivering in the huge stairwell at the centre of the house, Godfrey de Clare knew that all his white-faced companions believed it. If there was a difference, it was that the gaol was run by warders from a book of regulations, St Goderick's Junior House was run by its senior inmates by rules they made up themselves, and coated with an impenetrable varnish of tradition that none dared challenge.

The young boys in their line, shivering in thin hockey shorts and shirts, were the new year's intake. Those of the two years' above them hung over the railed landing, howling joyous threats and abuse, the persecuted become persecutors. Godfrey was possessed of an advantage over most of his new companions in that he knew the nature of the ritual about to take place, since his brother Perceval, now in Senior house, had endured it before him, and had warned him of the unwritten rules contained within it. Godfrey knew what was to happen. He even knew the purpose of the enormous wicker wastepaper basket that dangled from a rope in the middle of the stair well.

The yelling and abuse that howled down on them, accompanied by a thin haze of spittle, suddenly stopped as the doors to the great hall crashed back. Five prefects stood staring at them with what appeared to be contempt and loathing. They wore black blazers marked with the red cross of St Goderick's and held in their hands thin bamboo canes, the mark of their authority.

With a stamp of boots on the bare floorboards they marched in. They went behind the new boys as the older ones on the landing looked down in gleeful anticipation. Godfrey was waiting for it, he stood completely still as the prefects went behind him, slashing at random at the posteriors of the young boys.

Somebody squealed in sudden, terrified shock. There was a collective snarl of pleasure from above as the prefects fell on the boy, dragging him out in front of the others. One appeared to be in charge, a burly, athletic youth of about seventeen.

'Who are you?' he shouted.

'W-W-Worsley, please,' stuttered the boy, small and puny, wearing glasses, through which he goggled in terror at his tormentor.

'You're a snivelling little weed, Worsley!'

'Weed, weed,' they roared.

'Bend him over!'

They shoved his head down between his knees and thrashed him. When they jerked him up, tears of pain and humiliation were running down his cheeks, but he had bitten his lips to avoid crying out.

'Thank God!' the prefect screamed.

'Th-Thank you, G-God!'

'*Deo Gratias*, weed!'

'*D-Deo Gratias*!' Worsley squeaked, and they kicked him back into the line.

'Right, scum. I'm Starnley, I'm head of house. You do what I say. We don't like wets at St Goderick's. We toughen up wets here. You all look wet to me.' He looked up and down the line of some twelve boys. 'We want a song. We want you to sing us a song,' he said, and the boys on the landing all yelled their approval. Starnley pulled a short list from his pocket and called out the first name.

'De Clare,' he said, and Godfrey stepped out. Starnley tapped the long cast-iron radiator that ran along one edge of the stairwell with his cane. 'Crawl,' ordered Starnley, 'from one end to the other, and sing us a song.'

'Yes, Starnley.'

Grinning, anticipatory faces looked down on Godfrey, but he disappointed them, because he knew.

'Oh Heavenly Word, Eternal Light,' Godfrey sang out, as loud as he could, and climbed on to the radiator. It was fearsomely, sizzlingly hot. He scrambled along it as they yelled down, and sang: 'Our hearts enlighten from above,' he howled out, 'And kindle with Thine own true love . . .'

He came to the other end and got off, still singing. 'Praise, honour, might, and glory be, From age to age eternally.'

Starnley slashed across his buttocks and let him go back to the line. 'Davis!'

Another small boy scurried out, and Godfrey stood in silence, feeling the blisters throb as they formed on the insides of his arms, his legs, his stomach.

It may have been that the others had seen from Godfrey how to do it. Each and every one managed to crawl along the boiling radiator, singing at the tops of their voices, even small, spindly Worsley, who went last of all. Starnley slashed him across the bottom discontentedly as he came off, and he went back into line.

It was a mood that seemed to be shared by the entire audience. They had come for a circus, a spectacle; they had not got what they wanted. As the other prefects scowled at them, Starnley prowled down the line. Godfrey stood as still as he was able. The prefect passed him by, and stopped next to Worsley. He leaned forward, and smiled wolfishly.

'You're trembling, Worsley,' he said conversationally.

'I'm n-not, Starnley,' Worsley said bravely. 'H-Honest.'

'He's shaking like a jelly!' Starnley screamed, and they all roared. *Basketim, Basketim, Basketim!*

They poured down the stairs like a tidal wave and stuffed Worsley head first into the huge waste-paper basket, half filled with rubbish. They yanked on the rope and he shot up into the air, thirty feet up to the level of the top landing.

They shoved the basket from one side to the other, faster and faster, the wicker cage with its prisoner lurching and bouncing over the void. Worsley shrieked in terror, his nerve completely broken, and they howled with joy.

When they let him down, the boy was shaking so badly he could barely stand. They tore off his hockey shorts and coated his bottom with boot polish. Then Starnley stood him up in front of the line of prefects. 'Well?' he demanded menacingly.

'*Deo Gratias*, Starnley,' whispered Worsley.

6

God Wouldn't do it, Otherwise

Ploegsteert Wood, Ypres Salient, April 1916

Robert, in his Captain's uniform, set up an ammunition box on the firestep outside his dug-out, brought out a leather writing case, his fountain pen and shooting stick, set up the latter and in the pleasant spring sunshine, sat and began to write.

> My darling Flick,
>   I am just off watch, Sergeant Furzegrove has brought me a tin mug of strong tea and I am settling down to my favourite activity out here, which is to write to the person I love most in the world. If I cannot be with you in person I can be in spirit! I have your photograph next to me in my dug-out where I can see it at any time. I am afraid that we have had our first casualty since arriving in the sector. George's brother Tim went out on patrol last night. There was a bout of machine-gun fire and he didn't come back. I had to tell George about 3 a.m. He just went very quiet, and then said prayers for his soul. George is a rock. He lives with us in the line. He calls his dug-out 'The Vicarage'. When he first put up his sign two of the men came by and said, 'Blimey! A bleedin' Vicarage!' George poked his head out and said, 'Yes! And here's the bleeding Vicar!' He gave them some Black Cat cigarettes, of which he has an inexhaustible supply, and they were well pleased.
>   There is an aroma of Black Cat cigarettes floating about, in fact. The men find tremendous comfort in nicotine, it even helps with the shelling. That and the letters, which we all live for. I have been on censor duty, which is somewhat embarrassing – one is a gentleman, and not used to the act of reading other people's letters – but also, I am finding, a most valuable experience, as it provides me with such an

insight and knowledge of the poorer classes. They write with simplicity, humour, steadfastness and sentimentality, but also with humility – it gives me, their commanding officer, renewed confidence. When I return to the Commons after the War I feel I shall be a different man. The old days of class consciousness will be over.

I must mention, in fact, a letter I read from Corporal Simkins to his wife – you remember Simkins, head groom at the castle. Always rather taciturn – although Uncle likes him, which is always a good sign – and very good with horses. But you should see into his heart! A passionate fellow! The letter recalled details which would not, I assure you, be allowed to be published in a novel, the last time he and his young wife were in bed together! I do not know how I shall be able to address Mrs Simkins when I next meet her, knowing her and her anatomy as personally as I now do! He says he misses – after his young wife – beer and her steak and kidney pudding, sends his assurance that he is in the pink and hope she is too, promises her a *pickelhaube* when he can get near enough to a German to get one, and asks for some socks, lavatory paper and her damson jam, since the army apple and plum is, he says – quite rightly – inedible. The wood has been christened Plugstreet, by the way. The troops refuse to become Frenchified, or Belgified. What's funny is that when the Huns indulge in a brief hate and lob a few shells over, it goes 'Whizz . . . bang . . . cuckoo' – the birds sing all the time, in the middle of a war! The nightingales sing when the machine guns are firing in the night. I know which I prefer.

The boys are all well. Freddie is terrific. A born fighter. Fish is proving a grand soldier, despite his stammer – the best sort. I think anywhere for him is better than being with his ghastly parents. What a pair! I feel sorry for Cromwell with that vulture of a mother. He was plucked from us before we got up to the line, he's somewhere on the staff. Everybody could see the hand of Lady Constance working through the Brigadier. Poor Cromwell, the icy claw of his mother closes about his testicles by the year, soon there will be nothing left. Fish was very embarrassed, and has become rather reckless in trying to compensate for the smirch upon the fraternal honour. I'm going to have a word with him – I don't want him having to make up for his horrid mother with some nasty wound or even worse.

Darling, darling Flick, I do love you so. I cannot wait to have our children. It will be wonderful to have the castle alive with young voices.

I shall go now . . .

He was interrupted by the sound of someone running up the trench, and of Fish's voice calling: 'Rob! Rob!'

He quickly put his head out. 'What is it?' he asked quickly.

'It's Tim!' Fish gasped. 'We've seen him. He's crawling in. Looks like he's hit in the thigh, but he's pulling himself across no-man's land.'

They ran down the trench towards the look-out post. Freddie was there, and George. They passed Robert a periscope, and he peered out through it. The no-man's land on their sector was grassy and largely unshelled. Looking through the little square tube of mirrors he could see the German lines opposite, edged by breastworks and protected by barbed-wire. There were some stumpy trees, what was left of a copse. Nothing moved.

'Over there,' Freddie hissed, 'coming down the little ridge.'

'Got him,' said Robert. Through the glass he could see the image of a man, crawling towards him, pulling with his hands, dragging one leg. He had lost his hat. He could see Tim clearly. He was about fifty feet away.

'I'll g-go out and help him in.'

'No, wait,' Robert ordered. 'In daylight? Jerry'd get you before you were half way over the wire. Quick, someone bring a rope, and a can of bully.'

They lashed the rope round the tin, and with an expert cricketer's action, Robert lobbed it over their own breastworks. It fell just in front of the wounded man, and they saw him grab hold.

'Pull him in, nice and steady.' They began to drag him across the ground.

'Hold on, Tim!' George urged. 'Nearly there!'

As he came down the thin lane cut in the wire, George stood up, ready to help his brother in. There was a thud, like a pick-axe hitting through sand, a crack like a branch snapping. George jerked back, his face suddenly covered in gore, falling to the side of the trench.

'George!'

He clawed at his face, trying to clear the blood and brains from his eyes. 'Not me!' he gasped. 'Not me! I'm not hit.'

They turned, and Tim lay still on the grassy ground. His face rested on the dirt like a discarded mask, the back of his head blown clear away.

'Sniper,' Freddie said grimly. Stretcher-bearers had taken the dead man away to the rear, and George had gone with him. The three officers had been joined by Hopcroft, the former head gamekeeper, and Furzegrove, the poacher.

'Look,' Freddie said. He pointed to the splash of blood on the trench side, turning a dark brownish red. 'Line that up with where Tim was hit. What can you see?'

Robert peered through the periscope. 'A tree,' he said.

'A hollow tree?' said Fish.

'I think so. Look. I've got an aerial photo of our sector here. Take a look. There's a slight shadow on the ground by that tree.'

They all peered down at the large black-and-white photograph, and Hopcroft, the former head gamekeeper ran a thick finger along a faint shadow. 'There be a trench running up towards it, Mr Robert. Covered over with branches, I'd say, perhaps some sacking.'

'Like a gamekeeper's pit,' said Furzegrove, and the two old rivals smiled.

'I think you're right,' said Robert.

'Be like a hide, sir,' said Furzegrove. 'He be firing from inside cover, through a little tiny hole in some sacking, more'n likely. Tree'll hold any steam or smoke from gun if weather be cold or sweaty; be in shadow, so there be no glint on his sight. He be a countryman, I'd say.'

'So would I. Well, gamekeepers have ways of dealing with poachers.'

'Listen,' said Robert, 'word's come down from Division. They want a raid. Want us to capture a German for them to talk to. What do you say? Let's get the sniper.'

'My feelings exactly. I'd say he gets into position before dawn. Well, so will we,' said Freddie. 'What do you say to this? I'll go out with Sergeant-Major Hopcroft. I shall break into the tunnel and be waiting in the tree when the sniper comes to do his work. The Sergeant-Major will replace the covering so that he does not suspect. I shall bludgeon him as he come in, and then I and Hopcroft will pull him out into the long grass. Fish and Sergeant Furzegrove will take up a forward position and help us pull him in. You will be here with a Stokes mortar ranged on their trench.'

'Good. I want that swine, Freddie. Dirty trick, shooting poor Tim like that.'

'I've b-been thinking of s-something else,' said Fish, 'once w-we heard of the r-raid being ordered. If w-we raid them they'll almost c-certainly have to raid us back, especially now if we s-steal their sniper. They'll do it at night. Be m-murder going out there in daylight. But if we knew they were coming, we could catch them out in the open. So on our way out, we're going to set up a trip wire system, about fifty yards from our line. Sergeant-Major Hopcroft had the idea.'

'Be an old gamekeeper's trick, sir,' Hopcroft said to Robert. 'There being a deal of land to be watching when a poacher be about. Set alarm guns. Put one by a footpath or a ride, and stretch a wire across it high enough to be avoided by a fox or a hare. A poacher come along, he sets it off, and you know he's out there. There be variations on this, like the double gun, which goes off fifteen seconds after the first, and the counter-weighted trigger, in case you get clever customers like Sergeant Furzegrove here cutting your wire, but that be the theory of it.'

'We're going to p-plant Verey flares out there. Different colours,' said Fish. 'Each colour denotes a zone, we'll call them Piccadilly, Haymarket, Oxford and Regent.

'The colour of flare will show us where the Hun is. Then we cut him down with grenades and machine-gun fire. I've got a big box of these new Mills bombs. Just like a cricket ball, and any one of us can throw a cricket ball fifty yards.'

'Very good,' said Robert. 'Let's do it.'

The long grass was uncut close to the wire. Hopcroft led Freddie the final fifty yards to the tree, the two men crawling on their bellies. As they went, they pushed the grass to each side, flattening it so they made a path. If they had to leave in daylight, the waving grasses would not give them away. Fish and Furzegrove were at the mid point of no-man's land, in a dry shell hole. Behind them they had marked the gap in the line of flares they had laid on their way through.

Silently, moving with the care required to stalk deer, the two countrymen made their way to the tree, poking dark against the faint starlit sky. Their faces were blacked up with burnt cork, they were armed with coshes, knives, pistols and Mills bombs.

The German lines were about thirty yards away behind the hedge of wire. It was very quiet. Once or twice they heard a man cough further down the line. A sentry. Amidst the smell of crushed grass and disturbed soil Freddie suddenly smelled tobacco smoke. Lying flat on his stomach, inching along, he was afflicted for the first time by a most tremendous desire for a cigarette.

Hopcroft led the way to the rear of the tree. He delved with his hands, Freddie heard the rustling of sacking. Very carefully, the gamekeeper made a hole in the light roof that covered the trench, and Freddie lowered himself into it, feet first. Crouching down, he was below the level of the roof. It was completely dark. He reached up, and silently squeezed Hopcroft's hand, then moved into the pitch black of the tunnel, his hands feeling the sides, hearing Hopcroft gently rearranging the cover behind him. Somehow, the scent of tobacco was still in his nostrils and he found himself unable to stop thinking about it. He had smoked one cigarette in his life, a Woodbine, at school, and had greatly disliked it. Now he craved one.

There. His slowly waving hands brushed something in front of him. In the total silence he could hear the thumping of his heart, the breath rushing through the hairs of his nose. He could see nothing.

His hands found flat slats of wood, a ladder. In slow-motion, he rested a foot on a tread, and began to climb. It was a short lift up. Feeling with his hands, he found a flat base of concrete and a hollow metal shell all about him. He was inside the tree. Standing up, feeling gently about him, he worked out that the tree was equipped with a seat, some five feet up, a rest for a rifle, with sacking hiding the small aperture, just as Furzegrove had suggested. Looking up, he could see that the hollow trunk was masked with more sacking, although there was a faint light of stars coming through it.

The ladder that had brought him up led into the centre of the tree. He squatted down behind it, and waited. His eyes so adapted to the dark that he could dimly make out the interior of the tree in the faint phosphorescent glow of his wrist-watch. He waited, patiently, as he had done so often for flighting duck or roosting pigeon. He had a leather-covered, lead-filled cosh in one hand, held by a strap about his wrist, an antler-handled gralloching knife in the other, razor sharp.

What was that? Tobacco. He could smell it.

There. A faint scuffling. A rabbit, coming down the warren, its nose twitching. The soft patter of boots, of a man crouching down as he came down his familiar ways in the dark. The brushing of a hand on the tunnel wall. A faint red glow from below, a man pulling on the last fragment of cigarette, a butt-end nipped between the nails of finger and thumb. A long, drawn-out exhalation. Freddie smelled the tobacco swirling about him.

A clearing of a throat, very soft, a man feeling that he was getting into enemy territory. A spit. The cautious placing of a boot, the creak of a tread taking the strain. Freddie sensed a kind of darkness pushing up from the tunnel into the tree, smelled the man's breath, heard him grunt softly as he pulled himself up. He lashed out with his cosh, smacking into something with a noise like hitting a sandbag.

He grabbed onto him, feeling rough serge under his fingers and, as he dragged him further in, the German began to snore, a rattling sound in the back of the throat.

Freddie paused for a second, the breath tight in his chest, his heart thudding in his ears. Then he lowered himself down into the tunnel, his boots creaking on the steps.

'*Hans?*' A hoarse, guttural whisper from inside the tunnel. Freddie bit his tongue in the effort not to shout out.

'*Was ist los?*'

He could smell him. Sausage, and bread. Tobacco. He'd had a smoke to steady his nerves.

He was close.

Freddie slashed the air with his knife, felt it rip into something. Hot blood splattered his hand, a man grunted in sudden pain and horror. Freddie grabbed him, they staggered inside the tunnel, Freddie stabbed him again, and again, in a frenzy of fear, until the man slumped against the side, and slid to the floor.

The roof moved. He could see faint light, smell fresh air. Hopcroft. Quickly, he reached up inside the trunk and dragged down the man he had knocked unconscious. Reaching down into the tunnel, Hopcroft helped pull him up. Together, they dragged him down the little lane they had made in the grass. The German lines were still quiet. Above them the stars had gone out; in the west, the sky was lightening to a faint cinnamon-grey. So nearly back to safety, Freddie peered up anxiously, looking for the arc of sparks above him that would signify the bursting of a star-shell.

Fish and Furzegrove were waiting at the shell-hole, they took on the burden. Near the wire, they called the password, heard Robert reply. They crawled the last fifteen yards through the lane cut in their own wire, where Tim had died, rolled over the parapet of sandbags, fell down into the dog's-tooth of a trench, and lay gasping on the duck-boards. They picked themselves up just in time to avoid Fish and Furzegrove falling on top of them with the captive.

Fish shone his torch down onto the German, and they all stood looking at him, the first they had seen. A pair of binoculars was about his neck, much muddied and stuffed with grass from his journey across no-man's land.

'Observer,' said Robert.

'Mr Frederick got the sniper in the trench,' said Hopcroft.

Freddie turned him over, searched him with urgent hands, filthy with a cake of mud and gore. 'For God's sake, the bastard's got some gaspers somewhere,' he muttered. He found them in a breast pocket, a thin card packet. He shook one out, put it in his mouth. 'A light,' he mumbled. 'How do I light it?'

A match flared in Furzegrove's cupped palm, he bent and dipped the cigarette into the flame. Wonderful, soothing tobacco filled Freddie's head with tranquilising dizziness.

'You d-don't smoke.'

Freddie looked back to an age when he didn't smoke. It seemed a very long time ago. He watched himself, not smoking, like a man looking down from a high mountain top. 'Yes, I do,' he said.

The German moaned, and moved on the ground. He was suddenly sick.

'Take him to Division,' said Freddie, turning away. 'He's what they wanted.'

Fish was orderly officer. The sector was quiet, they had heard a certain amount of shouting from the other side of the line about an hour after dawn, and they had surmised that the Germans had found the dead sniper at the bottom of the ladder. Since then it had been quiet.

Lunch had come and gone – tins of beef stew, biscuit and mugs of tea. With the sector quiet the rations were coming up as they were meant to in regulations. Fish had gone down the line, checking fields of fire, the condition of the trenches and stores. Furzegrove had detailed jobs to the men. The fire trench closest to the enemy was manned by sentries every twenty-five yards. Another third of the men had gone back for rations. The last third was resting. This meant doing jobs: digging, filling sandbags, carrying ammunition, draining water, resetting duck-boards, and at night, strengthening the wire. A trench was voracious, it had a life of its own, it consumed things – wood, sand, ammunition, men.

Still, it was quiet, and it was not wet, nor cold. The wet and the cold wore them all down, like tramps sleeping rough, but on a warm April day it approached the level of camping out. From the support line, Fish could hear the excited voices of some of the soldiers organising a rat hunt. Sergeant Furzegrove had brought ferrets to France with him and the battalion now had a pack of them, the Windstone ferrets. The rats enjoyed the trenches, with its scattered food and dead men to eat. Those men still living returned the compliment with ferocious ferrets and clubs, and organised hunts, betting on the result.

From time to time, Fish inspected the opposing lines with a periscope. It was quiet. Nothing moved. Primroses were growing amidst the hedge of wire; he wished he could go and pick some, push his nose deep into a posy of them and smell something other than his own grime. The orchards and meadows of the castle would now be a patchwork of wild flowers, a Persian carpet of green and yellow and red and blue.

He wished he could see Violet. Maybe there would be a letter from her.

As he was thinking this, a man came round the edge of the dog's-tooth. It was Corporal Simkins. He grinned cheerily at Fish.

'Hallo, Simkins. Get the H-Hun to Division all right?'

'Yes, thank you, sir. Well pleased with him, they was. Gave me a meal and let me join in with some chaps what was going to the bath house. Lovely, it was. I took that 'uns belt and 'is cap, didn't think he'd be wanting them. Swapped the cap for a new Elinor Glyn with some quartermaster bloke, real good read it is, sir. This is 'is belt. Thought I'd send it to the wife. What's it mean, 'ere, sir?'

'*Gott Mit Uns.* God With Us.'

'Which God'd that be, sir? Be Satan, I suppose.'

'I suppose . . .'

Both Fish and the corporal suddenly stiffened in alarm. They looked up at the sky, anxiously.

Whoof, whoof, whoof.

'Mortar!' Fish screamed, and all along the line men scanned the sky in sudden terror. The German trench mortar was a 200lb canister like a huge rum jar full of marzipan-smelling paste. It blew a hole in the ground the size of a rich man's living room.

Whoof whoof whoof.

Fish was suddenly back on the cricket pitch, fielding deep and waiting for a skyer. His outstretched hands were shaking.

'Th-there!'

A brief glimpse of something dark, tumbling in the air. The air went black. A fog of dirt and smoke, a noise so loud it was painful, cracking into Fish's ear drums.

Then the filthy fog lifted. Dirt was in Fish's teeth, his eyes ran with tears from the stench of explosive. His steel shrapnel-helmet had been blown off, his head was bare. A huge smoking hole had been blown in between the fire trench and support. Men were shouting, a rain of dirt and mud was pattering down.

Corporal Simkins was lying on the duck-boards, holding his neck, wounded across the side, as though it had been slashed with a cleaver. Bright red blood was gushing out into the dirt.

'Stopped one, sir,' he said, in an aggrieved voice.

Fish scrabbled for the field-dressing stitched into his battledress, cut it free, clamped it over the wound, holding it tight. 'B-Blighty one, Simkins,' he said. The shock and fear in the young man's eyes eased a little.

'That's it, sir. Blighty for me.'

'G-Get you b-back to the c-castle. There's a h-hospital there.' Fish put his head back and shouted. 'M-Morphia! W-Wounded man h-here!'

The field-dressing was turning scarlet.

'I wouldn't say no to a gasper sir,' Simkins said conversationally.

'Sh-Shell d-dressing! Th-This one's too s-small.' A crowd of men had assembled. 'G-got a fag for him?'

A Trumpeter was quickly lit and placed between the corporal's lips.

'Lovely.'

Somebody brought fresh dressings, Fish took off the first, sodden red, and the blood splashed over his hands, hot and steaming. He clamped on another, holding it tight, trying to staunch the bleeding. The bandage became warm under his fingers as it changed colour.

'Feel a bit tired,' Simkins commented. ''Ere, where's me Hun belt gone?'

Fish pulled off the dressing, squeezing and reaching into the wound, fumbling in the flesh to try to find the spurting artery. Blood spouted contemptuously past his fingers in jets.

Simkins's breath became shallow, he looked up at the blue sky. 'Dad'll be getting the hay in,' he said, to nobody in particular. The blood was slowing. Fish put on a fresh dressing. Simkins was as pale as the belly of a fish. The blood showed up like poppies on a sheet. He took in a deep breath, looked up at Fish.

'Where are the bearers?' Fish demanded, over his shoulder. He looked back at Simkins, and the young man was staring at him.

'What is it, Simkins?'

A thin trail of smoke was rising up from the cigarette.

'Simkins?'

Fish became aware of Sergeant-Major Hopcroft, kneeling down beside him. He reached out and shut the young man's eyes with gentle fingers. 'He's dead, sir.'

'He can't be dead . . . we were . . .' Fish looked at the debris of blood-soaked dressings, the spattered duck-boards. He stood up. The crater was still smoking, there was still a stench of burned marzipan in the air.

'P-People shouldn't d-do that kind of thing,' he said, in a disjointed voice. 'B-Bally dangerous.' He turned away. As he did so, he heard a voice mutter behind him: 'Poor fucking bleeder.'

Fish whirled about. 'Wh-Who said that?' he demanded. Standing by the dead man a soldier looked up sheepishly.

'I did, sir. No offence meant, sir.'

'Who are you?' Fish shouted furiously. 'I don't know you. You m-must be f-from the b-blasted town. W-We don't speak like that. I w-won't have it. Sergeant-Major!'

'Yes, sir!'

'P-put this foul-mouthed p-person on a charge.'

'Yessir.'

Fish turned, and stumbled away down the trench, his blood-soaked sleeves flapping stickily from his arms. He halted by the great crater. 'It's d-dangerous, doing th-that sort of thing,' he said. 'It ought to b-be s-stopped.'

A red flare soared in a high arc, blotting out the diamond stars.

'Piccadilly!' shouted the sentry, and Freddie came tumbling out of his dug-out with a bag of Mills bombs. He and the other two subalterns arrived at the fire trench at the same time. A sentry was pumping a stream of flares into the sky from his brass-barrelled Verey pistol, a small blunderbuss. No-man's land seemed empty.

'Buggers are hiding in the grass,' said George.

They began to fling grenades into the sector, rifles started to pop and crackle along the line. The bombs exploded in the dark grass like firecrackers, brief mouths of flame. A machine-gun started up its typewriter rattle. From the rear came the flashes of a Stokes mortar, followed by the banging of the bombs landing in the German lines.

Bullets began to whine and crack over their heads; little pinpricks of light showed in the grass where the Germans were lying. Freddie had a Lee-Enfield to his shoulder, each time he saw a flash he fired, like a man knocking over tin ducks at a seaside shooting-gallery. An arc of crackling light suddenly went across the sky and a star-shell blossomed, swaying slowly down on its parachute.

The darkness over the German line began to sparkle with artillery fire. Shells started to whizz and roar over their heads, squalls of shrapnel beat on the rear. Coloured rockets shot up from both sides, red and green and yellow. In their light, Fish saw a man rising from the grass, running forward, shouting in German – others rising up at his urging, yellow and red and green men from hell – and Fish shot him. He staggered on, and Fish saw a froth of yellow-looking blood spraying from his mouth as he exhorted his men. Fish shot him again and the top of his head came off, carrying his *pickelhaube* with it.

Germans were yelling in the wire, running up and down like rabbits seeking a hole, and they shot them all.

The noise slowly died down, the sky became dark again. Dry smoke drifted across the line, reminding them of stubble burning at home. The dry grass was on fire, the flames licked gradually along the sector, and the wounded out there screamed as they burned. 'P-Poor b-bastards,' said Fish.

Robert was standing next to him. 'Yes. Poor bastards,' he said. He jumped up onto the parapet. 'Hoy! I say, you German chaps!' He turned to look down the line. 'Cease fire, everyone. The Huns can come and get their wounded. Do you hear me, over there?'

'*Ja*. You will not shoot?' came a voice through the dark.

'No. Go on, before they burn to death.'

Flares arced into the sky; in their light they could see soldiers climbing out of the opposite trenches, finding men in the smoke, carrying them away.

A big man came over near to them, a Saxon officer wearing the Iron Cross. He was a handsome man, with a fair moustache. He saluted across the wire entanglement, and Robert did likewise.

'Thank you gentlemen, one and all. I thank you very much. Good night.'

'Good night.'

The Saxon walked away into the smoke and a ragged cheer went down the line.

Freddie sat in the dappled shade of a crab-apple tree. He was reading the Bible. Nearby, Fish was darting about the little glade of the wood with a butterfly net, moving in fits and dashes as he pursued a multi-coloured butterfly. Through the trees came the sound of men singing, and a faint, warmish, soapy smell. They were in rest, the bath house was in full operation, steamy from seven in the morning to seven at night, a very happy place.

'Got it!' Fish cried in triumph. He came over to Freddie, holding the net, and gently turned it over. A handsome reddish butterfly with white and black tips to its wings sat on the folds of net, seemingly unperturbed.

'Painted Lady,' said Fish. 'I've seen Brimstones, P-Peacocks, Red Admirals, Garden Whites and Wall butterflies so far this morning.'

'Bit early for Red Admirals, isn't it?' Freddie objected.

'I've seen Chaffinches and White Throats in their nests with eggs. Red Campion's out and the Hawthorn. I ate some this morning – bread and cheese! Maybe it's an early summer.'

'Mmm.'

'What are you reading?'

'The Bible. You know, Fish, God would be quite happy out here.'

'What do you mean?' Fish sat down and pulled out a silver cigarette case. He offered Freddie one, and lit it for him with a Dunhill lighter. 'Only Arf a Mo's,' Fish apologised. 'I ran out of N-Navy Cut. I seem to be smoking a lot, I don't know why. Why would God like it here?'

'Well listen to this: "The Lord . . . slew them with a great slaughter at Gibeon, and chased them . . . and smote them to Azekah. And it came to pass as they fled . . . that the Lord cast down great stones from Heaven upon them . . and they died. The Lord delivered up the Amorites before the children of Israel, and the sun stood still, and the moon stayed, until the people had avenged themselves on their enemies." I mean, Fish, God must like it here.'

Fish looked quizzically at his cousin. 'Are you saying the Bible's wrong?'

'I don't know. I just don't see how it makes sense when you're told on the one hand to be Christian and good, and on the other that the Lord approves of us handing it out hot. A lot of things don't quite make sense to me at the moment, Fish. Why am I smoking all the time? Why am I thinking of girls all the time?'

'Are you thinking of g-girls, Freddie?' Fish said, amused.

'Well, I am now. I didn't when we were in the line. But now we're in rest I am. I never used to, girls were just other chaps' sisters. Now I can't get them off my mind. Do you, Fish?'

'W-Well, I think of Vi a lot.'

'Vi's frightful! So bossy. Do you really like her, Fish?'

'Yes. Lots.'

'Oh, well you can have her.'

'Th-Thanks. I'm sure she'll be grateful.' Both of them smiled at the thought of strong-minded Violet adding her views to the conversation.

The ground where they sat was covered in crab-apple blossom and Fish picked up a handful. He was suddenly very homesick.

'If we're still in this p-part of the line in the autumn we ought to make crab-apple jelly.'

'Nice on toast,' Freddie agreed. They descended into silence until an approaching figure came into view. 'There's George. What's he want?' Freddie said.

'Hallo, chaps,' George called. 'Guess what? I've just seen the Colonel.'

'A pleasing sight in spring-time,' said Freddie.

'He's giving us three days' leave!' George said. 'And he's putting you in for an award, Freddie.'

'Oh, I say. What're we going to do?'

'Let's go to the Hotel de la Poste in St Omer,' said Fish. 'I might ride the Indian over to see H-Henry.'

'You love that motorbike! Come and stay at the Poste anyway.'

'All right.'

'When does the leave start?'

'Now!' said George. 'So come on and stop lounging about. If Fish's going on his contraption we'll take the Standard, Freddie. We can stock up in Omer. I want to do a Woodbine run for the men.'

'I need some fags.'

'Come on, let's go!'

Fish parked the Indian by the kerb in the main square. Well behind the lines, the town was both undamaged and alive with activity, the hotels, bars, *estaminets* and restaurants doing a great trade. He switched off and the big V-twin engine thumped to a stop. He sat on the sprung saddle and pushed his goggles up, giving the great red fuel tank in front of him – emblazoned with its Red Indian head in full war-bonnet – a polish with his handkerchief.

The Hotel de la Poste occupied most of one side of the square. He sat on his motorcycle, quite content to wait in the sunshine and bustle of life for Freddie and George in the little car to catch him up. A black Renault taxi spluttered to a halt beside him, and not one, but three young women got out. Fish goggled delightedly, and opened his mouth to shout. Nothing came out. At the second try he managed.

'V-V-Vi!'

Violet whirled. Her face broke into a huge smile. 'Fish! You got my letter.'

'N-No. We've just c-come out of the l-line. What are you doing here?'

'Nursing. I've been given a post in the RAMC hospital here.'

'We're staying in the Hotel de la Poste.'

'So are we. Here, let me introduce you. Clarissa, Carlotta, this is Fish – the one I have told you about. Fish, Dr Clarissa Townall and her sister Carlotta.'

'Very pleased to meet you,' said Clarissa, in a soft American accent. Fish shook their hands. 'How-de-do?' he said. 'Are you a real doctor?'

'She's real,' said Violet. 'Come out to help in the hospital.'

'I'm a surgeon,' she said.

'Ah. P-Plenty of practice out here. And you, Miss Townall, are you a doctor?'

'Oh, no,' the American said softly. 'I'm just here for the ride. Tell me, why do they call you Fish?'

'My n-name. When I was born my father took one look at me and said, "Odd sort of fish. Christen him Fish." So they did. Fish Gawain Bohamond Henri de Clare. That's me.'

'Do you get on with your father by any chance?' laughed Clarissa.

'G-Golly no. We loathe each other . . .'

There was a tootling of a horn behind them and the Standard drew up, ejecting Freddie and George. 'I say,' Freddie said admiringly. 'Fast work, young Fish. Oh, it's you, Vi.'

'Yes, it's me. I take it you're glad to see me, Freddie.'

'Um, heaps,' he said pecking her on the cheek all the while staring at her two companions.

Fish put him out of his misery, 'The Misses Townall,' he explained, 'from America.'

'Oh, yes, indeed,' Freddie breathed.

The table contained the wreckage of a fine meal. There were wine bottles and empty glasses, the peel of fruit left on small plates, a cheese-board of soft, white and yellow French cheeses, some wrapped in green leaves. There had been plates of fried sole and tenderly casseroled beef, of prawns and yellow mayonnaise, of wobbling chilled *vichyssoise*, of sizzling *allumettes* and long cold green beans. The restaurant buzzed gently, Clarissa and George occupied opposing sides of the table, the seats each side of them, where Freddie and Carlotta, Violet and Fish had sat, now empty.

'A poet and a man of God,' said Clarissa, smiling. 'You're a soldier-poet-priest. You must be from the Renaissance.'

'There's quite a few of us out here,' George explained. 'We're only amateur soldiers. If there wasn't the war we'd all be at home doing something else.'

'What would you be doing?'

'I'd be in the East End. Of London, that is. That's where my parish was. I worked among the poor.'

'And now you're here?'

'The poor have come to the war. The men. Therefore I must come too.'

'You mean that,' she said quietly.

'It's a holy war,' he said. 'God's sent the war to make a better world afterwards. There'll be no prejudice, no class hatreds, when it's all over. We shall all be as one. You'll see.'

She was quiet for a moment. 'Poetry?' she questioned.

'This is a war that's seen through poetry. Even the men write poems. I've always loved it. My father, he loves limericks. He knows loads and loads. I suppose he started me off.'

'Tell me one.'

'Oh. Well, it's a little bit risqué, you see. But it gets a good chuckle from the men.'

'The best ones are.'

'Are you sure?'

'Try me. If I'm too shocked I'll call for the waiter, have you removed.'

'Right. Here goes. "Lady Lowbodice":

> Every time Lady Lowbodice swoons,
> Her bubbies pop out like balloons,
>   But her butler stands by
>   With hauteur in his eye,
> And lifts them back in with warm spoons.'

Clarissa clapped her hands together and laughed. 'That's great! I wish I'd known it when I was training.'

George refilled their glasses. 'You do?'

'I was the only girl in the class,' she explained. 'When you are in this situation you had better be as good as the boys, if you want any respect at all. I have probably committed damage to two-thirds of my liver by drinking as much as they could, and rhymes, however risqué, cannot bring a maidenly blush to my cheek any more. I do like them to be funny, though. Any fool can be rude.'

'Oh yes . . .' George fumbled for his cigarette case. 'Fag? Wills on the left, Churchman's on the right. Good show.' He lit their cigarettes and stared into the smoke he made.

> 'Now, God be thanked Who has matched us with His hour,
> And caught our youth, and wakened us from sleeping,
> With hand made sure, clear eye, and sharpened power,
> To turn, as swimmers into cleanness leaping,
> Glad from a world grown old and cold and weary . . .'

George stubbed out his cigarette and drank some wine before lighting another Churchman's. 'That's Brooke,' he said, 'though I don't think he knew quite how much we were going to have to pay for the new world.'

'What are you poets writing now?'

'Me, I just scrawl away, but there are some fine fellows out there.'

'Can you recite for me?'

'Oh, oh, yes. If you like. I'm very fond of Sorley. He wrote this last year. Friend of mine, we were at Marlborough together, for our sins. We'd have been at Oxford now, if it wasn't for the war. He was offered a place at University College.

> When you see millions of the mouthless dead
> Across your dreams in pale battalions go,
> Say not soft things as other men have said,
> That you'll remember. For you need not so.
> Give them not praise. For, deaf, how should they know
> It is not curses heaped on each gashed head?
> Nor tears. The blind eyes see not your tears flow.
> Nor honour. It is easy to be dead.
> Say only this, "They are dead." Then add thereto,
> "Yet many a better one has died before."
> Then scanning all the o'ercrowded mass, should you
> Perceive one face that you loved heretofore,
> It is a spook. None wears the face you knew.
> Great death has made all his for evermore.'

'"Great death" . . .' Clarissa said quietly. 'That's very good.'

'It is,' George agreed pleasantly. He felt that he was getting slightly drunk, but it was an agreeable feeling, so he poured more wine.

'I'd like to meet him one day.'

'Sorry. Not sure where he is.'

'Just if the opportunity arose,' she explained. 'I like artists.'

'So do I. He's in Loos, somewhere.'

'Serving?'

'No, no. Done his bit. Mixed up with the mud down there. *Napoo.*
Fini. Kapout. Au revoir. That kind of thing. Dear God, what am
I doing? I spend all that time in the trench wishing for civilised
company, and when I get it, and beautiful to boot, I start getting
maudlin. This won't do. Let me see, do you know the one about the
young fellow of Kings, who cared not for whores and such things?
No? His secret desire was a boy in the choir, with a bum like jelly
on springs.'

'Before you could start at my medical school you had to pass a
Latin exam,' said Clarissa.

'Of course,' George nodded. 'Got to prescribe, what?'

'That's it. The Latin tutor had quite a sense of humour. As a part
of the exam we had to translate a poem by Marcus Argentarius. I've
never forgotten it. I think he did it to see if I'd be embarrassed.

Normal sex is best, for the man of a serious turn of mind . . .'

'True,' said George.

'But here's a hint, should you fancy the other,
Turn Menophila round in bed, address her peach of a behind,
And it's easy to pretend you're having her brother!'

'Oh, I say. Jolly good. You must recite it to me again, when I'm
sober. Where are the others, anyway?' George peered over the rim
of his glass at the empty chairs. 'I mean, I can guess where Fish and
Violet are, but what about Freddie and your sister? Hm. Strolling in
the moonlight, what?'

'Carlotta is doing her bit for the war effort,' her sister said drily.

Carlotta Townall was wearing a shirt. It was Freddie's shirt; she lay
on her back in it and watched through half-closed eyes and with some
concealed amusement, as he lost control of himself above her. It was
not unlike a big hunter getting away from its rider and bolting, she
thought.

He collapsed in a gasping and ecstatic heap beside her on the bed, and she lit cigarettes for them both. 'You were just magnificent, darling,' she assured him. 'I sure am glad these French beds are strong. Cigarette?'

'Oh, yes. Thanks.' He turned over and they lay side by side, watching the smoke trails rising up towards the ceiling.

'I saw an aeroplane doing that,' he said. 'I think it was one of ours. It was flying along above the trench and a smaller one came up behind it. It made a small popping sound, and the one in front started to burn. It went all the way down to the ground, and left a sort of corkscrew of smoke behind it.'

'A machine-gun,' she said knowledgeably. 'I read about it in the paper. The Germans have an aircraft – a Fokker? – that can carry a machine-gun, and fires it straight forward.'

'Yes. Bloody machine-guns.'

'You're like a machine-gun, Freddie,' she said lightly.

'Oh, thanks.' He blushed slightly, much to her joy.

She reached down and fondled him gently. 'Tell me about the guns,' she suggested. 'Here we have an artillery piece.'

'Oh, no,' he laughed, 'Verey pistol at most. Sends off nicely coloured flares.'

'You made me see coloured flares. So what do you have?'

'Officer – a "barker": Webley Mk VI .455 revolver. OR's get a "bandook" – Rifle No. 1, Short Magazine, Lee-Enfield Mk III '

'I think that's what we have here. Some kind of rifle.' She sat up, put her cigarette into the ashtray and straddled him. He slid his hands up under the shirt. 'What about the artillery?' she asked.

'Two types,' he gasped. 'I say ...'

'Keep your mind on the things that go bang, Freddie,' she instructed him. 'I'll handle the rest of it. Now.'

'*I'll* go bang.'

'Not 'til I'm ready, you won't. The artillery, Freddie.'

'Guns and howitzers.'

'Hooo ... what's the ... difference?'

'Gun fires flat. Fast shell. Howitzer throws a big shell in an arc, slowly.'

'That's it, slowly ...'

'You play golf? Gun's like a driver, the howitzer's a niblick. Gun goes *whizz-crack*. Shrieks in your ear. Big howitzer ...'

'Not yet! Come on, Freddie, the howitzer ...'

'The ... howitzer ...' he gasped. 'It whacks you over the head with a walking stick.'

'Good, good.'

'Rolls across the sky. A man out for a ride on his bike. Whistles to itself.'

'Yes, yes.'

'Then it speeds up.'

'Quickly, yes.'

'It's an express train, rushing through a tunnel. Whistles and roars . . .'

'Oh, God, I'm coming.' Carlotta seized the cigarette from the tray, took a deep gasp as the feeling rushed over her, a shell bursting inside her. She allowed herself to be turned over, lay content as Freddie ravished her on the bed. Fragrant smoke drifted about her head, like explosive.

'It's a good job we're in France,' Violet commented. She and Fish were sitting up in bed, having piled bolsters behind their backs. They were eating candied grapes. 'We couldn't do this back home,' she explained. 'Not unless we were at the castle. The French expect people in love to go off and make love. Back home we'd be told to go and take a cold shower until we were married.'

Fish laughed.

'We're terribly stuffy,' she assured him. 'My aunt was *arrested* in 1885 for walking with a gentleman friend at night in London, not wearing gloves and hat! She was clearly a prossie.' Violet chewed a grape. 'Things *have* got better, Fish. It's not so long ago that I wouldn't have been supposed to enjoy doing it at all. Only loose women did that. Aren't you glad, Fish? Would you like me to lie there like a cod doing nothing?'

'Oh, no. Much nicer like th-this.'

'It is, isn't it?' She leaned a naked shoulder up against him. 'I do love you, Fish.'

'And I l-love you too.'

'Don't get killed, Fish.'

'Do my b-best.'

'I've got to start work at the hospital. Wonder how it'll be.'

'Why are you doing it, Vi? You're a lady. You could be at Cambridge.'

'Same as you,' she said. 'You could be at home, being a gentleman. We're the de Clares. *Noblesse oblige.*'

'Where are you going?'

Violet giggled. 'RAMC hospital number four. The troops call it Bandagehem!'

'I'll write to you at Bandagehem. We'll see Henry tomorrow. I wonder if he'll take me up for a trip . . .'

'There'a war on,' Violet objected.

'Can't be as dangerous as being in the t-trenches,' Fish retorted. 'The flying field's well behind the lines.'

'You did enjoy that flight at the castle, didn't you?' she said sympathetically.

'I'll say.'

'Fish, what're you doing?'

'You k-know what I'm d-doing,' he mumbled happily.

'It does feel nice,' she admitted. '*C'est la guerre, Fish. C'est la guerre.*'

George navigated along the corridor at Clarissa's elbow. It was decorated with faded prints of Louis XIV's court. He was singing, quite softly:

> 'Oh, another little drink,
> Another little drink,
> Another little drink wouldn't do us any harm.'

He stopped, and peered along the corridor. 'I say, Clarissa. Is it me, or is the corridor not straight?'

Clarissa looked down it. 'Bit of both, I'd say.'

George fell on one knee, and began to sing again:

> 'If you were the only girl in the world,
> And I was the only boy,
> Nothing else would matter in the world today,
> We would go on loving in the same old way . . .'

'This is my door, George,' Clarissa said gently.

'Oh, I say. So it is. Well, night night, what?'

'Night night, George. I loved our evening.'

'So did I. So did I. My room's somewhere along here, I'm sure of it. All the best, then.' He turned, then paused, and turned back. 'My brother Tim died last week,' he said in a voice that was quite sober. 'A sniper shot him. So you see, however horrible it is, it must be worth it. God wouldn't do it, otherwise, would he?'

'No,' she said quietly. 'No, I'm sure He wouldn't.'

George made his way unsteadily along the winding corridor, and she heard him break into song again:

> 'I don't want to go in the trenches no more,
> Where whizz-bangs and shrapnel they whistle and roar.
> Take me over the sea,
> Where the alleyman can't get at me,
> Oh my,
> I don't want to die,
> I want to go home.'

The meadow stretched out in front of them. Here and there it was stained with oil, in some places gouged so that the earth showed, grassing over as it healed; there were patches of charred soil where nothing would grow for a while, but in the main it was green. Behind them was the farmhouse taken over for the Squadron headquarters, and along the tree-line the bessoneaux hangars and the huts and tents of the men who flew and serviced the collection of aeroplanes.

'We're lucky to have the farmhouse,' said Henry. 'Makes life a lot more comfortable. Spent half the winter on a forward cinder strip cut through some farmer's turnip field and it was frightful. It was bad enough coping with the blasted Fokkers up there without getting soggy feet when you came down. Nothing worse than damp socks at fifteen thousand feet, let me tell you. If someone develops a device for electrically heated socks, I shall press for him to get the Military Cross, I really shall. It used to take me ages to thaw out my toes – I found that a mixture of three fingers of brandy to two tablespoons of Colman's mustard powder in two quarts of warm water was the only way.'

'Wh-What on earth do you d-do with it?' Fish enquired.

'Drink the brandy and stick your plates in the mustard, of course. Pity it isn't as easy to get rid of the Fokkers.' Henry patted the side of the biplane he was standing next to. Its engine was behind the cockpit, and so was the propeller. 'Didn't have these then.'

'What is it?'

'DH2.' He pointed to the Lewis gun mounted in front of the pilot's cockpit. 'That's the important bit. Doesn't need interrupter gear slowing it up, so you can really blast away. Get good and close and let them have it.' He gestured at what lay behind the gun. 'The rest of it's not great. I wish we had Pups like the Navy. The bloody Germans are bound to come up with something now the Fokkers aren't what they were.'

Henry had got thin, Fish thought. His eyes seemed too large for their sockets, the flesh had fallen away from his neck and his hands, you could see the bones and sinews and muscles under his skin.

The airman suddenly smiled at his cousin. 'Still, mustn't complain,' he said. 'It's not allowed. What about you lot? Good to see you all, and what a treat to bring these lovely girls with you.'

'We're fine. On a qu-quiet sector. Freddie went out and captured a prisoner with Hopcroft. George and I hung about in no-man's land while they were doing it, which is why we got this leave. We'll have to think up s-something else if we w-want any more!'

'Jolly good . . .'

'I s-say, Henry,' Fish said quickly. 'Any chance of a flip? You know, like we did at the castle?'

'A flip?' Henry smiled quizzically at his cousin. 'They shoot at you up there, you know.'

'They th-throw b-blasted great b-bombs like f-footballs at us in the line.'

'A flip. Well, we can't go in this one, we need a bicycle made for two, don't we?'

Henry walked down the line of hangars, and stopped beside an aeroplane that looked not unlike the DH2's father. 'I suppose we could take this,' he said.

Fish looked at the aircraft with its near fifty feet of double wingspan in some awe. 'What is it?'

'FE2b. Only had it a few days, I wouldn't mind going up and getting familiar with it. It's not bad. See the observer's nacelle at the front with the Lewis gun – it gives a great field of fire, they shot down Immelman with one of these.'

'When can we go up?'

Henry looked up at the sky. 'No time like the present. We can get back down in time for lunch. Come on, I'll lend you some gear, it gets cold up there.'

They found the others talking to a young pilot in the mess. 'I see you've met Pemberton. Pemberton has a unique method of landing aeroplanes which he may show you, one day, if you're lucky. I'm taking the FE up, Fish's coming as observer. You want to take the DH2 and come with us?'

'Jolly good.'

The two pilots went off to their huts, taking Fish with them, and he soon found himself swathed in the kind of boots, gloves, jacket and helmet most unsuited to the warm day. The ground crews had prepared the two aeroplanes, and Fish watched as the two walked round them in inspection.

'Don't get up to anything stupid up there,' Violet muttered in a low voice.

'It's just a sight-seeing tour,' said Fish.

'Pemberton, what's this punt-gun you've got attached to your aeroplane?' Freddie called, peering at the blunt muzzle like a small drainpipe sticking out from under the cockpit of the DH2. Looking inside, he could see part of the cockpit flooring taken up with the mechanism of the gun.

'Vickers one-pounder pom-pom gun,' said Pemberton. 'We're experimenting with weapons. Henry's such a good shot he was knocking them down with a hunting rifle strapped to the side of his scout, but most of us – certainly me – aren't crack shots like that. We've been trying out this pom-pom gun. Goes "bam bam bam" and damned nearly shakes the aeroplane in half, but it's a good gun.'

'Jolly good for ripping up a train,' Henry called. 'Went out a few days ago at dawn and had a snoop about over their side of the lines, caught a train breaking cover and planted twenty rounds into the engine. It went into a ditch, the driver ran like a rabbit. Only problem with it is its weight. Hampers the performance.' He pointed to a pile of boxes stacked up neatly at the side of the hangar. 'I think we'll do best with Lewis guns for air-to-air. We've got a stack of them.'

Freddie was still looking at the pom-pom gun. 'I'd like one of those,' he said.

George yawned. 'I plan to have a little rest in the shade while you are gone,' he said, lying down under a tree. 'For some reason I am slightly fatigued.'

'I'm going to go for a walk in the countryside,' said Freddie. 'You coming, Carlotta?'

Carlotta smiled blandly. 'Any time,' she said demurely.

Violet sat down on the grass under the tree with Clarissa. 'I'll wait for you here,' she said.

Fish climbed up into the observer's position. It was like crouching in a coracle. Most of the space was taken up by drums of ammunition in boxes, and a large black machine-gun. Above and behind him was Henry. He leaned forward round his small glass aero-screen. 'I don't expect any trouble. It's pretty quiet on this sector. If we do see a Hun, blaze away with that. Remember the shoot? Just like that. Lead the target just like a partridge. Try not to hit Pemberton while you're doing it.'

Fish examined the weapon in front of him. It was about four feet long, its barrel encased in a thick black radiator cover. It had a conventional rifle-style stock, but with a pistol grip incorporated into the trigger. Behind him he heard Henry calling out to someone else.

'Switch off. Petrol on. Suck in.'

The aircraft rocked gently, making a noise like a tramp drinking soup.

'Contact!'

There was a sudden cough, a thrum and an oiled, machined clacking from behind him, and he saw the ground crew moving away from the propeller they had swung. The thin bicycle-type tyres began to roll and they waddled out over the grass, the long wings swaying. Behind and to one side, the smaller DH2 was also on the move. Fish pulled down the goggles over his eyes. Violet waved, and he waved back.

The thrum of the engine behind him increased into a full-blooded bellow, the meadow rushed under his feet, the air swirled about him, fresh and cool in his face, the wheels bumped, tapped, rolled still – they were flying.

Henry climbed up into the sky, weaving slowly in a snake-like pattern. Fish leaned against the rear of his cockpit. Through the array of struts and shiny bracing-wires he could see the smaller biplane of Pemberton holding formation. As he flew, Henry looked about him constantly, his head rotating and gyrating up and down and around like a new form of exercise. While he did so, under his urging the aeroplane also flew in an erratic course. Fish realised that Henry was watching every part of the sky about him, even the space behind and underneath, which on a straight course would have been blotted out by the big six-cylinder engine behind them.

The ground below had lost its features, becoming a blurred area of greens and browns without movement. The air was chill. They flew on for some time. Fish had no idea where he was. He slowly became cold. He watched the ground below, saw that it contained straight grey lines – the French *pave* roads, lined with tall poplars. There were winding threads through the countryside, along one he saw a faint wisp of white steam moving – a railway. Those patches of dark brown and black, they must be woods, almost merging with those patches of reddish brown and green – the fields. Cloud shadows moved across the land, darkening patches of it, throwing others into high relief. He looked up and saw that they were flying just under the clouds, which passed overhead, like the bellies of whales.

Pemberton's DH2 was flying alongside them, perhaps one hundred yards away. The muzzle of the pom-pom gun stuck out below the cockpit like the tusk of a feral beast. Henry grazed through the bottom of a cloud and damp mist filled Fish's lungs, blotting out his view. Pemberton vanished from sight.

The grey became white, then they shot out into the clear air. Sharks flashed across in front of him. Mad sparks of red and green flew through the air. He had a sudden glimpse of Pemberton's DH2 on its side, whirling in a circle, chasing and being chased by a yellow and blue monoplane, startling black crosses on its wings. He could see the two pilots straining up at each other with goggled gaze. The world suddenly turned on its side, the floor pushed up at him. An aircraft was side on, he saw the crosses, he pulled the machine gun into his shoulder and fired. The smell of propellant stung his nostrils, he swung the barley-corn sight through the white body of the aeroplane as it passed, seemingly in slow motion, scarlet flecks flying from his gun like darts from an air rifle, one after the other, stitching their way up the taut white fabric. They walked into the cockpit and he saw the pilot jerk, his head flying back, sudden scarlet streaks painting the dove-white of the fuselage, and then he was gone.

Pemberton's DH2 shot by, just behind another German aeroplane. They seemed at some crazy angle. The whole front of Pemberton's craft was suddenly enveloped in rhythmic flame and the German disintegrated into tumbling, burning wreckage, staining the sky.

The world whirled back the other way, he heard a loud tearing, like a great cloth of canvas ripping; the structure of the aeroplane shuddered all about him, like a dinghy hitting a harbour wall. There was a clang, a hammer smacking into an anvil, someone hit him with a red-hot chain over his shoulder, he tumbled down into the coracle.

It was quiet, suddenly completely quiet but for the buzzing in his ears, and the whistling of the wind in the wires. He looked up from the wooden floor. Henry was slumped against the back of his cockpit. His face and his flying helmet were coated in gore. Fish pushed himself up onto his knees. The sky was empty. Behind him the propeller whirled uselessly. A thin trail of smoke in the air indicated their passage. They were coming down in a spiral. Below him the earth turned, getting ever closer.

Fish stood up, and the air rushed over him. He clawed at the fuselage rising above him like a swimmer scratching at the side of a boat. He swung a leg out into the gale of air, straddling the side like a bareback rider, and got a boot onto one of the rigging wires. The gale rushed up his jacket, blowing it over his head, roaring in his ears. He leaped upwards, fingers lunging for the aero-screen and its bracket. The huge wind caught him, blowing him across the front of the aeroplane, tumbling him over the little aero-screen and towards the still whirling propeller behind.

His foot caught in the cockpit, jammed into a strap. Frantic fingers grasping onto struts, he heaved himself back down into the main cockpit. A foot squashed into the control column and the aircraft jerked like a bucking horse, almost throwing him back out. Henry slumped against him, he pushed him back, took hold of the control stick, pushed it gently away from the steepening turn. The ground stopped its gyration, he pulled back as Henry had once shown him how to do, and the dive became less steep, the howling of the wind in the wires lessened.

The ground was still visible: smoke from a train was white against the darkness of the trees; horses were pulling waggons along a road. Fish sat squashed up against Henry in the little cockpit. Below, men looked up in alarm as the silent shadow raced over them.

A field. Thick green lines of something. A hedge of trees, cows running, the shadow of the aeroplane racing underneath, the ground rushing up at him. He pulled back, the aeroplane lurched up into the sky before falling again. A crash, a gigantic spray of dirt and foliage. The twanging and smashing of metal and wood breaking up, the world rising up at him as the biplane stood on its nose, a crash as it fell down, kicking him in the back. Steam, torn earth, oil.

Winded, Fish lay gasping on the floor. From somewhere he could hear voices shouting. Henry moaned through the blood spilling out of his helmet over his face, leaned suddenly over the side of the cockpit and was sick.

7

One Pound of High Explosive

June 1916

'We've been here before, Fish,' Freddie said cheerfully. The morning was cool and pleasant, the battalion was marching along a straight road cut through chalk downland, open countryside of farmland marked by woods and copses of mature trees. Elms planted along the road cast shade as they walked along the path of a river, all of them young and fit, the battalion cookers rolling with them. Victorian cooking ranges on wheels, pulled by horses, they offered coffee and tea when they stopped, and the promise of hot stew at noon. It was not an unpleasing way to spend the morning.

'You m-might have b-been,' said Fish. 'It's all n-new to me.'

'We de Clares did,' Freddie grinned. 'Rather a long time ago. Don't you know what's over there?' He took a folded map out of one of his large pockets, and pointed beyond some woods to where the ground fell away into a valley. 'I'm cheating a bit,' he said. 'I went to the Map Room in the castle and borrowed some charts. Earl Rufus brought a lot back from the Napoleonic Wars. They don't have the railways but everything else is there. Jolly useful. That's the Somme river over there. This one next to us must be a tributary. Earl John marched along its southern flank with King Henry in 1415. October, it was. Five hundred years and seven months ago.'

'Agincourt,' Fish said in understanding. 'Of course. We ought to go and see the battlefield.'

'I think we're going to see our own first.'

'Wh-What do you mean?'

'I've been watching the land since we entrained. What have we been doing since we left Plugstreet?'

'T-Training.'

'Right. Rest and field exercises. Advancing in line, trench attacks, capture and consolidation, wood fighting – the Colonel put his foot into a rabbit hole and broke his leg, that's why Robert's acting battalion commander. Obviously we're to see action somewhere. I think it must be up here.'

'Yes?'

'On our march I have counted items of the following: new hardened roads; railway spurs; water-pumping stations; hospitals; boards indicating supply dumps – mainly for artillery ammunition – and transport actually bringing it all up, in quantity. Transport parks. All of these things are newly-built. We are marching alongside an air-line for telephone and telegraph communications to and from HQ. When we get closer to the front it will sink into the soil and become a land-line, well buried against shell fire. I have seen cavalry units, and large, even-sided holes about six feet deep, which I take to be mass graves waiting to be filled.'

They passed a large pile of yellow stone at the side of the road. 'The ground's too soft to take weight here. That'll be for a railway siding. Bringing up the stores.'

Fish glanced quizzically at his cousin. 'You've been making a study of it all.'

'Dad's in the Sappers, you know. He taught me a lot. Observation is crucial.'

'Why didn't you follow him in?'

'I was going to, but the war started. I was booked to go to Woolwich. You need a lot of training to be a sapper. He says – I can quote him – that to be a sapper you need to be an astronomer, geologist, surveyor, draughtsman, artist, architect, traveller, explorer, antiquary, diver, soldier and sailor, ready to go anywhere and do anything. I thought the war would be over by Christmas and didn't have time. I studied quite a bit, though. When it's over I'll go to Woolwich, learn the theory of some of this stuff we're doing in practice.'

They marched on for a while, through the pleasant countryside. The river left them and came back again, wandering on its way about copses of poplar and willow, splitting into channels where water weeds streamed like mermaids' hair, spreading to wash about bulrushes and sedge. Wild duck and coots paddled purposefully about its surface. A heron creaked overhead.

'I think you might be right, you know,' said Fish. 'I got a l-letter from Henry, they've been taken out of the line, to re-equip. They're going to be in our sector. He says some of them have been given cameras and morse transmitters. Artillery observation, photography and contact patrol. And setting balloons on fire.'

'How's his headache?'

'Better, he says. Also, he doesn't have to part his hair any more. He's got a scar all the way from the crown of his head to the temple.'

'Born to be hanged, the pair of you.'

'I s-say,' Fish said, frowning, we're going to take up duty in this sector, won't we b-be with Rawlinson's Fourth Army?'

'Rawly? Yes, I should think so. We're taking over from the Frogs.'

'J-Just hope we don't get put under XII Corps. Father's Brigadier there.'

'How is the old bastard?' Freddie said casually.

'I don't know,' Fish said tersely. 'No-Nor do I w-wish to.'

They marched on. Soon enough, as Freddie had predicted, the aerial communications lines on their poles sank into the ground and vanished. The countryside was thickly strewn with the accoutrements of the army – bivouacs and men were everywhere, the roads choked with transport, troops, guns and ambulances. They found their camp above the small ruined town of Albert with its famous statue of the Golden Virgin hanging from the basilica, blown from its moorings by a German shell the previous year and still leaning precariously over the town square.

The next day they went up to the line, and like the communications cables, sank into the earth as they went up the sap trenches into the three rows of reserve, support and fire trenches, some six hundred yards in depth. With chalk just under the surface soil, the trench systems and their spoil could be seen stretching like bridal ribbons into the distance.

As the Windstone Yeomanry came in, the French went out, the *poilus* each laden with what seemed like the entire contents of a French corner shop on his back. They clanked as they moved, pots and cookers and rolled mattresses swaying and colliding like the instruments of a one-man band, their multitude of pockets stuffed with candles and coffee and tubes of aspirin, string and scissors and hexamine tablets for their cookers, pencils and paper and cloves of garlic, onions and carrots, pans and mugs and bottles.

Their lieutenant was on hand to show Freddie and Fish, the platoon commanders, the company headquarters. George came with them to find a home for his vicarage. They descended into the chalk, down a wide set of concrete steps.

'Like the grand staircase at the castle,' Freddie joked. Bays had been cut at intervals.

'Here you can put ammunition and machine-guns,' the Frenchman explained, 'in case of an attack. If you are shelled, you see. Then you leap out and massacre the swine.'

'Good thinking,' Freddie agreed. 'It's a pretty active sector, then?'

'Oh, *non.* Ver' quiet. We and the Germans, we have routine. Send over a shell or two after breakfast, and then ever'body happy. But you can still put the machine-guns ready up there in case. That is what the bays are for.'

They went down and down, and emerged into a fine, large room, perhaps sixty feet by twenty, lit by electric lamps, equipped with tables, chairs and communications equipment. Curtained bays held beds, high up in the walls were vents for fan-driven ventilation.

'I say . . .' George breathed. 'All the comforts of home, what?'

'Oh yes,' the French officer agreed. 'Is ver' pleasant, and ver' safe. You are thirty feet down, here, and are protected by concrete.' He indicated some five entrances and exits, and the tunnels that communicated with other dug-outs. 'One cannot be . . . *enterre,* how do you say that?'

'Buried,' said George. 'Entombed.'

'Buried, yes. You will not be buried in here, whatever the shelling.'

'Damned good show,' Freddie said approvingly. 'You French certainly know a thing or two about fortification.'

The Frenchman smiled in a slightly embarrassed fashion. 'I 'ave to confess, it is not ours. This part of the line was captured from the Germans. They pulled back to the 'igher ground, you see. The Germans, they love the 'igh ground. They left these dug-outs behind them. These are all German.'

Freddie looked up the high stairway with its areas for ammunition and machine-gun storage. 'The Germans must have a lot of automatic guns,' he commented.

'*Mais oui,*' the Frenchman agreed. 'More and more.'

'What about you?' Freddie asked curiously.

'Ah . . . we have the St Etienne light machine-gun and the heavy Hotchkiss. Here, in my battalion, one light machine-gun for every twenty men, and one heavy for every twenty-five.'

'*What?*' Fish said in amazement. 'Why, that's about . . . four times what we have.'

'I would like more,' the Frenchman said simply.

They heard footsteps coming along at a pace, and Robert came bustling along the wood-floored corridor, his little cricket bat tucked under his arm. 'Have you seen all this?' he demanded in delight. 'No more wading about in blasted mud up to our knees.'

'German,' said Freddie.

'I don't care whose it is, just as long as we've got it. We can stack the claret in one of these bed places. Right, chaps. First lot of signals just through. You can all jolly well salute and call me sir. I'm battalion commander, they've upped me to Lieutenant Colonel.'

They all cheered.

'Freddie, your heroics must have impressed somebody, you've got the MC for that do with the sniper. Sergeant-Major Hopcroft's got the MM. They've promoted you to Captain, Freddie, so you can have my old company, C Company. And we've all got to go up to Corps HQ to get briefed on the battle.'

'Told you,' Freddie said to Fish.

'Who are we attached to?' Fish demanded.

'XII Corps,' said Robert.

'Oh, n-no,' Fish said in disgust. 'F-Father.'

The four of them came up the château driveway in George's Standard. The morning was fine, and they had the hood down.

They pulled up outside the splendid Sun King château with its well-tended flower beds. Red and purple and white roses were breaking out of bud, filling the air with their perfume. The multi-coloured tiled roof shone in the sunshine.

'See Sir Hubert's brought his Rolls,' George noted, parking not far from the gleaming limousine.

'Windstone Yeomanry?' called a waiting staff-officer with a smile.

'Yes,' Robert called. That's . . . oh, I say, Cromwell!'

'Hallo, chaps! I saw you were coming, I've been waiting for you.'

'Nice d-digs,' said Fish.

'We manage. Come on, the briefing's inside. They do say that Napoleon stayed here overnight on his way to Quatre Bras . . .'

They went up marble steps and through high double doors. Cromwell led them through a great hallway into a ballroom over-looking a small ornamental lake. Chairs had been set out in rows, other battalion-level officers were seated, smoking and chatting. On a stage, a large map had been placed upon an easel.

'Sir Hubert will be briefing you,' Cromwell explained. 'If you want more detail come and talk to me afterwards. Father's on hand if you want to ask questions.'

'H-How are you g-getting on with him?' Fish asked his brother.

'Well enough, I suppose. Sir Hubert keeps us busy. He's a good general.' Cromwell grinned, and fished in one pocket. He brought out a small ivory-handled penknife. 'You know how big he is? He also has terrible blood pressure. The MO has given us penknives, and if he goes too red in the face we have to cut and bleed him! It hasn't happened yet, but we're all ready to pounce.'

'What about F-Father?' Fish commented sourly. 'How ab-bout opening *him* up?'

'Shh. Here they are. Good to see you, Fish.'

'Y-You too . . .' Fish sat down with the others as Cromwell went up to the stage, where Sir Hubert Mordaunt and Brigadier de Clare were now presiding.

'Good morning, gentlemen.' The General took a pointer and moved it across the map. 'Well, here it is, the reason all you splendid New Armies were brought into being – the great assault that will end the war.'

There was a pleased murmur of spontaneous approbation from all the young men assembled.

'This is Fourth Army's part of the line. We adjoin the French on our right. We comprise eleven front-line divisions, they some fifteen divisions.'

Robert, Fish and the others were already doing sums in their heads. A fully equipped division was comprised of three infantry brigades with their own supporting artillery and engineers. At full strength, some twenty thousand men.

'Our sector is some fifteen miles long, divisions will attack on a front of approximately one mile, with two brigades up and one in reserve. What this will mean to you, the men on the ground, is that two battalions each of one thousand men will, on the day chosen, form the leading wave of the brigade. You will climb the parapet at Z-hour using scaling ladders, and extend your soldiers into four lines a company to each, giving you a separation of about two to three yards between men. Your lines will be fifty to one hundred yards apart, and you will proceed at a regular pace towards the German lines. When your first wave gets there it will proceed through the former wire and take possession of the first line of trenches. Shortly afterwards the reserve waves will pass through and capture the German second position.'

Sir Hubert paused for effect, and smiled down at the young men with their expressions of concealed anxiety. 'That's all very well, I hear you say, but haven't you forgotten one rather important thing? What about the Germans!' A gust of relieved laughter swept the room. 'Well let me tell you, to begin with, you'll outnumber them seven to one. This is a quiet sector. But after what we're going to do to them, there simply won't be any Germans in the front trenches. Not live ones, anyway!'

The young men all started to sit back in their seats, finding more comfortable positions, beginning to relax. They smiled up at the big, fat, confident general. 'What we're laying on for you, gentlemen, is the greatest artillery bombardment in the history of warfare. There won't even be earthworms alive in the soil on the German side of the line after what we're going to do.'

He looked around the faces. 'Any of you have relatives at Waterloo, a hundred years ago?' A respectable thicket of hands shot up, including those of Freddie, Fish, George and Robert.

'Good show. Napoleon gave our chaps a pretty nasty few hours with his artillery. Fired off some twenty thousand rounds at us during the battle. Those of you who had relatives there will know that they had a bruising time of it. Cannonballs and canister-shot made carnage.' Sir Hubert paused. 'Twenty thousand rounds from muzzle-loaders in a few hours. What would you say if I told you we were going to fire over one and a half million shells onto the German positions over six days?'

A gasp of astonishment went up, and he beamed down at them. 'It's true,' he assured them. 'And not just iron cannonballs but modern shrapnel and high explosive. Not only field artillery – though we have plenty of that, eighteen-pounders and 4.5 inch howitzers that Napoleon would have given his eye teeth for – but also medium artillery: sixty-pounders and six-inch howitzer, and heavy guns all the way up to fifteen-inch howitzers firing 1400lb shells. Not that many of such monsters, admittedly, but if I say that the artillery will be practically wheel to wheel behind the front you'll see the kind of fire that we are going to put down for you. You will have twice as many guns as we had at Loos, and six times as many shells. We shall fire more shells in these six days than we fired in the first twelve months of the war.'

The young men in their uniforms looked at one another with impressed and pleased expressions. It was good to know that such effort was being expended on their behalf.

'When you go back to your battalions, your companies, your platoons, you may tell your men that we have assembled enough artillery that there is one mortar, one gun or one howitzer for every seventeen yards of enemy line. Furthermore, each of these weapons is serviced by crews day and night, and has a pile of ammunition behind it as high as a house. And it's all going to land on the heads of the Germans! Yes!'

They laughed at that. No-man's land was too wide to walk across with hordes of live Germans on the other side. The tip of the General's pointer darted here and there on the map, raking through the German lines and their rear.

'The field artillery is mostly assigned to wire-cutting. As you know, the German entanglements are very thick – you can't push through them. So we're going to scythe 'em flat for you. The eighteen pounders will fire shrapnel until the ground's as open as a meadow. They'll be supported by the smaller mortars firing directly onto the German trenches, which will help entomb the enemy in them.

'The heavy guns are reserved for material destruction. They will smash up communications trenches, approach roads, railway spurs – anything that aids the enemy in moving men and material. They will also destroy strong-points and machine gun posts.'

The pointer darted about on the map.

'Here and here, for example. The Germans make a speciality of fortifying these ruined villages, like Thiepval and Pozieres. These revetments are the most important elements in the German scheme of defence, and they contain what will be, from your point of view, his most dangerous weapon of defence, his machine-guns. He sets these in emplacements, and it is the destruction of the emplacements and the entombment of the machine-gun crews in their places of shelter, that will be one of the artillery's most important tasks.'

Sir Hubert removed his pointer, and held it up like a lance.

'Ah, I hear you say again, but what of *his* artillery? Won't *that* be firing at us as we walk forward?' Sir Hubert pursed his lips, and shook his head. 'I promise you, that as you walk forward over no-man's land on Z-day, the only noise you will hear will be from our artillery, exploding ahead of you onto what little will remain of the heads of dead Germans. Whole elements of our artillery forces have been designated for counter-battery fire. We shall simply have blown the enemy artillery apart into so much scrap-metal well before we send you forward.'

Brigadier Gervase de Clare and his team of staff officers sat at the sides of the stage as their general paced about in the middle. They radiated silent confidence, and that, too, increased the morale of their fellow officers in the audience, the ones who would actually lead the attack.

'Now, to your own part,' Sir Hubert went on. 'You'll be able to practise as much as you want. We have areas behind the lines specially chosen to represent your own sector of attack, and there you will form up by platoon, company and battalion; advance, capture your position and consolidate as succeeding waves pass through your line into the devastated German areas. Your men will be carrying full packs – we

don't want to waste any time while we go forward. They'll have
to carry ammunition and food and water with them, though we'll
re-supply as quickly as we can. You see, gentlemen, the point of this
great attack is to be this . . .'

Sir Hubert placed his pointer onto the big map like a lance thrusting
through the German lines. 'Here. From the Ancre to the Somme
river. At the Somme the French will form an infantry flank guard
after breaking through. You gentlemen are to their left, all the way
up to Gommecourt.'

He slammed the lance up to the far side. 'To the left – infantry
exploitation. To the right, gentlemen, the cavalry! Some famous names
will be forming up behind you as you wait to go forward on Z-day.
Have you heard of the Dragoon Guards, the Life Guards, the Royal
Horse Guards?'

He grinned down at them, enjoying their pleasure. 'To be sure you
have, gentlemen. The Poona Horse, Hodson's Horse, the Hussars?
Yes! Give them a big cheer as they go through. Three full divisions will
be riding through the hole you drive in the German line, gentlemen,
so let's be sure to make it a big one!'

From somewhere Freddie had acquired some tin soldiers. They were
rather old, their paint was chipped, the tips of their rifles were bent,
and they were from a bygone era, but they resolutely faced the enemy
in line. He had arranged them along a model of the waiting battlefield
he had made in the chalk on top of their bunker, mined deep into
the soil.

The model was a good one, with two sets of trenches cut into the
chalk, both guarded by barbed-wire, and the stretch of no-man's land
in between. The soldiers had left their own trenches, and had arrived
at the ones of the enemy. They stood poised in front of his trench,
ready to attack.

'Here we are,' said Freddie to the others. The four of them all
stood round the model, distinctive in their officers' uniforms. Their
Sam Browne belts were polished, as were their boots.

'This is us,' Freddie explained. 'We have left our trenches at Z-hour,
and have walked across no-man's land.'

He picked up the barbed-wire he had placed there. 'If the wire is
cut, and if the artillery has buried the Germans in their dug-outs, then
well and good. We occupy as planned, and hold as those behind us
move forward to their objectives.'

'That is the plan,' Robert pointed out.

'Of course. But things don't always go to plan, certainly not in a war, so I want us just to think about what to do if it doesn't. We have a lot of our men's lives to consider. People we know, people who live near us at home.'

'Fair enough,' Robert agreed.

'It seems to me that in order for us – the infantry – to do our job, then the artillery must do its job. If we are to walk across that land out there and take the German trenches then the artillery must have done two things: first, it must have flattened the wire – torn great holes in it that we can walk through; second, it must have killed the Germans – especially the German machine-gunners. If it hasn't done both those things, then this is what will happen. Ready, Fish?'

Fish was standing beside a stirrup pump. One end of a rubber hose was in a full bucket of water, the nozzle in Freddie's hand. Fish had his boots on the feet of the pump, and prepared to push and pull. Freddie bent down.

'I am a German machine-gunner who has survived the bombard-ment. I come out to find that the enemy – that's us – has advanced over no-man's land. The bombardment has failed to cut the wire. Pump, Fish.' A stream of water came out of the nozzle, and Freddie ran it along the line of soldiers, blowing them over. 'Stop,' he said.

He rearranged the soldiers and moved the pieces of barbed-wire to make a gap. 'Or, just as good, it has blown a narrow gap in the wire. Here we all are, trying to scramble through. Pump.' The water shot out, and in one brief squirt all the soldiers were blown down into a pile.

'Yes, but why don't you think the wire will be cut?' demanded George looking down at the little diorama anxiously.

'Some of it may be. But I think there's a good chance it won't be.'

'Why?' Robert asked stiffly.

'The eighteen-pounders are tasked with cutting the wire, and they're firing shrapnel. Shrapnel's good for killing soldiers. Blows holes in us. No good for cutting wire. For cutting wire you want high explosive, and there's not enough of it.'

'I didn't know you were a blasted expert on artillery, Freddie,' Robert said, sounding exasperated. 'Personally I place my faith in those who are.'

'That's something else,' Freddie said, unabashed. 'The chaps firing the artillery pieces are like us – not so long ago they were hunting, or farming, or going to work in an office somewhere. What I'm saying is that they aren't professionals. Good chaps, who will do their very best, but can they really whack a shell into a target the size of a tree stump from four thousand yards?'

'What rot are you talking now?' Robert demanded.

'Well, that's what you have to do. A machine-gun nest is small, as is the entrance to a dug-out. To destroy a fortified machine-gun post, or to get a shell down the tunnel into a dug-out and kill the occupants, you have to be fearfully accurate. You have to shoot like Henry. I went stalking with Henry last—'

'I have to warn you, Freddie,' Robert said dangerously. 'I find tall shooting stories as irritating as fishing ones when I am trying to help win a war.'

'. . . last autumn,' Freddie continued unperturbed. 'And you know, Henry *hand-loads* his rifle ammunition. He *weighs* the charge, examines the bullet under a magnifying glass, rejects for the slightest flaw.'

'Henry is a crank,' his brother said dismissively.

'He knows a lot about guns,' Freddie retorted. 'And the ones behind us – the artillery pieces – are not made by Holland and Holland. They suffer from wear. One shell differs from another in casing and powder – they're made in factories by unskilled labour! The maps the artillerymen use aren't perfectly accurate. Once fired, the shell is affected by wind, temperature and air pressure.'

'These technicalities are tedious,' Robert said grimly.

'That machine-gun encasement up on the spur. If we had a field gun right here we might be able to hit it. But from four thousand yards back . . .'

'I think you're wrong to disparage the gunners. And anyway, you're missing the point. Pinpoint accuracy won't matter. The whole German line is going to be flattened by sheer weight of shell.'

'Yes, but *is* it?' Freddie persisted. He produced a small pad from his pocket and peered at it. 'I've been doing some sums. Excluding the propellant that drives the shell up the barrel of the artillery piece, if Sir Hubert's figures are correct, which I am sure they are, then some twenty-one thousand tons of shell will land on top of the Germans from the bombardment.'

'Exactly,' Robert said, with deep satisfaction. 'They are not supermen. They will be so much fertiliser.'

'Yes, but wait a minute,' Freddie said, looking again at the neat columns of figures he had written into his pad. 'Twenty-one thousand tons will be fired into an area about twenty-five by two thou . . . it works out at thirty shells per thousand yards . . . but let's take out the shrapnel . . . which leaves us with HE from the howitzers and heavies . . .'

'Do get on with it, Freddie. I have told you how tedious this all is,' Robert said irritably.

'If my figures are correct—'

'I doubt it. Good at arithmetic, are you, Freddie?'

'Look, the point is that you can't take the figures for shell weight as they are, you have to use weight of explosive.'

'Yes?'

'A shell has to be dashed strong, to survive going up the barrel without blowing up. It has a strong steel case. Heavy. A thirty-five pound shell from a 4.5 inch howitzer only contains four pounds ten ounces of explosive. The rest is casing.'

Robert yawned ostentatiously. 'This is extremely boring,' he said. He moved off to the entrance to the dug-out.

'What that means,' Freddie called after him, '. . . what it means is that we are going to put only one pound of high explosive onto each ten square yards of German line.'

Robert turned. 'Freddie and Fish,' he said seriously. 'The only thing to bother yourselves with is having our soldiers ready, equipped and trained to get across no-man's land and occupy the German trenches. There we shall fortify them in such a manner to beat off any counter-attack the Germans may be able to throw at us, and get ready to support the cavalry in the breakthrough that will follow. George will then walk across and hold a service of thanksgiving.'

He looked directly at Freddie. 'I want no more of this waffle. Is that understood? If I didn't know you better I would say you were simply being defeatist. Now let's get on with this war.'

He vanished down the entrance to the dug out. Fish and George stood looking thoughtfully at the small pile of lead toy soldiers.

'Wait here a moment,' said Freddie. He went off down the trench and a few minutes later reappeared with a small box.

'What's that?'

Freddie placed it in the middle of his model of the battlefield. He opened the box and began to pay out a light electric cable. 'It's one pound of Ammatol,' he said. 'Same as in a shell.'

They followed him off down the trench and into his dug-out. There he connected it to a small electrical generator with a T-shaped handle.

'Take cover!' Freddie shouted, poking his head out, and the sentries all crouched down. He pressed in the handle and there was a colossal roar as the explosive went off. As they came out into the open the air was black with smoke, and chalk dust and fragments rained down all about them.

As it cleared, they saw Robert scrambling up out of the dug-out. Chalk dust covered his hat and his shoulders. 'What the hell was that?' he shouted.

'Where you've come from, that was a German dug-out,' said Freddie. 'They built it, same as the ones over there.'

'So?' Robert yelled furiously. 'What about this blasted explosion? Blew the damned lights out down there. What was that?'

'One pound of high explosive,' said Freddie.

8

An Obstacle Race with the Germans

Fish was peering intently over the parapet, through the entanglement, wide and grey in the sunlight.

'What is it?' Freddie asked, coming up. Fish did not reply, but continued staring, and a note of urgency came into Freddie's voice. 'What have you seen, man, what is it?'

'Shh. There's a lark nesting in the wire.'

'A lark . . .'

'Yes, the birds like it out here. Behind the line the French put them in the pot. There's a pair of swallows nesting in the overhead traverse by Karno.'

Freddie looked at his friend in amused exasperation. 'The way you were staring I thought it must be at least the Kaiser coming over at the head of his army. Are you actually with this war, Fish?'

'It can stop tomorrow as far as I'm concerned.'

'Well, that's what I want to talk to you about. Our little bit towards making it stop. Let's go down into the bunker a mo'.'

The two went along the trench. A dim buzzing was in the sky, Fish glanced up.

'Spotter plane,' said Freddie. Sure enough, the cough of an artillery piece came from the rear, and as they watched the lines, a puff of lemon-coloured smoke appeared in the air not far from the ruined farm on the spur.

'Ranging the guns for the bombardment.'

'*Look*!' Fish cried out, in sudden excitement. Seemingly from nowhere in the pale-blue sky another aeroplane was swooping down. 'Fokker.'

The RFC spotter aircraft was turning and twisting like a pigeon, the German scout on it like a pursuing hawk. They could hear the light ripping of the machine-guns in the still air. The Flying Corps craft was being forced lower and lower. It barely cleared the farmhouse opposite, flew through the yellow drifting smoke, the Fokker hard on its tail.

Something was falling out of the sky like a black stone.

'One of ours!' Freddie yelled.

The German scout saw it too, broke off suddenly. The RFC two-seater staggered groggily over their heads. Over the line the Fokker was trying to climb, to mount into the sky, but its pursuer had speed, had height and position. They heard the short, sharp bursts of a Lewis gun firing without interruption.

The Fokker flattened out. It left a thin trail of black smoke behind it, flying in a level fashion towards the lines, as if filled with bravado. The RFC biplane climbed up above it, watching warily for any companions. The Fokker came over the line, not more than fifty feet up, a pretty thing: a monoplane, dove-grey underneath, and green on its top, the large Maltese crosses very black on white panels. They saw the pilot in his cockpit, leaning back in his seat, staring up at the sky. It went over their heads, vanished behind the wood. A few seconds later they heard a loud crump, and dirty black smoke began to climb up into the air. Over the trees the RFC biplane waggled its wings, and climbed away into the sky.

'Funny thing, isn't it?' said Fish. 'The chap who did that, he'll get a medal, and we all think he's a fine fellow, buy him a jar, if we could. If he did that in peace-time, machine-gunned some poor soul in the back, well, he'd be hanged.'

'It's not the place to think that way,' Freddie observed.

'No. Here you do it to him before he can do it to you.'

'That's exactly it, actually.'

'I bludgeon, you bludgeon, he bludgeons. We bludgeon, you bludgeon, they definitely bludgeon.'

The two went into the dug-out entrance and down into the depths of the ground.

'You ever go in for the obstacle race at school, Fish?' Freddie asked.

'Oh, yes. Quite good at it, I was. I've got long legs, I could scramble over things.'

'Where'd they have it?'

'Oh, outside. Not in the athletics ground, I mean. We had to clamber over gates and stiles, crash through hedges, wade across running streams, slither down hillsides, crawl up valleys. All that sort of thing. Most rugged, it was.'

'Well, welcome back.'

'What do you mean?'

Freddie offered him a cigarette and lit for both of them. He drew the scented smoke into his lungs and spoke through the exhalation: 'As I see it, at Z-hour we shall be engaging in an obstacle race with the Germans. First one to the German parapet wins.'

'And what do you get if you win?' Fish asked, folding his arms, his cigarette tucked in the palm of one hand.

'Oh, it's a jolly good prize. Same as our airman just now. First one there gets to massacre the loser. First one to the parapet gets to shoot, hack, machine-gun, bomb or bayonet the one who comes second. Fearfully good fun, I'm sure, but the point of it is that first one to the parapet gets to live. Whoever comes second doesn't.'

'Unless our artillery scratches the Germans from the race altogether.'

'Well yes. That's Rob's view, isn't it? I'm afraid he doesn't think much of my estimates about pounds of high explosive per square yard. He may be right! I know that getting hit by a shell from a fifteen-inch howitzer will give you more than just a headache, even thirty feet down. That's 1400lb of shell and 200lb of Ammatol. That certainly will spread the Germans into mole-fodder. Only problem is there's only six of those monsters on our sector, they take for ever to reload, and have an aiming error of over twenty-five yards even with a professional behind them. Not many of those left, Fish. Not real Gunners from Woolwich with two years training behind them. Far more chaps like us, whose idea of an artillery duel is shooting at each other with champagne corks.

'But yes, if Rob's right, then we're fine. It's if Rob is wrong that I'm worried. Getting back to our obstacle race, the starter's gun is when the artillery barrage lifts off the German line. According to the plan as given to us by Sir Hubert, we then climb out of our trenches with all our equipment and walk across no-man's land towards the German line. In our case, some four hundred yards. If there are live Germans left in their dug-outs, they then run from the bottom of their steps to the top, carrying their rifles and machine-guns with them, and spread out along their fire trench.'

Freddie looked at Fish for some moments, through the silver smoke.

'Who's going to get there first, Fish?' he asked quietly.

'They are,' his companion said in a steady voice.

'Right. Unless we do something about it.'

'I would like to do that. There's this stretch of water back home. Dashed big trout in it, been trying to get him for ages. Always beats me. Drifts up to the surface and sneers at my efforts. Sworn I'll outwit him yet.'

'Jolly good,' Freddie said, absently. On the wall of the dug-out he had placed a large aerial photograph of their sector. He got up and went over to it. 'The battalion's objectives are split. A and B Companies are here, on the left. They advance on a fairly flat, rising slope. This spur here is the division line, it's really steep. The Germans have simply put entanglements up the side of it. There's no trench as such. That starts again with *our* objective, at the top of the spur. There's a ruined farmhouse up there and the Germans have certainly fortified it. There'll be machine-gun posts in there.'

He turned back, and fumbled in his jacket for his cigarette case again. 'Because it's split, Robert's agreed to let me lead C and D while he leads A and B. It means I can plan for my own attack.'

'Robert won't object?'

'Rob's a splendid chap,' Freddie said slowly, having found his case. 'He's the sort you always looked up to at school. He's honourable. Plays a straight bat. One of the first to be made a prefect. Head Boy. I'll bet if the head wanted something done, he knew if he asked Rob to organise it it was as good as done. He's the kind that's made our empire great, is Rob.'

'So why aren't you planning to attack the way he is?'

'I've always been a difficult sod,' Freddie said frankly. 'I suppose my dad has to answer for that. He always told me – and Vi – not to take things at face value. He taught us not to believe it was necessarily so, to work it out for ourselves. By my calculations, this bombardment isn't going to kill all the Germans in the trenches over there. To Rob, that makes me an insubordinate so and so. I'm not following orders, not going with the plan. I've pointed out to him that Haig's own directive states that GHQ will select the strategic objectives, but not anticipate details. The chief duty of higher command, as he sees it, is to prepare for battle, not to execute on the battlefield. They will indicate to subordinate leaders – that is, us – our respective missions, but will leave the execution to us.'

Freddie turned back to the photograph, and tapped his finger on the site of the old farmhouse and its buildings. 'Very good. They want C and D companies to take that. They say I can do it how I want. Robert's going to walk over to take his side of things. I'm not. Fish, go to the companies and find out how many miners we have. There must be quite a few from the Windstone Colliery. I want them. Get picks and shovels and have them bring up the materials for a light tramway to take away spoil. I want unrestricted use of a sap for our companies. Toad or Hole will do. Toad. Put the tramway down Toad. What date is it?'

'The twenty-second.'

'Right. The bombardment starts in two days' time. We'd better have the company concert tomorrow night, we won't be able to hear a thing once the barrage starts.' He reached out to the table and pushed a sheaf of papers to one side.

'Look at all this bumf,' he said irritably. 'Just look at it. As a company commander I am obliged to make returns to Brigade at 3.30, 8.30, 11.30, 3.00, 3.30 – three of the buggers at 7.00! – at 10.00, two indents. Meanwhile, they bombard me with incoming orders and circulars in foolscap! Yes, foolscap. My uncle Harry was Governor of Nyasaland and he ran the whole place with a couple of chaps from Charterhouse and a secretary from the Punjab. Worked a treat it did. *He* didn't bombard poor sods like me with great piles of bumf. They must cut down a medium-sized copse once a week for all this. Bum-fodder it is and bum-fodder it becomes. I put it all on a nail in the latrines, Fish. When did you last see anybody from Brigade up here? No fear of that, they're all in their blasted château sending me orders taking my heavy machine-guns away from me.'

Freddie stared angrily at his cousin. 'Did you know that, Fish? We are about to fight the biggest battle of the war and our battalion machine-guns have been taken away from us, and given into the control of somebody not here, so that not only are the guns not available for direct and opportune fire, they aren't even under our command. They now fire at hypothetical targets from the map at Brigade, and bury hundredweights of lead into harmless banks of soil somewhere in no-man's land. You ask me why I'm not prepared to believe them when they say all the Germans will be dead? Let me tell you, the bloody Germans aren't so stupid as to take their heavy machine-guns away from the company and battalion commanders.'

He picked up one of the phones that led via buried cable to air-line and into the dense communications network behind the trenches.

'Who are you c-calling?'

'Henry. Hallo? Yes, I want Number Twenty-four Squadron RFC. They're over near St Omer. Yes, I'll hold on.' Freddie tapped ash from his cigarette, heard Fish's boots clattering up the stairway of the bunker.

'Twenty-four Squadron? Windstone Yeomanry here. Is Henry de Clare about? He is? Tell him it's his cousin Freddie. Henry? Hallo . . . just got down, have you. A Fokker . . . jolly good. Over our way? That must have been you we saw. Crashed over by the wood. Good chap. How many does that make? Twenty-three, I say . . . Listen – what? The gorgeous Miss Townall? I don't know. I had to have a rest when I got back to the line. I was quite exhausted. Yes, that's right. Frightfully fit. Captures subaltern scalps like you get Fokkers. Listen. You remember all those Lewis guns you had in crates, and the Vickers one-pounder pom-poms? Right. Can you lend some to me? Will you get them back? I should hope so. If you don't get them back it's because *I* didn't get back. Yes, that kind of thing. You will? Sharoshie! I'll send a lorry for them.'

Freddie put the phone down and went back up into the open air. He walked down to the communications sap known as Toad. Men were moving there, bringing up wood for the tramway. He stood up on the firestep of the trench and peered out. Inside the entanglement a lark sat on her nest looking at him. In the distance he could see the enemy line. The thicket of barbed-wire snagged over its white posts stretched dull and grey across the spur.

24 June 1916

'Fish? Fish, are you ready?'

'I'm h-here.' Fish came out of his dug-out already shaved and dressed to find Robert waiting for him.

'Good chap. I thought you might like to see the show start. Curtain's about to go up.'

They went out and down the fire trench. It was not yet 6.30, but the morning air was clear.

'Look over there,' said Robert, pointing back behind them. In a great arc about the ruined town of Albert to their rear they could see artillery balloons flying, plump as Christmas turkeys, swaying gently, one thousand feet in the air, as though slightly inebriated. Small specks moved about the sky above.

'The RFC's driven the Germans from the sky here,' Robert said proudly. 'Look at that. Fourteen observation balloons. One for each division.'

A man came along the trench at a steady pace, a sandbag over his shoulder. It was Spyker, one-time footman at the castle, now the post corporal.

'Morning, Spyker,' said Robert. 'Post's early.'

'Yes, sir. Came up with the rations. One for you both, sir.'

'Thank you. How's your wife? Has she had the baby yet?'

'Midwife came to see her a few days ago, sir. Says it'll be any day now.'

'Good show. Let me know when you hear, and we'll all raise a glass to mother and child.'

'I will, sir.' He went off down the trench with his sandbag full of letters.

Fish had opened his, a solemn and thick manila, and extracted several pages of documentation.

'I s-say, what on earth is th-this, Rob?'

'Well, what *is* it?'

'I d-don't know. It s-says it's from the Inland Revenue.'

'Tax. Must be income tax.'

'Income tax? What's that?'

'The government's introduced a tax on incomes. You're worth, what?'

''Bout eight hundred a year.'

'Right. The government wants some of it.'

'What for? What does the g-government do for me?'

'Not much. We don't *want* the government to do anything, except provide the Navy and the law. It's the war, it's to pay for all the shells and such.'

'I d-don't see why they want me to pay for it. I'm here fighting for the country as it is. Not for the government.' Fish peered at the lists of questions and sections he had to fill in with increasing anger. 'L-Look at all this! It's n-none of their dashed business, asking me these qu-questions. D-Do I ask anything of th-them? No I d-do not.'

He crumpled the forms up and threw them over the parapet into the entanglement. 'Damn their eyes! Bally imp-pertinence, the lot of it.'

From behind him there was a sudden rumbling and drumming, a crashing and banging that spread down the front, from side to side, from north of the Ancre to south of the Somme. A howling, a roaring, a screeching as of a million express trains thundering by came over their heads. As they watched in astonishment, the entire German line erupted into an inferno of smoke and flame. White, black, lemon explosions played up and down the trenches. Great fountains of earth, of rocks, smoke and debris hurled up into the air. The trench system vanished into this great curtain, within which orange and red mouths of flame glowed and faded, like the smile of the Cheshire cat.

'It's begun,' Robert breathed.

Fish stared across at the devastation in progress, as it roared all about him, like some terrible mythical storm, possessed by dark forces. 'P-Poor b-beggars.'

'Yes, well, rather them than us,' Robert said briskly. 'Right, Fish. Remember I'm going to inspect all four companies this morning. Plenty of shiny buttons and gleaming boots, please. When we go over the top in five days I want us to look smart. Don't want any of those regular battalions showing us up.'

'Dear Jesus in heaven . . .' Robert breathed in disbelief as he stared at the line of men in front of him. Their boots were liberally caked with chalk, their puttees and trousers thickly dusted with white. At their head stood Freddie, and he was dressed as they were, in the rough serge of the ranks, only his captain's badges on the khaki epaulettes indicating the difference.

'Dammit, Freddie, come here!' Robert burst out, completely forgetting military protocol.

'Yes, Rob, what is it?' said Freddie, coming over.

'What is the meaning of this exhibition?' he demanded furiously. 'I want to inspect soldiers, not Irish navvies!'

'You *are* inspecting soldiers,' Freddie said, unrepentantly.

'Not the kind *I* wish to know,' Robert retorted. He was very cross. 'What in God's name will the regulars say when we turn out in no-man's land looking like that?'

'I'm not going to turn out in no-man's land, and nor are they.'

Robert's eyes bulged. 'And why not, pray?'

'We are going under no-man's land. That's why we're all covered in chalk. We're digging a shallow tunnel to the bottom of the spur. By Z-hour we shall be fifty feet from the German line, ready to rush them the moment the barrage lifts. D Company will go down the tunnel too, and be safe from enfilading machine-gun fire.'

'There will be no . . .' Robert began angrily, then stopped himself. He took a few deep breaths. 'I believe that you are suffering from some kind of mania, Freddie,' he said quietly. 'It breaks out from time to time within the de Clare family, I do know that. Viscount Gilbert in his dresses . . . I suppose you have been afflicted by some sort of dementia, that is why you are dressing up as a private soldier. You look dreadful. I hope nobody from Whites or Boodles sees you. Not even a Conservative would dress like that.'

He sighed, and then seemed to brighten. 'Still, our eccentricities have never stopped us performing our duties. Gilbert died at Naseby fighting like a de Clare, even if he was sidesaddle . . . I'll tell you what I'm going to do. When we have performed our attack, and once we are out of the line, you will parade your entire battalion, and I want to see them fit for Guardsmen. Not a speck! Is that understood?'

'Understood,' Freddie said quietly. 'Can we get on with digging our tunnel, now?'

'Were you stopped from playing in the mud as a child, do you think?'

'Perhaps. Rob, don't you want to know why I'm in a soldier's uniform?'

'I'd prefer not to,' Robert said austerely. 'It's not the kind of thing gentlemen talk about.'

He walked away, to inspect the other companies.

'The snipers know what we look like,' Freddie said quietly, almost to himself. 'They shoot us first.' He turned on his heel and walked down to the sap known as Toad. Sergeant Furzegrove and a squad were attempting to disentangle two trucks on the tramway, one full, one empty.

'What about it then, Sergeant?' he cried, and began heaving with the others.

'Good job we've got a navy, eh, sir?'

The wheel slipped back onto the rail and the truck began to roll to the rear, the men singing to 'Auld Lang Syne'.

> 'We're here
> Because
> We're here
> Because
> We're here
> Because we're here . . .'

9

Above the Clear Blue Sky, in Heaven's Abode

The Somme, 1 July 1916

Flying up to the lines, a light drizzle, the last of the rain that had delayed the attack by two days, made Henry Clare's DH2 colourfully shiny and slick, like a special boiled sweet. The biplane was heavy, laden with drums of ammunition and, on the outer wing struts, tubes containing large barbed rockets, four to a side, each containing fat explosive heads. The air was cool at four thousand feet – below the great arc of observation balloons sitting on top of their blanket of mist told him that he was over Albert. The distance to the lines was short; he came over the front and began his patrol.

He was to stay out for two and a half hours, to watch the opening of the attack and then co-ordinate the infantry flares as the battalions advanced through the German lines before being replaced by a second machine.

He began to sing, loudly and somewhat tunelesly, as he scanned the sky and the ground below:

> 'Madame, have you any good wine?
>   Parley-vous!
> Madame have you any good wine?
>   Parley-vous!
> Madame have you any good wine,
> Fit for a soldier of the line?
> Inky pinky parley-vous!'

Below the soft white haze was beginning to thin, and through it like a layer of dressing over diseased flesh he could see the devastation of the week-long artillery barrage. Square miles of countryside in one long strip were ripped and torn and blasted into desolation.

As he watched, the air itself began to vibrate with sound. Below, the
bank of mist rippled like a lake into which thousands of stones were
being thrown. The mist thickened, a whole salient from Beaumont-
Hamel to the Somme marshes covered with white smoke. It was the
greatest bombardment in history. Four thousand feet in the air, its
thunder beat upon Henry de Clare, slapping his face with its fury.
It was 6.25 a.m.

> 'Oh yes I have some very good wine,
> Fit for a soldier of the line,
> Inky pinky parley-vous!'

In his dug-out, Robert was shaving. His servant had brought him
hot water. A pot of tea steamed on a table, the scent of Darjeeling
was in the air. He made his chin smooth with one last stroke of his
Solingen steel cut-throat razor, wiped it clean and gave it a few strops
on the leather sharpening belt, keeping it keen for the next day. Then
he closed it and put it away in its small leather case. He washed the last
traces of foam from his face and dried himself. In the mirror he could
see where his razor had nicked him – a dab with a styptic pencil and
the tiny flow of blood ceased.

He drank some tea and carefully tied his silk tie. He was wearing
his dress boots with the silver spurs, polished the evening before by
his servant, Figgers. He put on his jacket, fastened his gleaming Sam
Browne belt and shoulder strap, and placed carefully his hat. Figgers
gave him a final brush before he set off up the steps.

Robert took his small cricket bat and tucked it under his arm. On
the floor was a full-sized bag containing stumps, bats, pads, balls and
all the paraphernalia necessary for a game.

'Now don't forget to bring the bag, Figgers,' he instructed. 'Once
Sergeant Kaye has taken our photograph at the German trench we
shall occupy ourselves with a suitably celebratory match.'

'I won't sir, don't worry.'

'I shall breakfast at the other side, Figgers. Sergeant Norwood's men
will bring the cookers forward for us all once we have consolidated
our position.'

'Very good, sir.'

'Bring up some bottles of the ninety-six Cliquot, too. I think we'll
all feel like a glass of something refreshing.'

'I shall, sir.'

Robert climbed up into the light. He took a good lungful of the fresh air. The mist had burned off, the sun shone from a cloudless sky. A tremendous racket assailed his ears: the dull boom of the heavy guns in the rear just audible beneath the sharp incessant cracking of the 4.7-inch weapons and eighteen-pounders closer to his line. Above his head there was a continual stream of shells rumbling and whining over to the German positions, bursting there in flame and smoke and noise. The howitzers and 9.2-inch guns were laying on the wood in the distance; whole trees were uprooted, flying flaming and tumbling into the air. Smoke was beginning to cover the area. It was seven o'clock.

Twelve thousand yards back from the line, and outside artillery range, the fearsome barrage assumed the qualities of a nearby thunderstorm, grumbling and growling to itself, shaking the air but not the ground. Violet stood at the end of the lane in her nurse's uniform, red cross vivid against the white of her apron. The morning air was pleasing, birds were singing in the trees, the sun was drying the damp of the previous day's drizzle, bringing out the fragrance of the countryside.

She stood by a large white sign, painted in red letters with an arrow, guiding people to Bandagehem Casualty Clearing Station. Behind her large white tents had been pitched in the meadow, as though in preparation for a large garden party. Beyond the tree-line a canal glittered in the sun, some barges moored to its bank. On the slight breeze she heard the shriek of a train's whistle, the slow clatter of carriages arriving at a railhead. As the noise ceased she heard the puttering of a car's engine, and a little black Renault came into view along the recently paved road. She waved and a hand inside fluttered back.

The small car pulled up, and Clarissa Townall smiled out. 'Made it!' she said. 'I'm not late?'

'Not a bit!' Violet said cheerfully. 'Look, park over here under these trees, and no eager ambulance driver will run into you by mistake.'

Clarissa moved the car and climbed out. The two girls gave each other a hug.

'It surely is good to see you,' said Clarissa. She was dressed in a functional outfit of white shirt and riding breeches tucked into boots.

'I wish I was dressed like you,' Violet cried. 'This affair is so cumbersome, and you get so hot in it.'

'Well, I suppose that's the uniform, and you have to wear it.'

'You do, you do.'

'What are you doing out here? I thought you were in one of those big hospitals in the rear.'

'Oh, I was. But I managed to have a row with just about everybody that mattered, so I applied to come up to a CCS team.'

Clarissa grinned. 'Tell me about it.'

'I will. Listen, we've got time for a gasper before I introduce you to Dr McKay.'

Violet brought out a packet of Player's Navy Cut, and lit cigarettes for them both with a gold Dunhill.

'What's that say on it? Oh, I see.'

'Fish gave it to me. Isn't it nice? That was something else. We weren't supposed to smoke. That with all the other things . . .'

'What?'

'Oh, I'm sure Mummy would say it's my de Clare blood coming out. I just can't stand all that institutional stuff, all the bureaucracy, all these little, little people making up rules to make other people's lives miserable. But you combine it with incompetence and I'm afraid the famous de Clare temper got the better of me! I'd read all those books you gave me, and I was amazed. I knew more than they did! They bled patients – as if they hadn't lost enough blood already – and with what? Leeches! They treated soldiers unfortunate enough to catch syphilis by mosquito bite! They used chloroform to knock them out for operations and in such quantities that some died and the remainder turned yellow with jaundice.'

'Liver damage,' Clarissa said soberly. 'I'd heard things were bad in some hospitals, but that's awful.'

'It's good out here. The closer to the front you get the better things are. The surgical techniques in the CCS are pretty efficient. We have the usual problems – septicaemia from battle wounds where fragments or bullets remain in the body – it's hard to locate the bits. But at least we don't treat it with rhubarb purgative like those dopes . . .'

'We're developing a photographic technique for that. X-ray they call it. But I haven't seen one yet.'

'Haemorrhage is fatal too. There's no way of replacing the blood.'

'Oh, but there is!'

'Really?' Violet said with interest. 'That would be marvellous. We get a lot of men who just die, you know, from shock. If we could put blood back into them they'd live.'

'I've read about it in the *Lancet*.' Clarissa affirmed. 'A man called Keynes has developed an apparatus for transfusing blood taken from donors. But you have to type it first.'

'Type it?'

'Yes, blood comes in different types, and some aren't compatible.'

'You couldn't find out about it, could you? It'd make such a difference. It's no use going through official channels. If you want something done you need to do it yourself.'

'I will,' she promised. 'Did you hate the hospital terribly, Vi?'

Violet drew on the stub of her cigarette, and then ground it into the dirt. 'They made the dying men sit up in bed and smile when inspection time came round,' she said grimly. 'The awful power of the institution over the individual, you see. I remember one chap, he came in having lost both legs, but for some reason, he was hungry. He came in at night and we were forbidden to serve food until breakfast time at eight. He was hungry. He died hungry, because he didn't make it until eight. That was the day I applied to join a CCS.' In the distance the growling thunder of the barrage continued without cease.

'Come on,' Violet said. 'I'll introduce you to Angus.'

Outside the tents nurses, porters, surgeons and anaesthetists were sitting and standing in the sunshine, waiting for their tasks to begin.

'There's about a hundred of us per unit,' Violet explained. 'All doing our assorted tasks. We provide six separate surgical teams, of which two are always on duty.'

Clarissa produced a pad and pen from her bag. 'I'd better start noting things down,' she said. 'Oh, and you wanted to know more about the blood transfusion business.'

She wrote in a neat hand and colourful blue ink.

'Here we are,' said Violet. 'Angus, may I introduce you to my friend Dr Clarissa Townall? Clarissa, Dr McKay.'

McKay was a young man in his twenties, from Edinburgh, casually dressed in shirt and flannels. 'Would that be a degree of philosophy now?' he enquired, shaking her hand.

'No, I am a surgeon, the same as you are, Dr McKay,' Clarissa said levelly.

He smiled. 'Well, now, this is an occasion to be valued for its rarity,' he said pleasantly. 'We don't see many female doctors. Please call me Angus, we don't stand on formality here.'

'My father is Senator Townall. He's asked me to write him a report on the Royal Army Medical Corps way of handling the battle casualties out here. He feels that we Americans might benefit from your experience.'

'I'll be happy to tell you what I know,' he agreed. They were standing under a large chestnut, on which conkers were setting. The meadow was a Persian carpet of crane's bill, loosestrife, orchids and innumerable other flowers. Tortoiseshell and Meadow-brown butterflies flew amongst them, and down by the stream the banks were alive with rushes in flower, white with campanula.

'Just to begin with, why are these little temporary hospitals so close to the front?'

'Very simple. We discovered from experience earlier in the war that some types of wound travelled badly. Chest and abdomen, most notably. Secondly if all dead and injured tissue, together with battle debris was removed from the wound within thirty hours of damage then much sepsis and gangrene could be successfully controlled. For both these reasons, it makes sense to bring the treatment as close to the patient as possible.'

She nodded thoughtfully, and made some quick notations in her book. 'Perhaps you could describe a man's journey from the battle-field to treatment,' she suggested.

'Why not? A man hit on the field can get off it in two ways, he can walk, if he is not too badly wounded, or he can be carried off it by stretcher-bearers. There are thirty-two of these brave men to every thousand soldiers.'

Clarissa wrote rapidly and clearly in her notebook. 'Whom do they take? The first they come to?'

'Not exactly. They are under orders to take the less badly wounded first.'

There was a short silence while she digested this. 'You mean the ones who need treatment with the most urgency get taken last?' she said, in disbelief.

'Yes.'

'Why?'

'The army is possessive about its men,' McKay said drily. 'It wants them, as far as is possible, patched up and back with them so that they may go and fight again. You see, the army's reason to exist is to win the battle, win the war. For that, it needs to get the most use from its raw materials. We are a kind of reconditioning plant.'

'And the badly wounded?'

'Many die out there, if there is a battle in progress,' McKay said frankly, in his quiet burr. 'But if they do get off the battle-field they are taken quite rapidly to treatment in the rear, by train or by barge, which is very good for the most badly wounded, and quite a lot of them to proper medical facilities in England itself.'

'Who sorts them out? Which ones are treated here, which ones need to go to England. You do?'

'That's right. The *triage* system.'

'*Triage?*' Clarissa asked, looking puzzled. 'I don't think I've heard of that. *Triage* ... does it mean division into three?'

McKay seemed suddenly to need a cigarette. He fumbled in his pockets until he found his packet, and lit one, looking older than his twenty-five years. 'That's it. You see, there tends to be so many casualties in a big battle. You can't treat them all. You have to make a decision on each one, when he comes in. Do I operate? Do I send him further to the rear for treatment? Or ...'

'Or do you let him die,' Clarissa whispered.

'Yes.'

'We have a moribund ward,' Violet said quietly. 'We shield them from the fact that they are dying. It is not a horrible way to die.'

'That's awful,' Clarissa objected.

'What's *awful* is being left out on the battlefield to die in agony. Maybe for days,' McKay said soberly. '*That* is beyond description.'

'What proportion of the soldiers do you expect to become casualties?' Clarissa asked suddenly.

'I was at Neuve Chapelle. These CCS hospitals are mobile, you know. We can arrive and set up in a day.'

'Neuve Chapelle?'

'They estimated sixty per cent of the attacking force, before the battle started.'

'Were they right?'

'That time, yes.'

Clarissa pointed to the growling of the distant barrage, through the trees: 'Sixty per cent?'

'They say not,' Violet said quickly.

In the clear blue sky, an aeroplane droned overhead, heading for the front.

'Not long now,' said McKay, and dragged some smoke urgently into his lungs.

The Russian sap with its closed, curved roof smelled strongly of bacon sandwiched in fried bread. As each man had come down the tramway to the entrance of the tunnel his water bottle had been filled with a mixture of cold tea and lemon, and he had been given two thick sandwiches, one of bacon and fried bread, the other thickly spread with raspberry jam. Cook Sergeant Norwood had prepared dinners for fifty, six courses at a sitting, for the Earl at the castle – it had been little problem for him to set up his range in a small culvert dug into the side of the trench. As the men went forward with their rifles and packs of ammunition, each was given sustenance.

As they came through, Sergeant-Major Hopcroft directed them into the bays where they would wait, before breaking out at the foot of the German lines. Here, close up, the very ground was vibrating with the shelling.

'Here we go lads. You all right, Squisson? Yes? You look a bit, you know?'

'I'm all right, Sergeant-Major. Be just fine when we get going, you know what I mean?'

'That's it, lad. Come on, Lurton lad, you and your lot sit here and finish your sandwiches while Mr Frederick opens the trench up ahead.'

'Be good to get it over, Sergeant-Major.'

'That's it, lad. Let's push them back to Berlin, and then we can go home and chase Sergeant Furzegrove about again, a-poaching his lordship's pheasant.'

'I'd like that, Mr Hopcroft.'

'You look out for them new boots you're wearing, young Harold, you haven't had a chance to break them in.'

'Climbing up that hill will do that, Sergeant-Major.'

'I dare say you're right, Harold. Safety-catch on that rifle till we form up, now.'

At the head of the long sap, there was air and incredible noise, as the spades ripped open the entrance and the two arms at the end of the trench. Furzegrove was there, as the miners emerged into the air. Pushing aside the last of the chalky turves, he and his men brought up the sandbags, and began to fortify the gun emplacements they had cut at the fists of the two arms. There they mounted the two pom-pom guns, and began to bring up the boxes of ammunition.

Freddie scrambled out into the rough grass and scrub of no-man's land, four hundred yards from his own line. The soldiers were carrying twenty-foot lengths of steel piping. The pipes were stuffed with ammatol – they were land torpedoes.

The noise was fearsome. At the top of the slope that led up the spur shells were bursting, white and black and yellow. Metal fragments screamed in the air, raining down mingled with dirt. On the spur the entanglements of barbed-wire stood snagged, dull silver on their posts. Here and there the posts sagged, the ground was churned to the consistency of porridge, but the wire remained.

'Bloody wire's not cut!' Freddie screamed above the din. Shells howled overhead, stinking smoke stained the morning breeze. Freddie led his team up the hill at a trot. As shells burst in front of them, whining and thundering, the men shoved the bangalore torpedoes into the heart of the entanglement. They paid out cables as they ran back down.

Freddie connected the wires to his box. They all crouched down in the trenches, and he shoved vigorously on the T-handle, feeling the generator whirr under his fingers. The noise was such that the roar of the explosions was almost obliterated. Only a rain of metallic fragments on their steel helmets told the story. When they looked up, they could see wide lanes blasted clean through the wire above them.

The gun emplacements were ready. The fire trenches were sand-bagged, the Lewis gunners were filing up, their weapons on the strong leather slings over their shoulders. Boxes of ammunition stood ready next to each man. The air of the trench was scented with rum; each man had a shot, thick and treackly and sweet, fiery in the stomach, real over-proof Navy rum, neat and giving of courage. The men tossed it down, and within seconds they laughed and grinned madly at each other, their eyes wild in the harsh light of the trench. Behind them came the bombers and the knobkerrie men. Freddie led them out to lie down at the bottom of the spur. Lewis gunners and riflemen followed, the sunlight glinted on the fixed swords of the rifles.

Still the shells howled and shrieked overhead. The infernal cannon-ade seemed suddenly to increase in rage as every available weapon behind the British lines hurled its explosive at the enemy crouching somewhere beneath the earth in front of them.

It was 7.20.

The mist had cleared. Henry de Clare knew exactly where he was over the lines. He was not far short of the northerly end of the attack – he could see below in the clear air the ruined fortified village of Beaumont Hamel, occupied by the Germans. Nearby was the redoubt of Hawthorn Ridge, from which the German troops were able to lay down a fearsome level of fire at anyone attempting to cross no-man's land. Hence, the British had arranged for miners to dig a tunnel underneath the redoubt, filling its end with several tons of high explosive. The mine was one of several, three large and seven small. The pilots on patrol above the lines had been warned of the presence of such dangers.

Henry was still singing, another verse of an endless song of the mademoiselle from Armenteers:

'Madame have you a daughter fine,
Fit for a soldier of the line?
Inky pinky parley-vous?'

His watch, mounted on the dashboard, told him it was 7.20.

As he watched, the ground heaved and glowed scarlet and orange. A magnificent and enormous column of earth reared high into the sky. In his open cockpit, four thousand feet up, Henry heard an ear-splitting roar that drowned out the thunder of the artillery. A great hand threw him sideways in the vibrating air. The column rose, higher and higher like some great cypress tree, its upmost branches reaching his own altitude. For a few seconds it hung there in the sky, and then disintegrated into a great and spreading cone of dust and debris.

In eight minutes, the remaining mines would be blown. In ten, the troops would go over the top.

As his machine steadied, like a calming horse, ponderous in the air with its racks of rockets mounted outboard on the wings, he scanned the ground below. Like flowers sprouting in the desert after rain, observation balloons were rising into the air from the German rear lines. As he watched, shells from their artillery began to fall upon the British positions and in no-man's land – white and black and lemon puffs of smoke that sent red-hot splinters of steel screaming through the air.

He could see the nearest balloon, floating three thousand feet below him, a monstrous tadpole. He could see the lorry it had rushed in on from the safety of the rear, that held its gas tanks, its winch and steel cable. Underneath it was the basket containing the observers, with their direct telephone line to the artillery batteries that were now shelling the British line. What he could not see were the men who could see him, the ones crouching about in hiding, next to all kinds of ordnance, all designed to protect the balloon from him.

Henry put the nose down, and dived. As he did so, the archie, the anti-aircraft fire, began to explode all about him, orange flashes that blossomed into stinking woolly-black smoke. As he went through the explosions grunted at him, like angry pigs. The balloon still flew high in the sky, the Germans making no attempt to pull it down. The sight annoyed him. Near vertical, he howled out a final verse of his song:

'Oh yes, I have a daughter fine
Far too good for a bloke from the line,
Inky pinky parley-vous!'

Something burst very close to him, kicking the aircraft sideways, snapping his head back, making it smack into the cockpit coaming. The air was now grimy but somewhere in there was the balloon.

'Fuckers,' he gasped.

He flew out into clear air and something rained on him, slapping and plinking and puncturing his fabric, popping dimples and gashes in its skin. Something very hot and sharp screamed about in his cockpit, slicing through his boot and burying itself, burning hot in his leg.

'*Bastard*!' he shouted. 'Bastard fucker!'

The ground was coming up close, dirty and scarred, stinking like a rubbish dump. It prickled with the orange and yellow flashes of fire directed at him. His controls felt sloppy and disconnected as the little biplane staggered across the sky.

They were hauling the balloon down: it attempted to run away from him as he hurtled down in his headlong dive. He touched the trigger of the Lewis gun and scarlet blobs streaked away from him, plucking at the fat shiny grey bag of gas. He could see two men staring at him from the heavy basket underneath, swinging like an udder. He pressed the electrical button that fired his rockets and they whooshed away from him in a filthy yellow glow. He banked away, felt the heat as the balloon ignited, turned back to see the sky filled with its light. It roared as it burned, like a great acetylene lamp. Two parachutes, white as dandelion seeds were floating away on the breeze.

Machine-gun-fire popped and spattered about him. Things flew off the bracing wires with a whine and a scream. Something smacked into his intrument panel and hot liquid sprayed across his face, making him shout out in rage. He was in a steep bank, explosions filling the air with blast and vacuum that smacked him up and then down, first one wing pointing at the sun then the other, his body hanging from its seat strap and then crunched into the floor.

'Oh, God, fucking Jesus.'

The great fire bag roared at his ear, he felt its heat. The air was suddenly smooth, the white parachutes floated gently by in front of him. He machine-gunned the observers with harsh, vivisectionist strokes, blew them into bloody bits dangling from the parachute straps. Balloons were easily replaced, artillery observers had to be trained. The parachutes crumpled, drifted idly, freed of their weight.

Slumped down in his cockpit, he staggered round in his turn. Below men were running, stumbling in panic over the rough shelled ground. Howling at full tilt, the powerful winch dragged the balloon down, and the great furnace of gas fell on top of them.

Henry de Clare lurched across the lines. A disgusting taste of oil and propellant and burning filled his nostrils. He spat gobs of it out over his boots, grimy and stinking. The very air was filthy but he could see the stains of the great mines that had blown. His leg hurt, his whole body was shaking. Spittle was running down over his chin, blood was filling his boot.

He heard a strange voice warbling; he looked about to see who it was before he realised it was his own croak:

> 'Mademoiselle from Armenteers,
> She hasn't been fucked in forty years,
> Inky pinky parley-vous . . .'

Shells of one sort or another blew him this way and that, bursting over no-man's land in sudden coloured puffs of smoke. The attack had begun. The first wave of British soldiers had left their trenches. Staggering for home in his battered aeroplane Henry passed over waves of them, lying down in khaki lines in no-man's land.

Pegs were hammered deep into the trench side, scaling ladders were hooked over the parapet. The barrage beat upon the men standing there like a force of nature, a hurricane. Waiting for the first wave to climb out, Fish could not hear any single gun or explosion, only a vast symphony of destruction, myriad groans and blows, sighs and cries. It roared over him like gigantic breakers smashing upon a beach.

He had checked his men: they stood waiting either side of him, packs and ammunition, bombs and picks and spades, Verey lights, flares, sandbags to consolidate the enemy trenches, round drums of Lewis gun ammunition, rolls of barbed-wire. He knew they all watched him, took their lead from him, and he took care to stand up straight, imperturbable and confident. He could see Robert strolling up and down the trench amongst his men, smiling, his little cricket bat tucked under his arm, and he began to do the same. The noise was so great that nobody could speak, but he caught the eye of the men and smiled at them. Corporal Roberts, who had been in the stables; rifleman Thomas, of the little property by the brook; Sergeant Groves, so proud of his marrows and sweet peas, which won prizes. There was rifleman Hinchwood, the only son of old parents, they would be needing him when he got home. Lance Corporal Davis, from the kitchen: active soldiering had made him lose weight. He was chewing something, and Fish grinned at him.

There were Nevil and Walter, the brothers, so good with the herd.

Their huge hands, that could grip a cow's nostrils like pincers, clasped their rifles like a boy's popgun. Clifford the farrier's son: Dorothy the pretty daughter of the stationmaster was waiting for him. There were Reg and Herbert, the firemen from the branch line; there Gilbert the organist from the church, who played so sweet for them whenever they could find a piano.

All in rough and ill-fitting serge, dull-green iron helmets, all loaded like mules, ten feet down in the earth, as the barrage roared above them. Sweat beaded their parchment faces, the air smelled of it, and of over-proof rum – one sixty-fourth of a gallon, a small coffee cup of potent treacly courage.

Robert was looking at his watch, his hunting horn in his hand. The sky was dirty, dust and debris and smoke from the mines staining it like chalky mud. It was 7.30. He put his horn to his lips and blew. The sharp sounds of the tantivy sounded clear. The shelling had stopped, as though cut off with a switch. Behind the lines the gunners were raising their sights for the first lift. All along the trenches the first wave were heaving themselves ponderously from their trenches.

Robert was the first to climb out, turning left and right, encouraging the men with his cricket bat, waving them forward as he marched into no-man's land.

The silence was shattered. Shells began to fall into no-man's land, the sky punctured by woolly black clouds, the air splintered by screaming steel.

Fish was furious. 'Bloody gunners!' he yelled. 'Bloody shorts.'

His twenty seconds were nearly up. He stuck his whistle between his teeth. From out over the ridge, he heard Robert's horn.

Time.

He blew hard and loud as he scrambled up the ladder and stood on the parapet. The sudden exposure, coming out of the trench, was like diving into icy water – for a second his breath was taken away. He made himself move, reaching down to help his heavily laden soldiers out.

'Here we go, Nevil. That's it. Come on Reg, here give him a shove. That's it. Get them in line, Hubert. Two yards spacing.'

Absurdly, he wondered why he wasn't stuttering. He reached down and grasped little Clifford's wrist, felt the young man from the farrier's grip him hard as he heaved him up.

'There we—' Something exploded just in front of him. He was wet, wet and warm, he had some muck all over his face, he wiped it out of his eyes with his free hand. He couldn't see Clifford.

He found he was holding his arm – only the arm, still in khaki from shoulder to wrist. His ears were singing, they echoed to the flat crack of a whizz-bang. He was soaked in blood and ordure. Fragments of bone stuck from his serge uniform. The trench in front of him was filled with offal, dead men strewn like a butcher's yard all over the duck-boards, stuck to the sides, mixed up with mud and equipment. He let go of the arm, and it clung to him, the hand gripping his wrist. In horror, he flailed it about, trying to release its grip, and red blood sprayed bright against the sun. He dragged it off, dropped it, turned away from the carnage.

The men were in line, rifles at the port, moving towards the German trenches.

'I s-say, wait for m-me!'

He ran forward through the wide gap cut in his own wire. Something exploded next to him without warning, blew him sideways, knocked the wind out of him like a rugby smother tackle, left him gasping for air, all tangled up in the wire as the men walked on. From somewhere, he heard a steady popping sound.

With thirty seconds to go Freddie led the two companies in a rush up the slope. Above them the barrage still pounded the trenches and the ruined farmhouse. Dust and debris filled the air, coating their teeth.

Suddenly, it was quiet. The roaring of the tempest that had enveloped them was gone. They came over the smashed parapet in a yelling horde. They found Germans streaming up from the deep dug-outs; they bayoneted them and flung grenades down the shafts. From below they heard the rattle of the Lewis guns and the syncopated clamour of the pom-poms as they massacred the machine-gun crews attempting to man their weapons in their fortified positions.

Then it was quiet.

'Sergeant! Bring up the wire and the guns from below. Secure this position,' Freddie ordered. 'Sergeant-Major! C Company will come with me. Have everyone re-equip with ammunition and grenades. Look lively now! We have to keep up with the barrage.'

Peering over the rear of the trench he could see the artillery fire playing on the second line of fortifications, some three hundred yards distant. The pom-pom crews staggered gasping up the slope with their small artillery pieces, the Lewis gunners set themselves ready with their ammunition. He blew his whistle, and the company went forward, moving in small groups, rushing from one set of cover to the next.

* * *

The breath rasped back into Fish's lungs. He crawled from the entanglement, feeling his uniform ripping on the barbs, and pushed himself to his feet. He couldn't see the men of his company, he simply ran after them towards the German lines. The brief moment of silence was over – once again the air roared and screamed all about him. The very ground quaked under his boots and he could not see. He tripped and stumbled on freshly dug earth. He thought he could see some men moving ahead like jerky figures in a moving picture, figures popping up and down in the strange subterranean murk. The dirty light flashed scarlet and orange, it howled at him through fountains of black smoke. He thought he heard someone yelling orders.

He tripped over something and fell beside it. A man. Lying in full battle order. A great sense of relief came over him as he saw the shiny brass of the Windstone Yeomanry on the epaulettes. Looking through the smoke, he saw them all lying down in a line. He had managed to catch up with his men.

He stood up, so that they might see him better.

'All right, chaps!' he yelled. 'Forward!'

Nobody moved, except one man, who turned his head, hearing a voice. Blood was running down his face. Fish thought it was Gilbert, the organist.

'Come on, Gilbert!' he shouted. 'It's no good lying there. Get the men up. Come on, chaps, for shame.'

Gilbert was mouthing at him in the roaring murk. Fish bent down to pull him up.

'Dead,' he said. 'All fucking dead, sir.' Blood poured from his mouth, and he slumped forward into the grass.

Fish ran to and fro along the line. He found a few wounded, one or two paralysed by fear. He got them to their feet, took a rifle and ammunition pack, led them forward.

In the howling steel rain he found himself singing. A hymn, a hymn from his childhood. He felt insanely cheerful. The prep school chapel organ roared in his head, he bellowed out the words. The shells burst about him, scarlet and orange and yellow, beautiful lights amidst the driving smoke. An aeroplane came by, its machine-guns rattling among the heavier booming, just like stage effects. The sky and ground was fused into grey and green and brown in the early morning light, and he thought he had never seen a more lovely spectacle.

'Above the clear blue sky!' he howled, 'In Heaven's abode . . .'

He raised his voice in song and marched on into the smoke.

*   *   *

'Here,' said Violet, and passed Clarissa a stiff, starched white smock, stencilled with the message 'RAMC Property'. She tugged on her own, and they did up the tapes behind them.

'Here they come.'

The puttering of an engine that Violet had heard emerged as an ambulance, khaki with red crosses on its boxy sides, coming into view at the end of the meadow. Clarissa pushed her notebook away.

'It's no good,' she said. 'I'm trained for this work. I can write up the notes later. What do you want me to do?'

'How about helping get them ready?' Violet said gratefully. 'It gets to be quite a crush. You'll have to cut away their uniforms so we can see the wound. Don't lose the luggage label.'

'Luggage label?'

'Wound description and particulars applied by the Regimental Aid Post. Cross on the forehead with an indelible pencil means a morphia injection's been given.'

'Okay.'

'I'll go inside and get ready to help Angus.'

Clarissa stood waiting, suddenly nervous. This was bizarre. What were they all doing, standing about in a field, preparing to do major surgery. Where was the certain, reassuring routine of investigation, ward, thorough notes, antiseptic operating theatre – all the facilities of a hospital?

The ambulance pulled up, a rattling Austin. A crow was disturbed from its tree, cawing derisively. The doors were pushed back, and a crew of two began unloading the first stretcher.

'Where'd you want it, mum?' the driver asked her.

'Over here,' she said, pointing inside the tent.

They put the first stretcher down, and she knelt beside it. He was a young boy, very white in the face. His uniform was caked with a filthy stiffening of blood and dirt. A two-and-a-half yard field dressing was barely visible in it all, wrapped about his thigh.

'Where are you hurt?' she asked.

He gestured silently to the brown luggage label attached to a button, and then opened his mouth, saving all his energy for what mattered.

'Got a fag, miss?' he whispered.

'Yes, yes, of course.'

She fumbled underneath her smock, and found her gold cigarette case. She took out a tipped cigarette and put it between his lips, lighting it for him.

'All right?'

'Proper *bon*, thank you,' said the faint, thin voice.

With her scissors she cut away the stiff cloth, the blades making a crunching sound. She had never seen such a wound, it was not like anything she had ever come across: huge, rough-edged, occupied by ragged and purple fragments of flesh and mud, bits of rough and bloody serge, amidst which vessels of different sizes leaked and twitched. A jagged edge of glistening white bone poked out of the mess. Whatever had done it had caused such impact that the blood had squirted away from it under enormous pressure. She could see bleeding tracks, destroyed roads of pulped flesh under the swollen skin that would require investigation.

She fumbled for the luggage label. 'Private Conyers, East Yorkshire Light Infantry. Regimental Number. Hit by a whizz-bang fragment.' She cut the uniform further away. Some secondary damage. Mentally she planned the operation, the moves required to save the leg. Certainly three hours work, with further operations to follow.

'Clarissa!'

She looked up, her thoughts interrupted. Violet was gesturing at her from the operating tent.

'Get him in, we need to get going,' she called urgently.

Clarissa scrambled to her feet, went over. The reception tent was filling up, nurses were working quickly, examining the wounded. 'He has a very serious injury,' she said.

Violet looked over her shoulder at the young man lying quietly, smoking his cigarette with stoic endurance, and assessed the wound with an expert, immediate glance.

'That's an amputation,' she said brusquely. 'Let's bring him in.'

'Who says so?' Clarissa said, shocked.

Violet pointed soberly out of the entrance, down the lane, along the road.

'*They* do,' she said.

The road from the battle, only a short while ago empty, was filled with men and amulances: Men on foot staggering wearily, stumbling along, wrapped in blankets or coats, limping, held up by comrades, their only sustenance the cigarettes in their mouths; ambulances pulling up in line to unload their damaged cargo. The tent was full, nurses were lying the wounded down on the grass, bringing water, attempting to arrange shade.

'We don't have time,' Violet said quietly.

Clarissa bent down, and helped Violet carry Private Conyers inside the operating tent, where the surgeon was waiting.

*   *   *

It was quite quiet. He was lying in a shell-hole. There were some other men there, asleep. The sky was clear, a clear blue. He was hot. He could feel the sun on him. His hands were sticky – when he looked at them his palms and fingers were ripped by three corner tears, oozing slowly coagulating blood.

'Was it some water you were saying you had, sir?' said a voice, an Irish voice, and Fish looked up from his damaged hands to see one of the sleeping men watching him alertly. He had taken off his kit, the wounded man's privilege, and it lay neatly beside him. He held up an empty water bottle.

'A bullet straight through it sir. Would you believe that?'

'Here.' Fish fumbled with his own water bottle and passed it over. They both lay below the lip of the crater. At some time earlier he had lost his peaked hat. An iron shrapnel helmet lay on the ground nearby, he picked it up and put it on.

'Lemon tea,' the Irishman said in amazement. 'What a fine lot you must come from.'

'W-Windstone Yeomanry.'

'Is that so?' the other said politely.

'What am I doing in this h-hole?'

'Well now. I saw yez running at the wire over there with the other lads, only it wasn't cut, you see. The Germans over there, they shot your fellows with a machine-gun. And while they were doing that you shot them with your rifle, and threw bombs at them. Shouting you was. You ran out of bombs and rounds for the rifle, and I called to yez to come over here, before some of the others shot you. I would have come to your aid, you see, only I have this.'

Looking at him, Fish saw that his left foot had been blown clean off below the ankle. The Irishman had improvised a tourniquet tight about his calf.

'Is it all right?'

'Ah, yes sir, doesn't hurt at all. A good Blighty one that is.'

'Well, thank you . . .'

'I'm Corporal Coogan. Pat Coogan.'

'I'm Fish. Honestly. Fish de Clare. I have a lot of other names too, but Fish does.'

'To be sure it does.'

From somewhere ahead of him there was a shouting and laughing, interspersed with the flat crack of a pistol going off. Somehow, it offended Fish.

'What's that damned noise?' he demanded.

He edged up the crater to peep through the grass. Behind the barbed-wire, a German soldier was capering about on the ruined parapet. A man's body was hung up on the entanglement and the German was shooting at it. The explosions turned it around, jerking at the corpse, and Fish saw that it was Groves, who had the little house by the copse, where the stream went under the old bridge.

'I say,' he said, enraged. 'That's dashed bad form.'

He looked about him. A rifle lay by one of the sleeping men.

'Do you think your chaps there will mind if I borrow that bandook?'

'Why no, sir,' Coogan said gently. 'They don't mind anything at all.'

Fish pulled up the weapon and checked the magazine and chamber. It was loaded. He pulled it into his left shoulder and settled the front blade sight into the notch of the rear tangent leaf. The German in grey was calling down to someone else in the trench, laughing. He fired into Groves' body again and a part of his head flew off.

Fish squeezed the trigger. For a second, the German stood on top of the parapet, blood spouting a yard and a half into the air from the stump of his neck, his head blown back over his shoulders. Then he fell, and vanished. Fish slid back down.

'That's enough of his d-dashed nonsense,' he said.

A few moments later there came the flat crump of a grenade going off and steel splinters whined over their heads. It was followed by some more, and then silence fell again.

'No sense of h-humour, your J-Jerry,' Fish observed.

'You know what I'd like, right now, sir? A long glass of Murphy's, all dark and cool with a head on like whipped cream.'

'It'll not be long,' Fish promised. 'The next wave'll be along soon. I'll get you back then.'

'I think I was the next wave, sir. We're all lying out there in the grass. Yes, a glass of Murphy's and a smoke.'

'I t-tell you what. All the platoon and company commanders, Robert gave us all a cigar to smoke when we got there. Proper Havana, in a tube.' Fish searched carefully inside his jacket and brought out a shiny aluminium tube like a torpedo.

'See? When we get back you can smoke it for me.'

'A proper cigar . . .' Coogan breathed. 'Just like the rich folk have . . .'

Fish tossed it across to him, and he caught it, looking at it reverently.

'All them funny words, that's be Spanish, I suppose. Makes you wonder why they can't talk properly, doesn't it? Poor benighted foreign folk.'

'Benighted foreign folk out there with g-guns, Pat.'

Fish peered along the front. He realised he had no idea where he was. Over in the distance there was a wood, ragged and shelled, partly occupied by a dust cloud. From somewhere inside it a mad drummer was beating a great drum.

'This isn't Mash,' he said. 'Our codeword, Mash. This isn't right.'

'Why no,' said the Irishman. He began to sing, softly:

> 'I have no pain, dear mother, now,
> But ho! I am so dry.
> Connect me to a brewery,
> And leave me there to die.'

He chuckled gently. Behind him Fish could see something moving. No-man's land was littered with rubbish. Torn and bloody field dressings. Dud shells like tree stumps in the soil. Paper. Letters, postcards, wrappings from parcels. Dead men. Scattered all over, pathetic heaps of khaki, some with upturned rifles to denote the wounded. One of the khaki figures was moving. Slowly, he turned himself, and began to crawl towards the British lines in the distance. A shot cracked nearby, he jerked, and was still.

'Bastard,' Fish muttered furiously. He took his rifle, and edged up again to the rim of the grass. Very carefully, he began to scan the line opposite, peeking under the flat steel brim of his helmet. Below him in the crater, he could hear Coogan singing quietly again:

> 'Here's to the good old rum,
> Mop it down, mop it down!
> Here's to the good old rum,
> Mop it down!
> Here's to the good old rum,
> That warms your balls and your bum,
> Here's to the good old rum,
> Mop it down . . .'

A British BE2 came down low over the lines, as though looking for infantry flares. It went off into the distance, weaving about like a hound that had lost the scent.

'Here's to the good old porter,
That slips down as it oughter . . .'

Fish watched the line intently, only his eyes moving. It was like waiting by the hen-house for the fox to come. In the shell-hole, Corporal Coogan was hitting his stride:

'We are the boys who fear no noise
When the thundering cannons roar.
We are the heroes of the night . . .'

In the trench there was a quick flicker of movement, an upraised arm, half a helmet.

'And we'd sooner fuck than fight . . .'

Fish fired, the arm jerked and vanished. A second or two later there was the flat crump of an explosion, and fifty yards away, a sudden pall of white smoke and dust rising from the trench.

'We're the heroes of the Skinback Fusilers . . .'

Fish heard the whistles blowing for stretcher-bearers. He put down a clean handkerchief and laid out some ammunition on it at his side. His hands streaked it with blood. An embroidered 'F' was on one corner, Violet had given it to him. The rounds in their clips shone bright of brass and copper in the sun. Very still, he peered through the grass.

'S-Sing another, Pat,' he suggested . . .

Smoke. Scented smoke was drifting across the position. Looking upwind, Fish could see that the wood was ablaze. From behind him Fish heard a ragged succession of thuds, like a board being hit by a cosh. All about small shells began bursting, like paper bags going off 'pop'. Thick grey smoke puffed out, drifted over the ground, obscuring the German trenches ahead.

'Qu-quickly, Pat!' he cried out.

The Irishman had taken a little of the morphia Fish had given him and was dozing. Fish lifted him up to a sitting position.

'The rations, they aren't fit for dogs, sir,' he said, half coming round.

'N-Not for dogs,' Fish agreed. 'Look, Pat. They're putting down smoke. I'll carry you to our lines.'

'Aye, to be sure, I'd like that.'

Fish put the sling of his rifle over his shoulder, and managed to get Coogan over the other.

'I've got my cigar,' he said. 'I'm ready, sir.'

Fish began to stagger back over the shelled ground. In the murk he saw others, some alone, some helping each other.

'You're not light, Pat,' he gasped, as he trudged.

'That's what my mother said, sir. I was a big baby. Twelve pounds. It took me two days to be born.' The smoke was clearing somewhat. 'I think we must be close to the lines.'

Somebody was calling. 'Over here, over here.'

A passage had been cut in the entanglement. Dead men hung in the wire. A lone redcap was calling the survivors through the cut. Fish eased Coogan down onto the parapet, and dropped down into the trench. With some help, he got him in, and sat him on the firestep. The trench was chaotic: wounded and unwounded men simply collapsing where they could, dazed and exhausted, their eyes glassy, staring somewhere into the distance. All were filthy, some bloodstained, some wrapped as best they could in field dressings, some slumped unconscious. Only the military policeman in his clean uniform, with his clean face and hands stood out, and he met the eyes of nobody.

Fish could see no officers, only a corporal and a sergeant.

'I m-must take c-command, Pat,' he said. 'You s-sit and have a s-smoke.'

The Irishman pulled out his aluminium tube in triumph. He unscrewed the lid and tucked it carefully away. He bit off the end and held it ready. Fish lit it for him with the Dunhill that Violet had given him. Fine tobacco smoke scented the air.

'So that's what the rich folk do . . .' Coogan breathed.

'I'll be back in a m-minute of two,' said Fish. 'Sergeant!'

A haggard face looked up from the duck-boards. Old habits reasserted themselves.

'Yes, sir.'

'L-let's get these ch-chaps organised. W-Wounded to the rear.'

Slowly, some sort of order was made of things. Stretchers were found, those unable to walk were carried to the casualty clearing stations, the walking wounded staggering and limping as best they could. Fish found himself manning a section of trench with a small force of about fifty, all made up from different units. He made contact with units on each side of him, and obtained water and a tin of dark tea leaves. The sergeant, from the West Yorks, improvised a fire with some petrol he found and boiled water for tea.

'Lads'll be better after a brew,' he confided.

They drank it any way they could, from canteens, tin mugs, helmets.

'What the 'ell 'appened, sir?' he asked.

'I d-don't know,' Fish said honestly. 'What time did you g-go over the t-top?'

'After the big mine went up. 7.30 ack emma.'

'Yes, us too.'

It seemed several years ago. He wondered what time it was. He looked at his watch. It said it was a few minutes short of eleven o'clock.

'B-blasted w-war's broken my watch,' he complained, suddenly angry. Violet had given it to him, it had her name engraved on the back. 'Wh-what time is it, Sergeant?'

The Yorkshire sergeant looked at his own watch. 'Got this off a dead Gerry sir,' he confided. 'Up at the Aisne, that was. Just comin' up for eleven, sir.'

Fish held his watch to his ear, and heard it ticking steadily. Looking down the trench he saw Coogan, still lying on the firestep.

'Oh, I say, dash it, they've forgotten Corporal Coogan. We must get him to the CCS.'

The sergeant followed Fish's eyes. 'Nay, sir. He was dead, so we just left 'im.'

'Of c-course he's not dead, damn you. I b-brought him in.'

Fish went along the trench. 'See, he's still s-smoking his cigar . . .'

The Yorkshireman reached down and gently closed his eyes. All along the firestep was a pool of dark blood. Shiny, multi-coloured flies had appeared from nowhere to feast on it. The tourniquet on the stump of the leg hung loose.

The trench seemed to be filling up with soldiers, men in clean uniforms, in full kit.

'Wh-what's going on?' Fish demanded. 'Wh-what are you lot doing in my t-trench?'

'Hulloa!' a voice called. Looking through the scrum of men fixing scaling ladders to the walls Fish saw a lieutenant-colonel.

'Colonel Rivers, sir,' the Yorkshire sergeant said quickly. 'CO of the East Yorks.'

'Sorry to barge in on you chaps. Oh, hallo, Sergeant Beardsley. What are you doing here?'

'Lieutenant de Clare, sir. Windstone Yeomanry.'

'You look like you've been over the top already.'

'Yes, sir. I've collected these men from no-man's land, and sent the wounded to the rear. Our own attack was repelled with heavy losses.'

'Well, we're here to put that right,' the other said cheerfully. 'Orders just down from brigade, y'know. Enemy line's weakly held. We're to advance and capture in five minutes.' He looked Fish in the eye. 'Could do with a veteran like yourself along.'

Horror flooded Fish's whole being. It was not possible that he was being asked to go over the top again. Not twice in one day. He stared at the Yorks commander in silence, unable to speak, paralysed by his stammer. The man clapped him on the shoulder.

'Good man. Any tips?'

'It's v-very simple,' Fish said thickly. 'You g-get out of the t-trench and w-walk f-f-f-f—'

'Good chap. Got a whistle? No? Oh well, just listen for mine.'

He went off along the trench, organising his men.

'F-F-forward,' Fish stuttered. 'And then they sh-sh-shoot you.'

Shortly, Lieutenant-Colonel Rivers came back, looking at his watch. Fish was peering over the parapet.

'Wh-When does the bloody b-barrage start?' he asked, anxiously.

'Oh, no time for that. Brigade wants us to move out in a hurry. You set? Jolly good.' He stuck his whistle between his teeth, looked each way down the trench at his men, and blew.

Matching command with act, he seized the sides of the scaling ladder and climbed out. Fish took his rifle in one hand and scrambled up behind him. For the second time that day he had the fearful sensation of being flung into icy water. It took his breath away – he gasped, looked each way to see the men climbing out, funnelling towards the gaps cut in the wire, so clearly marked with white tape.

In the distance he heard the steady tapping of a machine-gun, first one, then two, and three. In the lane to his right men suddenly spun and jerked and tumbled. Fish had played with skittles on the castle lawns: the men looked just the same as skittles hit by a fast-moving ball, jerking, falling, tumbling over each other. Skittles did not bleed, the men fell spouting scarlet blood, it came out as though from hosepipes.

Something smacked into his rifle like the kick of a carthorse. It knocked him over backwards onto the ground. As he lay gasping for breath, men fell over him. A bayonet jabbed his leg, he struggled to push the man on top of him off and his hand went through his guts.

He pushed himself up onto his hands and knees and somebody ran over him, screaming. Fish looked up and saw that half the back of his head was missing. The man ran into the wire and fell over, his legs kicking as though he was running the hundred yards. Soldiers were still climbing relentlessly out of the trench. Colonel Rivers lay dead on the wire, a huge ragged hole in his back. Fish ripped the shiny whistle from his neck and blew it, again and again.

'Back!' he screamed. 'Get b-back in the trench! Get back!'

The men turned, tumbling back into shelter, and Fish scrambled after them. Behind him the machine-guns popped mockingly.

They had opened up the back of the tent, but the sun still beat down on it. It had been wet from the night's rain and it had dried yellow. The damp it gave off was turning it into a hothouse. Clarissa Townall attempted to wipe the sweat that was running stinging into her eyes with the back of a bloody hand and failed.

'You wouldn't wipe me down, Vi, would you?' she entreated. The two of them paused as they bent over the wounded man on the table. Violet swabbed her face with a wet cloth, gave her a drink from a bottle wrapped about with bandage against breakage. It had become bloodstained from her hands.

They had set up another operating tent where the reception had been. Clarissa had flung herself into surgery on the wounded and McKay had given her Violet to assist.

Clarissa moved forward again, and tripped over a pile of things under her feet. She looked down and saw the amputated arms and hands, legs and feet, all the evidence of her work lying scattered on the sticky, bloody grass.

'Margaret,' said Violet to the nurse, 'take these out, will you?'

As the young girl picked them up like logs, green and blue flies buzzed about her face.

'Get the flit gun and hose us down when you come back,' Violet ordered. 'I hate those things.'

The sergeant had been hit in the forearm. The machine-gun bullet had struck the bone and tumbled, leaving a massive, explosive exit wound. Fragments of bone had scattered through the flesh of the arm like miniature pieces of shrapnel. She began to inject local anaesthetic around the elbow.

'I'm sorry I can't put you out,' she apologised. 'We're out of general. But this will stop it hurting.'

'Give me more time for another gasper,' the sergeant said softly. Violet produced a cigarette, and lit it for him. He lay quietly smoking as Clarissa removed his arm. She sewed up the flap over the stump with neat stitches and Violet wrapped it in clean white bandage. The man sat up.

'Where shall I go, miss?' he asked.

'That's a Blighty one,' said Violet. 'Can you walk?'

'I can walk as far as you want, if it's to Blighty, miss.'

'Let's take a short break,' Violet suggested. 'You can keep going longer that way.'

They helped him off the table and went outside. The meadow was filling with men.

'There must be three thousand there,' said Clarissa, in horror. Violet went to a table, and wrote rapidly on a chit. She gave it to the one-armed man. 'Go down there to the barge. They'll let you sit on deck,' she said. 'And hold on to that. It'll get you back to Southampton.'

Some other wounded were preparing to pick up a stretcher, taking a severely injured man down to the barge.

''Ere, chum,' he called, 'I'll give you an 'and with that.'

He picked up one handle, one empty tunic sleeve swinging, and they shuffled away down the path.

'Come on, then,' said Violet, and they went back inside.

'What the bloody hell are you d-doing here?' Fish demanded furiously, coming into the dug-out down the steps. A rifle he had taken from among the dead outside the trench swung from one hand, its bayonet still attached. The weapon was sticky with blood and dirt, as was he. His father looked up abruptly from the battalion desk, at first furious at being so addressed and then horrified at the sight. Fish was filthy with the stains and debris of battle, he stank of blood and ordure and propellant. Only by his voice did Brigadier de Clare recognise him at all.

'That's no way to address me,' he said, as mildly as he could.

'I don't f-fucking care.' The sight of his father in clean, pressed uniform, immaculately shaved, a pile of papers in front of him seemed to infuriate Fish. He brandished his rifle with its half yard of steel menacingly. 'That's m-my f-f-fucking desk. I'm the b-battalion commander, at the moment, as f-f-far as I can see.'

Brigadier de Clare got up quickly. 'Then you had better have it,' he said smoothly. Fish slumped in his chair and propped the rifle next to him.

'You have splinters in your hands,' said the Brigadier.

Fish looked at them. Large splinters of varnished wood stuck out of the flesh. He began pulling them out, seeming to feel no pain.

'A Jerry machine-gun hit my rifle,' he said. 'In the second attack. It must have shattered the butt.'

'*Second* attack?' the Brigadier asked intently. 'You see, Fish, we don't know what's happened. We seem to have lost most of the battalion, but we don't know where they are.'

'In b-bloody no-man's land, dead, most of'm. Freddie was right. The barrage didn't kill the Germans. They machine-gunned and shelled us the moment we went over.'

'Wait here a minute,' his father ordered. 'Sir Hubert's trying to make sense of things next door.' He went quickly down the corridor. 'Sir Hubert! We have one of the company officers back. Fish. Come and see what he has to say, sir.'

There was a creaking of floorboards, and the large figure of the Major-General came in. He was accompanied by Cromwell.

'Well, Fish?' Sir Hubert demanded. 'Tell me what happened. We've had no communication from the attacking troops at all: visual, flares, telephonic, nothing. That's why I've come up to the front, to try to see for myself. There's another attack ordered by Corps for this afternoon. Your sister battalions, the third and fourth Windstones. I need to know what the conditions are.'

'B-Bloody awful,' Fish said laconically.

'Make a proper report, damn you!' his father snapped. Fish had got to his feet when the General had come in. He reached out for his rifle again, as if it held some sort of comfort.

'I don't know where A Company is. They went out in front of us with Robert who was battalion commander at their head. I was knocked over by a whizz-bang. There was a h-hell of a l-lot of noise and smoke. I found most of B Company lying down in the grass. They were dead. Machine-gunned. I gathered up some survivors and went f-forward. The w-wire wasn't cut. Most of us got m-machine-gunned there. I shot the crew and b-bombed them. I hid in a shell-hole and sniped at s-some others through the w-wire. Somebody p-put down smoke and I got back. I didn't know where I was, but a Yorkshire battalion turned up for an attack. They w-wanted me to g-go with them. There w-was no barrage. We g-got out and the Jerry machine-guns were trained on the lanes. They shot us to bits. The Yorks lost two hundred and twenty men in ab-bout a minute. I ordered the attack to s-stop.'

'*You* ordered it to stop? Why?' the Brigadier demanded.

'I w-was the only officer left. I organised the evacuation of the w-wounded, and a Yorks captain left out of attack turned up. I gave the Yorks back to him, and m-made my way here.'

'Good lad,' Sir Hubert said. He was pale, and seemed shaken by the account. 'I'm sorry, my boy,' he said sincerely. 'We thought . . .'

'It w-wasn't,' Fish said succinctly.

His father's mouth tightened and his cheeks flushed slightly with anger, but he said nothing, keeping himself in check. Sir Hubert spoke next.

'You'd better get yourself to the Regimental Aid Post. I can see you're wounded.'

Fish pulled a splinter from his palm and added it to the little pile. 'There are ch-chaps out there with th-their legs b-blown off,' he said, quite calmly. 'I d-don't feel I qualify.'

'Cromwell! Get a stretcher-bearer down and have him dress the wounds, at least.'

'Very good, sir.'

In a corner was Robert's own tantalus. Sir Hubert went over to it and took a square-cut glass decanter, pouring a big shot of whisky into a matching tumbler. He splashed some soda on top.

'Have a drink, man. You've earned it.'

'Thank you, sir,' he said gratefully.

'Why don't you sit there and drink that while you mind the phones. I have to decide what to do about this attack. General Snow is pressing me hard for results. He wants Pigeon Wood captured by tonight. The push is stalling.'

He went back down the corridor, so solidly made thirty feet down by the Germans, and into the room he had taken over. On the wall was the map he had brought forward with him from the château. The line of attack up towards Pigeon Wood was clearly marked in chinagraph pencil.

'What the hell am I to do, Gervase?' he muttered anxiously. 'As far as I can make out the first and second battalions have ceased to exist. If I throw the third and fourth up this line of attack they will almost certainly meet the same fate. But that is what General Snow is directly ordering me to do.'

'We can't be certain of that, sir,' de Clare demurred. 'Simply because we haven't heard anything yet doesn't mean that substantial elements of the battalions may not have achieved their objectives. Heavy casualties, yes, but we may have expected that. As for communications we must accept that the fog of this war is even worse than in Wellington's day. The borders of the battle are so wide we can't possibly know everything.'

'I know that, dammit. But nothing at all . . . and we have your boy's own report. Fish saw them out there, Gervase. Dead in lines of advance.'

'Fish always was over-imaginative . . .' the Brigadier murmured.

'Highly strung, you know. I wouldn't place too much weight on what he says.'

'Didn't you see him?' Sir Hubert exclaimed. 'Over the top twice...'

'That's it. Cracked under the strain. I don't think we have any option, sir. The third and fourth Windstones will have to attack as ordered.'

Sir Hubert stood staring at the map in silence for a long time. Brigadier de Clare watched him, patiently, as though standing on a river bank, waiting for a fish to take the fly.

Along the corridor, a stretcher-bearer came down the steps carrying medical supplies.

'H-Hallo, Dooley,' Fish said, looking up. 'G-Good to s-see you.'

'Good to see you too, sir. Let me look at them hands of yours. Any other wounds, sir?'

'Don't know,' Fish said frankly. 'I f-feel like I've b-been at the bottom of a scrum. C-Can't be anything serious, else I'd not be here. S-Suppose I'll find out when I g-get my clothes off.'

'I'll do them hands then.'

Dooley, Marked by his SB armband, poured warm water and added antiseptic, making it go milky-white. The air smelled pleasant.

'Your uniform's a bit messy, Dooley. You've been out getting people?'

'Why yes, sir. When we saw the boys falling down we went out and got them, when the shelling calmed down a bit.'

The water was rapidly becoming murky with dirt and blood. Dooley laid one clean hand down on a dressing, the tears and gashes purple and red-edged, and very visible. He picked at fragments of wood and cleaned inside the three corner tears.

'Mustn't leave anything nasty in there, sir. Hope I'm not hurting too much, sir.'

'Oh, n-no.'

'It will in a moment, sir. Got to put iodine on.'

'Very good. Jerry shoot at you, while you were out there?'

'Not so you'd notice sir. There was a whizz-bang or two, but 'e wasn't having a proper bash, if you know what I mean.'

'Anyone stop one?'

'Figgis got a Blighty one, sir. 'E was well pleased. Hold on now, sir.'

The stretcher-bearer began to dab the wounds with iodine. The pain was quite sudden and severe, it made Fish break out into a sweat. He reached for his drink and made himself stay quiet. In the silence he heard his father's voice coming through the wall from the room next door.

'V Corps? This is Brigadier de Clare, of General Mordaunt's staff. Let me speak to General Snow.'

There was silence, only the sound of stretcher-bearer Dooley hissing a tune through his teeth as he worked.

'General Snow, sir? Brigadier de Clare. The attack on Pigeon Wood? Yes, that's why I've called. I'm up at the front, in the Windstone's battalion HQ. Yes, with General Mordaunt. He's going to call you, but I thought you had better get the news from me first. General Mordaunt is refusing to order the third and fourth battalions to attack this afternoon.'

Again, there was a silence as General Snow at the other end of the line talked.

'Very simple, sir,' Brigadier de Clare said, in his clipped voice. 'General Mordaunt has cracked. The sister battalions took some heavy losses taking their objectives this morning, and it appears to have affected his judgement. Yes, sir, I know we expect heavy losses. Yes, General Mordaunt does know that it is a direct order that they attack Pigeon Wood. I did point that out to him. When was he going to call you? I think after the attack was due to start. Yes, sir, I did point out that it would then be too late to restart an offensive. Yes, I think he knew that.'

There was a methodical clinking as stretcher-bearer Dooley put his equipment away.

'I'll have General Mordaunt call now. Yes, I will. Thank *you*, sir. You may count on me.'

'Thank you, Dooley,' Fish said quietly.

'My pleasure, sir. Be best to get them hands done proper at the Aid Post later, sir. Need some stitching, they do.'

As Dooley went up the steps, Fish heard the clatter of boots, a brief word of greeting between two men, and a runner came in, muddy and dishevelled. He bore an envelope in his hand. He saluted and passed it to Fish.

'Message from brigade, sir.'

'Th-Thank you.' The envelope was bloodstained. 'Did you have an accident?'

'Not me, sir. My mate Nobby, sir. We was sent in a pair, sir. 'E stopped one at Windy Corner.'

'Blighty?' Fish asked, hopefully.

'No, sir. Woolly bear. Bit took 'is 'ead off. Is there a reply, sir?'

'Oh . . . let me see.'

Using the free tips of his bandaged fingers Fish opened the envelope, and read:

PORK AND BEANS

> Certain complaints have been received that no pork can be found in the tins ... Troops must not be misled by the name 'pork' and beans and expect to find a full ration of pork; as a matter of fact the pork is practically all absorbed by the beans.

Underneath was an indecipherable staff signature.

Fish stood staring at it until the runner coughed.

'Any reply, sir?'

'Eh? No ... no reply.'

'Is it important, sir?' the man asked anxiously.

'Yes. Yes, very important. Thank you.'

Fish stuffed it into his pocket, and got up. He went to the tantalus and splashed whisky into a tumbler.

'Here,' he said, and gave it to the runner. 'Tip that back, it'll help you get by Windy Corner.'

The man drank it down and his eyes watered.

'Well, that's something to tell the wife,' he breathed. 'Thank you, sir. I'll be off now. I'm glad that was important, I'll tell Nobby's missus when I write.'

He clattered back up into the outside air. Once again, Fish heard his father's voice coming through the wall. Now it was harsh with command: 'Third Windstones? This is Major-General de Clare, commanding brigade. Yes, I am in command. General Mordaunt has been relieved. You will attack this afternoon together with the fourth battalion as planned.'

Fish did not hear the phone going down, but when he looked up his father was standing in the doorway watching him.

'You've b-been promoted? Now you're a g-general.'

'Sir Hubert's been degummed. Not up to snuff.'

'Are you up to snuff, Father? Will the third and fourth Windstones take Pigeon Wood?'

'They had better, or I shall want to know the reason why,' de Clare said menacingly.

'You can't court-martial dead men,' Fish pointed out.

'I expect casualties. I *want* to see casualties. An attack without casualties is an attack that has not been pressed home with vigour. I also want my objective.'

'How do you p-plan to attain it?'

'I shall . . .' He stopped himself. 'No, *you're* obviously an expert now,' he said sneeringly. 'You've been over the top twice. *You* tell me how you'd take Pigeon Wood.'

'No warning,' Fish said, without hesitation. 'The Jerry generals, you gave them seven days to g-get used to the idea that w-we were going to attack. No w-wonder they were exp-pecting us. Bombard without warning. Concentrated fire, not spread out. Infantry right behind. Machine-guns hosing the parapet. Aircraft overhead as the barrage lifts, bombing and machine-gunning. Be all over them like a bare-kn-knuckle fighter. Don't even give them time to think. Sm-Smash them up.'

'Smash them up . . .' his father sighed in contempt. 'Like a bare-knuckle fighter. I can tell you've never been to staff college. Does five hundred years of military theory mean nothing to you, Fish?'

'Five hundred years of military theory lies d-dead out there in r-rows,' Fish retorted.

'I can't stand about here talking to you,' the Brigadier said briskly. 'Even if you did go over the top twice.' He looked curiously at his son. 'Why *did* you go over a second time?' he enquired.

'I'm a de Clare!' Fish said furiously. 'That's why.'

His father opened his mouth to say something, then closed it.

'Yes?' Fish demanded. 'Yes? *Yes?*'

'Nothing.'

'Then mind your f-f-fucking insolence!' Fish screamed. 'My friends are dead out there and you're going to kill more this afternoon!' He scrambled to his feet, reaching with padded, bandaged hands for his rifle.

'I'm leaving,' said his father. 'As you can see.'

He went smartly up the steps, and Fish slumped back into his seat. He found he was sweating – rivulets of it ran down through the filth.

'Sir. Mr Fish, sir?'

He looked up. Another runner had arrived. He knew him, it was Corporal Woods, nicknamed Slinger. He had been in the stables at the castle, and was now in C Company. He was as filthy and grimed as Fish.

'Woods! What are you doing here?'

'Message from Captain Frederick, sir. We're cut off, under attack on three sides. Jerry's shelling the fourth. Running low on bombs and ammunition, sir.'

'But . . . what about A and B Companies, the second battalion? They were due to support you through the tunnel.'

'We got a few survivors with us, sir. See, parts of the tunnel fell in, what with the Jerry shelling in no-man's land. While they were trying to clear it Brigadier de Clare – that was him what I just saw – he ordered them to attack across no-man's land and they got caught in the Jerry barrage, sir.'

Fish jumped up. 'How long does Mr Frederick think he can hold on?'

'For a bit, sir. We blew in sections of trench, made a stockade. But we need support.'

Fish grabbed his rifle, and went up the steps.

'G-Gather round, chaps.'

A woolly bear shell came over from the German lines, rolling in a seemingly leisurely fashion towards them – a man on a bicycle whistling pensively. It was high overhead. The men blinking and pushing themselves up in the assembly trench as Fish came to stand amongst them took no notice of it.

The shell seemed to speed up, so you felt you would have to run to keep up. Then it was an express train, screaming through a tunnel. It passed over their heads to the rear, they heard it hit with a whistle and roar, heard the faint pattering of the debris coming down in dirty rain. Filthy black smoke smirched the clear blue sky.

'Hallo, chaps,' Fish said to the soldiers in the trench.

They were all as grimed as he was and looked at him through exhausted, twitching faces, reaching for cigarettes to soothe their pain. They waited to hear what it was he wanted.

'I'm g-glad to see you all here. I k-know you all, you live near me. We're the Windstones. Wh-When we go home we'll talk about these days.'

'Roll on!' said an anonymous voice, and they all laughed, Fish with them.

'I k-know you all went over the t-top this morning. The attack failed, but it wasn't your fault. Only p-problem is, some of us are over th-there and c-can't get back. C-Can't hold on for much l-longer, apparently. Not without support. Once it g-gets dark they can get across no-man's land. Slinger Woods managed to get back to tell me, you all know him. He says that Mr Frederick and Reverend George are over there holding on, with Sergeant-Major Hopcroft, Sergeant Furzegrove and some others, but they're very low on ammunition and bombs. They're stripping Jerry dead to keep fighting.'

An RFC observation two-seater came over about three thousand feet up, droning like a bee, zig-zagging its way along the line. Below it, nothing moved.

'I'm going to go over there and take some ammunition and bombs, help out a bit until it gets dark if necessary,' Fish said. 'With a bit of luck we can help them w-withdraw by counter-attacking. I've arranged for motor ambulances to be standing by to take wounded to the CCS in the rear once we get back.'

'Jerry's shelling no-man's land, sir,' a voice pointed out.

'I kn-know. I can hear him! The t-tunnel got a bit blocked, so I've got miners from the colliery clearing it. It brings us out at the bottom of the spur. That's the worst bit taken care of. Once we're at the spur we will attack the Germans enfilading our men with two groups.' Fish reached in his pocket for a cigarette.

'Anyone g-got a l-light? Thanks. I'd like some of you to come with me. V-Volunteers, only. I'm g-going down to the qu-quartermaster to get the supplies.'

Fish dragged at his cigarette, and went off down the trench. Slowly, in ones and twos and threes, the men pushed themselves to their feet, tightening the belts they had loosened, hawking into the dirt of the trench bottom, lighting cigarettes. They went along after him, leaving a bluish-grey haze of smoke behind them.

Someone was blocking the entrance to the tunnel. Fish had led the men down the trench, treading over the layer of scattered fresh white spoil that the miners had cleared away. They were all heavily laden with boxes of bombs, wound about with bandoliers of ammunition, draped with sacks of Lewis gun magazines, hung with water bottles. Fish looked up to see who it was. It was Sir Hubert. Standing to one side was his brother Cromwell.

'I hear you're going over there again,' said the General.

'Y-Yes, sir,' Fish agreed politely. 'Freddie and George and the boys are relying on us.' He waited for the fat man to move. 'We'd best be getting on,' he said. 'I don't suppose Gerry has called a t-truce.'

'Of course. Only I'm coming with you.'

Fish looked at him puzzled. 'St-Staff officers aren't allowed,' he said. 'The regulations say so.'

'I've been degummed,' Sir Hubert said quietly. 'I'd like to do something worthwhile before I go back, if I may.'

'Y-You're asking my p-permission?' Fish said in amazement.

'Yes.'

'Then of c-course, sir. Do try to keep your b-bloody head down.'

'I will. I'll carry those bombs, if you like.'

Fish led the way into the tunnel. The miners had cleared the passage. The ground underfoot trembled as shells landed in the ground about them, chalk dust filled the air, the bare bulbs above their heads swayed. Somebody behind relieved him of a sack of Lewis gun ammunition – he turned and realised it was Cromwell.

'You're not supp-posed to be here, Crom,' he said.

'I know.'

'T-Try not to get killed. Mother will moan so. I'll never hear the e-end of it.'

'I'll do my best.'

He could smell fresh air, see sunlight. He poked his head out. The spur was above him. Shells were bursting behind him. He climbed out, began to heave men out. They were a little band some fifty strong. The slope was marked where the companies had gone up in the morning. Fish put his head down and scrambled forward.

'Come on, ch-chaps,' he called.

They scrambled into the ruins of the old German trench and Fish peered out. 'Woods!' he shouted. 'Where's Slinger Woods?'

'Here, sir.'

The corporal scuttled down the trench like a monkey, keeping his head down. Two men heaved the bulk of General Mordaunt and haversacks of bombs over the parapet.

'Right, Woods. Wh-Where're they holding out?'

The ground was not as despoiled as no-man's land – its features remained but in it nothing moved.

'Over there, sir, in the ruined farmhouse. Got to watch out, there's a machine-gun nest in the copse, sir. Mr Frederick went to silence it, but I don't know if he got there.'

Fish looked across the rolling land to the smashed-up bricks and stone of the farmhouse, assessing it for dead ground with a horseman's expert eye.

'R-Right. Listen, chaps. General Mordaunt will occupy this trench with Corporal Woods, and riflemen Soffis and Haze. Take four Lewis guns and plenty of ammunition. When you see us signal, lay down heavy covering fire for us to come back. L-Listen to me, chaps. We'll come back the same way as we go. See the line from here across to the ruined wall. There's a ditch along there, we'll hug that to the orchard. Corporal Woods says that some of the party are holding out in the farmhouse.' As he spoke, a shell burst in yellow smoke over the ruins, they heard the scream of the shrapnel blasting out. 'We all know what they sound like when they're coming our way, so keep your heads down. You ready, General?'

'Very good,' Sir Hubert grunted.

'Stay near me, Crom,' Fish ordered. 'All right, let's go.'

He thought it must have been an old farm track – he could see that it had been in constant use by the Germans, bringing supplies up to their front trench – and they all reached the broken wall in safety. As Fish had guessed, there was a dry drainage ditch only partly blocked with rubble, and he led them down it, their loads banging on their backs and clattering against the stones.

At the corner of the orchard he peered round. He could see the copse where the machine-gun was said to be; the entire breadth of the orchard could be enfiladed if it was still active. He thought he could see a steel helmet in the ruins of the farmhouse. It wagged, as though somebody was talking. He thought he could see a flicker of white at the throat, like a parson's dog collar. He picked up a stone and hurled it as though aiming for the stumps on a run-out. There was a clang, the helmet ducked down, and then slowly reappeared with a face under it.

'I might have known it would be you, Fish, throwing bally stones in the middle of a war,' George called.

'I've got some chaps here and more ammunition,' Fish said across the twenty-yard gap. 'What about the blasted machine-gun?'

'Still active. But if you've got ammunition we'll loose off at it while you run across. Wait a minute.'

George vanished. A few seconds later a concentrated roar and clatter of rifle and Lewis gun-fire broke out, blue smoke rising up from the ruins, and they all dashed across in safety.

'Hallo, Fish,' said George, from inside the ruins of a byre. He was filthy, and bleeding from a number of small cuts. 'Yea, truly we are become hewers of wood and drawers of water today. Are those Lewis gun magazines? Jolly good, I'll have a few of those.'

'Why aren't you in church?' Fish demanded.

'I could see it was all hands to the pumps. God won't mind.'

There were perhaps fifty of George's men scattered in the ruins. Fish's party went amongst them, distributing ammunition.

'I've got a party in the old German trench to cover our withdrawal,' Fish told George. 'Where's Freddie?'

'He went forward to try to link up with Sergeant-Major Hopcroft's company. Got pinned down by that machine-gun.'

Cromwell moved forward to the edge of the old house, where he saw Furzegrove.

'Here, Sergeant,' he said. 'Bombs and ammunition.'

'There was me thinking you had a cup of tea, sir. Thank you.'

'Where's Mr Frederick?'

'Went forward, sir. In a shell-hole up there, near those sycamore trees.'

'Right,' said Cromwell, in a determined fashion. Furzegrove bent to the box of ammunition he had been given and began filling empty clips. When he looked up again, Cromwell was striding across the empty ground, still laden with bandoliers and haversacks.

'In the name of the Saints . . .' said George.

'Wh-What?'

Fish looked up.

'What the fuck's he *doing*?'

Nobody moved in the ruins. There was a terrible fascination about watching somebody going to certain death.

'Oh, sh-shit.'

Fish leaped up, and bounded out after his brother. The air cracked and whistled, there was a crackling like twigs beginning to take the flame.

'*Crom*!' he screamed.

His brother half turned, waved, continued on his way. Fish pelted after him, tripping and stumbling, always just keeping his balance, his sacks bouncing and slamming into him.

'Get . . .' – a whizz-bang went screaming by, Cromwell glanced up, as if expecting rain – 'fucking . . .' – a mortar burst nearby, it sent up a spray of dirt, Cromwell hunched his shoulders – '*down*!'

Fish slammed into his brother in a rugby tackle, and they fell into a shell-hole. There was a roar, filthy smoke enveloped them and dirt rained down through it.

'What was that?'

'Jesus fucking Christ, Crom,' Fish said weakly. 'Don't you know what goes on out here?'

His brother looked furiously at him through a faceful of mud. 'That is the most disgusting blasphemy I have ever heard.'

Fish rolled onto his stomach. 'This whole fucking thing is a blasphemy,' he gasped. 'Crom, they are *shooting* at you.'

'I don't see anyone.'

'It isn't Waterloo. They hide in holes like we are doing, and shoot at you from there.'

'I saw Freddie. I think. He was waving from a hole.'

'He was trying to tell you to get into cover, you stupid prick.'

'You have become extremely foul mouthed. I could have been there by now.'

'You could have been spread like strawberry jam!' Fish yelled furiously, enraged that his brother did not understand what was happening to them. 'Which hole?' he asked, more quietly. 'Yes, I think I see it. Look, there's dead ground along this old stream bed. F-Follow me and k-keep your fucking head down. Say after me, Crom, I will k-keep my f-fucking head down.'

Cromwell looked seriously at his younger brother. 'I don't know what's happened to you. Yes, all right, I will keep my head down.'

'Your f-fucking head down!' Fish shrieked. 'You don't understand, this whole thing is f-fucking obscene. Say I will keep my f-fucking head down!'

'I will keep my fucking head down,' Cromwell said quietly.

'Good.'

Fish crawled out of the hole and along the stony stream bed. Cromwell followed. They found Freddie in the shell-hole.

'Cromwell, you're fucking mad,' he said.

'I know, I know.'

'Right,' said Freddie. 'Oh, sharoshie, you've got bombs and a Lewis gun. Cromwell, you provide suppressing fire when Fish and I throw bombs at the machine-gunners. They've been annoying me all afternoon, I'm fed up with them. Here, Fish, a bayonet. No rifle I'm afraid.'

Freddie and Fish both took a bag of bombs and began to crawl along the little stream bed. The Germans were aware of them, machine-gun bullets began to crack over their heads, hitting the ground just above them, spraying them with dirt. Freddie halted their progress on the dead ground of a small ridge, invisible except from the level of a crawl.

'Fifty yards, Fish,' he muttered. The sharp stones of the stream had torn the elbows out of his jacket and he peered at one for a moment. 'Must get Hodge and Frisket to put bally leather on next time,' he observed. 'Fifty yards, Fish. Can you throw that far?'

'Of c-course.'

'Got to be right on the stumps, mind. Salvo of three bombs each to blur their vision a bit, then a jolly old sprint across before they can get their breath back. Fast as you can. That all right with you?'

'I p-played on the w-wing.'

'So you did. Ready, then?'

The two cousins took the serrated bombs from their bags, each like a small pineapple, and prepared to pull the rings. Freddie looked back.

Cromwell was just visible to him on the lip of the shell-hole. He signalled with his hand, and Cromwell sat up, just like a jack-in-the-box, his Lewis gun on the sling, firing in bursts. Freddie and Fish stood up, slinging their bombs like cricket balls. The black bombs were still in the air as they sprinted across the rough ground.

The bombs went off with a crump and a flash, orange in the dirty white smoke. Tracer bullets from the Lewis gun snapped by like speeding fireflies, only feet away. The gun was set up in a dug-out crater, protected by a sandbagged parapet. They could see the shining machine on its tripod through the smoke. Somebody was screaming in there. They leaped the parapet and landed in the middle of the crew.

Fish knocked over a small, balding German in grey uniform who had been feeding a belt into the gun. Fish stabbed him with his bayonet and the German howled like a wounded rabbit. The gunner was still at his post so Freddie shot his revolver, blowing him backwards, fired again, shot someone else in the smoke.

A man lunged at Fish with a spade – he slashed at him, hacking off a hand. He saw the blood spouting out in a stream, lunged in his turn, took the German soldier in the throat. He fell, pulling Fish with him, the blade stuck in bone. Fish bent over the gargling man, heaving to get it out. It came in a great gout of blood, then he turned to see something blow Freddie off his feet, knocking the legs from under him.

They were being fired on. Fish saw suddenly that the machine-gun had been sited at the end of a hidden trench and men in grey were firing erratically at him. He jumped down into the pit, falling on top of the dead gunner, grabbed at the Spandau gun and heaved it round on its sled mount. He took both the grips in his hands, and thrust his thumbs into the trigger. The gun took off with a chattering roar, spraying spent cases and sucking in its long belt. In the trench men spun and jerked and fell. He ran the fire up and down the trench until the gun suddenly fell quiet.

Freddie was lying tumbled amongst the dead Germans. He was clutching his leg, blood squirting through his fingers while he fumbled for his field dressing, sewn into his tunic.

'No time!' Fish shouted. 'Grab on, I'll get you back.'

He lifted him over his shoulder, and began to stagger as fast as he could in the direction of the ruined farm. In the rough grass Cromwell stood up, changing a drum of ammunition on the Lewis gun. He fired past him.

There was a sudden shriek over Fish's head. A shell burst in the air, and Cromwell flew sideways, as though kicked by a very large horse. Fish reached down as he got to him, not knowing if he was dead or alive, and began to drag him along by the belt of his Sam Browne, Freddie still over his shoulder.

Two men were running from the farm, George and Furzegrove. They picked Cromwell up between them, ran, collapsed into the cover of the ruins. Behind them a shell burst petulantly, sending splinters screaming through the grass.

'Apcott,' called Sergeant Furzegrove, holding the roll.

There was no reply. Filthy and exhausted, the men stood in ragged ranks. They sagged and bent this way and that, like a copse that has been hit by a fierce storm. The ambulances had taken the wounded away, the dead and the missing lay where they lay. Sergeant Furzegrove counted those who remained.

'Apcott? Has anyone seen anything of Apcott?' he asked again.

'I seen 'im,' called a voice. 'A whizz-bang got 'im this morning, after we got out the trench.'

'You sure of that, Coombe? You sure it was Apcott?'

'I saw 'im,' the young man insisted. 'A whizz-bang blew 'im to blazes just after we passed through the wire, 'e was a chum of mine and I seen 'im just blown to blazes.'

Furzegrove made a note on the sheet fixed to the clipboard. 'Arthmore.'

'I seen him. He was hanging on the wire, he was.'

'Sar'nt Furzegrove,' Fish called quietly.

'Yes, sir?'

'There were eight hundred and sixty other ranks and eighteen officers of us here this m-morning. I don't think we need to make the men stand here while we call out n-names. J-Just go down the line and have them c-call out their name to you.'

'Yes, sir.'

Furzegrove went over to the first rank, and went steadily along, the men quietly identifying themselves. Very soon he was finished, and came up to Fish.

'One hundred and fourteen men of the Windstone Yeomanry present, sir. And yourself.'

'Yes,' Fish said quietly. 'I s-seem to be the CO.'

He stepped forward and raised his voice. 'We're coming out of the line and into r-rest. We won't be going back for a b-bit. I'm b-bloody proud of you.'

They formed fours and began to march to the rear in the gathering gloom, leaning forward against the weight of their packs, heads down. There was no ring of their feet striking the paved road, their shoulders did not swing. They staggered, broke step, they swayed to and fro in their ranks like a flock of sheep.

The setting sun reflected on the cambered road and Fish felt that he was walking along a long, round, smooth and well-greased pole. He could not rid himself of the notion that if he lost his footing on its slippery surface he would fall into some fearful gulf below. He weaved about as he staggered with his men, attempting to maintain his balance. As it became dark he became more fearful of falling off the road into the pit below.

It was very noisy. His shoulder ached fiercely – he thought that he must have sprained it when he had rugby tackled his brother. He moved one of the rifles he was carrying to his other side. They marched in past a blacksmith's shop, a hammer striking sparks, the furnace shockingly bright. It was just calling out for a bout of hate from the Jerries.

'Cover up that light!' Fish shouted, and the man in his heavy apron just waved. Motor repair shops, a supply column, horse lines, all alive with sound and light, they blasted in on Fish. The smell of unshelled trees, the soft feel of turf under his boots.

'We're here, sir.'

Fish found Furzegrove staring at him. 'So we are, Sarn't.'

He realised that he was standing outside the orderly room tent, that they were back in camp. The men made a brave attempt to dress ranks. There were a few men watching – those left out of battle that morning, camp details, cooks, a handful of unfit – they watched silently, tactfully keeping back.

'Dismiss,' Fish ordered. He saluted as they turned about, struck their rifles. Then they slackened like puppets released from their strings, lurched and staggered slack-faced towards their tents.

Someone came out of the orderly tent, some officer he didn't know.

'Which company are you?'

'We aren't,' said Fish. 'We are the battalion.'

The man was looking strangely at him. He found it annoying.

'Wh-Who are you st-staring at?' Fish demanded. 'M-Mind your f-fucking insolence.'

'No offence, old boy,' the other said gently. 'I just wondered if you knew you'd been hit, that's all.'

'Hit?'

'Yes. Come on in and sit down, your men are looked after.'

Fish found himself sat down, and people were taking off his tunic, stiff with blood and dirt.

'Flesh wound. Shell fragment. Not in the wound.'

'Sprained it when I tackled Crom,' he mumbled.

They brought the doctor from the aid post, but by the time he arrived Fish had gone to sleep sitting up. The doctor cleaned his shoulder as he slept, packing it with gauze. All field wounds went septic within hours. They put him down on a cot in the tent.

The acetylene lamps hissed. Violet had one on a stand, which they hung over each case as they moved round the dark tent. Cigarette smoke drifted through its harsh light, in the shadows red tips glowed on and off. Patient eyes of men in pain watched them from stretchers, waiting like run-over dogs in a ditch for their turn to come.

'This one's dead,' Clarissa said suddenly. 'Oh, bloody hell, Vi. I've been operating on a dead man.'

There was a quiet commotion by the door, men and women in clean white smocks were coming in.

'You can stop now,' Violet said quietly. 'The relief team's arrived.'

They went slowly to the door of the tent, stiff and numb.

'Don't do anything to that one,' she said as she passed. 'He's dead.'

Outside a fire was burning. In its light men lay in rows stretching into the darkness. They helped each other undo the tapes of their smocks, tight and swollen with the blood that drenched them from neck to ankle. Violet threw the stiff, stinking garments on to the flames.

'They will never get clean,' she said.

10

You're a Very Naughty Bishop

September 1916

Fish had brought the trestle table out of the orderly room tent and was sitting in the sunshine. He had paper and pen to hand on the grey army blanket which served as a tablecloth but he left them alone, and sat watching a small swarm of goldfinches in a thistle patch, their red heads bobbing as they pulled out the seeds from the fat round heads. He held out his hands in the sun, turning them occasionally. They were marked all over with half-healed scars from the barbed-wire, red zig-zag patterns as though decorated for some primitive rite. He had formed the belief that exposing them to the sun would help the flesh knit whole, and held them out like a beggar at intervals. Finally, he picked up his fountain pen and unscrewed the top.

> Dear Mrs Hopcroft,
>
> Yesterday the division finally completed their advance through the ground we attacked on the first day of the battle. I very much regret to tell you that among the dead found from that day was Sergeant-Major Hopcroft and all those of his company that he had led. They were found at and about the site of their objective, over one thousand five hundred yards inside the German positions. They had died fighting to the last man, led by your husband.
>
> I am writing to let you know this so that you may not learn of his untimely death through an official telegram. He and his comrades are to be buried later today by us of the battalion, with full honours.
>
> Sergeant-Major Hopcroft was a fine man, a first-class gamekeeper who took on the role of shepherd and friend to the many men of Windstone who have been fighting with us out here. I shall myself greatly miss his steady support and cheerful demeanour at all times.

When I return to the castle on leave I will come to see you, and we can remember him.

Sincerest regards,
Fish de Clare (Captain)

Fish read it through, and put it in an envelope, which he sealed. He had a small pile of paper, held down by the polished base of a shell. There were many letters to be written. He took another sheet and wrote again.

Dear Uncle,

I'm just writing to let you know that we found Mr Hopcroft and his party yesterday. All killed, I'm afraid, about fifteen hundred yards into the German positions. We had hoped that they'd been taken prisoner. The Jerries had buried them all together, and marked the grave. We identified them by their identity discs.

I'd better give you a full list of the names so that you can visit their families. I'm writing to them myself, as are Freddie and George. Freddie is up and about, if still on crutches. They're having some problem getting the bones to mend properly. George and I are the only officers left of the original Windstones. We have been brought up to strength by various drafts – from London, Wales, Somerset, all over. They have been rushed out here after very skimpy training. Most of them have trouble knowing which end of a rifle goes bang. Some have only fired five rounds in training! A far cry from our wonderful country fellows like Hopcroft and the others. I hope to God we do not have to fight too soon, because the new men simply don't know how, although we are doing our best to educate them.

With a bit of luck I may get a bit of leave and be able to come back to the wonderful old castle. Crom has beaten me to it. I got a letter from him: he is plastered from ankle to hip, he says, but may get on his feet in a month or two. Mother has him in a private hospital in Belgrave Square. When I got winged I got a bit of sick leave and went over to Amiens to be near dear old Vi. She got a spot of leave herself having worked so hard and long at the CCS during the first days of the battle, and we spent it together, which was wonderful.

Thank you for sending me the Walter Scotts from my

room. I keep one about my person all the time and dip into it whenever I get the chance.

Here are the names of those you should visit. I gave you all those of the 3rd and 4th Windstones that father killed on the afternoon of the first day attacking Pigeon Wood. (The army would not want me to say that but since I am battalion censor this week then Yar Boo Sucks to them!) We took Pigeon Wood last week, for what good it might be. Nasty lot of charred matchwood, it was. But anyway, these names. I have a list here . . .

London

The trees in the railed central garden of the great square were beginning to turn red and gold. Horse-drawn cabs mingled with internal-combustion powered taxis, drays with lorries. Were it not for the preponderance of men in smartly cut uniform, gabardine not serge, there would have been little hint of war.

A private Napier motor car, dark green with red trim, came around the square, turning off into Wilton Crescent, where it drew up outside one of the houses. Switching off the engine the chauffeur, in uniform and cap, got down from the part open to the elements and opened the door to the part protected from them. Lady Constance de Clare climbed down.

'Wait for me here, Purvis,' she commanded.

'Very good, my lady.'

She went inside. There was an immediate smell of antiseptic, an assurance that this was a place of modern healing. Lady Constance swept past the nurse who waited at reception, and mounted the stairs. The corridor above was wide, as had suited the shipowner and merchant who had lived there, in Victorian days, and coming along it she saw a slim young nurse. Even wrapped in the voluminous garb of her profession, it was clear that she was very attractive. Her slender ankles were just visible under the long hem of her dress. She smiled at Lady Constance, showing white teeth and sparkling green eyes as she bobbed in a curtsey.

'He's looking very well today, my lady,' she said pleasantly.

'I am glad to hear it.'

'He asked for the new copy of *Punch* and I heard him laughing when he read it. It's so good when they can get above their problems, isn't it, my lady?'

'I'll be the judge of that,' Lady Constance said with an icy edge to her voice. The smile faded from the girl's face.

'Get about your duties.'

'Yes, my lady. He has a visitor with him, you know.'

Lady Constance watched as the young girl tripped away down the corridor. Patches of colour flamed briefly high on her cheeks as she controlled her anger. What in the name of God Above did Dr Mellis think he was doing, employing young hussies like that? Girls no better than prostitutes, flaunting their young bodies and charms in front of boys.

The thought of her pressing herself on her son as he lay immobile in his hospital bed – perhaps straightening a pillow, adjusting the sheet, she knew that kind, any excuse would do – made her mad with fury. Then she took control of herself. She could handle girls like that, see that they were kept away from her dear Cromwell. She was paying enough. A quiet visit to Dr Mellis in his room before she left the building, that was all it would take. The good doctor was ambitious, this private hospital must have cost him a fortune. He needed to keep in with people who mattered. She'd see to it that the young nurse was out on the street without references before the day was out, see if she didn't. It was the place for her, a slut like that.

She turned, and continued towards her son's room. A frown marred her alabaster forehead. He had a visitor. She hoped it was somebody respectable. Young boys were so vulnerable to the wiles of young women.

'Ah, Roderick,' she said, as she came in, and Roderick de Clare, Bishop of Windstone, smiled a wintry greeting.

'Good morning, Mother,' said Cromwell, from the bed. His leg was raised in the air, encased in plaster, attached to weights running over a pulley. 'Uncle Roderick came by to see me.'

'How kind. Unusual to see you up in town, Roderick.'

'I come up from time to time,' he said vaguely. 'I trust you will soon be up and about, Cromwell.'

'Me too, sir.'

'But you must have plenty of time to convalesce, my darling, musn't you?'

'Of course, Mother,' he said dutifully.

The Bishop glanced at his sister-in-law from under his brows. His expression had a venomous edge.

'Yes, yes,' he agreed. 'Get fit soon, young Cromwell. They will be wanting you back at the front to win the war, you know.'

'No, no!' Constance cried quickly. 'Cromwell is a hero, he has done all of his duty.'

'Perhaps Gervase will give him a job on the staff,' he said smoothly.

'Very possibly. Now were you not leaving?'

Roderick de Clare smiled to himself as he went down the corridor. He was poor, compared to his brothers, he knew it. His brother, the Earl, was rich because he was the Earl. His brother Gervase was wealthy because he had married Constance. What a price! And they had two sons! How the good Lord in Heaven had managed that he would never know.

In the hall he encountered the same young nurse that had so attracted the venom of his sister-in-law. He paused, pretending to examine an oil painting on the wall, as his eyes ran over her form, stripping away the wrapping of blue and white to see in his mind's eye the luscious young body underneath. Sudden desire inflamed him. He knew that he would have to visit the special club he frequented once again before he left. He was a far more regular visitor to London than his sister-in-law ever imagined. There was a strain of fearsome lust that ran through the de Clares, from Berthold the Bold, it was said – they all knew it, and it surfaced in the most unlikely places.

She went up the stairs and he caught a glimpse of a well-turned ankle. He headed for the door, and once outside made for the cab rank in the square. He wondered, as he put on speed, whether he had passed these driving desires on to his two sons, and how they would cope with them if he had. At least they were locked up in St Goderick's, that grim establishment. Cold baths, team sport and the ever-dominant presence of Jesus would sort all that kind of thing out.

Roderick, Bishop de Clare, slipped gratefully into the cab at the top of the rank and murmured the address. The younger generation could take care of itself when the time came. He knew how to manage things from his side.

In the hospital, Lady Constance smoothed her son's forehead.

'Wretched man . . .' she murmured. 'I hope he didn't tire you out, my darling.'

'Of course he didn't, Mother. You mustn't fuss so. It's good to get visitors.'

'Of course it is, darling. I just don't want you tired out.'

'I wish Fish and George and Freddie could come. I got a letter from Fish, would you like to read it?' Cromwell reached for the little cupboard at his side.

'Oh, trying to decipher Fish's terrible scrawl would give me a headache . . .'

Lady Constance looked at her son with excited eyes.

'Actually, Cromwell darling, *I've* got something I want to read to you.'

Cromwell stopped trying to shuffle through his letters. 'Oh?'

Lady Constance reached into her handbag, and drew out an official envelope.

'What is it?'

'It's your citation, darling,' she said, with barely concealed joy. She cleared her throat, and began to read. '"The Military Cross has been awarded to Captain Cromwell de Clare for coolness under heavy enemy machine-gun-fire, devotion to duty and disregard for his own life while coming to the aid of his comrades."'

Cromwell lay in his bed, his face a study of disbelief. 'What is this, Mother?'

'Let me go on. I *had* to be the first to let you know. Where was I. Comrades. "While leading a rescue party across no-man's land on the afternoon of the first of July bringing ammunition and bombs to comrades trapped in the ruins of Leblanc farm on the Somme front—"'

'Mother, Mother!' Cromwell cried out. 'Stop, please!'

'Why, what is it, darling?'

'That's all wrong. Fish led us across. I wasn't even supposed to—'

Lady Constance looked reprovingly at him. 'Darling, I know how you've always tried to help poor Fish, but the idea! Fish leading them? No, darling, it was you, of course it was. Now . . . on the Somme front. "Learning that a party of his battalion was trapped further out into the German positions he immediately set out carrying ammunition and bombs to their aid."' Lady Constance looked up. 'Now, you're not going to tell me that isn't true, are you?'

'No, that bit's true enough,' Cromwell said, suddenly weary. 'But you don't understand, Mother. I didn't *know* the enemy was out there. You can't see them. I didn't know that. It was Fish who saved me. Fish came running after and knocked me down—'

'Oh, Fish, Fish, Fish,' she said irritably. 'If you're not going to be pleased when I bring you this marvellous news I—'

'What did they give Fish?' Cromwell asked steadily. 'What did they give Freddie?'

'Darling, it isn't something that's just handed out with the . . .

rations or whatever. You only get medals like this for outstanding courage.'

'Which is what Fish and Freddie have. Not me. I was just a bloody—'

'*Cromwell*!'

'A bloody incompetent. I nearly got Fish killed. He and Freddie went on and destroyed a machine-gun nest. Freddie stopped one and Fish carried him back. When *I* stopped one Fish grabbed hold of me and began dragging me in too—'

'Nobody has ever denied that Fish has a measure of brawn—' she cried.

'I won't accept it,' Cromwell said obstinately. 'I shall send it back.'

'You will bring disgrace on the very name of de Clare,' she hissed, in a low, furious voice.

'Very well. I will accept—'

'*Good.*'

'Accept, *provided* you go through whichever channel produced this Military Cross for me, and arrange for the same to be awarded to Freddie and Fish. I shall write out the recommendation myself.'

She sighed in exasperation. 'There you go again, trying to help the wretched boy.'

'It ought to be the Victoria Cross,' Cromwell said quietly.

His mother laughed, and then cut herself short when she saw the expression on his face.

'Darling, darling, I've tired you out,' she said, sounding repentant. 'I'm a naughty, naughty mother. And I so wanted to talk to you about parliament.'

'Parliament?' Cromwell said bewildered.

'Why yes. With poor darling Robert dead, dying a hero's death out there, then Windstone needs a new MP.'

'Yes, I suppose it does.'

'We de Clares have held the borough ever since the Long Parliament. It is time for someone else to pick up the torch.'

'Yes . . .'

'*You*, darling.'

'Me?'

'When your leg is better, of course . . .'

'But I'm in the Army . . .'

'And you can stay in the Army . . . there'll be lots for you to do in Windstone as MP. Recruiting, looking after the wounded, serving on the committees . . .' Lady Constance was watching him carefully through her smiling, concerned mask, saw the tiny relaxation of muscles that betrayed his relief. 'You will have served with honour, darling . . .' she said softly.

'What about all those social affairs? Meeting people, garden parties . . .'

'Oh, the old ladies will love you darling! Nothing like a handsome young man to warm their hearts . . . and I'll be there to help you. You know you can always count on me, darling . . .'

'Of course I can, can't I.'

Lady Clare rose, and kissed him on the cheek. 'Oh, you know you can.'

'And you'll do that for Freddie and Fish.'

'Oh, if you insist,' she sighed.

'I do.'

'Very well, then. I'll let you rest, darling. I'll be back this afternoon, I'll see if there are some new magazines for you.'

'Nurse Robbins brought me *Punch*,' he said brightly.

'Did she darling? How kind of her.'

Lady Constance de Clare went downstairs and knocked on the door of the office. A voice bade her enter, and Dr Mellis rose quickly as he saw who it was.

'My dear Lady de Clare . . . do be seated, please. Such splendid progress Captain Cromwell is making. A sherry?'

'I must be going . . . I am having a small gathering next week, Dr Mellis, General de Clare is back from the front for a few days. Some quite . . . interesting people. You might like to meet them.'

'Oh, Lady de Clare—'

'Constance, please.'

Dr Mellis flushed with pleasure. 'Lady Constance . . .'

'So we shall see you? Next Tuesday, seven-thirty for eight?'

'I shall be delighted.'

A small frown marred her forehead, and he leaned forward attentively. 'Yes?'

'A new nurse . . . Robbins, is it?'

'Nurse Robbins, yes?'

'Not the right sort, Dr Mellis. I'm afraid she has been disturbing Cromwell.'

'I'm shocked! Shocked, Lady Constance . . . I shall see to it that she is dismissed this day.'

'Please do. I don't feel that references would be in order.'

'I obtained her through the agency, they're normally very sound. I'll let them know.'

'Good,' said Lady Constance. 'Very good.'

Bishop Roderick de Clare sat in a silk-covered spoonback chair. Outside, through the white silk gauze of the curtains he could see the autumnal garden. The very special club he belonged to owned a fine property. The room he waited in had high ceilings, thick carpet on the floor. A wood fire burned in the grate, a gold silk counterpane was turned back on the bed. By his side a bottle of champagne rested in a frosted silver bucket, and he sipped on a flute of golden wine. He rang a small bell beside him.

A few moments later the door opened and a very pretty girl dressed in a nurse's uniform came in, carrying a small tray. The idea had come to him in the hallway of the hospital, as he had watched the young nurse. Mrs Tompkins, the ever-obliging proprietress of the club, had as always been ready to provide. The bishop was an old, and valued customer.

'Time for your medicine, Bishop . . .' the girl purred. She put down her tray – there was a pot of scented cream on it. She began to undo his clothes. Her uniform rustled with starch, which he found deliciously stimulating. He reached under the crisp dress, she was wearing silk stockings and, he found, a garter belt, but nothing else. She giggled, and slapped his other hand, which was feeling her breasts.

'You're a very naughty bishop,' she said severely. 'I can see you need your medicine. Lie down on the bed.'

He did as he was bid. She climbed gracefully on top of him, and lifted the hem of her skirt. There was pleasure in heaven, the bishop knew. What it was, to be better than that obtained so on earth, he could not imagine. He cried out for joy.

It was worth every guinea. There were many, many guineas . . . He had tried, sometimes, to stop. He had prayed, back in the past, but that had proved of little strength when pitted against the fire of lust that rose up in his loins.

It was very expensive . . . he thanked God, sometimes, for St Goderick's, which imparted the love and fear of the Lord into its pupils and gave members of the cloth such a substantial discount. He didn't know what he would have done with his two sons Perceval and Godfrey, otherwise. Eton was far beyond his purse after Mrs Tompkins had been through it.

11

Happy Christmas

Ypres, December 1916

The flat glare of the setting sun came over their shoulders and painted the opposing wire entanglements. It could do little about the grey, frozen mud, nor did it light up the khaki of the dead men hanging on the wire.

Fish went down the trench with Sergeant-Major Furzegrove, and the duckboards crunched the ice in the drainage like gravel. Their breath hung frozen in the air. Fish came round the traverse and peered through the hard light at the sentry at the other end. The trenches they held were in the shape of a squashed semi-circle, with the ruins of a wood and a small village at each end, a bulge in the line disliked by the staff in the rear, who preferred straight lines on their maps. The ground sloped up to the wood and to the shattered village. The curved salient came out from the German line into the British one, a relic of the 1914 first battle of Ypres that had not subsequently been disturbed. It was a sector all of its own, not overlooked on either side.

Fish peered through the glare. 'Who is that tall chap down there, Furzegrove?'

'My brother, Amos, sir. Just joined us, you remember.'

'Oh, yes. He volunteered in July, didn't he?'

'After the battle, sir, yes. He got very upset when he realised that so many in the village and around those parts weren't coming home, sir. He said to me the women, the mothers and the wives of the dead, they were looking at him. Said he felt their eyes on him, didn't think he could stay at home, see.' Furzegrove squinted reflectively through the setting sun. 'I rather wish he'd stayed, sir.'

'Oh, why's that?'

'Amos's a bit ... slow, if you remember. But still, he'll probably be well enough if I'm around.'

'There's still a good core of we W-Windstones. We can l-look after each other,' Fish agreed. They came up to the big man and Amos smiled slowly to see his brother and commanding officer.

'You all right, Furzegrove?' Fish asked him. 'Cold not g-getting to you?'

'Oh, no, sir. I be used to the cold, back home.'

'Well, you won't be used to a m-machine-gun bullet through your head, if you don't keep it down.'

'I knows that, sir. My brother here, he told me.'

'Good. Now l-listen, Furzegrove. About dusk J-Jerry over there fires off a few belts from a machine-gun he's got s-sited. Goes from one end of our line to the other. Bit of a h-hate, you see? Anyhow, he got rifleman Roberts last night and I'm a bit p-peeved with him.'

Fish reached into his pocket and pulled out a length of cord attached to two rifle bullets, one at each end. 'When he goes b-by, I want you to range this on the noise. Understand me?' Fish held it stretched out in front of him so that the length of cord pointed at the German line.

'See? So that it points at the line. Thump the bullets into the earth. They w-won't go off. Then we'll sandbag r-rifles along the line of the c-cord and when he changes belts and starts up again we'll give him five rounds rapid, the lot of us.'

'You understand Major de Clare, Amos?' his brother demanded.

'Oh, yes, yes,' the big man nodded. 'I knows what to do.'

'And k-keep your head down,' said Fish. 'Rifleman Roberts didn't and he hasn't got it any more.'

Fish and Furzegrove went down the line, arranging the details with the sentries. About half way they met George.

'All d-done?'

'Ready my side. Damn but it's cold.'

'Just going to set up a rifle myself, sir,' said Furzegrove, and went towards the traverse.

'Want something to heat the inner soul?' George asked, and produced a hunting flask. He shook it next to his ear. 'Hmm. Wretched thing seems to run out between fills quicker than it did.' He put it back in his pocket. Fumbling inside his British warm he produced a second shiny silver flask and pulled the top off in triumph. 'Always prepared . . .'

Fish took a gulp of the neat whisky and felt it burn all the way down.

'I don't know what Mummy will say,' said George. 'She used to be quite vicious about the vicar. "He *drinks*, you know." Poor man only liked sherry. She found him buying a bottle in the village stores. "He drinks . . ." I don't suppose she'll be very pleased to find her only son's a soak . . .' He took another pull and wiped his eyes. The sun slid behind the frozen sludge behind them.

'R-Right. First belt, they range on him. Second belt, sandbag the rifles. Third belt, five rounds r-rapid on the whistle.'

As if hearing its cue, the rapid stutter of a machine-gun started up from the German line. Fish and George ducked down as it came to them, the metal rain stabbing into the rear of the trench, expertly aligned, sending shards of frozen earth flying like shrapnel.

'D-Damn,' said Fish, sucking a finger. 'Bugger's n-nicked me.'

The gunfire moved on, and he pushed himself up, pulling one of his lengths of cord and bullets from his pocket.

'Right. Let's get this organised,' he muttered. He cocked an ear, and thrust the bullets into the earth, thumping them home with a small rock. 'That's it, w-wouldn't you say, George . . . George?' There was no reply. He turned, George was lying with his knees tucked up under him on the duckboards, his head cradled in his hands.

'George?' Fish said in alarm. He bent down. Further away along the front some flares went up, a machine-gun began firing. It took little to inflame the front.

'Are you all right?'

'Yes, yes,' George said, his voice muffled.

'You're not hurt?'

'No . . .'

The machine-gun opposite finished its belt, and there was a pause.

'C-Come on,' Fish said gently, and began pulling George up.

'Yes, I'm coming.'

'George, you're not. You're l-lying on the b-bloody duckboards.' Through his mittens Fish could feel the trembling of his friend's body. 'Come on, old bean. The men w-will think we're playing l-leapfrog. C-Come on, let's shoot the Gerry gunner and we'll have a d-drink, eh?'

Slowly, George looked up at Fish, his face very white in the dark. He smiled, shakily, and Fish helped him up.

'Sorry, old man,' he muttered. 'Don't know what came over me. Bit windy these days. I pray to God and there's no answer.'

'H-Here. Let's line the rifle up. May as well all join in. You can blow the whistle.'

'All right.'

The machine-gun started up again, and George wrapped his arms about himself in reflex, leaning back against the solidity of the firestep.

'Where's God, Fish?' he demanded. 'Who's in charge?'

The bullets went by, they both tilted their heads forwards and frozen earth tinkled against their iron helmets.

'How do you keep going, Fish?'

'I suppose I have my parents to th-thank,' Fish said without emotion. 'I'm t-trained for it.'

'Your parents must be out of the book of Revelations. Those things surging about in the sea of flame, eating living flesh.'

'Th-that sort of thing.'

The gun halted its firing, and Fish called softly along the trench. 'All right, chaps! On the whistle. Five rounds rapid, pass it on.'

They heard the quiet call go down the line. Fish stood up, cuddling his Lee-Enfield to his left shoulder.

'Get the whistle ready, George.'

George fumbled for the silver whistle about his neck with hands that trembled like an old man's. He felt a sense of self-loathing, and stuffed it in his mouth. His fluttering breath made the pea roll about with a gurgling sound.

'Not yet, George.'

In the dark, the gun started up its inhuman, even, industrial rattle. '*Now.*'

George blew with all his might, a shrill shriek that echoed his terror, and from along the line of the Windstone fire trench there came a concentrated blast of sound. Above him Fish whipped the bolt back and forth. A hot casing fell on George's hand and he brushed it away in fear.

'Cease fire!' Fish called. 'Cease fire.'

In the sudden silence the front was quiet. The machine-gun had ceased its clatter. A few seconds later they heard the German whistles blowing for stretcher-bearers. Fish slung his rifle under his arm like a shotgun after a drive of pheasant. He reached down and heaved George to his feet.

'L-Let's have that drink,' he suggested. They went down the trench towards Fish's command shelter.

'Well done, chaps,' he said, as they went past the sentries. A smell of propellant was in the air, as always, mixed with corruption and death. George felt his stomach churn.

'Well done, chaps. G-Got the bugger, wh-what?'

A small candle burned inside the shelter, an affair about the size of a small stable dug out to the water table, which was about four feet down, and roofed over with an iron frame over which was a layer of sandbags.

'T-Take a pew.'

George slumped into a wooden chair. On a shelf dug out of the earth Fish had Robert's tantalus. He slopped about four fingers of whisky into tumblers and topped up with water. He gave one to George and he dipped his face towards it eagerly. Fish sat down behind his table, covered by its grey blanket, and took a gulp himself.

'You know, Fish,' George observed, 'I'm getting like a bloody meths drinker: I move my head to the glass, instead of lifting it up to my mouth. My bloody hands shake too much.' He shook himself, as though trying to get rid of dirt. 'So bloody morbid . . .' he complained. 'Watching oneself disintegrate and noting down all the symptoms in detail . . . I was all right when . . .'

'When what?' Fish asked quietly.

'When . . . when God . . .'

'You need to go h-home,' Fish said.

George felt the whisky seeping into his bones. He tipped the glass back and found it empty. He helped himself to another.

Above their heads came a clatter of machine-gun-fire. The whisky slopped in his glass, but he was sufficiently anaesthetised not to drop it. There was something curious about the gun-fire, it was firing with a stuttering rhythm. Peering out, Fish saw tracer passing high above their heads in scarlet streaks.

'B-Buggers are firing over our heads,' he said in surprise.

George began to tap against the frame of the shelter, beating out the rhythm of the bullets. He suddenly laughed in a cloud of whisky fumes.

'Meet me down in Pic-ca-dill-y,' he chanted. 'That's it, Fish! Meet me down in Pic-ca-dill-y!'

'Piccadilly?'

'Yes, it's what the whores call out, don't you know?'

'I've led a sh-sheltered life,' Fish said drily.

'Where's our gun?' George said, stumbling and weaving along the trench, bouncing off the sides, his fear temporarily forgotten. He came to the Vickers they had appropriated, and began to pull bullets out from the belt, muttering under his breath. Drunk, he sat down at the controls. The machine-gun opposite had stopped, and he squeezed the trigger with his thumbs, sending a stream of tracer sparkling high into the night. As he fired, he laughed like a madman, singing out at the top of his voice. 'Yes! With-out my draw-ers on! Yes! With-out my draw-ers on!' The belt slapped through the gun and the firing stopped. George stared into the darkness with suddenly vacant eyes. His lids drooped, he fell forward over his gun.

Behind Fish a man shuffled his boots. He turned to see a corporal standing with a line of burdened men behind him, a supply column.

'Give me a h-hand, Corporal. Get the vicar into his flea bag.'

'Yes, sir.'

'What have you there?'

'Beef, sir. Milk, flour, eggs.'

'Beef?'

'Yes, sir. What you had sent from the castle, sir. And the puddings.'

'The puddings . . .'

'Why yes, sir. The Christmas puddings what you had sent.'

'Oh yes . . .' Fish said, remembering. 'Of course. I want us all to have a d-dashed good meal for Christmas. Even if we are st-stuck out here in this blasted Ypres m-mud.'

'We is all looking forward to it, sir,' the man said appreciatively.

'Why y-yes . . .'

They put George into his sleeping bag as he was, boots and all.

'I say, when is Christmas, Corporal?'

The man looked strangely at Fish. 'Why tomorrow, sir.'

'So it is,' said Fish. He watched them go off down the line to the half-buried cookhouse, vanishing into the dark. 'Isn't it?'

They swept over the rolling ground in a great yelling mass of grey and khaki, their breath like steaming mist in the air, smelling of schnapps and gravy and brandy and fruit cake and pudding and beef and blood. Occasionally the big heavy stitched-leather football rose high out of the mob, turning over and over, the swirling men beneath changing course like a shoal of fish in its pursuit, grunting and yelling, elbows flying, tripping and stumbling, knees grazing, lips swelling, swirling all over the great patch of land in between the entanglements. There were no goals to shoot at, but that was not the point.

The Christmas sun was going down, casting its flat light over the battlefield. A new chill was rising up from the freezing earth. The two sides had withdrawn each near to its own wire, where they stamped their boots, and waited.

The relief companies had arrived, George could hear them. He slipped into his cubby hole, possessed by a sudden urgency, and lit the stub of his candle. Where was it? Quickly now, or there would be no time. The troops were gathering up their kit, getting ready to move.

Ah, there it was. His hands weren't shaking at all now. He found his cleaning kit in its little wooden box, opened it up, spread the flanelette patches on his bed, opened a bottle of gun oil. Scent suddenly filled the little earth dug-out. It was like being back home, cleaning his twelve-bore. He smiled happily. Not long now and he would be back, a hot bath waiting, supper cooking, a cheery fire burning in the grate. Not long now.

He arranged his little cleaning cloths with care. This was all right. No shame now. They wouldn't rib Father at the club, his sisters could go out without hearing people snigger, they'd put his name up on the board at Harrow – it was all perfectly honourable. Sympathy. Man of God. Front line. Simple accident.

He slipped his big, heavy, black Webley revolver from the holster at his waist, broke it quickly. A circle of six huge brass .44 rounds shone in the candlelight.

It was all right now. His mother wouldn't have the shame of seeing him drunk. Nobody would know. Chaplain. War poet. Tragic accident. One of our old boys today . . . Up on the board.

George snapped the revolver back together. Quickly, now. They would leave without him. He was going home.

He put the barrel up to his head. He smiled as he pulled the trigger.

The heavy mechanism whirred, the hammer smacked home. There was silence in the little earth hole. He pulled the trigger again and again but it would not fire. He dropped his arm, the pistol fell to the ground, he bent over the bed, weeping.

'I c-cut the firing p-pin out,' Fish said from behind him.

'You bastard . . .' George sobbed. 'You unutterable bastard . . . I was going home.' He looked at Fish, the tears pouring down his face. 'How can you do this to me, Fish?' he whispered. 'Now they will all know . . .'

Fish gave him a big white handkerchief. 'Here. The m-men won't know. It's dark. Come on, we're going out of the line. Blow your nose.'

'You see, Fish,' George said quietly, seriously. 'There is no God.'

Later, George suffered himself to be led through the darkness. he stumbled, here and there, but Fish was at his elbow. Fish made him sing, carols about holly and stars and wise men. Somewhere he stopped him in the darkness and George could hear the men marching into camp. Fish gave him a big drink, made him swallow it down, fiery and hot. He lay him down, and he slept.

When he woke the bed was swaying. He was in the back of a

lorry. He got out, and smelled salt. He was unshaven, unwashed. He climbed some iron stairs, blinked in dawn sunshine. He was on a ship. In the distance, white cliffs shone. In the wind of the steamer's passage, something flapped from his wrist, tied to him with string.

It was a brown manila envelope. He opened it. It held orders for a posting, signed by Fish under his title of battalion commander. He saw the name of Windstone Castle on the travel warrant.

12

Your Mater is a Leading Light in the Primrose League

St Goderick's, March 1917

The boys in their black jackets and wing collars oozed out of the chapel, slowly dissipating about the school. It was Sunday. Entertainment of any description was forbidden on the Lord's day. Instead there was two hours of compulsory psalms, prayers and hymns in the morning; the bleak day being broken by a cold and practically inedible lunch to mark the Lord's disapproval of enjoyment on His day, followed by a further two hours of the same in the evening.

Godfrey came out into the open, and blew on his white fingers. The chapel was floored with stone, upon which they knelt, and was completely unheated. The sun was watery but it almost seemed warm after the dismal gloom inside the building.

The boys were slowly drifting away, like disconsolate penguins. Godfrey hung about near a dark red-brick buttress, as though waiting for somebody, and watched Worsley. The small, rather pretty boy was killing time. He was standing over under the arches of the colonnade, reading the noticeboard.

Godfrey knew he was killing time. He had seen him do it the previous Sunday. And he had vanished somewhere afterwards. He Had also shown a faint lightening of spirit at the hideous cold lunchtable. Sundays at St Goderick's were not meant to produce any lightness of spirit. Godfrey wanted to know what it was that produced it in Worsley. Nobody else seemed to have noticed. He had. He was a de Clare, and the de Clares were hunters, bred to it over generations. Godfrey sometimes wondered if he was not bred to hunt people.

The boys were nearly all gone. There were enough left to disguise Worsley's progress. He drifted casually away, almost like a leaf in the stream. Using the cover of the buildings and the heavy, dark green shrubs with which the grounds were infested, Godfrey followed. Worsley seemed to be going down towards the river. The school buildings were away behind them, hidden by the trees.

He vanished. One second he was tripping along the path that went by the thick rhododendrons at the edge of the wood and the next he had gone. Warily, Godfrey slipped into cover behind some rotting brown bracken. A few seconds later he was rewarded by Worsley's elfin face peeking out, checking the path both ways before it vanished once more.

He padded quietly down the mossy path. Worsley had gone between two of the huge bushes. Some leathery leaves on the branch were still trembling slightly where he had brushed against them. Godfrey went into the wood. It was very overgrown, and he had to move carefully to avoid breaking twigs. It was difficult to see more than a few feet in any direction – he might not have found Worsley at all had it not been for the sudden whiff of tobacco.

Godfrey was a de Clare, the de Clares were hunters: they understood spoor and scent, they knew where the wind was. He spotted Worsley sitting almost hidden in a bracken-covered gully. He was sitting on a fallen log, and he was not sitting alone. Next to him was a bigger boy. They had a cigarette, and passed it between them.

Godfrey knew who the big boy was; Brophy, one of the rugger players and a prefect. He waited patiently, concealed in cover. He did not believe that smoking a cigarette in a wood could on its own account for Worsley's improved humour of a Sunday. He was right.

Brophy took a last pull at the stub of the cigarette and carefully put it out under his boot on the damp wood floor. Then he turned round, put his arms round Worsley, and kissed him.

They enjoyed it. The kisses became more passionate, their heads moving first this way and then that, their mouths locked together. Their hands moved into each other's groin, rubbing at their trousers and fumbling with their buttons. Godfrey saw them, exposed to the air as they felt each other. Hidden in his cover, he became stiff himself. His eyes glittered as he watched.

It was finished suddenly. He heard them gasp, saw Brophy rise, adjust his clothing, look furtively around. Godfrey saw him smile at Worsley, say something and pass him a lighted cigarette before he slipped away through the wood.

Godfrey watched him go, saw Worsley remain on his log, sitting smoking while he waited for Brophy to leave the wood and be well clear before he himself emerged on the other side. Godfrey well understood their caution. What they were engaged in was the ultimate sin of St Goderick's which led to automatic expulsion, an act preceded by a most ferocious flogging to drive all such evils from the body of the culprit.

Godfrey too waited, until he was sure that Brophy was well clear, then he slipped out of cover like a fox. Worsley only saw him when he was a few feet away, looking up in sudden alarm.

'Oh, it's you!' His face, suddenly pale, quickly flushed pink.

'What are you doing here, de Clare?' he demanded fearfully.

'I don't have to ask you that,' Godfrey said silkily. 'I *know* what you're doing here.'

'It's none of your business.'

'It would be Reverend Rose's business,' Godfrey pointed out, referring to their bleak, severe housemaster. 'I don't think he'd approve, not at all.'

'You wouldn't blab . . .'

'Who am I to spoil anyone's enjoyment?' Godfrey said lightly. 'I take it you do enjoy it . . .'

Worsley stayed silent, the smoke of the cigarette rising straight up into the canopy above them.

'Well, *do* you?'

'It's hell here!' Worsley burst out. 'All the rotten bullying . . . it's cold and horrid and . . . beastly. Freezing baths and horrid food and being . . . beaten . . . and those stupid rituals . . . I hate it, I *hate* it . . .'

Godfrey pursed his lips. Many indeed were the rituals, all unpleasant for the victim. They invariably involved humiliation, degradation and pain whilst exciting coarse and vicious amusement from those responsible. Godfrey had himself had the handle of a small broom rammed up his backside and been forced to sweep a floor with it while singing a music hall song, simply to amuse some of the prefects, led by the fiend Starnley. It had excited within him a burning desire for revenge.

'Yes, yes,' he agreed. 'But I fail to see why that leads you to creep into a wood and get tugged off by Brophy.'

'He *likes* me,' Worsley hissed. 'He . . . protects me from the worst of it.'

Godfrey thought for a second. It was true. He had not seen anything really nasty happen to him for some while, whereas Simmonds had had his balls blacked twice in a week out of simple malice.

'I see . . .' he said thoughtfully. 'But you still haven't answered my question. Do you like it?'

'There is very little to like here,' Worsley said bitterly. 'I don't mind it.'

'Jolly good,' Godfrey said languidly. He was still stiff. 'You can do it to me then.'

'Why should I?' the smaller boy protested.

'Because I feel like it, and because I hope your parents never get to hear about it.'

'What about yours?' Worsley squeaked.

'My mother's dead and my father would not be surprised, I assure you. Whereas your mater is a leading light in the Primrose League and would be shocked.' Godfrey undid his fly buttons. 'Do you like Starnley, Worsley?' he enquired.

'I *hate* him!' Worsley said vehemently.

'Well tug me off then while I think of something – you've given me an idea . . .'

Godfrey liked it, he liked dominating the smaller boy. Worsley was pretty; Godfrey thought there might be other things he could make him do in time. He had a sudden vision of Starnley with his trousers down, bent helpless over a form, screaming in agony as he was flogged, and delicious pain stabbed through his groin.

'That was nice,' he said, as he did himself up. 'We must do it again.'

13

This Line Needs Straightening

Ypres

'I hope I'm not making a muck of this,' the Prince said to Fish, poking the pin of the medal through his tunic. 'You'd think I'd be better at it with all the practice I've had.'

He clipped the pin home and stepped back. The cross on its duckboard ribbon gleamed even in the dull winter light. In the small parade of officers at Prince Edward's back Fish could see his father. As he looked over the prince's shoulder he saw him glance at him, with a strange blank expression.

'There,' said the prince. 'I think that's it. Good to see you, you know. I met your cousin Henry last week, went to see his squadron. I've asked the King for permission to go up.'

'It's great f-fun, sir,' said Fish.

'What of the rest? All safe? Hard to keep up sometimes, with the casualties . . .' He glanced past Fish at the company drawn up behind him. 'I'll go and inspect them in a minute . . . What do you think of Lloyd George being prime minister then? Squiff had to go . . .'

He made a gesture as of a man tipping back a glass.

'He lost his s-son at the Somme,' said Fish. 'The first day.'

'When you got your medal, what? I'm glad that bugger Churchill is out.'

Fish remained tactfully silent.

'Know anything about Russia?' Prince Edward demanded.

'Very little, sir.'

'The King is worried that the Russians will stop fighting now they've had this revolution.' The Prince stared at Fish with horrified eyes. 'Revolution! The Tsar is now Citizen Romanov! Can you imagine it? It's a worry . . . I don't suppose such things could happen in our own race: we have too much good sense, don't you think.'

'Abs-solutely.'

'I'd better inspect your chaps . . . talking of inspections, I had a look at the new land submarines, you know? Tanks, they call them. I don't think they'll ever work . . . Do you like spaghetti?'

'Spaghetti?'

'It's muck, let me tell you. I've been in Italy. The Italians run like rabbits – I think we should let the Germans have them. Oh, well. Let me see some real troops.'

They went over, and he began to inspect them. He paused opposite Amos, Sergeant-Major Furzegrove's brother.

'I say, you're a tall one,' he said in a friendly manner. 'Do you find it difficult in the trenches?'

The simple country boy flushed with pleasure at being spoken to by royalty. 'Not if I keeps my head down, sir.'

'Oh, yes! Jolly important to do that I should think.'

'Oh, it is sir. The colonel didn't, and he lost his.'

'Did he now?' Edward said thoughtfully. 'Did he really . . . dashed forgetful of him, what?'

'Yes, sir.'

The Prince completed his inspection and paused before going back to the patient group of staff officers waiting for him.

'You're off to the front now, then?'

'Yes, sir. It's not far. About a twenty-minute march.'

'I make them let me come within shell range, you know. They won't let me fight, but I get shelled, occasionally. It puts the wind up me quite awfully!'

'It puts the w-wind up me too,' said Fish.

'Oh no, you're a hero . . . Oh well, I'd better let you go.'

'Thank you, sir.'

They marched away, towards the front. The ground was muddy from the rains and the black of their boots, shined for the inspection was covered over by sticky grey clay within a hundred yards. As he marched, Fish could feel somebody's eyes on his back, and he knew it was his father.

They entered the trench system, sinking lower into the ground, and the water came up to meet them. They were soon sloshing along through the icy liquid mud, up to their knees. They took over their sector again and Fish stared in disgust at the water.

'Th-this is no bally good, Furzegrove,' he said angrily. 'Everybody'll have t-trench-foot within days. Can't we dig more drains?'

'No good, sir,' said Furzegrove, with the countryman's eye for land. 'This be nothing better than a marsh.'

'You're right . . . Very well, let's build up the trench sides, this rain's done it no good at all. I want the parapets . . . what's the depth of this filth we're standing in, two feet? All right, let's put the parapet up three feet and raise the duckboards the same amount. Send a detail for sandbags, boards, dug-out frames, girders and nails. Let's get going now: it'll keep the men warm and maybe we can be half d-dry by the time it's dark.'

'Very good, sir.'

Furzegrove sloshed away and Fish heard him shouting out orders. He found his commander's shelter near knee-deep in the freezing water. He lit candles and stuck them in the little alcoves cut into the walls. Then he sat on his table and removed his boots, hanging them upside down to drain. He took off his sodden socks, dried his feet and began to rub grease into them to counter the rot known as trench-foot. He was still doing this when he heard someone wading up the trench. A staff major in smart but now dirty uniform put his head round the entrance with an expression of extreme distaste.

'Major de Clare?'

'Yes.'

'Your father the general wants to see you.'

'D-Does he,' said Fish, and massaged more of the thick white grease in between his toes.

'Well come on, man!' the staff officer said irritably. 'Do you imagine I'm standing in this for my health?'

'Try a week of it,' Fish said indifferently.

'Mind your bloody tongue! Who do you think you're talking to?'

Fish clasped his Military Cross between finger and thumb and waved it at the man. 'I'm talking to someone who doesn't wear this.'

The messenger flushed with anger. 'Just come with me. The general wants you.'

'The g-general can b-bugger himself.'

The man stood staring at Fish with bulging, disbelieving eyes.

'I'm not coming,' Fish explained clearly. 'I command this sector. If the general wants to see me he can wait seven days until we come out or he can come down here. It makes l-little difference to me.'

'You're mad . . .' he breathed. 'Completely mad!'

'Oh yes. I'm th-that all right. And I'm still not coming.'

Fish heard his father's minion splashing angrily away. He wrung out his socks, and pulled them back on, together with his boots. He was very cold.

Later, he heard his father's voice outside.

'This it?'

'That's it, sir,' the messenger said.

'Go and wait at the end of the trench.'

Fish heard the man splashing away, and then his father came in. It gave Fish a perverse pleasure to see his shiny boots soaked, his cavalry breeches sodden to the thigh. His father cared about his clothes.

'You're an insolent little pig, Fish,' General de Clare said dangerously.

'If you s-say so,' Fish said laconically. He hung a report on a nail.

'But not for much longer.' There was a sinister note of satisfaction in his father's voice that made Fish look up.

'Oh?'

'Oh, no. Not much longer at all. You're going to be dead soon, Fish.'

'Oh, I k-know.'

'You do?' his father said, momentarily disconcerted.

'Of c-course.'

'Who told you?' he said peevishly.

Fish spoke to his father as if to a child. 'Don't you know where we are? This is where you die. Stay here l-long enough *you* will die.'

'Ah! So you *don't* know,' General de Clare said with renewed satisfaction.

'Know what?'

'What I am going to do to you, Fish.'

Fish raised his eyebrows.

'I'm going to court-martial you. You're a snivelling little traitorous coward, and you're going to pay the price for it.' There was silence in the icy, sodden little bunker, and then General de Clare went on. 'You've been collaborating with the enemy, Fish,' he said with a vicious satisfaction. 'On Christmas Day you were witnessed doing it. Do you deny it?'

'No,' Fish said wearily.

'Then you're going to be shot. I shall see to it.'

'Do what you want,' said Fish. He sounded very tired. 'I have some parapets to see to.'

'No you don't,' his father retorted. 'You have a court-martial and an execution to attend. I estimate we should be able to shoot you by Wednesday at the latest.'

Fish said nothing. He picked up some reports and began to sort through them. General de Clare stared at him with mounting rage.

'Well?' he demanded. 'What have you got to say?'

'I have n-nothing to say. We played football on Christmas Day. On Boxing Day we shot at each other again.'

'Don't you want me to intercede for you?'

'You want me to b-beg for mercy, is that it?' Fish said contemptuously. 'Stick it up your b-backside.'

'Very well,' his father rasped. 'You know I can't have the family name brought into shame like this. "Death Before Dishonour", damn you!'

'I won't shoot myself, if that's what you want.'

The general sloshed over to the wall. He was beginning to turn blue from the cold. There was a map of the front there. He traced the outline of the salient bulging into the British sector.

'This line needs straightening,' he said abruptly. 'See to it.'

'An attack?'

'Straighten the line, Fish. Do it before you come out. It's that or be shot for cowardice in the face of the enemy.'

'I'm a de Clare,' Fish said, finally stung. 'I am not a coward.'

'Straighten the line then.'

'What if I refuse?'

'Then we'll add dereliction of duty and another charge of cowardice in the face of the enemy to the first crimes and shoot you twice,' General de Clare said with relish. 'And what is more I shall order your successor to do it.'

'There'll be very high casualties.'

'If high casualties bothered me, Fish, I would not be prosecuting this war.'

Fish heard his father splashing away along the trench. He lit a cigarette, and sat on his table for a long time, thinking.

Furzegrove put his head round the entrance. 'Parapet's raised, sir,' he reported. 'We'll lift your roof when you're ready.'

'Very good,' he said. 'G-Give me a moment, I've got to speak to s-someone on the telephone.'

Fish lifted the receiver of his field telephone. 'Hallo? Major de Clare, First Windstones. I want to speak to 56 Squadron. Henry de Clare. Yes.'

He waited while the laborious connections were made. 'Henry de Clare. Yes, it's his cousin. Henry? I'm having a party over here, I wondered if you could come.'

14

I Don't Want a Bayonet up my Arsehole

Ypres

At a thousand feet the wind whistled through the bracing wires and behind his head the propeller freewheeled like a sewing machine. Ahead of Henry de Clare the German salient bulged out into the Windstone position like a hernia. They came overhead, eight DH2s in line abreast, noses down, at over a hundred knots. They had dived from altitude, engines off, the bright sun at their backs.

Seated in the very nose of his aeroplane, Henry de Clare held the nose down, the little dark shadow of the biplane racing along the ground below towards the trenches. He caught a glimpse of men running beneath him, carrying great lengths of pipe.

Even in its shallow glide the DH2 maintained its speed. It was heavily laden, as were they all. In racks under the wings 50lb and 100lb bombs hung in clusters and packed about his feet were boxes filled with drums of ammunition for the Lewis gun in front of him.

They had practised this. They had dug dummy trenches at the end of the aerodrome, had come out of the sun in a shallow dive. The airspeed indicator was steady on 105 knots. The little racing shadow flashed across the fire trench and Henry pulled the first lever. The fighter lurched, suddenly light as the cluster of bombs went away. He saw men frozen in sudden horror, blinded by the sun, the aircraft silent in their dive.

He cut in the power, the engine caught with a blast of noise and thrust behind him, he pulled the biplane round in a tight turn, fifty feet above the ground, and felt the very air tremble all about him as the bombs went off. The turn squeezed him down in the seat, but he managed to peer over his shoulder and saw dirt and smoke blasting up into the air from the bombs, filthy against the bright sun. The flight banked hard over as it followed him.

The air rattled and cracked, the ground twinkled with light. The people down there were beginning to fire at him. He began to sing loudly and tunelessly against the roar of the engine and the bombs:

> 'I don't want to be a soldier.
> I don't want to go to war . . .'

He came out of the 270-degree turn running parallel to the trench system. Dirt was still falling on the fire trench as he came down the support at ten feet, seeing men in grey running, firing, scattering as best they could – he dropped the rest of his bombs on them. From out in no-man's land amongst the entanglements he felt a great buffet of blasting air, which rocked him sideways. He corrected with a bootful of rudder; the trench slid under his nose and he began firing down it.

A scarlet smoke marker was burning at the top of the hill: it signalled the end of the German system. He pulled up and around in another turn.

> 'I'd rather stay at home,
> Around the streets to roam,
> And live on the earnings of a well-paid whore . . .'

Smoke streamed from the three lines of trenches. Men were running into it from no-man's land through the great gaps blasted in the entanglement. A DH2 was weaving in and out of the smoke at twenty feet. It vanished for a moment and then there was a great sheet of flame that lit the trenches around in sharp relief.

Henry pulled off his empty drum with one hand, slapping a new one in its place. His breath was rasping in his throat. The DH2s were swirling about the fight below like buzzards, black in the setting sun. He counted five in one sweep of his eyes. Two gone. Above them a great black thundercloud loomed, dragging a wall of grey rain beneath it. He put the nose down and heard the rising shriek of the wind in the bracing wires.

'I don't want a bayonet up my arsehole,' he screamed, and began to fire at the dim, running, grey figures. Rain as hard as hail rattled over the aeroplane as he dived into the storm.

'I don't want my ballocks shot away . . .'

Something whined off a wire, something twanged, the aeroplane seemed to sag under his hands, something very hot sliced across his face.

'*Bastard . . .*' he yelled. He fired again and again, flashing through the smoke and sheeting rain. The blast of the wind pushed running blood into his mouth. It emerged in a spray as he shrieked out his song.

> 'I'd rather stay in England.
> In merry merry England . . .'

Something enormous hit the engine behind him, the aircraft went one way and, it seemed to him, he another. Lightning flashed in the gloom, its thunder crashed like cannon in his ears.

'And fuck my bloody life away.'

He felt warm – he wasn't sure why.

Furzegrove watched as his brother tipped back the little mug of rum.

'That be more powerful than Uncle Nob's plum gin,' he said appreciatively.

'That's right, Amos,' said Furzegrove. 'It'll warm you nicely. Now listen to me, Amos. I'm going with the torpedo men.'

'Ah. I knows that.'

'Watch me. You follow me, Amos. Easy to get lost out on the battlefield. Follow me. What are you to do?'

'Follow you,' said the big slow man.

'That's it. And you see a Jerry, bayonet him.'

Amos had never been certain about that. He'd done it on the practice ground, of course, but really sticking half a yard of steel through a man . . .

He was going to ask his brother about it, but by the time he'd thought what to say Furzegrove had gone, was shepherding the running men with their long pipes across the ground in front. Shadows flashed overhead, a line of aircraft came above him, going like the wind, just a whistling of air rushing over them, knifing towards the German line. And there was the officer, Mr Fish from the castle, up on the trench parapet, waving them forward. He remembered, there was to be no noise, no whistles.

Amos clambered out with the others, set off across the rough ground at a run, the officers sweeping them forward. The sun suddenly went in as the great thundercloud rolled over them. A cold gust of wind blew, and the rain swept across. Ahead the trenches suddenly blossomed with flame; dirt and smoke blew high in the air. The aeroplanes were zooming like scattered crows, black against the sky.

He remembered to look for his brother. There he was. Wasn't he? Amos lumbered clumsily over the ground, rough as a ploughed field, clutching his rifle like a pitchfork. The entanglements erupted into flame, he saw stakes flying through the air, spinning about like matches. Men ran through the gaps – he heard bombs going off, rifles and Lewis guns cracking and rattling, he heard people scream.

The thunderstorm crashed in his ears, rain roared down over him in torrents, in sheets. He slipped on the wet clay, winded himself. Pushing himself up under the load of his equipment, he found himself alone in the storm. The grey gloom was illuminated by sudden flashes of light, the echoing crump of explosions, the scream of men dying. Bewildered, he stumbled forward . . .

Furzegrove's men had gone through into the fire trench. A DH2 shot by twenty yards further on, firing into the support line, its pilot crouched over the stick, his Lewis gun fluttering flames. Fish jumped down into the trench with his team behind him. He could hear Furzegrove's bombers to the left. He lobbed a bomb over the traverse, counted the five and a half seconds before it exploded. He ran round the dog's tooth with his Lewis gunner and was in time to see some Germans running away along the trench. The Lewis gunner sent a burst after them, then Fish led them at a run along the trench, his bag of bombs banging against his back, a bomb in one hand and his revolver in the other.

The rain swept over in an icy grey sheet, the thunder smashed overhead. The gloom suddenly erupted in bursting orange fire – something huge and burning smashed across the trench, hurling Fish into the side . . .

Amos saw a trench beneath him. He landed with a crash, and from a small dug-out in the trench wall somebody cried out. He saw something move, saw a grey sleeve, not a khaki one, saw it clutching something. He remembered what his brother had told him, lunged at it with his bayonet.

Something screamed, something thrashed on his bayonet end like a big fish, but it screamed, it screamed like a wounded hare. In horror he heaved at his rifle, trying to pull the steel out, and dragged a man onto the duckboards – a young man who cried out, a bandage in his hand, a wounded young man who had crawled inside his dug-out, away from the fighting. He cried out pitifully at Amos, the giant who had stabbed him in the darkness. In terror, Amos pulled as hard as he could at the rifle, jammed inside him. It came free, and the boy's guts spilled all over the trench.

Fire exploded suddenly all around him. He threw his rifle away, screaming. He scrambled up the side of the trench, and ran into the darkness, howling like a dog . . .

Fish found himself lying on the floor of the trench. Burning petrol was floating along on the surface of the water, it was burning his leg. He slapped at it. The wreckage of an aeroplane filled the trench behind him: tangled wire and wood and linen. Mixed up in its ruins were dead men. Squashed to a pulp in the cockpit was the pilot, transfixed by his own Lewis gun. Dazed and bleeding, Fish stared at him for several seconds. Out in the rain he could hear the boom of bombs. After a while he realised he was looking at Henry.

They were fighting, somewhere out there. He staggered along the trench. His revolver was still on its lanyard, he gathered it in, grasped it in his fist.

Something moved, there in the rain, he turned, staggering, his gun outstretched. The bayonet took Fish in the side, below his arm. He felt no pain, only a sudden heavy weight pulling him down.

He was lying on the ground, on the streaming duckboard. He was looking up at the German. The rain swept down the trench in blinding, shivering sheets. Suddenly he was gone.

Fish felt blood bubbling up hot into his throat. It was difficult to move, something was holding him down. He pawed at his side with his free hand, felt the bayonet jammed hard through his ribs.

The darkness shrieked and crashed. Something exploded in coruscations of icy white light. The side of the trench blew in over him in a torrent of mud.

He couldn't move. A small river of icy water came running down the gash in the trench side, it streamed over his back and neck. He was lying with his head in some sort of hole. The rain ran over his face, and began to fill it up. He cried out, calling for help. Shells were falling in the darkness. Blood foamed up from his chest, gagging him with its hot gore.

'Help . . .'

A whizz-bang screamed overhead, Verey lights painted the storm red and yellow and green. The rain streamed off the trench side over him, running in his eyes, in his mouth, in his ears.

'Help . . .' he whispered.

He was drowning. The rain had stopped, but the water was on the move. It ran in rivulets, it found channels, it sought the low ground, and there it made puddles, that grew into pools.

With an enormous effort he dragged his right arm underneath him, and pushed. His hand sank into the mire, came up against something hard. He pushed into the bog, and raised his face out of the water. He gasped in lungfuls of precious, stinking air, before he had to drop into the water again.

He was not going to last. He dragged his hand back out of the mud, and pawed at the edges of the pool that was drowning him. He scooped away handfuls of mud. *There.* Suddenly, the water was draining away. Voices. He could hear voices. Someone calling his name.

'Here!' he croaked. Louder, he must be louder, they would never hear him over the noise of the shelling.

'Here!' he shrieked.

'In the trench.' It was Furzegrove. 'There 'e be.' Furzegrove. Two stretcher-bearers. 'Soon 'ave you out, sir.'

'Steady, Ned,' Fish gasped. He could feel them digging at the earth that kept him pinned. 'There's a r-rifle and bayonet in there,' he explained. 'The sharp b-bit's in me.'

'Careful there, lads.'

He felt Furzegrove gently clearing away the mud and soil.

'Going to have to pull that out, sir. Can't move you like that.'

'Go on. N-Not with a t-twist, I beg of you.'

'No, sir.'

From the corner of his eye he could see Furzegrove arranging himself against the mud wall of the trench. He was filthy, soaked in liquid mud and blood. He felt his boots against the side of his chest, felt a great pulling on him, something dragging at his very core. It was jammed hard, through bone and cartilage, the muscles and blood vessels tightly clamped around the blade.

Furzegrove pulled with a steady pressure. The sky above sparkled and a white flare burst over no-man's land, swaying under its parachute as it came slowly down.

Fish felt something break, felt the long, sharp knife sliding out of him. He coughed convulsively, and hot blood gushed out of his mouth.

'Quickly now, lads. Get the major on to the stretcher.'

Hands lifted him and he was suddenly up on the trench parapet, lying on his stretcher. The lights whirled and bumped in the sky as they hurried back across the ground they had charged over only a little while earlier.

It was still. Without turning his head Fish could see that his stretcher was resting on the ground. He knew where he was. A tarpaulin was stretched over a shell-hole. Light from an acetylene flare was leaking out underneath it. It was battalion aid post. Wounded men with field dressings starkly white on their filthy uniforms were queuing up patiently. He knew them, they were his own men. A smell of tobacco was in the air – it caught in his lungs suddenly and he coughed in a fresh convulsion, blood bubbling up hot in his mouth.

Somebody was feeling him, looking at his wound. It was the MO, a Scotsman not much older than he was. He was in a bloody smock. Furzegrove was by him.

'Hallo, Sandy.'

'Hallo, Fish,' he spoke in a soft Aberdeen accent. 'You just lie here a minute, old boy.' He made a sign to Furzegrove, motioning him to one side.

Fish snatched at him with his right hand, seizing him by the wrist. 'You can tell me what you're telling him,' he rasped. The effort set him coughing again, and more foaming blood spilled up from his chest. He felt as though he was drowning, gasped desperately for air.

The doctor hesitated, and then knelt back down on the mud. 'I can't help you, Fish,' he said softly. 'I'm so sorry. The bayonet's opened up an artery in there. You're bleeding to death.'

Fish released his grip. 'G-Get on with treating those who can live then,' he ordered. McPhail hesitated, then nodded and got up, going back to his task. The queue of walking wounded slowly started to move.

Furzegrove bent down beside him.

'Get you anything, sir?' he asked quietly.

'Yes,' Fish whispered. 'Take me to Vi. She's in the CCS. I want to see Vi.'

The sky behind them was still flickering and glowing, like a far-off display of fireworks as they came up the path. The tents of the clearing station were illuminated from within, as though luminous. The stretcher-bearers stood patiently by the waiting walking wounded as Furzegrove went in.

He put his head round a canvas flap. Hissing white acetylene lamps lit up a table around which men and women in bloody aprons clustered.

'Lady Violet,' he called urgently. 'Where is she?'

'Just gone off duty,' the surgeon grunted, without raising his head.

Metal clinked in his hands, blood fanned the air in a fine spray, as though he were engaged in a terrible cannibal feast.

'Try next door,' he said.

Furzegrove went out and across to the adjoining tent. He found Violet bent over a ceramic sink. She was in a white gown and was washing her hands and arms beyond her elbows and the water was running a dark red. She glanced at him, very weary.

'Are you wounded?' she asked, not unsympathetically. 'They'll look after you across the way.'

'It's me, Lady Violet. Ned Furzegrove.'

'Ned?' she said in surprise. 'I didn't recognise you under all that dirt. What's happened? Have you been fighting?'

'The battalion 'ad to straighten the line,' he said. 'The general ordered us . . . but that's not it, Miss. I've got Major de Clare here.'

'Fish?' she said in alarm. 'Is he hurt?'

'The MO says 'e's dying,' he said steadily. 'Bayonet wound.'

'Bring him in!' she cried, and jumped for a flap leading to another tented room. 'Clarissa!' she shouted, and a dark-haired young woman lying flat on a cot, exhausted, opened her eyes.

'Clarissa, come quick! Fish's been stabbed.'

They returned as the bearers were bringing Fish in.

'Put him on the trestle table,' Clarissa Townall ordered. There was a tray of instruments by a steriliser in the corner. She grabbed two pairs of bent-bladed scissors, and she and Violet quickly cut away the mud and blood soaked tunic and shirt. Violet wiped Fish's chest with a wet cloth, and the wound was visible: a blue-edged rent in his side, quite small, no more than three inches long. The gash was livid against the dead white of his skin. His chest moved in short, shallow gasps, his eyes were closed.

Clarissa spread one hand on his chest, tapping her index finger, making a noise like hitting wood. She moved it over to the other side and it was suddenly hollow.

'Pleural cavity's filled with blood,' she said. Violet had wrapped a cloth cuff about his arm, and with a stethoscope was checking his blood pressure. 'Ninety over fifty,' she said.

'The bayonet's gone through an artery in there,' said Clarissa, looking at Violet. 'I need to operate and close it off.'

'Do it now!'

'I can't,' she said quietly. 'He's lost so much he's practically in shock already. Opening him up will just finish the job.'

'Fish's tough. He'll make it.'

'Not on what he's got left.'

'Then give him some more. That equipment that was sent . . .'

'But we haven't tried it yet . . .' Clarissa faltered. 'We don't know . . .'

'I know Fish's going to die if we don't.'

'But Vi, we haven't supplies of blood yet. It's not yet underway . . .'

'We've all got blood!' Violet screamed.

'If you put the wrong type into somebody you kill them,' Clarissa said frantically. 'It's all different types . . .'

'That kit,' said Violet. 'That kit, where is it . . .' She ran across the tent and began pulling at boxes. 'Here. Here it is. All right, blood, we need a sample, then we mix it with this on the dish . . .' She opened a small bottle and took a glass petrie dish. 'Blood, blood . . .' she said intensely. She passed a dish to Clarissa. 'Get some of Fish's.'

Fresh red foam was bubbling from his mouth. She scooped it up and passed it back to Violet, who mixed it with some fluid. She consulted a chart.

'A,' She said. 'It says Fish is A.'

'Then we have to have type A to put in him. Or O.'

'Why O?'

'Universal donor,' she said shortly, pulling bottles and tubes from a box. 'I read about it in the *Lancet*. You can put O in anybody.'

'*Can* you?'

Without hesitating, Violet picked up a short-bladed scalpel and cut across the back of her forearm. Blood rushed out, bright and red in the acetylene lamps, and she caught some in a dish. She added some drops of fluid, and once again consulted her chart.

'I'm O,' she said triumphantly. 'Quickly, Clarissa, let's get some out of me and into Fish.'

'Go next door and say I want some nurses and an anaesthetist from number two team,' Clarissa ordered Furzegrove.

He went out, and she sat Violet down. She tightened a cuff about her upper arm and flicked the skin until she saw a vein rising. Expertly, she slid in a needle attached to a tube, and blood began to flow into a glass bottle.

'Read that little book there,' Violet ordered a girl who came in, rubbing her eyes. 'We want A or O.'

'A or O?'

'Mix a blood sample with the fluid.'

''Ere,' said Furzegrove. 'Try me.'

The bottle was soon full. Clarissa hung it from a stand and inserted a needle into Fish's arm.

'I'm not sure if I'm doing this right,' said the sleepy nurse. Violet glanced at her, took a new bottle and allowed the blood to continue to flow out of her.

'Where are the spreaders?' Clarissa demanded. 'I'll need to open that wound up if I'm to get inside.'

'No, you're B, I think . . .' the nurse said doubtfully. 'If I'm reading this right . . .'

The blood was draining rapidly into Fish.

'Take this,' Violet ordered, and they took the second bottle and hung it up. There was still confusion over by the table, and Violet put the drain in her arm into a new bottle.

Clarissa was scrubbing her hands and arms. The anaesthetist had arrived with a black bag of equipment.

'He's only got one lung working,' said Clarissa. 'I don't want him to drown while I'm stitching him up.'

'Atropine, then.' He busied himself with preparing an injection. 'You'll have to be quick,' he said. 'He won't stand much. I'll use chloroform.'

He injected Fish in his upper arm, and stood listening to his heart with a stethoscope. 'Not too good,' he said doubtfully.

'The cavity's filled with blood,' Clarissa said quickly. Stepping over she inserted a hollow silver speculum into the tight edges of the wound. Dark blood poured out over the floor in a thick jet. It slowed, and became a dribble.

'Yes, better.'

'Here,' Violet called weakly. 'You'll need some more.'

She indicated a full bottle at her side. She was slumped in the chair, a dead, chalky white.

'Violet!' Clarissa cried. 'Is that all yours?'

'I'm O!' a nurse yelled from the table. 'I'm O!'

'Fish . . .' Violet called. 'You're not to die . . . do you hear me? That's my blood going round inside you. You die on me now and I'll be really cross with you . . .'

Violet took the needle out of her arm, got up from the chair and crumpled to the ground.

15

Desertion in the Face of the Enemy

Ypres, April 1917

The sun had risen and for once there were no scudding clouds in its way, dropping rain upon the bog beneath. The tent was drying in the heat, turning yellow as it did so, and making its interior like a Kew hothouse. The smell of the boy in the end bed was nauseous, they were all glad when one of the nurses pulled back the flaps, letting in clean fresh air, and a view of the fields. The boy was, they all knew, dying by degrees. He had legs that were rotting away.

The surgeons had not been quick enough: the gangrene spores played leapfrog with them up his legs, reappearing higher up after each piece had been whittled away – calves from feet, knees from calves, thighs from knees, the body under the sheets becoming shorter and shorter. He would soon be dead, but still talked cheerfully in his weakening voice of the rugger matches he had played for the school First XV the previous year.

Fish sat quietly in a chair near the open flap, grateful for the fresh air. He wore his officer's boots and trousers, his hat and tunic on the bed next to him with his swagger stick. His shirt was loosely done up.

The nurses were coming down the canvas ward. Dressings were to be changed, conditions assessed, maintenance and repair work done on these items of army property which it wanted back in working order.

Fish was very familiar with the routine of the ward. He knew that the first team were changing dressings, the second were drawing off fluid from the lungs of the men with chest injuries. All battle injuries became infected, went hotly septic: thereafter it was a question of plugging with gauze, packing with lime chloride and draining off the wound to allow slow healing from the bottom up. The lungs produced

fluid at an alarming rate, threatening to drown their owners, and it was
drawn off by the nurses using long, sharp needles that were driven into
the back without anaesthetic. The purulent fluid was then taken out
by a black suction mechanism like a large bicycle pump.

Fish was very familiar with the pump. Daily he had felt the sharp
pain of it as they had sat him up. He had come to dread it. He had
longed for a cigarette to ease the fear, but tobacco was not allowed
those with chest injuries.

There was a subaltern opposite who had come in a few days before
with fearful shrapnel wounds across the top of his body. He was still
alive after five operations – they had begun to think he might make
it. The nurses were changing the dressings. He couldn't take any more
anaesthetic – he was already yellow from jaundice, his liver protesting
at the effort of ridding him of the chemicals. When he was waiting,
as he could see them coming he kept up a cheerful chatter about
anything at all, only his constantly moving hands on the coverlet
betraying his fear.

They gently took off his white cotton smock with its RAMC
stencilling. The wounds were sliced into his upper arms and shoulders,
the stubs of stiff gauze stuck out like sprigs of rosemary in a joint of
lamb. The nurses bent over him and Fish saw his mouth tremble for
a second. He was eighteen, and an embodiment of the current slang
expression, 'one star, one stunt'. The star was a subaltern's insignia,
the stunt an attack.

'I say, Courtney!' Fish called over. 'Where did you say that girl of
yours is?'

Bright, grateful eyes looked at him as the nurse took hold of the
first stiff dressing, jammed inches deep into his flesh.

'Dash it, Fish, I've told you three times already!'

His voice wavered only slightly. The nurse had to lean back, the
gauze crackling under the pull of the forceps, blood and pus leaping
out from the cavity. Fish held his eyes steady as they moved to the
next, and blood began to flow down the boy's chest.

'I think I must have got a bang on the head,' Fish said. 'What was
it, past the post office on the left?'

'No, no. Past the village shop! You'll find the rectory about a
hundred yards past the shop.'

'Oh, that's it. And you want a box of Abdullahs. In return you'll
bring her flaming passion just as soon as you can!'

The boy blushed. 'Oh, I say, Fish, it's not like that! I've only
been able to see her when her mater's been around. Fearful old
harridan . . .'

'Oh, but love's fetters burst asunder when the conquering hero returns, old chap. Don't worry, I'll pave the way for you.'

Soon the nurses had finished, the filthy long strings of gauze were in the bag of rubbish and they were packing his wounds with fresh. Without saying anything, one of them gently wiped away the sweat that drenched his face. They plumped his pillows and let him sink back, his face white from the pain. He still managed to smile across at Fish.

'I'll soon be off like you,' he promised.

'Of course you will,' said Violet, coming down the ward. She was dressed in a tweed skirt and a crisp white blouse. The wounded men's eyes followed her – in their suffering it was like balm to be able to look at pretty young women.

She undid his shirt, used a stethoscope to listen carefully to his chest.

'You can't leave if you aren't fit,' she said, strictly.

They watched anxiously as she moved the head of the stethoscope to various locations about his torso.

'Lift your arm,' she said, and they saw the livid red scar of the bayonet wound.

'Oh, do say he can go!' the dying boy in the end bed called.

'Come on, nurse! Let him go . . .'

Violet stood up, taking the instrument from her ears. 'He can go,' she said, with a smile, and a wave of weak cheering broke out.

Fish dressed himself, and went down the two lines, shaking hands, wishing them well. 'Your turn soon, Charlie,' he said at the end. The smell of putrefaction was terrible.

The boy smiled faintly. He seemed to be going in front of Fish's eyes. 'Not me, old chap. I'll go with you in spirit.'

''Bye, Courtney. Get yourself f-fit for that girl of yours.'

'I will, Fish.'

Then he was out in the fresh air. Violet was standing by her little Renault. He got in and they drove away down the lane. As they headed away from the line the signs of war slowly vanished and they were driving through the flat countryside. It was covered in spring foliage and flowers and Violet saw colour returning to his cheeks. She put her hand affectionately on his knee.

'Better?' she said. He nodded.

'I'm so g-glad to be out, Vi. There were times I th-thought I was going to die in that tent, like poor Charlie.'

'You've got my blood going round inside you. You can't die.'

'I k-know. Can I have a fag, Vi?'

'Poor Fish! You must be so fed up with me prodding and poking you, and sticking things in you, and telling you what to do ... When we get home I want *you* to do things to me, and tell me what you want me to do. I'll do anything you want, Fish ...'

They looked at each other with shining eyes, and laughed happily.

'Can you wait?' she said, suddenly anxious. 'I'll stop if you like ...'

'I can wait,' he smiled. 'But if I've got to wait, I'd better have a fag.'

He took out his cigarette case, and lit two Player's Navy Cut for them both.

'God,' he said, breathing out the smoke. 'That's so good ...'

They rolled down the empty road towards the sea, and the port, the waiting ship that was going to take them home.

'I can't go b-back, Vi,' he said.

'No,' she said quietly. The little engine thrummed steadily under the black bonnet, pulling them away from the front.

'N-Not like that. The W-Windstone's are f-finished. N-Not enough of us left to reform the battalion. I d-don't want to go to some other b-blasted hole with a lot of people I don't k-know. I don't k-know if I could take it. P-Probably go w-windy like poor old George ...'

He took another deep pull on his cigarette. The tobacco seemed to loosen the tight feeling in his chest.

'I'm going to join the RFC,' he said quietly. 'I like it up there. And there's nobody to see you if you start to s-snivel ... P-Poor George, he was so afraid that people would s-see he was afraid ... if I wh-whimper a bit nobody'll know ...'

'You wouldn't want to go on the staff,' she said, in a neutral voice.

'Henry's dead,' he said flatly. 'I k-killed him. It's the only d-decent thing to do.'

'They found Ned's brother.'

'Who? Big Amos?'

'Yes.'

'His body, you mean?'

'No, he was still in it,' Violet said steadily. 'It seems he ran away during the battle.'

'I thought he was dead.'

'They found him out in the country, about ten miles behind the line. An old Belgian widow had taken him in. He was working for her as a labourer.'

'They should have left him there.'

'Didn't he desert?'

'These b-bastards don't know what it's l-like, being in a battle. It's horrible . . . Poor Amos is slow, you can't expect somebody like him to . . .'

Fish stared through the little flat windscreen at the unfolding flat black road, trying to explain himself.

'P-People like me, we're trained,' he said. 'We go through all those years of school, we believe in K-King and Country, we're used to giving orders, we play g-games which g-get you ready for it . . . When they tell us to go, we go . . . Poor Amos, he's a simple boy, he should never have been out there.'

'They're charging him with desertion in the face of the enemy,' she said.

'I w-was his c-commanding officer. I'll recommend m-mercy.'

Violet was silent for a long time, driving the little car along the small Belgian road.

'Your father's going to make the final decision,' she said, at last.

16

You'll Hear Something Very, Very Nice

St Goderick's

Starnley tossed two tin mugs in the air like an amateur juggler, and grinned at the row of boys standing nervously by their iron-framed beds in the dormitory. They did not smile back. He had his cane thrust under one arm; behind him lounged a few cronies. Standing next to Worsley, Godfrey could see the smaller boy's friend, Brophy, who was affecting not to know of his existence.

'Who's for a hot pot?' he enquired.

Nobody replied. They knew he was not referring to a stew.

Godfrey realised that Worsley was trembling. Starnley smiled wolfishly.

'*Worsley!*'

The little boy bit into his lip to stop his mouth from quivering.

'Drop 'em, Worsley.'

Starnley glanced round casually at his friends. Brophy smiled back at him. Slammed up inside their walled school prison for months at an end they lived in an extremely dangerous sexual and political minefield. Brophy was very fond of Worsley. To overtly protect him was to commit suicide. He smiled, therefore, as the head of house prepared to torment his little friend.

Worsley undid his trousers, letting them fall to his ankles, and pulled down his underpants. Grinning hugely, Starnley stuffed some crumpled paper into his tin mugs. He lit the first and when it was well ablaze, clapped it over one buttock. Tears shot into Worsley's eyes as the paper inside continued to burn, until it had consumed all the oxygen, and had clamped itself firmly to his bottom. Starnley then repeated it for the other side.

'Forward – *march*!' Starnley yelled, like an OTC sergeant, and Worsley tripped forward, his trousers round his ankles, the cups on his bottom swaying like a pair of pendulous breasts.

Starnley watched through narrowed eyes. 'You're an obscene little swine, Worsley.'

'But Starnley, you said to—' Worsley wailed despairingly.

'*And* insolent,' the big boy said in judgement. He whirled round and stared down the row of fearful faces.

'*Bum-shaving*!' he screamed. He went down the row, looking into their eyes. Godfrey stared impassively back. 'You're an insolent little swine too, de Clare. Drop your bags.'

He yanked off the tin cups, revealing two bright red circles on Worsley's buttocks.

'Come along, then. Touch your toes.'

Standing back to back, Godfrey and Worsley bent over, touching their toes. Their bottoms squashed up against each other. Starnley swished his cane in the air, and Godfrey could feel Worsley trembling. He heard the blow coming and ground his teeth hard together, staying stock still.

He felt Worsley jump away in involuntary reflex just as the cane sliced across his buttocks. He didn't stir, stayed bent over like a statue.

'You *moved*, Worsley,' Starnley said in a soft voice.

'I didn't, Starnley, I *didn't*!' he bleated, terrified.

'*And* you're a liar!'

Starnley whirled on the rest on the dormitory.

'Bend 'im!' he screamed, and they siezed Worsley, two to an arm and a leg, spreadeagled him on the hard bed, face down, and Starnley flogged him until his bottom rose up in scarlet weals.

Then he stopped, tucked his came under his arm.

'Pull up your bags, de Clare. You've left my study like a rubbish heap. Come and clear it up.'

Godfrey hurried after the head of the house. For the next hour he busied himself about the senior's room, making toast and tea, lighting his fire, polishing his boots, tidying up. Fagging for the prefects was an integral part of the harsh existence of the house.

Godfrey often found himself doing jobs for Starnley. He had made it his business. While the rest of his year simply went in fear of the older boy, Godfrey made himself agreeable. He had a certain charm that was pleasing, a nice smile, a cheerful way of talking that hid sexual undertones.

He was precocious, he knew things about Starnley that he did not know himself. Starnley was crude and boorish, but he was also prudish and repressed. Brophy thought that Worsley was a substitute for a girl and treated him like one. Starnley did not know that he found beating the young boys' naked bottoms exciting and stimulating. Godfrey did.

'Your bum glowing, de Clare?' he enquired, as he came into the study.

'Does a bit,' Godfrey said, smiling at him as though they were sharing a joke. He slipped his trousers down, and his underpants, in an easy movement, trying to peer at his bottom. 'What does it look like?'

Starnley laughed, and gave him a slap. Godfrey giggled, and Starnley ran his paw over his bottom.

'We could use you for a lamp in the dark!' he said. Godfrey moved his weight from one foot to the other, leaning gently against the bigger boy.

He knew, for he felt it himself, just how the prison conditions of the school, the cold and the forced exercise, the fear, the beatings, the total absence of female company simply inflamed desire among boys. Somebody like Starnley, who had no imagination and lacked knowledge was simply prey.

He felt him stiffen, saw the grey trousers bulge. He stood still, let him feel his naked buttocks. The hand sought him out, felt between his thighs, where he was hard, ran up and down him, the breath coming in quick gasps.

There was a clattering down the corridor, somebody's voice calling out, and Starnley jerked away. Godfrey quickly pulled up his trousers, and went to the door. Starnley was breathing hard.

'*Tomorrow.*' Godfrey whispered intensely. 'During prep. I'll come to the study then.'

The big boy nodded eagerly, and Godfrey slipped out. He went up to the dark dormitory and into bed. Worsley was crying softly into his pillow.

'Got to go to the bogs, Brophy,' he said, going up to the prefect's desk in the big hall where they ate, studied and did their prep. Brophy nodded indifferently, and he hurried out. The school food was so bad that attacks of diarrhoea were more the norm than exception.

The corridor was dark. He paused outside Starnley's study for a moment, peering into the gloom, then tapped on the door and slipped inside. The room was lit by a bare bulb.

'I didn't know if you'd come,' Starnley said hoarsely. He got out of the chair, and embraced him clumsily. Godfrey took the opportunity to rub his palm over the bigger boy's groin, felt him harden in moments and gasp in surprised pleasure.

Godfrey quickly undid his buttons, dropped his own trousers and underpants, squirmed round, as lithe as a cat, bending over the chair, making Starnley rub himself against his bottom. He could feel him, as hard as a poker.

Starnley's big hands were gripping his hips, thumping into him with grunting strokes.

'*No!*' Godfrey squealed, his voice a sobbing falsetto. 'Please, Starnley, don't! Please . . .'

He whimpered pathetically, pinned over the chair, and there was nothing Starnley could do, driven by the rushing joy through his groin.

The door slammed back, crashing against the wall – the bare bulb of the ceiling glared down upon him as he buggered the sobbing boy beneath him.

'*Apage me Satanas!*' the Reverend Rose roared, and whipped Starnley across his own bare bottom with his cane.

'Now you've got to be very, very quiet, Worsley,' Godfrey said. 'But if you are, you'll hear something very, very nice.'

The little boy smiled like a savage elf, and nodded his head vigorously. The school was a jungle, and any kind of news travelled round it at great speed. Something like the fall of the fiend Starnley was transmitted almost by telepathy.

They took off their shoes and Godfrey led Worsley over the rafters in the half light. They were deft, made not a sound, and came to the platform by the wall where pinpricks of light showed up the shape of the plaster rosette of Jesus. Peeping through, they could see the thunderous form of the housemaster, dressed all in black but for the white collar of his calling about his neck.

A wooden form stood solid in the centre of the room. On it lay a fearsome device: not a rod, not a cane but a birch, whippy, springy, savage, its tendrils bound together with black leather to make a handle.

'How did he find out?' Worsley whispered, very softly.

Godfrey smiled.

'I *told* him,' he mouthed back. 'He was *waiting*.'

They were just in time. A knock came at the door.

'Enter,' the reverend commanded in a harsh voice. The door was swung back and Starnley was marched into the room by those who only hours before had been his fellow prefects. They stood him up next to the form and the master stared at him with loathing from the other side.

'Wretched and evil boy,' he rasped. 'Corrupter of the young, violator of mind and body. Truly there are few lower than you in the sight of God. When you leave this place the recruiting sergeant will take you to be trained for the fighting in France. It may be that there on the field of battle you will find expiation for your hideous crime.'

He took the heavy birch and stepped back.

'Prepare him,' he ordered, and the prefects took down Starnley's trousers before bending him over the wooden form. They held on to his arms and legs, pinioning him so that he could not move.

In the half light Worsley grinned at Godfrey in delight. Godfrey let him see the first blow. The man of God raised the birch with a muscular arm and it whistled awesomely as it whipped through the air. Starnley's buttocks were suddenly striped in scarlet – he jerked in agony, his head rising up, his teeth bared in rictus.

'What do you say to your God?' Rose demanded.

'Deo gratias . . .' he gasped.

Godfrey was suddenly as hard as rock. He quickly undid his fly buttons and pushed Worsley to his knees. The smaller boy took him in his mouth as the second blow whipped through the air.

Starnley whimpered in pain, and Godfrey saw delight on Worsley's face. His mouth was warm and slippery, it was quite delicious. He peered through the little hole beside Jesus's arm, and saw another blow strike his enemy's buttocks. They were red with blood, which ran down his thighs.

'Deo gratias . . .' Starnley moaned.

Worsley's trousers were undone, he was pulling at himself as he sucked on Godfrey and listened to the magical cries of agony from below. In the half light, Godfrey grinned in savage triumph.

'Deo gratias . . .'

17

I Was Feared They Would Shoot Me

Ypres

Major-General Gervase de Clare came through the door of the château and a soldier-servant took his cape.

'General Snow is waiting for you, sir, through the door there.'

De Clare frowned. He hadn't liked the sound of it since he got the summons. He harrumphed, straightened his shoulders and marched in. His superior officer was standing by the long windows, looking out at the garden.

'Hallo, Gervase,' he said, turning round. 'Saw you arrive. Drink?'

'Whisky, thank you, sir.'

Like de Clare, Snow was a cavalry general. He was a marvellous horseman and had managed to lose the 1908 Aldershot manouevres to Sir John French: ideal qualifications for high command.

'I'm being moved,' he said shortly. His eyes flicked up to see his companion's reaction. 'No, not degummed. Not quite. Sideways, if you like. Going with the Egyptian Expeditionary Force.'

'Why?'

'I was French's man. Haig's been looking to get rid of me for some time. We failed to take Boyson Wood last week, it's given him his excuse.'

De Clare was familiar with the attack, had played a part in its planning. One of the few remaining complete Pals battalions had been used. Rain and a bad barrage had dislocated movements that had seemed excellent on paper and all the young women of a small town in Lancashire were going to have to look elsewhere for husbands.

'Who's taking over?'

'Warrender,' Snow said, watching him carefully.

'I see,' de Clare said, appalled.

'Yes. *You* won't last long.'

'No. Dash it, Harry, it was a long time ago . . .'

'He's got a long memory. You'll have to go, Gervase. There's this business of this attack of yours, you know, the one your son led. Bit irregular. I can cover it up, but Warrender won't. Better go.'

'To Egypt?' de Clare wailed.

'No. Can't take you anyway. Been thinking. Best for you to get well clear.'

'Where?'

'Flying Corps?'

'The RFC? I don't know anything about aeroplanes.'

'What difference does that make? I spoke to Tubby Warren the other day, he's one of their generals. Can't tell a balloon from a dirigible. Doesn't make a jot of difference. The offensive spirit's the thing.'

De Clare thought hard for a few moments while Snow sipped on his drink. He knew he was being offered a lifeline. Fish's damned attack . . . it was true, questions were being asked . . . he hadn't the authorisation . . .

'I'll do it,' he said promptly.

'Jolly good! You get a pilot to fly you about. Your own chauffeur!'

'Thank you, sir.'

'I'll make the posting. Listen, before you go. What about this damned deserter of yours.'

'Furzegrove.'

'Yes, ah . . . Amos Furzegrove. What ghastly names these peasants have. Court-martial's sentenced him to death. Do we commute?'

'Bad lot, the Furzegroves. I gave his brother five days without the option before the war for poaching my brother's pheasants.'

'Simple soul apparently – this Amos.'

'Broke under fire!' de Clare barked. 'Brave men died marching forward as ordered. Furzegrove cut and ran. Shoot him.'

Snow fingered the piece of foolscap, heavy with official black print, suitable for the ending of a man's life. He hesitated, put it down.

'I'll think about it.' he said.

St Goderick's

It was Sunday in the town. Godfrey stood in the shadows of a closed shop doorway. From somewhere came the sound of people singing a hymn. He had walked through the woods from the school, had changed out of his uniform into flannels and jacket, had made his way into the town.

In his doorway he felt excitement prickle in his stomach, raise hairs up his spine. He should not have been there. He was because he was a de Clare, and the de Clares had honed the taking of calculated risks into a way of life. He was there also . . . well, he would find out. Godfrey accepted himself as he was. He had no desire to change what he was. He simply needed to know how far he extended.

There was somebody else in the street. A man in a grey overcoat. A middle-aged man, sitting on a bench by the park smoking a pipe and reading a paper. Except he wasn't. Godfrey knew he wasn't reading the paper, he was waiting. He was sitting on the park bench near the black and white imitation Tudor public lavatory and waiting.

Godfrey came out of cover, and walked casually across the road, and into the park. He felt the man's eyes on him, watching him across the top of his paper. He went past the public lavatory and paused, looking out over the mown grass and formal flower beds.

When he turned round the man had gone. As if suddenly assailed by the need to relieve himself, he turned and went inside. It smelled of coarse disinfectant and urine. The floor was tiled, a row of black-painted doors, with brass boxes on them to receive the single copper penny required for entry, stood opposite the wall with its runnel. Water was dripping steadily down the wall from a tank above. His shoes clattered. A door opened a crack.

'*Here*!' a desperate, anxious voice hissed. 'Over here.'

There it was. He could turn, relieve himself, go . . . the alternative was very, very dangerous. Homosexuality was against the law. The law did not like it. Society did not like it. It punished people for being homosexual. It put them into gaol, it broke them.

'Here . . .' A voice frantic with need.

There was nobody else in there. Godfrey went quickly to the door, it opened. The man was sitting there, with the seat down. His eyes were as pleading as a dog's. Godfrey undid his fly buttons, and thrust himself into the man's waiting mouth.

A few moments later, he felt him buckle and bend, grunt pathetically. Godfrey took the man's sweating ears in his two hands and contemptuously ejaculated into him. He turned and went out, and behind him he heard the man frantically wiping himself with the coarse brown paper on the roll, each sheet marked 'Council Property'.

Godfrey hid himself behind a tree in the park. A few minutes later the man came out. He had composed himself, slicked his hair with water. He paused to light his pipe, and walked away into the town.

Like a huntsman, Godfrey followed him at a distance. He turned into a row of small, semi-detached houses, all very respectable, with small, mown front lawns. Half way along, he went down the little front path, and into a house. Careful not to look to either side, Godfrey went down the road. 'Bide-a-wee'. The home was called 'Bide-a-wee', in small, wrought-iron letters.

Godfrey smiled savagely to himself. He turned the corner and directed his steps to the road that led up to the wood. He knew a little bit more about himself. He liked it. It had been pleasant, humiliating the balding, futile, middle-aged, sweating man. He put on some speed. If he hurried he might have time to bugger Worsley over the dead tree in the thicket before lunch.

Windstone Castle

The Earl shuffled into the breakfast room, peering apprehensively around the door. The sole occupant of the room was his youngest and only son, Aylmer, who was getting outside bacon, sausages, fried bread and eggs. A book was propped up against a milk jug, and he was reading.

'Good morning, Father.'

'Morning, m'boy. What're you reading?'

'*The Riddle of the Sands.* It's jolly good. I'd like to go sailing like that myself.'

'Fish was saying that to me. Thought he might get *Parma's Pride* back in the water once this blasted war's over, take her round Britain. Follow Rodney's voyage.'

The Earl foraged amongst the dishes, and helped himself to devilled kidneys and some bacon from his own sties.

'I hope he does! That's the big sailing boat laid up in the yard on the water, isn't it? Why's it called *Parma's Pride*?'

'That was Rodney's little joke. He was Earl in Elizabeth's time. One of the few of us who've taken to the water. He was a privateer like Drake and Hawkins. We were a bit hard up in those days, and he went out to plunder the Spanish treasure fleets. Had to give Elizabeth her due, y'know, she was as much of a brigand as they were. But there was plenty left. Among the plunder on one ship was a whole set of gold plates – the Duke of Parma's own! We've still got 'em somewhere . . .'

'What happened to him?' Aylmer asked eagerly. He already knew, but liked the story.

'Ah . . .' the Earl said, through a kidney. 'The Spanish invasion fleets massed, the great Armada swept down the channel. Drake and Hawkins, and Earl Rodney, they fought all day. When they ran low on powder and shot they put in for more. Rodney savaged 'em all the way round the channel, and up into the North Sea. A terrible storm got up, blew them all to the north, scattered ships right up to the Shetland Isles. They never heard of Rodney again . . . His son Francis was a favourite of the old Queen for a while, had the sense to spend a lot of time down here hunting when Essex was being foolish. Hung on to his head, that way. Bit of a scholar: King James had him in when they did the new Bible. Got a copy somewhere, so'm told.'

The Earl looked about the empty room.

'Dash it, where is everybody?' he demanded peevishly.

'Fish had to go back to France. He left early this morning.'

'France, France? What for, the boy's done his bit, he's got to recover from his wound, dammit.'

'Something about one of his men. Furzegrove. He's being court-martialled. Fish said he had to do something about it.'

'He's a good egg. Bad business. Poor Amos . . . well, where's George?'

'We're going fishing. He doesn't eat much breakfast.'

'No . . . your mother?'

'I think she's in the chapel,' Aylmer said carefully.

'Ah . . .'

He peered hopefully at the place set for the Dowager Gwendolyn.

'I don't suppose your grandmother . . .'

'I went to see her in her room yesterday.'

'Did she say much?'

'No.'

'No . . . I suppose I'd better see if she wants something taking up on a tray . . .'

He peered about the table. The papers were laid out in a row, left by Foskett, and he found *The Times.* He went out, and was almost run over by George, who was riding a bicycle down the corridor.

'Hallo, Uncle! I've been thinking that this is the way to get about. We ought to fit it up with a trailer and have Foskett deliver the food that way. Keep it hot, don't you know.'

'Sound idea, m'boy.'

The Earl shuffled off and made his way up the grand staircase, his paper in one hand. He tapped on the yellow door in the corridor of the Glorious Revolution. The Earl of 1688, a staunch Protestant, had played a leading part in ridding the country of James II, whom he considered to be an agent of Satan, and had celebrated the arrival of William III by putting up a new wing.

There was no reply to the Earl's knock, so he opened the door, and went in. It was gloomy, the curtains were not drawn back.

'Mother?'

'Yes, dear,' a quiet voice said, from the bed.

'I've brought you the paper,' he said, forcing a cheerful note into his voice. 'Shall I open the curtains?'

'No, thank you.'

'Can't read the paper in the dark, what?'

'I don't want to read the paper, Cuthbert.'

'Interestin' letters today. Some fellah says he's heard a cuckoo, don't y'know. Suppose he might have: had a look in the bird book meself, we had a cuckoo in King Richard's Tower, April 6, 1872, only it might have been Earl Gilbert himself, he was somethin' of a mimic. What do y'say, mother, shall I pull back the curtains? Fascinating stuff.'

'No, thank you.'

'Why not, dammit? Can't simply wallow here, it ain't good for the soul.'

'My soul is my own concern.'

'Interestin' idea. Don't think Roderick would agree, bein' a bishop.'

'Go away, Cuthbert.'

'No. Not until you read the paper.'

'I don't want to read the paper. I do not want to see page upon page of black type, row upon row of fine young men, all of whom are dead.'

'Then let me get you some breakfast.'

'Cuthbert, I want you to do something for me. Contact Roderick, as bishop, ask if he is free next week.'

'Eh? What for?'

'To perform the rites.'

'What rites?'

'My funeral, Cuthbert.'

'But you're not dead, Mother.'

'I'm going, Cuthbert. I do not want to live any more. One can live too long. I wish I had not lived to see all the young men die.'

Ypres

The Austin lorry pulled into the farm yard, its yellow acetylene lamps lighting up the walls. A single window glowed in the building.

Ned and Amos Furzegrove climbed out of the back. The big man stood, a little bewildered, and his brother the sergeant-major went to the cab. A major in provost-marshal's uniform sat there next to the driver.

'He's in your charge,' he said severely.

'Officer's here soon,' said Furzegrove. 'We'll take care of him.'

'You'd better. On your head be it. I'll be back in the morning. At dawn.'

'I hears you,' Furzegrove told him, steadily.

'I hope you do.'

The military police officer motioned to the driver. With a rattle of the gears, the little truck jerked forward, turning around over the cobbles and down the road.

'Here we are then, Amos,' Ned said cheerfully. 'Let's make ourselves comfortable, shall we?'

'It be quiet out here.'

'Like being at home, eh? That's where you'll be soon.'

'What if they shoots me, Ned?'

Furzegrove could feel the unknowing fear in his brother's voice.

'Major Fish, he's appealed for you, Amos,' he said reassuringly.

'I wasn't cut out for this soldiering, Ned . . . I should've stayed at home . . .'

'And that's where you're going. The major, he wouldn't let them shoot you, you know that.'

'Ah, I always trusted Master Fish.'

'Come on, let's go inside. See if they've left us anything to eat and drink.'

The yellow window beckoned. They went over and inside the door. Two simple beds were made up and an oil lamp cast a cheerful glow. Some bottles of British beer stood on the table; Furzegrove pressed his thumbs against the heavy wire holding the stopper in, it swung out with a pop and he poured dark brown beer into a glass.

'Well, this is friendly,' he said. 'Here, Amos, you hold this one while I fill mine. Like being down in the Hawk and Partridge, this is. Home from home.'

'I wishes I was,' the big man said forebodingly.

'Now listen to me, Amos,' Ned said, seating himself. 'When you gets back, you has to go out to the hop field, first off. With both of us gone it'll be that overgrown. You knows what to do, same as always.'

'Ah.'

'Well drink up, Amos. When you gets back you has to reach into your pocket for a pint – this one is free, the Army give it to us.'

'I can't drink it, Ned,' his brother said miserably, holding the glass. 'Won't go down right.'

Furzegrove cocked an ear.

'Hold on, now, Amos. What's that? That be an engine, bain't it.'

The big man looked nervously towards the door. Lights swept across the wall.

'They be coming to take me away, Ned.'

The engine stopped, a door clanked, they heard boots coming across the cobbles.

The door opened, and Fish came in. He went straight over to Furzegrove, sitting fearfully in his chair.

'Th-they granted the app-peal,' he said directly, and beamed down at him. 'You're a free man.'

Colour rushed into the big man's face. 'Free, sir?' he said uncertainly.

'Free. You're discharged from the Army. They're sending the documents over in the morning. Then you can go home.'

Amos got up, shaking his head in bemused happiness, the glass still in his great paw. 'I was feared they would shoot me . . .'

'I told you, Amos,' Ned said with a big smile. '*Now* will you have that drink?'

'Oh, ah. I can drink it down, now.'

And so saying, he raised it to his lips and drank.

'Fill that up again, Ned,' Fish ordered. 'I've brought a kind of shooting picnic with me.'

Amos drained his glass, leaving just foam sliding down the side, and his brother refilled it as Fish went out to the little van. He reappeared with a wicker hamper, and unpacked cold chicken, a loaf of crusty bread, yellow butter, pickles, cheddar cheese, smoked ham and some honey in a comb.

'I'll have a bottle of that, Ned,' he said, and began to cut the bread. When it was poured he raised his glass.

'Here's to going home, Amos,' he said.

'Going home, yes . . .'

'Going home.'

They sat down around the table, and began to eat.

'Now, Amos,' said Fish, munching a chicken leg, 'I have a message from the Earl. He's most concerned that the hops are gathered this year. We can't gather the harvest in without proper Windstone beer.'

'I is going right away, sir, just as soon as I gets home. Ned here has been telling me what to do,' Amos reassured him. He washed down a big cheese and pickle sandwich with a draught of beer and his brother refilled his glass.

'You got some catching up to do, Amos,' he said.

'I has, Ned. I has been that worried I haven't been eating or drinking properly.'

'Your w-worries are over now, Amos,' Fish said.

Ned Furzegrove heard his brother stir in the darkness. The window was showing the light of dawn. Outside, they heard the van door clank shut.

'You awake, Amos?' he said.

'Oh, ah. Can't wait to go home.'

'Let's get up, then. I can hear the major.'

They went outside. Dawn was breaking. Fish was standing near the fence, looking out over the meadow. He turned as they came out into the farmyard, they saw that he had a twelve-bore shotgun in the crook of his arm.

'What ho, chaps,' he said. 'I say, Ned, I thought I might bag a couple of rabbits for the pot while we're waiting. Look down there.'

The two brothers inspected the meadow below with expert country eyes. Rabbits were out in the grass, feeding.

'Be best if me and Amos go down below, sir. Drive them towards you.'

'Good idea.'

'Amos, you take the path on the right while I go this way. Send them up towards the major, like.'

Amos swayed slightly on his big feet. 'I's still a bit fuddled,' he said, rather amused. 'Right, Ned, I be going down this way, then.'

Very faintly on the air they heard the sound of a truck engine coming up the road.

'That'll be your discharge papers,' said Fish. 'Just be time to bag a couple before we're off.'

Amos stepped forward, moving away along the fence. Behind

him Fish swung the shotgun up to his shoulder in a single, fluid movement.

He fired, pulling both triggers at once.

The heavy load caught the big man between the shoulder blades, blowing him forward like a sledgehammer, dead before he hit the ground. Ned Furzegrove ran forward, checked his neck for a pulse. Amos was smiling.

'He was going home, sir,' he said to Fish.

Fish broke the gun, the empty red cartridge cases flew in the air.

The sound of the lorry engine came up the lane, an army six-tonner pulled up, and a squad of troops with rifles clambered out. The front door opened, and the provost-major got out.

'Very good,' he said. 'Where is the prisoner?' He gestured to the wall. 'Firing squad opposite that wall, Sergeant.' he ordered.

'He's over th-there.' said Fish.

The major took a few paces forward, and then halted. He whirled on Fish.

'He's dead!' he said in outrage.

'Of course he's d-dead,' Fish said coldly. 'The court-martial sentenced him to death. General Snow confirmed the order.'

'But, but,' the man spluttered. 'He had to be shot *properly.*'

'Orders say a condemned man must be sh-shot with members of his unit there as w-witnesses. We were here. He was shot. We're the Windstones. We don't let other people murder our men.'

'By God! I'll see you pay for this.'

'I d-don't think so,' Fish said indifferently. 'Just fill in the papers, that's your job.'

He put his shotgun into the back of the van. Furzegrove helped him pull out a plain wooden coffin, rather large, and they carried it over to where Amos was lying on the ground.

'We'll take him home, now,' said Fish.

St Goderick's

It was Sunday. Godfrey turned in down the road of small, semi-detached houses with their neatly mown front lawns. He held a tin in his hand: a screw-topped jar that he had wrapped about with white paper and coloured with a red cross. He had cut a slot in the tin top.

There was 'Bide-a-wee' in small wrought-iron letters. He opened the gate and went down the narrow front path. He tapped politely on the polished brass knocker.

The man opened the door. Godfrey had seen him go down the road and into the house, earlier. He held out the tin and rattled it, smiling mockingly at the man.

'Africa Cross Day, sir,' he said, in a fair impersonation of a Cockney whine. 'Please 'elp little black boys in Africa.'

The man blanched sheet white. Desperately, he reached inside his pockets, pulled out a note – a real white Bradbury, a fiver – and frantically stuffed it into the jar.

'Go!' he hissed. 'Get out—'

A door behind opened: a middle-aged woman looked out at them, her face instantly suspicious, old lines of unhappiness and anger marking her prematurely.

'What's this?' she demanded, taking in Godfrey's youth, his good looks.

'Charity, Margaret . . .' the man bleated.

Godfrey rattled his tin.

'Little black boys in Africa, mum. Please 'elp save 'em from a life of yoomiliation and crime. Little black—'

'Go away,' she hissed murderously. 'Go away, you digusting . . . you filthy little pervert.'

The door slammed in his face. Inside Godfrey heard the man whimpering, heard the woman shout, the crack of a blow, the noise of things breaking, the man crying out.

Godfrey strolled down the road. As he turned the corner, he put his head back and laughed.

London

Bishop Roderick de Clare had been feeling a little peaky. A bit lack-lustre. He wasn't sure why – put it down to the effects of the overly long winter. Now that spring was here he felt certain he would soon buck up and, on the principle that nothing bucked him up like a visit to Mrs Tompkins' establishment, there he was, ensconced in a wing chair by the window. He wondered what girl the madam would send in; he had told her of his need for a little rejuvenation, and had requested someone new. She had, she assured him, just the one.

He sipped on a nice, light, dry sherry, pale gold in its crystal glass. He was feeling better already. There was something about Mrs Tompkins'. She was not cheap, of course. As always a stab of guilt went through him at the thought of how much he had spent with her, over the years. As always, the brief moment of pain passed. There would be no money for the boys, of course: the bishop's palace was the property of the Church of England, the living went with the job. What was left he had largely pushed up a succession of young women in this very establishment. He sighed, and drank some more of his sherry. It was God's will.

She was French! A can-can dancer! She swayed into the room in a wave of perfume, her petticoats rustling, and the sound made him as hard as iron. He could barely get out of the chair. He sat there, the breath catching in his throat, his hands suddenly slippery with sweat, his eyes gleaming, and she offered an elegant hand.

'*M'sieu* would like to dance?' she murmured, curtseying so that he could see right down the decolletage of her top, filled with her round breasts, her nipples just showing, and he was on his feet. The gramophone whirled, the horn sent forth the sounds of Paris, the dance hall, the band, and they swayed incongruously about the room. Her bosom popped out from her top – he slipped his hands into the glorious rustling foliage of her skirts and she was naked underneath.

Champagne exploded like a howitzer, it foamed over the sides of the glasses and they drank it laughing. She wound the handle of the gramophone and they were off again.

They fell to the floor, the music pounding in his head. She slipped her legs about his neck as he thrust into the white lace skirts. He caressed her breasts, arched on his knees, his head thrown back; a saxophone howled and he felt the glorious, fabulous pain shooting up from his very toes, wringing him out like a mangle: he had never felt it so strong, stabbing through him like a sword. He gargled insanely for joy, his eyes bulging almost from his head, his very tongue swollen with effort, and slumped forward over her.

Bien, the girl thought. *Le vielle cochon est fini. Quelle* . . .

'*M'sieu?*' she cooed. A tip was in order – she had given the old goat the time of his life.

He did not reply. *Merde*, but the old swine was heavy. Get off, you dessicated pig, I am not a mattress.

'*M'sieu?*'

The awful truth dawned on her. With some difficulty, she managed to wriggle out from under him. He was crouched over on his knees and elbows, his hands still in front of him, his head resting on the floor, his clerical black trousers about his ankles. His body was as he had died, stiff in spasm.

She was a girl of resource and had an apartment in Paris she planned to retire to, when she had made enough. The bishop's jacket hung neatly on the back of the chair. She quickly found his wallet, relieved it of some seventy of the ninety pounds inside. You never took the lot. She had it squirrelled away in seconds, stuffed herself back into her clothes, and went to find Mrs Tompkins.

The two women stood looking at the man of the cloth.

'Gawd bless us,' said Mrs Tompkins. 'You've killed the old bugger.'

'You told me to make him happy,' she objected.

'Not *that* 'appy. Nah, then, 'e can't die 'ere, it ain't good for business.' She looked shrewdly at the dead man.

''E looks like 'e's praying don't he?' she said thoughtfully.

The church was always open. Those who sought God could come in at any hour of the day or night to receive His comfort.

The little door to the nave creaked, and the verger came in carrying a candle to light his way. He lit two of the large candles and light suffused the choir stall, lit up the altar. To his surprise he saw a man at the rail praying. Since the war had started they got more people coming in, but it was unusual to have someone communing with the Lord in pitch darkness.

He coughed. The man still did not move.

'Evening prayer will soon begin,' he said helpfully. He went to stand by the man. A cleric, surely? He could see by his clothing. Ah . . .

'When the wicked man turneth away from his wickedness that he hath committed and doeth that which is lawful and right, he shall save his soul alive.'

There was a loose board up by the altar rail. He stepped on it as he came up, and it lifted the man under his knee.

Bishop Roderick de Clare fell sideways before his God, as stiff as though he were frozen.

18

Doolally Tap

Windstone Castle, July

At three thousand feet Fish picked up the Windstone Water where it ran to the sea, a dull glint of silver in the haze. He was proud of himself: he had navigated across half England and found his destination.

To his left a thunderstorm was brewing dark and malevolent over the channel; somewhere beyond it was France, and the lines. He wasn't going there today, he was going to the castle.

He eased in some aileron and the cumbersome biplane tilted a wing. He came back on the throttle, the steady thrumming of the engine decreased, and the nose fell, giving him a better view of the land ahead. He picked up the Water, and came down to a few hundred feet, where the haze vanished, and he could see the corn ripening gold in the fields, the orchards and woods cool and green, the streams flowing into the great river.

The Riviera Express came thundering over the long iron bridge across the water, leaving a white trail of steam and smoke on its way to Cornwall. The ancient town of Windstone was over to his right. He allowed the aeroplane to drift over that way, so he could see the old medieval streets, the open Broad of the Sheep Market, the terraces, squares and crescents, all picked out with trees and grass; the long promenade and the parades leading to the spa and the pump room. They slid under the wings, were replaced by the chequered pattern of fields and hedgerows and meadows, of woods and streams and paths; and there at the centre of it all was the great castle, sitting in mighty splendour amongst its sprawling land.

He passed by the battlements, drifted down towards the pasture by the big barn. He edged into the breeze, the grass came up at him, he felt the wheels rip softly through it, touch down; he bumped, rolled, taxied in towards the big long barn, and Freddie got up from the tree stump where he had been sitting.

Fish let it roll inside, and cut the engine. The big four-bladed propeller thwacked to a stop, and he sat for a moment in the smell of oil and hot metal, dust and old hay. He pushed up his goggles, undid his wide belt and clambered down.

'I say!' Freddie grinned. 'This beats taking the train!'

Fish clapped his cousin on the shoulder. 'Are you well?' he said.

'Am *I* well? What about you? My sister says you've got to make an honest woman of her now, you've stolen her blood. You're a bally vampire, Fish!'

They went out into the sunshine, and Fish pulled off his leather flying helmet, undid his white silk scarf. Freddie picked up a haversack.

'I thought you'd be thirsty,' he said. 'So I brought a drop of Windstone scrumpy.'

He produced a large stoppered stone jug and two glasses, and poured out the golden cider. They sat on his tree stump and drank.

'I say,' said Fish. 'What's that cap badge you've got on? I don't think I recognise it.'

'*Fear Naught.*' Freddie said proudly. 'Tank Corps.'

'*Tanks?*'

'I had a long chat with father,' Freddie explained. 'He's a sapper, you know. What's going on out there – the front – is simply medieval seige warfare. At the moment neither side has the capability to break through. To get back to mobile warfare you need modern cavalry – armoured cavalry. Tanks. Tanks and aircraft, and trained infantry to go with them. Making men walk into machine-gun-fire simply gets them killed . . .'

'So you're a t-tankie . . .'

'And you've got your wings. A dashing RFC hero . . .'

'Hah!' Fish grunted explosively. 'That was f-funny . . . an RFC general came down to Brooklands to award us our wings. It was b-bloody father! 'I thought you were dead' he said to me.'

'What did you say?'

'I said I knew he wasn't but I lived in h-hope,' Fish said bleakly. He tipped back his scrumpy. 'Give me another sp-splash and then we'll waddle up to the castle. Anybody there?'

'Pretty quiet. Uncle's there, of course.'

'Aunt Maud?'

'Well yes . . .' Fredie said hesitantly. 'I mean she's there, but she isn't . . . Spends a lot of time in the chapel.' He stared out over the meadow to the dark green of the chase beyond. 'Went in there yesterday, thought I'd better say hallo, don't you see. She was polishing Robert's gravestone with her hair. That's what it looked like, anyway. Making a fearful racket, wailing and so forth. There's Charlie and Robert and Henry all there side by side, y'see.'

'The chapel's full of dead de Clares, all ab-bout our age,' said Fish. 'A thousand years of them.'

There was a silence for a while, and they lit up cigarettes. Fish coughed noisily.

'You all right?'

'First lungful catches me a bit. George up at the castle?'

'No, he's in town. Seconded to the Royals.'

'Oh yes?'

'The King asked Uncle if he'd lend out a few of his relatives to lend a suitably English air to the court. Worried about people thinking they're German.'

'Well, th-they are,' Fish objected. 'The whole lot of them.'

'Not a good thing to be when you're in the middle of the most ghastly conflict with the entire Boche nation,' Freddie pointed out. 'Anyhow, they're not the Saxe-Coburg-Gothas any more, they're the Windsors and as English as roast beef. So George has gone off to add tone to it all.'

'J-jolly good.' Fish coughed again and turned an alarming purple. 'You *sure* you're all right?'

'Fine . . .'

'It doesn't sound it.'

'It doesn't make any d-difference,' Fish said resignedly. 'As long as I can drag enough in for the time being. What about Uncle Roderick, then? Praying for forgiveness, what?'

'Got given the old celestial verdict, eh? Uncle's putting up Perceval and Godfrey here. When they're not at that ghastly school of theirs.'

'Right ho . . . I meant to get down for Dowager Gwendolyn's p-planting party. My dashed lung started playing up. How did she d-die like that? I thought she'd live to be a hundred.'

'Gave up,' Freddie said simply. 'Told Uncle to summon the bishop as she intended to die. And she did.'

'I w-wish she wasn't dead. Not m-many of the old s-sort left. Her father was at Waterloo, she used to tell me about it.'

They looked out over the great de Clare lands in a ruminative, rather tired fashion.

'Your leg all right?'

'Aches like billy-oh in the mornings. But worse things could happen. I was in the next bed to a chap had all his spare parts whipped off by a moaning minnie. Poor bastard had just got married.

Soon as he could walk he went into the bog and hanged himself. So I don't bleat about my wretched *jambe* too much; at least I can keep my girlfriend happy. So she tells me, anyway. She's a kind girl. What's that aeroplane of yours like?'

'Should've been junked on the designer's board,' Fish said dismissively. 'It's a Quirk. R-Royal Aircraft Factory rubbish. Finest machine ever made for k-killing young RFC pilots – the Boche just loves it. I w-wish I was in the N-Navy.'

'Why?'

'Navy won't use Royal Aircraft Factory stuff. They use private firms like Sopwith. Sopwiths are the w-works. J-Jerry doesn't like coming to p-play if you're in a Tripe. Still, the RFC's getting Sopwith Camels now. I m-may be lucky.'

'How many hours have you got? It is hours, isn't it?'

'Hours, yes. I've got thirteen. L-Lucky thirteen. I'm a veteran.'

Freddie looked at him doubtfully.

'It doesn't seem very much . . . we were trained for months in the Windstones.'

'The RFC needs us. C-Can't afford to w-wait until we know what we're doing. Father told us. The off-ffensive at all costs. G-Got to keep the planes over the front. Have to g-give Richtoven and his ch-chums something to shoot at. Ain't fair to let them wander about up there without any t-targets.'

Freddie drained his glass.

'We'd better get up to the castle. I know Uncle wants to see you. Listen, I'm going to come the upright brother. When are you going to make an honest woman of our Violet?'

Fish shook his head. 'C-Can't. S-Sorry.'

'Why not?' Freddie said, perplexed. 'She thinks the world of you, you know.'

'I w-worship her,' Fish said frankly. 'I g-go about kissing the g-ground she w-walks on. But I can't m-marry her, it wouldn't be fair.'

'Don't talk rot. Get on with it.'

'C-Can't,' Fish said quietly. 'Look, Freddie, I'm not right in the head, you see.'

'What do you mean?'

'I'm doolally tap. Screwy. I'm *mad*, Freddie.'

'No, you're not . . . no more than any of us who've been out there.'

'I killed Furzegrove's brother Amos the other day.'

'What? He was killed by a firing squad.'

'No, no. Furzegrove didn't want him to suffer, he asked me if I couldn't do it another way . . . We pretended he'd got off on appeal, we gave him a slap-up supper, told him he'd be going home in the morning. Then before the firing squad came I shot him in the back.'

'Well good for you . . .' Freddie said sincerely. 'Better that way . . .'

'I dream about him,' said Fish. 'He comes up to me in the dawn light and asks me to show him the w-way home . . .' Fish took off his hat and wiped his face with a handkerchief, suddenly slick with sweat. 'When it isn't him it's the patrol I sent out: they went down the ditch like I told them t-to, only there was mustard gas pooled there from an attack, it was waiting for them, it got them all as they came back, a d-dozen of them, they coughed their lungs up while we w-watched . . . I have a thousand dreams, Freddie, all of them real . . .'

He looked up, his eyes suddenly desperate. 'So you see I c-can't marry Vi, Freddie, it wouldn't be fair . . . And I'm dangerous to know. Vi nearly died giving me her blood when I was bayoneted . . . Her heart nearly stopped she lost so much . . . she could have *died*, Freddie . . .'

'She *loves* you. It's that simple.'

'Oh, I love her, Freddie, more than l-life itself. That's why I w-won't saddle her with looking after a l-loonie . . . and what about the children? It might be hereditary . . .'

'Fish, Fish, you're not thinking straight,' Freddie said gently. 'It's the war . . . look, with your record you could get a home posting. Training, the staff.'

'No, no!' Fish shouted vehemently. 'It's not l-like that. The w-war's what's m-made me the w-way I am. I d-don't like it but I c-can c-cope with it. It's n-not the war I can't cope with . . . it'll solve all the th-things in my head . . .'

'What do you mean?' his cousin asked steadily.

Fish tipped back his cider.

'Th-Thanks for the scrumpy.'

'Fish, what do you mean, it'll solve the things in your head?' Freddie repeated.

'Oh, you know wh-what I mean . . .'

'No, I don't.'

Fish got up and looked at his aeroplane. 'Junk, Freddie, don't let them t-tell you otherwise. Ought to be put down, really. Bit like me. What do you do with a winged pheasant, eh? Don't let it suffer, it ain't fair. Wring its neck, what? A quick snap and it's done. The little chap's problems are over, it don't hurt any more. That's what I mean, Freddie. I'll go and do my bit again, feel I owe it to Henry, really

– it was me that got him killed, and then when the war feels like it it'll snap *my* neck for me, it won't hurt any more. Then Vi can get married to some decent chap and have her children instead of having to look after a loony . . .'

They began to walk up to the castle, that looked down over its lands below.

'Aylmer and George set up a real tennis court in the Crecy Hall,' said Freddie. 'Let's crack a bottle and have a couple of sets.'

'G-Good idea . . .'

'When are you off?'

'Two days' time. G-Got to fly the Qu-Quirk over there.'

'Two days? We'll get the girls over, have a party. I'll get on the blower soon as we get in. Oh, I forgot. Some weasely little man from the tax office came to the castle looking for you. Said you hadn't paid your income tax or even been in touch with them. They wrote to you in June last year.'

'Tax?' Fish howled. 'In J-June last year we were getting ready to do something else on the S-Somme. What do they w-want? Why don't they bring our bodies back when we get killed in their b-bally war and use us for fertiliser? Eh?'

'I told him to put his beastly little forms where the monkey put the nuts,' Freddie reassured him.

'Let's h-have a drink. And play tennis. I w-warn you, my forehand is in pretty good sh-shape . . . and . . .'

'What?'

'Let's see the girls.'

19

Lots of Us Carry Automatics

La Gorgue, France
3rd August, 1917

My Darling Vi,

Would you believe it, here I am back on the Ypres front! The good news is that a) I'm above it looking down (instead of in it looking up, ha ha), and b) when I do so I'm in a Sopwith Pup. Yes, I handed the ghastly Quirk over to the Aircraft Depot at St Omer and haven't seen it since. The squadron has just been re-equipped with Pups, which is one of the few scouts we have that the Boche has respect for, and Pemberton, who is squadron commander since Henry died, is letting me build up some experience. The sector is quite quiet, thank goodness.

I do love you, Vi. I don't know why you love me, though.

10th August

My Darling Vi,

We went over to Hunland today. An OP (observation patrol) of four, led by Pemberton. A gorgeous clear morning. We climbed up to twenty thousand feet, well past the lines. No Huns. So high the cumulus below was like great icebergs in a blue sea.

When you're up so high you feel like you're not a normal human being. I sit there in this little tight cockpit, the whirling prop ahead, the wings reaching out either side of me, miraculously sustaining me, and it's as though I'm motionless in the sky among three other motionless winged machines, the roar of our engines somehow unnoticed.

If you look down from four miles up the earth is a huge

bowl, with the horizon curving up to me. The ground below a patchwork of colours and shapes, veins and lines. The ghastly lines where millions of men are fighting each other in dank holes like rats in sewers. At twenty thousand feet I feel so grateful to be a part of the sky and clouds, and completely cut off from the hideous butcher's shambles beneath.

Furzegrove got the DCM. I do hope he makes it.

I'm feeling much better, Vi. I can cope now I'm busy and learning how to be a good scout pilot. I still don't know how I'll adapt to peace . . . Maybe Uncle will let me have a room at the castle. Oh, I know, *us* a room. I still don't know why you want to have me. Perhaps we'll go round the world on *Parma's Pride.* That would be fun.

26th August

Dearest Vi,

My first air battle yesterday. I shot a German aeroplane down. We were up early on OP in a near cloudless sky. Just a sheet of mackerel cirrus very high up. Led by a splendid Scot called McCann, only nobody calls him that. His favourite expression is Hootsmon, so that's his nickname. He wears his kilt to fly!

We were over near the Houlthust Forest when we got bounced by a flight of Jerry D-IIIs, or would have, only Hootsmon had spotted them and we turned inside their tracer. My reactions are good now: the minute I hear the rapid rak-ak-ak of Spandau or see tracer I kick rudder and skid out of the way.

A red and yellow V-strutter whizzed past, I had to dive under Jock who was mounting up in front of me like a lift, saw a Hun whizz across my front, let him have twenty rounds deflection, he zoomed up in a loop and another D-III shot by, a red and yellow one. All a terrific mix up, he came at me and I turned with him, both of us trying to get into position to fire. I was slightly surprised to find I was quite calm and collected. The Pup is a sweet girl: I could turn inside the target without losing height while his nose kept on dipping, and within four turns I was behind and a little above him.

I was really close, I could see the bullets pocking his fuselage as I fired. I aimed at the cockpit, and the D-III rolled onto its back and went down streaming smoke. The sky was suddenly empty, nobody about. I saw my D-III crash near a wood and went home on my own.

The boys were really pleased for me and threw a party last night when we got back from evening patrol. Lots of singing and too much to drink. The words of 'Some Girl's Got to Darn His Socks' were still going round in my head when I woke up. I went up on patrol this morning – it cures the hangover!

When Hootsmon comes down his knees are blue with cold and the hairs stand straight out like bristles on a hog!

I don't think of the D-III as having anyone in it. It's a big mechanical bird. It's the only way. I *know*, inside my head, that it's nothing else than murder, but if I allow myself to *think* that way, then sooner or later I won't be able to get in the aircraft at all, and I am a de Clare. All that great roll call of past de Clare warriors all staring disapprovingly if one begins to snivel . . . So it's stiff upper lip all the way. I couldn't bear it.

I heard from George, he's well in at the Palace. Good for him. Crom wrote to me too, he's going to be elected MP for Windstone.

I love you, Vi, I think about you all the time when I'm not ratcheting my head about on my neck looking for Huns . . .

5th September

Bestest Vi,

Pemberton's made me leader of 'A' Flight. I wish I felt happier about it. Hootsmon was shot down yesterday. Not hurt, but his Pup was set on fire. I followed him down. He was trying to sideslip it to blow the flames away from the cockpit but they crept to him. He got up in the cockpit, I saw his kilt burning. He climbed out of the side in the gale and tried to fly it with one hand but the cockpit was like an inferno. He lost his grip, he tumbled away, and fell all the way to the ground. Another flamer. Lots of us carry automatics on us. They're good for shooting the frogs in the nearby canal, of which there are thousands, but really they're not for that.

If only Hootsmon had had a Calthrop – that's a parachute

– he'd have been all right. I miss Hootsmon's blue knees and the hog-bristle hairs.

We went up this afternoon and I got two V-strutters. Could have had a third but I helped a new chap, Thomas to get it. It's important to build up their confidence. He was pleased as punch and will be a good pilot now he's got his first. I'm a bit worried about Carstairs, who has all the sensitivity of a tractor driver, which he probably has been, since he's a sheep farmer from Convict Hollow or some such place in Australia. He took the undercarriage off his Pup yesterday trying to land it. I ought to send him home but we are so short of pilots. Three new boys in my flight. A quiet chap called Fortin who's got a scholarship to Balliol waiting when the war stops. I worry about them when we get into a scrap and am always rushing about trying to see that my little flock does not get savaged by horrid Huns!

I'm trying to teach the young chaps (there I go, at twenty I'm a veteran!) how to do it. I've worked out some principles that seem to work for me, and if I can instil them into the new boys it may a) keep them alive and b) shoot down Germans, which is what we are here to do.

I love you, Vi, but you know that.

9th October

Most darling Vi,

Thomas is dead. We had a huge scrap with Richtoven's circus. Their aeroplanes are painted all bright colours, just like a circus. I had a brief bout with the Baron myself but he's a cunning soul, he's ready to fight again another day if he comes up against someone who can handle themselves, as indeed am I. But by the time he'd gone off poor Thomas was battling very bravely against three triplanes. I shot down two and the third ran off. His engine was hit, he was gliding home. I went with Thomas to look after him. He was trailing smoke, and suddenly yellow flames started licking about the cowling. Within a few seconds the cockpit was filled with flame. He put his automatic to his head and shot himself. The blood blew all the way back over the fuselage.

Why don't the bastards let us have parachutes like the observation balloonists have? Thomas could've jumped. We were over our side of the lines, he'd have been back with us by now. He was a good chap and very brave and he's dead and I've got to write to his wife, who's expecting their first.

I'm so angry about the parachutes. First Hootsmon and now Thomas.

I love you.

11th November

Most dear Vi,

I hope this letter doesn't smell of petrol. We had a scrap with Richtoven's lot again and I got shot down. A bullet through the petrol tank, which is thoughtfully placed in front of the pilot so that when it bursts you get soaked in the stuff. We were at twelve thousand and I came all the way down in a complete state of blue funk. I've never been so scared: I had to change my trousers when I got back and not just because of the petrol. Sorry! (The castor oil from the engine doesn't help. That's my excuse, anyway. The truth is I was so frightened I had as much control over my bowels as a baby.)

Got down, thank goodness.

Went up again this afternoon to test the old nerves. Got a Halberstad. The poor bastard burned.

I'm starting to dream about people burning. I wish I didn't.

Thank you for going to see Thomas's window. She sounds very nice. I'm glad the baby is well, and I'll be godfather. I may be able to come over some time. I'm due some leave, but we're so busy.

I got the bar to my MC.

I love you so much.

29th November

Dear, dear Vi,

Pemberton got shot down. He's alive, and may survive. They should have replaced him ages ago, his nerves were completely shot. I'm the most experienced man in the squadron now, so they've made me CO.

I went to see him in hospital and while I was away poor

Fortin was killed. Flamer. He jumped. If he'd had a parachute he'd have been all right.

I feel very guilty, if I'd been up there I might have saved him. I'm trying to fly with the boys as much as I can.

I'm a bit tired. I think I'll organise a binge for the boys – the weather's shut in for tomorrow, it'll do them good. I wish I could sleep. I keep getting this dream. It's a face. It's vague and rather distant, but it comes closer and closer. When I can see it it's burned, all black and charred, I can smell it, but it's alive, it looks at me. I never know who it is.

Thanks for the records from the shows. It helps the boys when we have a new supply of songs.

I heard from Freddie. His tanks were in the thick of it at Cambrai. They gave him a bar to his MC. It was a rotten place to use tanks. The high command should have picked good ground where they could have made a proper breakthrough. What do you expect? All the brass knows how to do is slaughter young men in ever-greater quantities.

I've put Furzegrove in for a commission. I want him to transfer to ground crew tradesman for the RFC. If he stays in the line he'll only be killed. He'll train in Blighty, too.

I love you Vi, as always.

5th December

Most wonderful Vi,

A mixed day. I'm being allowed to go home for a bit. The doc says I'm tired. My concentration's gone rather. I wrote off two Pups on landing last week. The ground wasn't where I thought it was.

Carstairs is dead. He was the last of the old hands. He burned. He shot himself with his automatic. I was there. He was due to go on leave. He had his girlfriend waiting for him. All he needed was a bloody parachute.

I wish I could take the RFC brass, all the bloody generals up and drop them from twenty thousand feet. Alight, if possible.

I'm being sent back for a bit of leave and to form a new squadron. We've been promised Bristol Fighters. The Pup is totally outclassed now. I'll be a major again! Had to drop rank when I got into the RFC.

I'm so angry about the parachutes.

The French gave me the *Croix de Guerre.* With all this tin on my chest I walk lopsided.

Can you get away for a bit to be at the castle with me? I long to see you, and there's something I have to do. You can help me.

I love you, Vi.

20

Because They'll Use Them

Windstone Castle, January 1918

'What the devil's going on?'

Standing on the bank of the Torrent, as it widened and slowed after rushing through the Windstone Gorge, Violet turned. Two bemedalled figures, one great in bulk, one lean, both heavy with braid, the winter sunshine gleaming from their cavalry boots, were climbing from a limousine.

'Good morning, General,' she said pleasantly.

'Never mind good morninging me, young lady,' General de Clare said biliously, 'What's going *on*? Who are these blasted people?'

'Photographers, Gervase,' said Sir Hubert Mordaunt reasonably.

'I can see that, dammit, Hubert. What are they doing here? Why have I been brought down here?'

Violet pointed high above them, to where Brunel's Iron Bridge carried the railway across the gorge. Somebody was standing in the middle of its span, up on the ironwork. He waved.

'He's going to jump,' she explained.

'Who is?'

'Fish is,' she said levelly. She was watching him closely, and saw a brief flash of hideous joy cross his face. Then it was gone.

'Fish? That's Fish up there?'

'Yes.'

'What's happened to the boy?' Sir Hubert asked anxiously. 'Splendid feller. Brave as a lion. Fought with me on the Somme. First day, don't y'know?'

Violet raised her voice so that everyone could hear, and the waiting journalists looked up at her to listen.

'Major de Clare – that is him up on the bridge – is a much decorated hero of the war. After the most gallant service on the front, in which he fought at the battle of the Somme and on the Ypres front, he was severely wounded and transferred to the Royal Flying Corps. In the space of six months on the Western Front in the air he has shot down some twenty-three enemy aircraft, four balloons and has made numerous attacks upon ground targets. He has been brought down twice himself. He has been awarded the bar to his Military Cross, the Distinguished Service Order and the *Croix de Guerre*. He has risen to command his squadron, and has been sent to form a new unit to take back to the front.'

'Get on with it,' de Clare snarled. 'We can do without a blasted eulogy.'

'During his time in the RFC,' Violet continued clearly, without looking at him, 'Major de Clare has become very upset at the unnecessary casualties being caused to extremely brave pilots by the dogma of their higher command.'

'Oh, dear,' sneered Gervase de Clare, 'the boy's cracking up. We're running a war, not a garden party for the RSPCA.'

'Major de Clare *knows* that the war effort is being greatly harmed by the needless loss of these experienced fighting men. It is his wish that the matter be brought to the attention of the highest authority.'

De Clare yawned. 'Is that it? How long do we have to stay here on this freezing river bank? Is he going to jump, or not?'

He looked up to the great silver span of the bridge, some three hundred feet above them. 'Jump, damn you!' he bawled. 'Jump!'

Fish stood on the bridge, looking down at them. His father grunted contemptuously.

'The boy hasn't even got the guts to commit suicide,' he jeered. 'When he gets off that damned bridge I'll have him committed.'

All those looking up at the bridge cried out in sudden horror.

Fish had jumped.

He didn't tumble, his flight was graceful. It was as though he had taken a swallow dive off the bridge.

'No!' Sir Hubert called out in anguish. 'The poor boy——'

Something white streamed from Fish's back. It blossomed like a flower. Two hundred feet above them, Fish floated down under a pure white silken parachute. They cheered in spontaneous relief, those standing below, and Violet saw de Clare's face twist.

There was a light breeze flowing down the gorge. It caught the parachute like a dandelion seed, drifted it away from the icy river. Fish came over their heads as the cameras clicked like machine-gun-fire, and landed with a thump on the wide bank. The silk collapsed, and he drew it in. Violet ran over to him and began unstrapping the strong leather harness from him.

'Well done, darling. I'm so proud of you.'

'Congratulations, sir!'

'Well done, Major! Wonderful feat!'

Fish stepped out of the harness.

'The p-parachute, gentlemen. Designed by Mr Calthrop, and as you c-can see, it works!'

'It certainly does!'

'Dashed good show!'

'If we pilots in the RFC were allowed to wear parachutes like this one – as gunnery officers in observation balloons do – then literally hundreds of lives would be saved, and skilled and experienced pilots returned to their squadrons in fighting order, to continue the war against the enemy. As it is, brave and valuable pilots who are themselves unhurt, but mounted in damaged or burning aeroplanes, are killed every day on the front, for simple l-lack of a parachute. The h-higher command might just as w-well sentence them to death.'

'What do *you* say to that, General de Clare, sir?' one of the journalists demanded, turning to him. 'You *are* a senior officer in the Flying Corps, are you not?'

De Clare's face was slowly turning a purplish red with fury. He spoke clearly, however, taking hold of himself and avoiding looking at his son, who was watching him with interest.

'The matter of issuing parachutes to pilots has been discussed at staff level several times. There are a number of sound operational reasons why – spectacular propaganda exercises like this aside – it has been deemed unsuitable for pilots to have parachutes.'

They waited expectantly.

'Er – the parachutes themselves are bulky and cannot fit into the cockpits.'

'Major?'

Fish shook his head. 'Not so, I'm afraid,' he said cheerfully.

They looked back at the general.

'*Furthermore,*' he grated, 'a smashed aircraft generally falls with such a velocity that there would hardly be time to think about using a parachute.'

'Major?'

'Not so again,' said Fish. 'In f-fact, that's one of the most horrid things about many combats where an aircraft is damaged – the time it takes to fall. S-some chaps go to their deaths quite unh-harmed themselves, but simply p-passengers in a craft that no longer answers to the controls and flutters down through the sky like a leaf before smashing on the ground. I f-followed one of my chaps down from fifteen thousand feet and it took over five minutes.'

Fish looked round the grim faces.

'It's a long time to wait to die, you know,' he said gently. 'His nerve went before he got there. He shot himself.'

They turned accusing gazes on General de Clare.

'We don't let them have parachutes because they'll use them!' he yelled furiously. 'They'll jump at the first sign of danger!'

They looked at him in disbelief, and then at Fish. Standing by him Violet silently ran a finger over the line of medals on his chest.

'Well, let me tell you!' Sir Hubert said loudly. 'I don't believe a word of that and I shall raise the matter at the highest level.'

'Thank you, sir,' said Fish.

'You're a degummed has-been, Hubert,' de Clare said viciously. 'We got rid of you on the Somme.'

'You mean I wouldn't slaughter young men like chickens,' the fat man said quietly.

'Listen gentlemen!' said de Clare, forcing a smile on to his face. 'I am just passing on the current opinion of the higher command. Rest assured that after this amazing demonstration, I too will be raising the matter at the highest level.'

'Thank you, Father,' Fish drawled. 'Said in front of witnesses, too.'

21

The Parson Came Home Drunk Last Night

Fayetteville
17th February, 1918

Most Darling Vi,

The squadron is here. When I say the squadron, I mean the squadron. All eighteen Brisfits (that's what we call the Bristols) landed safely. Brigade sent a query asking me how many had arrived and how many crashed en route and I was dashed pleased to send back a stiff note saying all eighteen proceeding with the war. They're used to people cracking them up. Not in *my* outfit we don't.

It was a wonderful flight over. Everyone kept marvellous formation, and we came across the Kentish Weald in style. The weather was crisp and sunny, and how beautiful the land looked below us! The fine woods waiting for the green kiss of spring, the sparkling silver rivers, blue smoke curling up from the cottages. We could have been flying over the Windshire, with all of it after four years of war still intact and undamaged, standing just as it had for centuries. Such a happy contrast to the hundreds of square miles of devastated France. I looked down at the shining Channel with the toy boats ploughing white furrows and blessed it. We owe so much to that narrow strip of water. I felt so proud to be English, I would do anything to defend that land as it passed below us.

We came over the Leave Boat gliding out of Calais on its way to Folkestone, with its escort of destroyers and the little airship hovering above, looking out for submarines. We landed at Marquise for tea and new maps, and were in Fayetteville before dusk. The ground crews and observers/rear gunners were waiting for us. Guess who was with them? Ned Furzegrove!

Ned got his commission, but turned down the maintenance training for a chance to be a gunner. Guess who's flying with me! I feel very confident. Despite the fact it's so big you fly the Brisfit like a fighter – it's very powerful and very strong, and the gunner acts as a sort of rear armour. God help the Hun who gets on *my* tail! Ned can hit a snipe in a gale with a folding .410, so whacking all kinds of hell out of a pursuing Hun with twin Lewis guns is right up his street.

I'm taking people up tomorrow to begin training.

I love you, Vi. Good news that you're coming out. Find a field close to the CCS and I'll be able to whizz over and see you.

Did I tell you I love you? Oh, yes. I see it above.

Fayetteville
3rd March

Dearest Vi,

De Clare and Furzegrove 4, Germans 0. There is this German airfield about ten miles behind their lines. One of the much-vaunted 'circuses' of Fokkers has moved into it, all brightly painted. I saw the aerial photograph, and we thought we'd welcome them!

Got up before dawn and came over just as they were running up and taxiing out. Strapped to the side we had a long sack we'd made, filled with footballs painted bright scarlet, with flaming yellow streamers on each, about fifty feet long. I came over the line of Fokkers and Ned cut the rope.

Aerial bombs! By George they came screaming down, bouncing everywhere, streamers howling, mechanics running like rabbits, machines going all over the place trying to get out of the way. Two lots of two taxied into each other in the confusion! Much splintering of props, much Teutonic shouting, no doubt.

I laughed so much I could hardly fly.

We saw a Halberstadt trainer, all black crosses, on the way back, instructor and pupil earnestly ploughing along. Buzzed him from a range of about three feet. Hadn't the heart to shoot him down. He fluttered off, looking pale.

The Huns take their lady friends promenading at Ostend when the weather is fine. I know: we had to go and take photographs for this seaborne invasion thing (which let me tell you is never going to come off) and there they were, all decked out in their finest. We've bought a big sack of oranges and we're waiting for them to get really oozing ripe. Then one fine afternoon we're going to roar along the prom at twenty feet and fling ripe fruit at the lot of them!

Sometimes I feel about twelve, Vi. But I do love you.

Nobody's been killed yet. I want it to stay that way. I've introduced a policy that everybody has forty-eight hours without a mission coming back from leave, to get their hand back in. Even a week away makes you rusty.

Fogged in today, so we organised a rat hunt. There are far too many about, large and Hunnish-looking, and remind those of us who were there of the trenches, where their cousins breed in quantity. Lots of us have hounds – uncle sent me two of the staghounds – and we got them all together and armed ourselves with clubs and Verey pistols. The procedure is simple: you fire a Verey cartridge down a suitable hole and wait. Final bag: forty-six rats, two walking wounded dogs, the padre who got in the way of someone's cudgel and has had to go off and lie down, and a farm building which is still smouldering.

Fayetteville
21st March

Dearest, darling Vi,

I don't know if this letter will get to you first or me! I'll write it anyway – when I'm writing to you it's as though I'm talking to you. Can't wait to see you in Paris. I'll be busy in the day with this squadron commanders' conference but we'll have the evenings to ourselves. There's some talk of making me a lieutenant-colonel but I don't know if I want that. It'd mean leaving the boys. I can go for the conference: things are quiet at the moment and Harris, my A Flight leader will stand in for me. He's a sound chap, came to us from Camels.

Heard from Crom. He was returned unopposed at the by-election. He quite likes going in to the House of Commons, he says. Frightful row brewing about Lloyd George selling honours, he says. The man's quite barefaced about it. There's even a tariff! £10,000 for a knighthood, £30,000 for a baronetcy and £50,000 upwards for a peerage! What's worse is that he's giving these honours to the most ghastly crew imaginable. Crom says in the new list coming up there's one man who's in there for 'untiring work with various charities'. He's a Glasgow bookmaker who's been in jail! Crom says that most of the new arrivals in the Lords would be – and probably have been – blackballed by any respectable London club. (At least we de Clares hewed off the heads of the King's enemies in battle to get *our* baubles!)

Ah, me. Hold on. Somebody's pulled up outside in a smart car. It's Pemberton! Vi, darling, I'll finish this later, I'd better go and welcome him.

2 a.m. Most darling Vi. Been having a great time with Pemberton. Gave him a party in the mess. We were singing a lot of the old favourites – 'The Parson came Home Drunk Last Night, as Drunk as he Could Be' – sung to the tune of 'While Shepherds Watched Their Flocks', and I can't repeat the words. Nor to 'Barnacle Bill the Sailor'. Pemberton is in great form, and recovered from his wounds. The RFC's turning into the RAF, by the way. We shall have our own uniform, a kind of sky – of course! – blue.

I'd better get to bed. I'm not flying tomorrow, so a late night and 'another little drink' won't do me any harm. Let's catch a show in Paris.

4.45 a.m. Darling Vi. In haste. I'll get this off. No Paris, that's scrubbed, I'm afraid. The Boche have been quiet these past days just to fool us. The most colossal bombardment has broken out. Brigade says they are coming at us with fifty divisions, led by their new *sturmtruppe* – stormtroops. Freddie was telling me about them. It's still pitch black and foggy, but as soon as it clears we're to attack them on the ground. Much low flying.

Vi, darling, I must go and get the chaps ready. I love you so much. Paris when it's quiet again.

22

The Chaps on the Ground Will Be Waiting for Us

25 March, 1918

The ground below was a filthy brown and green. The green was not the fresh colour of spring, but the decayed tint of corruption, pock-marked with shell craters. The dawn light occasionally glinted dimly off suppurating water. Leading the flight at fifty feet Fish realised they were over the old Somme battlefield. He caught a glimpse of some khaki-uniformed troops digging in on the west bank of the river, attempting to make a stand. To his left and right were two other bomb-laden Brisfits, one flown by Pemberton and the other by a new boy, MacLeod, straight from flight training.

Flying low along the trees marking the east bank of the slow, muddy river, he spotted field grey cavalry and troops, supported by lorries bringing ammunition on the Matigny road. He pointed them out to Furzegrove, behind him, and to the other two pilots. Racing at 130 knots over the ground he led them up in a zoom climb to fifteen hundred feet, checking for enemy fighters. The steel grey sky was clear. At the top of the parabola he put down his nose. The wind screamed through the wires as the heavy aeroplanes accelerated to over two hundred knots.

They arrived over the road like a clap of thunder. The road was congested with troops and horses, grey lorries moving slowly. The Bristols were in line, with Fish in the lead. He raced over their heads, dropping the twenty-pound Cooper bombs from his racks. When they were all gone he switchbacked along the road, firing with his Vickers, hearing the rattle of the twin Lewis guns behind him.

Over the village he pulled up in a steep turn, looking back behind him. The young boy, MacLeod, was racing through the smoke, and Pemberton some hundred and fifty yards behind him. There was tremendous chaos, with lorries burning, overturned, on their sides in the ditches, men and horses milling about, dead men and animals scattered everywhere.

From the top of his turn he could see the erupting smoke of shellfire from the wood and houses of the neighbouring village. Men in khaki and men in field grey seethed about its streets, clustering close to the walls and firing at each other around corners, and he realised that a fierce fight was taking place there. A column was filtering off the main road, outflanking the British troops in the village, infiltrating a large green field by the canal. He dived towards them with the others behind.

He almost brushed the poplars as he shot into the field. The troops were looking the other way until he began firing. He walked the rudder pedals, sending his fire along the column. They seethed like ants prodded with a stick. Over the village he pulled up in a steep turn, coming back, and saw the other two Brisfits streaking over the grass. The air was filled with noise, with the whipcrack of bullets, and the thudding of them striking home into the aeroplane.

Fish dropped it low through the main square, and shot over the bridge at ten feet, coming back at the troops from a different direction. A house on the canal side silently erupted into smoke, and collapsed. There was a sudden, enormous roar right beneath him, and the Bristol was blown vertically upwards.

For a moment he couldn't see, the impact was so great. A shell, it must be a shell. Chunks of shrapnel blasted through the fabric, through the frame. The outboard struts were collapsed, the wings twisting. The stick in his hand was slack, the whole aeroplane was wobbling about him. Only the big green field was ahead. He shut the throttle and switched off. There seemed to be some kind of control fore and aft, so he brought the stick back as the grass rushed up at him. Something broke as they hit; he heard the twanging of snapping wires. Earth fountained about him, the lower wings vanished. Hot oil suddenly burned him, and a stench of fire, of animal manure, surrounded him.

He was still. He sat in the cockpit, dazed. Smoke gushed all about him. Somebody was heaving at him, dragging him from the blazing wreck. It was Furzegrove. Blood was spilling down his face from a cut on his forehead.

Function came back to his limbs.

'I'm all right, Ned,' he gasped.

His ears were singing, he didn't understand why Furzegrove suddenly pulled him down on to the grass.

'Jerry's having a go at us sir.'

Peering through the smoke Fish could see the flash of a machine-gun over by the tree line. Some field grey figures started to advance towards them.

'Bloody hell . . .' The thought occurred to him that the men in grey would probably be extremely cross with him.

With a crackling roar the ammunition in the Bristol began to cook off. There was an explosion as the Lewis guns went up and they started to stagger across the grass away from the German troops.

Something huge swooped over their heads, in a blast of oil and burned petrol. A Bristol touched down, rolled to a halt. Pemberton hung out of the cockpit, yelling.

'Come on, you chaps!'

The air snapped and cracked as bullets clattered about them. There was a roar overhead as they ran to the aeroplane, the huge propeller ticking round, and MacLeod's Brisfit came over, firing at the advancing troops, golden brass casing spraying through the air. He zoom-climbed above them and his gunner hosed them from behind.

Fish heaved Furzegrove up into the observer's cockpit and the gunner pulled him in. Fish scrabbled up the wing, hauling himself on by the inner strut. He wrapped his arms and legs about it, and Pemberton opened the throttle. The huge twelve-cylinder engine bellowed, they rolled over the grass, the tail lifting, and they were airborne.

As the ground fell away Fish saw MacLeod making a last pass over the troops, a toy aeroplane knocking down tin soldiers, and then he was climbing away after them into the steel grey sky. The old Somme battlefield was still filthy. The British troops had finished digging their hasty trenches. A man with a Lewis gun waved at them as they came overhead.

The land changed: it bore the green imprint of spring. It came closer and closer, a line of trees painting in under the trailing edge of the wing where Fish hunched about his strut in the hundred-mile-an-hour gale. There was a thump, a bounce, a roll and they were taxiing in towards the line of big hangars. The engine thrummed, and then tocked around a last turn like a grandfather clock. Fish began to unclasp himself. He had difficulty making his hand let go of the strut, and when he did, he slithered down the smooth, doped linen to fall at Pemberton's feet. He staggered upright.

'Thank you,' he said hoarsely. 'Thank you very much.'

'My pleasure,' the other said drily.

'I'm going to put you in for an MC.'

'Already got one.'

The new boy, MacLeod, had taxied up next to them. Most of three bushes were wrapped about his undercarriage. He climbed out, and Fish went over to him.

'Good lad,' he said, and the boy flushed with pleasure. He looked as though he had just made a century in the house match. He was no age. 'Very well done,' Fish said again. 'The both of you.' He clapped pilot and gunner on the shoulder.

'N-Ned! Go and get your wound dressed. S-Somebody get us all a d-drink.' Fish went to his office. His adjutant came in and poured him a large scotch.

'Th-Thank you, Charlie.'

He took off his flying coat and mud and dirt showered down on to the boards. 'Am I v-very filthy?' he enquired.

'Very.'

'I need a new Brisfit, Charlie.'

'They brought four in from Candas.'

Fish poured back the neat whisky as though it was cold tea.

'Give Mr Pemberton a shot, Charlie, here he is. Mr MacLeod too. Mac here has invented a new way of trimming hedges with his prop. It will probably prove very p-popular when the w-war's over. I'll have another of those.'

Fish put a boot on the table and excavated a dead frog from it. He looked up to see two young men in very new RFC maternity jackets watching him with horrified fascination from a post by the wall.

'I say, who are these f-fine young chaps, Charlie?'

'Replacements, sir,' said Charles Cordell. 'Stephens and Horris. Just joined us.'

'Dashed good . . . give'm a drink, Charlie.'

'We don't drink, sir,' one of the boys said hesitantly. 'The instructor forbade it.'

'What rot!' Fish said hotly. 'Look at me, I can't fly *without* a drink! What do you say to that, eh?' He fumbled inside his jacket for his cigarette case. When he found it it was bent almost in half. He stared at it in annoyance.

'It's too dashed bad, Charlie,' he complained. 'This bloody war gets in the w-way of everything. Give me a gasper, will you?'

'Gold Flake?'

'Anything.'

Fish lit up with his trench lighter and coughed violently for some moments, turning purple. He drank some scotch and the fit subsided.

'Anything in from Brigade?'

'Yes, sir,' the young adjutant said. He picked up a signal from the desk with his one good hand. He had left the other in the mud at Passchendaele, still attached to his arm up to the elbow.

'From the big white chief, actually. Salmond himself. We're to fly to a designated line west of Bapaume. Us and other squadrons. "These squadrons will bomb and shoot up everything they can see on the enemy side of this line. Very low flying is essential. All risks to be taken. Urgent.' Just came in, sir.'

'All r-risks . . ." Fish looked up at his adjutant. 'What's happened, Charlie?'

'Fifth Army's crumbling. Jerry's trying to annihilate it.' He coughed. 'Also, we're to move. Jerry's expected to come through here about four o'clock. Our new base is Bertangles.'

'Bertangles?' Fish's face brightened under the dirt. 'We c-can have d-dinner at the Savoy in Amiens. Book us all a big table, Charlie.'

He looked at the two replacement pilots. 'How much time have you got?'

'Thirty-eight hours, sir.'

'Thirty-five and a half hours, sir.'

'On Brisfits?' Fish asked hopefully.

'Solo, sir. Three and a half on Brisfits.'

'Ah . . . Well, let's see . . . Mac, you're a veteran now, aren't you?'

'If you say so, sir,' MacLeod said with a smile.

'Oh, I do. You go to B Flight with Pemberton. Mr Stephens and Mr Horris, you fly with me.'

The rain was sweeping across the country, grey sheets of it; when Fish put his head over the side to try and see where he was it blinded him, slashing at his face. The cloud whipped overhead, though they were at no more than two hundred feet. The rain had soaked the white bandage about Furzegrove's head, so it was slowly turning pink. To his left and right, a little behind, swaying and lurching in the foul weather, but hanging onto him gamely, he could see Stephens and Horris, both their heads turned to him, following his lead. The racks under their wings were clustered with bombs, the water streamed back off them into the murk.

Fish couldn't see through his goggles so he pushed them up on to his forehead. The big fighter vibrated to a staccato thudding in the air. He bent it over onto its wingtip and there right below was a battery of sixty-pounder guns blazing furiously into the murk.

The river. Fish straightened it out, the two young pilots lurching and swaying after him, and they dived under the rolling cloud into the little valley. German troops were massing on the west bank, piling up in the village by the stone bridge. Everywhere was smoke and flame as the artillery pounded the villages. German field guns were lining the river bank, and he felt the percussion as he twisted and turned. The big fighter was taking hits – an outer strut went, snapped like a match. He could see the Germans in a mass, pushing over the bridge. British artillery shells were landing in the water, sending up columns of spray, very white in the gloom. Fish reached down and pulled his Verey pistol out, firing it in an arc over his top wing. A scarlet flare seared through the murk. The guns seemed to take it as a signal: the monstrous orchestra increased its pace, the very air shuddered all about them as they hurtled down the valley. He rammed a big green cartridge into the pistol.

The Lewis guns behind him opened up as Furzegrove started to fire at the artillery men on the bank. Fish reached down and grasped the lever for the rows of Cooper bombs. The wingtips were shredded, bending and flapping, the Bristol staggering through the rough, blasting air. Missiles and shells and shrapnel whined and howled all about them. Glancing to left and right he could see Stephens and Horris bent forward over their controls, their big biplanes swaying and lurching like toboggans on a rough slope. He fired his Verey pistol and a bright green light arced down towards the bridge. The roar and blast of the artillery seemed to reach a crescendo.

They came over the men at twenty feet, and let the bombs go. Something huge blew up underneath him, the fighter bucking like a horse. He pulled back the stick and the cloud swallowed him up. For a moment it was quiet, and then behind them the grey murk turned bright orange.

He put the nose back down and they came back out into the violent, sleeting rain. The orange light faded behind him, the noise of the guns died away. He was on his own.

He paused over the town in the half light. He could see the wide open space of Bertangles in the clearing drizzle, as he flew over the trees and cut the throttle. For a second the Bristol rolled on the grass and then it gave way with a twanging of wires, and snapping of wood and metal, sagging onto the wet grass, slithering round in a ground loop as it left pieces of itself behind. The propeller disintegrated into an arc of flying wood, the engine howled and sent pistons and connecting rods hurtling into the air. Fish cut the switches; they clambered from the wreck.

Outside the hut that was their new mess a strange aeroplane stood:

a gleaming silver-blue triplane with black Maltese crosses on. Fish staggered into the hut.

'Pour us a drink, Charlie. Stephens and Horris back yet? What's the tripehound d-doing here?'

'We captured it!' the adjutant said proudly. 'Well, sort of. Pilot got disoriented in the murk. Low on fuel. Saw the field and landed. When I waddled up to him with revolver in hand and stuck it in his ear he was peering at a map.'

'Where is he?'

'Gave him a few drinks and sent him off to the cage.'

'We'll k-keep it. S-Spoils of war, what? Put it in the hangar. You g-got that t-table booked? Where are the other chaps?'

'Seven sharp, sir. Stephens and Horris aren't back yet.'

'I lost 'em over the bridge. Stout boys, stayed with me the whole way. Stupid shell blew me into the clouds and by the time I'd g-got down I'd lost them. Hope they haven't got lost in that weather. I n-need a new Brisfit, Charlie, that other one broke. They aren't making them as s-strong as the old ones. I th-thought you were g-getting me a drink.'

Cordell poured some more whisky into the glass without comment. 'We'd better get on, sir,' he said.

'Leave a message for Stephens and Horris. They can catch us up.'

Pemberton parked the Crossley tender in a side street and the pilots poured out of the back. They surged down the little street and onto the main boulevarde. The lights of the Savoy showed bright in the darkness.

A small group of soldiers was coming the other way, singing soulfully of sweet Molly Mallone in Irish voices, and Fish suddenly halted, looking eagerly at the corporal at their head.

'I s-say! It's Corporal Coogan, isn't it? Pat Coogan.'

The singing died away, and the men stopped, looking at Fish in a puzzled fashion.

'Sir?'

'You r-remember me, what? First day on the Somme. We sh-shared a shell-hole . . .'

The corporal shook his head.

'I t'ink you're mistaken, sir. I was not at the battle of the Somme.'

'Well I'll be dashed . . . spitting image, you are. Might be b-brothers . . .'

He reached into his pocket and took out a note.

'Here, you and your chums have a drink for me . . .'

'Why, t'ank you, sir. We'll be pleased to do that.'

Pemberton had waited with Fish, was standing in an amused fashion watching. 'Friend of yours, Fish?'

They walked on towards the hotel, and Fish suddenly clicked his fingers. 'Silly me,' he said. 'Couldn't possibly have been him. Poor old Pat had his foot blown off.'

Pemberton gave Fish a worried glance but the other was bounding up the steps.

'We'll have some bottles of each,' he said breezily to the waiter, seating himself at the top of the long white table in the buzzing dining room. 'No plink-plonk, I want to see a château on the label.'

Fish knew the effect that hot food and a few drinks could have on young constitutions temporarily exhausted by the missions of the day. By the morning, with some sleep, they would be fresh again. He peered down the table, through the blue haze of a hundred cigarettes. On a dais a small orchestra was playing selections of light opera.

'Do you know, Charlie, I can't recognise half these chaps. Are you sure this is our table?'

'Replacements, sir,' Cordell said briefly.

Fish shook his head, and came back to the conversation running up and down the pilots. Fresh bottles came, old ones vanished. Fish had got onto his plans to sail *Parma's Pride* round Britain.

'Going to follow his course, all the way up to . . . oh, I say! Thomas! Thomas, old chap!'

Fish half got out of his seat, waving at a passing RFC lieutenant, who stopped, looking puzzled.

'Thomas, old boy. Haven't seen you in ages.'

'Sir? I'm Lee, sir.'

'You are? 'Strordinary thing. You look just like Thomas.'

The boy went on. Pemberton leaned towards Fish.

'Thomas is dead, Fish,' Pemberton said quietly, so that the others did not hear. 'He burned. He shot himself. You saw him.'

Fish looked at the bustling, busy dining room with unfocused eyes. 'Are we all dead?' he asked. 'Perhaps this is hell. We died and didn't know it. I wake up in the night and I'm sure I'm dead.'

A mist covered the aerodrome, but through it they could see the glow of the sun that would soon clear it from the sky. Fish came into the office carrying a mug of coffee.

'Capital binge, Charlie,' he said. Two young men in very new

RFC maternity jackets stood by the wall. They looked eagerly at him.

'Who are these young chaps, Charlie?'

'Replacements, sir.'

'Replacements?' Fish said, sounding puzzled. 'Sorry, chaps, don't think we need any replacements.'

'Jamieson and Ford,' the adjutant said firmly.

'Oh. How many hours?'

'Thirty-two, sir.'

'Twenty-eight and a half, sir.'

'On Brisfits?'

'Solo, sir. Two on Bristols.'

'One and a half, sir.'

Fish fumbled for a packet of cigarettes, and lit one. He coughed for some seconds and the telephone rang.

'De Clare. Eh? The bridge at Marieux? Yes, that's right, I attacked it yesterday. The entire centre span, Brigadier? Jolly good. Held the Boche up a bit, what? Anything to help. You've got them? Stephens and Horris? You found them. What do I want you to do with them? Send'm back, of course, I need'm.'

Fish listened in silence for a few moments, then put the telephone down. 'They didn't get lost,' he said absently. He glanced out of the window. The mist was beginning to clear.

'Charlie, this coffee is filthy. Give me a scotch.'

'Yes, sir.'

'What about you chaps?'

'It's a bit early sir . . .'

'Is it? What s-strange habits they teach you young pilots these days . . .'

Fish rummaged in the drawers. 'It's going to be a nice day. Do you fish?' he asked brightly. 'You can go fishing if you like.'

'We've come to *fight*, sir.'

'Of course. To be s-sure. Ah, here it is. The manual on the Brisfit. Read up on that and I'll ask you questions when I get back.' Fish suddenly tipped back his beaker of whisky and made a dash for the door.

'*Signal* from Salmond,' the adjutant snapped, and Fish stopped.

'What?'

'All squadrons will assist our ground forces by incessant attack of the enemy. All risks to be taken. Utmost aggression.'

'Yes, yes, I know, Charlie,' Fish said in a wheedling voice. 'I'm just off to do that very thing. Now if you'll give these chaps a seat and they can study the manual while I'm gone . . .'

'*Replacements*, sir,' Cordell said firmly. 'Without Stephens and Horris we are under half strength. I've assigned Jamieson and Ford to you. Mac's to lead C Flight, and Pemberton B Flight.'

'Mac's leading C Flight?'

'He has more experience than anyone else except you and Pemberton,' the young man explained.

'Two days. He's a veteran.'

'Yes.'

'We'd better go, then,' Fish said quietly to the two young pilots. 'The chaps on the ground will be waiting for us.'

They went outside. Some new Bristols stood waiting in the clearing mist.

'You see, our chaps down there are very grateful to us for shooting up the huns like this,' Fish explained. 'It's making a difference to the war. S-Stopping the Jerry advance, that sort of thing. Jerry doesn't like it at all, so our chaps want us to hammer them as much as we can.'

'Oh, we will, sir, we will!' the two young men said enthusiastically, their faith in their veteran commander instantly restored.

'Oh, I know you will,' Fish said quietly, sadly. 'I know you will.'

The two young pilots ran over to their machines, and began to prepare them for flight.

23

Welcome to St Goderick's

The junior house had a new boy. His parents were missionaries, bringing the love of Jesus to Africa, and he had been living with a maiden aunt in Bournemouth. The aunt had caught a winter chill that had turned to bronchitis, transporting her first to a nursing home and then the grave, and the decision had been made, far away in Nyasaland, that young Matthew Paul Cromer should attend boarding school. It would, the Christian ones so far away felt, make a man of him. It was important to them that it be an Anglican foundation, and if possible, cheap. St Goderick's, which catered for the sons of the clergy and offered them a handsome discount, beckoned. They arranged the fees by telegraph, and went back to instructing Africans to pray thrice daily and abstain from sexual desire with light hearts.

Matthew Cromer was taken to London by the vicar, and outfitted in the Army and Navy Stores in an uncomfortable black suit, stiff black shoes, three shirts with detachable starched collars and a tie. What he did not wear was placed in a large trunk which when stood on end was slightly taller than he was. The vicar gave him a bible and put him on a train that took him to St Goderick's.

He was the only new boy that term. Everybody else in his year had arrived the previous September. They stared at him with chill eyes, as lean as wolves from the icy winter. Somewhere in the huge, draughty red-brick building was the housemaster, the Reverend Rose. So he believed. He never saw him. The junior house was run by the prefects, big boys armed with whippy bamboo canes.

His dormitory mates rifled his trunk for sustenance and, enraged to find only two shirts, three underpants, a pair of rugby shorts, five collars and a bible, poured icy water over him while he slept.

At the end of the week they paraded him in the great hall. He stood down there on his own while they surged on the landing above yelling promises of violence. The terror he had felt since arrival, that had ensured the total immobility of his bowels, increased even further. He trembled all over and they howled. They tormented him by whipping around him a great wicker basket, suspended from a rope, and screeched with laughter when he flinched.

Suddenly, the noise ceased. The doors were flung open, and a cohort of prefects marched in. Their leader was tall and handsome. He smiled at Matthew Cromer.

'Welcome,' he said pleasantly, 'to St Goderick's.'

'Thank you, sir,' Matthew whispered.

'De Clare,' the prefect corrected him. 'I am Godfrey de Clare. You must get things right, here, Cromer. St Goderick's is an establishment of fine old traditions, it punishes people who don't get things right.'

'Sorry, de Clare.'

'Good . . . do you know any songs, Cromer?'

'Yes . . .'

They made him crawl along the great cast-iron radiator, burning with heat. His mind had gone a complete blank and he could only remember the first line of an evangelical hymn. He screeched out 'Raise my soul from darkness and degradation, Lord' eight times as he crawled desperately along the huge radiator. They were not contented with his performance and pelted him with rubbish while they made him crawl back the other way. He fell, so they tore off his trousers and put them over his head before stuffing him in the basket and whirling him about the hall thirty feet up.

They painted his face with whitewash and his bottom with boot polish.

'Welcome to St Goderick's,' Godfrey said pleasantly.

'*Deo gratias* . . .' he whispered.

24

I Want You All Back

Bertangles, 23 April

Pemberton came into the mess in a sky-blue uniform, holding a kind of casing.

'I say, Fish,' he said cheerfully, 'look at this.' He placed the casing on the table and Fish peered at it over his coffee mug. It was a dark mud colour, like the outside of a man's torso or the upper half of a suit of armour and it stood upright on its own.

'What is it?' he enquired.

'It's my old tunic.'

'I say . . . mine was getting a bit stiff too.'

'Well, I crashed twice and got a lot of mud on once and a dosing of petrol the second time.'

'And you've been spilling more than you d-drink.'

'That too.'

The jacket stood on the table, as if worn by an invisible pilot.

'How's Reynolds?' asked Fish.

'I called the hospital last night. He's going to make it.'

'G-Good show. Who've you got as your observer?'

'New chap. Gould. I've had a chat with him.'

Other pilots began to come in, cradling coffee mugs, breathing in cigarette smoke, twitching, scratching or performing whatever involuntary actions their overworked nervous systems commanded of them. They were all in the sky-blue of the RAF. The RFC and the Royal Naval Air Service had been amalgamated on the first of the month. By now, everybody had their new uniform.

'G-Gather round, then, chaps,' Fish commanded. 'First off, we're winning this w-war.'

They cheered, in a weary kind of way.

'We even sh-shot down the Baron. Ludendorff's offensive has stalled, and it's in no small part thanks to us. It's cost us. We've lost about a thousand machines this past month, but h-here we still are.

You'll be pleased to hear that we're g-going back upstairs. J-Jerry can't t-take it down low, and he's gone up again. So we're going too! Now, most of you only know low-level strafing and bombing since you got here. Let me say that I prefer air fighting. Far nicer.'

'Me, too,' Pemberton agreed.

'There are some simple rules. Fly the Brisfit like a scout. Observers cover the rear. Attack with height, attack out of the sun. Don't fly straight and level. Keep looking over your shoulder. Jerry's taken losses, you'll be better than most of his pilots. However, if you come up against some tough old veteran who really knows how to fly – run away. The Brisfit is the fastest aeroplane in a dive on either side. Stick forward, full throttle and let your observer hose him as you run for it. I w-want you all b-back, I've g-got used to your ugly faces.'

Fish tipped back his coffee, they picked up their helmets and gloves, and went out into the bright morning sunshine. Fish wrapped the silk stocking that Vi had worn round his neck, checked that he had the lucky handkerchief she had given him, looked at the small photograph of her and went after them.

A red light curled away from Fish's Bristol, and the squadron about him swayed and moved as the pilots shifted throttle and rudder like a pack of hounds hearing the warning horn. Leading B Flight, Pemberton looked down and saw what Fish had already spotted: eight scouts, four thousand feet below. Black crosses. He pointed them out to Gould right behind him, and the two prepared their guns.

Fish swayed sideways, the signal to go, and suddenly dropped, hurtling away into the icy air with the others in close pursuit. The earth raced up at them. The crosses broke, startled, wheeling like disturbed crows. Fish fired, one tumbled, like a shot pheasant, learning a tail of smoke streaming towards the green ground below.

Pemberton tightened his zooming turn, grunting as the forces pushed the air from his lungs. Suddenly, a blast of firing from the cockpit behind as he strove to bring his Aldiss sight onto the fleeing Halberstadt. Gould. He glanced behind him: *where the hell had that come from*? A red and blue Albatros.

He broke away from his quarry, snapping over into a reverse turn. Gould was crouching low, firing in short bursts from his twin Lewis guns. There. Smoke. The Albatros jerked like a hooked fish, and plunged away into the blue.

Pemberton rolled it straight, and suddenly something struck him a terrific blow in the leg. Simultaneously the petrol tank caught fire, and a furnace blew underneath his seat. The wooden floor was on fire, the heat scorching his boots. He rolled it over into a diving turn, and saw the yellow triplane behind him. Enveloped in smoke, Gould began firing at their killer.

The flames were roaring about his calves, his blue uniform was on fire. His seat ignited. He yanked at his belt, cut the throttle and climbed out of the burning chair onto the lower port wing. Hanging onto the strut with one hand in the gale, he flew with the other, manoeuvering the stick to set the doomed fighter into a crabbing sideslip that kept the flames away from him and Gould. The observer had straddled the fuselage, and was still firing at the triplane that darted about them.

A thunderbolt came out of the sky: the triplane jerked and rolled, its top wing came off and it disintegrated into flying wreckage. Fish's Bristol came out of its dive and pulled alongside. Hanging on, Pemberton gave a half wave.

The ground was coming up; they were at five hundred feet. It was open country. Pemberton manoeuvred the stricken biplane as best he could towards a large field. The Bristol was pouring with smoke, the fabric about him was on fire. Gould had climbed up and was standing on the cockpit coaming, supporting himself on the trailing edge of the wing. A twisting, trailing path of dirty black smoke marked their passage through the air.

Fish watched as Pemberton set it up for the landing. He straightened the blazing, gliding machine and smoke and flame gushed up through the cockpit like a furnace door opening.

At fifty feet above the grass the port wing folded up, its spar burned through. The upper wing tore off, the wreck tumbled over twice before it hit the ground, throwing the two men off like dolls.

25

Please

'This is Major de Clare,' Fish said into the telephone. 'Squadron Commander. I w-want to speak to General de Clare. Yes. Same name.'

He waited patiently, sitting at the desk. On the table, Pemberton's tunic stood, worn by a ghost.

'This is Fish,' he said unemotionally, as he heard his father's voice come down the line from the château. 'I want parachutes.'

'Want all you like,' the general said brusquely. 'I am not aware that policy has changed since the RFC became the RAF. No parachutes.'

'I want parachutes,' Fish repeated. 'Pemberton and his observer died this morning. They caught fire. If they had had parachutes they could have escaped. They died.'

'I see no point in continuing this conversation.'

'The wrong people are getting killed,' Fish persisted. 'You're alive in your château, Pemberton is dead.'

There was a dangerous silence on the other end of the line.

'Do I take this to mean no parachutes?' Fish asked, with exaggerated politeness.

'No – bloody – parachutes,' his father ground out.

'Then you'd better get back to your lunch.'

'Mind your damned impertinence!' General de Clare screamed at his son.

Fish put the telephone back on its cradle.

He went outside. The fitters and armourers were preparing the machines for the afternoon patrol. He walked over to the hangar. In one corner, the captured Fokker triplane stood, shiny blue and silver. He went over to it, and stood looking at it for a while, noting the twin Spandau machine-guns, the short bomb racks. The senior ground tradesman in charge of the maintenance came over, seeing his squadron commander, and stood quietly next to him.

'Hodge, do those racks take Cooper bombs?'

'I don't see why not, sir.'

'Jolly good. What about ammunition for the Sp-Spandaus?'

'Plenty, sir,' the man said, slightly puzzled.

'J-Jolly good,' Fish said again. 'I'll want it all ready for tomorrow morning, before dawn. Bombed up and full ammunition. Incendiary bullets, Hodge. Fill the magazines with incendiary bullets.'

The countryside below Fish was soft and green in the gathering light. He was miles behind the lines. The Fokker's nine-cylinder rotary engine hummed sweetly in front of him. He was three hundred feet above the French landscape, following a road. He made a couple of S-turns, admiring the taut response of the little fighter aircraft to its controls. The doped linen of the wings stacked in front of him was as tight as a drum, the silver-blue paint shone in the early morning light.

A crossroads. A farm labourer, walking alongside a horse and dung-cart towards his place of work, glanced curiously up at the speeding machine as Fish swung down the poplar-lined road that led to the château.

There it was. He could see it set quiet in its green grounds, like a fairytale house. Mist drifted gently on the lake and ponds, fringed with fresh green reeds. It was a small château as they went, the country home of an aristocrat of perhaps slightly straitened means, not a Versailles imitation. A comfortable place to be.

Fish knew where the bedroom was, it was in the west wing, on the second floor, under the gaily enamelled tiles. He flew straight over the west wing, and dropped his Cooper bombs straight through the tiles.

He made a flat turn over the ornamental wood, bright in its spring foliage, and went back the way he had come. The air was as smooth as silk. Smoke was gushing up from a huge hole in the roof of the château. Fish commenced firing, the twin Spandaus ripping out their bullets, walking the rudders back and forth and the incendiary shells stitched into the fabric of the building. He shot overhead as it began to burn.

He repeated his turn, squinting back over his shoulder as he saw people begin to run from the blazing structure like ants.

There he was. He knew his father's night attire. Always the same. Pale blue silk pyjamas. Fish knew there would be a monogram on the breast pocket. He hadn't had time to put on his dressing gown with the scarlet trim. Fish assumed it was there in the burning bedroom, somewhere.

He was rather irritated. What right had his father to be scuttling about on the lawn like a demented rabbit? He ought to be spread all over the walls of the bedroom like raspberry jam.

Fish fired a long burst all about him as he crouched amongst the statuary, and sprayed the area with blazing fragments of marble. He looked down at him as he roared by at twenty feet and he laughed. Over the green lawn he pulled back the stick, letting the little triplane hang on its prop. At four hundred feet he looked over his shoulder and saw his father running away towards an ornamental summer house.

He pushed in right rudder. The torque of the rotary engine whipped the nose over in a hammerhead turn and he came down upon the running figure below like doom.

General de Clare looked despairingly up at the fighter screaming towards him. He tripped, fell to his knees, held out his arms in abject surrender.

'*Please . . .*' he shrieked.

The wash of the triplane blasted all about him, hot and oily. It was suddenly quiet, just the sound of its engine dying away, the crackle of the flames taking hold of the château, men shouting. General de Clare knelt trembling in the middle of the garden.

The Bristols came over the trees one by one, the big twelve-cylinder engines fluttering as the pilots cut the power, wheels rumbling on the grass, undercarriages squeaking, tailskids sliding, quiet as they taxied in and switched off. The metal ticked softly as it cooled.

There was a strange aeroplane there, Fish saw it as he glided in: a BE2, the sort of pool transport the generals used to take themselves about their domains, flown by pool pilots, instructors and old fighter pilots seconded to such duties.

He cut the engine nearby, climbed out with Furzegrove.

'Isn't that your father?' he enquired. 'He looked like that when he was giving me ten days without the option for taking one of his hares.'

'S-So it is,' Fish drawled. 'So it is.'

General de Clare stood by the hangar glowering at him. Fish went over.

'Good day, Father.'

'I'll have none of your insolence,' the general snapped.

'Then how can I help you? I'm a busy man.'

'Not too busy to come to try and kill me.'

'You've been trying to kill me half the war, while you crouched behind the l-lines,' Fish said reasonably. 'I thought if you wouldn't come to the war, then the war should come to you.'

'I'll have you shot!'

'I don't think so,' Fish said, indifferently. 'Now are you here just to s-snivel, or can I get on with my duties.'

'You're being transferred,' de Clare said sullenly.

'Oh?'

'The King wants you. You're to do three months as an equerry. He wants . . . war heroes.' His father's face twisted bitterly. He reached in his pocket.

'You're to have this. You ought to be hanged, but you're to get this instead.'

He passed over a small box covered in blue silk. Inside, on a ribbon was a cross.

'The Distinguished Flying Cross. That must be new. Why bring it yourself?'

De Clare hunched his shoulders inside his coat. He's small, Fish thought in surprise. A little man.

'I had to know,' his father said intensely. '*Why?*'

'Why what?'

'*Why didn't you do it?*' his father screamed. He wiped some spittle from his mouth. 'I saw you, Fish! You went by and you laughed. I know what killers look like! You were going to do it!'

'I was,' Fish agreed.

'Why didn't you, then?'

'You shat yourself,' Fish said coldly. 'You were kneeling in it and you begged me not to kill you. I thought I'd leave you there.' He turned and went into the mess.

General de Clare heard the roar of approval go up from the pilots inside as Fish showed them the medal. He climbed into the BE2. He sat staring straight ahead and the pilot flew him away.

26

They Might Not Be There By the Time I Get Back

17 May

Fish saw the tents, a pale yellow pitched on the meadow. A farmer had lit a bonfire nearby, sending a stream of acrid white smoke towards his neighbour's property. Fish judged the breeze and let down over the trees. The wheels of the little triplane ripped softly through the grass, rolled on the hard earth with a rumble, the prop spinning with a flash of gold against the sun. Violet was standing by the tree. The prop kicked and stopped, with a sucking sound from the cylinders. Fish undid his belt and vaulted out.

They spent some time kissing each other, and then went and sat on the soft grass by the tree.

'Sorry we can't go any further,' Violet giggled. 'But I'm supposed to be on duty as it is.'

She smoothed her nurse's apron and Fish brought out the cigarette case that Violet had given him.

'It got bent,' he apologised. 'But one of the armourers mended it. He's a jeweller in civilian life.'

They lit up, inhaling the fragrant smoke with pleasure.

'What's that?' she said, pointing at the triplane. 'It looks different.'

'That is the famous tripehound, favourite m-mount of the dreaded Baron Richtoven. One of his ch-chaps got lost and landed at our aerodrome in it. It's a good aeroplane. Very good indeed.'

'Your father's château was destroyed by an aerial attack,' she observed.

'It was me,' Fish admitted cheerfully.

'You? Why?'

'Well, why not, eh?' Someb-body should have given h-him the p-push ages ago. He w-walks about asking for somebody to wring his neck.'

'What has happened to you, Fish?'

'Am I being unreasonable? People try to kill me every day, it seems. I kill them first.'

'You didn't kill him.'

'He wasn't *worth* killing, y'see. He was covered in shit and snivelling. So I left him there. He was without honour. We're the de Clares, dammit! Our motto means something. It means if it's got your number on it you put your head up and take it. You don't grovel and wail.' Fish took a deep drag on his cigarette.

'I don't ask for much. All I want is to buy a farm somewhere near the castle, do a bit of fishing and hunting, marry you and have children, dine with the neighbours a few times every year, get old and eccentric. Have b-bloody people leave me alone.'

She regarded him with quiet amusement. 'Thank you,' she said. 'And I accept your eloquent proposal of marriage.'

'I've g-got to sail *Parma's Pride* first, mind.'

'I'm twenty-one,' she said. 'I think I can wait a little bit.'

'J-Jolly good.'

'The things in your head have gone away?'

'A b-bit. Seeing father grovelling in orduere bucked me up immensely. I realised he was n-n-nothing . . . I don't think you'll have to t-take me to Colney Hatch.'

'I'm so pleased . . . so it's off to the Palace?'

'Suppose so . . .' Fish said gloomily. 'I'd rather stay here. I don't like it back home much at the m-moment. All the best people are out here, all the best types from all over the Empire . . . when you go back all you run into are bolt-holers, profiteers, strikers, fake conchies pretending their consciences won't let them fight when they're just gutless. Them and ponces and other r-refuse. "How many Fritzes have you got old man?" They don't care that it's some poor b-bastard shot to bits in a Camel or a Fokker . . . Being with the R-Royals won't be m-much fun, either. It's so st-stultifyingly boring, and their idea of a subtle j-joke is to put a bucket of w-water on a door ajar and summon you in. G-George told me. They d-did it to him three times in one weekend. G-Great-uncle Rodney was at court in Queen Victoria's day. D-Drank himself to death from b-boredom, p-poor old soul. Still, it's only for three months. I should think they'll give me a new squadron then.'

'You're flying this . . . tripehound back?'

'Yes. Going to take it to the castle. S-Spoils of war. See, I've got the black crosses painted out and nice roundels on. Don't want to get shot down by our own side.'

'Leave it here,' she said, her voice suddenly urgent. 'Why don't you? I'll take you to the station . . . I'll drive you to Calais, even, if you like, and you can catch the boat.'

'I'd rather take the hound. Vi, I've survived all this being shot at, nothing's going to happen to me pootling over the water to the castle.'

'Is it armed? Do those black guns have bullets in?'

'Oh, of course. I have bullets in my revolver when I go down Regents Street, Vi.'

He finished his cigarette. 'I'd better get on, darling. I'll write this afternoon from the castle.'

'All right. I'll miss you so much. I'll try and get leave to come and see you. We have to move the CCS in a couple of days. The Germans are starting to go back.'

'We've won,' Fish agreed. 'The March offensive was their last chance. Now we just have to push them back all the way to Berlin. Smash the b-bastards, make sure they never do it again. Sh-shatter Germany back into the old princeling states. That's what we have to do.'

'Write to me. I'll get that leave. We can stay at the Savoy and be quite decadent.'

'It s-sounds good to me.'

He got up, helped her to her feet and kissed her. Then he set the controls of the triplane, went around to the front and swung the propeller with a practised hand. The rotary spluttered to life, and settled down to a sweet, gentle purr. Fish clambered into the cockpit.

'I'm going to climb up to about six or seven thousand,' he said. 'Take a last look at the b-blessed lines. They might not be there by the time I get back.'

The breeze had almost died away. He turned the triplane with a burst of power, pointed it down the slight slope to the trees. The engine hummed, the tail came up and he was skimming over the grass before climbing away into the blue sky. She stood watching him, growing ever smaller as he ascended in a series of wide circles. The lines were not that far away, a matter of five or six miles.

She glanced over at the tents that made up the little temporary hospital. It was quiet: they would be packing up and moving forward to follow the troops soon. She looked back up at the sky. Something tiny glinted up there, a silvery blue. Then something else flashed. A wing, against the sun, higher than the silvery blue. Something else. A dozen, two dozen, falling down out of the sun.

* * *

The lines straggled away in both directions, dirty and jagged. In the distance Fish could see the white streamer of smoke of a train. Still climbing he turned the triplane round, and the compass in its little bowl of alcohol went round and then back as though suspended on rubber. He levelled out and cut a course for the channel.

He banked over to get his position, and eight thousand feet below the little pattern of yellowish white tents slid under the wing. Cold air scented with hot oil whipped over his head; he straightened up and from habit his head rotated around, checking the blue sky.

He hardly saw them. Diving down on him, their thin wings were practically transparent – but the glare of the sun fluttered, and he knew. At full power he turned straight into them, slapping the cocking levers of the two black Spandau machine-guns.

The sudden manoeuvre caught them by surprise. Tracer flashed to his side, where he would have been, a red and white Fokker roared towards him and he fired at thirty-feet range. A ball of flame enveloped it, and it tumbled past his wing, ablaze.

A green and white striped DVII was behind him. Crouched forward in his cockpit he banged in rudder, skidding sideways, whipping the stick back and over, and the stripes were under him. He completed the half-roll, chopping the throttle, and hung inverted. The Albatros seemed to slide underneath him as slowly and smoothly as a big salmon making its way upstream. He pulled the stick gently back and squeezed the trigger. The twin guns sounded like a great sheet of canvas ripping; the bullets picked a line all the way back from the engine of the Albatros, exploding with small puffs of smoke, explosions of oil, fragments of metal, gouts of blood, and the machine with its big black crosses fell slackly away into the haze below.

Fish completed the roll and pulled back on the stick. The triplane rose up and away from the shark-like fighters coming at him.

They came running from inside the empty tent when they heard her scream. She was sprinting towards her little car. As they saw her bend to crank the handle, she pointed desperately up at the sky and jumped in. She crunched the gears, shot off down the lane, her head frantically looking up to see. They too peered upwards. In the blue above, two trails of spiralling black smoke stained the air. The sun flashed on a dozen, two dozen wings as they went this way and that in a dance of death.

*   *   *

The triplane could outclimb anything else. Fish knew it. You had to dive on a triplane. Dive and zoom back up to him. You couldn't live with him in a climb. The Fokkers below went away from him. They were still there, staying with him like sharks, their pilots looking up at him, but he was above them and safe.

What was above him?

It flashed out of the sun. A huge blow smashed into his leg like a sledgehammer. He jerked back the stick as the blood blew back into his face and fired a burst. More, there were more, another dozen above him, zooming down and climbing.

Rak-ak-ak-ak.

Bullet-holes stitched across the fairing in front of him. Something smashed into the machine-gun bracket with a scream. Somebody kicked him in the back when he wasn't looking, throwing him forward against the gun-butts. He felt a tooth break, tasted blood hot in his mouth.

They were all about him as he twisted, turned, skidded across the sky. Groups of five and six, first to one side then the other, above him, behind, below. He looped, surprised the rear guard, blasted the engine and cowling with bullets, saw the top wing disintegrate. At the top of the loop, inverted, the bullets smacked across his cockpit, a white-hot flail that smashed his leg and wrist and arm in a single crunching blow.

The triplane fell slackly away, and began to spin.

A crossroads. Violet stopped with a squeak of brakes, looked frantically up at the sky. Dirty black smoke billowed up not far away, where an aircraft had crashed. She knew it wasn't Fish, because the savage twisting combat above had not stopped. Another one was tumbling down. Red, she could see red.

In the distance she heard the clanging of a bell. The ambulance. Somebody had got the ambulance.

The aeroplanes were swirling down like a shoal of bright fish, all the colours of the rainbow. They were pursuing something. Something that tumbled over and over like a leaf. A silver-blue leaf.

Over there.

Violet rammed into into gear and accelerated up the road, her engine screaming.

It was the unfamiliar gyration that brought Fish conscious again. That and the pain and nausea that racked him. He was slumped at the side of the cockpit as the ground went round and round and blood washed about his feet. He shoved in rudder and forward stick, the triplane flew, and they were on him again.

Bullets lanced up from under his feet, something hit his arm like a cricket bat and smacked it into his face. A Fokker skidded in front of him and he pushed the stick forward, screaming with rage, trying to ram it. There was a thump as his undercarriage tore its wing away, he saw it tumbling down out of control.

Rak-ak-ak-ak.

He was going to die. He lunged savagely over the sky as they swarmed over him, trying to fly the triplane into them. His ammunition was all gone. He screamed in fury, they cut at him with knives of fire.

A white-hot chain smashed across him, throwing him across the cockpit. The nose jerked up, and fell, spinning towards the green ground close below.

He saw them leave him, watching him die from above. The woods and fields snapped across in front of him, whipping round and round. Blood sprayed up, streaming back in a scarlet banner. A road. A field. A small racing car hurtling along.

Blood filled his mouth. In one last, enormous effort of will Fish straightened the little doomed aeroplane with rudder. Screaming out with agony as shattered bones ground against each other he pushed the stick forward to check the stall and she flew again.

He was just over the trees. There was the field. A little car racing along the road. With his good left hand he cut the switches, and for a moment as he went into the field it was quiet.

He hit the ground at great speed. The lower wing came off, the propeller shattered, the aeroplane skidded on the turf like a toboggan, smashed through a hedge. The impact threw Fish forward into the gun butts, then back.

It was silent. Just the noise of hot fluid hissing and steaming. The smell of torn earth and petrol, oil and blood.

A click. A *whoomph*. The wreckage caught fire.

The little engine screamed as she hurtled down the country lane with the springs protesting, the wind whipping her hair. Something came over the trees, hurtled past her into the field. A silvery-blue flapping and streaming fabric and smoke, bits dangling and banging in the slipstream. She heard it break as it hit the ground.

She lost sight of it behind the hedge. A gate, there was a gate. The triplane shot along the ground, shedding pieces of wing, wood and linen, spars and wires, hit the hedge and was thrown up in the air, vanished from sight. She swung the wheel recklessly, smashed through the gate in a shower of wood, crashed over the field.

Behind the hedge, there was a billow of smoke, the crackle of flame. She crashed into the hedgerow, scrambled out and through the torn gap. The wreck was blazing, she could see Fish in the cockpit – he was thrashing weakly, trying to pull himself free with one bloody claw.

She ran into the flames. He was held in by the belt. She heaved at the buckle, tore it loose. With her uniform scorching, her hair ablaze, she heaved him from the inferno with incredible strength, dragging him clear.

From somewhere, an ambulance bell was ringing.

27

Around Here

St Goderick's

Godfrey stood at his study window, looking out. The spring had clothed the grounds of the school in green, and he watched the Reverend Rose walk away from the house, over the cricket pitch towards the chapel, where he was to prepare for evening service. A man of habit, he left and returned at the same time every day.

The inmates of the house were at prep. Worsley was in charge. Down the corridor came light, timorous footsteps. A hesitant hand tapped on the door.

'Come,' he said, without turning round.

'You w-wanted to see me, de Clare.'

Godfrey whirled, and Matthew Cromer blenched.

'I did indeed,' Godfrey said with a silky menace. 'You're a nasty little sneak, Cromer, and you tell lies.'

'L-Lies?'

'Yes . . .'

Godfrey reached out a hand to his desk, and picked up a letter. He shook it open and out dropped three pages of closely packed handwriting.

'Lies, Cromer, lies. You've been blubbing to your mummy, haven't you?'

Cromer stared in horror at the letter. 'B-But that's . . .'

'A whining lot of lies, isn't it Cromer?'

'No, it isn't!' the young boy burst out with sudden spirit. 'I *do* hate it here! I want to leave . . .'

'Your mummy is in Africa, Cromer. It says so on the envelope. You can't go there. Where do you stay in the holidays?'

'With the vicar . . . my parents pay him for a room there . . .'

'You are surrounded by God, Cromer,' Godfrey observed. 'God here, God there, God overseas. But let me assure you, of these the most important is God here. Have you read the Old Testament, Cromer?'

'Yes, de Clare.'

'That is the kind of God that rules in St Goderick's, Cromer. A jealous God. A vengeful God. A God who demands you fear and love him. A God who insists you do not tell whimpering little lies about him in letters.'

It rarely got warm in the icy barn of the Junior house, and Godfrey had a coal fire burning in his grate. He tossed Cromer's letter on to it and watched it burn.

'Your mummy has given you up into His care, Cromer. Now drop your bags.'

'Wh-Why?'

'Lesson one in learning to love your God, Cromer,' Godfrey said pleasantly. As the boy watched fearfully, fumbling with the buttons on his trousers Godfrey selected a cane from his collection, swishing them experimentally in the air before choosing. 'Pants as well.'

Godfrey bent him over the desk. Somewhere in the dark, gloomy barn they called the chapel the Reverend Rose was preparing the evening service.

Godfrey whipped him six times, raising six evenly-spaced weals across his bare buttocks, and by the time he had finished he was stiff with pleasure. He put the cane down and shoved the boy's head back on to the desk as he tried to get up.

'Lesson two in learning to love your God, Cromer,' he said. He undid his fly buttons and buggered the young boy with a fierce excitement as he squirmed and whimpered.

'Around here,' he told him, 'God and I are one and the same.'

28

I've Got a Jolly Funny Story for You

Amiens, France

Clarissa came into the room. Violet was lying in the bed that stood between the two windows. Her hair had been cut back, a white bandage circled her forehead, ran down under her chin like a nun's cowl. One arm lay bandaged on the white sheet, her fingertips just poking out. They had brought flowers, and anemones smiled sweetly at her from the little bedside table.

With her free hand she had been reading. She put the volume down on the coverlet.

'I was hoping you'd come,' she said with a smile. 'I'm out of gaspers. Light one for me, will you?'

'There's somebody here to see you,' said Clarissa.

'I can still have a fag, can't I?'

'He's from General de Clare's headquarters.'

'Then I definitely need a fag. What does he want?'

'He asked to see Fish. I told him it wasn't possible.'

Violet stuck the lit cigarette between her lips and levered herself up on the pillows with her good hand. 'I'll speak to him, then. I can always pass the message on to Fish when he wakes up.'

'Vi . . .' Clarissa said hesitantly.

'What is it, 'Rissa? Come on, spit it out instead of shifting from one foot to the other like a virgin deb.'

'I don't think Fish is going to wake up,' she said in a low voice.

'Twaddle,' Violet said shortly.

'Vi, he's dying.'

'Fish is *not* dying. He can't die, I'm not finished with him. I shan't be finished with him for about another eighty years. We've got far too much to do.'

Clarissa's eyes suddenly glittered with unshed tears. Violet stared at the wall and drew on her cigarette.

'Send this blasted man in,' she ordered.

Fish was in a room with three windows, two behind him and one to the side. The walls were painted a dingy brown up to shoulder height, at which point they became a dingy cream. He lay completely inert, both legs encased in plaster, his feet attached to weights by means of wires that ran over pulleys. His right arm was wrapped in plaster, the tube from a glass bottle suspended on a metal stand ran into his left forearm. His face on the pillow was the colour and texture of candle wax; only a faint movement of his chest indicated that he was alive.

Clarissa pumped the bulb of the sphygmomanometer about his upper arm, listened with her stethoscope. She released the pressure, the mercury slid back down the tube. She slipped her earpieces out and went round to the chart that hung from the bottom of the iron-framed bed.

As she stood noting down his blood pressure the door opened, and Violet came in. Her bare legs showed beneath the simple shift, her arm rested in its sling.

'*Vi!*' Clarissa protested.

'Don't be so wet,' Violet said, and found the chair by Fish's bed. She sat down in it, and looked at him for a long time. She took his free hand in her own good one.

'He's still alive,' she said levelly.

'He's incredibly strong. He ought to be dead.'

'Fish! Fish!' Violet said loudly. 'Clarissa thinks you're going to snuff it. Well, you're not, do you hear? If you give up the ghost now I shall be jolly cross with you. I forbid it, in fact.'

Fish lay silent, without moving.

'Listen, Fish,' she went on, leaning forward. 'Listen, darling, I've got something to tell you. First off, though, enough of this lolling here doing nothing. I've got lots to talk to you about, and just hearing the sound of my own voice won't do, so I want you to snap to, now. I want to get you out of this morgue and back to the castle, for a start, and I can't do it while you lie there like a side of pork. Then we have lots of things to do. We'll have to choose our first child's name. Shall we keep it in the family? If it's a boy we could call him Perch or Flounder. What do you think?'

Watching Fish closely, Clarissa thought she could detect the faintest movement of a pulse in the still, waxy skin of his temple.

'Anyway, listen. I've got a jolly funny story for you. Best I've heard in ages. Once upon a time – yesterday, actually – a general went off to inspect the troops. Being a thoroughly modern general he didn't take his charger, he went by aeroplane. Yes, it was your father! The old bastard climbed in and the chauffeur behind him duly took off. Away through the mist they trundled. Did I tell you it was a drizzly sort of day yesterday? Well, it was. Couldn't see very far. They got lost. Yes. That must have been it, because your father hasn't been near the lines since they were dug in 1914, and that is just where they wound up. They did. And the German anti-aircraft gunners couldn't believe their luck. A droning old BE2 overhead.

'Now, it seems that these Germans must have been to an old, slow aeroplane shooting school because they peppered it. About up at eight thousand feet it was, according to the reports. Did I tell you it was a dull day? Yes, well, it lit up the sky when it went up, a lovely rose red it was.

'He jumped,' she said quietly, her eyes very intent as she stared at him. 'He was on fire, and he jumped. He burned all the way to the ground.'

For a few seconds there was no sound in the room, and then a faint gargling came from Fish's chest, a rattle and gasp that opened his lips.

'He's dying!' Clarissa exclaimed in alarm.

Violet gripped his hand with a fierce possession. Fish's lips had tinged a faint pink.

'He's laughing,' she said in triumph.

29

Strike me Pink

Amiens, 8 August 1918

Mist was drifting across the land in the dawn light. Through his vision port Freddie could see tanks moving forward, some big Mark Vs with their six-pounder naval guns poking from their sides; others smaller Whippets like his own, their boxy turrets bristling with their four machine-guns. Clustered about each tank, and following up, were groups of Australian infantry.

There were the two of them in the turret, himself and Gunner Symes. The driver, Corporal Taylor, was in the front, between the two separate engines that ground away, propelling one track each, and filled the iron hull with noise, stench and dreadful heat. Even in the cool of the dawn, they were all sweating profusely.

'There's the railway, Taylor!' he bellowed, over the din. 'Run parallel.'

The Amiens–Ham railway line followed their line of attack, and they set off across country with their accompanying infantry. Fighting in the trenches was a thing of the past. The Germans were going backwards, the army of the British Empire at their heels. The bellow of an engine ripped overhead – peering out of his port Freddie saw a Camel dive onto a nearby wood, saw smoke billow out from some target.

They ground on. Despite its name, the Whippet was not fast. It boasted no suspension at all, and inside its dark hull they hung on grimly as the bumps threw them from one side of the iron turret to the other.

The ground became smoother and Freddie was able to peer out once again. They were approaching a village. Flashes of light and dust blasting into the air told him that a gun battery was situated there. Glancing to his right he saw a Mark V suddenly billow with smoke, the little figures of its crew tumbling out of the hatches, and infantry falling under the effects of shrapnel.

The Whippet suddenly rocked, a rasp of noise scraped across its skin and the interior was filled with the stench of earth and explosive.

'Near miss!' Freddie yelled. 'Half-left, Taylor!'

The Whippet jerked diagonally across the path of the battery, some six hundred yards away. Taking the right-hand Hotchkiss, Freddie began to lay fire onto the position, seeing the tracers leaping through the air at them. Heat and propellant assailed him.

The small tank passed behind a belt of trees. A road was there and they jerked parallel to it, approaching the battery from the rear. Looking out of the swaying vision port he could see the lean Australian soldiers loping alongside like wolves, teeth and eyes gleaming savagely.

He could see the battery firing on the approaching Mark Vs. As they came alongside there was a gap in the trees.

'Hard right, Taylor!' he screamed, and the little tank's gears crashed as it swung roughly in a right angle. The guns were pointing the wrong way, and he and Gunner Symes commenced firing. Within seconds the thirty-odd men of the battery were dead under the fusillade of machine-gun-fire. Above the beating of the engines he heard the savage howling of the Australians' approval.

They pushed forward into the village. It was a half-ruined place, brick and rubble scattered over the road. The Whippet slowed as it clambered over the debris. Freddie caught a sudden glimpse of a dark figure darting at him from a ruin and then suddenly the interior of the tank was filled with fire.

Somehow, he was tumbling out of the hatch at the rear, he and Symes. He was not sure how, or which of them had opened it. They fell to the ground, rolling over and over to extinguish the flames. Some Australian soldiers were beating them with capes.

He clambered up, his nostrils filled with a fearful stench of burning oil. His clothes were charred and his hair singed away, but miraculously he seemed unharmed.

Suddenly, a fearful thing flapped screaming, black and on fire, from the tank. It ran howling in the street until it fell over. They smothered it with a cape. It was the driver, Corporal Taylor, charred as though he had been tossed on a barbecue.

At the front of the tank some soldiers were savagely kicking a German. A black tank and nozzle lay on the filthy ground. A *flammenwerfer*.

'Hold it, boys!' the Australian lieutenant, Digger yelled. 'Bring the bastard here.'

On the turret of the Whippet were spare cans of petrol, carried according to orders but much disliked for the risk they posed by their crews. Digger vaulted athletically onto a track and released a can.

They dragged the man forward, two of them, and the lieutenant undid the cap.

'*Nein! Nein!*' the man screamed.

'*Ja, ja,* you fucking square-head,' the lieutenant said grimly. He poured the petrol all over the man and tossed the can aside. From his pocket he took a box of Swan Vestas, and lit one. As the phosphorus sizzled into flame he flicked it onto the soldier as his captors let go of him.

He ran screaming through the flames, knocking into walls, tripping over rubble, blazing like a torch, and the Australians laughed.

Freddie bent over Corporal Taylor. He was still breathing in short, agonised breaths. Raw flesh showed bleeding through the cracked charring of his skin. He pulled out his Webley and shot him through the temple. Blood and bone and brains sprayed over the dirty ground.

The German firebug was lying nearby, still flapping. His skin sizzled under the blue flickering flame, he screamed hoarsely. Freddie fired into him once and then twice, and he was still.

'Waste of fucking bullets, mate. Strike me pink I hate these Kraut mongrels,' Digger said. 'All right, lads! Let's go ratting!'

The company spread out through the ruined village, tossing grenades into rooms, flushing out Germans hiding there.

'*Kamerad*! *Kamerad*!' Freddie heard a boy scream, saw his hands raised high.

A bayonet took him in the throat, his eyes bulged out like a prawn's as he died.

'Too fucking late, mate.'

The Australians chased the shrieking survivors about the ruins, running them down and bayoneting them. Occasionally one of their own number got shot, and this increased their fury with the remainder. Finally they had killed everybody there was to kill. They reformed into a loose pack, their rifles and bayonets sticky with blood and ordure, and prepared to move on.

Freddie got back into the tank with Gunner Symes. It stank of burned oil and charred pork. Symes got into the driver's seat, started the engines. Freddie shut the iron hatch and they ground forward towards their next objective, with the Australians loping alongside them.

12 November, 1918

He sat at a table outside the café. It was getting dark, inside the lights glowed as men and women celebrated the end of war. He could hear the racket inside pumping through the windows. Yesterday the Germans, now on their way back to their fatherland, today the allies. It made little difference to the proprietor.

Freddie had a glass in front of him, but could not summon enthusiasm to drink it. He felt depressed. The Australians had gone off on a gigantic binge after which they intended to descend upon the red light district.

'We're going to fuck 'em free tonight!' Digger had promised, and they had all snarled happily, like a bunch of wolves.

Freddie sat at his table. In his pocket he had his papers, confirming his place in the regular army. All he had to do was sign. Nearly everybody he knew that was still alive was going to be looking for their free suit and cash gratuity. He was a soldier, now he didn't know if he wanted to continue as one. It was getting dark, but the sky was lit up by Verey lights and flares.

A small train of carts drawn by donkeys and manned by nuns in black and white habits came up the street, and drew up outside an old building with large black wooden gates, which stood open. Freddie realised that it must be a convent, and one presumably used, but now abandoned, by the Germans pulling back to the Rhine.

The nuns dismounted, and stood for a few moments waving their arms and crying out their thanks, Freddie presumed to God, or Jesus, or since they were Catholics perhaps Virgin Mary, for the return of their establishment. Through the gates he could see a stately, cobbled courtyard.

The nuns began to unload their carts, carrying what were clearly precious possessions inside. Some seemed heavy, and Freddie got up, leaving his drink. He felt he would rather do something useful than sit about. Now that the war was over its memories crowded too closely about him.

Without being asked, he started helping them carry the objects inside, everything from tables and chairs to graven images of the Blessed Virgin, rescued some four years earlier as the Germans of the Schlieffen Plan attempted lightning victory over the French. They piled everything up in the courtyard as their leaders went inside to assess the damage.

Suddenly, there was an explosion. Glass shattered, smoke gushed from the gaping windows. Nuns staggered outside, blood streaming down their faces, their habits blown into tatters. As Freddie ran forward, two young nuns came tumbling down the steps with their clothes on fire, screaming. He knocked them down, beating them with his jacket on the cobbles to extinguish the flames.

The engineers came in. The Military Police took away the two dead girls. A doctor and some nurses from the nearby CCS tended to the wounded. The engineers found three more booby-trap bombs in the convent.

Freddie went back to his table. His drink had gone, he ordered a fresh one, and when it came, he tipped it down in one. He took the papers from his inside pocket and signed them with his fountain pen. They smudged with dark, sticky blood from the dead girls.

30

Does it Go Far Enough?

Windlesham-in-the-Hedges, January 1919

Dusk was gathering like pools under the bushes and trees, the icy clear waters of the stream were turning to ink. George stood at the edge of the pool, and cast an imaginary fly. It fell straight and true in his mind, just short of the old tree, whose snags of branches stood clear of the water. In his mind, the ancient trout that lurked there took the bait – a green-bodied Mayfly, his own tying – and his hands, held out in front of him, played the powerful beast all across the pool, the lacquered rod bending at its tip, first this way then that, until it was tired, and he played it all the way into the shallows.

He stood at the edge of the pool, and slowly, he came back to the present. He shook his head, clapped his gloved hands together against the cold. He could see the lights of the house shining bright and hurried along, crossing the river by the old stone bridge, his breath puffing like smoke in the fading light, the hedgerow still frosted like icing beside him. Over his shoulder, the sky was slowly starting to brighten under the artificial lamps of London in the distance.

He came through the cottage garden, where straw lay strewn about on the frozen ground. He had opened the clamps that morning and taken out potatoes, carrots, Jerusalem artichokes, parsnips, all perfectly preserved.

The lights were bright through the kitchen windows – old Mrs Babbage from the village had come up to do for him, as it was a party. The big wicker basket was waiting for him by the chopping block in the woodhouse, and he set to filling it up with the logs he had prepared that afternoon. He hefted it up in his arms and carried it inside. The fire was getting a little low in the big hall. He tossed on a few logs of apple wood and the flames played against the cheerful, shiny ornaments of the Christmas tree standing there on the marble flags in its great earthenware pot.

Appetising smells were drifting through from the kitchen. Mrs

Babbage's apple crumble and treacle tart were famous in those parts and won prizes annually. Soon there would be the fine aroma of beef roasting in the great Victorian iron range, the scent of potatoes beginning to brown, like fine polished wood, then gravy, and golden, risen Yorkshire pudding.

He hung up his cap and scarf, put his gloves away. He poked his nose round the corner of his dining room: the long oval table was spread with the Irish linen cloth, as white as snow. Small vases of snowdrops which he had picked that morning dotted its surface. Silver shone at each laid place, fine yellow candles stood ready in candlesticks. Claret and port the colour of ruby, decanted from his cellar, glowed upon silver salvers. A company of polished glasses stood ready to be filled. A fire flickered pleasingly in the grate. He went over and tossed on another log.

He went upstairs. His black evening suit was laid out upon the bed. He conducted a quick tour of the bedrooms: all was tidy and welcoming – Mrs Babbage's niece, Nancy, had come in at lunchtime and arranged everything. A fire burned in each grate, the counterpanes were turned back and freshly aired towels hung in the bathrooms.

Lights shone against a wall, swinging across the room, and he bounded downstairs. Two big, powerful saloon cars were drawing up on the gravel. He switched on the great carriage lamps, one at each corner of the house, and went out to greet his guests.

They piled out, all young and bright, calling out his name as he moved among them, clapping him on the shoulder, and he they.

'Aylmer! They didn't let you drive, did they? What a brave lot you are . . . Perceval! Good to see you, and you too, Godfrey. Last year, what? Jolly good show . . . bring your bags inside: this is the new age we live in, don't you know. No bally servants! Drag it all in ourselves, eh?

'Freddie, Freddie! Ah, better and better, beautiful women, that's what we need around here, lots of beautiful women. Vi, darling, so lovely to see you. Clarissa . . . and you brought the poems! A poor thing but mine own. Siegfried was too generous to me in the review, he really was. Felicity, Flicks! Well well, this is lovely . . . And is that you, Crom? I say, this is a full house . . . Fish, Fish! Are you caught up in there? Eh? Bally sticks, such a nuisance what? Bless you, Aylmer. You sound like I did last week. Blessed colds this time of year . . . Come in, come in, let's all have a glass of something cheering and stand by the fire . . .'

Beaming with pleasure, he soon had them all gathered inside like an amiable sheepdog, and was splashing and gurgling drinks into glasses.

'Gin and it, Vi?'

Violet glanced up from collecting Fish's sticks as he lowered himself into a chair. 'Lovely, George,' she called.

'Flicks?' he said to the slight, elfin girl.

'Gin,' she said with a smile. 'And a bit of it.'

Felicity was holding up well, George thought. And she was. Not a day passed by when Robert's face didn't swim before her but each day her grief got a little easier to bear. Besides she was a de Clare now. Robert would have wanted her to be strong. She wouldn't let him down.

'Clarissa . . .'

George went around all his friends, quickly assembling drinks, proffering and lighting cigarettes.

'What about you young rascals?' he asked, coming to Aylmer and Godfrey.

'Scotch,' said Aylmer. 'A toddy, if you will. I have a nasty snuffle.'

'I can tell. Godfrey?'

'I haven't,' the tall young man said boldly. 'So I'll have cold water in mine.'

'You must be finishing up at school soon.'

'Ah, the dear old Alma Mater . . . My last year.'

'And then?'

'Cambridge.'

'You must have a chat with Vi. She's going as well.'

'These women are everywhere!' Cromwell cried, from near the wide fireplace. 'We even have them in the House.'

'So you should,' said Felicity. 'Shake you stuffy old men up a bit.'

'I think that's happened even without the ladies,' he said, rather ruefully. 'What a crew . . .'

'What's so d-different?' Fish called from his chair. The hand with which he held his tumbler of scotch was marked with a livid purple scar that vanished up under his cuff. 'The p-politicians are all swine. You excepted, Crom, of course.'

'Thank you, Fish,' his brother said drily. 'What's the matter with them? Baldwin summed them up rather well, I thought: "A lot of hard-faced men who looked as if they had done well out of the war." And they did, Fish, they did . . . the sort we know, old-fashioned country gentlemen like us, why there's hardly any of us left, just me and a few others. The dashed benches are packed with brewery, shipping and munitions millionaires on the one side and blasted socialists and revolutionaries on the other. A chap hardly knows where to sit.'

'Up with the revolution!' Perceval cried out.

'Revolution?' George asked, puzzled.

'Perceval has become a socialist,' Violet explained coolly. 'He has joined the coming age, or so he says.'

'You're a dashed turncoat!' Cromwell said hotly. 'Things are bad enough without our kind breaking ranks.'

'Oh, don't take on so, Crom,' said Perceval. 'The old world is dead and it was devilish unjust too. Under socialism there will be freedom and plenty for all.'

'Well I do take on so. Our sort fought the war, and for what? So that Bolsheviks could march down the Mall? So that bally trades unionists can sit in flat hats in the Commons?'

'I find myself caught between two stools,' Freddie said smoothly, defusing the approaching row. 'I too want the old days back – but not as a soldier!'

'Why's that, Freddie?' Clarissa asked, helping him along.

'The higher command sees the war just past as some sort of aberration,' he explained. 'One of the first things my general said to me was, "Thank God. Now we can get back to proper soldiering." By that he means no tanks or aircraft, and lots of cavalry.'

'There's a m-move afoot to disband the RAF,' Fish said in disbelief.

'There's *more* than a move afoot to get rid of the tanks. "Tanks is tanks and tanks is dear, there shall be no tanks this year." Thank goodness we've got General Fuller fighting our corner. The whole future of land warfare is tanks and aircraft, in my opinion.'

'Freddie!' Clarissa said, her face shocked. 'How can you talk like that? How can there possibly be another war after all the horrors we've been through? It was the war to end all war.'

'When the world is socialist there will be no war,' Perceval chipped in. 'Brothers in socialism can never fight each other.'

'I rather d-doubt that,' said Fish. 'British workers gutted German ones with a will, and vice-versa. Nationality counted more than class.'

'Exactly! Under socialism there will be no class! We shall all be equal.'

'How frightfully boring,' said Felicity. 'George, my glass is dry.'

'Oh, I say, let me come to your aid ... well who can that possibly be?'

He peered out into the dark, where the lights of a small car were drawing up. Clarissa, standing near the window looked out.

'It's Carlotta,' she said in surprise. 'I didn't know you'd invited her, George.'

'Nor did I,' he said, and went out to the door.

'This is awful!' she said, beaming. 'I must be gatecrashing. I called the castle from Southampton and they said you were all gathered here, so I thought I'd drop by.'

'Come in, come in!' George said hospitably. 'You're just in time for dinner.'

He ushered her into the long, high reception room.

'I feel awful pushing in like this!' she said with bright insincerity. 'But when I heard what was going on I just knew I had to come. Clarissa, darling, so lovely . . .'

She brushed past her sister, ignored Freddie and went straight over to Fish. Violet, standing nearby, watched her warily from behind a bright smile. From the corner of her eye, Carlotta noticed it.

'I don't know what to say . . .' she breathed.

'S-Sorry I can't get up,' said Fish. 'Bit of an operation at the moment.'

'All those medals, and now the Victoria Cross!' she said reverently. 'I just don't know how you survived . . .'

'It was none of my doing, I assure you.'

'Awarded by the King . . .'

'He's not a bad old stick, by all acc-counts. So George t-tells me.'

'George?' she said, turning to him as he brought her a martini.

'I work there, for my sins,' he explained.

'With the Royal Family?'

'Yes, I'm a sort of aide, you know. Guardian of the back staircase is my title, I think. Look, chaps, shall we all stagger upstairs and prepare for dinner? Let me show you to your rooms . . .'

They gathered themselves up and he led them up the grand curving staircase.

'Perceval,' he said. 'You're looking rather seedy. Are you hungover or something?'

'I think I feel something coming on,' he confessed.

'Probably got what young Aylmer has. I'll get you a grain or two of aspirin. Right now. Carlotta, if you'll wait for a moment while I get everybody sorted out, then I can organise a room for you. We aren't short of space, here.'

'I can see,' she said admiringly.

'The gaffer put on a wing just before the war. Now then. Clarissa, the green room is yours, right here, and Vi, you're next to her with Fish here.'

Fish arrived, having hauled himself up by the banister one leg at a time. 'I f-feel like a bally octopus,' he said.

'He won't let anyone help him,' Violet explained. 'He's so obstinate.'

'I have to get ab-bout on my own,' said Fish. 'And the sooner I g-get rid of these w-wretched sticks the happier I shall be.'

Slowly, George's guests vanished into their rooms to change, and he was left with Carlotta, patiently waiting.

'Tell me, where does the master of the house sleep?' she asked.

'Me? Oh, I'm over the other side of the landing there with that blue door. That's always been my room. I suppose I should have moved into the great bedroom when the gaffer died, but I didn't see the point ... look, I'll put you along here if it's all right with you ...'

He led her down the corridor and opened a door. 'Here, I'll get the fire going and that'll be a start. Sheets are on the bed, I'll ask Mrs Babbage to come up and put—'

'Don't bother her, honestly. I'll do it.'

'Oh, would you? Here, now ...'

A fire was already laid, he bent and put his lighter to the balled newspaper. The flames took hold of the kindling, and he cautiously set on a few small logs.

'Feed it once it gets going,' he told her. 'Shall I see you downstairs? The noise you'll hear in a moment is the dressing gong. My grand-father got it in Cawnpore and took it with him everywhere, even the African jungle. He dressed for dinner every night in his tent. Must keep up standards, what?'

He smiled cheerfully at her and went out. A few moments later the gong boomed melodiously. As her fire began to crackle in the grate she set her suitcase on the unmade bed. She took out a smartly cut dark suit, with white blouse and hung them on hangers near the fire to air, together with a dark blue coat and court shoes.

There was a tap at the door, and her sister came in.

'Hallo, darling, isn't this fun?' she said brightly. 'You must be so pleased to see me.'

'I thought you were still in America,' said Clarissa.

'Such a bore, darling. A self-righteous spirit is abroad. They've just banned alcohol. I prefer decadent old Europe.'

'Did you get into trouble?' Clarissa said directly.

'Trouble and I are old friends,' she said breezily. 'Now look, I must get changed.'

'You're not taking any more of that stuff, are you?'

'Of course not.'

'You think it's just fun, but it isn't. It does nasty things to your head, sweetheart. I'm a doctor, I know. Makes you think strange.'

'I told you.'

Clarissa shrugged. 'Don't say *I* didn't tell *you*.'

Her sister went back out. Efficiently, Carlotta changed into a black silk evening dress, decorated it with a gold brooch, put pearls about her neck, scented herself, adjusted her hair and lipstick, and gave herself a small dusting of powder.

She glanced at the door, listened for footsteps. Then she opened her handbag and her long fingers rifled through its contents: powder compact, lipstick, cigarette case, scent, gold lighter, small silver automatic pistol. She took out a small silver snuffbox. She carefully raised the lid. Inside was a little silver spoon resting on the pale powder. She dipped it in, and raised it to first one nostril then the other, taking in the powder with a sharp, practised inhalation. Her eyes suddenly sparkled, her cheeks were flushed with colour. She slipped a silk square about her shoulders. Very carefully, she checked the combination lock of a small, oblong leather-covered case, to make sure it would not open. Satisfied, she went out into the corridor. Godfrey was emerging in evening dress from the room he was sharing with Perceval. He stepped back, smiling charmingly.

'After you.'

They meandered gently towards the stairs. 'You must be leaving school soon.'

'Upper sixth. Two more terms.'

'And then university. I hear all the young people are becoming Bolsheviks. Are you?'

'I don't know. Perceval is a red-hot socialist. Thinks it'll solve all the world's problems. I'm not so sure.'

'No?'

He grinned at her in a disarming way, but with eyes that glittered.

'No. We're extremists, our side of the family. I ask myself, does it go *far enough*?'

'I'm always interested in extremes. Your father the bishop, I suppose he believed in some rigorous form of God.'

'Only in a manner of speaking. Sexually available young women were his poison.'

'Hah!' she cried in amusement. She looked up at him with calculating eyes. 'And you, you've inherited his tastes, have you?'

'What a forward lady you are. Most refreshing.'

'I'm American.'

'Yes, so I gathered. His tastes? Again, only in a manner of speaking.

Have you heard of the love that dares not speak its name? That's what I am.'

She looked at him in frank amusement. 'And you said I was forward. You're a homo. Isn't that rather dangerous? And should you be telling me such things? You hardly know me.'

'Oh, I've heard what they . . . say about you. I feel sure you're my kind of person.'

'Is that a compliment? I shall take it as one. Do they know about this at your school?'

'Of course not. The ultimate vice. Anyhow, how shall I say it . . . relations within one's own caste are less exciting than outside.'

'Ah, the famous English class system. Working class boys?'

'For preference.'

'Why?'

'As I said. Forbidden fruit. Much more exciting. Like my father's sixteen-year-old whores. You aren't meant to do it. I told you my side of the family liked extremes. Do I shock you?'

An expression went over her face that for a moment made her seem much older. 'Honey, it takes electric voltage to shock me.'

As they came down the stairs George bounded out from the dining room and beat the polished Indian brass gong again. He beamed at them.

'Dinner,' he said proudly, 'is served.'

Soon they were all around the long, oval table, unruffling snow-white napkins as George filled the wine glasses.

'I'm moving with the times,' he claimed proudly. 'Apparently it's far too expensive to have servants waiting at table. You spend what you save on the wine, what? Fish, are you all right, there?'

Fish was folding himself onto his chair. 'Oh, y-yes. I've got rid of one stick. Dashed nuisance. Once I get my new kneecap I'll chuck the other away too.'

'A new kneecap?' Carlotta enquired.

'Why yes. Metal, don't y'know. W-Wretched Jerries shot off the one God gave me with a machine-gun. I say, George, this is a spread . . .'

A steaming tureen of mulligatawny soup arrived, and they were soon spooning it out in the soft light of the candles.

'What time do we have to be off tomorrow?' George asked.

'Palace says to be there for ten-thirty,' Violet said.

'It's an easy journey in. Forty minutes to Buck House. Allow an hour . . . let's say on the road at nine-thirty. Breakfast at eight? Sausages, bacon, eggs?'

'Is it hard work being an MP, Cromwell?' Clarissa asked, across the table.

'It didn't used to be,' Felicity said drily. 'Robert used to arrange his schedule around his cricket matches.'

'It's not so much hard work as a bit of a bore,' Cromwell confessed. 'All those bally speeches, so frightfully dreary. And getting elected! I swear it is the most ghastly process ...' He put down his spoon to emphasise what he was saying. 'A *nightmare*, I assure you. You aren't your own master, you are pushed about from place to place, making speeches, having to smile all the time, rubbing shoulders with the *polloi*, having to shake their hands, admire their babies ... It's quite loathsome ...'

'It's called democracy,' Perceval said delightedly. 'This is at last the era of the common man.'

'Well I wish it wasn't,' Cromwell said shortly.

'Well why do you *do* it?'

'It's traditional,' Freddie explained. 'The de Clares always have one of their own as MP for Windstone.'

'Mother wanted me to do it,' Cromwell said, rather plaintively.

'It's a new age,' Perceval said again, with a triumphalist edge to his voice. 'No time for dilettantes. Politics! Think it, breathe it, live it! We're going to change the world!'

'How quite ghastly, Perceval,' said Felicity. 'You seem to think that society can be shovelled about like ... wet concrete.'

'Exactly! Building! We'll create a new and just world, instead of crouching in the ruins of the old!'

'I doubt it,' she said sharply.

Small, golden, roast partridges arrived, one for every person.

'Got these myself,' George proclaimed. 'Went out last week with the dogs and got six brace before dusk.'

'Godfrey tells me he is set to go to Cambridge,' Carlotta said to Aylmer, expertly dissecting his bird. 'What are you doing?'

'Spending some time at the castle with father,' he said frankly. 'Because all my elder brothers have been killed I shall be the next Earl of Windstone. Nobody would have expected it ... I might have gone into the Guards, gone to university, perhaps served as an ADC in the Empire ... but now I have to learn how to be the Earl, to manage the great estate, there is so much to do. Apart from anything else we have to plan how to pay the taxes of the future while trying to pay the taxes of the present.'

'But your father is the Earl,' she objected. 'He is wealthy beyond dreams.'

'It's more complicated than you think,' he said with a worried frown. 'We were very rich when land meant wealth. We had a lot of land, it was valuable in itself and the crops and beasts raised a lot of money. That isn't so now. Hasn't been for perhaps forty years. Huge prairies, the outback, fast refrigerated steamships ... The real rich are the plutocrats, those in railways and mining, iron and steel, city property, chemicals, machinery ... men like Rockefeller and Mellon. You must know about all that. Wealth is liquid, not tied up in land.'

'I hadn't realised ...'

'I like Lady Bracknell's summary of land,' Violet called from the head of the table. '*The Importance of Being Earnest*? The duties expected of one during one's lifetime, and the duties exacted after one's death. Land gives one a position and prevents one from keeping it up.'

'I don't follow,' Carlotta frowned.

'The government,' Aylmer said savagely.

'What about it?'

'D-Don't talk to me about the government,' Fish muttered, and drank some wine.

'Tax. Death duties. Ten years ago – eight per cent. What right has the government to steal from you at your death anyway? But now – forty per cent! Let me put it to you this way. Had my father died in 1914 and my brothers inherited the title in turn – and been killed, as they were – then the entire estate would now be dissolved.

'That's just death duties. Income tax while you're alive. Super tax on ten thousand pounds and up. Levied on gross rather than net income. That hurts us especially because we have to spend so much on maintenance, and because people look to us for charity. Father says he's become nothing more than a bally tax collector for the government.'

'We sound like blasted convention of accountants,' said George. 'Let's talk about something more cheerful. I do think, Fish, that when you get your new gong tomorrow you'll have trouble standing up straight, you've got so many. What uniform are you wearing? The RAF?'

'D-Don't think so. The only one I had g-got a bit damaged. I'm going to put on my old Windstones one. S-Sort of do it for all the chaps who volunteered with us in fifteen.'

'Jolly good ...' Freddie said quietly.

'So tell us about the great voyage. When are you off in *Parma's Pride*?'

'In the summer. Flick's been getting her ready for me. Flick knows about sailing.'

'What about you? What do you know?'

'Not m-much,' Fish said with a disarming smile. 'But having been a soldier and an airman I'm sure I'll learn.'

Mrs Babbage, a strong country woman cleared the small plates and brought in the beef on a great salver, to cries of admiration. A silence fell over the table as they attacked their plates.

Aylmer sneezed into a large white handkerchief at about the same time as Perceval put his knife and fork together over a half-finished meal, looking rather waxy. Aylmer peered at his cousin over the linen. 'Is this a gesture of socialist solidarity with the less well off?' he enquired waspishly.

'I feel rather seedy,' Perceval muttered, 'and the point of socialism is to bring roast beef and Yorkshire pudding to everybody, young Aylmer, not just privileged swine like us. George, I'm frightfully sorry, I think I shall have to go up.'

'Take the aspirin with you,' Violet advised. 'If you wake up in the night in a sweat take the same again.'

'I will,' Perceval said slightly shakily, and rose from the table. 'Sorry to leave you.'

'We shan't be far behind you,' George promised. 'We don't want to be too late if we're to get Fish to Buck House in the morning.'

After dessert, there was just room for brandy or port as they sat back and lit up cigarettes and cigars. Slowly, they began to drift to bed.

'Fish, what the devil are you doing?' Violet said suddenly, sitting forward in her chair. Fish had hobbled to the fire; it flickered with a fresh flame.

'Burning my blasted stick,' he said triumphantly.

'You're so obstinate,' she said. 'How are you planning to waddle backwards after you see the King?'

'I shan't,' he said. 'I shall explain that the wretched Jerries have left me with only forward gears. George, that was one of the finest meals . . . by the way, my room, whose was it?'

'Young Tim's. You remember?'

'Oh yes . . . poor boy . . .'

George saw all his guests to the foot of the stairs, one by one. He went round all his rooms. In each he paused, looking about him, quietly and pulling the door to after him as he left. The kitchen was clean, still warm from the range, mingled scents of cooking and washing up hanging in the air. Mrs Babbage was gone.

Finally, he went upstairs to his own room. It was lit by the glow of his fire in the grate. He undressed in the soft red and yellow aura, hanging his evening clothes on the rack. His pyjamas were there, ready. As he reached for them a voice spoke from the bed.

'Don't bother with the jammies, George,' Carlotta said. 'I haven't.'

'What—'

'Just get in,' she insisted.

George paused for a moment, naked in the firelight, then reached for his pyjama trousers and tugged them on.

'Hallo, Carlotta,' he said, and went to sit on the edge of the bed. 'What a pleasant surprise.'

Carlotta raised herself on to one elbow, and the sheet fell away.

'George, darling, I want to make it much more pleasant than that,' she purred.

'Why, yes, of course,' he murmured. 'Tell me, did you enjoy the meal?'

'Of course. What's—'

'Like the house? You should see the grounds. One hundred and eighteen acres, give or take a pole piece or two. That's what's on the title deeds, y'know.'

'Oh?' she said, slightly warily.

'The gaffer bought the estate in ninety-three. It's important to have somewhere to live that matches one's position in society, don't you think?'

'Why of *course*,' she said, sounding enthusiastic again.

'I love the stream down by the stone bridge,' he continued. 'I've fished there from being a boy.'

'Uhuh.'

'I shan't be fishing there any more.'

'No?'

'No. In fact, nobody will. They're putting in a great concrete pipe the length of the estate; it'll go through that.'

Carlotta sat up, pulled the sheet irritably about her nakedness. 'George, what the hell are you talking about?' she demanded.

'The gaffer's dead. Just as well, really, the bank was moving to make him bankrupt. The bank owns all this, they've sold it to a property company. The business was pottering on, y'see, but the war did it such damage . . . Father was offered chances to get into things that made money from the war but he said it wasn't right to profit from death, not while so many of us were being killed . . . I'm afraid banks don't record Christian sentiment as interest on their books. In a year's time the estate will be covered in rows of semi-detached houses built for people to commute into London from, and the sewage will all flow into the concrete pipe.'

'What about this grand party?' she asked, annoyed.

'A last hooray. For the way things used to be. I have to move out in March. I'm going to live in town for my sins. I have a job, working for the royals. I shall be a kind of superior grade flunkey.'

There was silence in the bedroom. The fire spat a small, glowing cinder on to the tiles.

'I am broke,' George said quietly. 'I can say I was there on the first day on the Somme, I have a decent hammered twelve-bore my grandfather had, a Standard car, a library of books I have to move by the sixteenth of January, a volume of poetry published, and seventy-eight pounds in the bank. Oh, and a brace of pheasant hanging in the coldhouse.'

'I see.'

'I thought you should know. Now if you would still like me to get into bed, I will.'

She pushed back the sheet and climbed out. A man's dressing gown was at the end of the bed where she had left it, she picked it up and went over near the fire. The red light played over her beautiful body.

'I'd have been fucking your brains out if you hadn't made your little speech,' she said evenly. 'You could've had fun and let me know later.'

'It isn't right to take advantage of a lady,' he said, as though pointing out that the sun rose in the morning. 'Not the done thing at all.'

'Where I come from,' she said acidly, 'you profit where you can. Your father could've left you rich.'

'Ah, but you come from America. There are no gentlemen in America.'

'Gentlemen will soon be extinct. Look at you.'

'One knows how to behave,' he said mildly. 'What will the world be like if men are not courteous towards women, if the strong simply oppress the weak?'

'George,' she said exasperatedly, 'you're broke and you're talking like this? You ought to be going out and robbing a bank.'

'Oh, no,' he said, with a slight smile. 'I've always thought that if one did that you'd find your old housemaster there cashing a cheque or something. Frightfully embarrassing. One would be cut in society, end one's days as a remittance-man in Cairo. Oh, and I have a couple of good tweed suits from Jervis and Croke. Last a lifetime, they will.'

She tugged the dressing gown about herself, and went angrily to the door.

'Good night,' George said politely. 'Sleep well.'

In the dark corridor she paused outside her door, stiff with fury at the failure of her plans. She had taken some more of her little white powder before going to wait in George's room; now it rushed about her veins under the influence of her raging emotion, tipping her reason. They were all against her, she knew it. For a moment or two she thought of simply going downstairs and stealing some of the silver ornaments she had noted, and driving off. She forced herself to take some deep breaths, and think it through. She had created a plan, she would simply have to modify it, be patient, start again. She swallowed hard, and went into her room.

It smelled of cigarette smoke. Near the dimming fire, a tip glowed in the dark.

'Who's there?' she asked abruptly.

'Me,' said Godfrey. 'I thought you'd be back soon.'

'You did? What damned business is it of yours?'

'Wrong door,' Godfrey said pleasantly from the gloom. 'You went to the wrong room. George is on his uppers.'

'I *know*,' she said bitterly, 'now. Why didn't anyone mention it when we were eating and drinking down there?'

'Tut tut,' Godfrey said reprovingly. 'That wouldn't be the done thing at all. No, you should have talked to *me*.'

'Oh yes?'

'Yes. I am correct, am I not, that you are an adventuress? What in your home country would – I think – be called a woman on the make?'

'I'm what they want,' she ground out.

'I don't doubt it. What you don't have is a suitable target.'

'Are there any?' she asked gloomily. 'The way they were moaning about taxes down there you're all in the same boat.'

'Oh, no,' Godfrey said quietly. 'Oh, no. George is broke, yes. I and my brother are not wealthy. Fish is well off. Aylmer is the heir to a mighty fortune, death duties or not.'

'Cradle-snatching is noticeable.'

'Too obvious,' he agreed.

'You've left out Cromwell.'

'That's right. I've left out Cromwell. MP for Windstone. Elder son of Major-General Gervase de Clare, recently deceased.'

'He got his money?'

'Why, yes,' Godfrey said smoothly.

'What's he like?' she said intently.

'Crom? Decent sort of cove. Bit of a mummy's boy. Led a sheltered life, don't you know.'

'Weak?'

'Oh, yes. He's not Fish. Fish's a very different chap. At the end of the day, Fish is . . . *dangerous.*'

'He has enough of those medals. Cromwell, is he a ladies' man?'

'Nooo . . . I wouldn't say he has a lot of experience with . . . *younger* women,' Godfrey said judiciously. 'I wouldn't display – how shall I put it? – the full range of your expertise to begin with.'

'Softly, softly, catchee monkey,' she said with a savage note of anticipation in her voice.

'Why yes,' Godfrey said imperturbably. 'I couldn't have put it better myself.'

He pulled at his cigarette, and tossed the stub into the grate.

'Why are you doing this?' she asked.

'Oh, in *our* kind of world, allies are always useful, don't you think? Look, I must be going. I have to travel back to the frightful St God's tomorrow.'

'I'll let you know how I get on,' she said.

'I'll know,' he said. 'We're the de Clares. We get to hear everything.'

He went out, and back into his own room. He stood by the door for a moment or two. Outside, a floorboard creaked softly. He put back his head and laughed silently in the darkness.

A thin line of light showed below the door. She tapped softly, and pushed it open, slipping inside. Cromwell was sitting at a table near the bed, reading. He was dressed in pyjamas and a striped dressing gown.

'Oh, hallo,' he said pleasantly, rising to his feet. 'Can I help?'

'Am I interrupting you?' she asked. She held the collar of her dressing gown up, closing it demurely about her throat.

'No, no. I was just reading a detective story. I like a chapter or two of a good mystery before bed.'

'Do you?' she said enthusiastically. 'So do I. I was trying to read myself, but I got so cold. There's a terrible draught in my room.'

'Oh, I say . . .'

'I couldn't sit in your bed and get warm, could I?'

'Why, of course,' Cromwell said courteously. 'You hop in and I'll finish my chapter.'

'You're so kind.'

She slipped off the dressing gown and got quickly into the bed in her night-dress, showing a brief glimpse of her long legs. She sat up, and rubbed herself. Then she smiled at him.

'I'll bet the butler did it.'

'Eh, what? Oh, yes. Jolly good. No, in fact, I think it's Lord Chendelshea's long-lost cousin, Archie. Definitely seems to be a frightful bounder.'

'I'm still freezing,' she said plaintively. 'Come and read next to me. We can be like brother and sister and warm each other up.'

'Do you think we should?' he said doubtfully. 'My mother once found me in bed with my cousin Violet when I was about ten, she made a frightful fuss.'

'We aren't ten,' she pointed out.

'Eh? No, I suppose not. Well, why not, eh?'

'Why not,' she agreed patiently.

Cromwell took off his dressing gown, and came over with his book. He climbed into the bed next to her.

'I say, you're warm as toast,' he said.

She slithered herself next to him.

'See how quickly it works,' she murmured.

Violet came awake suddenly. Her room was dark, only the faint glow of the embers of the fire lighting it at all. What had woken her? Some cry of pleasure echoed in her ears. It was cold in the bedroom, she could feel it creeping about her ears. She tugged the bedclothes around her head and went back to sleep.

She was awake. It was pitch black. What was it? She sat bolt upright in bed. It came again, a strangled cry from the room next door. Throwing the sheets back she fumbled for her torch in the darkness, found it, splashed a pool of light in front of her and hurried to the connecting door.

In his bed, Fish thrashed desperately. Putting the torch on the chair she grabbed hold of him.

'Fish! Fish, it's me!'

Terrified eyes suddenly snapped open in a face like chalk, streaming with sweat.

'He's dead, can't you see? The bastard blew his head off—'

'I'm here Fish. Violet. You're having a dream.'

He held her tight with shaking hands, the breath sobbing in his throat. 'Oh, God . . .'

He was drenched, his pyjamas sodden with sweat.

'Let's get you changed, Fish, darling,' she said gently, and he allowed himself to be taken out of bed and sat in the chair by the fire, with its high wings. She tossed a few split logs on to the embers of the fire, and the dry splinters began to crackle as they caught.

'G-Give me a Scotch, Vi,' he said quietly. In the gathering light of the fire she poured three fingers into a tumbler from the bottle, and topped it at the tap. His suitcase lay open on a stand. She gave him his drink and took some fresh pyjamas out.

'Stand up,' she ordered. He did so, obedient as a child, and she began to undress him.

'It was young Tim, Vi,' he said. 'This used to be his room. He got caught out in no-man's land one night by a machine-gun burst. R-Reconnaissance, we were learning the ground.'

She took off his top, and rubbed him with a towel. His body was marked as though he had been whipped with a red-hot iron. Massive dents and slashes showed in the brightening flames.

'We thought he was dead, only the next morning we heard him crying out. Then we saw him, he was crawling in. The machine-gun had smashed his leg. He was dragging himself to the lines, one hand at a time.'

She took off his trousers, and dried him. The surgeon's knife had made geometric lines amidst the torn, scarred flesh. His knee was concave where the cap had been.

'He made it to the lane in the wire and the sniper blew his head off. George got his brains all over his face.'

She did up the cord of the trousers and he took a swallow of his drink.

'Freddie went out and killed him. Don't know why we bothered. We should've stonked him with artillery. W-We hadn't realised people got w-wiped out by the battalion, back then.'

'Do you want to get back into bed, darling? It's a big day, tomorrow – today, now, I suppose.'

'I think I'll sit by the fire, Vi.'

'Are you sure?'

'I'm t-too frightened to go back to sleep, Vi,' he said, in a small, sad voice. 'The d-dead are w-waiting for me.'

'I'll sit with you, then,' she said. There was another chair there; she fetched their dressing gowns and they sat quiet together. After a while he noticed she had gone to sleep. He got up stiffly and pulled the blankets off his bed, putting them around her.

When she awoke in the dawn, he was still sitting there, staring out of the window.

'Vi! Vi, can you come?'

She answered the tap and call at her door. It was Godfrey.

'What is it?'

'Take a peer at Perceval,' he said. He seemed vaguely amused. 'He looks like a hamster.'

Watery-eyed and flushed, Perceval lay miserably in bed, his face swollen up as though stung by a hiveful of bees.

'Mumps,' Violet said. 'You have mumps, Perceval. You'll have to stay in and keep warm. Take plenty to drink. I'll get you some aspirin.'

'Aylmer's not looking too good either,' said Godfrey.

'I'm all shivery,' he complained, as Violet came into his room. 'I keep going hot and cold.'

'Maybe you've got mumps too.'

'I think I've had it.'

'I'll get the doctor to come round. He's got to see Perceval as well.'

As she went down the corridor she passed Carlotta's room. On an impulse, she tapped on the door. There was no reply. She opened it. A suitcase stood neatly closed on the bed, next to a set of crisp, starched sheets from the laundry. She looked thoughtfully at them for a moment, and then went back out, closing the door behind her. There was a smell of frying sausages and bacon in the air; she could hear cheerful voices coming from the kitchen.

Aylmer heard the crunching of feet over the gravel below, heard their voices and car doors clunking shut. With an effort, he pushed hismelf up and got out of bed. He went to the window, and watched as the cars went away over the old stone bridge towards the village, and London, their exhaust pipes steaming white in the frost.

He felt short of breath, and rather dizzy. He made himself walk to the door, and down the corridor. In his room, Perceval was lying in bed looking at the ceiling from watering eyes. His face was very swollen, his breath coming in pants.

'You all right?'

'No,' Perceval gasped. 'My balls ache like hell. Feel like some bugger's got them on a hob.'

'You made everybody else's balls ache last night with your socialist rubbish,' Aylmer said unsympathetically. 'It's probably justice.' A fresh spasm of shivering swept over him.

'I don't feel very clever myself,' he said. 'I hope the bally doctor gets here soon.'

Godfrey got out of the taxi, stared expressionlessly at the forbidding red brick of St Goderick's. Its inmates were scurring in and out, small boys in black and white.

'Smithers,' his voice cracked, and a boy hurried towards him, fear in his face. He paid the cabman.

'My things,' he ordered. 'Put them in my study and make tea.'

'Yes, de Clare,' the youth said quickly, and began to gather up the belongings.

'Careful with those canes,' said Godfrey with a pleasant menace. 'Unless you want them tried out on your backside.'

He selected one, the wand of office, and strolled into the building. A fire was burning in the grate of the great hall, ineffectually attempting to combat the icy air. He paused to look up at the gold-lettered boards. 'Our Glorious Dead', the biggest was headed, in bright fresh capitals.

They had put up Starnley's name at last. Godfrey approved. A bit of buggery shouldn't stand in the way of acknowledgement of a man's death. Caught the blast of a potato-masher grenade in a trench near Ypres and bled to death by the time they found him.

'Hallo, de Clare.'

He turned. It was Worsley, his own cane tucked under his arm.

'Hallo, Worsley. Good hol?'

'Not bad. You?'

'Rather good, actually. I did something quite disgusting in London, I must tell you about it.'

Worsley was looking intently at him. 'Cromer isn't coming back,' he said.

'No?' Godfrey drawled. 'Dear old St God's too much for him?'

'So it would seem.'

'I also went to the Matisse exhibition. Now that wasn't disgusting at all. The *fauves*—'

'He hanged himself, de Clare.'

Godfrey stayed very, very still, staring over Worsley's shoulder.

'He did?'

'Yes.'

'How very silly of him.'

All about him, the boys seemed to be moving as though in glue. He did not look at Worsley.

'He say why?'

'Why?'

'Yes, damn you,' Godfrey hissed. 'Did he leave a note?'

'What would it have said, I wonder?' Worsley mused. 'Enough to have you strapped to the flogging bench, I fancy.'

A sheen of sweat suddenly broke over Godfrey's face. He smiled. He had the sensation of galloping at full speed, just missing a branch as the horse jumped.

'Never said a word, eh . . . silly boy,' he said. 'Just strung himself up, did he?'

'That's it. Tied a curtain cord to the cistern pipe and stepped off the seat.'

'They should investigate the vicar,' Godfrey said, beginning to walk to his study. 'Didn't he live with a vicar? These parsons are all pederasts. Damn but it's cold, Worsley. Let's go and beat the junior dorm to warm ourselves up. Then I *must* tell you about the Matisse exhibition . . .'

The big car turned in at the driveway, rolled over the old stone bridge. As the house came into view Violet sat forward, stiff and suddenly worried.

'Freddie, look!'

Freddie turned the wheel, pulling up by the white-painted ambulance, with its great red crosses on the side. A nurse was just closing the rear door. Violet jumped out, ran over to her.

The second car drew up just as the ambulance was pulling away. George poked his head out anxiously.

'I say, what's up?'

'It's Aylmer,' Violet said, worry creasing her face. She twisted one of her smart dark-blue gloves nervously. 'Doctor Bates was delayed getting here. Aylmer's got Spanish flu. They're taking him in with pneumonia.'

31

Countess of Windstone

Windstone, 1919

She came down the narrow, grey-paved street, a little old lady in a fawn mackintosh, an oiled-cloth shopping bag slung over one arm, a scarf tied about her white hair. She moved in a jerky, frenetic manner, her eyes darted about the road and its inhabitants; she muttered to herself in an angry, desperate fashion as she went along. Nobody took any notice of her. She looked what she was, a mad old woman, and the war had created plenty like her. They were no novelty to anybody, any more than the blind man on the corner with his tray of matches and bootlaces, or the one out in the square with a medal bar but no legs, who said it made it easier to draw his pictures with broken chalk – he didn't need to bend down, no more.

There were no cars in the narrow lane, they did not penetrate that part of the town. Nevertheless, it was an important little street: it held a place with a sign of three orbs, there since the eighteenth century, and it was up the narrow curving wooden stairway, rather dark and certainly dirty, that the old woman darted, her feet hurrying and scraping on the treads.

She pushed open a door that had once been white and which sagged rather on its hinges. Beyond it was a row of thin doors, all next to each other, and it was through one of these that she went. Inside it was like a cupboard, only open at the front where she faced, with a worn wood counter. She could hear a woman's voice in the next cubicle, a pleading sound, a man's voice in reply, cold, indifferent. There was a chink of money, a few coins, and he appeared, a middle-aged man in a brown overall carrying a man's suit on a hanger. As he saw the old woman a chill glint came into the back of his eyes. He put a brown luggage label on the suit and hung it up on a rail next to a row of others: demob suits in grade-three cloth, but serviceable, and the woman would be back for it when her husband next tried for a job only she would have to pay 8d instead of the sixpence she had received.

'Can I help you?' he asked.

The old woman had it ready; she thrust a silver tray over the counter.

He took it away into his little office, where he kept his jeweller's glass and scales, and she shifted from one foot to the other in her impatience as he examined the hallmarks.

'How much do you want?' he asked, when he returned.

'Five pounds.'

It was a lot, when a working man might take home six and sixpence at the end of the week, but the tray was solid silver. The Rajah of Mysore, who had given it as a gift, was not aware of the existence of plating.

'No.'

'*I must have five pounds!*'

The pawnbroker stared at her impassively, silently, a man who knew all about people's desperations.

'*Here then,*' she said, her hand darting into the shopping bag. She pulled out a gold ring set with small green emeralds, and this too he took away to examine. When he came back he passed over a white Bradbury note. She snatched it from his hand, and was gone, only her feet clattering on the stair.

Now she hurried, as quickly as her feet would carry her. The streets were all alike – narrow, grey-paved – but she knew her way. At a door she stopped, knocked upon it. A woman of gypsy appearance answered it, a shawl about her shoulders.

'Come in, dear, come in,' she said. 'We were expecting you . . .'

Lady Maud, Countess of Windstone, was not accustomed to being called 'dear' by anyone, but she seemed not to notice, only hurrying inside, and sitting down at a round table in a darkened room.

'I'm not too late, am I?' she asked anxiously. She held up the five-pound note and the woman took it, tucking it away inside her clothing with a practised movement.

'Of course not, dear, the spirits are always there, it's just a question of whether they'll come . . .'

'Oh, I do hope so . . .' Maud said desperately, twisting her fingers with their bitten nails.

'Let's see, shall we dear?' the woman said placatingly, and sat down on the other side of the table. She closed her eyes, her hands spread out flat.

'Is anyone there?' she called out. 'It's Maud who's asking . . . is there anyone there for Maud . . .'

There was a silence in the room.

'Will anyone come through for Maud . . .'

Maud's face was twitching, some saliva had escaped her mouth and was trickling down her chin.

'*Pleaase* . . .'

From somewhere there came a faint sound as of tiny bells ringing.

'Who's there?' the woman demanded confidently.

'Robert . . .' said a deep voice. 'I am Maud's son Robert . . .'

Maud raised up her hands into the air, her face transformed with joy.

'Rob, Robbie darling . . . are you well?'

'I am well, Mother,' said the voice.

'Are you all there?' she cried out.

'Not Charlie . . . not today . . . Henry is here, Henry and now Aylmer . . .'

'Just say the word and I will come!' the old lady shrieked. 'Let me join you . . .'

'No, Mother,' said the deep voice. It paused for a second, seeming to clear its throat. 'No, Mother, do not come until you are called . . .'

'Aylmer, are you there, darling?' she howled.

There was a pause and then a voice spoke, a voice quite like the first voice. 'I am here, mother, I feel no pain . . .'

Lady Maud had begun to sob, tears pouring down her ravaged cheeks. 'I so want to be with you,' she wailed, 'please tell me to come . . .'

The voice began to fade away. 'Only when it is time . . .'

'Don't go! Don't go darlings!' she shrieked.

The gypsy woman opened her eyes, looked at the demented, weeping creature opposite her.

'Did they come for you, dear?' she asked brightly.

She watched with cold eyes as Lady Maud staggered away down the street, and went back into the room. She crossed it, pulled back a curtain and jerked open a hidden door, one with holes drilled into its surface. Behind it a man sat in a chair, taking beer from a bottle.

'You lay off the drink until she's gone next time!' she shouted furiously. 'You think I didn't hear you belch?'

'The old bitch don't notice nothing,' the man said surlily. 'She give you the money?'

'She's coming back tomorrow,' the woman said in satisfaction. 'Always remember, don't have them all there at once.'

'What if the old cow knocks herself off? My gawd, she's crying out to get to the other side all the time.'

'Well she ain't going yet. She must have thousands in that place of hers . . .'

London

Carlotta heard the wheezy rattle of the taxicab downstairs, the thud of its door, Cromwell's distinctive voice as he paid the driver. She had time to check herself in the mirror and dab fresh perfume behind her ears as his steps came up the stairs and the cab crunched its gears and went off into Pimlico.

She flung open the door before he could knock on it, and smiled dazzlingly.

'Darling!'

'Hallo, my love,' Cromwell said. He had a briefcase in one hand and a bouquet of flowers in the other. She kept the smile fixed to her face. Cromwell was predictable. Flowers normally meant he was about to let her down.

'Come in, darling Scotch?'

'Oh, God, yes. What a day. Half of it spent listening to Balfour and LlG waffling. LlG made a rotten speech. Then I had to serve on the committee, and on top of that I'm supposed to make a speech next week.'

'That's marvellous!'

'No, it isn't,' he said gloomily, sinking into a chair. 'Oh, thank you, darling, I don't know what I'd do without you and a drink at the end of it all. *I* don't want to make any bally speech, but Mother says I must. Now that poor Aylmer . . . well, I shall be Earl when Uncle dies, and Mother says I must make my mark in politics . . .'

'Must you?' She sat on the arm of her chair so that he could see her long legs under her charleston dress.

'Well, I suppose so, dash it,' he said feebly. 'We de Clares have always been involved in politics, we always have at least someone there. That's how I got my name . . .'

'How is your mother?'

'Still in the clinic . . .'

'Strange, isn't it? She lives, Aylmer dies. You'd have thought it would be the other way around.'

'Oh, don't . . . I couldn't bear the thought of Mama dying, she's been so good to me . . .'

You're a drip, Cromwell, she thought viciously.

The flowers would wilt. She kept the little flat warm against the ghastly English weather. At a guess, the weekend down on the coast was off. Cromwell sucked on his drink mournfully. She concealed her irritation and reached for one of her cigarettes to calm her down. She lit it, and inhaled gratefully. Out of obsessive habit she checked the combination lock on her special oblong leather case. It was shut. She went over to the sink in the little kitchen and his eyes followed her like a hound.

'I say, that's that funny tobacco, what?'

'Special Russian,' she agreed. The reefer was soothing her. She began to sort out the flowers. They were good quality, glasshouse grown. Cromwell was generous, he would give her anything she wanted – when he was able to.

With her back to him she could feel his eyes caressing her figure. She did her dance exercises religiously.

'Cromwell, he was some kind of great general, wasn't he?'

The de Clares, she knew, had a great store of history in their heads, and never minded displaying it.

'Oh, absolutely! More than just a general. He was a great *man*. One of the greatest men who has ever lived.'

'You don't say?'

'Oh, yes,' he said sincerely. 'If it wasn't for him, the world would be a very different place. He broke the old order, he and his kind, they smashed it all up, let in light and air, let new ideas flourish.'

'Uhuh?' she said, encouragingly.

'We did it, you see, we English. The old order was the order of Rome, it was like . . . those fossils that scientists dig up, ancient extinct creatures whose bones have turned into rock, well all countries were like that, just as immovable and lifeless and cruel as that. No new ideas. The sun going round the earth. The earth flat. God's vicar on earth the Pope. And if you disagreed with them they simply trussed you up with a bundle of logs and set fire to you. It'd still be that way, you know, if it hadn't been for we English. And my namesake.'

She carried the vase in and set it on the table.

'The English, the English,' she said, half-mockingly. 'You think you're God's people.'

'Oh, we are,' he said, quite seriously. 'Nobody else could have made the world like it is except us. We're an island, for a start. Evil can't cross running water, did you know that? And we have miles and miles of running water, it's called the English Channel.'

'Are you serious?'

'Dash it, yes! You Americans ought to be grateful to us – we made you the way you are. We've always loathed what went on in Europe, and we made America, not the Frogs or the Boche or the Pope, so you be jolly thankful.'

'President Lincoln is suitably grateful,' she said.

'So he should be.'

'And you English, what else did you invent, apart from America?'

'Everything,' he said smugly. 'Cricket, tennis, polo, golf, rugger and baseball, for a start.'

'You did not so invent baseball.'

'We did. It is a game played by small girls called rounders.'

'Oh, ho. Anything else?'

'I told you, everything,' he said, quite serious again. 'Most of it in a small church in Putney.'

'Now I know you're joking. These flowers are fine, by the way.'

'Thanks. Honestly. The Church of St Mary, Putney. One of my ancestors was there. He was one of Cromwell's young colonels, he became Earl Henry. The war had been won, the New Model Army had smashed the armies of King Charles. The country was theirs. They met to decide how they should arrange things from then on. It was quite an occasion. Just forty of them standing and sitting about the bare communion table for a couple of weeks. We have Earl Henry's account of it, in the library at the castle. It was a General Council, and they had the generals like Cromwell and Ireton, colonels like Henry – and Rainborough, who had risen from humble origins in the war. There were some ordinary soldiers, there were some civilians – Levellers, they called themselves. We'd probably call them Bolsheviks now. Between them all they invented modern society: you name it, old girl, democracy, communism, republicanism, socialism, free medical treatment for all – though we're still waiting for that one – the new learning in the sciences, printing, books, newspapers, modern finance like we have in the City of London. If Cromwell had lived a little longer we'd have had the industrial revolution beginning in about seventeen hundred . . . I tell you he was a great, great man.'

He stared across the room, lost in his thoughts for a moment, and then sighed. 'I sometimes wish they hadn't named me after him. It's a great responsibility, they expect you to live up to him . . .'

She sat back down on the arm of the chair and stretched out her long legs in front of her.

'So, darling, are we on for this weekend?'

'Something's come up . . .' he said weakly, shifting uneasily in his chair. 'Got an invitation to stay with the Dugdales. Mother thinks it's a good idea. Help me along in the House.'

'Of course,' she said smoothly. 'Contacts are useful. What time do we leave?'

'But you see, Carlotta, darling . . .' he bleated. 'It's difficult . . .'

The reefer had calmed her down, her frustration had left her. She put her plan into motion.

'You're worried about what your mother will think,' she said in a friendly fashion.

'Well yes,' he admitted, relieved. 'Mother is frightfully strong willed, y'know.'

'Fish doesn't do what she wants,' she pointed out.

'She and Fish don't *talk* . . . and anyway, nobody can make Fish do what he doesn't want to, except Vi. But Mother counts on me, y'see. I'm all she's got . . .'

'There's nothing like a mother's smile, darling. But seriously, you need to strike a blow for freedom here. They won't respect you if you're just a mummy's boy, you know.'

'I know,' he said feebly. 'But . . .'

'Just think of the respect you'd get at the Dugdales if you turn up with a hot number like me on your arm. Say hey, they'll say. Cromwell's a stallion!'

'Oh, I say . . .'

'I'll tell you what you're going to do,' she said, with ruthless charm. 'You're going to make two telephone calls. One to the Dugdales, inviting me as well. Then one to the Ritz, booking a table for dinner and a room. We're going to have one heck of a dinner and then you're going to take me upstairs and make me cry out with ecstasy.'

'I am?' he goggled.

'I told you, you're a stallion. And I'm even going to make it easy for you.'

He looked at her, wide-eyed. 'How?'

'With something made in America. Not England.'

'What is it?'

She got off the arm of the chair and went to her handbag. She opened it, and her fingers rifled through the contents. A small shiny automatic pistol slid out onto the table.

'Oh, I say. I didn't know you had a little gun.'

She picked it up, and popped it back into the bag.

'It's a pretty little thing. Beretta thirty-two.'

'Why do you have it?'

'Oh, a girl has to be able to protect herself, Crom darling. There are people out there waiting to get you, you know.'

'I understand!' he laughed like a donkey braying. 'Lloyd George is one of them!'

'Just waiting to get you,' she repeated. 'I *know* . . .'

She took out her small silver box, and opened it.

'What is it?' he asked, intrigued.

'American magic powder. It gives you confidence. That's all you lack, Crom. A bit of confidence.'

'Oh, I do,' he agreed. 'Always been a bit backward in coming forward. But what do you do with the . . . powder?'

'It's a kind of snuff,' she explained. 'Look, I'll show you.'

She took the little silver spoon from the top and scooped up some of the white granules with it.

'You do it like this.'

She held the spoon up to one nostril and inhaled sharply, with a snort. She blinked away a tear and did it again. God, that was good. She felt the pleasure rush through her. Marvellous. She'd even be able to cry out in ecstasy, like that.

'Here,' she said. 'You try.'

Gingerly, he filled the spoon and she helped him put it next to his nostril.

'Now' she commanded.

He inhaled nervously.

'Again. There's a bit left.'

His eyes goggled, his face was suddenly flushed. He ripped in air, and the white powder vanished up his nose.

'Now the other. That's it, you've got the hang of it . . .'

'By golly!' he trumpeted. 'That's marvellous. God, I feel like a new man.'

'I told you,' she purred. 'Now . . .'

'Yes, yes,' he said masterfully. 'The Dugdales . . . I'll ask if I can bring my girlfriend . . .'

'Fiancée,' she said. 'Fiancée sounds so much better.'

'Oh, I say!' he chortled. 'We are a couple of gay dogs, aren't we?'

He picked up the telephone, and dialled. Standing behind him she slipped her hand round to his fly. He was already stiff, she massaged him gently.

'Hallo? Fruity? Yes, Crom here. Mind if I bring my fiancée? Eh? Didn't know I had one, eh? Dark horses, what? Yes, we'll see you then.'

'Now the Ritz, darling,' she murmured. She slid lightly to her knees, took him in her mouth. Countess of Windstone. The very thought made her moan with ecstasy. Cromwell gasped – she felt him shudder, jerking in her mouth.

Countess of Windstone. She couldn't wait.

Windstone Castle

Lord de Clare, Earl of Windstone, took his twelve-bore from the rack in the gunroom. From somewhere in the castle a grandfather clock boomed out the time. It was midnight. He took a handful of red cartridges from a drawer, slipped two into the breech and the rest into his pocket and went out. He padded along his great corridors in the half-light of the moon filtering through the long, tall windows, until he came to his wide, airy entrance hall with its high double doors, and its sweeping grand staircase.

Then he sat down in a chair, hidden away in the shadows next to the enamel plate of lighting switches. He thought of himself as a custodian, as of one who kept in trust the possessions and acquisitions of his ancestors for those who were to come, and he had noticed that things were going missing. Just here, and there, little and not so little trinkets, ornaments and valuables were vanishing. Somebody, it was clear, was stealing them. The Earl, trained as a soldier and a hunter, had decided to trap the thief. He had set himself a vigil every night. So far he had had no luck, but he was a patient man. He sat silently in the darkness, his shotgun resting upon his knee.

The clock boomed once. One o'clock.

The Earl yawned. He wished he could light a cigar, but the aroma would give him away.

Up above, a board creaked.

He stiffened in his chair, took a firm grip of his weapon. Very carefully, he craned his neck. There. In the pale moonlight somebody was stealing along the upper floor.

With a roar of righteous anger, he swept his hand down the array of switches, and the whole atrium burst into blazing white light. Smoothly and professionally he whipped the shotgun up to his shoulder, and found himself staring down the barrels at his wife.

Her face contorted in madness, she was carrying a small wooden, brass-bound chest. Inside it, he knew, was priceless crystal.

'*Maud*!' he bellowed. 'What the devil do y'think you're up to?'

She teetered at the head of the staircase, her old dressing gown trailing on the ground.

'You shan't keep them from me!' she shrieked.

The old woman lost her balance, her gown tangling itself about her ankles. She tripped, stumbled, dropped the crystal and tried to catch it. She fell in a screeching tumble down and round the curve of the great staircase.

32

It's All a Bit Unusual

York House, St James's Palace

George marched down the corridor. He came to a tall door, left slightly ajar, and knocked on it.

'Enter.'

He pushed open the door. As he stepped forward a book fell some eight feet downwards and struck him on the head. A small figure waiting on the sofa burst into peals of laughter. Gritting his teeth against the sudden pain George put back his head and laughed too. He bent and picked up the book, a bound volume of the *History of the Roman Empire*.

Edward, Prince of Wales wiped his eyes.

'Jolly good sir,' said George. 'Catches me by surprise every time.'

Edward got up. 'Sorry to hear about Lady Maud.'

George put the book down on a table as the Prince went to a Queen Anne desk.

'We were all very sad,' George said. 'We shall miss her very much. I have to say that her last days were very . . . unhappy.'

'Lost her boys, didn't she?'

'Yes. Three in the war, and then the youngest, of Spanish influenza.'

'Too bad . . . know much about Wales, George?'

'Very little, sir.'

The Prince took a Coutts cheque book from a drawer and began to write.

'I have to go on a tour there. I suppose I shall have to ask LlG.' He signed the cheque, and gave it to George.

'There you are. Sorry you've been a bit embarrassed. You'll get your place organised now?'

'Thank you, sir. Yes, I'll go down and sign the lease today.'

Edward lit himself a cigarette. 'Good show. A man's got to have his own place. That's why I moved out of the pile along the road.

Mind, neither of us will be here for very long later in the year. The word is I'm to embark on some great tours of the Empire. Canada, India, Australia, South Africa ... We want to present the throne as a binding point for our heritage of common aims and ideals, shared equally by all sections, parties and nations within the Empire.'

'Excellent, sir. An inspired choice.'

'I hope so ... I wish my darling Freda could come too, but they don't think it's a good idea. Just because she's married!' Edward said, slightly petulantly. Then he brightened. 'Lord Louis is coming, anyway, he's a good sport. You know him?'

'Lord Battenberg's boy?'

'Don't be so damned tactless! We got rid of the Boche names. Mind, I sometimes wonder why, don't you? All the blood in our veins is as German as the Rhine ... No, Dickie's Mountbatten. Don't forget it or he'll get frightfully cross with you; his father got booted out of the Admiralty at the beginning of the war for being too German. So tell me, what's your new place like?'

'A flat, sir. In Kensington. Rambling sort of thing, but I need a bit of room. Not used to small places. Like to have guests to stay.'

'Jolly good. Lady Maud, she was very fond of her sons, I take it. She bring them up then?'

'Yes, I believe so, sir. She didn't like nannies. The de Clares are a close family – all of us.'

'I say. What a thing. Never saw much of my parents when I was young. Busy job, you see. I remember waiting with my brother Bertie when they came back once and he didn't recognise our mother. I suppose she had been away a while. Yes. I was brought up by nannies. Were you?'

'No, sir. Though our house parlourmaid looked after us if my parents were away.'

'She pinch you?'

'Not that I remember, sir.'

'No. Dashed odd thing, I remember; I was small, of course, and my nanny used to pinch me before showing me to my mother. I used to bawl, of course. Nothing my mother hated more than a bawling child so back I would go, and then she'd cuddle me to make me stop howling. The nanny, that is. Not my mother. No. Dashed odd, wouldn't you say?'

'I would, sir.'

'Oh, well. Ever been to a whorehouse, George?'

'Not recently, sir. Like ... most of us, I suppose I was taken to one by some more experienced friends when they considered I

had remained ignorant long enough. In more recent times I have
been fortunate enough to enjoy the company of similarly inclined
girlfriends.'

'Oh, yes! I love the ladies, don't you? In fact I love them so much
I always like to have more than one on the go, if you know what
I mean!' Edward laughed uproariously. 'Freda's such a good sport.
She knows I love her to death . . . it's only harmless, having a bit of
extra fun . . .'

Freda Dudley Ward was clearly extremely tolerant, thought George,
but said nothing.

The Prince eyed him surreptitiously through his cigarette smoke.

'Tell me, George, what do the others do?' he asked.

'Others?'

'Yes . . . poofs, you know.'

'Homos? I . . . really don't know, sir. It's against the law.'

'I know it's against the law. But it obviously goes on. People get
arrested in the park out there at night, don't they? Men together.'

'So I believe.'

'It's Prince George. You know, my youngest brother. Can't seem
to make up his mind. Men or women, you know.'

'Oh. No, I didn't sir.'

'Just between you and me, now.'

'Of course.'

'Can't have a prince getting arrested in Green Park, what? Mother
would have a fit.'

George could barely imagine what Queen Mary would think.

'Find out, eh?'

'You want . . . someone obliging? Some man.'

'A young man, yes. In fact, probably more than one. Discreet,
what? There must be a . . . what's the word I'm looking for, where
these people congregate?'

'A *milieu*?'

'Yes.'

'Paid, you mean, sir.'

Prince Edward looked at him with suddenly cold eyes. 'Of course
I mean paid. You pay, you get. It is understood by both sides. I
wouldn't want any of it getting out. I had a little trouble with
a French whore when I was George's age. Some letters . . . my
equerry went along to her, took a couple of rough gendarmes with
him, made it clear what would happen to her if she didn't close her
mouth.' He laughed, with a braying sound. 'I think the gendarmes
amused themselves. She did what she was told.'

He stubbed out his cigarette. 'Find out about it will you, George?' he said languidly. 'And, oh, he might want to borrow your flat some time.'

'Very good, sir.'

On leaving the palace, George took his cheque down to the bank. He signed his lease and went back home to the country, driving past the site where the builders were piling up materials, putting up their cement plant. The removal men were coming in the morning. He sat down at his desk, took out paper, and began to write.

> Dear Godfrey,
>   I was so pleased to hear that you have got into Cambridge. I am myself moving house, as you know, which is why you will see the London address above.
>   Well, I certainly am getting to do some strange things in this job. I wonder if you can help me? There is something I have to find out about which is taking me somewhat out of my depth, but not, perhaps, if I understand you correctly, out of yours.
>   It is like this . . .

Carlotta sat at her dressing table. She had her little chrome-plated pistol on a napkin in front of her. It had flat mother-of-pearl handles each side of the butt. She pressed the catch and the small oblong magazine popped out. She tugged at it with her long nails and it slid smoothly free. She pulled the cocking mechanism as she had been taught and it obediently spat out the bullet in the breech.

From the bathroom she could hear sounds of splashing. She took all the bullets out: short, fat, deadly little rounds of death, tipped with lead domes, felt them heavy like marbles in her hand. Then she put them all back, slid the magazine into the butt, cocked it so that a round was in the breech. She held it up, peered down the barrel at her reflection in the mirror. It would be nice, she thought, to kill somebody she really hated. Yes, it would really be so very nice. Bang. A scream. Blood and that hateful person thrashing in agony on the floor.

Bang, bang, in fact.

She held up the little gun, lost in her dream, her breath quickening with excitement.

Bam bam bam bam.

'I say, old girl, what are you doing?'

It was Cromwell, out of the bathroom. She carefully put her pistol down.

'Just practising,' she said carefully.

'It isn't a war, dash it,' he complained.

'You never know when you might need it,' she said, quite certainly. 'I told you, there are people out there trying to harm me.'

'Oh, honestly,' he said, rather irritably. 'Who?'

'People . . .' she said quietly, darkly. 'People look at you, and you know . . . you mark them down . . . enemies . . .'

He half-laughed, twisting his head about, as though his neck were very stiff.

'Name one.'

'Violet,' she said, with a malevolent edge to her voice. 'She hates me.'

'Dear old Vi? Don't be silly.'

'I saw the way she looked at me, at George's house. I knew then . . .'

'What?' he said incredulously. 'Vi's a really good sport.'

Carlotta turned to look at him. He was sitting on the sofa, moving about, first shifting one foot then the other, sitting back, sitting up. His eyes were feverishly bright.

'I can't settle to anything,' he complained. 'I'm so . . . *tight*. My skin feels like scratchy leather, I'm hot, then I'm cold . . . that bath didn't do a bit of good . . .'

'You had a lot of my magic powder over the weekend,' she observed.

'Yes, but I *need* it, darling,' he said, suddenly anxious. 'I don't know what I'd do without—'

'Of course,' she said soothingly. She got up, and stood behind him.

'Do you want mama to make it better?' she asked softly. 'Shall I take the nasty feeling away . . .'

'Yes, yes . . .' he said querulously, like a small sick boy.

'Let mama get the medicine then.'

She went over to the wardrobe, took out her small, oblong, leather-covered case, put it on the table, and carefully adjusted the circular combination locks. When it was done she pressed the catches, and they sprang up. She opened the case, and sorted through the various packages and items inside.

'What's in there?'

'Oh, this is where mama keeps her very best things,' she said. She poured a little powder into a spoon, put a candle on the table, lit it. She had water, a small bottle of medicinal alcohol, cotton wool.

'Oh, I say. Is that a syringe? I do so hate injections.'

'This won't hurt a bit,' she assured him. 'And it'll make you feel much better.'

Expertly, she melted the powder in the spoon, sucked the liquid up with the needle into the syringe. She flicked it for air bubbles.

'Give me your arm,' she ordered. She wiped his shoulder with an alcohol dab, and quickly slid the needle into his skin. She carefully pressed down the plunger until it was home, and rubbed the flesh.

'There.' She watched him with practised eyes. 'How does that feel?'

'Oh,' he said, his voice filled with relief. 'Oh, that's much better . . . oh, it's really wonderful . . .'

'Sit back,' she suggested.

He did as she bid, his eyes goggling with the sudden change in his feelings.

'See, mama *knows*,' she said softly. 'Mama knows how to look after you . . .'

'Oh, yes . . .'

'We must get married soon, Crom,' she said quietly by his ear. Traces of alarm went over his face.

'Eh? But dash it, what will Mother say?' he bleated anxiously.

'Don't you *want* me to look after you?' she asked softly, dangerously.

'Of course, darling . . . you know I love you more than life itself . . .'

'Soon.' she said intently. 'Soon, Crom . . . You wouldn't want mama to go away and leave you, would you?'

'No! No!' he cried out, in sudden fear.

'That's good, then,' she said soothingly. 'You lie there, Crom. Enjoy yourself. Soon, though . . .'

'Yes . . . yes . . .' he agreed, sounding rather dazed. 'Soon, darling . . .'

'Good . . .'

Carlotta got back up. She went and washed out her implements, drying them and putting them away in her case before revolving the combination locks shut once again.

She sat back down at the dressing table, and lit one of her special cigarettes. She picked up her little pistol and pointed it at the smoky reflection in the mirror. She wondered what it would be like to shoot Violet. Bang. Or even better, *bam bam bam bam*.

Bits of Violet. Violet's blood, Violet screaming, thrashing on the ground in agony.

She put her head back and laughed.

'You all right, darling?' Cromwell asked, slurring his words slightly.

'Oh, yes,' she giggled. 'Never better.'

George left the palace and walked up the sloping hill towards Hyde Park Corner, with the wall of the palace gardens on his left and the trees of the park across the road. The lights were on in the gloaming, the cars and buses rattled past him as he crossed around the cream stucco of the great hospital, and down into Knightsbridge. Harrods was lit up ahead of him. A troop of the Household Cavalry clattered by on their way to the barracks they shared with the Guards on the edge of the park.

He crossed the street, found the road. There it was, a London pub, just as he had been told. The Packenham. He took a deep breath, and went in. It was busy, a buzz of male voices, the air tinged with silver cigarette smoke. Someone waved a languid hand from a corner. Godfrey.

'Hallo, Godfrey. Good of you to come.'

'Not at all, I assure you. A pleasure,' Godfrey said, smiling pleasantly. 'Gets me away from the tedious St God's.'

'No problems?'

'Oh, no. Last term. Exams over.'

'Cambridge.'

'Oh, yes.' Godfrey smiled, somewhat smugly. 'I'm a Trinity scholar.'

'Well done! What are you studying?'

'Mathematics.'

'Good Lord . . . I have trouble understanding my bank account . . . why maths?'

'It is intellectually rigorous, and I have a first-class mind,' Godfrey said arrogantly.

'If you say so,' George said, looking around, and missed the flash of anger in the younger man's eyes. 'Get you a drink?'

'Of course. Scotch.'

'I remember.'

When George returned from the bar, Godfrey spoke first, with a sly grin.

'I heard a rumour of Prince George—' His cousin's face twitched, and he knew he was right. 'But of course, that's none of my business,' he murmured, feigning indifference.

George sighed. 'It's all a bit unusual,' he said.

'Of course,' Godfrey said patiently. 'Why don't you tell me what it is you need, and let's see if I can arrange it for you?'

There was something in Godfrey's voice which made George look up, and just for a second he saw an extraordinary chill at the back of his cousin's seemingly friendly gaze. Godfrey smiled plesaantly at him.

'You can trust me,' he said.

'Dear God . . . you shouldn't know so much at your age.'

'This . . . *milieu* is founded on youth, George,' Godfrey explained quietly. 'It's what the ones *buying* want . . . the one's for *sale* are young, they become . . . knowledgeable very quickly . . .'

'Yes, I see . . .'

George paused before speaking, his mind temporarily distracted. 'Godfrey, an avuncular word of advice . . .'

'Ah?'

'You would do well to dissociate yourself from this world if you're to do well in Cambridge.'

'I have the ability to split my life up into compartments,' Godfrey explained.

'You'll have to take Cambridge seriously, you know. You're a big fish at St God's. School prefect, head of house, all that sort of thing. You'll be a minnow there.'

'I'm sure I can cope,' Godfrey said with a confident smile, almost amazed that George should think otherwise. 'Now what did you . . .'

'Oh, yes. Well, the . . . requirements are somewhat detailed,' George said slowly.

'How exciting!' Godfrey said brightly, then stopped as he saw the expression on George's face.

'Sorry,' he said, appearing contrite. 'What kind of details.'

'The . . . *bugger* has to be working class.'

'Not a problem, I assure you,' Godfrey said efficiently. 'But can we be clear as to the terminology. Your, ah, client wants to do it? Or have it done to him?'

'It is slightly more complicated than that,' George said . . .

George left the pub, and strode fast down towards Knightsbridge. A cab was passing, its light candle-bright yellow. He hailed it and climbed in. He felt extremely unclean; he wanted a bath.

33

Stupid Pooves

Bill 'Chalky' White alighted from the omnibus as it slowed to turn up into Kensington Church Street, and caught his bearings. He'd got to know the better parts of London quite well ever since he'd joined the Brigade of Guards in the middle of 1918. Just missed the war – not entirely a matter of regret to him: he'd seen the husks of strong young men littering the streets of his Peckham neighbourhood. His brother Harry had come back with his privates burned away by mustard gas. With two paternity orders to his name, you knew what Harry liked to do in his spare time; couldn't face it, spent the last of his disability pay on a bottle of gin and a ticket on the District Line. Swan-dived in front of the first train and made a lot of people late for work in the City, spoiling his good looks into the bargain.

Chalky White was a handsome lad too, and no less fond of the girls, but girls didn't pay, did they. Some of his mates in the Guards had quickly alerted him to the possibilities of extra-curricular earnings to be had by frequenting pubs like the Bag o'Nails or the Packenham, where older homosexuals hung around on the look-out for trade. So Bill had got to know parts of London like Mayfair, Kensington and St Martin's Lane that a working class boy like him would not normally have seen, not from the inside of the fine houses, at any rate.

He made his way to a square of smooth-stoned mansion flats, all with shiny glass-panelled doors and brass fittings, set about a railed central garden of grass and trees and shrubs. In the pocket of his jacket were two keys that the young toff had given him along with the first Bradbury. Little – well, he was tall, but young – aristocratic bleeder had taken a free one behind some bushes in the park as his commission too. Still, a tenner was good pay for the work, he had to admit.

As he checked the numbers he ran through the instructions in his mind. He was a conscientious soldier, always followed orders, did what the sergeant said. You certainly got some strange things to do. Not in the army, with the queers. Still, it was good for a laugh with his mates back in barracks. What he'd had to do to the old queen in Soho last week had left them all in stitches. Mind, he was to say nothing about this one, the young toff had been very clear about that. Pulled him up off his knees seconds after he'd done it to him and there had been something in his eyes that had almost frightened Bill White. He decided to do as he was told and keep stumm on this one.

Here he was. He took his keys and let himself into the mansion block, went down the clean red carpet in the hall, ignored the open trellis of the lift, loped up the stairs. He made no noise – the walls were thick, the treads carpeted, held in place by polished brass stair-rods. On the third floor he checked the number to make sure he had the right flat. Give someone a terrible fright if he got in the wrong place and did his bit, he thought, and it brought a brief smile to his face.

Now then, the main lock was undone, of course, the door just on the latch, so he put the shiny yellow brass Yale into the lock, and turned it smoothly. The flat yawned dark inside as the door swung open, and he stepped in. He closed it with a click behind him. All the curtains were drawn, just enough light to see by filtered through.

He was in the hallway, which extended through the flat, split at the end; rooms furnished with antiques and soft chairs and sofas branched off, paintings and drawings on the walls.

A silver box gleamed in the half-light, standing on a crescent-shaped card-table by the wall. He picked it up; solid, not plate. These appointments with queers in their own houses could be quite lucrative – pocketing the odd item brought an extra profit when passed through the fence who operated at the Packenham. The implicit threat of a thrashing was always enough to subdue any old queen who might whine. Bill White's face sneered in the half-light. Stupid pooves, he thought.

The thought of thrashing made him reach inside his jacket and take out the riding crop. His own, used to manage his horse. Then, the thought of the expression on the young toff, de Clare's face made him put the silver box back. De Clare was a poof, but he was certainly not an old queen. Bill suspected he would enjoy doing something very nasty to him if he stepped out of line.

Remembering Godfrey brought his attention back to the job in hand. He put the whip down and quickly got undressed, folding his clothes neatly as the army had taught him, and putting them on the silk-covered spoon-backed chair in the hallway.

The flat was quiet. He felt the hairs on his body rising up in the sudden cold air. He picked up the whip and slapped it menacingly against the wall.

'I knows yer 'ere!' he called out, in a rough voice.

He went into the first room, a sitting room. An Indian carpet was soft under his feet. He padded softly about, looking behind the Chesterfield, peering in the half-light around the tall Chinese silk screen. A toff's place, no doubt about it; all kinds of things from the Empire. He swished his crop through the air and went further into the apartment.

A dining room, twelve hand-carved chairs set about an oval table. He glanced underneath. Nothing there but the carpet.

A bedroom. He doubted it. Him, now, he liked to be comfortable. If he was with a girl from Peckham, they'd have a few beers and a knee-trembler in some quiet alley. Your poof, here, he liked it different, and he was paying for the privilege, so who was he, Bill White, to complain?

He swished the crop again, and went on.

A storeroom. What's that the respectable folks called it? A box-room. Where he come from nobody had enough to want a box-room, but here it was. On impulse he slashed at a tea box or two in the darkness.

Somebody squeaked, something white ran for the door. He lashed out, copped him across the buttocks and he squealed. Bill caught a glimpse of the black silk hood over his head and then he was gone.

'I'm coming arter yer!' he roared, and ran out. He was just in time to see the naked figure run into another room, the buttocks white as a rabbit's scut.

'I knows where yer are . . .' he called, in a sing-song voice, play-ground menace.

The figure was hiding behind the bed. He chased him out, in and out of the rooms, down the corridors, the whip whistling through the air, making tingling contact. He caught him by the big bedroom, pushed him down, whipped him across the buttocks as he squirmed and squealed.

Their breath panted in the silence. He pulled the hooded figure up, onto his knees. The hood had holes for the eyes, a slit for the mouth. He forced himself through the gap, made the gasping figure perform on him.

When he was ready he pulled him up, bent him over the end of the bed and buggered him. Reaching around he felt his victim as hard as a rod.

When he had finished he did as he had been bid, went out and down the corridor. He dressed quickly, let himself out, shut the door behind him.

In the neatly tended central garden of the square, Godfrey stood silent and still behind the camouflage of a large viburnum. He watched as Bill White came out of the door, turned back the way he had come, walking quickly away. He would be waiting for him at the Packenham later, wanting the rest of his money.

Godfrey waited patiently. A few cars were parked about the square, polished and shiny. One had caught his eye: a discreet, dark blue Lagonda with a patiently waiting chauffeur in uniform.

The doors of the mansion block flashed briefly as they opened. A small figure hurried down the steps, in overcoat and trilby hat, pulled well down over the face. A hand held a scarf up over mouth and nose. The chauffeur had jumped out and held open the door; the little man jumped quickly inside.

Godfrey watched, as alert as any of his ancestors hunting. Prince George was tall, well-built; this was not he.

The chauffeur slid into his seat, the big six-cylinder engine swung near-soundlessly into life. The long limousine swept from the kerb. Godfrey watched its occupant settle back in his seat, reaching for a cigarette. The scarf fell away from his face, and Godfrey saw Edward, Prince of Wales.

34

We Want to Have a Word With You

Windstone Castle, July

From the mullioned windows of the Cadiz room – where Drake and Hawkins had met with Earl Henry to plan their raid – Cromwell could see *Parma's Pride* in the Windstone Water, tied up to the dock. The furled white sails shone in the sunlight, her paintwork was bright and fresh. He could see Fish moving about on deck.

From the bathroom came the sounds of running water. He tapped on the door.

'Darling?'

'What is it?' called Carlotta's voice.

'Freddie's here. I'm going down to look at Fish's boat with him.'

'Don't be long,' she said.

'No, darling,' Cromwell said obediently.

Freddie watched him expressionlessly.

'Washing her hair,' Cromwell said, by way of explanation.

Inside the bathroom, Carlotta looked out at the ship lying by the quay. There was a savage expression to her face. She felt a deep, instinctive sense of unease at being in the castle. At Cromwell being in the castle. With his relatives. She didn't need Cromwell getting away from her, she needed him where she could control him.

She had not been able to stop him coming down. Fish was off on his voyage. The good part was that *they* were going too: the hated Violet and her brother Freddie. She hoped they all sank.

By the time they got back, if they did, it would all be too late. Lady Constance, his mother was in the convalescent home, too weak to put up strong resistance. She and Cromwell would be married. No society wedding. Registry office. There. Legal, unbreakable.

As she stared malevolently out of the bathroom window she saw Cromwell and Freddie emerge from the great house and wander across the lawns. She hoped that Freddie enjoyed it. Once she was Countess of Windstone it would be the last time he set foot in the place. *Any* of them. She'd put the dogs on them.

There was the small matter of the old Earl dying first, but frankly she didn't see him lasting long. The deaths of his sons, the death of his wife had aged him greatly. He looked like an eighty-year-old. She was confident he'd be pushing up the daisies within a year. And then . . .

She frowned. She had better get the marriage organised just as soon as *Parma's Pride* set sail. Cromwell would not dare oppose her now. Even his fear of his mother wouldn't get in her way. His last puny act of defiance to her will she had used to lock him in a cupboard for a day and a night. When she had let him out she had made him crawl and lick her feet. She no longer bothered to use sex to control him. She was not interested in sex for its own sake, only as a means of power.

Out by the water, Fish waved, his two relatives went down the gang-plank and on board.

She took off her shirt and bent over the sink to wash her hair. The sooner it was done the sooner she could get out there. It was settled in her mind. As soon as the ship sailed, they would get back to London. She needed that document in her possession.

As she bent over she felt something run hot inside her nose. The running water was suddenly stained red with blood. She cursed viciously and reached for her swabs. Her nosebleeds were becoming very regular.

In the big bedroom outside, with its aquamarine walls, the door silently opened. Freddie had left it ajar. Very carefully, Violet put her head around. She could hear the noise of water and activity from the bathroom. She slipped inside. She was dressed in a loose shirt, culottes and boating shoes.

Two suitcases stood upon stands, opened. No, not there. Carlotta's handbag lay on the bed. She did not bother with that. Moving as quiet as a cat on the soft carpet, Violet went to the wardrobe, with its large mirror set into the door. She eased it open; a savage smile glimmered across her face, and she reached inside.

Its weight surprised her. She pulled out the oblong, leather-covered case with its combination locks and, clasping it to her went silently out and away down the corridor.

Behind her, Godfrey was watching. He had seen Cromwell go off with Freddie, had begun himself to go to the Cadiz room. Carlotta was somebody he wanted to talk to. Cromwell had become her prize, her whimpering poodle. Godfrey was always interested in people who had that kind of destructive power over others – he had it himself. He had thought that a little chat with Carlotta might prove mutually beneficial, but then who should he see slipping down the corridor but Violet. Godfrey might not like Violet, but he had a high opinion of her intelligence. She looked intent upon action, so he had concealed himself behind a marble bust of the eleventh Earl and waited.

He had not had to wait long. For there, and putting on speed as she went away from the bedroom, was Violet, now clasping a small leather suitcase to her bosom. Keeping her in sight, padding along as quietly as he could, Godfrey followed.

Violet headed directly to the great library, which looked out over the water. When she went in the Earl was waiting for her, standing grimly by the long table. Sunlight was flooding in through the high windows; it fell upon a silver-grey mace in front of him. Unseasonally, a fire was burning briskly in the great grate.

'Is that it?' the old man asked.

'I believe so,' she said levelly.

'Damned bad thing, breaking into people's property,' he observed.

'If I'm right you'll see I'm right about what she's done to Cromwell,' Violet said steadily. 'She has reduced Cromwell to a puppet who does her will.'

'The boy was ever weak,' he said. 'His mother's responsible.'

'He will be Earl when you are gone,' she pointed out. 'Do you want Carlotta in control of all we are?'

An expression of marked distaste went across his worn face.

'Certainly not. The gel ain't suitable, ain't suitable at all.'

'She would finish it all. She's mad, you know.'

'Don't doubt she is,' he said despondently.

He sighed, and picked up the mace. It had been made for Bishop Henri, who as a man of God was forbidden to spill blood, so it was blunt; a skull-crusher rather than a splitter. At the end of its eighteen-inch iron haft it was hooked, for fastening to the bishop's weapon belt. The Earl slid the point under the first catch of the briefcase and levered it upwards. The metal fixings of the case came asunder; another pull and the lid opened. He tipped it forward on the table and oilskin packets fell out, heavy and packed, amidst the paraphernalia of syringes, needles, spoons.

'What the devil is all this?' he demanded, his face curdled with disgust.

'What I told you it would be,' Violet said quietly. 'Drugs. Cocaine and heroin. Poppy juice. Cromwell is a drug addict.'

'Dear God,' Lord Windstone whispered. 'Have we not had enough suffering without this?'

'So you approve of what we're going to do?' Violet demanded, searching his face with her eyes.

'Yes, yes!' he cried. 'Do it. Do it now, while I still live.'

'We'll burn this filthy stuff,' Violet promised. 'I'll do it now.'

Quiet as could be, peering through the open jamb of the door at the scene inside the library, Godfrey had seen all. Quickly, he slipped away, and went back the way he had come, straight into the Cadiz room.

'*What the hell*—' Carlotta snarled. She was naked from the waist up, and was attempting to stem the flow of blood from her nose.

'No time!' Godfrey assured her urgently. 'Have you got something valuable in a blue leather case?'

The expression of savagery that sprang into her face was so great that he took a prudent step back.

'I saw Violet with it,' he said quickly.

'What . . .' she breathed. Her face was dead white with fury. Scarlet blood ran down from her nose as if over snow.

Godfrey stepped to one side as she ran out of the room, and to the wardrobe, slamming the door back. It was empty.

'Where is she?' she screamed. Blood spattered down over her breasts.

'In the library,' he said. 'She was opening your case.'

She gave a terrible, eldrich shriek, a sound of killing, of murder, and seized her handbag, tearing it open. She pulled something from it, and ran from the room. Following her, Godfrey saw that she had a small glittering pistol in her hand.

In the library, Violet threw the oilskin packets on to the flames. They burned vigorously, throwing off a noxious grey smoke. Violet stepped back, put a handkerchief over her nose.

'Pooh,' she said in disgust. 'Better get back a bit. That stuff smells foul.'

'What are you going to do now?' asked de Clare.

'Fish and the others are going downstream to the sea. I'm going to motor down to Exmouth and meet them there.'

She went over to the high window, open to the summer air and looked out. She could see Fish at the wheel, Freddie moving along the quay.

'They're casting off,' she said. 'I'll go and have a word with Carlotta now.'

From above came a fearsome screech, a scream of insane rage.

'She seems to have found out,' Violet said calmly. She glanced at the fire, then over her shoulder. Freddie hopped from the quay on to the ship, just moving from the shore.

'Too late now,' she said.

Something howled behind her. She whirled round and saw Carlotta framed in the doorway. She was half naked, and blood spattered her face and body like warpaint. She pointed her fist at her and it blossomed into flame.

The great sheet of glass shattered as the bullet went past her head, and cascaded down all around her.

'*Die!*' Carlotta shrieked. 'Die-die-die-die—'

The Earl threw his heavy mace at her; the gyrating iron handle slammed into her arm as she fired and the next bullet went wide. As more glass shattered about her Violet leaped up onto the window-sill, and jumped.

Carlotta fired again at nothing and screamed in fury. She whirled round, and ran out, making for the garden.

Violet landed with a terrific whack in the flower bed, the breath all knocked out of her. Her ankle was gone, she could feel it. She began to stagger away across the grass towards the boat. It was starting to move away from the quay. A bullet cracked past her.

Carlotta, standing in the doorway, her little gun smoking, saw Violet's hobbling progress and smiled in insane delight. She loped forward towards her. Violet took another painful step and fell down a slope into a dried-up stream bed, vanishing from sight.

When she looked up, Carlotta was standing above. She held the little pistol up in the air.

'This is wonderful,' she crowed, and laughed.

Violet's arm snapped foward as though she were throwing a cricket ball. The smooth stone from the stream-bed flew straight and true, smacking Carlotta straight in the mouth. She fell backwards with a terrible scream, the gun flying from her hand.

Violet hobbled painfully towards the quay, as fast as she could. The boat was beginning to catch the current, ten feet out. The crack of gunfire had made Fish look up from the wheel.

'Behind you!' he yelled desperately.

Carlotta was running after her, blood pouring from her smashed mouth, screaming incoherently, the gun in her hand. The Earl was in close pursuit, the mace flashing in the sunlight.

Violet flew herself into the river and swam powerfully underwater towards the white outline of the boat.

Shouting insanely, Carlotta fired again and again at the vanishing figure. As she raised the gun to shoot at Fish, the Earl beat her over the head with the mace.

Fish bent down, pulled Violet up as she clung to the small ladder and drew her in, water streaming from her. From below, Freddie appeared with Felicity. Finally, Cromwell, looking bewildered.

'Go on,' the old Earl shouted. 'I'll see to this mess. Go!'

The breeze caught the sail, it bellied out, foam hissed at the prow of the ship. Slowly, the castle became small behind them. Gulls wheeled above the mast.

'I say . . .' Cromwell said feebly. 'What's going on, chaps?'

'You're coming on a t-trip,' his brother informed him, from his seat beside the wheel.

'We want,' Violet said grimly, her sodden clothes plastered to her, 'to have a word with you.'

'I thought you wanted to talk,' Cromwell muttered querulously. He huddled against the side of the cockpit as though feeling the cold. They were out to sea, the sails filled and white. To port they could see the green of the hills behind the shore, the golden ribbon of the sand. Fish sat in his chair by the wheel, and Violet on the other side of the cockpit. She had changed from her wet clothes into a pair of Felicity's shorts and a shirt, her hair drying in the sea breeze. Her heavily strapped ankle she had up on the cushions.

'Plenty of time,' she said.

'Well no there isn't,' Cromwell objected. 'I have to get back, you see.'

He shivered, and wrapped his arms about himself.

'You look cold,' Violet said solicitously.

'Well yes, I am cold, I'd like to get back to shore, it's jolly good to have this trip but—'

'Put a s-sock in it, Crom,' said Fish. 'You aren't going anywhere.'

'Dash it! You can't just kidnap people and—'

'Crom,' Fish said, almost indifferently, 'we can do what we p-please, and r-right now we p-please to have you on b-board.'

'Well, what is it you want to talk about?' he said, admitting defeat.

'Don't you know?' Violet asked. 'But it will keep. Not just yet.'

There was a fine smell of frying bacon from below, and soon Freddie and Felicity came up, bearing fragrant plates of food.

'I s-say!' Fish cried with delight. 'Bacon and egg sandwiches! There's nothing like the sea air f-for giving one an app-petite, what? And you've fried the bread! This is heaven . . .'

Freddie went below and came up with mugs of beer.

'Real Windstone bitter,' he said proudly. 'Nothing but the best.'

There was silence for a while as they champed on their golden sandwiches, and the ship made a steady five knots through the water.

'Wonderful!' Fish cried, and wiped his chin. 'The troops' favourite, though we didn't often get an egg thrown in as well. Wh-what's the matter, Crom, you not hungry?'

'Not very . . . I . . . I think I must be coming down with something. Feeling a bit seedy, what?'

He half rose to his feet, putting his untouched plate down on the cushions.

'Think I'll go and lie down,' he muttered.

'S-sorry,' Fish said expressionlessly. 'You s-sit there, where I can see you.'

'What gives you the right to order me about?' Cromwell cried hotly.

'I have the Military Cross,' Fish said, and smiled faintly.

'So do I!'

'I have the Military Cross and bar.'

'Look, I haven't – I haven't time to sit here playing silly games. I demand that you take me back to shore.'

'I have the DSO and the DFC. I have fifteen holes of varying sizes that have been blown in me.'

'What has this to do with anything?' Cromwell howled.

'I have the Order of St Sebastian. An Italian Cardinal gave it to me for protecting purity.'

'I want to get back!' Cromwell sobbed. He had gone a nasty waxy colour, like decomposing fat.

'The *Croix de Guerre*, the 1916 star and one kneecap,' Fish continued.

'The blasted war is over!'

'I did not do it to have you hand over all w-we have to a madwoman.'

'You keep Carlotta out of this! I shall do what I want!'

'You won't, you know.'

With a tortured howl, Cromwell sprang at his brother. Freddie, who had been watching him, knocked him down, and sat on his struggling body in the well of the cockpit.

'T-tie him to the mast,' said Fish.

✳   ✳   ✳

'I think it's time for a d-drink,' Fish said. He was down inside the ship. The lamps were on, the sea about them was black. He poured tumblers of Scotch for himself and the two girls, and cocked an ear.

'He's not making so much noise now,' he observed. 'I'll go and see how he's getting on.'

He took a second tumbler for Freddie at the wheel, and went above. The sea was dark all about, to port some lights from the shore glimmered faintly. The ship went steadily onward.

'S-strange to think of Drake and Hawkins and Earl Henry all pursuing the galleons out here,' he said, passing Freddie his glass.

'A great storm . . . it blew some of them all the way to the Shetlands. At least it's good weather for us.'

'How's he d-doing?'

'Ranting and raving an hour or two ago. Calmed down a bit now.'

Fish made his way forward carrying a small storm lantern. A boxed shelf was about the place the mast was stepped, and they had sat Cromwell on it before lashing him in place.

Fish sat down on the coaming, and put the lantern next to him. Cromwell raised his head to peer at him. His eyes seemed to have sunk back into his his skull. Some spittle hung from the corner of his mouth, and his brother reached over and wiped it with a handkerchief.

'In the name of God, Fish,' he moaned. 'Have a heart, take me back now.'

'And what would you d-do?' Fish asked reasonably. 'You'd be snuffling up powder and injecting that other stuff into yourself . . . it isn't on, old man.'

'You don't understand . . .' Cromwell whimpered.

'Silly boy.'

'You can't imprison me on this ship for ever!'

'You could fall overboard,' Fish suggested.

'You may not threaten me! I shall be the Earl of Windstone, one day!'

'Ah,' said Fish. 'I was wondering when you would manage to get round to the point.'

'What do you mean . . .'

'You are going to be Earl. I am not. I don't want to be Earl anyway, I am all used up by the w-war . . . there isn't much of me l-left. The p-problem is, as we see it, Crom, that you will make a pretty poor Earl.'

'That's my business!'

'No it isn't. We are the de Clares. We have been at Windstone since three months after the Battle of Hastings. We have always made sure that the Earl, whoever he may have been, is the custodian of our interests. You, Crom, are not up to it.'

'I'm going to die!' Cromwell moaned. 'I'm dying out here on this hulk and you babble about Windstone . . .'

'We want somebody to look after you,' Fish continued mercilessly.

'What the hell do you mean?' muttered his brother.

'You're not safe on your own. Look how that madwoman Carlotta chewed you up. Have you no sh-shame? Crawling for the sake of some powder to snuffle up your nose.'

'I need it!' he cried. 'You don't understand, you're strong, you're a hero, you don't know what it's like to be weak. I *need* it . . .'

'Well you aren't getting it,' Fish said brutally. 'You are j-jolly well staying strapped to that mast until you think straight. And then—'

'Then what?'

'Then you're going to get married,' Fish said triumphantly.

They had streamed some lines astern in the afternoon and towards dusk had caught a number of shining cod. Sitting in the stern Felicity had gutted and filleted them, throwing the remains into the sea, to the delight of the trailing gulls, and now Violet was coating them in batter before frying them. Fish had peeled and prepared potatoes for thick-cut chips, and was looking at the chart on the table.

'Where are we?' asked Violet.

'Eight nautical miles south-east of Folkestone, if my navigation is correct, wh-which it might not be,' Fish answered. 'I'm more used to being above it and l-looking down. Earl Henry was last seen not far from here, having p-put in for shot and powder.'

From above an awful moaning began again. Fish lurched over to a hatch and pushed it up.

'S-stop that whimpering, Crom,' he said severely. 'It won't do you any dashed good.'

Felicity unfolded herself from a corner where she had made herself comfortable with a book.

'He probably feels awful,' she said kindly.

'Of course he feels awful,' Fish said unsympathetically. 'He's p-put more f-filth through his body in the past months than a s-sewage plant.'

'I'll go up and chat to him,' she said. 'He's probably lonely. Will you be all right, Vi?'

'Of course. Supper in twenty minutes?'

'Eight bells!' Fish cried. 'Or th-that sort of thing. I'd better pull a c-cork or two. Uncle let me raid the cellar.'

She went forward. Cromwell was making gargling noises in the dark. She sat down on a hatch cover.

'You all right, Crom?'

'Ooh, God, of course I'm not all right,' he moaned. 'I've never felt so ill in my life. I think I'm going to die.'

'I don't think so. We checked with Clarissa, she says you'll feel pretty rotten for a couple of days.'

'You're all bastards! I hate all of you . . .'

'It has to be done. We can't afford to have you on drugs.'

'Let me do what I want . . .'

'Well, yes, if you were just Crom de Clare. I suppose we could just let you sink into the gutter and die. If we didn't care about you at all, which we do. But you're not. You're going to be the Earl of Windstone.'

Cromwell made a heaving sound in the darkness that suggested his body was trying to be sick on nothing.

'So . . . bloody what?' he rasped.

'So everything. Then you're head of the clan. Then your life isn't yours to do with as you please. Then you take up duty. To us. To the de Clares.'

'I hate the fucking de Clares, I hate the lot of you.'

'They kept Earl Raymond locked up for six years in the Grim Tower when he went mad,' she remarked severely. 'He died there.'

Cromwell remained silent.

'You do understand me, Crom, don't you? We de Clares are almost unique, we go back a thousand years. Baron Bohamond married Ethelreda, cousin of King Harold, in ten sixty-seven. That united the Normans with the ancient English. We have survived. Where is the house of de Puy today? Where the Earl of Wessex? Where a hundred other great lords who once rode tall? All gone, Crom, all gone, cut down by history, cut down in battle, died out because they couldn't produce enough men, murdered on the scaffold by their enemies. But not us. We're the de Clares. We survived, we must survive another thousand years. And you're going to play your part.'

'I can't,' he muttered pitifully. 'It's too much.'

'We'll help you.'

'You'll push me about, you mean. Fish's already told me, he's not letting me go until I marry some woman of his choosing. Oh God, oh God.'

'Is it so terrible? I thought you were fond of women, Crom.'

'Oh, I *am*. But God Almighty, this one's going to keep me in line, be some sort of gaoler.'

'Well, you have to admit you've been very silly. She can't allow you to get up to your old tricks again.'

'But can you imagine her?' Cromwell moaned. 'Some ghastly broom-faced harridan. About six feet tall with a voice like a sergeant-major. Something like my Great Aunt Griselda. She used to sing hymns in the bath; the natives were terrified of her on two continents.'

'I'm quite small,' Felicity said quietly. 'And I promise not to sing hymns anywhere, if you don't like it.'

'But what . . .' he said feebly.

'You're going to marry me,' she said firmly. 'You're not as useless as you think. What you need is a good woman. And that is me.'

'You?'

'Follow my advice and you won't go wrong,' she said briskly. 'Why not start now? Try and eat some fish and chips. It'll make you feel so much better.'

'All right. I'll try.'

'Good boy.'

'The de Clares have always turned out steel-framed bitches,' he remarked, without rancour.

'As I said, we go back a thousand years,' she agreed. 'Somebody has to do it.'

She went back down. Fish was decanting claret into glass. It shone ruby clear in the lamplight. Violet was turning golden chips, leaning against the side to favour her sprained ankle.

'A plate for the shaky one upstairs,' she said.

'Well done,' Violet remarked.

'We'll have him licked into shape in no time,' Felicity said confidently. 'A good supper and an early night. Does wonders. I'll feed him.'

She curled up in her corner and took up her book. 'I'll just finish my chapter while we're waiting,' she said. 'I bet the butler did it.'

'H-here, Crom,' Fish said, opening a drawer. 'I brought ties for us. You can have Eton, the Windstones or this one with pink elephants on it.'

The bright sunshine glittered on the calm water of the Scottish harbour outside, and ran in bright patterns on the roof of the cabin.

'By golly, I saw blasted lizards when I was on that mast. Crawling all over me they were. I'll have Eton.'

'All right. Here you are. Freddie can have the Windstones, he'd better look respectable if he's best man. I'll have the pink elephants. Ah, here you are, Freddie, this one's yours.'

They went up on deck where the two girls were sitting in their best frocks.

'I s-suppose we should have brought our morning dress.'

'Don't imagine the natives do, when they get married,' said Violet. 'Stout tweed seems to be more their line.'

'When in Rome . . .'

The tender was tied up to the side. They carefully climbed in, Fish undid the painter and Freddie took the oars, propelling them across the little harbour, with its high-sided, beamy trawlers and shrimp boats tied up to the grey stone walls, ochre nets hanging from the rigging. The fishing village was all about the tiny bay, its narrow streets and white-painted houses climbing up the sides of the slope. At the top there was the square kirk, free of decoration.

They tied up at the quay, going past fishermen mending their nets and sails and strolled up the hill. Fish made slow progress, Violet staying back with him while the others went on ahead.

'I hope it will work,' she said.

'Flick's our best bet,' he said. He laughed. 'You know, we ought to make *her* Earl instead of Crom. Or you. You'd make a good Earl.'

'Hah!' she cried in amusement. 'Generations of de Clare men revolving in their graves at the thought.'

'Why not? Crom's not up to it, you know.'

'You would be.'

'I'm damaged, Vi . . . When I remember the boy I was, it's like looking at a portrait of a long-dead relative . . . No, we'd better do our best with Earl Flick.'

'I've booked a trunk call to the castle,' she said. 'Once it's *fait accompli* we can tell the world.'

'I shall look forward to seeeing M-Mother's face,' he agreed.

'She won't be pleased,' Violet warned.

'Pleased? Vi, darling, *nobody* was supposed to get their hands on her baby Crom . . . m-mad Carlotta only managed it because Mother's been flat on her back for so long.'

'Your mother is as dangerous as Carlotta. More so, since she's under control.'

'There won't be anything she can do, once Crom's tied up. Dear God, is this it? What can it look like on a rainy day?'

'The Scots like their religion grim,' she observed.

'By g-golly they succeed,' Fish said, and they went in. 'Freddie, have you got the b-bally ring?'

He peered inside the small church.

'I s-say, Vi, we have an audience. The place is filled with hairy-knit jersey.'

'We're an attraction,' she said. 'They'll probably talk about the mad foreigners who sailed in to get married for years. And I promised a round of drinks for everybody at the inn afterwards.'

'B-by golly,' Fish said. 'This is like waiting for the whistle to blow and go over the top. You ready, then, Crom?'

His brother gave a sickly smile. 'Here we go,' he agreed.

'I declare ye man and wife. Ye may kiss the bride,' the pastor said, from behind his beard.

Cromwell kissed Felicity while all looked on in approval. They went back out while the woollen-clad fisherfolk sat and waited, marvelling at the antics of the mad foreigners.

'R-right,' said Fish. 'All ch-change.' He turned to Violet. 'I do love you, darling.'

'I love you too,' she said. 'Is this my posy? I'm glad it's small: nobody will think I'm clutching it to my tummy to conceal my illegitimate offspring.'

'Vi!' Felicity giggled.

'Well, they must wonder what on earth we're doing up here all getting married.'

Inside the kirk the Scots fisherfolk crashed into a second rendition of 'God's Sea'.

'Go on then, darling,' Violet urged. 'I've had to wait about three years for this.'

'S-see you inside, then.'

'I've told him not to put in "obey",' she said, as he and Freddie stepped forward. 'Is that all right?'

'I'd have been am-mazed,' he said drily.

'I didn't want to lie to God,' she explained.

'Good. Can I go in now?'

'Of course. See you in a minute. I shall be late. The bride always has to be late.'

The two men vanished and she stared at Cromwell and Felicity.

'I'm completely panic stricken,' she said.

'Lady Violet?'

The landlord of the King's Oak called from the doorway. Violet was sitting on a bollard in her best frock, looking out over the harbour, the water shimmering in the sun. Not far away, Fish was attempting to teach some fishermen the Eton boating song.

'Yes?' she called brightly.

'Your trunk call to the south,' the landlord explained. 'It's ready.'

She went inside and he wandered over to where Freddie was sitting with Felicity. Cromwell was visible in the distance, walking round the harbour wall.

'What's Crom doing?' asked Fish.

'Stretching his legs, he says,' said Felicity. 'He's probably staying away from me.'

'He'll get used to it.'

'I'll jolly well see that he does,' she said spiritedly. 'In fact I think I'll go and get him now.'

She got up and went briskly off in pursuit.

'Do you think Earl Henry got this far?'

'P-Probably not. It was one heck of a storm that blew, and the ship had already taken battle damage. I think it broke up at sea.'

'What do you want to do now?'

'I was th-thinking of going all the way round the top and back down the other side.'

'Good idea. Oh, here's Vi.'

'What's the m-matter, darling?' Fish asked, as he saw her face. 'What's happened?'

'It's Uncle,' she said, still shocked. 'I spoke to Godfrey. Uncle's dead. He fell from the battlements last night.'

'My God . . .'

Fish looked across the harbour. Felicity had caught Cromwell, they were standing talking.

'My God,' he repeated. 'Then Cromwell's Earl.'

35

We Are As We Are

Windstone Castle

The great white sail came down at the end of the last tack across the Water, and the ship drifted gently towards the quay. Freddie jumped nimbly from the prow, tying her up, Violet threw him a line from the stern. Fish centred the wheel and they began to bring up their belongings and pile them on the quay while he went about preparing the ship for inactivity.

'There's your mother,' Violet said laconically. Across the lawns Lady Constance was proceeding at full speed. Fish limped forward to meet her.

'So inconsiderate of you, Fish,' she said as she came up. 'You should have returned the minute you heard the news.'

'We did.'

'Not by that boat! Why didn't you put Cromwell on the train? He is the Earl! He has his duties to take up.'

'We're here in time for the funeral,' Fish pointed out. 'That's why you're here isn't it, Mother?'

'Certainly not. I have moved in, of course,' she said, as though amazed at his stupidity.

'Oh,' He looked at his mother. She had recovered from her illness, clearly. A glittering necklace caught his eye.

'Been down to Garrards?'

'What? No, no.' She seemed temporarily flustered. 'Hermione . . . she had some pieces for sale, from the Russians, you know.'

She looked her son in the eye. 'I decided to help her out,' she said.

It was so manifestly untrue that Fish smiled.

'Don't gawp at me! *Where is Cromwell*?'

'He's coming. Vi, darling . . .' Violet came to stand by Fish. 'Mother, Violet is my wife.'

'Your *wife* . . .' Fish seemed temporarily to have got her attention.

'Yes. We were married in Scotland.'

'Good Lord . . .' She pulled herself together. 'Well I hope you don't expect me to support you. Times are very difficult since your father died . . .'

'Two can live as cheaply as one, Lady Constance,' Violet said sweetly.

'You'll have to, my dear,' she said acidly. 'Where is . . . ah, *there* you are, Cromwell, darling . . .'

Cromwell had put his head up from below. He smiled sheepishly at his mother, and vanished once again.

'Lady Constance, where is Carlotta?' Violet asked sharply.

'That madwoman?' she cried angrily. 'In hospital, I am glad to say. When I think of her and . . .'

Felicity appeared from below and a wintry expression passed over Lady Constance's face.

'Well, well, you all seem to be underemployed, don't you? Gallivanting off like this. I hope you're not thinking of wasting any more of Cromwell's time. He's a very busy man now, you know.'

'Oh, we know, Lady Constance,' Felicity said pleasantly, jumping on to the quay. 'We've been discussing it all on the journey south.'

'Discussing? How very presumptuous . . . ah, Cromwell, darling. You'd better come with me. With Cuthbert's funeral tomorrow and . . . there's so much to do.'

Quietly, Felicity slid her hand into Cromwell's, and prevented him from moving after his mother. She turned, sensing something wrong, saw them all watching her, saw Cromwell beginning to blush with anxiety.

'Yes?' she said sharply. 'What is it, what is it you have to say to me?'

'Mother,' Cromwell said hoarsely. 'Meet my wife. Felicity and I are married.'

All the colour drained from her face. Her hand went to her throat, she gasped for air.

'Married? *Married*? Oh . . .' She clutched her bosom. 'I think I may be having a heart attack. I must lie down.'

She held out an imperious hand. 'Help me to my room, Cromwell,' she ordered. He scuttled to her side and mother and son made their painful way across the lawn. Cromwell's head began to bow. Violet glanced across at Felicity.

'I think war has been declared.' she said.

*   *   *

Through the glass in the door Violet could see Carlotta sitting up in bed. A white bandage was wrapped all the way around her head. She was reading a magazine.

'She could not possibly have been at the castle the night Lord Cuthbert died,' Clarissa said to Violet. 'I know that it's probably your first thought after she went crazy there, but she was in fact still unconscious right here. The Earl certainly inherited the knack of swinging a mace from his ancestor. He fractured her skull. I'm not saying she didn't deserve it, but there's no way she could have pushed Lord Cuthbert off the rampart.'

'I thought I'd check,' Violet said seriously. 'I was very fond of Uncle, I'd be tempted to do something quite nasty to anyone who'd killed him.'

'The coroner thinks accidental death. He was an old man, he lost his balance and fell. He liked to go up there of an evening, to watch the sunset. They think he didn't see properly. The change from very bright light to dusk as he turned round.'

'Hmm. Perhaps. He certainly didn't throw himself off.'

'He lost his entire family . . .'

'He had the rest of us. We're the de Clares. And only the failures commit suicide in our family. Uncle wasn't a failure. He was a tough old man.'

'She wants to see you, if you will,' Clarissa said hesitantly.

'Carlotta?' Violet smiled faintly. 'Has she got a gun?'

'No, of course not. Violet, are you going to press charges?'

'For trying to kill me? I don't know. Is she still mad?'

'She took an awful lot of dope,' Clarissa said seriously. 'It warped her mind. She's off it now. She'll never do it again.'

'All right. Listen, I want you to come up to the castle. Aunt Constance is in the process of warping Cromwell's mind. He married Felicity up in Scotland, you know.'

'Really? I never thought he'd have the guts to defy his mother.'

'We gave him a bit of a hand,' Violet admitted. 'But Aunt Constance is carrying on rather. I want you to give her a sedative.'

'I'll come up and see her.'

Violet pushed open the door and went into the hospital room. Carlotta looked up, putting her magazine down.

'Violet, I am so sorry,' she said sincerely. 'I was completely insane, right out of my mind.'

'You're also a bad shot,' Violet said pleasantly. 'I take it you won't be taking any of that stuff again.'

'You have my word.'

'Better stay away from Cromwell too.'

'Of course.'

'Then there's no more to say. I hope you get better soon.'

'Thank you.'

'I have to get back. Lots to attend to. You'll be up soon, Clarissa?'

'Within the hour.'

'See you there, then.'

Violet went out. Clarissa stood beside her sister's bed.

'She's a very good person. She's not going to pursue it.'

'I'm grateful,' Carlotta said levelly.

'Carlotta, I'm a doctor. You had an awful lot of cocaine and heroin. More than you could use.'

She said nothing, picked up her magazine again.

'You were supplying other people.'

Carlotta turned a page.

'I'm your sister, I know you.'

'Little Miss Goody-Two-Shoes,' Carlotta said, mockingly.

'You're bad. Bad through to the middle.'

'We are as we are,' she said indifferently.

'I want you to go away. Leave the country. I'll give you some money.'

'Oh, I'm going,' Carlotta said lightly.

'Good,' Clarissa said, in relief.

'When I'm ready,' said Carlotta, and her eyes, which were not reading her magazine, glittered.

36

You Ought to Be a Spy

Cambridge, May 1920

The late afternoon sun glittered on the surface of the river. In the dappled shade of the bank Godfrey strolled along, his Oxford flannel bags swinging about his ankles, a tweed jacket cast casually over his shoulder, held by one finger. He was in the company of a striking young woman a few years older than himself. She was Carlotta. Behind them the spires and towers of the university stood up against the sky; in the distance they could hear the cadenced call of a cox commanding his crew, the rhythmic clopping of oars.

'You're giving up maths?' she queried. 'Why?'

'I believed it to be a discipline of purity,' he said loftily. 'My mind is attuned to symmetry and order. I identify with the aesthetic principles of modern art. Mistakenly, I thought that mathematics as taught here in the leading university of the world would be in agreement with me.'

'It isn't?'

'I am taught by a fat pig who qualified for his post by working out the dynamics for the improvement of spinning projectiles whilst recovering from wounds received from one, namely a shell. My dear, I am not interested in spinning shells.'

'You don't think you'd get top marks,' she said shrewdly.

'I have a first-class brain,' he said chillingly. 'I will not be humiliated by less than the best.'

'So what are you going to do?'

'Modern languages. I speak fluent German, you know. I don't know why I didn't think of it before. It is not simply the language; one covers literature, art, history and thought. But what of yourself?'

'I'm . . . going abroad for a while. Shanghai.'

'How exotic . . .'

'I have friends out there.'

'Isn't there a civil war going on in China?'

'Yes. My friends . . . profit from disturbed times.'

'Let us retrace our steps. I shall purchase suitable refreshment for us at the Dog and Gun.' They turned back the way they had come.

'How is your cousin Cromwell?' she asked neutrally.

'The Earl?'

'*Yes*,' she snapped.

'Well, he *is* the Earl, isn't he?' Godfrey said, sounding slightly amused.

'Yes . . . and the others?'

'Well, Violet's pregnant, and Perceval's MP for Windstone. The electorate is so conditioned to voting de Clare they failed to notice he was standing for the Socialist Party. Rather a joke, eh? But you were asking about Cromwell. He is in an unfortunate position. He is caught between two formidable women. His mother Lady Constance on the one hand, and his wife, Felicity. Both wishing to force him in differing directions.'

'God,' she said viciously. 'And it could have been me!'

'You came within an ace.'

'It was that bitch Violet. She did it.'

'You failed to realise how protective the de Clares are of their own interests. They got rid of you, just as they are in the process of trying to eliminate Lady Constance, whom they also see as an outsider.'

The ghastly situation appeared to amuse Carlotta. 'She's a tough customer. How's she coping?'

'She has moved herself into the suite of rooms directly above those of the Earl and Countess. She exercises considerable moral authority over her son, as if by telepathy.'

'Crom's as wet as they come. How's he taking it?'

'He drinks a lot, so they say. Felicity doesn't care for it.'

She held out a slender, clenched fist. 'I had him *here*.'

'You used drugs. So American. English women are more subtle. A finely honed streak of cruelty runs through the de Clare women; it emerges when they come up against a weak man. The de Clares abhor weakness. But it does all have a rather interesting result.'

'Ah?'

'Felicity's position – as Countess – would be considerably enhanced should she be able to produce an heir.'

'Can't she do it?' she asked eagerly.

'It appears not.'

'She got problems?'

'A rather specific one,' Godfrey said, with waspish delight. 'Cromwell.'

'Mmm?'

'He is unable to . . . ah . . .'

'He can't get it up?' she crowed.

'So delicately put. Yes, he appears, under the pressure of his mother above and his wife of arranged marriage at his side, to be quite unable to perform, um, at all.'

'Well, well. Let me tell you, he was no stud at the best of times, but it did work. But not now, eh? Limp as boiled spaghetti, huh?'

'You have such a way with words,' Godfrey said charmingly.

'I wonder if he's gone fag,' she said, suddenly.

'What's that?'

'I had a cousin back in the states. Real mama's boy, like Crom. Tried to break loose, went on the sauce, married a showgirl. Boy, did his mama crack his nuts when she found out. She made him feel that he'd betrayed *her*, you know? The full guilt trip. Anyhow, a while later I read about Hank in the paper, been arrested in a fag nightclub. Turned into a closet queen.'

'How fascinating,' Godfrey murmured.

'They know you're a fag round here?' she asked sharply.

'Why no,' he said smoothly. 'It isn't advisable. Not if you want to rise to the top of your academic tree.'

'You can conceal it?' she said disbelievingly.

'My dear, I can seem to be anything I want,' he assured her. 'I even dally with young ladies, who are suitably impressed by my youthful good looks and charm.'

'You ought to be a spy.'

37

Somebody Here Murdered Cromwell de Clare

The Savoy Hotel

'I'm sorry about dinner with the Crawfords,' Cromwell said. He shut the door behind them, and slumped on to the side of the bed. 'My bloody headache just won't go away.'

'That doesn't matter, darling,' Felicity said sympathetically.

'I don't know what's the matter with me these days,' he muttered. 'I just don't seem to be able to face people.'

'Our social circle is quite small at the moment,' she said lightly.

'I let you down all the time,' he said abjectly.

Felicity took off the skirt of her dark blue suit, and put it on a hanger with the jacket. She undid her blouse and stood in her cream silk slip and stockings.

'Darling, we've been through this before and you know what the problem is,' she said gently, but firmly. 'You have to decide who you want on your side. Me, your wife, or your mother. I understand how it is for you. You're a nice man. You're used to doing what your mother says. When you are with her you bow to her wishes, you see things from her point of view. Which is, mainly, that I am a vicious and heartless intriguer who has wormed her way into your affections. Having married and lost one heir to the Earldom I have managed to scheme my way back by marrying you. When she manages to spirit you away you come back filled with this black view of me, and we row until I once again convince you that it is not true. Then the skies lighten, and you are once again the good man I know and am married to. Until the next time.'

'I know, I know . . .' he moaned. 'You don't understand how—'

'Oh, I do,' she said sharply. 'Believe me, Crom, I do. Darling, Robert told me what was going on ages ago, back in the war, when your mother fixed you with your staff job to keep you out of the line—'

'I was there, on the first day at the Somme!' he protested. 'I was wounded fighting!'

'I know you were,' she said softly. 'Left to yourself your instincts are all fine ones. You were brave, you volunteered to go and fight with Fish and the others. I *know*. But I also know what Robert told me. He said that your mother's icy claw was about your balls, and slowly squeezing them away—'

'You mustn't talk like that!'

'It's true!'

'My head aches.'

She stood looking thoughtfully at him for a moment.

'Here,' she said, 'take off your jacket and tie. Give them to me. In fact, take off your shirt as well. I'll give you a massage. You know that helps your headaches.'

'All right,' he said.

She went to the bathroom.

'I'll just get changed, and then I'll do it for you. Lie down and rest a moment.'

In the bathroom she pulled off her slip. Underneath she wore cream silk French knickers and a matching brassiere. She unhooked the bra and squeezed the bulb of her glass bottle, giving herself a brief spray of eau-de-cologne. She put on a lacy negligee, tying it by a single silk ribbon at the front. From her small case of make-up she took a pot of French skin cream.

'Here we are, darling,' she said cheerfully, emerging into the bedroom. 'That's much more comfortable. Now, let's see to you. Lie on your tummy.'

He turned obediently over, and she put a little cream on her fingers. She began to rub and squeeze the tense muscles of his back and neck. Slowly, they began to loosen.

'That's better,' she said encouragingly. She undid the silk ribbon of her negligee.

'Now the other side,' she said, and he turned over again. She began to rub the muscles of his chest and neck with both her hands, and the light negligee parted so that he could see her beautiful round breasts.

'Is it better?'

'Much,' he mumbled.

'I would so love it if you kissed me,' she said softly. She leaned forward over him, and gently put a nipple into his mouth. He began to suck at her breast like a small child.

'That's so lovely . . .' she murmured. She resumed massaging his skin with one hand, slippery with the cream. She rubbed his stomach, slid her hand down under the band of his trousers, gently took hold of him, her hand slippery and smooth.

She grew in his mouth as he sucked her breast, she felt him stir, begin to grow in her hand. Let it happen this time, she prayed.

'Mmmm . . .' she murmured encouragingly. She rocked a little on the bed to stimulate them both.

For a moment she thought she had succeeded, as he began to stiffen, and then as suddenly as he had shown signs of life he drooped to nothing. In the same instant he screamed something incoherent, and hurled her from him. She tumbled backwards from the bed, landing in a heap on the carpet. The fall half-winded her; she pushed herself up on to her knees, and tried to gather her negligee about her. Her hands were trembling, she was shocked by the suddenness of his violence. He sat on the edge of the bed, his face in his hands. She got up, and went into the bathroom, closing the door behind her.

Turning the taps on hard she ran water into the bath, hot. She believed in the powers of a bath to soothe pain. She thought she could hear Cromwell crying in the bedroom, great sobs of agony.

She took all her clothes off, got into the bath, stayed there for a long time. When she emerged, the bedroom was empty. She pulled her dressing gown about her, went to her bag, took out her cigarette case and lit one. Inside the bag was a photograph in a little Liberty frame. She took it out and looked at it.

Two young people smiled out from the monochrome print. In sailor's cord trousers and boots, in short-sleeved shirts she and Robert, Viscount Windstone, grinned happily at the camera, sitting on the side of their boat. They were on honeymoon.

'Oh, Rob,' she whispered unhappily. 'How I hate the war.'

Cromwell stumbled down the staircase. His tie was askew, his shirt roughly shoved into his trousers.

'I say! Crom!' a voice called. He peered wildly about the lobby. A tall, slim figure waved cheerfully. It was Godfrey.

'Crom!' he said, coming over. 'I say, you look awful. Nothing wrong is there?'

'Is anything right?' Cromwel rasped.

'You know,' Godfrey said reassuringly, 'what you need is a drink.'

'I need a bucket,' Cromwell muttered.

'Yes, yes,' Godfrey murmured thoughtfully. 'I can see extreme measures are called for, eh? Come with me, I know a jolly good little place not far from here.'

He took Cromwell's arm, and led him out of the hotel towards the Strand.

'What am I doing here? Oh, I often come up to town of a weekend . . .'

Cromwell wasn't sure what time it was. It was quite dark in Godfrey's club. A small but powerful band occupied a stand at one end; small round tables were populated with couples and little groups intent on enjoying themselves. They made energetic forays on to a polished dancing floor, where they jigged and bucketed about in a manner he had never seen before, returning to their tables for refuelling stops. Cromwell had sunk several whiskies, which had reduced the pain to a kind of numb ache.

'What about a dance, old chap?' Godfrey yelled encouragingly, over the combined noises of the club.

'With you? No thanks.' Cromwell laughed, inanely. 'No, not with me. With her.'

'Who?'

'That girl there. She wants to dance with you.'

Cromwell peered through the smoke, silvery in the small lights. A tall, slender woman was standing at the side of the dancefloor, wearing a short fringed dress.

'I don't think—'

'*Go on.*'

Somehow, Cromwell found that Godfrey had propelled him onto his feet and towards the woman. As he came up, she turned to him and smiled a very intense smile.

'Hallo, Crom darling,' she purred.

It was Carlotta.

She pulled him to her, onto the floor.

'Oh, God,' he said, almost weeping. 'I've needed you.'

'Don't worry,' she said, into his ear. 'I've got it. I'll arrange it all. I've got what you want.'

Light came through the windows, pierced his closed lids, made him groan, even through the last of sleep. He turned away, and a stab of real pain pulled at his face. He opened his eyes, found himself stuck to a pillow by old blood and dried slime from his nostrils.

He peeled himself free, managed to sit upright on the edge of the bed. He hurt, he hurt most dreadfully, worse than when Fish had tied him to the mast. A fit of shivering racked him. He put his arms about himself against the sudden chill, looked in horror at the bruises there. Oh yes . . . it came back to him, Carlotta and her soothing needle.

He was half naked, he had on only a pair of soiled underpants. Stubble was heavy on his chin.

'Awake, are yer?'

A rough voice sounded from the doorway. He looked painfully up. A young man with short blond hair stood there.

'Who are you?' he croaked.

'You didn't say that last night,' the boy said with an unpleasant snigger.

Oh, God. His hands were shaking, he put them on his knees.

'Well, where is it?' the youth demanded.

'What?'

'The money. You ain't got nuffing in yer wallet, I looked. How you going to pay me?'

'Bugger off,' Cromwell said.

'You ain't going ter pay?' the boy demanded.

'I owe you nothing. You've obviously emptied my wallet already.'

The flicker that went over the boy's face told him he was right.

'Get out.'

'You'll be sorry,' the boy said.

Cromwell pushed himself to his feet. Madness went over his brain in waves. He found himself standing in front of the boy, looking down at him. His hand snaked out, grasped him at the crotch, squeezed, made him buckle over.

'Why will I be sorry?' he grated.

'She's going ter get yer,' the boy moaned, frantically trying to remove Cromwell's fist from his groin.

'Oh? Speak up, or I'll make you a contralto.'

'She took photographs of yer doing it ter me!' the boy howled. 'She's going ter send 'em to the coppers!'

Cromwell's fist clamped down and the youth buckled double, vomiting onto the dirty floor. He dragged him to the door, threw him out. Then he dressed. When he went out the boy had gone.

'Hallo, Flick,' he said. He sat on the edge of the bed, by the telephone. He had cut himself shaving and blobs of dried blood stuck to his cheeks.

'Oh, God, Crom darling!' Her relief flooded down the line. 'Where are you?' she asked frantically. 'You've been gone days, I've been so worried about you . . .'

'I went back to the Savoy.'

'I'll come down . . .'

'No, no. I'm coming back to the castle. Look, I'll meet you and the others in the library. About three.'

'Why the lib—Crom, what others? What are you doing?'

'About three.'

There was a silence for several long moments.

'Are you all right, Crom?' she asked quietly.

'Oh, yes,' he said calmly. 'Never better, I promise you. I've got it all worked out now.'

Windstone Castle

Felicity came round the library door, quickly, anxiously.

'Oh, God. Darling, you're here. I was looking out for you.'

Cromwell carefully placed one of the leather-bottomed library chairs at the end of the bow he had made in front of the long table. On the table was draped a white cloth which obviously concealed a number of bulky objects.

'There,' he said with satisfaction. 'I came in the back way . . .'

'Oh. You look terrible—'

'Yes, yes,' he said easily. 'I know. Now, Flick, darling, you sit here.'

'Why?'

'Because I ask you to,' he said reasonably. 'Ah, Vi. I'm so glad you could come.'

'We've all been worried about you, Crom,' she said.

'Have you? Look, do sit down. Is there long to go before the baby arrives?'

Violet looked at him, worried. 'Not long . . .'

'Ah! Mother.'

Lady Constance came rushing into the room, ignoring everybody except Cromwell.

'Darling!' she shrieked. 'Where have you—'

'Not now, Mother,' he said. 'Sit next to Violet. Has anybody seen Godfrey? Perceval, have you seen your brother?'

Perceval had entered, obviously bothered. 'What's all this about?' he asked peevishly. 'I'm supposed to go and inspect slum housing in Windstone. I'm putting forward proposals for the government—'

'To spend loads of lovely taxpayers' money!' Cromwell guffawed brightly.

'Yes,' Perceval said sullenly. 'Since you ask.'

'Sit down, Perceval,' Cromwell said dismissively. 'Or isn't it Percy, these days? Percy de Clare sounds a bit funny, doesn't it?'

'He's changed his name,' Lady Constance said acidly. 'He goes about calling himself Percy Clare.'

'I saw you in a flat hat the other day, Perceval,' Felicity commented.

'What about Godfrey?' Cromwell demanded. 'I left a message for him to be here.'

'*I* haven't seen him,' said George, coming in with Fish, who was limping heavily.

'Hallo, Fish,' said Cromwell. 'Leg giving you gyp?'

'Some days are better than others,' Fish agreed.

'Take a pew,' he suggested. 'Take the weight off it.'

'Don't mind if I do.' Fish sat down, lit a cigarette and eyed his brother thoughtfully through the smoke. 'You all right, old man?' he asked quietly.

'Never better, never better.'

'He's sat us all down here and won't tell us what's happening,' said Lady Constance. 'I think you should lie down, darling, you—'

'Don't look well at all,' her son finished. 'Ah, Freddie.'

Freddie came in with Clarissa. He glanced at Cromwell, went over to the window, peered casually out. He glanced at his nails, moved along the outer wall past the serried volumes.

'Sit down, Freddie,' said Cromwell, from behind the table.

'Eh, what? Oh, I say, are we going to play charades?'

He took a quick look at Cromwell from under his brows, continued to move casually towards him.

'Bags I have first go,' he said. 'Crom, Crom, you whisper your word to me and I'll act, eh?'

He stepped towards Cromwell who reached under the cloth, pulled out a twelve-bore shotgun with one smooth action, pointed it casually over Freddie's head and pulled the trigger. There was a shattering roar, and Lady Constance screamed through the noise of shattering glass.

'Sit down, Freddie,' Cromwell said, through the singing in their ears.

'Whatever you say, old man,' Freddie said carefully.

'I'll bet you all thought the butler did it,' Cromwell said affably. With an expert flick of his wrist he broke the weapon, the empty cartridge flying behind him, slid another into the breech and closed it with a snap. A servant poked his head anxiously around the door, and Cromwell pointed the gun at him.

'Bugger off, Figgins,' he ordered, 'and close the door behind you.'

'Cromwell,' Lady Constance wailed, 'what are you doing?'

'It's a murder mystery,' he explained. 'The detective always has everybody into the library at the end of the case and tells them how he found out which one of them committed the murder.'

He reached again below the cloth, retrieving a tumbler and a bottle of whisky. He pulled out the cork and poured himself a hefty measure. He took a swig.

'I'm not going to offer you lot any,' he said. 'You don't deserve it.'

'Cromwell, dear,' said Clarissa concernedly. 'Nobody has been killed.'

'Ah. That's where you're wrong. Somebody here murdered Cromwell de Clare, and I'm going to find out who it was.'

'You're not dead, Crom,' George said quietly.

Cromwell took another gulp of his whisky and waved the barrel of his shotgun at him. 'Only in a manner of speaking I get up, I dress, I eat, I . . . drink, yes I certainly drink. I bathe, I go to bed. I walk about and people say there goes the Earl of Windstone, but actully I was killed ages ago. Murdered. Yes.'

He looked cunningly along the row of anxious and wary faces.

'The only question we have to answer is who?'

'Crom,' Violet said clearly. 'May I leave?'

'Leave? Leave? Why should you want to leave?' he said querulously. 'We haven't finished yet.'

'I'm pregnant,' she said. 'I very much fear that something very horrible is going to happen. I am frightened.'

Cromwell peered at her, pursing his lips, and then shook his head.

'Sorry,' he said. 'Look upon it as the little bugger's first test of being a de Clare. We de Clares value courage more than anything else; that's why we destroy those of us who haven't got it. see if the mite can take it. He might as well get used to it early.'

He looked down the row again. 'Now who's to blame?' he asked. 'Empty chairs, here . . . let's go through the ones who're present. Freddie and George . . . one a good soldier, one not so good, and a failed vicar to boot. But you're a better poet than Freddie is, George.

I don't suppose you've either of you done me any harm. No, it's not you. I can't blame Vi either. Vi wanted Fish from being young and now she's got him. How single-minded of you, Vi. I wish I'd wanted something like that. So we're narrowing it down . . . Ah! My wife! Flick. Take a bow. Why did you marry me, Flick?'

'Because she's a—' Lady Constance snarled. Her words were cut off by Cromwell firing another barrel over her head. Plaster rained down from the wall.

'Do shut up, Mother. I wasn't talking to you.'

Lady Constance clutched at her heart in astounded horror.

'Flick?' Cromwell said again.

'I married you because I'm a de Clare,' Felicity said clearly, grittily. 'You've got no backbone, I have.'

'Admirably put!' he cried. He refilled his glass.

'But why have I no guts?' he murmured. 'We must look closer to home.'

He pointed at Lady Constance with his shotgun. 'Mother. Why do you love me so?'

'A mother should love her child!' she wailed, spreading her hands. 'I mean . . . look at Violet, she—'

'You hate Fish,' he said brutally. 'So did Father. Why?'

'Wh-what a jolly interesting question,' said Fish.

Lady Constance's face was white, she clasped her trembling hands together, clamped her mouth shut.

'I'm serious . . .' Cromwell said softly. 'I want to know.'

'It's none of—'

'I'll blow your head off,' he said sincerely.

'I – your father was – we . . . it didn't work!' she shouted incoherently. 'I met another man, your father, he . . . I . . . he was a far greater man than Gervase. Gervase never knew. About you that is. I wanted a divorce. Gervase was unfaithful . . .'

'So why didn't you get one?'

'I become pregnant with . . . him. Your brother. Gervase wouldn't let me leave. Said no other man was bringing up a de Clare. That damned name. He hated us both anyway, afterwards. Said it was God's punishment on me that Fish was a cripple. I could have gone with *you* Robert, but Giles didn't want Fish either. Her head turned savagely to look at Fish at the end of the row. He had gone very pale.

She turned back, looked at Cromwell and once again her eyes softened. 'He didn't wait for me. But I had *you*, darling,' she said entreatingly. 'And you did become Earl. Ha! If Gervase had known.

Come, now, as Violet says, let us stop this before something terrible happens . . . you can let Fish have the Castle and we'll go away. Just you and me.'

'Mother,' he said stonily, 'I told you, I'm looking for the murderer of Cromwell de Clare.'

'Y-you know, old man,' said Fish, it's not a bad idea to call it a day, what? Clarissa's here, she can give you something, make you feel better . . .'

By her side, Freddie eased himself casually forward in his seat.

'Freddie, if you get off your chair I shall blow a hole in you.

'If we *all* die here in this room, who gets to be Earl?' he enquired.

'Godfrey,' said Violet.

'Good God. What a frightful thought. I damn well told him to be here.' He reached under the cloth yet again and pulled out a razor, his other hand, still clutching the shot gun.

'Come here, Fish,' he said pleasantly.

'Wh-whatever you say, old boy . . .' his brother agreed, and levered himself from his chair, shuffling across the floor.

'I want you to lean over the table and put your head *there*,' he said precisely.

'Crom no—' Violet cried out in agony. 'You wouldn't.'

'It's all right, old chap,' said Fish. He leaned forward. 'Take it steady.'

'Look up at me,' Cromwell insisted. Fish twisted his head as he lay across the table, so that their eyes met. Cromwell's were strangely glazed, Fish's unreadable. 'Not like me at all. Not at all,' Cromwell said. Suddenly, he squeezed the trigger and the machine-gun erupted with a roar. Bullets flew, glass flew, someone screamed.

Then, quite gracefully, Cromwell held up the razor, and buried it in his own throat. Blood spouted from the gaping wound in his neck, and he fell forward onto the table.

38

He Fell Into Bad Company

Windstone Castle

George drew up outside the castle in his small Austin, and plucked a suitcase from the back seat.

'Hallo, George,' called a voice, and he looked up to see Violet emerging from the cut-flower garden.

'Hallo. Not gone pop yet?'

'Three weeks to go, according to my chap in Harley Street. The little passenger can't wait. Thumps away like a boxer.'

'Got a name?'

'Well not yet. Have to see which brand it is. At the moment it goes by the name of Algie.'

'Algie?'

'Yes. You know, like in the rhyme. Algie and the lion went for a walk together and when they came back the lion was bulgy and the bulge was Algie. Down for the weekend?'

'Try to, whenever I can. My Royal masters like to keep the lower classes busy.'

'You sound as though you're wearying of it all.'

George sighed. 'The Prince of Wales ... he *is* very trying to be around. Rather relentlessly puerile at times.'

'Not quite as dashing as presented? Aren't the ladies all over him?'

'He has a nasty habit of treating the married ladies he meets like prostitutes,' George said disapprovingly. 'That and ...'

'What?' Violet said, smiling.

'Oh ... nothing. You get asked to do things that ... make you feel dirty, I suppose. Where are you off to anyway?'

'Going for my walk. Damned if I'm going to sit about and get fat ankles, I'm far too vain. I march up to the Oak Bridge over the Torrent every day, there and back again. Then I treat myself to a gin.'

'Good for you. I'll unpack and have a couple ready. Fish about?'

'Yes, he's inside.'

'How does he like being Earl?'

'I think he could have done without the method of selection.'

'By golly, we all could. Crom was absolutely barking. I'm not surprised Lady Constance gargled and turned blue. They must have arrived at the Pearlies at the same time.'

'Yes . . . a kind of awful justice to it all. But Fish didn't need all that blood and gunfire. He's damaged, too shaky still.'

She stared angrily over the Water. 'Godfrey. Cromwell was asking where Godfrey was. He wasn't there . . .'

'He was at Cambridge,' George said mildly. 'We all just happened to be at the castle.'

'I have a very suspicious side to my mind,' Violet said grimly. 'I don't necessarily believe that bad things happen by accident. Look, let me have my walk. You get a gin waiting for us.'

'Jolly good . . .' George said amiably, and hefted his bag up the steps. Violet stepped out across the lawns towards the distant Torrent falling down the hillside towards the weir.

Where the fast-running stream erupted from its narrow channel in the stone and swirled dangerously down towards the polished curve of the weir, there was a bridge that curved across to the other side, its dark oak lichened with age. As she came up the slope she saw somebody bending nearby, gathering wild flowers. It was Godfrey, casually dressed in flannels and an old loose hacking jacket.

'Hallo,' she said. 'What are you doing up here?'

'Hallo, Vi! Oh, I've let my art suffer so studying. I've decided to really put in some work again. A simple still life. Wild flowers in a jug, a plain linen tablecloth. All next to a French window, throwing in the light. It's more difficult to do properly than you'd think.'

'Oh, I believe you. Godfrey, why do you think Crom killed himself?'

Godfrey straightened up, clutching his little bouquet, his face concerned. 'Such an awful thing . . .' he muttered.

'It was,' she said crisply. 'But why do you think he did it?'

'You want my opinion?' he asked, looking candidly at her.

'Yes.'

'I think he'd found out he was . . . a homo.'

'*You* haven't cut your throat.'

'I'm happy about it,' he shrugged. 'For somebody like Crom, it would have been a mortal sin.'

'He vanished for nearly a week. After a scene with Felicity.'

She walked slowly up onto the bridge. She always went to the centre, where she paused, leaning on the rail and looking out over the Water while she gathered her breath and thoughts before going back to the castle.

'I don't like that bit,' she said. 'Crom couldn't have done that on his own if he'd tried. He might have got drunk, but he'd have staggered back to the hotel. He vanished because somebody was waiting for him.'

'Maybe he fell into bad company,' Godfrey suggested, watching her expressionlessly.

'Oh, he did,' she said, with a set face. 'I know it.'

Her back ached furiously, as it always did. With a sense of relief, she leaned herself against the rail. For a fraction of a second it stood firm, and then it snapped. Her arms flailed as she fell forward, off balance. She almost seized the broken end of the heavy rail, and then she fell, plunging ten feet down into the turbulent, dark water.

She vanished, and then a few seconds later her head reappeared above the surface. She seemed to be trying to strike out for the bank. The powerful current swept her along, towards the surging weir that fell into the Water.

Displaying remarkable reflexes, Godfrey sprinted down from the bridge, along the Torrent bank.

'Hang on, Vi!' he yelled. 'Hang on, I'm coming!'

The winter gales had blown an ancient willow down into the water, some fifty yards from the weir edge itself. Long tendrils spilled back from the half-sunken boughs like the hair of a great mermaid.

Godfrey raced down the bank towards it. He overtook Violet, who was struggling feebly in the water, scrambled out along the trunk, and forced himself out along the submerged branches into the Torrent waters themselves. He could see Violet's head, sweeping along towards him.

'Here I am, Vi!' he yelled. 'Here!' He ripped off his jacket, swinging it in one hand. 'The coat Vi!' he shouted, above the steady roar of the weir. 'Grab the coat!'

She was just going to go by. He swung his jacket by one sleeve; it fell into her desperately clutching grasp. He swung her inwards, managed to seize hold of her arm, dragged her into the safety of the ruined tree and helped her onto the trunk. She crouched there, huddled up and bent over, water streaming off her.

'Oh, Jesus, Godfrey,' she gasped, clutching her stomach. 'I'm having my baby.'

39

Heroics

Windstone Castle, January 1923

The man stood patiently at the small side-door. A pantry window was to one side; through the gauze he could see some pheasants hanging up. He was not that old, in his thirties. He wore the army tunic he had been given free upon demobilisation, its serge worn shiny in parts, and somebody had patched the elbows with some leather for him. A grubby medal bar was still across his chest above the pocket. He stood at ease, occasionally moving his weight forward and then back, wriggling his toes as the sergeant-major had taught him to, so as not to faint on parade. They were just visible through the gap where sole had come away from upper, poking through his socks.

From behind the door he heard a shuffling, and then the handle turned. It opened, to reveal a tall young man in tweeds.

'Hallo,' he said amiably. 'Corporal Franks?'

Franks whipped his greasy hat from his head.

'Beggin' yer pardon, sir,' he said quickly. 'It was the cook I was looking fer, thought she might have some scraps . . .'

Fish had run his eyes quickly and expertly along the line of medals.

'Mons star, eh?' he said. 'You were out there before I was then.'

'Oh yes, sir,' Franks said quietly. 'A duration man, I was. But I didn't—'

'I ask to see any old s-sweats if they come to the door of the castle, Franks,' Fish assured him.

'You're . . . the Earl, sir?'

'That's me,' Fish agreed. 'Well, come on in, man, don't stand there. Where did you get your Military Medal?'

'Passchendaele, sir,' Franks said, following Fish inside, and up a staff staircase.

'Did you now? N-Nasty place that, glad I never went there. Now then, those boots of yours have seen better days . . .'

'Wore 'em in Passchendaele, sir.'

Fish showed him into a storeroom. Boots and shoes were piled up by one wall, tied together by their laces. There were teaboxes full of vests and socks and shirts, piles of mufflers and gloves, coats, trousers and jackets.

'Been having a bit of a clear out,' he said. 'My brother left an awful lot of stuff when he went. He must have spent a frightful length of time at the t-tailors. He was a bit taller than you, but same shoe, I fancy. There's quite an array, why don't you see what you need?'

'Why thank you sir,' Franks said with alacrity. Moving quickly amongst the clothes he began finding things that would fit him, holding them up against his lean frame.

'Out of work, Franks?'

'Yes, sir. Had a job as a brickie, but the building trade's taken a bad turn . . .'

'Have a tie,' Fish suggested. 'People always like to see a man in a tie when he goes for a j-job.'

He tossed him a dark blue tie, and Franks put it in his haversack.

'Show them your medals too,' Fish urged. 'It can make a difference. A Military Medal . . .'

'I doesn't talk about it much, sir,' the man confided. 'Not to people what wasn't there . . .'

He paused, an Oxford blue-striped shirt dangling incongruously from one hand, his eyes far away.

'Orders come down from brigade, see?' he said suddenly. 'New lot of Jerries moved in our sector. The major, he said for me and Smudger to go out that night and patrol. He was a good sort the major, always give yer a gasper and a nip of rum when you got back . . . Smudger and me, he knew we knew our way about in noman's land, see? Quick with a knife or a club, we was. So we went out, see? Black as a coal bunker it was, just the Verey lights in the next sector . . .'

'Yes,' Fish said intently. 'The lights.'

'Out there we was, me and Smudger, picking our way to the wire, quiet as mice, when blow me down if we doesn't run straight into a group of Jerries coming the other way! Nasty do it was. Me and Smudger, we flinged a couple of Mills bombs into the lot of 'em, scuttled as quick as we could for the ditch. Old drainage ditch there was, from the days when it was a farm, see?'

'Yes,' Fish murmured. 'Get down, get down . . .'

'Smudger was in there first and I come after 'im. The bombs went off then, and Jerry was making a nasty amount of noise in the dark, so we was all right, except I smelled it. Gas it was. Mustard. See, Smudger, 'e had a cold, couldn't smell a thing, and the last lot of Jerries, they gave us a hate before they left, flinged a few gas shells over, and it had settled in the ditch like. Nasty sweet smell it was. Smudger, Smudger, I sez, gas, gas, get out of 'ere, and 'e's right down there, 'is head down, see, so I drags him out, and Jerry's letting off 'is Spandau gun and there's lights and bombs and that going off, and a Jerry what doesn't know where 'e is, right there in front of me and so I club 'im on the nut and grabs 'old of 'im.

'Smudger's there and 'e can't see! Blimey, I sez, what a carry on. So I drags the Jerry with one hand and pulls Smudger with the other and we get back to the trench. Dead pleased, Brigade was.'

Fish was sitting on the chair by the wall, his eyes staring unfocused at the wall.

'Smudger, 'e started to cough, and the major, 'e sent us to the clearing station. Me arms, they came all up in blisters like, from the gas . . .' He pulled back a sleeve, showing shiny purple scarring all up his forearm. 'I 'ad to carry Smudger, he was coughing so bad. Yellow it was, nasty yellow foam, pints of it . . . all gargling and rattling out of 'im like the village pump . . .'

A tremor had infected Fish's hands, he held them clasped together, but they shook on his knees. He had gone a waxy colour, his face sheened with sweat.

'Died, did Smudger. Died there on a stretcher, all blue like 'e was drowned . . .' The former soldier shook himself, came out of his reveries. ''Ere, you all right, sir?'

Fish slowly raised a hand, as though he was very tired, wiped the beading sweat off his face. He sat staring at his hand.

'Blood . . .' he whispered. 'So much blood . . .'

Franks stepped smartly forward, shook his shoulder hard. ''Ere! Snap out of it, sir.'

Fish looked up at him with hollow eyes. 'Is there blood on my face, Franks?' he whispered.

'Nah, nah, sir. It's a bit 'ot in 'ere, that's all. Sweating, you are.'

'Oh, good. Sometimes I th-think there's b-blood all over me, that's all.'

''Appens to all of us, what was there, sir.'

'Yes . . .'

Visibly, Fish made an effort to bring himself back to reality. Through the window he could see the station taxi puttering up the long road.

'I f-fancy this must be the man from the tax,' he said. 'You have problems with tax, Franks?'

'No, sir. When I 'ave work I gets me pay in an envelope.'

'Do you now?' Fish said, seeming intrigued. 'How ingenious . . . want a gasper?'

'Oh yes, sir. I never says no.'

Fish offered him his cigarette case. He took one, carefully nipped it in half and placed one section behind his ear for later. Then he accepted a light, and he and Fish puffed together.

'Very nice, I must say.'

'N-navy cut, what?'

Outside a small man got out of the taxi. He wore a blue serge suit and a bowler hat and carried a briefcase. He seemed to be asking for a receipt.

'He's the man from the tax,' Fish said positively. 'I m-mean, Franks, who else would ask for a receipt for a taxi fare? Eh?'

'That's right, sir,' the former corporal said stolidly.

'Got what you n-need? Jolly good. If you go back down those stairs you'll find the kitchens. Tell cook I said you were to have something hot to eat before you went.'

'Thank you, sir. Thank you very much.'

'I w-wish it could be m-more,' Fish said quietly. 'W-we didn't fight for this, did we?'

Franks smiled mirthlessly. 'Land fit fer 'eroes,' he said.

'Did you feel a hero when you got your MM?'

'No, sir. Bleeding scared, I was.'

'Me, too,' Fish agreed. 'Windy most of the time, I was.'

'You get any medals, sir?'

'Just what they s-sent round with the rations. Well, nice to meet you, Franks. I have to g-go and talk to this obn-noxious little man from the tax. I hope things improve for you.'

'Thank you, sir.'

'Franks. You're sure there's no blood on me?' Fish wiped his face and stood looking anxiously at his wet hand. 'Sometimes it's very red.'

'No sir,' Franks said reassuringly. 'Not today.'

The former corporal went down the stairs. His nose guided him to the kitchens. By a black iron range a formidable woman with a bosom like the prow of a battleship was stirring something in a pot. She tested whatever it was on the spoon and nodded in approval. He coughed.

'And what would you be wanting?' she asked.

'The Earl, 'e said I might find something to eat if I asked,' he said, with an ingratiating smile.

'And how does the Earl think I'm to run my kitchen if he sends every passing soldier down here to fill up his belly?' she demanded. 'Answer me that?'

'I wouldn't know, mum.'

'Here, sit yourself down,' she said, not unkindly. 'When did you last eat?'

'Day before yesterday, mum.'

'You'd better start with soup, then. It'll warm your bones. I might have some pie in the larder.'

'Thank you, mum,' Franks said sincerely. He took the chair nearest the range, and felt the heat begin to seep through his jacket.

'Master Fish won the Victoria Cross,' she said, putting a steaming bowl down before him, and a big hunk of brown bread and butter. 'Shooting at him they were, all those German planes. A hero on the Somme he was, before that . . .'

''E 'ad a funny turn with me,' the soldier said. 'Thought there was blood on 'is face, 'e did.'

'They kept him there too long!' the cook cried fiercely. 'After all the others were dead, too!'

'We was all there too long,' Franks said quietly.

'Mr Higginb-bottom, I p-presume?' Fish said, shuffling into the great room.

The small man in his blue serge suit jumped up as though out of a spring-loaded box.

'*Botham*, if you please, Lord Windstone,' he said sharply. 'Higgin*botham*.'

'Oh,' Fish said vaguely. He limped over to a chair and parked himself. 'It's not a common n-name in these parts.'

'A good Yorkshire name, that is,' the man said abrasively.

'Then wh-why aren't you in b-bally Yorkshire?' Fish cried. 'Why do they send blasted Yorkshiremen all th-this way to p-persecute me? Eh? Answer me that.'

'You haven't paid your taxes,' Higginbotham said grimly. 'You're a person of some standing in these parts, so we at the Revenue Authority thought it best to send somebody from outside. There was, you recall, that problem with our last summons, Lord Windstone.' He opened his briefcase, and drew out a formidable sheaf of documents. 'They all relate to you.'

'B-balderdash!' Fish said spiritedly. 'The magistrate found there w-was no case to answer and sent your b-bally documents back to you.'

'You did!' the tax inspector yelped. '*You* sent them back . . .'

'I'm the m-magistrate,' Fish said reasonably. 'I f-found I h-had no case to answer.'

'This will not do,' the small man muttered. 'It really will not do.'

Fish took out his cigarette case. 'F-fancy a gasper?'

'I do not smoke,' he said, arranging his forms.

'Really? How do you g-get through the day . . .'

'By doing my job,' Higginbotham said grittily. 'Now then, Lord Windstone, before we move to the really serious charges against you I would point out that this office has received no completed tax forms from you beginning in 1916 and leading to the present.'

'I was b-busy in 1916,' Fish said reasonably. 'Also 1917, and 1918. I was pretty busy in 1919 too. 1920 . . . yes, fairly active, and last year I spent sailing with my wife and son. So I wasn't here.'

'You are claiming tax-exempt status because you were not resident within the United Kingdom?'

'I simply wasn't here.'

'It won't do! Did you fill out form LK 202?'

'I am the Earl of W-Windstone. I don't fill out forms.'

'In that case, we had better move on. Criminal charges of tax evasion are being prepared against you. You have made no attempt to pay the forty-per-cent inheritance tax levied against your estate upon the death of your brother the Earl two years ago.'

'Crom already paid. We had to sell a lot of land.'

'He died. Now *you* pay.'

'Again?' Fish howled. 'You want me to pay *again*?'

'It is the law,' Higginbotham said complacently.

'Then what will be left of the de Clares if th-this goes on?'

'Perhaps you will have to earn a living, like working men do.'

'A living . . .' Fish muttered. He looked up at the taxman. 'What did you d-do in the war, Mr Higginbottom?' he asked quietly.

'I worked in the Authority. Some of us had to do the dirty work of finding the money to pay for the war. Not everybody can go off and perform heroics in aeroplanes, Lord Windstone. Some of us stay at our task day after day, week after week.'

'H-heroics . . .'

'Oh, aye. We know all about your medals. But don't think they count when it comes to paying back taxes, because they don't.'

Fish's eyes became unfocused. He semed to try to pull himself together, pushed himself to his feet, went over to a tray of decanters.

'Wh-what about a stiff one?' he suggested. 'Sun's over the yardarm somewhere.'

'I don't indulge.'

Fish splashed whisky into a tumbler, spilled some over the side, swallowed it. He put it down, and limped out of the room.

'Back,' he promised, over his shoulder, 'in a m-minute. D-don't go anywhere . . .'

Efficiently, the official laid out his forms and sheets of paper on the table. He looked irritably at the door, tapped his fingers, began to walk disapprovingly around the great room. He took a notebook from his pocket and began to note down the contents.

The door opened again, and Fish tottered in. He had changed his tweeds for riding breeches and boots.

'A proper inventory must be made of the entire estate.' Higginbotham said crisply. 'We at the Authority require an exact valuation of all you own.'

Fish ambled over to him and took him by the elbow. 'L-let's shuffle outside,' he suggested. 'Lots to sh-show you outside.' He was a pale, waxy colour, he mopped the sheen of sweat on his face with his hand and stared at it. He muttered something incomprehensible to himself.

His grip on the small man was insistent, and Higginbotham found himself out in the open air. He appeared to be in the stables. A horse stood saddled, suddenly huge piebald dogs surged about him. He squealed in alarm.

'Smell 'im,' said Fish, and to his horror the dogs thrust their snouts at him, poking him with their noses, snuffling and sniffing, their eyes bright and shiny, their fur bristly.

'Windstone stag'ounds,' Fish said. 'Been stag'ounds here since Berthold brought them from Normandy. All descended from Berthold's pack, these are.'

'I don't see the relevance of this!' Higginbotham said in a high voice. 'Now can we get—'

Fish staggered out of the yard, taking him with him. They looked out over the rolling fields and hedgerows. In the distance a train was puffing in miniature along its track.

'Ever p-play that game when you were young?' Fish enquired. 'You k-know, with your chums, you split up into two teams. One team tries to make it home, to a place of safety, d-don't you know, and the others have to try to catch them, hunt them down, what?'

'No,' Higginbotham said nervously. 'No, I didn't.'

'What a strange life you've led. Wh-what was it you did in the war again?'

A huge bitch thrust her slavering jaws into his crotch and he squealed, trying to push her away.

'*I collected the taxes!*'

'Why didn't you volunteer?' Fish asked softly, dangerously.

'It was a reserved occupation . . .' Higginbotham whispered.

'You could still have volunteered . . . do you see the villages dotted all about? So many with women in the houses, wives and mothers, little children with no fathers . . . we were the Windstones, Mr Higginbottom, we went to the Somme and we didn't come back . . . so why weren't *you* there? There was a Yorkshire battalion there with us, brave boys all of them, they got slaughtered in the second attack on the first d-day, I was there, I s-saw them . . .'

Fish held up a hand to the man, his face terrible.

'See . . .' he whispered, 'see the blood all over it, all down my arm. A whizzbang blew him to bits all over me . . . the blood, it won't wash off . . .'

'Lord Windstone . . .' Higginbotham said, his voice almost sobbing. 'The war is over . . .'

'No,' Fish said certainly. 'It isn't. Why weren't you there on the first day, Higginbottom? Why isn't your b-blood all over me? Oh y-yes, you s-said, you were collecting the t-taxes . . .'

He looked out over the fields, his fist gripping the smaller man's elbow like a vice.

'The station,' he said softly, 'is home. If you can g-get to the station, you're safe.'

'You're mad,' Higginbotham said certainly. 'Stark mad . . .'

'I th-thought you knew that,' Fish said dismissively. Higginbotham stared wildly about him, looking for someone, for anyone to call to for help.

'Everyb-body has someone they lost around here,' Fish said. 'What we see when we look at you, Higgins, is someone breathing our l-loved ones' air.'

He looked down the fields, assessing the distance.

'Wh-what do you think? Will a four-field advantage be enough for you? T-tell you what, I'm a sp-sporting man, I'll make it five.'

He released his grip, gave Higginbotham a push that sent him stumbling down the pasture.

The little man suddenly found himself running in panic, as fast as he could go, tripping and stumbling in the long grass. He pushed and scrambled through the first hedgerow. Thorns and brambles tore at his skin, hot blood suddenly began to run down his face. Looking fearfully over his shoulder he saw Fish mounted on his horse, the huge dogs surging about him.

He vomited near the third hedgerow, at the fifth he heard the rippling notes of the tantivvy as Fish blew his hunting horn, and soiled himself.

He staggered over the field, and heard the booming barking of the hounds grow ever closer in his ears, the thunder of the great horse's hooves, the rising notes of the horn as they rode him down.

In the station lane he fell and the dogs surged over him, huge, bristling, panting, Fish's voice shouting harsh commands. He lay in a ball on the ground, trying to push his face into the earth.

Fish looked down at him from the saddle.

'C-Come back,' he said, 'any time.'

40

Attention to Detail

London

George came into the club, gave the porter his bowler hat and umbrella, and asked for his post. He received a small sheaf of letters from his polished brown pigeon-hole, put them in his briefcase and went towards the bar. Inside, a figure seated under a large painting of the charge at Omdurman called out to him.

'George! Just the fellow. I was looking for you.'

Reaching out for his scotch and soda George turned to see his cousin Freddie waving *The Times* at him.

'Thank you, Harry. Freddie, what are you doing here?'

'Came up to town to see the match. Kent are making a fair fist of it. What about you?'

'Oh, I tend to shuffle by here quite often. Home from home, what? I find my place in Kensington rather gloomy. Might give it up.'

'I'll buy you dinner and you can tell me about it.'

George glanced at his watch. 'I'm supposed to be getting the train down to Cardiff. The little man's doing a tour, I have to check arrangements tomorrow. Oh, why not? I haven't seen you for ages. I'll get the early express.'

'Jolly good. Shall we take our drinks through? Have you been down to the castle lately? Young Gawaine's growing up a treat. Splendid little chap. Fish's done out the old Indian room as a playroom. Much better, I must say. Gawaine and I had a good time trying to knock over skittles with a miniature howitzer he's got. Fires marbles. He's a much better shot than I am.'

Freddie laughed cheerfully, and led them into the dining room, where they were shown to a table near the window which looked out over Green Park.

'How's Vi?' enquired George.

'Oh, improved. A bit down in the mouth because her girls' doctor thinks she won't be able to have more infants after that ghastly business in the Torrent. A serious haemorrhage, it was.'

'Terrible. I thought she was going to die.'

'Oh, Vi's pretty tough,' her brother said airily. 'What takes your fancy? I think mine's some of those potted shrimps and a steak and kidney pudding to follow.'

'Mm. Yes, I'll have the same.'

'Had a word with Vi, actually, when I went down to pot skittles with young Gawaine. She said you weren't in the best of spirits. I'd have thought you'd have been skipping about like a spring lamb, what with your engagement to young Frances.'

'Oh, I am, really. Though I don't see her as much as I'd like.'

'Breaking out, eh? We de Clares usually marry another de Clare from some other branch of the family. You're striking a blow for freedom.'

'Completely smitten, old man. I saw her across a room forty-deep in dowager duchesses and that was it. Handed over my heart that night.'

'So what's the problem?' asked Freddie as the food arrived.

'Oh, I get a bit dispirited. Working with the blasted Royals is a penance. Spent half the afternoon explaining to some impoverished Russian Grand Duchess why the Queen's only giving her about a tenth of what her tiara's worth. The poor old thing hasn't the faintest idea of what money *is*, anyway.'

'Get another job.'

'What? In the City? Only another form of hell. I was brought up to be a vicar, Freddie, and that line of work's closed to me.'

'Chap offered me a job the other day.'

'But you're in the army.'

'Oh, this was a sort of military job, only I didn't want to take it. I'm in the Tank Corps and it looks like we're going to get the Experimental Mechanised Force. Fuller's promised me a place in it. Churchill's very keen. We'll be working with low-flying aircraft. I wouldn't miss it for anything. So I told this chap I couldn't do it, but I said I thought I knew somebody who might be just right, cousin of mine.'

'Me? I hung up my uniform at the end of the war.'

'Oh, you don't wear a uniform. It's in intelligence.'

'What sort of intelligence? Plans for enemy battleships, that sort of thing?'

'Counter-intelligence, to be precise. Looking into subversives and spies here and in the Empire.'

'The war's over,' George objected.

'Well, yes. But while the Germans are beaten, for the moment, the new regime in Russia isn't. World's first communist state, old boy, and very keen to increase that solitary number by as many as it can. Starting with us, as the world's foremost power. We have a lot of Empire to protect.'

'How would they do that?'

'Undercover followers of this fellow Marx. Work through something called the Comintern. The chap I spoke to saw it all as a kind of cancer eating away at the very fabric of our society. Cheaper than force of arms, as my chap pointed out, and in the long term it could be more successful. Unless we put a stop to it. Which is what he wanted me to join in doing.'

'Who does this fellow work for?'

'It used to be called the Secret Service Bureau. In the war they split it up into domestic counter-intelligence and overseas operations, called them MI5 and MI6. He wanted me to join MI5. I suggested you.'

'It might be interesting,' George said, intrigued. 'Though I don't know if Frances would approve. She has an entirely erroneous view of the glamour attached to being at court. Look, can I think about it?'

'Of course. Give me a call, and I'll have him make contact with you, if you're keen.'

'But what sort of people would want to do all this?'

'You'd be surprised!'

Freddie pierced the steaming suet crust of his pudding and watched in satisfaction as fragrant meat and gravy burst forth.

'Really,' he continued, cutting a chunk and lathering it. 'Closer to home than you might think. He told me. You know Hermione's been going about selling off jewellery for exiled nobles?'

'Of course. Queen Mary bought a piece.'

'Bolshevik, old man,' Freddie said succinctly. 'The poor benighted aristos are all either dead or in jug over there. The jewellery pays for Lenin to run his blasted Comintern.'

'You're not serious! Does Hermione know about this?'

'Of course she does! Thick as thieves with Mrs Pankhurst. Founder member of her Worker's Socialist Federation.'

'But what does Hermione know about workers? She's never done an honest day's turn in her life and lives at the castle when she isn't being arrested.'

'Exactly! Thoroughly meddlesome. Plenty more like her, let me tell you.'

'I'll think about it,' George agreed again. 'Now then, what was the score at close of play?'

＊　　　＊　　　＊

George used his key and let himself into the mansion block. The hallway with its dark red carpet smelled of wax polish from the parquet flooring. He ignored the lift and went up the stairs. He'd thought of going down to Paddington for the late train but found himself unable to face the thought of Cardiff at midnight. It would have to be first thing. He decided to call the agent and apprise him of his change of plan.

He used the Yale and opened the door to his flat. He paused, in surprise. The hall lamp was on and further along the corridor a bar of light showed under the bedroom.

A surge of anger went through him as he put his briefcase down and picked up a knobkerrie he kept in the umbrella stand. Very quietly, he padded down the hall towards the door.

Outside, he stopped, cocking an ear. He could hear the faint murmurings of two voices. One was certainly a man's. He wasn't sure of the other, through the heavy wood.

Taking a deep breath he grasped his club hard in one hand and gripped the doorknob with the other. With a twist, a bounding rush and a roar he was inside.

Two men, a big one and a small one, were in the bed.

'For God's sake, de Clare!' Mountbatten said, anger replacing his shock.

'For God's sake to you too!' George said furiously. 'Use your own flat.'

The little figure suddenly sat bolt upright, twisting round, his tear-stained face purple with rage. George recognised his employer, Edward, Prince of Wales.

'*Get out*!' he squeaked apoplectically. 'Get out get out get out!'

George turned on his heel, went out and to the sitting room. He tossed the club onto the sofa. From the bedroom he could hear the Prince shrieking with rage. A few moments later he appeared, his clothes hurriedly pulled on, practically running down the hall.

'You're fired!' he screamed at him. 'Fired, fired, fired!'

The door opened and shut with a crash, and he was gone.

'I resign,' George said, to the air.

Louis Mountbatten appeared, nonchalantly doing up his tie, having recovered his composure, tall and as handsome as a film star.

'I say, de Clare, you do pick your moments,' he said. 'You were supposed to be in Wales, weren't you?'

'I changed my mind,' George said coldly.

'Cost you your job,' Mountbatten pointed out.

'I don't care.'

'I'll have a word for you, if you like,' he said, seeming to be generous.

'Lord Louis, taking favours from people and putting myself in their debt is how I am here in the first place.'

The other man shrugged. 'Suit yourself. I might not have managed it anyway. He was *very* cross with you. He's made a mess of your sheets.'

Mountbatten grinned cruelly.

'Though not much. They don't call him the little man for nothing.'

'What are you doing with him?' George burst out.

'Eh?' Mountbatten checked the setting of his tie in the mirror. 'It keeps him happy, de Clare. And what keeps him happy keeps *me* happy. It's useful to have friends at court. You may find that out now you don't have any.'

Mountbatten looked left, right and then centre at himself.

'The little man isn't much of a performer,' he explained. 'Something of a short-time boy. Know what I mean? All these pretty ladies who get to grips with him thinking they've found their demon lover usually don't get much more than stained underwear. He lasts better when it's done to *him*. That's why he was so cross when you came in doing your Tarzan king of the ape men impersonation.'

'I am not interested in this,' George said icily.

'Attention to detail,' Mountbatten said reprovingly. 'Very important in one's career.'

'You're married!' George said in disgust.

Mountbatten slipped on his beautifully cut jacket, ran a comb through his locks, looking deep into his reflection.

'What on earth has that to do with anything?' he asked, in amazement. 'It has certainly never bothered my wife.'

He looked at George and laughed contemptuously. 'Don't tell me you believe in being faithful,' he sneered.

'As it so happens, yes.'

'You'd better go and live in the suburbs, then, now you're out of a job,' he said dismissively. 'That's where the upright, boring middle classes live, screwing their boring, upright little wives once a week on Saturday night.'

'I am not middle class!' George said, stung.

'Heading that way,' Mountbatten said, spearing him on his scorn. 'Had to sell up your place in the country, didn't you? Now you go and sponge off your cousin down at Windstone to keep up appearances.'

'You are a bounder, Mountbatten,' George said angrily. 'And the world will find you out.'

'Not me, de Clare,' Mountbatten said confidently. He went to the door. '*I* pay attention to detail.'

The door shut with a casual, uncaring bang, and George stood by his sofa, shocked and furious. He splashed whisky into a glass, took a gulp, looked out of the window at the yellow lights of the city, then away again, pulling the curtain shut on them. He hated the place.

His thoughts were in a whirl. He made himself sit on the arm of the sofa, lit a cigarette, trying to get his world in order. One thing was certain, he wasn't going to go on living where he was. A place in the country, that was what he wanted. Frances. Children. The city was no place to bring up children.

His thoughts turned to Windstone. Maybe Fish and Vi would help, let him rent one of the small farms. A job, though. What he had in the bank was ear-marked for the wedding. Frances wanted to put on a bit of a show. He had to get a job.

Freddie. Bolshevik spies. Yes, it had a rakeish air to it all. Frances would think something of that. Make up for not being in with the Royals. He felt a twinge of dismay. Frances was impressed by the court. But she loved him for himself, he was sure of it. He loved her, he knew that, he would live anywhere with her. A frown creased his forehead. Frances was ambitious, she liked to keep up appearances. Maybe one of the smarter farms down at Windstone . . . yes, a manor . . .

He crossed the room, went over to the telephone.

'Hallo? Major de Clare still in the club? Yes? It's his cousin, George.'

George stood patiently for a few moments.

'Freddie. Yes, it's me. Look, been thinking about that job. What was it you said? Military Intelligence . . . MI5. That's it. I think I'd quite like to have a crack at it. You will? Good. I'm turning it in with the Royals. If your chap wants me I'll be at the castle. Going down for a few days.'

George stood for a few moments by the telephone, feeling relief flood over him. He went through to his bedroom, and began to pack a bag. He could be down there before midnight if he stepped on it.

Windstone Castle

Gawaine, Viscount Windstone came down the main straight at full speed, his feet pushing hard on the pedals. He passed his father and mother and rounded the statue of the fourteenth Earl, leaning hard out of the side of his car, a fruity humming of the engine emerging from his lips. He vanished around the gargantuan buttresses of the York tower, still pedalling furiously.

'You've bought him a new car,' said Violet.

'Railton Special. The Brooklands w-wonder,' Fish said proudly.

'Is there nothing you won't do for him?' Violet asked, smiling. 'You spent most of yesterday with him down on the river.'

'P-probably not.' Fish agreed. 'We h-had a d-dashed good time. Mud pies. It all came back to me. And I s-started him out on c-casting a fly.'

'He's three!'

'N-never too early to start. G-got the makings of a good w-wrist, he has. We c-caught a nice trout, about a pound and five ounces, grilled it over a fire we made for our l-lunch. Bit whacked after that, we were, so we had a snooze in the grass before coming home. Wearying work, making mud castles.'

'What about this tax thing then?' she asked neutrally.

'Buggers tried to tell me off for putting the frighteners on that one they sent – Higgins I think he was. Off sick, they said. I told 'em to send me another, if they felt like it. Listen, old thing, I was thinking, this racing of motors, like they do at Brooklands, going to be quite a thing. Popular, what? We might build a racing circuit, over near the Torrent Wood. Natural bowl. Easy for people to watch, what?'

'Moving with the times? Might make some money, help pay the taxman.'

'Exactly. Call it W-Windstone Park.'

'Agricultural prices are depressed, we might generate more by investing in such a thing. We already have the land. You talk to some of your Brooklands chums and I'll talk to the bead-pushers.'

'Jolly good.' Fish said comfortably.

'Now talking of money, what are you going to do about George? He wants to rent Todrington Manor.'

'He'll n-need a place to live. Getting married. What's she like?'

'I've only met her once,' Violet said frankly. 'She's not one of us. Seemed pleasant enough. I think she's ambitious, which is why

George is trying to placate her with the Manor, having chucked it in with the Royals.'

'He'd do better with one of us.'

'He's in love with her.'

'S-so let him have the Manor.'

'He can't afford it.'

'I'll set the rent so he can.'

'Are you going to help George out for the rest of his life?'

'The strong must help the weak. *Noblesse oblige.* You're one to talk, anyway. You fished about, trying to get him a job, and Freddie got him one.'

'Well, he was so miserable with the royals, poor thing. The court's simply too ghastly. He'll be better off chasing spies.'

'George's a decent ch-chap. Life just hasn't t-treated him quite right.'

Violet ran her hand tenderly over his shoulder, down his arm. He was filled with dents.

'Has life treated you right, darling?'

'I have you.' Fish said. 'And *him.*'

Gawaine de Clare shot through the Prisoners' Gate, and down the slope towards the Tudor garden.

'Fish?'

'Yes, darling.'

'These blasted taxes. We're going to have to pay, but we can structure it. I talked to old Penders in the City. He recommends an estate management company. Do you want me to sort out the details?'

'Yes. You do it, Vi.'

'We should cash in on your name. You're the Earl. Get some City directorships.'

'B-bit vulgar, what?'

'Fish,' Violet said quietly, 'you cannot hunt the entire Inland Revenue. They want theirs, and in the end, they will get it. We have to make the best of it and if it means you going into the City of London once a week to talk about banking or insurance you will jolly well do it.'

'Whatever you say, Vi.'

'The war's over, Fish.'

'If you s-say so, Vi. If you say so.'

41

A Lot of Bad Eggs
Having a Field Day

Windstone Castle, May 1931

Violet dug in her heels as her horse came to the top of the cherry lane. They were on the long ridge, the pilgrim way up from Cornwall to the west that followed its jagged path along the highest ground, mile after mile; the downs spread out like a map all the way to the sea as they fell down below, the Torrent shiny like polished silver in the sun, the great Windstone Water swirling powerfully as it went to the ocean in the distance. She cantered down the path, her hair blowing in the wind.

A man was ahead of her, and she reined in, clopping up and coming to a stop.

'Hallo, Ned,' she said, and Furzegrove raised his hat.

'Lady Violet,' he said smiling. He put his spade in the earth as Violet slid down and patted her horse. The animal began to graze.

'I've been watching you,' she said. 'From the lookout roof on the Traitors' Tower. I used the Admiral's telescope. Aren't I nosy? I realised that it must be something to do with the Earl, but he doesn't tell me anything. Anyhow, he called at breakfast. He and my son are off the ferry, they're driving up from Dover, so I decided I was entitled to come and see for myself.'

She looked at the two great posts Furzegrove had sunk deep into the ground. Attached to the stump of each was a huge coiled and plaited length of elastic, a vast rubber band.

'It's a catapult,' she said. 'An enormous catapult. I had one when I was a girl. I potted Uncle's pheasants with it when he wouldn't let me shoot. Only this is much, much bigger.'

'You was always wild, Lady Violet,' Furzegrove said, rather approvingly.

'So what's it for?'

'I doesn't know,' he said frankly. 'The Earl, he wrote to me from Germany and enclosed a plan, telling me what to do.'

'Well I jolly well wish he'd write to *me* and tell me what's going on!' Violet said hotly.

'Some parts arrived on the postal truck,' he explained. 'A large catch and a lever to make it go. You pulls the elastic back with a winch.'

Below, along a track, something was moving along. A car, towing something.

'Well here he is,' she said. 'We'll soon find out. And what about the hop fields? I'm expanding production this year, don't forget. The new brewery's finished.'

A few minutes later the car came into view, rolling along the way; a large, green, open-topped 4.5-litre Bentley, towing behind it a long, boxy trailer. It pulled up and Gawaine and Fish clambered out, grinning broadly.

'Fish, you complete rotter!' Violet cried. 'What have you been up to?'

'C-completing our son's education,' he said smiling.

'Oh yes? Art galleries? Baroque churches? The Grand Tour?'

'Dad's taught me to fly!' Gawaine burst out, unable to contain his news any more.

Violet looked at him gravely. 'Yes,' she said finally. 'Ten is probably exactly the right age to learn to fly.'

'Double figures, what?'

'Where did you learn to fly, darling?'

'Up in the German mountains! In a glider!'

'We fell in with a couple of decent coves from the w-war. One of them was in with Richtoven's lot. P-probably shot at each other, eh Ned? Interesting stuff, this gliding. Place like this, darling, where the wind blows up a ridge, you get what's called a standing wave. Air goes up, y'see? You can keep altitude. Great fun, eh?'

'It's the best!' Gawaine said, his eyes shining. Violet looked suspiciously at the long box on wheels behind the Bentley.

'What's in that, Fish?' she demanded. 'It's not what I think it is, is it?'

'It's a glider,' Gawaine breathed proudly. 'The one we learned on. Dad bought it for me.'

'Of course. Go to Germany for the bank, come back with a glider. Fish, you did go to those meetings at the bank, didn't you? They don't pay you just because they like the sound of your name, you know.'

'Of c-course. One of these ch-chaps, he was on their board. Once we'd established who we were we s-sloped off and let the others g-get on with it.'

'Lunch,' Violet said firmly. 'I want to hear all about it over lunch. Come on. I've got cold steak and mushroom pie and salad waiting with some bottles of our new Windstone Green Label. I want you to try it, it's rather good.'

'Young fella,' Fish called to his son, 'unhitch the trailer for me. We'll put the wings on after lunch and you can take your mother up.'

'Oh, may I?' he said excitedly. 'May I, Mummy?'

'There is nothing,' Violet assured him, 'that I should like more.' She quickly pushed away a memory of a burning blue plane fallen from the sky. 'Darling boy, you ride Mikado down for me, and I'll go with your father. I need to tell him off for not going to the meetings at the bank as he was supposed to.'

'Oh, but Mummy, it was so boring! Much more fun flying.'

'Life is not supposed to be just fun,' she said severely.

'Oh, pooh!' he said. She adjusted the stirrups, and helped him up into the saddle.

'Not too fast down the hill,' she said. 'He isn't an aeroplane.'

She watched fondly as he trotted away, and climbed into the Bentley.

'Have you got lunch, Ned?'

'Brought some with me, Lady Violet,' he said. 'My wife, she sends me out with it in the morning.'

'I knew you were looking better fed.'

Fish selected first gear and reached outside to release the hand-brake.

'We'll be up after l-lunch, Ned.'

They rolled gently along the ridgeway. As they came to the long track leading down towards the castle Violet put her hand on his arm.

'Let's stop here a moment, Fish. It's so lovely to see you.'

Fish obligingly stopped the car and they sat with the spring breeze blowing, looking down the Persian carpet of wild flowers. They lit cigarettes and the silver smoke whipped away.

'See?' said Fish. 'It goes up off the ridge.'

'Clever stuff,' she said. 'How are things over there in Germany?'

'P-pretty bad,' he said. 'A lot of people out of work. Bankrupt. Happened to 'em after the war and just when they thought they were back on their feet – this.'

'They're calling it a depression,' she said. 'It's hard here too.'

'Worst bit of it is that there's a lot of bad eggs having a f-field day over there. The B-Bolshies on the one hand and the Nazis on the other. They have full-scale street battles – Gawaine and I saw one – and of c-course all it does is make the government look ineff-fectual.'

'I'd hoped that little bastard Hitler was finished. But look, let's not rant on about politics. What's happened since you left? Oh, Freddie and Clarissa have had twins.'

'Oh, splendid! What make?'

'Boys. I volunteered you to be godfather. Freddie's finally made lieutenant-colonel.'

'Oh, good show! Promotion's so dashed slow. What's that toast in the army? 'Here's to a bloody war!' We must have them over, celebrate.'

'And Frances has left George.'

'I th-thought that might happen.'

'Gone off with an American film-maker. Taken the children too. Upped sticks a couple of weeks ago. George's very cut up about it.'

'Poor old chap. Where's Frances now?'

'In America. Los Angeles. Hollywood, or some such place. Poor George, he never liked Americans much anyway, and now he's rabid about them. Oh, I'll tell you who else's is back in town, so to speak. You'll never guess.'

'Who?'

'Carlotta.'

'Got her gun with her?'

'I don't know. Clarissa tells me she's with some American woman, a Mrs Simpson. They've managed to row themselves in on Thelma Furness's crowd.'

'I didn't know Carlotta batted on that side. Crazy and dangerous, but not one for other ladies.'

'Maybe she isn't.'

'Thelma is. Her and her sisters. Consuelo and Gloria. And the mad Russian, Nada. Very steamy, they say.'

'Never appealed to me, personally. But liking other pretty women doesn't stop Thelma from being the Prince of Wales's mistress, does it? Consuelo's married to that diplomat, and Gloria was married to the Vanderbilt heir, before he drank himself to death. Very versatile, these girls.'

'What about this . . . Mrs Simpson is it?'

'Frantic social climber, they say. Rabid. Wants to get in at court.'

'P-perhaps the little man will have a crack at her. He likes married women.'

'I think Thelma Furness has her claws sunk fairly deep into him.'

'Where did Carlotta meet this w-woman, anyway?'

'Clarissa says in Shanghai.'

'Then she's a bad lot. Nobody comes out of Shanghai but bad 'uns. Carlotta ran some high-powered brothel out there, Clarissa told me.'

'When she wasn't dealing in drugs,' Violet said grimly.

'Poor Crom,' Fish said unexpectedly. He rarely talked about his brother. He finished his cigarette, and restarted the car. They rolled down the hill.

'It will all end in t-tears, if Carlotta's anything to do with it.' he predicted. 'I'm more interested in seeing Gawaine f-fly the glider.'

42

He's a Secret Policeman, Darling

March 1934

'Hallo, Carlotta.'

She turned in her best frock, kept a polite smile on her face. Wasn't it always the way? There you were, waiting for the Prince, and the bores came up, the really pathetic ones, with their damp hands and ingratiating, simpering expressions, desperate to please.

'Hello, George,' she said politely.

'Pretty grand occasion, eh?'

It was, she had to agree. The Carlton House Terrace mansion had been refurbished, it was said, with cost no object. The Ambassador of Nazi Germany was housed in a style surpassing all his contemporaries. His parties were the best in London, and the cream of English society came, which was, naturally, the object.

'Very,' she said. George was dressed in a rather dull dinner suit cut in a fashion of twenty years earlier.

'That must be the evening dress you told me about. That and your two suits and a library,' she remarked waspishly.

'Oh I say!' he guffawed. 'What a memory you have!'

'Oh, there's nothing wrong with my memory.'

On a raised dais, the gypsy band of the Hungaria Restaurant played, at no doubt considerable expense. Fabulously dressed guests swirled about in the magnificent and glittering reception room created for the ninth Duke of Marlborough. George looked like a rather dowdy jackdaw.

'Here on your own, what?'

Oh, God, she thought. He wants to invite me out to dinner.

'No,' she said shortly. 'I'm with Wallis.'

'Oh I say!' he said again, sounding fatuous. 'You *do* mix in high society. They do say ... she may be the next one after Lady Furness ...'

'Watch this space,' she said. 'As they say.'

'Oh, look!' he cried. 'There's Fruity.'

She glanced up, and saw a man in full black military uniform, standing laughing with von Hoesch, the ambassador. It was all black, including the shirt.

'Full fascist fig, what?' George murmured. 'That's Fruity Metcalfe, you know. He has my old job, dogsbody to the Prince.'

He looked thoughtfully at the Prince of Wales's equerry, in his full-dress uniform of Mosley's British Union of Fascists.

'Bit much, turning up in that outfit, wouldn't you say?'

'Why?' Carlotta asked sharply. 'This *is* the Embassy of the German Nazis.'

'Think Edward minds?'

'Why don't you ask him? If Fruity's here then he must be close by. No, he doesn't mind. Why should he? Democracy's dying, George, dictatorships are the new way.'

There was a flurry of activity in the doorway, and George saw the Prince coming in, superbly dressed, with an equally magnificent Wallis Simpson close by. When he looked back, he found that Carlotta had vanished. A few moments later he saw her, amongst those circling around the Prince. An amiable expression on his face, clutching his untouched glass of champagne, George circulated. In a corner, looking out of place but interested, he found one of his relatives.

'Perceval!' he cried.

'Percy, please,' the member of Parliament for Windstone reproved him.

'What on earth are you doing here?'

'I could say the same to you,' Perceval said pleasantly. 'Does Herr von Hoesch know what you do?'

'The ambassador clearly does not read,' George countered. 'Not the Left Book Club, at any rate. I saw your new one. What was it about? These yellow jackets all look the same.'

'The Peace Pledge Union!' he said proudly. He beckoned to a passing waiter and snaffled some canapés with the inherited skill of an aristocrat. 'The people shall vote, George! They shall vote yea or nay for the League of Nations, for disarmament, for peace itself.'

'Very nice,' George said drily. 'What price Churchill's rearmament, then?'

'Rearmament? Nothing more certain to lead to war, let me tell you. Churchill, pah! A loose cannon on deck, a dangerous ideologue. Fortunately he has no standing, no standing at all, not in the House, not in the country. If ever I saw a politician with a past and no future, it's him. The future is with us.'

'You have an invitation here, I take it?'

Perceval grinned mischievously.

'Von Hoesch's invited all the aristocrats. I got in as a de Clare!'

George glanced across to where the Prince of Wales was holding court.

'It certainly seems to be working,' he said. 'Any news of the King's health?'

'No better, they say.'

'Then he'll soon be our monarch,' George murmured. Fruity Metcalfe was standing near the Prince in his jet uniform, grinning broadly in approval of whatever was being said.

'That's your route, Percy!' George said naughtily. 'Become a fascist like Fruity. Mosley was a Labour MP, you know!'

'I shan't answer that,' Perceval said with dignity.

George moved on. He waved at Freddie, in splendid Tank Corps dress uniform, and Clarissa, and insinuated himself into the loose crowd about the Prince.

'Good evening, sir,' he said pleasantly. Edward glanced across, looking rather frosty.

'Ah, de Clare. What're you up to these days?' he asked. He sounds more American than he did, thought George. A strange cockney American. Nothing. Something that doesn't exist. Wallis, never far away, raked him with a sideways glance.

'Oh, just a civil servant, sir,' he said boringly. He saw Carlotta sneer to herself.

'Like it here, do you, sir?' George said, suddenly the slightest bit aggressive. The Prince's eyes flashed, he was unused to people not toadying to him.

'I do,' he said, his voice slightly louder than it need be. 'I find German company most congenial.' Von Hoesch beamed. 'My own forebears were of Hanover and Coburg,' the Prince pointed out.

'The German government is very hostile to its Jewish people,' George said in a dull voice.

'It's none of our business!'

'No, I suppose not. But what about the pace of German rearmament, sir? Isn't that our business?'

Von Hoesch frowned, wondering which of his guests George was. Edward took the opportunity to look around, to make sure he had people's attention. Wallis smiled encouragingly at him, he seemed to swell.

'Let me tell you, de Clare, Chancellor Hitler is strong against communism, and that is something we must never forget. Only the fascists of Europe are strong against communist subversion – yet we have it here too! We are in great danger in this country, and Chancellor Hitler and *Duce* Mussolini are showing the way! I hope and pray – and believe – that we shall never fight a war again, but if we do – if we do! – then we must be on the winning side, and that will be the German, not the French. Fascism may well be the future. Dictators are all the thing these days, we may want one here too, soon.'

There was a spontaneous outbreak of applause, and Edward smiled, gratified.

George beamed back.

'May I recommend you for the post, sir!' he cried, and they all laughed in approval. Wallis's eyes shone briefly, like stars.

George shuffled off.

As they swirled about, like autumn leaves, Carlotta found herself next to her sister.

'Clarissa, darling!' she cried, insincerely. 'You'll never guess who I saw here, looking just like something the cat dragged in. George. George de Clare.'

'Oh, yes. We see George, from time to time. His wife left him, he comes for the weekend.' She smiled wryly. 'He has a rota. We see him once a month, he goes down to the castle one weekend, and another he spends in Cambridge with Godfrey. I'm not sure what he does the last one.'

'Godfrey . . . I always liked him. What's he doing nowadays?'

'Your sort, was he, Carlotta darling?' Clarissa asked, with a hint of malice. 'He's a don. Art's his subject.'

'I must look him up. George's wife left him? I'm not surprised. What a bore!'

Clarissa looked at her sister with a certain amusement.

'Yes, he's perfected the act, hasn't he?'

'Mmm?'

'Don't you know what he does?'

'He's a civil servant.'

'Yes. Something like that. He works for MI5. He's a secret police-man, darling.'

43

I Love Happy Endings

London, May 1936

Carlotta got out of bed, and pulled back the curtains. The morning sunshine flooded the room. It matched her mood. She was happy and there was a spring in her step as she went through to the kitchen to put a kettle on the hob to boil for coffee. She never drank tea, it was too English. God, how she loathed the English! That was in large measure the reason for her ongoing happiness. Revenge was sweet. The English were getting screwed and she was in on it. When Wallis Simpson had told her how she made him – now he was the *King*! – crawl she loved every second. Those de Clares may have thought they'd ruined her all that time ago, made her live in filth out in Shanghai, made her whore for her living, but she was back, she was at the top of society and there was nothing they could do about it. She flung the kitchen window open just so she could hear the sound of the English traffic rumbling away on the Mayfair street below. Underneath. That was the place for the English all right, grovelling away down there in the dirt.

She cackled maniacally to herself and went through to run a bath. She tipped in a dose of sweet-smelling bath salts; she liked to cosset herself. She was at one with Wallis there. Take as much as you could get for yourself.

She ran over the plans for the day in her head. The King was holding a party in the evening at Windsor Castle. That was the most important thing. Wallis Simpson would be holding court, of course. The Nazi von Ribbentrop was bound to be there. Carlotta giggled to herself. Now that was style. Simpson had the King crawling to her merest whim and on the side she was fucking a foreign diplomat for fun! She wondered if Wallis told the King about it, as she made him lick her feet. Probably. The more you gave these sickos the more they liked it. She probably described it in detail. Carlotta grinned savagely. She certainly would. Make 'em suffer.

She turned off the water just in time to hear the doorbell ring.

She frowned. She wasn't expecting anyone. Perhaps the postman. She went casually through her softly carpeted sitting room, and into the hall. She opened the door. A man stood there, an official man in a fawn raincoat. He had a rather crushed looking trilby hat in one hand.

'Mrs Carlotta Jacobs?' he asked, politely.

A policeman. She could recognise them anywhere, any nationality. A board creaked in the corridor; she saw a policewoman standing there, in frumpy black uniform.

'I am Inspector Morris.' he said. He reached inside his coat for a document. 'I've come to search your apartment.'

They came inside, and shut the door behind them. He had her sit down at her own table while the silent policewoman stood by the wall and watched her, and he disappeared into the rest of her flat.

He must have known, she thought, as he came back. He must have known where to look, and her heart began to beat very fast.

Morris put the bags of white powder down in front of her.

'I have reason to believe that what is contained in these bags are drugs, prohibited by the law,' he said. 'Am I right?'

'Yes,' she said, dully.

'You're a dealer,' he said, nastily. 'You're going to go to jail. Five years in Holloway, at least.'

'No! No, look. I'm a friend of the King.'

Morris smiled patronisingly. 'I don't think the King knows people who deal in drugs,' he said.

'No, you must believe me, he'll—'

'The King will do nothing,' he said implacably.

Her mind raced. God, this couldn't be happening to her. Not having got this far—

'George!' she cried, thinking furiously. 'This ... this isn't what you think.'

Oh, Jesus, why was that fat bitch standing by the wall? She could have fucked herself out of this one, she'd done it before. But yes, George.

'George de Clare,' she said, with a confidence she didn't feel. 'He'll explain to you. I'm not a drug dealer, don't be so stupid. I'm working for MI5.'

Morris's eyebrows climbed up towards his hairline.

'*Really?*' he said disbelievingly.

She took the initiative, got up without asking, found her bag, took out a cigarette and lit it.

'Call him if you don't believe me,' she said.

∗   ∗   ∗

'Hallo, Carlotta,' George said.

'George, darling.'

'Thank you for coming so quickly, sir,' Morris said, and Carlotta was intensely relieved to see he was extremely respectful. Thank God she still kept in touch with Clarissa, still indulged in family gossip. At the party, she had mocked him, such a bore. Clarissa's strange smile. Don't you know what he does, darling? *He's a secret policeman.*

George put his bowler hat down on the table.

'Would you mind waiting outside, Inspector?' he asked, politely.

'Not at all, sir.'

He and the policewoman went out, at his bidding.

'Oh George—' she carolled.

'You're stupid,' he said coldly. 'You're going to go to gaol for several years. Very nasty it is, in our gaols.'

'Get me off the hook,' she whispered.

'What have you got to offer me?'

'Anything you want,' she said desperately.

'I only deal in intelligence.'

'Huh?'

'Information,' he said. He sat down at the table and lit a cigarette without asking her permission. 'Hard, accurate information, not known to other parties.'

'I . . .' she faltered.

'Let us begin with Wallis Simpson, the King's mistress,' he said brutally. 'You seem to be well in with her.'

'I'm a kind of secretary, companion.'

'You clearly advised her as to the nature of our society.'

'I helped, yes.'

'Where did you meet her?'

'I . . . ah . . .'

'The judge will take a recommendation from us for a more severe sentence if we want it.'

'I met her in Shanghai.'

'When?'

'About ten years ago. I was . . . involved in business there.'

'You ran a brothel and were engaged in the drug-trafficking trade. Now, I don't care about you, but what was Wallis doing there?'

'She . . . well, yes, she was involved in dealing too. It was a very corrupt society, you understand. You made money, got power, forged connections in any way you could.'

'Mrs Simpson clearly learned well from her experiences,' George said acidly. 'She has done the same here. This involved sleeping with powerful men, I take it?'

'That's what you do,' Carlotta said, as if explaining the two times table to a child.

'I have a report that says Mrs Simpson was involved in espionage. What do you know about that?'

'Well, look, she got some naval information from some British officers, yes.'

'To sell to whom?'

Carlotta shrugged. 'There were plenty interested. England's the naval power out there. You Britishers, you have your great base at Singapore. Information about it was valuable to people like the Russians and the Japanese.'

'Mrs Simpson sold naval secrets.'

'Yes.'

'Would you say that she was expert in various sexual arts?'

Carlotta suddenly cackled with mirth.

'Various sexual arts . . . you crack me up, George! Of *course* she's expert, she's a high-class whore, you don't think these men played patience with her, do you?'

'How she chooses to spend her time would not concern me, if it did not have the potential to damage national security,' he said coldly.

'The King, you mean?'

'I do. She appears to be his mistress.'

'She doesn't fuck him, you know,' Carlotta said frankly. She crossed her legs and blew smoke into the air.

'Really?' George said icily.

'Says she doesn't have to.'

'We believe that while she does, one way or another, exert a wholly undesirable power over the King, whether by sexual artifice or not, she *is* having sexual relations with Herr von Ribbentrop.'

'So what if she is?' Carlotta asked indifferently.

'Herr Ribbentrop is a trusted and senior member of the German Nazi élite.'

'Yeah. So what?'

'Nazi Germany is a foreign power whose interests do not match our own,' he said grimly. 'The King is entitled to read state secrets of the day, they are sent to him in sealed red boxes. We have reason to believe that some of those secrets are making their way to the German government.'

She stayed silent.

'We are forced to the conclusion that Mrs Simpson is a spy,'

'Maybe the King wants her to be,' Carlotta said sullenly.

George gave an outraged laugh.

'One may not approve of everything King Edward does, but he is *not* a traitor. However, it is clear that Mrs Simpson exerts a considerable influence over him. He is no longer his own master.'

'So he follows her about like a dog. He does what she wants. So what?'

'He is the King,' George said, suddenly savage. 'His duty to his people comes first, before anything else.'

There was silence in the room for some moments.

'As Prince of Wales the King formed a number of liasons,' George said, after a while. 'Freda Ward, Thelma Furness foremost, but there were many others, brief, transitory . . . it suggests that he has been, for many years, looking for something . . .'

'Hey, I love happy endings,' Carlotta said brightly. His expression withered her smile.

'The King is not made for happiness,' he said bleakly. 'All we wish to be certain of is that whatever he has been looking for – whatever it is – that he has not found it in Mrs Simpson.'

He was silent again, sitting staring through spiralling cigarette smoke at the window.

'Does she want to be Queen?' he asked abruptly.

'I . . . ah . . .'

'Answer me!'

'Yes,' she said quietly. 'Above all else.'

He pushed back his chair, took his bowler hat up from the table.

'I'll take care of the police,' he promised. 'For the time being.'

'What do you mean, for the time being?'

'I'm going to be in touch with you,' he said enigmatically. 'There's something else I want you to do for me.'

He went out, closing the door behind him. Looking out of her window, she saw him go away down the street, an upright, trim figure in his dark, striped suit, his black hat and tightly rolled umbrella.

A few streets away, on the border of the park, he turned into a pub. The landlord was attending to his affairs behind the bar; only a couple of regulars sat at the small round tables on the burgundy carpet, reading the papers over a half of bitter. It was rather dark, a bit dingy. George ordered a gin and bitters and carried it with him over to one of the men.

Inspector Morris looked up from his paper.

'Get what you wanted?' he enquired.

'I think so,' said George. 'I'll know for certain soon.'

Windsor Castle

The Royal Buick stood huge, silent and shiny in the lights of the castle. The King was in residence. A stab of hatred went through George. He loathed all things American. What kind of King was it that imported foreign cars to ride in? There it was, yet more of the taint of the American woman, Simpson.

George showed his special pass to the policeman standing quietly by the lamp in his uniform, and the man saluted respectfully.

He opened the door, and George slipped inside. It was gloomy in the hallway. Carlotta came over to him quickly, her eyes very large and white.

'I thought you weren't coming,' she whispered. 'Quickly, if you must. Follow me.'

She led the way up a flight of back stairs, along a little-used corridor, up another flight of stairs.

'You must be quiet,' she insisted. 'There are no carpets up here.'

He bent and took off his polished black brogues, holding them in his hand.

'Good,' she said. 'I'm going to take you into a room. In the corner the skirting-board is loose. Lift it up and you can see through a little gap into the bedroom below.'

He nodded. They padded along the corridor. She paused, and very carefully opened a door. She pointed silently to the corner of the bare room: he could see the board she meant, faintly limned by light seeping up from below. He crept across and knelt down. The door closed behind him, and he lifted the board, propping it up with one of his shoes.

He could see the King. He recognised his former employer immediately, even though he was on his knees, and wearing a pair of grey flannel shorts and a grey shirt and school tie that a schoolboy might wear.

A woman stood in the centre of the room, a severe, forbidding figure in black frowning down at her charge. On the bed behind her was a jumble of disconnected things: what appeared to be a large baby's cloth nappy, a feeding bottle, a black rubber garment, a length of rope, an object like a policeman's truncheon.

*   *   *

Carlotta was waiting at the bottom of the stairs. She took one glance at his face, almost spoke, and thought better of it just in time, realising he would have struck her. She guided him down to the door, closed it behind him.

He found his car in the darkness, drove away down the long drive towards the distant glow of London. By the gate a spasm seized him. He opened the driver's door quickly, bent double, hanging out as he vomited up his disgust.

44

Sure as Eggs is Eggs

Windstone Castle, October 1936

Gawaine de Clare rolled the little glider to the left, pulled back on the stick and they were driven down into their seats by the G-forces. Fish felt himself greying out, looked across at the wing and saw the air compressing to mist over its edge.

'Good boy,' he grunted. 'And back.'

Abruptly, the horizon in front of the little open cockpit rotated through nearly one hundred and eighty degrees and went tearing across the little aero screen. Russet woodland, the downs, the castle and the Water, sweeping past.

'On your tail!' Fish shouted. Gawaine pulled the stick back and over and they shot up into the sky like a dolphin. He rolled it around like a barrel, came inverted, put the nose down and completed the roll.

'Rat-ata-tata-tat!' Fish called, banging a forefinger in front of them. 'There he is, right in front of you, so don't waste time, l-let him have it.'

For a few moments they drifted silently over the land below, and Fish savoured the trees and fields and streams of Windshire. Stubble stood golden in the cornfields, haystacks plump as new-baked loaves. Pigs were foraging in the oak wood for acrons, one of his men waved as they went without sound overhead. The Earl and his son in their white glider had become a part of the castle. Golden pheasant were pecking for grain in the stubble; once the leaves had fallen the shooting could begin.

The long road down to the staion meandered below. A little woodsmoke drifted across from the inn.

They were down to about two hundred feet.

'Forced landing,' said Fish. 'Wh-where are you going to put her?'

'Breeze is from the west,' Gawaine said confidently. He wheeled the glider round into an approach pattern, and pointed down to the cornfield below. 'I'll land her there.'

'Good. Just remember in a fighter you come d-down much faster than this. Have to p-pick somewhere straight ahead, give or take a little each side.'

'I will.'

The sixteen-year-old guided the glider round expertly, deftly slipping over the high trees that bordered the field with opposite stick and rudder. He straightened out ten feet above the ground and the skid kissed the stubble. Golden pheasant scattered, running as fast they could for the safety of the edges, where the wild weeds still grew.

The wing fell gently to the ground, and Gawaine sighed with pleasure.

'I do love to fly,' he said.

'We'll fit in one before evening, if Winston gives us time,' said Fish.

He could see the inn only a quarter of a mile away, towards the castle.

'F-fancy a half?'

'Love one, Dad!'

They walked out over the field, the short stubble crunching pleasantly under their feet. Fish fumbled in the pocket of his baggy jacket for his cigarette case and lit one. For a few moments he coughed violently as the smoke went into his lungs, turning a dangerous shade of purple.

'You all right, Dad?'

Fish dragged some air into his chest, and slowly became suffused with pink once more.

'N-never better,' he gasped. They arrived outside the inn and Fish sat down on a bench. He gave his son a small gold half-sovereign.

'Couple of halves of your mother's own,' he suggested.

His son went inside and Fish sat in the crisp autumnal sunshine. The rough scraping feeling in his chest died away and he leaned back with pleasure. A little while later Gawaine came back with a tray bearing two small barrel shaped glasses of clear brown bitter.

'Lovely,' said Fish. 'Well flown, darling.'

'Thanks, Dad.'

Fish wiped a little foam from his lip and peered at the tray.

'What have we got, then?' he said, interestedly. It was one of their favourite small amusements, looking through the change to see what they had, rather like fishermen dragging in the net of fish.

On the tray were round coins of copper and bronze, some polished, some dark with age, some smooth like stones from the sea, some still sharply stamped. There was shiny silver, some worn thin at the edges, some neatly bevelled, sixpence pieces of differing engraving, of differing reigns, the heads of William and Edward, of Victoria, both young and old, there were tiny silver three-penny pieces, there was a halfpenny, a small round farthing. Two big round silver half crowns were there, and a florin. They pushed them out flat, sifting through them.

'I say, I can hardly even see the date on this one!'

Fish held up a flat round penny. Faint markings on its surface, worn smooth by countless pockets and purses were all that remained of its sharp stampings. Fish licked a corner of his handkerchief and dampened it.

'It's a copper,' he murmured. 'Old King William, I'd say.'

The outline of Britannia seated with helmet shield and trident was faintly visible on the reverse, he turned it over and peered hard.

'Eighteen thirty-six,' he said triumphantly. 'Another year and Victoria was on the throne.'

'This is one of hers, Dad,' Gawaine said, picking up the florin with its young crowned head on the obverse. 'Eighteen forty-nine.'

'Forty-nine? Not Gothic?'

Fish pricked up his ears.

'Just the date, Dad.'

'Must be a godless. Let's s-see.'

Fish took it.

'Yes, look, no *Deo Gratias*. We'll hang on to that, it's rare.'

They both drank some beer.

'Your m-mother knows how to brew,' Fish said in praise.

'Lovely,' Gawaine agreed. 'Dad, why a florin anyway?'

'A t-two-bob bit?'

'Yes, two shillings. It doesn't go. Twelve pennies in a shilling, a sixpence, a threepence, a half crown – eight in a pound – a half sov and a sov. Why two shillings?'

'Because it's a tenth of a pound. It's decimal, like they do on the Continent. Very b-boring they are, over there, all tens and hundreds. Litres and kilos. No pints, quarts, pounds and ounces. No pecks and chains and bushels and poles. All very t-tedious, they are.'

'So why a two-bob bit?' Gawaine persisted.

'Oh, s-some fool tried to make *our* coinage decimal like theirs, back when Queen Vicky was first on the throne. The godless coin we have here was the first one. Of course, everyb-body laughed like h-hell and it came to nothing. Can you imagine g-giving up our h-history like that? M-might just as well pretend to be like them, all a ghastly mish-mash of Frogs and Jerries and Eyeties. I c-can't think of anything worse. We're far better than that.'

He tipped back his beer.

'We'll have to down these quickly,' he said. 'Better make sure everything's ready for Winston when he gets here.'

'You're taking a lot of trouble over this visit,' Gawaine observed.

'Winston has s-simple tastes. He only likes the best.'

'Old Smithers my housemaster says he's a warmonger.'

'Your old Smithers is a b-blithering idiot, like most of the rest of the people in charge of th-this country.'

'He says he's an erratic, dangerous adventurer.'

Fish winced slightly.

'Winston doesn't always get things in proportion. But on this one he's right. Totally right. L-listen, darling. There's going to be another war. Sure as eggs is eggs. Winston's simply trying to get us ready to fight it. You remember when we were in G-Germany that time, darling? When we saw them f-fighting on the streets, and all the blood? That's wh-what they're like, the Germans, and n-now they have this Hitler who's going to let them do it again to everyb-body else.'

'We had Nazis here, *they* rioted.'

'Mosley and his lot?'

They finished the beer, rose and began the walk back to the castle.

'All they did was take their pretty uniforms away and they folded up like paper dolls. We're English, we don't like that sort of thing, we leave it to the b-blasted Jerries. Everybody in G-Germany wears a uniform. W-we prefer flannel bags and an old jacket.'

Gawaine grinned. 'Will we fight the Germans like that?'

'If n-necessary. We'll be doing the fighting, that's for certain. We had to win it last time, it'll be the same this.'

'What about the French?'

'Winston thinks a lot of the French,' Fish said gloomily. 'I don't. I was over there last year, the place is f-falling apart.'

They came over the rise and the downs lay spread out, stretching to the sea, the castle on its great mound dominating the land about it.

'We'll win, young man,' Fish said certainly. 'We always win. In a thousand years some ancestor of ours will stand here looking at this and it'll be just the s-same.'

Jervis the butler signalled and the two footmen cleared away the plates of oysters, now so many piles of shells, and refilled the glasses with champagne. Fish had ordered a dozen bottles to be on ice in the butler's pantry. He had placed Churchill at one end of the table, himself at the other. In between were Violet, Gawaine, Freddie, Clarissa and George.

'Do your farms prosper, Lady Windstone?' Churchill asked winningly. He was dressed in a one-piece siren suit, rather like an enormous baby's romper suit. It was made from striped worsted and zipped up the front. He looked very comfortable.

'They have to,' Violet said drily. 'We are still paying the death duties.'

'You must come to Chartwell and give me the secret!' he exclaimed. 'I keep ponies, pigs, chickens, calves and sheep. I am determined to make it pay, whatever the cost!'

They all guffawed. Chartwell Manor, Churchill's home and court was his great love. He refused to stint on it, and it bled him white.

They brought in the next course, golden fried fillets of sole, wrapped in thinly-cut aromatic Scotch smoked salmon, liberally garnished with plump scampi. Silver platters of fried mushrooms and sautéed potatoes accompanied them.

'After my last speech advocating rearmament in the House, the Reverend Soper said that pacifism contained a spiritual force strong enough to repel an invader,' Churchill commented. 'What do you say to that?'

'Perhaps he has been to see Mr Wells's new film,' Violet suggested.

'Anti-tank guns have rather more effect,' said Freddie. 'The Germans are developing a rather good one, eighty-eight millimetres in calibre.'

'Ah, but nobody is expecting to invade Germany,' Churchill pointed out. 'The countries of Europe await in fear and trepidation the arrival of German tanks across *their* borders.'

'There is nothing to stop the Germans from fitting the gun to a tank,' Freddie pointed out. 'In my opinion the best anti-tank weapon is a superior tank.'

'Very good!' Churchill cried, washing down his food with champagne. 'And are *our* tanks of superior quality?'

Freddie hesitated.

'As a serving officer I probably shouldn't comment on that ... I could point out that the Army estimates for this year allow only £2 million in total for mechanisation; most of this going on trucks. Our potential enemies have enormously increased their tank corps in the past three years, whereas in the Royal Tank Corps no such increase has taken place. We have only one Tank Brigade, which in effect means that we are unable – with the Experimental Mechanised Force disbanded – to practise such fundamentals as tank-versus-tank combat.'

'Have another glass of this delightful bubbly,' George suggested with a sour grin, 'and tell our distinguished guest what you really think.'

'George is in military intelligence,' Freddie explained.

'Ah!' Churchill said pugnaciously. 'So what are *your* views?'

'I find the pace and quality of Herr Hitler's military build-up extremely alarming,' George said frankly. 'Like the Führer himself I share the respect of most professionals for the competence of the German officer corps, and he is providing them with excellent equipment to do the job.'

'But should Herr Hitler once more go to war he will find, as the Kaiser did before him, a most formidable alliance ranged against him,' Churchill pointed out. 'Not only the might of France, but the awesome resources of the British Empire, which spans the globe.'

'Leaving aside for the moment the competence of the French to fight,' said George, 'the forces Hitler is bringing into being do not seem designed for an extended war of attrition such as we here took part in last time.'

'Not me!' said Gawaine.

'Not you,' George said, with a sad smile. 'Your turn may come, I hope it won't. No – I think Freddie may bear me out – we fear a war in which combined forces of air and ground, linked by radio command, will deal out devastation in a conflict of short duration but terrifying intensity.'

'We s-saw that at the end of the Great War,' said Fish. 'When Ludendorff advanced in March. He used stormtroops, we savaged him with low-flying aeroplanes.'

'It is what the Experimental Mechanised Force was proving,' Freddie agreed.

'You made a disparaging comment about the ability of the French to fight,' Churchill observed. 'Can you explain yourself?'

'French society is in a state of decay from top to very bottom,' George said succinctly. 'It compares very unfavourably with the regeneration regrettably achieved by Herr Hitler's Nazis. I believe the French will barely fight, if attacked.'

'You are talking of a great nation!' Churchill cried angrily.

'All nations, great or otherwise, have their day,' George said obstinately.

'I went a few months ago with my general to France,' said Freddie. 'A courtesy visit, to inspect the 9th Army.'

Churchill shovelled in more sole and scampi, and grunted for him to go on.

'We inspected the guard of honour that had been drawn up for us. Seldom have I ever – not even Rumanian forces in the war – seen anything so slovenly and badly turned out. Men were unshaven, horses ungroomed. Vehicles filthy. The men ... there was no pride in themselves! They shambled, wore insolent and insubordinate expressions. I tell you, I would have clapped the lot in the guardroom! I certainly would not care to have to depend upon them in a battle.'

'Very gloomy you all are, I must say,' the old politician grumbled.

'We didn't go on any tour of inspection after that,' Freddie finished. 'General Corap – a great fat fellow with gravy stains down his uniform – took us off for a colossal and most lengthy lunch. He might not have known how to fight, but he was in a class of his own when it came to shifting food.'

'Hmm. So you say it will be the British Empire that will have to see to Herr Hitler?'

'If we re-arm!' Freddie drained his flute of champagne and, as George had known he would, finally launched into passionate speech. 'And even then, what arms shall we be given?'

'I have seen prototypes of the coming eight-gun fighters – the Hurricane and S-Spitfire,' Fish said quickly. 'M-magnificent machines.'

'They may be!' Freddie said hotly. 'What have I got? Undergunned junk that can barely stagger from the maintenance workshops to the practice range! The Germans are entrusting the design and build of their tanks to firms of high quality, such as Henschel and Daimler-Benz; their engines are made by Maybach. Our new prototype tank has its hull made by the London, Midland and Scottish Railway Company! Its turret is made by the people who make the Austin Seven motor car! The designer has only ever built locomotives and has placed the radiator of the tank inside the hull, where it cools the engine and roasts the crew. The turret has a gun capable of penetrating enemy armour only at short range.'

Freddie looked about the table, a forkful of cold fish in his hand.

'And I,' he said quietly, 'should war break out, will be required to lead brave men off to fight in this contraption.'

'We are importing great quantities of modern machine tools,' Churchill said quickly. 'This must improve matters.'

'Manned by old-fashioned craft unionists,' George said acidly.
'Ready to strike at the drop of a rivet.'

A somewhat sombre silence fell over the gathering as the servants
took away the plates, and brought in fillet of roast venison, stuffed
with paté de foie gras, and served with a truffle sauce. Churchill's
face brightened.

'Of course, I am familiar with our failings, but yet we are still a
very great nation.'

'Of c-course we are!'

'Of course,' Freddie agreed. 'But we have to keep pace with the
times, with our competitors. We shall only remain a great power as
long as we are industrially great. Much of our industry is crippled
by practices and habits of thought from the past. My wife Clarissa
is American, we go over there to visit her family – her father was a
senator, he arranges for me to see things I might not otherwise be
able to. I tell you, what goes on there boggles the mind! Fish, isn't
it so? You came with us last time. You remember we went to see the
Boeing factory.'

Fish shook his head in remembered disbelief.

'Like an H.G. W-Wells novel!' he exclaimed. 'Not a factory as we
know it. *Enormous.* So clean and tidy . . .'

'Efficient. A huge design staff – educated chaps with degrees.
Well-trained workforce.'

'All in s-smart uniforms. I f-flew one of the aeroplanes with a test
pilot. It was very good.'

'Hmmm . . .' Churchill looked over to Clarissa and smiled charmingly. 'How do you find the mood in America towards the dramas
that occupy us in Europe, Mrs de Clare?'

'I'm afraid that many of my countrymen and women are simply
appalled by what they see in Europe,' she said frankly. 'After the Wall
Street crash we chose protectionism. Last year Congress passed the
Neutrality Act. Intellectually there is a culture that wishes to praise the
traits which are seen as being *American*, not European. We don't like
the look of Hitler's Nazi Germany, but we're a very long way off from
it, a very long way indeed. Furthermore, many people see the British
Empire as a bigger threat to American prosperity than the dictators.'

Churchill scowled, and Violet broke into the conversation.

'My goodness this is all too gloomy!' she cried cheerfully. 'Let us
not talk any more about politics. Why don't we be thoroughly vulgar
and gossip about the King and Mrs Simpson?'

'Why y-yes!' said Fish, quickly moving to her support. 'What do
you think will happen, sir?'

Churchill pondered for a few moments as the empty venison plates were removed, and stilton, baked apple tart, port, biscuits and jugs of thick yellow cream appeared on the table.

'My own view is that the King is a man of fleeting passions,' he said. 'He has fallen in love often enough in the past, and fallen once again out of it. Let us give him time. Mrs Simpson will prove as ephemeral as many another *femme fatale* has been in the King's affections.'

'I am sorry to have to disagree,' George said quietly. 'My own view is that the King's emotional, physical and mental involvement with Mrs Simpson is complete and total, and will probably only end with his death.'

'Well!' Violet said.

Churchill leaned forward alertly. 'And is that the view of your superiors?' he asked quickly.

'It might be,' George said mildly. 'Frightfully good tart, Vi.'

'And do you and your superiors approve of Mrs Simpson?' Churchill probed.

'Freddie, do pass this cream to our guest,' said George. 'I believe he is partial to it. We do not think Mrs Simpson is a good influence on the King, no.'

'Isn't his relationship with her their own affair?' Churchill demanded, pouring the contents of the jug over his tart.

'No,' George said, without emotion.

'Better and better!' Violet cried, keeping a light-hearted tone.

'They do say her house is entirely furnished and decorated with valuables taken from the Palace,' Clarissa chipped in. 'To the value of tens of thousands of pounds.'

'Well, hasn't he given her some two hundred thousand in jewels?' said Freddie joining in.

'Three,' George said quietly. 'Mrs Simpson appreciates the concentrated value of jewellery. The King has just lavished a further one hundred thousand pounds' worth on her.'

'You could buy a fair-sized warship for that, couldn't you, Fish?' Freddie cried jovially.

'S-small squadron of f-fighters certainly,' agreed Fish. 'Either that or refurbish the castle roof.'

'So what shall he do?' said Violet.

'He must wait until Mrs Simpson's divorce becomes absolute next April, at the very least,' Churchill said wisely. 'With the Coronation having taken place, he shall be better-placed to make decisions.'

'He had better abdicate,' said George. 'Sooner, rather than later.'

'This is ruthless talk!' Churchill cried. 'We should not be talking of things that will damage the monarchy. The institution of monarchy is a great bulwark against the fearful depredations that have so damaged society in Europe. No King today, a dictator tomorrow.'

'That is a very valid point, sir,' George said politely. He drank some port. 'Nice vintage, Fish. However, I feel that the King will do sufficient damage to his institution, should he remain in it.'

'So you advocate abdication, let him make way for the Duke of York . . . as Albert the First?'

'I feel he is more likely to take the name George. George the sixth. But yes, I do.'

'I know his wife, Elizabeth Bowes-Lyon that was,' Violet chipped in. 'She's very bright. She'd make a good Queen.'

'He's very shy,' said Fish. 'T-terrible stutter.'

'*You've* got a stutter, darling. It hasn't done you any harm.'

'I'm not the K-King.'

'Well, he wears a good uniform, darling. That's important. And he's very dutiful.'

'As Edward is not,' George pointed out.

'We are hurrying on too fast!' Churchill protested.

'We live in queer times,' George said strangely. 'Here we are, gathered about the table with one of the great politicians of the age. Should we not let him talk?'

Churchill beamed. 'It is never a hardship to me to talk.'

'Jervis!' said Violet. 'The cigars, please. Romeo y Julieta, Mr Churchill?'

'My favourite, my dear.'

Churchill selected a long, perfectly formed cigar from the box offered to him by the butler. He pierced it with a long match, fumbled in his pockets for some brown gummed paper which he wrapped about its lower half, and lit it.

'Gawaine, see if Ned's got the glider up to the catapult,' said Fish. 'We'll fly before dusk.'

'That's super, Dad.'

The boy left the room. When she glanced out of the window a few moments later Violet saw her son pedalling hard on his bicycle up the hill.

'Is war inevitable?' she asked, turning to Churchill.

'I pray not . . . It is of course self-evident that Germany, led by a band of desperados, now seeks to subjugate the continent and establish a Germanised Europe under Nazi control. We British will be shirking our historic duty if we fail to prevent this calamity. We cannot afford to see Nazism in its present phase of cruelty and intolerance, with all its hatreds and all its gleaming weapons, paramount in Europe. Ever since the days of Queen Bess our task has been to oppose the strongest, most aggressive, most dominating power on the continent, and particularly to prevent the Low Countries from falling into the hands of such a power. Today that power is Germany. Increasingly, the weaker nations look to the British to ensure that law and freedom reigns among the nations and within the nations.'

Churchill's cigar had gone out, he took a fresh match and relit it.

'You appear to be describing a different government to the one we have, sir,' George said lightly, while watching him intently.

'I do indeed!' Churchill exclaimed, wreathed in new smoke. 'Hardly government ... decided only to be undecided, resolved to be irresolute, adamant for drift, solid for fluidity, all powerful for impotence!'

All around the table beamed, making mental efforts to memorise the phrases.

'What of Eden?' Freddie asked. 'Good war record, at least.'

'True. But I fear the greatness of his office will find him out. He is a handsome man. Within, I feel, is a man of straw. And he is a party man. He will put the Conservative party before nation – not thinking to do so, you understand – but nevertheless, it will happen. Party men do not make great national leaders.'

'Nobody could accuse you of being a strong party man, sir,' George said smoothly.

'Hah! The attitude of the present government towards Herr Hitler may be summarised as "Dear Germany, do destroy us *last*!" I do not think Mr Eden will alter that. The government wishes to appease Hitler; they do not appreciate that feeding the Nazi beast only whets its appetite. Yet this is just what they do. They have intimated that the Germans may have a free hand for treaty revisions where Austria, Czechoslovakia and Danzig are concerned. "Treaty revisions?" Herr Hitler does not take such phrases seriously.'

'What can we expect?' Violet asked quietly.

'For certain, Austria is Germany's, and Czechoslovakia too. Perhaps even without bloodshed. If we fail to prevent this then it is the turn of Poland.'

'Prevent . . .' George mused. 'We should fight for Czechoslovakia?'

'Once Germany annexes Austria,' Churchill said expertly, 'she acquires an extra twelve divisions. Should she disarm the Czechs, a further thirty – in fact, worse than this, for she will acquire the fine equipment of the Czech army, and their powerful armaments industry. The turnaround in forces amounts to some eighty divisions, or the size of the entire French army.'

'Is this what you fear most?' asked Violet.

'No,' Churchill said sombrely. 'I fear what I have feared since the Bolsheviks came to power in Russia: an alliance between Russia and Germany.'

'Preposterous!' George expostulated. 'Why . . .'

'Tell me, what is preposterous about it?' Churchill asked quietly. 'These are fearsome times. The rule of Stalin bears close comparison with that of Herr Hitler. Both are gangster-statesmen, they may yet come to the realisation that it could pay to co-operate for a while, to devour the weak democracies before they turn on each other. We must pray it does not happen. As it is, the government is bent upon appeasing the demands of Herr Hitler. I fear that we are close to the bleak choice between war and shame. My own feeling is that we shall choose Shame, and then have War thrown in a little later on even more adverse terms than at present.'

'I am to speak in the Lords next week on the s-subject of the rearming of the Air Force,' said Fish.

'Good! Excellent. They will listen to you; you have the cross of Queen Victoria herself, struck from the very metal of the Crimean guns.'

'I intend to support all your efforts,' Fish said quietly, sincerely.

'Thank you,' said Churchill. He smiled quizzically at Fish. 'My army of followers has now swelled to five! Brendan, Bob, Duncan, the estimable General Spears and now yourself. Against such warriors who shall prevail!'

His cigar was cold. He fumbled at his watch chain.

'So late? I must head for London, I am due to speak in the House tonight. Lord and Lady Windstone, I must thank you for your warm hospitality. If you will summon my coachman . . .'

The chauffeur duly brought the great gleaming Daimler limousine to the base of the steps. They gathered and waved as it bore Churchill away down the long drive to the massive gates.

'A great man,' said Fish.

45

Have an Imperialist Sandwich

Cambridge, 23 August 1939

Sunshine splashed the surface of the River Cam, making the little ripples glitter. Ducks paddled briskly about like small tugboats. Godfrey sat with his back to a tree, in its dappled shade. A wicker picnic hamper lay behind him; an ancient boneshaker bicycle was leaned against the tree. He was reading a book, and smoking a cigarette. In the warmth of the day he wore an old stained painter's smock, and baggy flannel shorts. From the distance came the puttering of a small car engine. It slowed; he heard a squeak of brakes, a silence and the clunk of a car door.

'Over here, George,' he called languidly. He heard the soft tearing of shoes coming through the long grass and looked up to see George, dressed in a dark suit, carrying his jacket over his arm. He was pale, but sweating.

'Goodness, you do look uncomfortable,' he drawled. He put a bookmark from Heffer's inside his book, and placed it beside him. 'Fortunately, I have recuperants at hand. As soon as I got your strange telephone call I went out and prepared a picnic. A nice bottle of Muscadet is cooling in the river. Do sit down, dear fellow, and loosen your tie, while I pour us a refreshing beaker.'

George slumped into the grass, and tugged at his tie, pulling his collar stud free. He sat staring at the slowly gurgling river as Godfrey went to the bank, and pulled in a bottle on the end of a cord. He took it out triumphantly, undoing the string and removing the cork. He plucked two tumblers from his hamper and filled them.

'Here,' he said.

George tipped back half the glass in one go.

'God,' he said. 'I've been needing that ever since I started out.'

'I rather think you have,' Godfrey agreed. He pulled up his knees like a stick insect, and clasped his arms about them. 'Why don't you tell me what's happened?'

'It began with the post,' George said. 'I think I'll tell it in order.'

'Do,' Godfrey said patiently.

'It's odd how small things and big ones can somehow have the same effect on you,' he said, in a disjointed fashion. 'I got a letter from America. From Frances. I knew it was from her as soon as I saw those filthy American stamps. I've been asking her to send the boys over they were supposed to come for the holidays but she found excuses . . . I suggested the Christmas holidays, I'd get some shooting organised, I thought it was her arrangements . . .'

George stared sightlessly over the water. A moorhen took off from the reeds, paddling frantically with red feet, dipping over the river to land further down in a small surge of white foam, like a small flying boat.

'They've taken out American citizenship,' he said, in an agonised voice. 'My boys, being turned into filthy Americans, with their foul accents and ways . . . she's not sending them, she says, not now, not ever. She wants them to be free of the European taint, she says. Free of taint! How can she say—'

He choked, wiped his eyes, drank off the remainder of his wine. He blew his nose, and Godfrey refilled his glass.

'I feel a bit better,' he said. 'Being able to tell somebody. And how much I hate them. The Americans. I can't say, you see, not at work. Mustn't let anyone know.'

'You must not,' Godfrey said, firmly. 'They might move you.'

'I have to deal with them, you know that. The FBI, the State Department.'

'Just think of the revenge you wreak on them, all the time,' Godfrey urged.

'I know, I know. It's hard, when it's your own sons . . .'

'All the more reason to fool them,' said Godfrey. 'Think of it like that.'

'Yes, yes, you're right,' George said. He was bringing himself under control. 'Just sometimes, Godfrey, you know, I feel like a mad person. Saying one thing and underneath, being quite another.'

'We all feel that, from time to time. You mustn't let it show, that's all. People . . . *watch* for that.'

George laughed, for the first time.

'Yes, we know what sort they are, don't we? I mean, dear God, that's my job. Looking for the spies . . .'

He drank a little more wine.

'Shall we break into the provisions?' Godfrey suggested. 'While you tell me the other news?'

'The other news . . . Oh, Jesus yes.'

Godfrey opened his hamper and unwrapped a greaseproof paper parcel.

'Smoked salmon sandwiches, to begin with,' he said. George took one, sat with it in his hand, pain once again suffusing his face.

'Godfrey,' he whispered, 'Stalin's signed a non-aggression pact with Hitler.'

Godfrey's head snapped round like a snake striking.

'*What*—'

'It's true. I got it off the wire.' He looked up at his cousin in agony. 'Dear God!' he cried. 'How are we to live if they're one and the same? How can Stalin betray us like this?'

Godfrey sat silent for a few moments, his thoughts racing.

'Betray?' he said finally, a mocking tone in his voice. 'Come, come, George, where's your faith?'

'What do you mean?' George whispered.

'You're one of us. A Marxist. Like me. We hide it from this decaying world all about us, work for the new order. Isn't that right? Let me hear you say it.'

'Of course. This country is sick, dying. It'll be a foul American colony or—'

'Or a shining new nation, transformed! But only if we work for it. Don't you think that's what Stalin's done? He knew what Chamberlain and Deladier were trying to do, push him into war with Germany to save their skins! Well, he hasn't done it! He's made a deal with Hitler to gain time, to strengthen the new Soviet order for the day when it falls upon the Fascist beast and tears it limb from limb! You know how *we* have to pretend to be one thing and do another. You don't think it's the same for Stalin?'

George shook his head, still deeply disturbed.

'I became a Marxist . . . I suppose . . . because it seemed to be the way forward . . . everything was so corrupt and disgusting here . . . but I tell you, Godfrey, it worries me . . . what they're doing in Russia, the show trials, the camps, the murders—'

'The price necessary,' Godfrey said icily, 'to build the future. You don't think we won't have some judicial murders here when the day comes? The Augean stables have to be cleaned out. You run the river of clean communism through them to do it. It runs red for a while. Don't you think we won't stand Edward and Mrs Simpson up against a wall on that day, for dealing with the Nazis? Won't they deserve every bullet we blow into their stinking, corrupt bodies?'

'They've killed millions,' George whispered. 'And now Stalin deals with Hitler . . . They had a ghastly junket in the Kremlin, communists and fascists together like a bunch of gangsters, all with blood on their hands . . .'

'Desperate times, George, call for desperate measures. You have to decide whose side you're on. Sit on the fence and get killed. You've made your choice, you made it when you joined us.'

'I don't know about that,' George muttered. 'I never signed any-thing.'

Godfrey stared at him with cold eyes.

'Let me put it to you this way, George. Either you serve us, or you die.'

'What?' he said, startled.

'As I said, run the river through the stables it turns red. Our side'll kill you for sure if you let us down.' Godfrey grinned, ghoulishly. 'We only want the pure in heart, George. And you know, our countrymen will kill you too, if they find out.'

'What do you mean?'

'Shall I quote?' Godfrey asked with malicious pleasure. 'I looked it up the other day. 'Any subject who is adherent to the King's enemies in his realm, giving them aid and comfort in his realm or elsewhere is guilty of High Treason.' A capital offence, George, for over six hundred years. They used to cut your head off. Now they'll hang you.'

George was very white. Godfrey leaned forward and tipped his glass towards his face.

'Come on, drink up. There's a nice bottle of claret waiting.'

George did as he was bid.

'Good. Just remember how stinking this place is. What about Edward, the Duke – didn't you tell me he's crawling about with Nazi sympathisers?'

'Yes. Bedaux, the millionaire, who lent them his château. The time and motion man.'

'An American, like that woman Simpson.'

'French-American.'

'The worst of both! Do the Windsors know he's a Nazi agent?'

'She does. For certain. He just does what she orders him to. They hang about with all kinds of Nazi sympathisers. Laval, Dietrichstein, Abetz, Wenner-Gren, the other millionaire, all degenerate scum. They see to it that all the women curtsey to Mrs Simpson and call her Royal Highness. The Duke is pathetically pleased by it all.'

'And Mrs Simpson's up to her old tricks?'

'My former employer's taste for humiliation does not seem to have lessened,' George said, his mouth twisting with distaste.

'Corrupt, decayed, rotten,' Godfrey sneered. 'And you want to support that? Come on. Let's get to business. This must mean war.'

'Yes. Hitler's cleared his back. Stalin's happy, he's going to provide the Germans with huge quantities of *matériel*. The German army's massing to attack Poland. Chamberlain's finally realised that pieces of paper from Munich are worse than worthless. He'll take us into war with Germany.'

'Will he last?'

'I doubt it. You know, I think they'll have Winston in. I was wrong about him. He isn't yesterday's man after all.'

'An appropriate leader for the end of Imperial England,' Godfrey sneered. 'Right. I have instructions for you, then.'

'What?' George cried in alarm.

'From our Moscow masters, of course. You don't think they just want a bit of information, do you? This is our chance to lay the foundations for the future. You're a senior MI5 officer, now is your opportunity. You're Deputy Director, B Division. What do you cover?'

'Counter-espionage, Enemy and Neutral, Commercial Espionage, Sabotage, Communications, Censorship Liason, Leakage of Information, Examination of Aliens Arriving in the UK.'

'That's right. With the war starting there'll be a massive increase in requirements. MI5 will expand its personnel dramatically.' Godfrey tipped back his glass. 'You're to get us in,' he said clearly. 'Me and Guy immediately. Philby too. I'll have other names. You're the gatekeeper, George. Once we're in we'll all help each other. There's no telling how high we can go . . .'

He stared dreamily across the Cam. A mother duck was paddling importantly along at the head of a small snake of fluffy ducklings, the water rolling smoothly off her polished feathers.

'Here,' he said, holding out his packet. 'Have an imperialist sandwich. I think, George, that you can give me a lift into town. Then I can fill in the requisite forms, and so can the others. I think I might go by the Packenham tonight and celebrate. I haven't done anything really disgusting in a while.'

He ate a sandwich with relish.

'You've got that, George?' he asked sharply. 'You're to get us in. I'll give you more names later. Continue to pass information through me. Nobody will think it at all strange, we are cousins, after all.' He smirked. 'And now, colleagues.'

He splashed claret into the glasses, and broke out some jellied chicken.

'They don't want Britain to lose,' he said.

'Who don't?'

'Our masters in Moscow. They want Germany well tied up in war in Europe. So while we tell them all, we're also to do our British duty.' Godfrey laughed, as though the notion amused him. 'It will help us rise up through the ranks.'

'We must develop real split personalities to do that,' George observed.

Godfrey drank deeply from his glass, his eyes glittering.

'This is it,' he whispered. 'At last, this is it.'

There was a sudden swirl amongst the polished, glittering ripples. The last duckling in the line vanished beneath the surface. George caught a fleeting glimpse of it, clamped in a pike's savage jaws. A stream of blood muddied the clear water. The mother duck paddled on, unaware.

46

Grovelling Would Be Pleasant

Paris, February 1940

Wallis went through the rooms of the mansion. Occasionally, in between her self-imposed duties – of checking switches, light bulbs in cupboards, cords of blinds for knots, the position of ornaments, clocks and vases, the possible presence of dust on horizontal surfaces, the exact positioning of flowers in vases and the posture of her servants – she glanced out of the tall windows, done in the style of Louis XIV. The bleak trees of the Bois de Boulogne waved in the winter wind; out on the Boulevard Suchet cars hissed by in the drizzle.

She went down through her floors, savaging the staff with her tongue as she went. In a bathroom she found that a towel had been placed on a rail with the embroidered Royal insignia and coronet facing in rather than out. She summoned the maid responsible, together with a footman in the red and gold livery of the British Royal household. She fired her on the spot, and had the footman show her the door. She stood at a high window, watching her walk away through the rain.

By the time she arrived at the ground floor the fresh flowers had been delivered. She had already received the attentions of her hairdresser, masseuse and chiropodist that morning, all of whom motored in from their salons. She considered whether to change her jewellery, to monitor the accounts presented every Tuesday by the staff, or to arrange the flowers.

Choosing jewellery from her collection was something pleasant. Catching the staff out in the presentation of their accounts and fining them had its satisfactions. Standing up to arrange the flowers had the merit of burning off some calories to maintain her figure. She dieted relentlessly. There was a certain joy in feeling permanently hungry, never satisfied. She stood, and began to arrange the stems and blooms.

She heard a noise, glanced up, out of the window. Not one, but two limousines had drawn up outside. She heard the footman open the door, and the sound of voices. Edward, Duke of Windsor came in, wearing the uniform of a major-general in the British Army. With him was their friend, Charles Bedaux.

'Charles caught me up on the Boulevard!' Edward exclaimed. He put his attaché case down by a chair. The footman stood waiting.

'Champagne before we go out,' Wallis ordered. 'The Rothschild '33.'

'How nice to see you, Charles. Do sit down.' She turned to her husband. 'Did your morning at GHQ go well, darling?' she enquired pleasantly.

'Well, I suppose so. I had the usual unsatisfactory conversation with Monkton in London on the telephone.'

He turned to Bedaux, suave in chalk-striped suit, who sat attentively.

'It's too damned bad, Charles. Here I am – we are – doing our bit for the war effort, and if I need to get through to my brother the King to sort out this ridiculous business of my wife's rank – or even ask for a bit of money, it costs a fortune to keep up a little style out here – can I do so? No! I have to talk to Monkton, who's a blasted lawyer. I was in the middle of telling him what I thought when that stuffy fool Gort sent word he wanted me to attend a meeting.'

'No movement on the question of rank then?' Beduax murmured sympathetically. Edward's eyes flicked nervously towards Wallis, like a hound's, but she remained impassive.

'It's so stupid!' Edward cried. 'It's *her*, you know, Elizabeth, the Queen. My brother's wife. That ice-veined bitch, she hates Wallis. All Monkton would say was "There's a war on". I know that! But what is more important than Wallis receiving what is due to her?' Edward stamped his foot in petulant anger. 'She *will* be Her Royal Highness! They *shall* curtsey and bow to her! They shall, they shall, they shall!'

Wallis smiled at Bedaux.

'Grovelling would be pleasant,' she murmured. Edward seemed relieved that his ongoing failure to raise his wife's status was not, at least at the moment, to result in a lengthy and vicious catalogue of his character flaws.

'Of course you will arrange it,' she said. 'But what of the war, this reluctant war, this phoney war? When will the Germans strike?'

'Soon,' Bedaux said confidently. 'Hitler waits only for the spring, do you not think, David?'

Bedaux was a trusted friend, he had won the right to call Edward by his more familiar name.

'Yes,' the Duke said frankly. 'That's what we all expect.'

'Another war of the trenches?' Wallis suggested.

'What do you think, David?' Bedaux said, deferring. 'You're on the British Military Mission here. You know the order of battle.'

The champagne arrived, in a silver bucket, condensation frosting its sides, and the footman poured it into flutes.

'That depends upon the German plan of attack,' the Duke said knowledgeably. He swallowed a little champagne.

'Did you bring the map I asked you for?' said Wallis.

'I have brought everything,' Edward said, pleased with his work. He opened his attaché case and took out a military map of Western Europe, opening it to show Belgium, the Netherlands and western France.

'The British Expeditionary Force is now in place,' he said. He ran his fingers across an arc of the map. 'We stand here. This line you see here is the French Maginot line, their extensive fortifications. Their armies are ranged across here.'

He cleared his throat importantly.

'A German frontal atack on the Maginot line is not a consideration. No, what we expect them to do, indeed almost their only option is to do what their ancestors did in 1914 – the famous Schlieffen Plan, a thrust from right to left. We expect Hitler to extend that sweep to invade Holland. Our response will be to move forward – like this – to advance into Belgium and meet the Germans half way across Belgium and in south-western Holland.'

The Duke reached into his case and drew out a document marked MOST SECRET, Plan D.

'I'm not supposed to take these out of HQ,' he admitted. 'But Wallis likes to discuss military strategy with me. You'd make a marvellous general, darling! Much better than that fool Gort!'

Wallis smiled. Bedaux watched carefully as the Duke put down the thick document on the table.

'That's the Allied plan of battle?'

'That's it,' Edward said proudly.

'Will it work?'

'There are some pretty alarming deficiencies in both the BEF and the French armies, let me tell you,' Edward said confidentially. 'But if the Germans invade as I have said, we should put a fair spanner in their works.'

'You said "almost" the only option the Germans had?' Bedaux said, seemingly vague.

'David has such a grasp of strategy,' Wallis said, and the Duke swelled in her seeming admiration.

'The Allied plan of battle has a potentially fatal weakness,' Edward said importantly. 'What if the Germans attack not from right to left but from left to right?'

Bedaux looked intently at the map to where Edward was indicating. 'A sort of Schlieffen Plan in reverse?' he hazarded.

Edward beamed.

'Very good! he cried. 'What a strategist you are, Charles! Yes, a rapid motorised advance across the hills of the Ardennes and across the Meuse, making straight for the Channel ports. If it worked it would cut off the British Expeditionary Force and the associated French divisions here in Belgium, forcing them back onto the French coast.'

His fingers pointed to the map, tapped it.

'They could bottle us up, oh, somewhere about here. Dunkirk, or somewhere close to there. Calais, Ostend. Absolute disaster. The Germans would be masters of France and Western Europe in weeks.'

'Will they do it?' Bedaux asked intently.

'Very risky! After all, they would have to know what was in here.'

The Duke tapped the document marked MOST SECRET significantly. There was a silence in the room for a few minutes.

'It's so stupid!' Edward burst out. 'The German and the British races are one. They should always be one! They are of Hun origin. Look at me, I could have been King of England or Emperor of Germany!'

'You may be King again,' Bedaux murmured. 'If events should turn out a certain way.'

'Yes, yes,' Edward muttered furiously. 'And my darling Wallis *shall* be Queen. They shall pay for their treatment of her, mark my words.'

'That will be pleasant,' Wallis said, smiling. She reached out and took the thick military document.

'I'm going to go up and change,' she said. 'Lunch at the Ritz, Charles?'

'I have the table booked,' he assured her.

'When does this Plan have to be back at HQ, David?' she asked.

'Tomorrow,' he said, sounding slightly nervous. 'I'd better put it back tomorrow morning. It's a court-martial offence to take it out of the building.'

'You will,' she assured him. As she rose, Bedaux did as well.

'I'll wash my hands, if I may.'

They went out together and up the grand staircase. By the wash-room they paused. She gave him the document.

'You heard what David said. He must have it back by the morning.'

'There is no problem,' he said confidently. 'I have a photographer standing by at my office. Hitler himself will have it by the time its back in the HQ.'

'Tell Ribbentrop I'm keeping my side of the bargain,' she said, her eyes burning. 'I expect him to keep his.'

'Don't worry,' he said, completely certain. 'When the British are smashed you can have what you want.'

'I know what I want,' she said. 'I'll make them pay, for treating me like that.'

Bedaux slipped the document under his coat. She went upstairs, opened her long wardrobe of Mainbocher, Schiaparelli, Chanel and Molyneux originals. In the courtyard below she saw Bedaux go out to his limousine, open the driver's door, poking his head inside. He passed over the document, which he had put into a large sealed manila envelope. She stood by her mirror, taking off her jewellery in preparation for the pleasures of putting on the new, and watched the great car accelerate away along the edge of the Bois de Boulogne.

47

She Knows That Already

France, 19 May

'You've been here before, sir?' asked Hoskins, the young lieutenant in command of the most reliable of the three Cruiser tanks standing in the main and only street of the village.

'Nineteen-eighteen, Hoskins,' said Freddie. 'The only difference was that we were going the other way.'

They were all filthy, and exhausted from the fighting of the past nine days. The Germans had come pouring through the wooded hills of the Ardennes, across the Meuse, in panzers and fast-moving trucks and half-tracks – the very latest in military technology – and his battalion had been going backwards ever since. In the deserted village, abandoned by all its inhabitants, he looked back down the road along which his small force had come. It emerged from a belt of plane trees in full yellowish bloom, to cross a gurgling clear river by an ancient stone bridge, before climbing steadily up to the little village with its single main street.

'Sticks in my craw, Hoskins, does going backwards,' Freddie remarked.

'Mine, too, sir.'

Two lorries carried the infantry, and they were pulling a field gun each. They had hitched ammunition tenders behind the tanks.

'Do you want to blow that bridge, sir?'

'The river bed looks fairly flat,' said Freddie. 'They can ford it. I think I'd rather shoot them up on the bridge itself.'

He put his head back.

'Sar'nt-Major!' he bellowed. A small, tough, regular soldier in khaki battle dress came running.

'Bren gunners and riflemen in the houses looking down on the road there. Mr Hoskins is going to put his tank into that hay store on the corner. When he fires into the lead vehicle – wait until he's good and close, Johnny, 'til you can see the rivets, the armour on these panzers is thick – that's your signal to open up into the soft-skinned vehicles. Have we still got ammunition for the mortar?'

'Yessir.'

'Set up the mortar team then to fire when they debouch. Catch them in the open. There's some nice stone walls down there, send some flints whizzing about. The other two tanks and the field guns will take out the other vehicles of the column.'

The other officers and sergeants had gathered round. Freddie pointed out the barns and orchards where he wanted them sited.

'I want them trapped on that road,' he commanded. 'Shoot them up from the front and the back. Tank commanders to take out any attempt to get off the road and down that slope to ford the river. My last report from the RAF was that they were about ten miles behind us, we should be able to expect them soon. Let's get into position.'

The village was a mass of moving men and vehicles, spreading out over its eastern edge. Freddie set up his command post in the Mairie, built of old stone, a metre and a half thick. On the wall of the room overlooking the meadow and fruit trees that led down to the river was a very old hand-tinted photograph of Louis XVIII. The room was musty; he opened the window and pushed back the shutter. He could see his men manoeuvring their tanks and guns, chopping branches, lifting hay, camouflaging their sites of attack.

'This is better,' he said, to nobody in particular.

The early morning mist had burned off, leaving a pale blue sky. As he watched from his window, he detected a faint darkening over the trees, a dirty smudging of the blue. He leaned out, cocking an ear. What he heard caused him to jog outside, and into the hay barn.

Hoskins had backed his Cruiser tank right inside, and had pulled the doors partly to. In the gloom he had created he had a perfect view down the road leading up into the village. He sat up in his turret, waiting.

'They're coming, Johnny,' said Freddie. 'I can hear them.'

The noise grew louder, soon they could all hear it. A grinding, a heavy roar of diesel engines, a rolling of numerous hard tyres, of rotating tracks.

Something poked its head out from the gap where the road cut through the trees, like a ferret sniffing the air. An armoured car: a powerful, fast-moving, eight-wheeled affair. Its turret and gun twitched to and fro. In the clear air Freddie could see its straight-sided black and white crosses. Wireless aerials on its hull whipped back and forth. With a plume of black smoke from its big exhaust, it moved forward. Behind it came dark panzer tanks, five of them, their black-uniformed commanders, in caps and earphones, head and shoulders out of their turrets. Half-tracks and lorries followed in a stream.

The armoured car rolled quickly over the bridge, followed by the tanks, black fumes staining the air.

'Cocky bastards,' Freddie muttered.

He heard the driver of the armoured car change gear, the powerful engine revving as it sent it up the hill into the village.

Hoskins' Cruiser tank fired, at almost point-blank range. The blast of the two-pounder gun blew the barn doors open; hay and fine dust billowed out into the air. The shell hit the armoured car with a huge clang, like a giant beating a saucepan. It smashed it sideways across the road, crashing into a stone wall, and it began to burn.

There was a fraction of a second's silence, just enough for his ears to sing, and then all the waiting weapons of his force burst into life. Through the sudden smoke he saw a young German commander smack back in his turret, lie across its top, half in, half out; saw a track suddenly spew out from under its cover, the heavy vehicle striking the wall of the bridge. A lorry burst into flames, men spilling out across the road in disorder, tumbling and falling under the heavy machine-gun-fire from the windows above him.

The dark panzer tank swayed in the gap it had made in the side of the bridge, propelled by its still-churning single track. One corner dipped and it tumbled over in the air, falling into the water with a huge white splash. In the orchard the two field guns were firing over open sights. Mortar shells burst down in the confusion, grey-uniformed soldiers fell like corn.

The small, deadly killing ground was wreathed in smoke. The short column of vehicles were burning.

'Pull out!' Freddie ordered. The tanks came wheeling from their hides, the lorries dragged the guns once more, the men came tumbling down from their shooting gallery.

'What now, sir?' Hoskins called, his face flushed with the excitement of the short battle.

'Good show, Johnny,' Freddie called. 'That should slow them up a bit.'

He felt a savage satisfaction. The Germans had had it all their own way ever since the shooting war had started, nine days earlier. It had been their turn.

'Where to, sir?'

'Dunkirk,' he said.

The small column, what was left of a regular battalion, hurried

away along the empty road, heading for the coast, the sky behind
them dirty with smoke.

'*There* you are,' Violet said. She stood on the quay, next to the big
white sailing vessel. Behind her the bulk of the castle loomed dark
against the fresh sky, in the green lawns the buttercups and speedwell
shone yellow and blue. The banks of the water were alive with marsh
marigolds and silver white ladies' smock.

'What are you doing? Dr Jennings called, wants to know why you
aren't at the hospital.'

Fish paused in his assembly, large wooden-handled screwdriver
in hand. He appeared to be fitting some kind of iron bracket to a
hatch cover.

'P-putting in the m-mountings,' he said, not very helpfully.

'Mountings for what?' she asked patiently.

'The g-guns, of course. I had Githers the blacksmith make 'em up
for me.'

'Where are you going in this vessel that you need guns?'

'Call's gone out,' he said succinctly. 'They want lots of small boats
to go over to the French coast, fetch the soldiers back.'

'Is it that bad?' she asked, quietly.

'Complete m-muck up, apparently. The F-Frogs have folded like
paper bags and we're going backwards as quick as poss. But not even
the British Army can swim the channel.'

'Then I'd better get provisions on board,' she said equably. 'The
chaps will be hungry, I expect.'

'Jolly good.'

'I suppose this means you're not going to the hospital for the
operation.'

'No . . .'

'You missed it last time.'

'Bring some g-gaspers with you, darling, will you?'

'Dr Jennings said you weren't to smoke any more.'

Fish tightened a last screw and looked at his handiwork with satisfaction. He picked up a Lewis gun from the deck and put it in place.

'I always kn-knew it would come in useful. Yes, well, what did
Alexander the Great say, eh? 'I am dying with the help of too many
physicians.' You know that fearsome muzzle loader of Uncle's? I'm
going to take it. I've always wanted to loose it off in anger. Shake
some Jerry's fillings, that will, a quarter-pound of lead coming the
other way.'

He reached inside his jacket and brought out a battered silver cigarette case.

'Found this old case you gave me. I've filled it up, but we'll need more. The chaps will be feeling like a gasper when they get on board.'

'You had that on the Somme,' she said quietly.

Fish helped himself to a cigarette and lit it with a gold Dunhill.

'You had that too.'

Fish coughed hideously as the smoke reached his lungs, bending almost double as the spasms racked him. After a few moments he straightened up and dragged in some air.

'That's better.'

'Dr Jennings—'

'Dr Jennings can g-get st-stuffed.'

'Fish,' she said suddenly. 'You're not to die, do you hear me? What am I supposed to do without you?'

The waxy pallor of his cheeks did not lift, but he smiled.

'I always do what you say, Vi, darling,' he said gently.

'Then you'll go in for this operation as soon as we get back?'

'The very minute.'

'All right, then. I'll go and organise the provisions.'

She walked across the lawns back to the castle. When she was out of sight, she took a handkerchief from her pocket and wiped her eyes.

'You're a good-looking woman,' the old man said appreciatively, turning from the window that overlooked the Thames, passing between the Houses of Parliament and the handsome Victorian buildings of Florence Nightingale's St Thomas's opposite.

'They gave me your name,' Lloyd George continued. 'I didn't know what you looked like.'

'Why, thank you, sir,' said Carlotta. She had been advised of the old statesman's continued interest in women, particularly good-looking ones, and had dressed appropriately in a bright spring frock.

'The Duke of Windsor sends his regards,' she said lightly.

'Does he now?' Lloyd George said indifferently. 'Civil of him, I suppose. You've come from him, I take it?'

'The Duke and Duchess have left Paris for the south, to avoid the fighting,' she explained.

He sat down on the chesterfield sofa of his office.

'Here, sit next to me,' he commanded. 'Not often I get the chance to be close to a girl like you these days. Different years ago, of course.'

Carlotta obligingly sat down next to him, and with long habit he put his hand on her knee.

'So what message do you have for me?'

'Chancellor Hitler also sends you his regards,' she said boldly. Lloyd George's eyes bulged slightly, he almost looked over his shoulder to see if anyone was listening.

'Does he, by God!' he said hoarsely. 'Seen him lately too, have you?'

'Both the Duke and I have contacts . . .' she said carefully. 'We are able to receive and transmit messages from and to the German authorities.'

'You can, can you?'

'Yes. Chancellor Hitler wished it especially known to you how he still reciprocates your regard for him. He was much honoured when you referred to him after your visit to him – before this conflict – as the greatest living German.'

'I know when I saw him, damn you,' Lloyd George said abruptly, with an irritation born of nerves.

'He himself reveres you as the greatest living British statesman.'

Lloyd George's head, with its mane of white hair went back, his vanity massaged.

'So much wiser than Mr Churchill,' she said carefully.

'Winston is prime minister.'

'For how long?' she murmured, and let the question hang in the air for a few moments. Lloyd George sat staring out of the window in thought, but the hand upon her thigh began to move again.

'The Führer considers this war against Great Britain to be foolish and unnecessary.'

'Let him stop fighting us then!' the old man exclaimed.

'The British Expeditionary Force is in full retreat,' she pointed out. 'Once it is back across the Channel there need be no continued fighting.'

'You don't know Winston,' he said grimly.

'It is precisely because the Führer *does* understand the needlessly aggressive nature of Mr Churchill, his belligerence, his love of war and slaughter, that he is seeking ways to bring this unnecessary conflict to a close. Churchill is a practised liar, an inciter and agitator, a blood-covered dilettante aristocrat.'

Lloyd George's mouth twitched faintly.

'Chancellor Hitler wishes to send a message to the wise men of Britain,' she murmured. 'If Churchill remains in power, then the war will continue. The Führer asks anyone who doubts the power of Germany to look at what his forces have achieved in mere weeks. The destruction of all who oppose him! The occupation of all his enemies in Europe! With what will Churchill make the British people fight when the Expeditionary Force returns beddraggled and without its arms? Their bare hands? All it will lead to is the destruction of the great British Empire – a destruction which has never been the Führer's aim.

'A continuation of this struggle, which Churchill is bent upon, will end only in the complete annihilation of one of the two opponents. It will not be Germany. But by then Churchill will be drunk and in Canada, with the great British people slaughtered in their islands. So this is why the Führer seeks out the men of wisdom in Britain. To stop this stupidity on which Churchill is bent before it is too late.'

'And the Duke of Windsor,' Lloyd George murmured, 'our recent and abdicated King, where does he fit into all this?'

'His brother King George is a stupid man,' she said dismissively. 'He does not appreciate, as the Duke does, the deep similarities of blood and culture between the German and British peoples. He supports the warmonger Churchill.'

Lloyd George eyes widened a little.

'He wants to come back?' he murmured questioningly. 'As King?'

'Head of a government of true national unity,' she suggested, 'not of Churchill's bloodthirsty clique. All that is necessary is for the removal of Churchill and his cronies.'

'Winston has asked me to join his government,' he remarked. Carefully, and with a certain relish, he pulled up the hem of her dress until he could see the tops of her stockings, the milk-white of her thighs. She sat calmly back and let him. Men were pigs – you could lead them about as though they had rings in their noses.

He sighed, and pulled the material back down.

'I wish I was younger,' he said. 'I shall not be joining Winston. I shall wait upon events.'

She smiled pleasantly, got up.

'Please do,' she said cordially. 'For the British, events will only get worse. Hammer blows will soon fall upon the people of Britain and their cities. Then they will look for wise men, to lead them out of their difficulties.'

He showed her to the door courteously, closed it behind her. Then he went back to the window, where London lay smokily in her vastness, under a milky blue sky, and stood staring out once more.

※   ※   ※

'All right, Ned,' Fish called, from his seat at the wheel of the ship. 'Best take up stations.'

Furzegrove went forward to man the twin Lewis guns, and Violet took down the mainsail. They had come across the Channel under full sail; now they were amongst the darting shipping going into Dunkirk and coming out – destroyers and trawlers and sailing boats and pleasure craft, minelayers and tugs and even riverboats, all loaded to the gunwales with troops, like khaki bees. Fish navigated in on the inboard engine, the diesel thudding away beneath him. He peered through the drifting smoke towards the beaches where men stood patiently, lines of them, thigh deep in the water, for the small boats to come and take them home.

A destroyer came out of the main port entrance, the Gare Maritime, zig-zagging at full power to avoid the bombs of the Stukas queuing up above the town, circling like buzzards, dark and bent-winged, sirens howling as they dived. Smoke swirled over the water, the pom-poms of the ship were blazing away. The water was pock-marked with the splashes of shells falling from the German guns and tanks outside the perimeter.

The destroyer came out and past them at nigh-on thirty knots, its decks thickly covered with men, and they all cheered. They could hear the howling turbines, the roar as they sucked in air. Bombs from a diving Stuka exploded in front of it and steel fragments whined across the water. The ship vanished in the huge cloud of spray, and then they saw it reappear, still going.

Fish, Violet and Ned were all dirty. The smoke was sticky, oily; they had been going to and fro across the Channel for five days. *Parma's Pride* was no longer white, but streaked and stained. Fish peered through the smoke for the stone jetty where they had tied up before.

A fishing vessel, a small crabber, was just casting off, its engine hunting in neutral, decks crammed, and Fish slowed, putting his screw into reverse to allow it room. Its skipper, a small person in blue fisherman's trousers and hair tied up in a scarf suddenly waved furiously.

'Ahoy there!' she shouted. 'Hallo, Vi! Hallo, Fish, Ned!'

It was Felicity.

'I say!' she yelled, as she began to make way. 'What a lark! I haven't had so much fun in ages.'

An artillery shell burst in the water near by, and spray soaked them all. As it cleared they could see the crabber beginning to turn, water swirling white about its stern.

'Silly bastards can't shoot straight!' Felicity yelled.

'Flick, darling!' Violet screamed across the bedlam of noise. 'Come down to the castle when this is all over, we'll have a drink.'

'God, yes,' Felicity shouted. 'Let's get completely squiffy.'

She vanished in the smoke and spray, and Fish manoeuvred up to the narrow stone finger pointing out into the sea. A line of men were marching up. They were very dirty indeed. From their black berets they were tankers.

'I say,' their leader said, 'you don't know how glad we are to see you. Hoskins. Lieutenant Hoskins.'

'Hop aboard, Lieutenant Hoskins,' Violet said hospitably.

The young officer turned to the men. 'All aboard, chaps,' he said.

'Wh-where are your tanks?' Fish enquired, as the ship began to rock with the arrival of the men.

'Out there, sir, out there,' the officer said wearily. 'We were the rearguard.'

'Have a gasper,' Fish suggested. 'You don't know my brother-in-law, Colonel Freddie de Clare, do you?'

'My commanding officer, sir! He ... stayed back to command resistance in Calais. I haven't seen him since.'

The last men piled on board.

'Cast off!'

'Hold on, darling,' Vi said quickly. 'Somebody's coming.' Through the smoke she had seen a lone figure running along the narrow jetty. He came up alongside, panting, a red-cross armband about his sleeve.

'H-hop on.'

'Are you coming back?' the young doctor asked anxiously. 'I've got some wounded men up there. The Germans are beginning to push through the perimeter. If you're coming back I'll get them down here ready for you.'

'We'll b-be back,' Fish assured him. 'Have them here. If you're still here we'll take you off.'

'Wonderful,' he said in relief. 'I'll be here.'

Fish put the screw in gear, foam hissed at his stern. He manoeuvred out into the smoke, fumbling in his battered cigarette case, pulling one out with his lips. He lit it. From the bow the twin Lewis guns hammered at a diving Stuka. Fish coughed hideously as the smoke dragged at his lungs. Water boiled alongside as the bomb exploded, metal fragments whined through the air. On the packed deck, nobody moved. They were all asleep.

The engine thudded, he headed for the open sea.

'Sail up, darling!' he called. The stained white canvas bloomed in the breeze, they emerged into the clean fresh air, heading for home.

The tall, handsome man standing with Carlotta stared in a disgruntled manner down the beautifully mown lawn. From beyond the high wall in the distance came but the faintest hum of traffic going about Hyde Park Corner. A large wall of sandbags had been built across the lawn. In front of it stood, life-size and realistic, but painted upon cardboard, a German soldier in coal-scuttle helmet and rifle. Some small bullet-holes marred his snarl.

'My brother and Elizabeth come down here every morning and practise revolver shooting,' he said contemptuously.

'The King and Queen?'

'Yes. They say if the Germans invade they will stay here and start firing when they see the first one coming up the Mall. Ridiculous.'

'I heard that the Queen said the children were staying with her, she with the King and he wasn't going anywhere,' Carlotta said. 'It's a good line. But you know it means she and the King are for the war.'

'Fools, the pair of them,' Prince George, Duke of Kent and the King's brother said irritably. 'How many times does one have to say it, we have no quarrel with Hitler's Germany. What we need is a bit more of it over here.'

He glanced over his shoulder.

'Not that one's supposed to say that sort of thing just now. Not with that windbag Churchill making these provocative speeches and whipping everyone up.'

Carlotta pursed her lips. 'Things might change,' she suggested. 'The news is all bad, you know. They may sling Churchill out yet. I heard he got a very poor reception in the House of Commons the other day.'

'They don't trust him!' Prince George cried. 'He's done nothing but betray the Tory Party for years. And here he is, in charge!'

'As I say,' Carlotta said smoothly, 'things might change. You and I and your brother the Duke of Windsor aren't the only ones who see that this war is senseless. We should be partners with the Germans, not enemies. The Führer wants peace, you know, he's bending over backwards to be reasonable to the British. It's just that bloodthirsty swine Churchill who stands in the way. Get rid of him and ...'

Prince George twisted the gold ring on his little finger, looking about the beautiful gardens of the palace.

'Who else?' he murmured.

'Lots,' Carlotta said quickly, eagerly. 'I've been sounding out a lot of people who matter. Of course we have the stalwarts like Mosley – all the fascists, of course – there's Admiral Domville, Captain Ramsay the MP, General Fuller . . .'

'Anyone else?'

'I think I've got Lloyd George,' she said quietly, significantly. 'The Führer wants men he respects in charge of the European countries – he wants Marshal Petain to be in charge of France, you know.'

'*Does* he?' the Prince said eagerly.

'Yes. He admires Lloyd George greatly, you know. He'd be very happy to have him lead Britain.'

The Prince looked up at the great bulk of the palace and his face became sour.

'*He* won't,' he said. 'Nor will she. Plodding John Bulls the pair of them.'

'Well yes,' she murmured, 'which is why your brother Edward is standing by. He wants your help, of course. The two of you, shoulder to shoulder. The King, your brother, he has no charisma, not like you two. You and he, and Lloyd George, on the balcony of the Palace, announcing peace with honour!'

His eyes glittered. 'What needs to be done?' he asked softly.

'A *coup*.' she said quickly. 'Churchill needs to be taken out. What happens to him isn't important. Shoot him, whatever. Mosley's fascists could do it. Like that. The country is in chaos as it is. Round up the old lot – Chamberlain, Halifax, Beaverbrook, all of them. Proclaim a government of national unity, headed by Lloyd George, to make peace with honour. The Führer will deliver his side of the bargain, I assure you.'

Prince George licked his lips, nervously.

'I can't come out publicly, you know that,' he said. 'But if it happened . . .'

'We can count on you?' she asked quickly. His eyes flickered about the garden, as though seeking out spies, and then he nodded.

'Now, look,' he said, quickly moving on. 'Want to see something special?'

'Sure,' she said amiably. They went towards the palace.

'A mutual friend is here,' he explained. 'Someone we both know. Godfrey de Clare.'

'Godfrey? I haven't seen him in ages.'

'I mentioned you were coming to see me. He said to bring you down.'

'Down?'

'He's one of our foremost art historians, you know. He's cataloguing the pictures in the vaults for the King. My brother is shipping them all out to some caves in Wales for safety,' he said disapprovingly. 'Keeping this war going, you see.'

As they went into the Palace he turned to her.

'Did you, ah . . .'

Out of sight, she opened her handbag and took out a package, slipping it into his hand. In a twinkling, it was gone.

'Thanks awfully,' he murmured. 'You've got no idea how difficult it's become . . . this wretched war has interrupted everything.'

'You can count on me,' she said. 'I know I can count on you.'

They came to a door where a liveried servant stood.

'This is the Yeoman of the Silver Plate,' Prince George explained. 'Take us down, please.'

The man produced a key from his waistcoat, opened the door and let them in. He locked it behind him and took them down some stairs. At the bottom was a metal grille. This too had to be opened, and then relocked behind them. On the other side was an ordinary industrial lift. They got in, and it took them further below ground. When it halted the Yeoman opened the trellis of the lift door.

'We'll ring when you're to let us out,' said Prince George. The lift hissed as it rose up again, and Prince George smiled mischievously at her.

'Here it is.'

She looked around her. A huge room was divided up by racks of shelving. Tarpaulins lumpily covered what was beneath. She lifted one.

A jewelled scabbard encased the blade of an ornamental sword, fully three feet long, chased with gold. A small zoo of Fabergé animals pinked diamond and ruby eyes at her in the light of the bare bulbs hanging down from the ceiling. Ivory decorated with jewels and gold lay in piles. He twitched the tarpaulin and it was covered.

'You have no idea how much of this stuff there is,' he said casually. He dropped his voice. 'Here. Can you get me more of that lovely powder?'

'Of course.'

'Have a look round while I have a word with Godfrey,' he murmured. 'Help yourself to a ring or something. There's loads about. Nothing too large. I'll take it out for you. You'll be searched, I won't.'

'All right,' she said, pleased.

'Back in a moment,' he said, moving quickly away. She saw his hand dip into his pocket for the packet she had given him and she smiled cruelly.

She found something she wanted quickly, lying with others on a shelf, rings and necklaces scattered haphazardly about. She took a beautiful ring, a huge diamond surrounded by fabulous emeralds, all set in gold, and slipped it in her pocket. She looked about her in awe: the place was simply stuffed with shelves, all of them piled high. The wealth was incalculable. She began to wander about over the floor of coarse carpet. Near a doorway, she heard the murmur of voices. Always curious, she peeked through by the hinges, where it was just ajar.

Prince George dipped a little spoon into the cocaine, and held it up to his nostril, snuffling it up eagerly. Godfrey stood watching him, an open catalogue on the table. He seemed slightly amused. The Prince's handsome face suddenly flushed pink, his eyes glistened and he smiled happily. He wrapped up the packet, putting it back into his pocket. He spoke quickly, his teeth flashing in a smile.

'Where is she?' murmured Godfrey.

'I let her have a trinket,' he said. 'Come on! Quickly, before it goes.'

She saw the front of his trousers bulging. He dropped to his knees, undoing Godfrey's fly buttons, taking him in his mouth. In only a few more seconds Godfrey pushed him face forward over the table, and she saw the Prince gasp with joy as he buggered him.

Moving quietly, she slipped away, stood casually admiring an entire row of golden chiming clocks standing silent under their sheeting by the wall. A minute or two later she heard the sound of voices. Godfrey and the Prince were threading their way through the maze of shelving towards her.

'Carlotta!' Godfrey cried cheerfully. 'How splendid to see you, George told me you were coming.'

'It's lovely to see you, Godfrey,' she agreed, smiling. 'This surely is an impressive place.'

'You won't find a greater accumulation of fine art and jewellery under one roof anywhere in the world,' he confirmed. He glanced at his watch.

'I think I've put in my eight hours,' he said. 'Do you want to come to a party with me? As soon as I heard you'd be here, I said, Carlotta *must* come to the party. Yes? Wonderful. Let's go upstairs and have a couple of scoops to get us in the mood.'

He smiled dazzlingly at her.

'There's somebody there who's dying to meet you,' he said.

The streets were very dark in the blackout; the hooded lamps of Godfrey's car hardly lit up anything beyond a dull yellow glow in front of them. She was quite lost, had no idea where she was. He stopped, wound down his window, talked briefly to somebody she could not see outside, drove on a short way and stopped.

'Here we are,' he said brightly. 'Let's go to the party, shall we?'

She got out. There seemed to be some kind of great building looming in the darkness. He took her arm, steered her, a door opened yellow in the gloom.

'Here we go,' he said. 'After you.'

She was in a windowless brick corridor, painted a dingy cream. Worn Victorian brown tiles were under her feet.

'What is this place, Godfrey?' she asked. 'Is it a college or something?'

'That's it,' he agreed. 'We're going to a sort of graduation party.'

'You'd think they'd have it somewhere nicer than this,' she complained. The place was making her nervous, for some reason.

'Oh, yes. I think they would,' he said enigmatically. They went up an equally gloomy stairway, smelling of ancient cabbage and potato. She turned, suddenly.

'Look, Godfrey, I don't think I've got time to—'

He urged her on, very much taller than she was.

'Oh, but you've been specially invited,' he said, smiling. 'You really can't leave, not now.'

He stopped outside a dark brown door. The varnish was bubbling.

'We're here,' he said, and opened it. He gave her a small push, she stumbled inside. It was a strange, horrid room. Stone flags, an unpleasant smell. A pit in the floor.

'Don't fall in the hole, will you?' he said from behind her. She turned to leave, to run from this place of danger, but he had her by the elbow. She was aware that he was very much stronger than she was.

'Stand here,' he ordered, and would not release his grip.

Feet suddenly crashed on the ceiling, she looked up in alarm. Bare wood rafters, the light shining through the gaps, people moving, roughly, quickly. A hoarse voice suddenly shouting out in terror. Brief, short hard words of command. A horrid gargling. Godfrey had her by both arms, forcing her to stand at the edge of the hole.

Suddenly, a terrible crash from above, and part of the ceiling fell in. A man fell through it. A rope was about his neck. She saw his face, contorted in terror, and then the rope snapped taut. He hung in front of her, stopping with a hideous jerk, a cracking of bone, the harsh hemp of the rope deep in his neck, his feet dangling in the pit, his hands lashed behind his back. A foul, dreadful stench of sudden death swamped her; his staring, open, terrified eyes stared into hers, inches away, and she screamed, and screamed.

Somebody slapped her. Smacked her viciously across one cheek, and then the other.

'Shut up, you bitch,' George de Clare said coldly. She cringed away from him in sudden fear, stumbled against the hanging man, whimpered in horror. A face appeared in the square gap of the trapdoor.

'You all right down there, Mr de Clare?' it enquired. 'If I let out the slack perhaps you'd lay 'is body flat.'

'Take his feet,' George ordered Carlotta, as Godfrey stood by the taut rope. She was frightened, very afraid indeed – she bent and did as she was bid. His feet were bare, the dead man's, bare and warm to the touch, but lifeless, unmoving. Above her the hangman let out slack, the man slowly folded along the flags.

'Up the stairs,' George snarled. He hustled her outside, almost at a run. She lost a shoe, started to protest, but he simply ignored her, dragged her upstairs like so much baggage. She found herself thrust into a room. The hangman was closing the trap, resetting the operating lever. He smiled.

'This the lady, Mr de Clare, sir?'

'This is the one,' George said.

The executioner stood looking at her for a moment, with almost cheerful eyes set in a ruddy face, clasping his capable square hands together. He looked like a village butcher accepting a side of beef from the supplier.

'About eight stones, I'd say,' he said. 'Here, Miss, step on the scales a moment for me, will you?'

In the corner of the room stood some broad butcher's scales, Victorian cast iron, red and green, with the maker's name on. She found herself standing on them as he expertly moved the weights in the bar.

'What's going on?' she shrieked hysterically.

'Length of rope, Miss. Varies with the weight,' he said knowledgeably. 'If we hang you with too much rope your head comes off. Makes a nasty mess down there. Too short and you strangles, see?'

'You can't do this!' she yelled. 'I'm an American citizen. I've done nothing.'

George jerked her off the scales, shoved her back against the wall so that her head banged on the brick. He was dressed in his old, unfashionable dinner suit. A black silk bow-tie was about his neck.

'You're a spy,' he said. 'A German spy. We can do anything we want to you, and we're going to hang you.'

He turned his head. The hangman was methodically measuring out a fresh length of hemp. At one end of it was the noose, already tied.

From the room below she could hear voices, rough men dragging the body out. One made a joke, they all laughed.

'Jolly good,' said George. 'When you're ready, then.'

He turned to Carlotta with indifferent eyes. Godfrey had come in, and was lounging against the wall as though attending a poor show in a gallery.

'Godfrey . . .' she wailed, entreatingly.

'Godfrey's taken on a second job,' George said. 'He's in intelligence, with me.'

Godfrey smiled at her, his eyes icy cold.

'We rounded them all up,' he said. 'Mosley and the others. All the fascist sympathisers. Domville, Captain Ramsay. All the ones you've been talking to.'

Her mind driven by desperate panic, as the hideous executioner carefully laid out his rope along the steelyard, she found what she was looking for.

'What about the Duke?' she blurted.

'Duke?' George enquired. 'Which Duke?'

The white cliffs stretched out into the distance, white in the late afternoon sun. The castle stood high above the crowded port, seething with troops, policemen, nurses finding and tending the wounded, NAAFI ladies serving tea and lemonade, with ambulances, with redcaps directing files of soldiers towards the station where the steam engines of the Southern Railway waited with their red carriages to haul them up through Kent. Fish brought *Parma's Pride* into the crowded quay under the directions of the naval sub-lieutenant waiting there, and they tied up.

Lieutenant Hoskins' soldiers stirred themselves, clambered off, formed up under the command of the small, tough sergeant-major, and shouted their thanks.

'That's it, sir,' the sub-lieutenant called. 'We're halting the evacuation; word from the others side is that the Germans are pushing into the town.'

'How many have come home?' Violet asked quickly.

'Over a quarter of a million of our own,' the young man said proudly. 'Plenty of French, too.'

'Just as well,' Fish said quietly. 'Or we'd have had no troops to fight with.'

'You don't know how well you did, sir, you chaps in the little boats.'

'Well, yes, but there's a ch-chap still waiting for us, over there,' Fish objected to the naval officer. 'With some wounded.'

'Sorry, sir. Orders are for it to be stopped today. Last boats went out three hours ago.'

'I s-see.' Fish turned to Violet. 'Darling, what about a c-cuppa, eh? Go and see if one of those nice NAAFI ladies will give us some. Ned, go and help her ladyship.'

Violet walked down the quay with Furzegrove. Her legs felt as though they were made from indiarubber.

'Are you tired, Ned? I am. I think I shall go home and sleep for a week.'

'The Earl, he looks none too well, Lady Violet.'

'He's got to go into hospital for this operation on his lung. Where he was bayoneted. He keeps putting it off.'

She paused, stopped in the middle of the crowded quay.

'Fish—' she said anxiously. She turned, began to push her way back, went towards the edge so that she could see.

In the harbour, the dirty, streaked shape of *Parma's Pride* was turning, making its way through the crowded waters towards the open sea, a streak of oily smoke coming from its exhaust, Fish bent over the wheel.

'*Fish*!' she screamed. 'Fish, you stubborn goat! Come back here this minute!'

Fish turned, straightened briefly as he waved – they saw him smile, then he moved forward. They saw the big main sail rise, fill with air, and pull the ship towards France.

They were waiting patiently, on stretchers, sitting on the jetty patched white and red with field dressings, when they saw the cutter pulling in through the oily smoke drifting from the burning town. They raised a ragged cheer. Fish laid up alongside, the engine hunting in neutral, and they began to limp, totter and drag themselves aboard.

'I didn't think you were coming,' the doctor said, in manifest relief. 'There's Germans up there in the town.'

'I th-think I'm about the last,' Fish admitted. 'I didn't see anyone else on the way over.'

'Where's your crew?'

Fish put the ship into gear, the jetty began to recede, and he turned the wheel.

'Making tea,' he said. 'They'll have tea waiting for us when we get back.'

The young battalion MO started to move among his patients, and Fish went forward to raise the sail. The pall of stinking smoke slipped behind them like a bank of evil fog, and they emerged into the fresh air. As they left the coast behind them the sail caught the wind, and they began to crash along through the waves at speed.

Fish was not the first to see it. A sharp-eyed corporal with a bound leg spotted the lean, dark shape knifing through the patchy cumulus, an aerial shark. It dipped a wing, turning.

''Ere!' he yelled in alarm. 'Jerry fighter up there, guv.'

Fish tied the wheel, and went as quickly as he could forward, where the twin Lewis guns hung on their mounting. On a pair of hooks by the coaming was the huge muzzle-loading elephant gun, still unused, but loaded.

He could hear the rising snarl of the twin engines, saw the sun flash on its wings as it left the clouds, straightening up on its run in. He put his shoulder to the wood butt, felt it warm from the sunlight, pulled the cocking lever back.

At about four hundred yards the hurtling bomber half-filled the ring sight, and he opened up, seeing scarlet tracer spitting away from him. The guns hammered, spilling golden cases into the sunlight. The aeroplane raced in, dark green; he could see the pilot inside the glass of his canopy, leaning forward.

Two black objects fell from beneath it, and it passed over the yacht with a ripping, tearing roar. The whole ocean suddenly boiled beneath the ship, white hot nails slashed Fish across the back.

He was on his hands and knees, looking down at the deck. Somewhere close by, a man was swearing, in short, Anglo-Saxon words. Blood was bubbling hot in his mouth. He looked up, half a mile away over the sea the German bomber was turning to come back. The boom swayed to and fro, slack, and then slammed forward under the wind, the sail filling again with air.

The elephant gun was in front of him. He pulled it from its bracket, resting the weight on his knees. He had the packet of percussion caps in his pocket. Quite casually, still watching the turning aircraft, he fitted the little shiny brass top, and pulled the hammer all the way back. Blood was filling his mouth, he spat it out in a gout of scarlet.

The bomber was returning on a second run. He propped an elbow against his knee and drew the weapon into his left shoulder. A vision came into his mind of pheasants, long ago, and he smiled to himself.

He could see the pilot clear: a young man, sitting crouched in his greenhouse, between his shining, whirling propeller blades.

He led the target, just a little, settling the foresight into the notch, and he squeezed the trigger. The huge rifle exploded with a massive roar, belching flame and smoke, and Fish's hunter eyes saw the glass shatter, the huge sudden blossom of blood as the pilot's chest was torn asunder. The bomber jerked, went overhead screaming like a dragon. He heard it crash into the sea in a crump and sizzle, and then it was quiet; just the rhythmic slap of the water running under the hull, and the same man nearby, cursing.

'You got him,' a voice said in disbelief. It was the doctor, feeling with quick fingers about his chest. 'You're hit.'

It was warm, in the sun.

'Wh-what about a gasper?' he suggested.

'I can't do anything on board. We must get you to a hospital.'

'G-got an app-pointment already booked, old man,' Fish said helpfully. 'Dr Jennings, what? You know how to sail?'

'No, no I don't.'

'Aim for the wh-white cliffs, dear chap. Run her up on the beach.'

'All right.'

Fish managed to bring his battered cigarette case out. It seemed very heavy to him. With difficulty, he put a cigarette in his mouth.

'Remind Gawaine that the buggers will come out of the sun,' he said clearly. 'And send my love.'

He lit the cigarette with bloody fingers.

He looked up at the young man with eyes as bright as a candle's last flame.

'I'm not to be buried at sea,' he ordered. 'I'm the Earl, I have to be with the rest.'

Very faintly, in the haze, he saw a glimmer of white where the sea met the land.

'Tell Vi that I love her,' he said. 'But she knows that already.'

48

New Jerusalem

London, July 1940

The door on the other side of the little office opened. She blinked, she had been far away. A portly figure wreathed in cigar smoke stood there.

'My dear Lady Windstone,' Churchill said, 'I have kept you waiting. I am so sorry. These are busy times, I have twice sent messages to the palace to say I shall be late to see the King, and now Lord Halifax has gone in my stead. Pray do come in.'

She found herself inside, clutching a glass of whisky. A small garden was visible through the window, the roses shining from the afternoon rain. The room seemed in some state of disorganisation, as though removal men were half-way through their work. A large Victorian map of the world with the Empire marked in pink hung on one wall.

'Mr Chamberlain and his wife have not long left,' he explained. 'I have moved from the Admiralty.'

He picked up a report from the desk, scowled at it, put it down.

'Edward, our former king,' he said. 'He is scuttling about southern Europe with that American woman of his. He is not behaving very sensibly, he keeps bad company.'

'He's a Nazi sympathiser,' Violet said frankly. 'Always was. We're much better off with his brother.'

Churchill winced.

'Let us say . . . he is misguided. He does not seem to realise what harm he can do us by his actions.'

'Perhaps he does,' Violet said levelly. 'Mrs Simpson certainly hates us.'

Churchill glanced sideways at her, then chewed his cigar ferociously.

'How do you find the people?' he demanded. 'Are they of good heart now that we are entirely alone?'

'I feel we are in some ways like a rather large and quarrelsome family, faced by a death in the house, and reunited by it.'

'Good, good,' he grunted.

'You've made my mother frightfully happy,' she said.

'I have?'

'Oh, yes. That appeal Mr Eden made for the Local Defence Volunteers on the radio.'

'I am thinking of naming them the Home Guard,' he said enthusiastically.

'Oh, yes. Very good. Well anyway, she and daddy had been niggling at each other as they do – she finds him a bit trying about the house all day – but when he heard Mr Eden he was off down to the police station to volunteer before he'd finished speaking! He's as pleased as a dog with two tails; they've made him a full lieutenant and given him a whole squad of other old boys. Now he's got plenty to do. Mother's delighted. If my brother Freddie will just get home everything will be perfect.'

'Where is your brother?'

'Well, he *was* in Calais, shooting at the Germans. He's a prisoner of war, but we don't expect him to remain one for long.'

'You are clearly a most enterprising family! How old is your father?'

'Eighty-two. He told them he was sixty-nine.'

'And what did he do, before he got on your mother's nerves?'

'Oh, he was a major-general in the Sappers.'

'Splendid! With such men on our side how can we do else than prevail! What is it, then, my dear Lady Windstone, that I can do for you?'

'We . . . have buried my husband, the Earl.' Again, she felt the tears prickle behind her eyes. She forced herself to keep her voice steady.

'He was a great patriot. We miss him. He spoke, many times in my support. In my darkest hour, you know, when I stood up in the House after Munich, I told them that it was no victory, that we had sustained a total and unmitigated defeat, that it was but the first sip of a bitter cup that would be proffered to us by Herr Hitler year by year. How they reviled me then, all my fellow members, so much so they began the process of removing me from the party, from my seat in Epping, and your husband the next day put on all his medals, which were very many, and included the cross of Queen Victoria, and went to the Lords and spoke in my defence, and none of them could say him nay, for he was who he was. I miss him dreadfully.'

'I . . . cannot go back to the castle, just yet. My son Gawaine has just joined his squadron. My husband rests with his ancestors. I want . . . I must have something to do. Something to help. Anything.'

Churchill took a pull at his large but weak whisky and soda.

'You are a de Clare,' he murmured. 'You come from a great family of warriors and statesmen. I have commanded that a most secret organisation be set up. Its task shall be to keep the flame of resistance alive in Europe now that the evil forces of Nazism have brought darkness to cover their lands. It shall bring hope to those people, from we people here in our free islands, and one day it will set Europe ablaze. Would this work interest you?'

'Yes,' she said. 'Very much.'

'I'll tell Colville,' he said. 'I can hear him creaking the floorboards outside to let me know I must see Mr Cripps before he goes to Moscow.'

A tall, handsome young man was outside.

'John,' Churchill grunted. 'Lady Windstone is going to help with Special Operations. See to it.'

'Yes, sir.'

'My dear,' Churchill said warmly, 'you may ask to see me whenever you wish.'

Then he was gone, and Colville smiled pleasantly and respectfully.

'If you're on board, you wouldn't help, would you?'

'Of course.'

'I have a de Clare waiting to see somebody. Perceval de Clare. No relation?'

'My cousin. He calls himself Percy Clare and goes about pretending to be one of the proletariat.'

'That's him,' Colville said in relief. 'You wouldn't see what he wants, would you? Mr Attlee said he could come and talk to somebody about reconstruction but we're all rather busy fighting the war.'

'Delighted,' she said. 'Show me to him.'

They found Perceval in a small room on the ground floor, clutching a sheaf of papers.

'At last!' he cried, jumping up. 'Violet, what are you doing here?'

'I am helping the prime minister,' she said. 'He asked if I would see you, as he is busy with other matters.'

'Well, few things matter as much as this,' he said enthusiastically. 'Let me tell you.'

Violet sat down at the oblong oak table that was against the wall and lit a cigarette.

'Why don't you do that?' she suggested. Through the window she could see a little of the green of the park. She thought she might walk through it when she left.

'New Jerusalem!' he said, so fervently that she jerked her gaze away from the trees.

'What's that?'

'What we're fighting for,' he said intensely.

'I don't know about you, Perceval, but I'm fighting to avoid having Mr Hitler and his cronies marching down the street outside. What are *you* fighting for?'

'A world without want! A world free from prejudice of class, free of greed and exploitation, a world of Christian community, a world that cares for its citizens, shares equally, fairly between all—'

'You get that when you die, if you've been good,' she said drily. 'It's called Heaven.'

'We can have it here on earth. Here, in this Britain. In fact, we are starting to plan for it, now.'

'We are? Who is?'

'Me, and people like me.'

'You and people like you campaigned for world peace and disarmament, so successfully that Herr Hitler and the Nazis have gulped up all Europe and we are in the middle of a most desperate war,' she said acidly. 'Do we really want to trust you with plans for a new world once we have won it?'

He flushed red. 'I don't think that's a fair thing to say at all.'

'Get on with telling me what demented piffle you have come up with this time,' she said bitterly. 'If you must. I'm the only one here you've got who'll listen to you.'

'We shall make them all listen, before we are through,' he said determinedly. 'You see if we don't.'

'Who will?'

'We will. Those of us who believe in a New Jerusalem, a new society where there will be no poverty, full employment, where the citizen will feel the beneficent care of the state about him from cradle to grave, where men will work hard for the good of all, in new, garden city communities, where—'

'You're cracked, Perceval.'

'Am I?' he retorted furiously. 'Is Archbishop Temple cracked? Harold Laski? Mr Carr? Sir Richard Ackland? Dorothy Sayers? Yes, and Mr Attlee himself? Mr Butler? George Bernard Shaw? Kingsley Martin and Victor Gollancz?'

'The old gang,' she said. 'The stage army of the good. The ones who saw to it we couldn't stand up to Hitler before it was too late. The ones who grovel before a little stone god of Lenin. Listen, Perceval, if you want to do something useful in this war why don't you join the Home Guard, or become an air-raid warden?'

He stood up, and clutched his papers to him importantly.

'Nothing,' he said pompously, 'is more important than the reconstruction of our society. And please don't call me Perceval. The world to come is classless, and I am Percy Clare.'

Violet got up, stubbing her cigarette out.

'I am the Duchess of Windstone, and I have to go and fight,' she said. 'So each to his or her own.'

'You will see me again,' he warned. 'And next time I shall come at the head of a host, all demanding their natural rights.'

'You're full of wind, Perceval,' she said, and they went out. 'You always were.'

She changed her mind about walking through the park. It was disfigured with zig-zag trenches. They were all six inches deep in water, with crumbling edges. She went out into Downing Street and to Whitehall. In the middle of the great boulevard the Cenotaph stood, commemorating the dead of the Great War. As they passed, men quietly doffed their hats on their way, in respect.

49

Takes It With Him Wherever He Goes

Biggin Hill

Gawaine de Clare undid his harness and clambered out of the little cockpit, jumping down to the ground, clumsy and heavy in his flying boots and Sidcot. He took off his gloves, and for a moment ran his hand over the aluminium of the wing. Although the day was hot it was cold, smooth and cold. Up there, the air was chill.

'Happy?' asked a voice, pleasantly.

He turned; Hedges, the squadron commander was smiling at him.

'Smashing job, sir,' he said enthusiastically.

A Fordson tractor arrived at the concrete bay towing a petrol bowser. An airman climbed down and began to unreel his hose.

'This is Corporal Wilson,' said Hedges. 'He's bowser king around here. Wilson, this is Pilot Officer de Clare. He's just joined us.'

'Sir.'

A small engine on the tank began to thud and the air was suddenly fragrant with the 100-octane fuel gushing into the tank.

'Let's go over to the Mess and I'll buy you a beer,' suggested Hedges. His uniform was clean but old, and well-fitting, with a short medal bar that included the DFC on his shoulder. The award was bright, and new.

'Thank you, sir.'

Hedges glanced across at his new pilot. Gawaine had grown a moustache, a blond handle-bar. Hedges thought it made him look about twelve. He smiled ironically to himself and said nothing.

'We're front line,' he said pleasantly. 'You do your job here properly you call me boss, skipper or Harry. Save the "sir" bullshit.'

'All right, boss,' Gawaine agreed. 'What do I get called if I don't?'

'Dust to dust and ashes to ashes,' Hedges said, and the young man laughed. They walked across the grass, away from the line of cold, primed Spitfires sitting with their noses in the air.

'We took some losses over Dunkirk,' Hedges told him. 'They sent us north to refit, but now we're back. You're the first of our replacement pilots – we're still a little understrength. How did you find the Spitty?'

'Wizard. Absolutely wizard,' he said reverently.

'Yes, she's lovely, isn't she? Anything you found strange?'

'Not feeling the wind on my cheek.'

'Yes, I saw your log book. You're a glider man. Loads of glider hours.'

'My dad bought me one when I was ten.'

'Did he now? What flying club did you belong to?'

'Well, I – er – didn't really. My dad was the Earl of Windstone. We owned all the land about.'

'Oh . . . he was the Earl?'

'Yes. He was killed near Dunkirk. Got bombed in his boat, picking up soldiers.'

'Oh, I'm sorry. Who's the Earl now?'

'I am.'

Hedges looked amused. 'Do people call *you* sir?'

'No, boss,' Gawaine said determinedly. 'They call me Pilot Officer de Clare.'

'Fair enough,' Hedges agreed with a chuckle. 'All right. I liked your approach. You got a good report from Cranwell. Let's go up this afternoon and have a picnic somewhere over the trees.'

'Love to, boss.'

'They tell you anything about combat?'

From over at the butts there came a noise like some giant ripping a sheet of calico.

'We practised against each other.'

'Good. Remember, don't fly straight and level. Keep your head moving. use your mirror. If you see a spinner it's time to chuck it all over the shop. Frankly, to begin with I'll be happy to see you go up with us and come back safe. But if you see a sitter then blast away. Get close. Forget long-range marksmanship. Get bloody close, stuff your nose into his cockpit and let him have it.'

They came up to the Mess, a long wooden hut. Outside a group of young men dressed in eclectic style lounged about on chairs and old sofas dragged from inside the hut. They sat playing draughts, reading, looking up at the sky, smoking, throwing darts at an old board.

'This is Gawaine de Clare, chaps,' Hedges called. 'Our first replacement.'

They looked up at him with interest, called out their names, asked him about Cranwell. A lanky young man in flying boots and a dirty white cableknit sweater stuffed a battered paperback into his boot and got up, smiling welcomingly.

'Morton,' he said. 'Frank Morton. I'll buy you a beer.'

A head poked itself out of a window holding a telephone receiver. 'Group, boss,' it said.

Hedges took it. Gawaine was suddenly aware that all the pilots had stopped what they were doing, were frozen as they stood, listening. Hedges said a few words into the receiver and handed it back.

'Stand by,' he said. There was a shifting about, a gathering of gloves and helmets. Hedges fumbled in his pockets for a packet of cigarettes, produced a battered pack of Navy Cut.

'What's up, boss?' the lanky Morton asked.

'Big formation showing up on the plot over the Pas de Calais. Looks like this is it.'

He turned to Gawaine.

'Smoke?'

'No thanks, I don't.'

'We've been waiting for the next phase,' Hedges explained. 'They can't invade without air superiority. They can't have air superiority without getting rid of us.' He gestured at the group of waiting young men crouched about on the battered sofas and chairs.

'I'm sorry,' he said. 'Your picnic will have to be the real thing. Feel up to it?'

'Yes, sir – boss.'

'Good show. You can be my wing man. Stick to me like glue.'

Hedges lit his cigarette. Above his head the tannoy suddenly sounded.

'Scramble! Scramble!'

Cigarettes flew in the air. A short flight sergeant came out of the flight hut like a jack in the box.

'Start up!'

Men were running. Gawaine found himself among them, dashing over the grass. He could smell it, sweetly crushed by the pounding boots. The Spitfires were booming into life, one after the other.

Where was his? There. Yes, that was his. An erk was in the seat. As he ran up he could see him, as if in slow motion, pushing the cocks down, stick back, mags on, pressing the button. He came pounding up behind the wing; there was an LACW waiting, a young aircraftwoman wearing an overall held in by a length of string, she was smiling at him, waiting.

The erk had pressed the button, the big propeller turned, jerked, caught life with a noise like thunder and blurred. The exhausts vomited long blue flames enveloped in black smoke and the whole aircraft began to vibrate like a boiler under pressure.

As Gawaine scrambled up one side the aircraftsman was scrambling out the other. The LACW was strapping him in, he plugged in his helmet and voices were sounding in his ears. A smiling face, she grinned cheerfully at him.

'Good luck, sir!'

Machines from the flights were turning, bumping out of the flight line, rolling over the grass to their take off positions.

There. There was Hedges, passing him, he could see the big white numbers, 509. He waved the chocks away, the aircraftwoman jumped down and out of the way, he fed in some throttle, opened his radiator wide against overheating, and followed, in the huge din of the squadron moving out to fight.

Hedges was in his place at the head of the vic. Gawaine saw him glance round, checking they were ready; he gave the signal, opened the throttle. Behind him the other eleven were moving, rolling, tails lifting, the huge swelling bellow of the engines beating across the grass to hammer against the huts and hangars, wheels lifting from the grass, bumping, rising up, the legs tucking up into the mainplanes. The ground crews stood watching, hands on hips, eyes narrowed against the sun, their part done, dotted about by their bowsers and trolley-accs and the fighters having their fifty-hour inspections, ears deafened by the noise, which slowly died away and wings glinted in the light as they turned on course, vanishing into the blue.

Gawaine held formation in the tight vic as they climbed. They were all at full throttle.

The radio-telephone had been quiet for a minute or two. Now he heard the voice of the controller behind them, down on the ground at Group, watching his radar plot.

'Hallo, Green Leader. Bandits angels fourteen crossing the coast over Dover. Vector one four five. Buster.'

Hedges' voice crackled briefly in his ears. 'Green leader here. Vector one four five. Buster.'

The formation altered to the new course, but kept their throttles wide open. Gawaine performed a quick check of his instruments: altimeter, rising steadily; artificial horizon, wings level; nose high; airspeed, pegged on one hundred and eighty knots; oil and cylinder-head temperature, pressure gauges, heading, warning lights. He checked his mirror, to reinforce the habit. He could see a lone Spitfire there: arse-end Charlie, guarding the rear.

There. There was the coast in the distance below. The sea shone gold. The ground was green and grey and wrinkled, unmoving.

'*Hallo, Green leader. Bandits coming up, one o'clock below.*'

He saw them. With a sudden rush of adrenalin into his stomach he saw them about four miles away, a big block of aircraft, bombers and fighters, punching its way inland, a swarm of insects.

Hedges held his course, crossing the sun, making it swing round to come behind them.

'*All right, chaps. Formation attack.*'

His wing tilted, the vic dived upon them. Gawaine released the safety catch with his thumb, switched on his sight and in its glow the enemy aircraft grew bigger.

He could see a few fighters peeling off from the bombers. With a sudden thrill he recognised Messerschmitt 109s and Dorniers, the one they called Flying Pencils. In front of him, at two hundred yards, Hedges opened fire, thin smoke and gold cases streaming from his wings.

'*Help yourselves.*'

Gawaine steep-turned with Hedges as he knifed into the formation. The green Dorniers were weaving and rearing like startled horses as the fighters cut into their even ranks.

There! There it was, right in front of him. He squeezed the trigger hard, jamming it into the stick and the eight guns roared, shaking the whole aircraft. The bomber was whizzing past him – he pulled the stick back into his stomach, through the grey it was still there, he fired again, inverted in his turn, bits flying off it. It was going down. Black smoke poured from one engine. He fired again, the guns hammering. Dark objects shot out of the bomber, tumbling black into the milky blue. Out of the corner of his eye he saw something white blossom, realised they were people. He fired again, and as it suddenly exploded, he pulled hard to get away from the tumbling rubbish.

A Spitfire shot by, seeming inches away, something hard on its tail. Two fish, streaking green and brown through the blue water. He felt the slipstream, saw the big straight-edged crosses, kicked hard left rudder, fired a sudden ripping burst, somehow felt no surprise as the Me 109 disintegrated, breaking up from just behind the cockpit.

'*Behind you Gawaine.*'

Where the hell was Hedges? He'd lost him. The sky was filled with swirling, tumbling aircraft, the clear air becoming stained with smoke.

'Break left! De Clare, break left. Behind you.'

God! That was him. Something smashed into his Spitfire behind him. There was a terrific crash as things started bouncing off him, he pulled the stick back so hard he passed out for a second.

The mirror was filled with a yellow spinner. Pieces of metal were streaming off his wing. He struggled like someone demented. twisting and turning all over the sky. His oxygen mask dragged down over his face, it skinned his nose, the blood streamed down into his mouth. He found he was cursing insanely, his head bouncing from side to side off the canopy. The sky was a hideous jumble of aeroplanes. Smoke was in his lungs from somewhere.

He thrust his nose down and dust and rubbish rose up the cockpit. He dived vertically for the ground. It was closer than he remembered.

The airspeed indicator went up and up – 410, 420 mph. Oil was smearing his windshield, streaming away like black rain droplets. He squinted over his shoulder, there was someone following him down. A black dot. It winked yellow flame from its centre, and the fuselage behind him screamed as a cannon shell howled off it.

The ground was very close. Roads and villages flashed under his wings. He came back on the stick, the air grunting from his lungs. The ground was no longer wrinkled, but alive and moving. Trees shot by, a church steeple. He saw tiles disintegrate, flying in the air as cannon shells ripped through it, doves scattering like snowflakes.

He managed to look behind him, and saw the Messerschmitt, black, a shark, three hundred yards distant.

He was at fifty feet, over the fields. Farm workers gathering hay into a wain ran for their lives as the two fighters shot over their heads. A hill, topped with a green copse, kept for the hunting, for the pigeons to flee into, rose up above him. He weaved to the right, and a line of explosions ripped up the hill, grass and dirt blowing high into the air.

He screamed round the side of the trees, his wingtip almost on the ground, the blast of his passage flattening the shrubs, the stick right back, and hauled the throttle closed, the Spitfire suddenly squashing in the air, cutting off speed. He shot round the back of the copse and then rolled it hard to the right, pushing the throttle wide. It caught with a huge bang, jerking the fighter forward, and the Messerschmitt shot by.

It all seemed slow motion. He fired and he could see the machine-gun bullets lash the enemy fighter from end to end. Pieces flew off, streaming away, smoke came out of the holes, followed by flames. The canopy blew away, tumbling glittering in the sun.

As he watched, the 109 rolled on its back, dense black smoke pouring from its engine. Flames gleamed yellow through the black. It went in inverted, hitting the ground at speed. Incandescent fragments sprayed in the air, as though from a firework, and it left a trail of blazing fuel along the ground. It ripped through a hedge, breaking up as it did so, and crashed into a bank in a blaze of sparks.

He began to climb away into the sky. A last glance below showed the skeleton of the Messerschmitt, burning fiercely, surrounded by a crown of blazing fuel.

At two thousand feet, something banged horribly in front of him. Hot oily smoke rushed all about him. He ripped back the canopy, undid his belts, his RT wires, oxygen. As he saw the first yellow flames in the smoke he rolled it on its back, and jumped.

The air was cold, blasted him, turned him upside down, filled his flying suit. He yanked at the ripcord and it came away in his hand.

For a long, hideous moment he thought it had broken. Then there was a huge bang, and a giant hand jerked him upright. He was floating peacefully through the air. Below there were green and yellow fields, a wood. A river glinted. It was very quiet. He wondered where the Spitfire had gone.

In the distance he saw a house, nestled amongst trees. The ground came up with a rush, thumped him hard. He scrambled to his feet in long grass, yanked at his parachute to spill the air, dragged it in, sat on it to stop it blowing away in the breeze.

He sat there for a few minutes, waiting for the feeling that he was going to be sick to go away. He had a sudden, intense desire for a cigarette, to get drunk, to lie in some girl's arms.

After a while, rather shakily, he got to his feet, and gathered up his parachute. It was RAF property – he had a feeling they wanted it back. He was hot; he unzipped his sheepskin jacket and took off his leather helmet.

He pushed his way over a hedge, and fell into a lane. he rather thought that the house he had seen was that way. He walked along. It was pleasantly cool and shady, a small brook babbled as it passed him.

He found a wicket gate, went in. A grey-haired lady was kneeling by the flower bed of a thatched cottage, a trug basket slowly filling with weeds at her side. She glanced up.

'Is that my parcel from Hatchards?' she asked.

'No,' he said, rather weakly. 'No, I don't think so.'

She slowly raised herself, and turned so that she could see him properly.

'No, of course it isn't. I thought you were Griggins, from the Post Office. Why are you carrying a bundle of washing about, young man?'

'It's a parachute,' he explained. 'I'm a pilot.'

'Pilot? Pilot? Where is your ship, then?'

'I fly aeroplanes.'

'Where is your aeroplane, then?' she demanded.

'It crashed,' he said clearly. 'I was fighting against Germans, and got hit. I had to jump out.'

'Fighting against the Germans?' she said. For the first time there was a note of hesitancy in her voice. 'You can't be old enough, surely?'

'I am nineteen!' he cried hotly. 'And I have just shot down three German aircraft.'

'Well!' she said. 'Good for you. You must come and tell Arthur.'

She swept around the corner of the cottage, and he followed in her wake. In the kitchen garden an old man was tending some canes.

'Arthur! This young man has just arrived from shooting down Germans.'

'Eh?'

He straightened up, peered at Gawaine through round glasses.

'Have you, by George? Quite right too. We don't want Mr Hitler and his nasty lot over here. What's your name, boy?'

'Gawaine, sir. Gawaine de Clare.'

The old man turned back to his canes, unfinished business on his mind.

'Know much about raspberries, Mr de Clare?'

'No, sir.'

'You know what the summer of 1940 will be memorable for?'

'No.'

'Raspberries!' he cried triumphantly. 'Best crop I've had since '28.'

'I need a drink!' Gawaine cried desperately. 'And a fag.'

'My dear chap,' the old man said reproaching himself. 'Of course you do. Thirsty work, shooting down Germans, no doubt. Come inside.'

The interior of the cottage was pleasingly cool and rather dark. Gawaine found himself with a whisky and water in his hand. The old man fumbled in a drawer.

'Smoke a pipe?' he enquired. 'Of course you do. Here. Let me fill this one for you.'

Somehow, he found himself wreathed in fragrant smoke.

'I must call my squadron,' he said, from around the unfamiliar stem. 'Have you a telephone?'

'Can't be doing with them,' said the large woman, whose name was Mabel. 'Such noisy things. What's wrong with a letter?'

'I have to tell them where I am,' he explained. 'So that they can pick me up.'

'To take you where?'

'Biggin Hill.'

'Biggin Hill? Arthur, doesn't cousin Lucy live over that way?'

'She does,' he said comfortably.

'Then go and fetch the car,' she ordered. 'We shall take this young man home and go and have tea.'

'You have a car, sir?'

'Oh yes,' said Mabel. 'We quite enjoy a run out from time to time. Now, you sit there and enjoy your drink while I lay the table. A cold collation is what we usually have at this time of the year. Have you finished that one? Let me give you another. Arthur! Young Mr de Clare would like to try some of your raspberries.'

The small black Austin Seven trundled slowly to a stop outside the main gate, and Gawaine clambered out. He was clutching his parachute, and a large bouquet of summer flowers wrapped up in a copy of last week's edition of the *District Advertiser*. Mabel put her head out of the window.

'Now don't forget to put those into water straight away, Mr de Clare, and cut the stems.'

'I will.' he said. 'And thank you again for—'

'Oh, don't thank us. Cousin Lucy will be ever so pleased. Arthur! Go down to the crossroads and turn left.'

He watched the little black car putter away down the road, and went through the main gate.

He trudged along the road towards the Mess. The sun was falling in the west, it was nearly early evening. From somewhere across the field an engine was running up, he could hear the note of it dropping and rising as someone checked the mag drop. A tractor was moving along the perimeter road. In a hangar he could hear the clink of tools, a clatter as a mechanic dropped a panel. Two Spitfires stood there with some of their clothes off. One of them was ripped and holed, two fitters were taking off its elevators.

He trudged up in the warm late sunshine, went into the Mess. By the bar a tall, lanky figure was just picking up a pint. He turned, beamed as he saw him.

'It's the brolly man! Look, chaps, de Clare's back.'

They crowded round him, slapped him on the back, thrust a pint pot into his hand. Morton held up his parachute, laughing.

'He's an umbrella man!' he cried. 'Look, takes it with him wherever he goes.'

Gawaine passed the wrapped flowers over the bar to the barman, clutched his new pipe between his teeth. Coming into the Mess, Hedges saw him, was pleased, thought he looked even younger than he had in the morning.

'You have to put them in water,' Gawaine said to the barman. 'And cut the stems.'

50

Some Suitably Ghastly Sinecure

Cascais, Portugal

Godfrey sat in the darkness. His car was parked at the end of the sandy track, where it meandered down and petered out at the beach itself. Behind him the Atlantic crashed rhythmically into a seething foam, faintly white in the starlight. Crickets creaked and shrilled in the pines. From time to time he rested a pair of large Zeiss binoculars on the surround of his door and focused on the brightly lit villa on the hill. The curtains of the great dining room were not drawn, and he could see inside. Facing him, with Wallis at his side, was Edward, the former king. He was dressed for the evening, as was she. When she turned to talk to one or other of the guests Godfrey could see her jewellery flash in the light of the great chandelier. The men were all in formal dress, and the women in silk frocks. The courses came and went, the air became tinged silver with cigarette and cigar smoke. Liqueurs circulated. He saw Carlotta, her head back, laughing.

Finally the powerful lamps of limousines lit up the grounds, splashing them with yellow as they made for the road. Godfrey sat silently, watching the great cars carrying their important passengers back into Lisbon.

Up on the hill, the lights winked out. He lit a cigarette of his own, shielding the flame with his cupped hand. He got out of the car, leaning against it as he smoked, watching the glowing phosphorescent foam of the waves.

Finally, he heard the crunching of feet coming down the sandy path.

'Godfrey!' a woman's voice hissed. 'Is that you?'

'Here,' he called softly, and she came towards him. It was Carlotta. She had changed out of her evening dress and was in jersey and slacks.

'God,' she said. 'Give me a fag. All this spying is killing on the nerves.'

He handed one over.

'Better than being hanged,' he observed. 'I don't think I've seen so many Nazis since I was at Nuremberg. What's happening?'

'Right,' she said, drawing in smoke and composing herself. 'You know that the Duke and Wallis are staying here with Santo e Silva. This is his house. He's a banker, and one of the chief local Nazi sympathisers. The Duke of Kent was here a few days ago, now he's gone and Edward's come.'

'So what are they up to? I saw von Hoyningen-Huene, the Nazi ambassador. Who was the man with him?'

'That's Schellenberg. He's Ribbentrop's man. He's head of the SD, the German Secret Intelligence. Wallis wanted him to be on hand.'

'So Wallis is still working actively with the Nazis?' Godfrey said quickly.

'She's been with them for a long time. She was fucking Ribbentrop when he was in London. You know that. Schellenberg is here because she sent orders for him to come.'

'She's more than an agent.'

'Of course. Look, she wants to give your country to the Nazis, that makes her fairly powerful, huh? What you might call a prime mover.'

'So what are they doing?'

'He's brought money, for a start. Fifty million francs in a Swiss account. Wallis always needs money. The Nazi authorities have guaranteed that Edward and Wallis's bank accounts in Paris won't be touched.'

'What has their lucre bought them?' Godfrey said, leaning back against the car and pulling on his cigarette, watching her closely in the gloom.

'Wallis and the Duke are working hard to destabilise the Churchill government. They think, and the Ambassador and Schellenberg seem to agree, that Churchill's political position is still very precarious.'

'It is.'

'The Duke has just sent a telegram to his brother the King demanding that he appoint a new pro-appeasement government in place of the Churchill coalition.'

'Who?'

'Lord Halifax, Sir John Simon, Sir Samuel Hoare. He proposes that Lloyd George be prime minister of a new fascist order in Britain which will become allied to Germany.'

'The King and Queen are both staunch patriots,' Godfrey observed. 'They will do no such thing.'

'Edward advises the Germans to commence heavy bombing of England, which he thinks will bring the people to their senses. They will demand the overthrow of Churchill. In the meantime, he and Wallis are going to go to America.'

'Oh?'

'Yes. You know how popular they are there. They plan to go from coast to coast on a peace platform, to stop the war with Germany.'

'Churchill and Roosevelt are planning for America to come into the war.'

'They know that. But this is election year. The Duke and Wallis will ally themselves with the isolationists. Roosevelt will have to come over to the peace platform or lose. If you Brits do badly in the air war that's starting Churchill will fall. The King and Queen will be kicked out with him and Edward and Wallis will return. Edward will take back his throne and Wallis will be queen.'

'It could just happen,' Godfrey said thoughtfully. 'All right. Is that it for the moment?'

'That's what I've got so far.'

'Good. There's something else I want you to do. Get in with Schellenberg. Point out your connections into English high society. You'll find that Wallis and Edward won't be going to America.'

'Where will they go?'

'They will go,' Godfrey said evenly, 'wherever we tell them to go. Some suitably ghastly sinecure will no doubt be arranged.'

'What if they don't want to?'

'The penalty for treason is death, as you yourself are aware,' he pointed out.

'Schellenberg is thinking of taking them to Germany.'

'Wallis does not have the mettle to gamble all on one throw of the dice. We'll see that she rots somewhere she'll hate.'

'Only if your fighter pilots win the battle,' she said acidly. 'If they lose she'll have *you* rotting in the Tower.'

'Yes,' he said languidly. 'Our brave boys in blue will have to do their stuff, won't they?'

Carlotta finished her cigarette, ground it out under her shoe.

'Why am I supposed to get in with Schellenberg?'

'You're going to be an agent for the Nazis in England,' he said smoothly.

'Oh, no . . .' she cried. 'I thought that doing this for you was it!'

'Oh, by no means,' he said smiling. 'Your life isn't yours any more. It's ours. For ever.'

When she had gone back up the hill he started his car, drove quietly away. When he got to the main road he switched on his lights, headed for Lisbon. The decaying capital was a place of bright lights, raffish and corrupt, a place of intrigue, secret police, refugees, spies and deserters.

Godfrey stopped his car at the side of the road, by a bar where people were still carousing despite the late hour. He sat down at a table outside, ordered whisky as he got his thoughts in order.

A chair scraped, somebody sat down beside him. He looked up, and into the grinning face of Freddie de Clare. He was thin, his battledress dirty and torn, he had not shaved.

'I'll have one of those,' he said. 'Hallo, Godfrey.'

'Good Lord, Freddie. You're supposed to be a prisoner of war.'

'Frightfully bad food, old man. I left the camp in a rubbish truck and I seem to have been walking ever since. Is this my drink? Bottoms up. I'm looking for suitable transport back home. Think you can arrange something?'

51

You Taste of the Air

Biggin Hill, 15 September

'Up! Up! Up!'

Gawaine stared uncomprehendingly at the flight sergeant. The cool air from his prop washed into his open cockpit, he ached, twisting and turning and fighting at thirty thousand feet, over seven miles high. He had landed, the flight sergeant was hopping up and down, his arms flailing in the air as though trying to pick the Spitfire up personally and fling it back up into the blue.

The tannoy was screeching something. Air punched his cheek. A gun. More guns. From somewhere nearby a Bofors was firing.

'Scramble. Scramble. All Green aircraft scramble.'

Jesus. They were scattered all over the grass, the ones that had come back. Hedges was dead, he had seen him go down on the first mission, a flamer. He had no idea who was leading the squadron.

He gunned the throttle, sent the Spitfire bouncing over the grass in a blast of dust. Jesus. The airfield was under bloody attack just when they had got down. He quickly checked his fuel state. About twenty gallons sloshing about. Still twenty seconds' worth of ammunition.

He scanned the field, gave it the fuel. On the perimeter the Bofors was firing steadily, red tracers streaming flatly over the land. They were low.

He got off quickly, light, tucked in his undercart. Full throttle.

There. There they were. There flashing up the valley, a shoal of them, green and grey, the fat bombers driving on, a swarm of fighters about them. They were so low he could see their shadows running dark over the ground.

He had no time to get altitude, to make a conventional attack. A hundred feet over the fields he banked steeply, and flew at them head on.

The reflector sight glowed brightly, he picked out the leading Heinkel and began firing in short bursts. Fire sparkled all over the canopy, armour glass shattered, glittered in the sun. Something exploded inside it and it reared sharply to the right. The bomber behind flew into the wreck. As he flashed through the formation Gawaine saw them tumble in locked embrace, felt the sudden huge buffeting of air as they exploded with full bomb load onto the ground below.

He pulled the Spitfire round in a savagely tight turn, right over the tree tops, screaming after the formation. Somebody else had got up; he saw another fighter diving into the shoal, saw yellow flame ripple along its wings. The German formation was streaming smoke. A Dornier was on fire, he could see its port engine belching flame. Bombs tumbled from it as the pilot desperately dumped his load, veering off from the formation, trying to put his stricken machine down before it burned.

Gawaine ignored him, he was gone. They were over the field. The bombers were attacking the buildings, the hangars. The flak was pouring in fire at enemy and friend alike. The first bombs went up, throwing huge gouts of brown earth and smoke high into the air.

He was in among them again. The buffetting of the slipstream was enormous, sending his wings flipping first one way then the other. The bomb blast beneath him lashed out at him like the kick of a mule. The Dornier in his sight had its bomb doors open. He squeezed the trigger hard against the stick, the whole fighter vibrating as he poured in fire. Pieces blew away into the air, the bomber suddenly dipped, dived, flew straight into the ground in a huge gout of orange and yellow flame.

A Messerschmitt came flashing across his path – he fired again, heard the scream of compressed air, the empty clanking of the breech blocks. He whirled away, back towards the field.

The air about him was suddenly empty. Smoke from the fires stained the clean morning air. He came over the airfield, saw the brown craters scarring the grass, saw some hangars burning, people running, fire tenders and ambulances racing. He dropped his gear, turned back towards the field, touched down past a big smoking crater, taxied in.

The flight line was still intact. He turned in at his bay, cut the throttle and switches, climbed out.

'Well done, sir!'

It was the flight sergeant again, beaming all over his face.

'That was lovely, that was. You give 'em hell, you did. Right where we could see it. Something to tell the missus, that is.'

Armourers were swarming about the aircraft. Corporal Wilson, the bowser king, drew up on his tractor, Gawaine smelled the sudden cold rush of 100-octane. Inside his gloves, his hands were shaking.

'My pleasure,' he said.

Violet opened the small door at the top of the narrow stairway and she and Felicity stepped out onto the roof. They were high up, the buildings of Mayfair were spread out about them, eerily unlit in the moonlight like a ghost town. To the west the park stood darkly, stretching to Kensington.

'Here we are,' she said cheerfully. 'Take a pew.'

The two women sat down on a small wall of sandbags. Behind them was a small hut made out of sandbags, sitting on the wide, flat lead roof.

'Is this where you spend your evenings?' said Felicity.

'Yes. I've appointed myself ARP warden at night, and Fergis the porter does it in the day. It's jolly nice at the moment, sleeping up here under the stars. Be a bit chilly later on, but we will have told Hitler to push off by then, so it won't matter. Gasper?'

'Please.'

They sat smoking for a little while. Down on the streets they could see buses crawling about with their dimly lit lamps on.

'You don't go down into the bomb shelters when there's a raid on?'

'Goodness, no. The buggers are spraying the place with incendiaries, you have to rush about chucking them off. Anyway, it's safer up here.'

'It is?'

'Oh yes. My Uncle Harry told me that, when he was in the Navy, got sent out to Japan – oh, turn of the century, it was – when we were teaching the Nips how to have a navy of their own. They decided to have a war with Russia and gave them a terrifically bad time, so the Tsar sent a fleet all the way round the world to give them a bloody nose for it. The Nips knew about it and were waiting for them – the Russians were led by some chap called Resudsky, and the others by Togo, and my Uncle Harry went out with Togo as an observer. He sat out on the foredeck in a camp chair taking notes all through the battle and only got up to change his uniform when some chap got blown to bits all over him. They all thought he was mad, but there was method in it, you see, as he said, because he could only get killed by a direct hit, whereas inside the ship you got all these splinters flying about chopping people up horribly. So

I consider I'm safer up here. Togo slaughtered Resudsky and his lot, of course.'

From somewhere in the depths of the city sirens began to groan and wail.

'Here we go.'

As the alert died away, they could very faintly here the sound of engines in the distance.

'But anyway, Flick darling, I haven't just asked you up here to talk about my Uncle Harry. How's your Frog? You do parlay, don't you?'

'Oh, yes. Marseille accent, I'm told.'

'Wonderful! Do you want something to do? I went to see Winston, you see, and he's given me a job. I need some people like you.'

'To do what?'

'Go over to France and do nasty things to the Germans.'

'Sounds my sort of thing,' Felicity said absently. 'Who do you work for?'

'SOE – Special Operations Executive. I'll take you in tomorrow.'

The noise of the bomber stream was becoming very loud. The darkness was suddenly lit up by flashes of yellow and scarlet towards Chelsea.

'Do you get frightened, Vi? I am, a bit.'

'Oh, God yes. I'm in a most fearful funk most of the time. I just can't stand the idea of cowering in some hole while those bastards fling bombs at me. I'd rather be up here doing something about it. What I usually do is retire into my hut and have a scotch while the swine come over. Then if we get any incendiaries I dash out and get rid of them. Scotch first, though.'

'Sounds all right to me.'

They went inside the little structure, and Violet lit a small storm lantern. They could hear the sound of bombs falling. The anti-aircraft guns were starting up, and light flickered in from outside as the shells hurtled up into the air. Violet poured them both large whiskies.

'Darling Fish swore by whisky when they were loosing off at you, and he was so right.'

'Lovely. How's Gawaine?'

'Down at Biggin Hill. I got a letter from him the other day. I think he's having a wonderful time, to me honest. Hurtling about up there.'

'You know, the whole war hinges on a few young chaps shooting these bastards down. The whole world, really. We're the only ones left fighting.'

'I know. I'm so proud of him, you know. I went down to
Fortnums the other day to get some tea and the doorman there,
he's an old friend, and he said 'Well, mum, we're in the Final.
Just us and 'Itler, but it's going to be played on the 'ome ground.'
I liked that.'

She gave Felicity an iron helmet. 'Here. I wear one of these. Fish
brought some home from the war. Shrapnel helmet. Stops your hair
catching fire.'

The lamp vibrated as bombs fell nearby. In a corner were some
large shovels.

'Look, darling, if the incendiaries fall we have to rush out and chuck
them off. I use a shovel and fling 'em over the parapet. Nobody's
about down there. They're like rather large fireworks.'

'Give me another scotch before they arrive, darling.'

The two ladies sat quietly inside the little hut. A bomb went off
not far away, everything rocked. There was a terrific clatter all about,
smoke gushed into the shelter.

'That's it!' Violet cried. She tipped back her drink, thrust a shovel
into Felicity's hand and they rushed outside. On the roof almost a
dozen objects smoked and hissed scarlet flames, like brands from a
bonfire. They ran through the smoke as the guns fired, scraping them
up, throwing them into the void.

'*Green leader here.*'

It was Morton. There was nobody else left who could lead. He
flew steadily at the head of the vic of five

'*Green leader here. Where are these bastards headed?*'

'*Looks like London again, Green leader,*' the controller down at
Group replied.

'*They came visiting us at home this morning.*' Morton said laconically. '*We told them they weren't welcome.*'

The little formation continued to climb on its course. Somewhere
out in the blue was another bomber force. London had been pounded
by day and night for two weeks. In his place next to Morton, Gawaine
glanced across at the others. He realised he didn't know who they
were. The squadron had virtually been wiped out: they had lost
eighteen pilots in three weeks, the CO that morning. On his tunic,
under his sheepskin jacket was a small fresh ribbon. His DFC had
come through the day before.

The morning was bright, the sky a shiny, polished blue. Below the
land was just beginning to take on the faintest yellow and red tint of

autumn. They went into a great bank of haze, and the woods and fields below disappeared into the blur.

They emerged a few minutes later, the visibility suddenly becoming crystal clear. Below, the Thames estuary lay spread out in front of them. Gawaine recognised Sheppey, and glancing to port he saw the winding signature of the great river going into London. The docks were crammed with shipping, a thin layer of blue smoke covered the mighty city.

The haze curved away over to sea, they were flying along its edge.

'Jesus bloody Christ!'

Out of the haze came an armada, a towering tidal wave of black aircraft, stacked layer upon layer, rank upon rank, climbing up into the sky. They darkened the sky, like some hideous migration of primeval insect life.

'Help yourselves, chaps,' Morton said laconically. They sat forward in their armoured seats, switched on their sights, turned up the oxygen, took off the safeties from their guns and flew at them, full throttle.

The air around him was suddenly full of whirling aircraft. A 109 flashed past, white plumes spuming from its wingtips. he fired a short burst, and missed.

A bomber. Dark green, yellow flashes winking at him from its gunner. He pushed in left rudder, hard, stitching bullets all along its body; it lit up, from within, began to roll. Another 109, streaming golden cases as it fired.

Head on. A 109, filling the windshield, at less than 100 yards. Its big red spinner and apparently slowly turning prop filled his vision. The wings and spinner lit up all over as it flung itself at him. As he fired there was a huge bang and his windshield splintered into an opaque wall. For a second he was frozen. Something huge ripped over his head in a blast of air and noise. Oil poured over his canopy as if from a hose.

For a fraction of a second all went black through the scarred, filthy hood. He could see nothing. He hit something with a crash that sent him smacking forward in his seat. His face, in mask and goggles, cracked into the instrument panel. In front of him there was a hideous scream as the propeller splintered to nothing and the engine exploded. Something tore at him, twisting the aircraft over and over as though cracked by a whip, and his head smacked off the sides of the canopy. He pulled frantically at his harness.

There was a tremendous bang. Air blasted all over him. He had a

fleeting a glimpse of his ruined Spitfire in a deathly embrace with a
Dornier. Two bodies spilled out of the wreck. he tumbled over and
over, clawing at his ripcord.

The parachute opened with a booming jerk, snapping him upright.
The sky was somehow clear of aeroplanes, though marked by dark,
smoky trails where they had died. The bombers and the battle was
above him. He was over London. He could see the river below. The
docks were on fire, shipping was burning.

The breeze was pushing him from the suburbs into town. Like a
huge white dandelion seed, he floated down, at the wind's mercy.
He could see the green of the parks. Bombs were hitting the West
End, he saw smoke and dust rising into the air, saw a building fall
in on itself, rubble gushing into the street.

The roofs were coming up at him, grey slate, sloping down towards
the street, chimneys poking up at him, wires crossing high over the
pavements below.

He hit with a crash, bounced off the roof in a shower of breaking
slate. He grabbed at a heavy pantile, missed, slid along the roof, still
dragged by his parachute. It pulled him off the edge and he fell onto a
small dormer window poking out. A hundred feet below people were
running in the street. He clawed frantically at the old black guttering
with his gloved hands. For a moment he hung there, dangling over the
drop, and then the rotten metal broke, flinging him into the void.

He fell, and then was pulled up with a jerk, slapping him hard
against the side of the building. Rough brick ground against his face
as he swung from his harness. He could see the cords taut above him,
vanishing over the roof. The parachute had caught on something.

He felt it rip. He fell a few feet, scrabbling futilely at the bricks,
trying to gain purchase. His feet felt a break in the wall below. As
he fell further he was grabbed, small furious, hard hands, seizing him,
pulling at him. He was half over a windowsill, a young woman had
hold of him. She was yelling something he couldn't understand and
had a foot up on the sill, heaving as hard as she could. he grabbed at
the windowframe and heaved, and fell inside.

They clasped to each other. From somewhere there was a rising shriek, a great explosion. The floor underneath them vibrated,
bounced as though it was an earthquake. She pulled at him, mouthing
something in the din. He yanked at his release harness, they scrabbled
across the floorboards, she dragged him under the bed, a big, brass-
framed bed. Another bomb howled down nearby, exploding with a
shriek and a roar of shattering masonry. They clung together in frantic
embrace. The third bomb in the stick went off further way; he could

hear the steady rise and fall of the siren, the clanging of firebells and ambulances, the shouting of voices.

They lay together, gasping. The raid seemed to have moved on, like a thunderstorm. They could hear the droning of aeroplanes becoming distant. She sat up on one elbow, her dress torn. He could see her breasts, smooth and pink and round. She smiled at him with white teeth and green eyes.

'I say,' she said. 'We haven't been introduced. Molly Francis.'

She held out a small hand, and he shook it, quite formally.

'Gawaine de Clare,' he said. 'It's very nice to meet you.'

'I think we can probably crawl out now,' she said, and they emerged. His parachute was still dangling half out of the window, and he went and pulled it in. The street below was covered in shattered glass.

She stood in front of him. She had done up the buttons of her dress.

'Do you make a habit of dropping in on girls like this?' she asked.

'I . . . was up there,' he said. 'I hit a Dornier, had to come down on my 'chute.'

'Do you make a habit of that?'

'Just recently,' he said, standing in front of her so that he could watch her. She was overwhelmingly beautiful to him.

'This makes the fourth time,' he said. 'In the squadron, they call me Brolly. I'm the umbrella man.'

'Brolly,' she said, repeating the word, as though it tasted very pleasant. 'Brolly. I shall call you Brolly too. Do you shoot down a lot of German aircraft in exchange?'

'Fourteen, at the moment,' he said.

'Well, it's a fair exchange. We seem to be doing better on the bargain.'

'Yes.'

She was so lovely all he wanted to do was stand looking at her.

'I must go to the hospital,' she said. 'They will be bringing in the casualties.'

'I have to go back to the station,' he said. 'Biggin Hill. The Germans will be coming back, the chaps will expect me to go up with them. We're very short of pilots, you see.'

'Then we must get together,' she said gravely. 'When we are not otherwise occupied.'

'Yes.' He thought for a moment, his face brightened. 'Come down and stay at the pub. I get off in the evening.'

'You don't fight at night?'

'No. Can't see.'

'Good show,' she said. 'I have some days off next week. What pub is it?'

'The King's Arms. They have nice rooms around the garden.'

'I'll find it,' she said. 'Come and get me on Wednesday.'

'I will.'

She moved, took a nurse's blue uniform out of a cupboard, laid it out on the bed with a belt with an ornate silver buckle.

'I must get changed,' she said. 'They'll be bringing them in.'

'Yes. I must get back.'

He folded up his parachute into a bundle, wadded it up under his arm, went to the door with her.

'Molly?'

'Yes?'

'I think I'm already in love with you.'

'Yes,' she said seriously. 'I know. Now go back to your aerodrome, Gawaine de Clare, and we shall find out all about each other on Wednesday.'

He bent, and they kissed.

'You taste of strawberries,' he said.

'You taste of the air,' she said. 'So high up.'

'Wednesday.'

'Yes.'

He went down a winding stair, found the hallway, went out into the street. It was covered in a yellow dust, and broken glass. A lugubrious man in a brown dustcoat was sweeping it into piles with a stiff broom. His shopfront was open to the air.

'If this 'Itler feller keeps on like this, 'e will get hisself much disliked,' he said disapprovingly.

He looked Gawaine up and down.

'You in the Raff?'

'Yes.'

'Give 'em what for then.'

'I will.'

Gawaine began to trudge down the street, his boots crunching on the broken glass. As he emerged into the main road a passing taxicab sputtered to a halt.

'British?' the driver enquired, staring narrowly at him.

'Of course.'

The man beamed under a flat hat.

'Where you going, then, guv?'

'Biggin Hill.'

''Ow come you're 'ere?'

Gawaine held up his parachute.

'Collided with one of theirs.'

''Op in then. You'll be needing a new aircraft.'

He got in the back, and they jerked away down the street. As they did so a man came hurrying down some steps from a house. He was smartly dressed, in a striped blue suit, His hair was oddly long, he pushed it off his forehead, and seeing the taxi coming he raised a peremptory hand.

'It's 'Arris.'

'It is?'

'The loony doctor,' the cabbie explained. 'Mind if I drop 'im off? 'E goes to 'is clinic.'

He slowed and stopped, and the doctor got in.

'Takin' the pilot 'ere to Biggin 'Ill.'

Doctor Harris peered closely at Gawaine, brushing his long hair out of his eyes.

'You're contused,' he said.

'I baled out.'

'You're a fighter pilot?' he asked keenly.

'Yes. I hit a Dornier, I had to jump out.'

'How is your mind? I see the bruises on your face, but what of those on your mind? I'm a psychiatrist, tell me about your pain.'

Gawaine looked sideways at him and said nothing.

'You see, you're typical!' the doctor exclaimed irritably. 'This sickening British stiff-upper-lip attitude. Look at you! You've almost been killed! In the name of God let your trauma out!'

'I'd rather have a pint, if you don't mind.'

'Bah!' Harris said in disgust. 'Recourse to alcohol merely masks the symptoms. We are all sick! Look! Look out there!'

They were passing a police station. It had been damaged in a raid, wooden shuttering blocked out its windows. On it a constable had painted: Be Good. We Are Still Open.

'Not bad, eh?' said Gawaine. He found his pipe and began to fill it from the tobacco pouch he had brought.

'More denial,' Harris muttered, throwing himself back in his seat. He looked at the pipe.

'Oral substitutiary comfort again, like your need for alcohol,' he said sharply. 'Did your mother breast-feed you?'

'I wouldn't know,' Gawaine said austerely. 'It is not a subject we have ever discussed.'

'Precisely!' he cried in triumph. 'All your problems are ones of repression! You are unable to talk frankly to your mother about your needs.'

The taxi drew up outside a drab building in the middle of an area that had clearly taken considerable damage from the bombers.

''Ere we are Doc.'

Doctor Harris peered out expectantly, and then his face crumpled with disappointment.

'Where are they?' he cried. 'The council has hired me, at great expense to the taxpayer, to provide psychiatric counselling for the trauma the citizens of this borough have suffered, and *nobody comes.*'

'They're prob'ly down the boozer, having a bit of a sing-song,' said the taxi driver.

'Our society is sick!' the doctor said bitterly. 'This denial of trauma, this perverse "we can take it" attitude. We should all be healthy, admit it, say, "I am in pain, I can take no more, help me." That's what I am here for, to help people, to say, "talk to me, I feel your hurt." But no. They are all, apparently, down the boozer, singing sentimental folk songs.'

'But we *can* take it,' said Gawaine.

The psychiatrist got out, paid the driver some money, and went angrily across the road, to his empty clinic. The taxi sputtered away.

'See what I mean?' the driver said, grinning in his mirror. ''E's the loony. The loony doctor.'

Gawaine filled his pipe and lit it, silvery smoke drifting out through the window. He sat back in the seat, thinking of Molly Francis. Soon it would be Wednesday.

He realised he was leaning against a kind of parcel, all rolled up in a blanket.

'I say,' he called, 'I think somebody's left something in the back here.'

'Eh? What's that, guv?'

The cabbie glanced over his shoulder.

'No, that's mine, guv.' he said. 'That's what I sleep in. Kip in the cab, I does, since we was bombed out. Come back home last week and found Jerry been there before me.'

'I'm sorry,' said Gawaine. He could still see her breasts, through the rumpled dress. 'Nobody hurt, I hope?'

'Just me Aunt Flo,' he said. 'Found her feet in our house and her head in the neighbours.'

He paused at the crossroads, headed south.

'Died 'appy, I reckon,' he said ruminatively. 'She was always inquisitive.'

52

You've Just Been Scorched

Banks of cloud hung over the land like gigantic ramparts. Clusters of flak appeared out of nowhere and hung black along their flanks. From the battlements fighters and bombers swarmed towards the climbing Spitfires like the defenders of a castle.

The first contact, the aircraft formations breaking up into a confused mêlée. A Heinkel exploding like an enormous flak shell, a dark expanding mushroom spreading out across the sky, incandescent debris spraying out across the white cloud. A Spitfire going down, belly up. Three parachutes suddenly smacking into view.

Gawaine twisted and turned in the swarm. The fighters swirled and snapped like demented predatory fish. Nothing but huge scarlet spinners, yellow bellies, black crosses and clipped wings, roundels and ellipses. Multi-coloured tracer striped the air, dazzlingly bright.

The red filaments of his gunsight encircled a grey and green Messerschmitt. They were turning tightly across the sky, he grunted as the air forced itself out of his lungs. His oxygen mask was loose, dragging itself off his nose and down over his mouth. He fired in short deadly bursts, pieces of debris flying off the German fighter.

There was a thunderclap of noise, a burning slap of fire across his face, a shriek that pierced his eardrums. A cannon shell smashed through the windshield. Hammer blows rocked the Spitfire, beating into its body, metal screaming off metal.

The cockpit exploded into flame, he was sitting in a furnace. He howled with the sudden agony. The huge 300-mph gale blew the fire into his face like a vast blowtorch.

He did as he had been trained, did it without thinking. He pulled the split pin out of his sub-harness with his blazing gloves, disentangled his oxygen and radio-telephone wires, yanked back the canopy and rolled the doomed fighter on to its back.

He was falling through the sky. His hands were somehow up near his face. Smoke streamed off the charred gloves. They hurt, fearfully. His face hurt. All of him hurt. He managed to pull the ripcord. The harness whipped him upright with red-hot straps, and he screamed in the sky.

He hit the ground without knowing it. He could hear voices, people running, somebody shouting to call an ambulance.

Somebody was talking to him. No, not talking, issuing orders. He focused on her. A severe woman with iron-grey hair drawn back under her nurse's hat. She was looking at him in disapproval.

'Sit up, young man,' she said. 'Mr Green is coming on his round.'

'Who might you be?' he asked. It hurt his mouth to talk.

'I am the sister in charge of this ward and you do as I say.'

'I'll have my pipe. Where is it?'

'Smoking is not permitted. When Mr Green talks to you you will lie to attention.'

'Who is he? Does he fly?'

'Certainly not. He is the consultant surgeon.'

'Doesn't fly? Balls to him then.'

The sister's mouth tightened grimly.

'He holds the rank of colonel in the RAMC. You will address him as "sir".'

'I am the bloody Earl of Windstone. He can fucking call me "sir".'

He felt unconsciousness welling up inside him again. He closed his eyes to shut the woman out, and as he went under he felt only slight surprise to realise that nothing came over his eyes.

'Hallo, darling.'

'Hallo, Mummy.'

Violet bent to kiss him. He smelled sweetish, like underdone pork and crackling. She smiled, and not for an instant revealed that she could not recognise her son. His name was at the end of the iron-framed bed.

'Pretty poky hole this, darling,' she said.

'Look, Mummy, there's a couple of things need fixing up. Firstly, the old cow who runs the ward won't give me my pipe. And I can't close my eyes. My eyelids have got stuck to my eyebrows or something.'

His eyelids were burned away.

'That's what I've come for, darling. I've found this frightfully good chap, specialises in unsticking eyelids, that sort of thing. Name of

McIndoe. He's over in East Grinstead. Nice place, much better than this.'

'Plenty of pubs?'

'Five for every church, apparently.'

'I just need the old eyelids fixing, and then I can get back to the squadron, you see.'

'That's it,' she agreed. 'Does it hurt?'

'It does a bit.'

'I ought to have brought some butter with me,' she smiled. 'We could have buttered you all over.'

She reached in her bag, took out a brand new Dunhill pipe and tobacco pouch.

'I forgot the butter, but I brought this. I think you must have lost your old one, so I've got you a new one.'

He stuck it into his mouth triumphantly with his reddened, weeping hands. Violet reached into her bag again and took out a hunting flask. She took off the top and filled it.

'Your father swore by a tot of whisky,' she remarked, handing it to him. 'It was his cure for everything.'

It went down like liquid fire as the sister of the ward pounded up in outrage.

'Alcohol is forbidden on—'

'I am Lady de Clare, the Countess of Windstone,' Violet said, cutting her off effortlessly. 'I have come for my son.'

They had covered half his face with some kind of gauze. It had solidified into a kind of armour, stuck to him in rigid sheets. He had seen only a town through the windows of the ambulance, red-bricked buildings and trees, hospital grounds, a group of temporary huts. The white Morris ambulance with its red crosses had pulled up outside the biggest of these. He had managed to get to his feet and walk in.

It was called Ward Three, he found out. Almost the very first thing they had done to him was lie him on a bed and begin to soak off the gauze bandages. Two young nurses did it for him; pretty girls, very pretty girls.

It hurt, it stopped him from trying to see what was going on. He somehow liked the noise about him, it was like being back in the mess. The bandages stuck to his face, and however careful the young nurses were they pulled and tore at his lacerated, burned flesh. Once he cried out, and he heard a voice by his ear.

'Oh, dear,' it said. 'You'll have me sobbing on the floor in a minute if you go on like that. Let me take a peer at you.'

Gawaine swivelled his eyes and found something looking at him. It had no ears, its lips were burned. A kind of sausage made its way from its forehead to where its nose had been. Looking further, he saw that it was mounted in a wheelchair, that its hands and feet were both burned as well.

'Oh,' it said dismissively, 'you've just been scorched.'

The burned man turned his wheelchair, as the girls finished their task and took away the pile of sodden gauze. He propelled himself with his burned hands over to the wall. A wooden chair stood there. He leaned forward and picked it up with his teeth, resting the legs on his wheelchair. He turned, and came back, slinging it alongside.

'Have a seat, old boy,' he said.

Gawaine climbed off the bed. He hurt almost all over, but with the torched man in the wheelchair watching him, he simply made himself smile.

'Gawaine de Clare,' he said, and held out his own burned hand. 'Though they call me Brolly. I keep jumping out of my Spit.'

'Bill Perkins,' said the wheelchair man. At the end of the ward stood a large barrel of beer. Not far away was a grand piano. Two men, with one pair of hands between them were thumping out a show tune.

'What is this place?'

'This is the Guinea Pig Club,' Perkins said proudly. 'I am the secretary.' He held up his hands gleefully. 'I can't write! Pete over there is the Treasurer.'

Gawaine looked to where a legless man was playing table tennis from his chair. Perkins watched him intently.

'He can't abscond with the funds?' said Gawaine. He thought that he was beginning to understand how this place worked.

'You'll do, laddie, you'll do,' Perkins said approvingly. 'Trot down to the barrel and get me a pint.'

'I think I'm going to like it here.'

'Wheels down, chaps,' said Perkins.

The old car came round the corner on two wheels, and Gawaine closed his eyes, partly for the sheer pleasure of doing so. He had eyelids. They lacked lashes, had previously been on the inside of his wrist and were too large, but it did not matter. They would shrink to size, and they went up and down at will. It was wonderful.

When he opened them, Perkins had pulled up with a screech outside the pub and the collection of men with Hurricane burns and an uneven number of hands, fingers and feet, with faces like patchwork quilts, were clambering out in a cacophony of rattling plaster casts, crutches, sticks and wheelchairs.

They piled into the pub.

'Just time for a couple, chaps,' said Perkins. 'I want to be in the theatre after lunch, the boss is putting Harry on the slab to do his hand and I want to watch. My turn next week.'

'I'll come too,' said Gawaine. He had got used to the fact that in Ward Three, the normal hospital regulations did not apply. If you wanted to get up in the night, you got up. If you wanted to have a drink, you helped yourself. If you wanted to see how the boss, McIndoe, was going to carve you, you put on a theatre gown and went in and watched him doing it to one of the others. A Hampden navigator with no fingers but two working thumbs cut out of his hands began playing darts with a Hurricane pilot who was blind, calling out directions. They both laughed uproariously.

Perkins took a small box from his pocket and opened it.

'Look at this, old man. The boss got them for me.'

He took a pair of remarkably lifelike ears out of the box and secured them over the puckered, scarred flesh where his own had been.

'Wax,' he said proudly. 'Until the boss can make me some proper ones.'

Gawaine sank the first quarter of his pint, and reached for his letters. The postman had arrived just as they were leaving.

'Oh, I say,' he said, pleased. 'My uncle's back.'

'He's been away?'

'Cook's tour, old boy. Calais, Stalag Luft something, Spain. He's a tank colonel.'

'We must drink to him,' Perkins said solemnly.

'We must, we must. Fred! Tee up two more of the same, my uncle's escaped from the Jerries.'

Gawaine peered at his mother's letter.

'He's going to Combined Ops, whatever that is. Good show.'

Perkins cleared his throat.

'I say, old man, there is a terrifically good-looking piece of knitting looking at us. Me, probably. I'm more handsome than you are. It's my new ears.'

Gawaine glanced up. His skin went ice cold, then hot, his heart began to pound. She was standing by the door.

She smiled, beamed at him, came forward, tripping over the carpet light as a feather. She put one slim and strong arm round his neck and kissed him. She tasted of strawberries.

'I say . . .' Perkins breathed in awe.

'Hallo, darling,' Molly said. She stood by him, took his hand in hers. 'It's taken me ages to find you.'

'But . . . what, how—'

'You stood me up, you rotter,' she said cheerfully. 'I turned up at the pub that Wednesday with my hair in a braid and you weren't there. I'll have that drink, now.'

'Fred!' he called hoarsely. 'G and T over here, please.'

Perkins goggled at him. 'Introduce me, old boy,' he urged.

'Molly, this is Bill Perkins. Don't have anything to do with him. He's a reprobate and can't even fly straight. Bill, this is my girlfriend, Molly Francis.'

'How do you do?' Perkins said, holding out his mutilated paw, and she shook it without a qualm.

'Very well, thank you.'

The light from the window became dim. They looked up to see a very large policeman standing there.

'There is a car parked outside causing an obstruction to the traffic,' he announced pompously.

'Mine, officer,' said Perkins.

'Why have you left your car outside, sir?'

Perkins removed his ears and stuck them to his forehead. He peered at himself in the mirror before turning back to the policeman, standing imperturbably waiting.

'Well, the bally car doesn't drink.' He hobbled to the door to move it, and Gawaine was left alone with her.

'How long can you stay?' he said. It was vitally important, every second with her was important.

'Oh, quite a while,' she said, smiling. 'I've transferred here. I'm on Ward Three.'

'Oh . . .' he said, and choked. Tears spilled up over his new eyelids, ran down over his patched face.

'Oh,' he said. 'Everything's all right now.'

53

The Master of Disaster

Plymouth, August 1942

'Oh, it's you, Freddie,' said the man with vice-admiral's rings on his sleeve. He was sitting at a table with Perceval de Clare. Through the immense window of his office the crowded port was clearly visible, packed with vessels of war.

'Hallo, Lord Louis. Perceval. What are you doing here?'

'Playing my part in the war, Freddie,' Perceval said, sounding pleased. 'I'm bringing Lord Louis up to date with the forthcoming Beveridge Plan.'

'All that New Jerusalem stuff? Pie in the sky. Don't you think we'd better win the war first?'

'We *are* winning the war,' Mountbatten asserted forcefully. 'Percy's right, we have to win the peace too. The people are going to win freedom from want, freedom from the giant evils of the past.' He picked up a printed sheaf of paper. 'It's all in here.'

'New Britain!' Perceval cried. 'Freedom of Want, of Disease, of Ignorance, of Squalor and Idleness.'

'Well I'll drink to that. But I'll believe it when I see it.'

'It's here, Freddie!' Louis Mountbatten said cheerfully. 'Don't be so hidebound. There'll be a new socialist order in Britain after the war, believe me. A new world.'

'I didn't know you were a socialist.'

'Oh, my wife Edwina's opened my eyes to a lot of things. I'm for the new order, all right.'

'I thought your wife was frightfully rich,' Freddie said drily.

'It doesn't mean she can't hold progressive views,' he expostulated.

'Insulates her from the pain of it all, what?' Freddie said genially. 'Well, if you've finished, Perceval, I'm supposed to be seeing Lord Louis about eliminating the giant evil of Nazism.'

'Oh, yes. Are you Brigadier Reynold's replacement?' Mountbatten enquired.

'That's it. Slipped off a Churchill tank and broke his leg, so you've got me.'

'I'll keep you up to date, Dickie,' said Perceval, leaving.

'Please do,' Mountbatten said sincerely.

'Back to the war,' said Freddie.

'Oh, yes. In fact, talking of the war, have you heard about this marvellous film Noël's made about me? I've been helping him, of course. He plays *me*. On the *Kelly*. When we were sunk and dive-bombed. *In Which We Serve*.' Mountbatten paused, savouring the title. '*In Which We Serve*. It's terribly good, you'll love it. I've already seen it a few times. You mustn't miss it when it comes out.'

'I won't. I believe I'm to be an observer.'

'Eh? Are you going to review it?'

'No. There's some operation you're planning. I'm to observe for the Tank Corps, see how the tanks get on.'

'Oh, yes.' Mountbatten lowered his voice, became serious.

'Operation "Jubilee",' he said quietly. 'We're going to smash the Germans in Dieppe.'

He made a fist, punched the air savagely.

'Bam. We're going to crash through them at dawn from the sea. An amphibious assault from two hundred and fifty craft. Five thousand soldiers, an entire division with tank and artillery support, smashing straight through the town. You'll witness a feat of arms the like of which you'll never have seen before. That's what we've been planning and preparing for here at Combined Ops. The latest in modern warfare.'

'It sounds impressive.'

'It is. It's the curtain-raiser for the invasion, you know.'

He tapped his brand new golden rings, and grinned boyishly.

'I'm allowed to wear a lieutenant-general's uniform and an air marshal's as well!' he crowed happily. 'I've been to the tailor's for them. The word is that the American general marshall is to be supreme commander and I'll be his chief of staff.'

'Wonderful,' Freddie said politely.

'Monty will be frightfully miffed.'

'What's the opposition?'

'Well, Monty, of course.'

'No, in Dieppe. The Germans.'

'Oh, we've got them fooled. Maury's run a first class intelligence operation – he's my head of intelligence – and the place is only garrisoned by a pretty battered battalion of infantry from the Russian front. Our boys are crack Canadians and they'll go through them like a knife through butter.'

He chuckled charmingly.

'Our only problem will be stopping them from driving on Paris! We've practised it until we could run it on Broadway, let me tell you.'

He looked musingly out of the window at the immense array of warships in the harbour.

'You know, with all the experience I've amassed here, I wouldn't be surprised if they make *me* supreme commander,' he said thoughtfully. 'Anyway, listen up, Freddie. Don't go too far. We're on our way soon. Can't tell you just when, all hush-hush, you know. Just don't stray too far away!'

'I won't. This should be something.'

'It will, dear chap. Look, I'll try to get hold of a copy of the *Kelly* film for you. You'll love it. I'm thinking of showing it to the troops here, before they go, put them in the right spirit.'

'Freddie!'

A black Rover that was moving off pulled up; somebody wound down a window, called to him. It was George. He grinned, went over to him.

'Good Lord, are all the de Clares here today? I've just seen Perceval giving Mountbatten a lot of bull about the glorious new order we shall all enjoy after the war's won. I personally think we'll all be too exhausted to do anything except order another round.'

George glanced alertly at him.

'You've been seeing Mountbatten? I've been giving a report to his intelligence chief, if you can call him that.'

'What do you mean?'

'Hop in. I'll buy you a drink.'

Freddie got in and they went away through the streets of the port.

'There's a decent pub down on the coast. Mountbatten's head of intelligence is a failed Cuban racing-driver-cum-playboy called Maury. One of his cronies.'

George turned onto the esplanade, headed out of the town.

'Mountbatten doesn't employ professionals,' he said savagely. 'He prefers his "Dickie Birds". They all tell him how wonderful he is. What are you doing here, Freddie?'

'I'm to be an observer. For an operation he's mounting,' Freddie said carefully.

'"Jubilee",' George said instantly. 'That half-baked idea to invade Dieppe.'

'Yes,' Freddie said, puzzled. 'I'm on stand-by for it.'

'Balls,' George said contemptuously. He turned into the forecourt of a pleasant hotel on the sea front. '"Jubilee" has been cancelled. Monty saw the fuck-up Mountbatten made of the rehearsals – absolutely everything that could go wrong *did* go wrong – and he's put a stop to it.'

'I don't think so,' Freddie said with a frown. 'Dickie told me it was ready to go ahead.'

'Sit over here, I'll get a couple of pints.'

He emerged from the hotel a minute later and joined Freddie at a white-painted metal table looking out to sea. White roses were climbing up the walls, and pink hydrangeas foamed about them.

'No, take it from me, it's off,' George continued. 'The planning's a joke and if you ask me there's serious opposition there. Casa Maury thinks there's a worn-out battalion in Dieppe. I don't. Maury trusts his French agents. I don't.'

'What do you mean?'

'This crap about the brave French resisting the Germans is fine for the BBC propaganda,' George said savagely, 'but crap is all it is. The bastards are collaborating to a man over there. I wouldn't trust any of them to tell me the time, let alone the truth. Dial in planning by Dickie Mountbatten and you've got the makings of a real mess.'

'He talks a good war. That pansy Coward is making a film about him.'

'God!' George cried. 'What a country ... only here could an incompetent like him get two ships sunk and be turned into a hero! You know what his comrades in the Navy call him? "The Master of Disaster"! The one thing Dickie's really good at – apart from promoting his own career – is killing people. The only problem is they're always on our side.'

'So how is he in charge?' Freddie asked, puzzled.

'As far as I can see, people promote him to get him out of their particular hair. This process has gone on so long that instead of doing what he is fit for, which is sending Aldiss signals with a lamp, he is running a truly enormous show like Combined Ops. I only hope they will promote him to some stratospheric post where he has no real command of anything before he manages to do some genuine harm.'

'I'm glad it's off, then. I'll hang about until the end of the week and claim business back at Aldershot. I'm going to young Gawaine's wedding then anyway. You be there?'

'If I can. Nice girl?'

'Lovely. Molly, her name is. The right sort, too. He's a lucky chap.'

'How's his face?'

'Patched up.'

'Still in the Raff?'

'Going to fly for SOE. Dropping agents, Vi told me.'

'Waste of bloody time,' George said viciously. 'Let the bloody French rot.'

Out on the sea a big boxy landing craft was going by, its powerful engines pushing it through the water at speed. They could see the American sailors of the crew, all in white, with their upturned caps, the stars and stripes flying from the short mast.

'God, it makes me sick to see them here, polluting our water,' George commented. Freddie frowned.

'At least they're here,' he said. 'We're winning the war, with their help. They're not bad chaps, the ones I've met.'

'I hate the lot of them, their filthy ways, their stinking culture.'

'You hate a lot of things, old man,' Freddie observed quietly.

'Yes, well, we're fighting a war,' George snarled, turning on him. 'A bit of hate comes in useful.'

'You started hating things a long time before the war,' he said.

George drained his mug. 'Life . . . oh, never mind. I'll give you a lift back. Come on.'

They got back into the Rover, drove along the sea front.

'I told you I saw Perceval. Filling Dickie up with his socialist guff, he was.'

'Can't have been difficult. He gets a diet of it from his wife.'

'So he said. What's she like?'

'She's a useless cow,' George said frankly. 'Rich beyond avarice, spent the last twenty years screwing as many chaps and girls as she could. Now she's thrown herself into progressive politics, good works and campaigning against the system that's made her rich. Hard to know in which guise she's more repellent. She and Dickie are made for each other, really. Here. This do you?'

'Fine. Thanks for the beer. See you at the wedding.'

'Brigadier de Clare!' a voice called. Freddie turned at the dockside. The destroyer he was about to board hummed with life. Out in the harbour the night was filled with whistles and clankings, with the sounds of command coming over loudhailers, the squeal of steam-powered derricks, all the noise of vessels preparing for sail.

'Yes?'

A messenger came hurrying down the quay.

'Important call for you, sir. You can take it down here.'

Freddie followed him down, was shown into a room with a green telephone. He picked it up.

'Brigadier de Clare here.'

'Freddie, it's George. Does your telephone have a scrambler button?'

'Yes.'

'Press it. Done? All right. Is it true, is "Jubilee" on?'

'Yes.'

'Jesus Christ. It's not even authorised. Look, the bloody Germans will know you're coming. You're going to sail smack into the middle of one of their convoys. I know. I can read . . . signals. I've been on to Mountbatten's HQ, but they aren't listening to me.'

'I don't see what I can do about it.'

'Dear God, man, just don't go! Stay on the bloody dock side.'

'I don't think I can do that, old man. Not on, really, is it? But thank you for telling me.'

Freddie put the telephone down, and went back out into the dark. Landing craft banged against their attack transports, chain cable rattled up through hawsepipes, warship bugles sounded. Out on the water, the first craft were beginning to move out to sea.

Freddie could smell burning. It came from a nearby destroyer that had been damaged in the firefight. They had run into the German convoy exactly on schedule. The sea was glossy with starlight, over at its far rim the coming dawn brushed it with the palest grey. The armada of over two hundred and fifty ships hung poised to attack. He could hear the young Canadians clinking as they climbed into their assault boats, heavy-laden with their weapons and ammunition.

Almost as one, the great wave of landing craft surged forward, and the air was filled with the roar of their engines. As they made their run into the silent, dark port their phosphorescent wake stood out behind like shining diamonds laid on blackest velvet.

Bells rang inside the destroyer, and it moved forward. The dawn was coming quickly. Freddie could see the narrow shingle beach of the town and its esplanade hiding behind its high sea wall, the brooding buildings of the sea front.

'For God's sake!' he suddenly cried out loud. 'Is there no bombardment? Where is the barrage?'

The assault craft swept in towards the shore. The leading vessels grounded on the shingle, the ramps went down. The soldiers pushed forward and the entire sea front erupted with fire, with machine-guns, with rifles and grenade launchers, with mortars and anti-tank guns pouring in shell over open sights. On the ramps of the landing craft the young men danced briefly, bloodily like puppets as the bullets and shrapnel tore them apart. They fell into heaps. The survivors had to crawl over the piles to reach the beach, where they were massacred in their own turn.

The big LSTs grounded, and the Churchill tanks ground down the ramps under the fearsome fire. One or two made their way towards the esplanade, others lay helpless, their tracks grinding futilely in the shingle. One after the other, they exploded in shards of flying armour, and began to burn.

Overhead, the sky was suddenly filled with the roar of aero-engines, the scream of the dive-bombers. The sea erupted into seething foam, the sky was striped with tracer and shell, acrid black smoke drifted through the air. On the flat water ships were exploding, burning and drifting without command. The beach was edged with brown and red where the young men in their battle dress lay dead and dying.

'It was a bad show,' said Mountbatten, in his vice-admiral's uniform. He shook his head regretfully, pursed his lips in censure. 'A bad show indeed. General Roberts was hardly the commanding officer I had been led to believe.'

Freddie suddenly felt a savage flame of anger ignite inside him, sitting among the staff as they reviewed the raid.

'I don't quite follow you,' he said, standing up. '*You* were in command.'

'I provided General Roberts with all the facilities at my disposal,' Mountbatten said smoothly. 'But of course, on the day, the force commander takes responsibility. He insisted on making a frontal assault.' He shook his head again. 'Very bad. And the Canadian troops were hardly of the highest quality, although he insisted upon using them.'

'I assume General Roberts was following the plan drawn up by your staff,' Freddie said. He had remained standing. He was very angry indeed. 'His troops were an élite force. They were massacred before they could even get out of the assault craft.'

'Freddie, Freddie,' Mountbatten said gently. 'I understand how upset you are. You were there, you witnessed it all. Such a combination of bad luck . . .'

'They knew you were coming, you incompetent bastard!'

Mountbatten looked left and right at his beautifully turned-out staff officers, seated each side of him, raised his eyebrows.

'I do hope you're not blaming *me*,' he said.

'There was no bombardment. There was no heavy bombing. Jesus Christ, man, the last time we let troops walk into sustained enemy fire like that, unsupported by anything, was the first day on the Somme. I know, I was there.'

'My dear chap! If you have criticisms of the ground and air forces please address them to the generals and the air marshals. I'm just a sailor who tried to help them with their plans.'

'They gave you a general's uniform, and an air marshal's one too,' Freddie said quietly. 'The boys who are dead and maimed today trusted you knew what you were doing.'

He pushed past the staff officers, went to the door.

'Poor chap,' Mountbatten murmured behind him. 'Taken prisoner, you know. Affected his mind.'

Freddie turned.

'The only one insane here is you,' he said levelly. 'Insane with ambition. You murdered those boys yesterday as sure as if you shot them yourself.'

'We have learned invaluable lessons. Lives, in the long term, will have been saved. When this little bit of bother is over people will see that I was right all along. Now, gentlemen, shall we get to work? We have already identified some of the causes of the failure on the ground. General Roberts and his men obviously take principal responsibility. Monty cannot be absolved, he attended the principal planning meetings. Bad luck, of course, attended the convoy, running into the Germans. MI6 must take its share of responsibility for misinforming us of the troop levels in Dieppe itself . . .'

Freddie went out and into the street. He stood breathing in the fresh air, until the sweat on him cooled and dried. He walked away, leaving the port behind him.

54

Personal Recommendation

London, April 1944

The King stood looking out of the window. His view of the skyline had been altered by a German bomber the night before and he watched, in the uniform of an admiral of the fleet, as people scurried over the ruins of a mansion block, cutting and extracting its wood, carrying it off for fuel. Godfrey came across the vast room, still chill from the freezing winter, and paused respectfully on a worn runner carpet, the gift of a Rajah to Queen Victoria. Geometric Asian pattern, changed course under his feet. King George looked round.

'Ah,' he said. 'De Clare. Th-there you are.'

'You asked to see me, sir,' Godfrey said smoothly, his hands clasped behind his back.

'I did. Yes.' The King picked up a half-drunk glass of whisky. 'Want a Scotch?' he asked. 'They s-send it down for us from Balmoral, you know. Help yourself.'

Godfrey glanced around. They were entirely alone in the giant room, filled with its ancient artefacts of empire. There were no servants at all – the door had been quietly closed behind him, leaving him secluded with the King. His interest quickened, he helped himself to whisky, and topped it up with soda from a glass siphon. They sat together on an enormous sofa stuffed with horse hair. The King took a quick pull at his glass.

'Got a special request to make of you,' he said. 'Damned useful, having you here in the Palace. R-resident art surveyor and MI5 man. Couldn't be better.'

'MI6 now, sir. I transferred. How can I help, sir?' Godfrey asked quietly.

'MI6, yes. That's it, see? You're in intelligence. And you're an art historian. Well known. Could be good c-cover, eh?'

'I'm sure it could sir,' Godfrey said patiently. 'What did you have in mind?'

'Invasion's coming. Oh yes it is. I know. See Ch-Churchill, y'see. Yes, invasion's on its way. Wouldn't be surprised if you aren't involved somewhere.'

'I have . . . certain duties,' Godfrey said cautiously.

'Good man. Don't want to know what they are. Must keep security.'

'Oh, yes.'

'It's afterwards. Once the great armies are advancing into G-Germany.'

'Yes, sir?'

King George cleared his throat. He succeeded in looking tremendously embarrassed and worried at the same time. Making a great effort, he began to speak.

'My b-brother David. Who was king.'

'King Edward,' Godfrey murmured.

'King Edward, yes. God knows, de Clare, I didn't ask to have this job, but I have d-done it to the best of my ability.'

'You are a great monarch, sir.'

'No, no. I'm not really. No good at speaking to people. But with the Queen's help . . . anyhow, that's by the by. I am k-king, and I do my best.'

The King got up, and kicked both feet hard a few times against the monolithic construction of the sofa.

'Damned cold gets in your b-bones, don't you find? Can't f-feel my feet sometimes.' He sat back down. 'Yes. David. King Edward that w-was. He . . . wasn't always sensible. Let that damned woman lead him on, I'll be b-bound.'

The King appeared to come to a halt. He snuffled up some whisky.

'In what way was he not sensible, sir?' Godfrey asked helpfully. The King turned to look at Godfrey and suddenly a hunted expression filled his face.

'The Nazis, man!' he said desperately. 'My brother collaborated with them, he was working for the overthrow of this country. He betrayed military secrets to them, he connived at our defeat . . .'

'I know,' Godfrey said quietly, firmly. 'I do know, sir.'

'Yes, I kn-know you do . . . you were involved in finding out.'

The King took a grip on his tumbler with both hands.

'What I most fear, de Clare, is that the German r-records of all this – and they do exist, believe me, they exist – will come to light. They will be uncovered by those who follow the advancing Allied armies. The whole terrible business will be exposed to public view. What my brother did was treat with the king's enemy in the hour of our most m-mortal peril, and th-that is High Treason. The penalty is death. In this hideous . . . in this nefarious affair he was aided and abetted by my other brother, Prince George. He is dead now, of course, killed in the aeroplane. But David is not. Even while shut up as g-governor in the Bahamas he c-continued his plotting with the N-Nazis. I f-fear for the very existence of the House of Windsor should such secrets ever become public knowledge.'

'Yes,' Godfrey agreed thoughtfully.

'I want you to find them, de Clare. All the relevant documents. Bring them to me here, they shall be shut up with the Royal Archives in Windsor. I h-have a cover for you. Yes. You shall be my personal emissary to recover the great correspondence conducted by my illustrious ancestor, Queen Victoria, with her many German relations, to bring them back to this country for safe-keeping. You shall be armed with whatever warrants you require, that will enable you to go anywhere, see whatever you wish. I shall see to it.'

'You will supply me with your own personal letter, as the King, describing me as your trusted emissary, acting upon your own orders?'

'I will.'

'Then I shall do as you ask, sir,' said Godfrey solemnly. 'Your secrets will be safe in my hands.'

'That's good!' the King cried in enormous relief. He went to the salver and splashed whisky vigorously into his glass.

'Another?'

'No, thank you, sir. I have to go to a meeting.'

'MI5, eh?'

'Yes, sir.'

'The invasion, I'll be b-bound. Well, I mustn't keep you. I'll get those letters to you.'

Godfrey bowed as he took his leave.

'Thank you, sir,' he said, in deep sincerity. 'You don't know how much it means to me to have earned your trust.'

'Well, well,' Godfrey said cheerfully. 'This is a family gathering, isn't it? Good morning Violet, Felicity.'

'You're late,' George grunted sourly.

'Taking whisky with the King.' Godfrey said airily. '*Droit du roi*, that kind of thing.'

'Well, let's get on with it. D-day itself. Finally, the invasion of Europe.'

It appeared that Violet and Felicity had only just arrived as well. Violet produced a solid gold cigarette case and offered them round.

'God but it's good to have real tobacco again,' she said. 'The poor French are smoking hay.'

'I like your fag case,' said Godfrey.

'We get given them. Solid gold, in case you need funds in a hurry.'

'Can we get down to business?' George asked testily. 'The Diamond Network.'

'Is ready and waiting,' Felicity said calmly. 'Violet and I have been in France for the past seven months seeing to just that. We were picked up last night from a field outside Caen. We are in place, we await instruction.'

'Good. Good. Now you must listen to me closely, just as the agents of the network must listen to you. There must be no, repeat no acts of aggression against the Germans before the word comes. The word is in fact a message, a line of poetry. You'll hear it on the radio. You know when. It will say: The chestnut casts his flambeaux.'

'Housman,' said Felicity.

'Yes. It's easy to remember. This is your signal to begin Plan "Violet" – not actually named after you, Vi, so don't look smug – which will disrupt German telecommunications.'

'We have the trunk cables, overhead wires, repeater stations all marked,' said Violet.

'Good. After that you move on to Plan "Vert", sabotage of rail communications, and "Tortue", the disruption of German road travel. I can't tell you how much it all matters. The Allied armies will have a tough job getting ashore from the beaches, the more we can slow up the arrival of the Germans the more help we'll be giving the troops to get established on French soil. There is something I want to say. Although your *resistants* have been armed by us with good quantities of Sten guns, grenades and so forth, you are to avoid actual fighting as much as possible. Your task is sabotage and disruption.'

He cleared his throat.

'There is, however, a possibility you may have to fight. If things get hard for the troops we may have to throw everything in to slow the advance of the German troops. If you hear the second line of the poem transmitted at your listening hour by the BBC, it is the signal for insurrection.'

'Our *resistants* aren't trained soldiers,' Felicity commented.

'I know. As I say, it will be in part a measure of last resort to help the invasion force. An effective one, if costly. Let's hope it doesn't have to happen. All right. I just wanted a quick briefing once you got back. Let's meet for a full session before you return to France. How long have you got off?'

'Two weeks leave,' said Violet. 'We're going down to the castle.'

'I'm going to go fishing,' said Felicity. 'Apparently the Water's seething.'

'Lovely. All right, Thursday fortnight then? Same time?'

The two women went out.

'When's Garotte due?' said Godfrey.

George glanced at his watch. 'Half an hour.' He glanced out of the window at the river, watched a procession of huge black barges being towed by. 'I had lunch with one of the Americans. OSS chap, seconded to Six. Name of Angleton.'

'I know him.'

'Hmm. Clever fellow, I have to admit. Seems to think that counter-intelligence can be turned into a science. Looking into the future, he sees the next contest as being against the Soviet Union.'

'Oh?'

'Yes. If I understood him correctly, which I think I did, even through a glass of the most hideous Algerian wine which was all the club could offer, the central axiom of his theory is that you must penetrate the enemy's counter-intelligence service. This is essential. You are then able to manipulate him into an unreal world where he in effect does as you wish.'

'Rather as we are doing to the Abwehr at the moment.'

'Quite. Garotte, for example. They believe her to be theirs, whereas she is ours, and tells them what we wish them to know. Looking into the future, Angleton proposes a similar penetration of the Soviet NKVD.'

'Well, well. We shall have to keep in touch with Mr Angleton, won't we?'

'I thought you would want to know. Being an astute man, he also raised the possibility of us being penetrated by them.'

'The Soviets,' Godfrey said, without expression.

'Yes.'

'What did you say?'

'I told him that it was quite impossible for the British secret services to be penetrated by a foreign power. I pointed out that the wrong sort of fellow would never be allowed in the door. That we only recruited from people with the right background. Chaps we knew personally.

Had been to school and university with. Knew socially. Met at the club. That we relied on personal recommendation from people of sound judgement, who had close acquaintance with the candidate.'

Godfrey looked blandly out of the window.

'Chaps like us, in fact,' he said.

'Isn't is grand to be back?' said Violet. 'What do you say we treat ourselves to lunch at the Connaught and then on down to the castle? We'll be in time for an hour's fishing before dusk.'

'Why not? Why don't we cut up through the park? I've missed seeing the English blossom so much.'

They paused at the side of the road to let an old red double-decker bus pass. It went by in an acrid cloud of smoke, filled with passengers. As they crossed Felicity suddenly grabbed at Violet's elbow.

'Vi. Look. Isn't that Carlotta?'

On the other side of the street a woman in a smart grey suit was walking, moving quickly, going the way they had come.

'Lord, so it is.'

'Should we say hallo, do you think?'

'Not personally,' Violet saud drily. 'Carlotta is nothing but very bad news.'

'Where is she going, in such a hurry?' Felicity asked, watching her. 'Let's follow and see.'

'Honestly, Flick! Spying's got into your blood.'

'Come on. Look, she's going down to the river.'

At a distance, they followed her. Suddenly, with the Thames in sight, she turned into a tall, drab, red-brick office building.

'Vi,' Felicity said quietly, 'we just left there. That's where George is. MI5.'

55

We'll Go Home Now

France, June 1944

The air rushed cold through the yard-wide hole cut in the bottom of the Halifax bomber's fuselage. Through it, looking down through the black night, they saw a steady flashing from the ground, long and short, Morse code.

'That's it,' the dispatcher shouted above the racket of the four engines and the roaring gale. He began to flash back the reply letter as the pilot wheeled gently round in the sky. Violet and Felicity pushed themselves up from the hard bench where they had been waiting, their parachutes, Sten guns and grenades weighing them down.

Violet sat down, made the awkward sideways shuffle, swivelled at the edge of the hole, dangled her feet out as she had been trained. Through the hole she could see the L-shape of bicycle lamps below, indicating the drop zone and the prevailing breeze. The pilot was bringing them back on to the field. They would drop in quick succession, the bomber would fly on to Caen a few kilometres further on, where the dispatcher would fling out a load of propaganda leaflets from the Political Warfare Executive, thus explaining the mission of the low-flying bomber. By then, Violet and Felicity, F-Section's two agents would be back in the heart of the Diamond Network.

'Coming up,' the dispatcher yelled.

The red light turned to green, the dispatcher's arm swept down.

'*Go!*' he cried, and she pushed gently forward, springing to attention as she did so. Like a guardsman, she fell straight down through the hole. The air whipped at her, the great bomber's dark belly rushed above her. With a snap and a jerk, her parachute opened and she floated down in the cool night air. She could see the lights of the drop zone, she steered towards them. The pilot had dropped her in the perfect place; the light breeze was blowing her directly at the field. Glancing back and up, she saw something dark drifting against the moonlit sky, and knew that Felicity had dropped successfully as well. The night was quiet, with just the grumble of the departing Halifax fading in the distance. Down near the lights she saw figures moving, it would be the reception committee, Gaspard, Arnaud and the others.

As she came down the breeze died, close to the ground. She was dropping short. The river ran between the fields there, with trees that poked their roots into the water. She did not dare risk getting caught up in their branches, accepted the logic of the wind and settled for landing on the other side of the river, and getting her feet wet when she waded across.

She landed with a thump in the long grass of the meadow, got to her feet to collapse the canopy, drew it in. Against the sky she saw Felicity landing by the lights, heard the soft exclamations in French.

She unbuckled her harness in the darkness. Suddenly, the night was filled with the clamour of automatic weapons. The hedgerow beyond lit up with the muzzle flashes of Schmeisser machine-guns, yellow and orange.

The burst of fire lasted but a few seconds. Then she heard harsh, shouted commands in German, the sound of somebody in the field beyond screaming hideously.

She saw the troops, dark figures pushing through the hedge, further commands, knew that they were coming for her. Desperately, she shrugged off the harness, dumped her sack of grenades. The water gurgled dark and swift by her side. She crawled frantically through the long grass, rolled into its current, and the river tumbled her away.

In the small attic room, Carlotta put her attaché case down on the table, set herself on a chair in front of it and opened it. Through the window she could see the sprawl of Victoria, going down to the river. Buses and military lorries were crossing Vauxhall Bridge, dirty smoke was drifting from the old factories south of the bridge. She reached out and tugged the curtains shut – you didn't need any nosy parkers peering across at her from some other garret.

Quietly and efficiently, she brought out her Morse key and plugged the radio set inside the attaché case into the mains with its round-pronged Bakelite plug. She switched on, and the little dial jumped to life. She took out a sheet of typed notepaper, and began to transmit.

'Have just returned from ports of east coast and south-eastern England,' she tapped. 'Saw with my own eyes the Army Group Patton preparing to embark. Came close to General Patton himself, heard him remark that now the diversion in Normandy was going so well, the time had come to commence operations around Calais. The King, Churchill, Eisenhower and Field-Marshal Brooke have all visited First US Army Group command post at Dover Castle. General Marshall of the American Army arrives here from Washington on the 9th or 10th of June to see Patton and the troops off. These assault troops comprise at least five airborne divisions, a sea force of ten divisions, and FUSAG itself will have over fifty divisions, most of which are here already.

'In the light of this must warn that Normandy invasion currently under way, known as D-day is a feint. The real invasion will take place on the Pas de Calais in a few days time. I transmit this in the conviction that the D-day assault is a trap set with the purpose of making us move all our reserves in a rushed strategic redisposition that will lead to our defeat when Patton and FUSAG invade unopposed at the Pas de Calais. Ends.'

She lifted her hand from the transmitter key, and flexed her stiff fingers. Silently, she switched off.

Godfrey got up from the chair where he had been listening and watching, and took the typed sheet of paper.

'Well done, Garotte,' he said. 'We'll send them more of the same tomorrow. Patton will have had a hold-up. The invasion will be delayed another day. They'll sit waiting there in front of empty beaches, waiting for a force that never comes.'

The message was coming through: F-Section had put in a new wireless operator to replace Felicity – Tony, who had worked in Vichy France in '43. Violet waited in the little farmhouse, while he wrote down the groups that came through from London, and watched out of the window. Somebody was coming up the dusty red lane through the vines. She sighted on him with the sniper rifle that had arrived in the big C-type canisters, packed in with Sten guns, cyclonite landmines that looked like cow droppings, soup plates, tobacco and chocolate. It was Gilbert, her *maquisard*. She put down the long rifle with its big telescope, and Tony came in, handed her a sheet of pencilled letter groups. She sat down, began to decode them.

She heard voices. Gilbert came in in his collarless blue shirt, baggy chambray trousers and beret. Tony poured *rosé* wine, sharp and acid, into chipped glass tumblers as Violet finished writing out the translation of the message. She looked up.

'I have some news,' said Gilbert.

'So do I,' she said. 'But tell me yours first.'

'Felicity is alive,' he said.

Sudden hope burst inside her, she bit on a knuckle to control the emotion.

'Injured,' he said.

'Of course. She was gunned down. Quickly, where is she?'

'The Gestapo have her,' he said grimly. 'She is in the prison in Caen. Tell me now, does she have knowledge of this place?'

'No. Nor did I. When we were ambushed I then assumed that all previous plans were unsound.'

'Good. Good.'

'We shall have to break into the prison and release her.'

'How?'

'We have a force of thirty *maquisards* under arms. We are well supplied with weaponry, with explosives. We *must* get her out.'

His mouth tightened, he stayed silent for a few moments.

'Do you know how we were betrayed?' she asked. He shrugged, his mind still on the fearsome prospect of having to attack a heavily defended German building.

'There are traitors,' he said. 'We shall find the one, and then – *zut.*' He ran a finger across his stubbly throat. 'But you have news,' he reminded her.

'Yes . . . yes. Our forces are still held up in the *bocage* country. They have yet to take Caen. The Germans are moving units towards them. One is the 2nd SS Panzer Division, *Das Reich*. It has had to come from Montauban. *Das Reich* is considered of the most formidable fighting units anywhere. Twenty thousand SS troops, seventy-five self-propelled assault guns, sixty medium tanks, one hundred heavy tanks, including Tigers.'

'General Montgomery will not welcome the arrival of this force on his battlefield,' Gilbert observed. 'Why is London sending us messages about it?'

'The division has been harassed by *maquisards,* Jeds and F-Section all its way. The railways have been made useless, it is travelling under its own power by road.'

'*Oui?*'

'It's coming through here,' she said quietly. 'They have asked us to assist.'

Gilbert smiled mirthlessly.

'Truly a tale to tell our grandchildren, should we have them. But I regret, there you have your answer. We cannot attempt to free Felicity.'

'No,' she whispered.

'*Violet,*' he said urgently, pronouncing it in the French way. 'Violet, the only news I have is that she was alive when taken into the prison. The Gestapo . . . and on a wounded woman . . .'

'They will have tortured her.'

'For sure. That is what these swine do.'

'Yes,' she said grimly. 'Then we must see what we can do to these other swine, the men of *Das Reich*.'

She hesitated.

'There is something I did not tell you. In revenge for the atacks made on them on their journey they have murdered six hundred people in a village they passed through. Oradour-sur-Glane. They are all dead.'

'Then why do we wait?' he asked. 'Let us kill some of them.'

Noises came through the dark. The moon had sunk, a white sickle, towards the far horizon, the sun had not yet painted the west. The hoarse grinding of huge diesel engines, the squeaking of tracks, the steady tramp of boots, the clink of equipment, it formed a whole, the sound of men and tanks on the march; it filtered out through the trees and over the hedges, it reached Violet on the steep hillside. The narrow, winding road below began to be lit by hooded yellow lamps, moving towards them.

'Now,' she said, and Tony spoke into his radio set.

'*Maintenant. Le feu.*'

There was a pause, then a short bang in the night, and flickering yellow flames that grew, until a blaze lit up the area below. A lorry, wedged across the road, was burning furiously. In its light a column of SP guns, tanks and infantry stood, the men deploying off the narrow, walled road. The shouting of orders was drowned by the rising bellow of the lead tank's engine. It pushed forward, black in the yellow light, ready to ram the truck from its way.

There was a second explosion, a burst of light under its tracks, it slewed sideways, slammed into the wall. On the road, in the flames, they could see a double line of circular objects.

Tanks were beginning to force their way off the road, but it was narrow, bounded by walls and ancient, deep ditches covered with primeval trees, bound together, hundreds of years old.

'Open fire,' said Violet, and the hillside erupted with guns.

Dawn sunlight coloured the stinking smoke that drifted through the valley. Violet could taste it as she lay in the bracken, high up on the steep hillside. A tank was burning, part of the scrub and trees on the far side was on fire. The rocks echoed to the sounds of machine-guns and grenades. She could see dim figures trying to push up the scree. The ambush had been well sited. The column was still out in the open, and not safe in laager.

She had the radio with her. Tony was dead. Blood ran down into her eye from her forehead, sliced open by flying shards of rock. Hidden in the bracken she switched it on, tuned to the frequency she had been given.

'Yellow leader, this is Team Oliver,' she said clearly. 'Team Oliver calling Yellow leader.'

'Yellow leader here, Team Oliver,' a voice replied immediately. 'Yellow section airborne, awaiting instructions.'

She spread out her map in front of her, and carefully read out the map reference.

'Leading elements of the *Das Reich* division are on the valley floor,' she said. 'Team Oliver holds the high ground.'

'Stand by,' the unseen voice said unemotionally.

She rolled on her back, peering through the drifting smoke at the polished sky above the valley. A few seconds later something flashed over the ridge, a fighter, a fighter-bomber. Its wings erupted in flame, rockets streaked through the air, screeching, ejecting fire, exploding with short vicious crumps. Through the stems she saw the turret of a Mk IV tank rip off, turning over and over, lazily, to crash into the hedgerow. The huge-nosed Typhoon leaped back out of the dim valley light into the dawn sunshine, climbing almost vertically, its huge engine howling, rays of sun glinting from the pilot's clear canopy, its black and white invasion stripes glowing.

'Thank you, Yellow leader,' she said.

They came through one after the other, a whole section, and the valley floor boiled with filthy, belching black smoke, lit from within by flickering yellow flames. The Typhoons cannonaded the survivors. Violet saw the troops running, falling. She crawled up through the bracken, and over the ridge, slipping away through the pine trees on the other side.

Caen

She had seen the great air fleet fly over from the fields outside, had heard the roar of an earthquake as the bombs fell, had seen the immense column of dust and smoke blackening the sky, rising up to the very clouds above.

Now she picked her way through the ruins, just one more refugee woman with a filthy, bloodied bandage about her head. The German troops pushing through the rubble towards the front line they had fortified from the wreckage paid her no attention. The roads were choked with rubble, pocked by great craters from the bombs the Lancasters and Halifaxes had carried. Great cubes of rock like enormous stone sugar lumps lay scattered everywhere, and all was covered in dust.

Here. It was here. The wreckage of the prison. It had taken a direct hit, maybe more than one. The upper storeys were entirely gone, ragged walls and empty window-frames stood up like stone hedges. She went into the ruins, calling.

'Flick! Flick!'

Something moved in the mess of wood and iron and stone. A dog, foraging for dead meat.

'Flick! Flick!'

Parts were entirely destroyed. A great crater marked where the bomb had struck, she could see the bare earth beneath the ruins.

'Flick, *cherie*! *C'est Violet*!'

What was that? A small, weak cry. It came again. She heaved at a wooden beam, moved it. Stone rubble slid down the man-made scree. There was a hole in there.

'Flick?' she called softly.

In the darkness, something whimpered. Very carefully, she climbed down. A stone wall, a bundle of rags in the corner.

'Flick, darling, it's me.'

She held her, she was hot with fever, her eyes were glassy and bright. She was huddled up, clutching herself. Through the torn prison uniform Violet saw hideous wounds. Burns, livid cigarette burns marking the white skin. No fingernails. Purple, bloody, pulped toes. Old injuries.

For a second, she seemed to know Violet.

'I didn't tell them!' she cried out, and her voice broke. Violet held her tight in the wreckage, and in the street, a column of troops tramped by.

'It's all right, now, darling,' she said softly.

In the darkness she heard a tank engine start up, heard the squeak of its tracks. She thought it was a Sherman. In the ditch she picked Felicity up again, staggered on along the road. She glanced up at the stars, she was still moving north-west. Suddenly the darkness was ripped open by a harsh voice.

'Who goes there?'

'Friend,' she croaked. The voice had been English. 'Friend. Please help me.'

She tottered forward, felt friendly hands on her, a light flashing in her face. The soldiers went to take Felicity from her arms, and she screamed, piercingly, clutching onto Violet.

'I'll take her,' she said, walking on. 'She was tortured by the Gestapo, she fears men. Find me a doctor, please.'

She passed through the front line.

'We'll go home now, darling,' she whispered, but Felicity made no reply.

56

Fast, Fast, Fast!

Kandy, Ceylon, August 1945

Major-General Freddie de Clare climbed down from the Dakota and walked across the tarmac to the airport building. It was very hot, the flight from Burma had taken a long time. He went underneath an immense white sign that proclaimed it to be Supreme Command Allied Forces South East Asia. A smartly turned-out military clerk was behind the desk when he went in, large wooden paddle-bladed fans turned on the ceiling. Outside, he suddenly heard the sound of sirens and engines, saw a vast white Cadillac limousine driving away from the airfield building through the palms and bougainvillea, surrounded by a flotilla of motorcycle outriders, their whirling lights flashing blue on the shimmering white uniforms of the riders.

'Who the hell is that?' he enquired. 'Has President Truman arrived, or is it Mae West?'

'Neither, sir,' the man said proudly. 'That's the Supreme Commander himself, Lord Mountbatten.'

'Does he always go about like that?'

'Always. He's come for someone important.'

'President Truman?'

'No, sir. Big-wig politician from London, sir. Man from the Colonial Office, Mr Clare.'

'Perceval?' Freddie said disbelievingly. 'I am General de Clare, are you sure he didn't come for me?'

The man consulted a list.

'No, sir.'

'How am I meant to get to headquarters?'

'I'll see if I can find you a jeep, sir.'

They were playing golf when he got there. He climbed out of his jeep outside the King's Pavilion and somebody shouted 'fore' over the music of a full orchestra playing. He went in, hot and sweating, and found himself in the middle of a reception. Pushing through, he came across his cousin.

'Freddie!' Perceval said absently. 'What *are* you doing here?'

'Having a conference with Dickie, I hope,' he said shortly. 'But first, a bath.'

'Join us for dinner.'

He was in time to find Perceval as drinks were being served before dinner. He took a whisky and soda from a uniformed, white-gloved steward and went up to his cousin as he moved through the crowd.

'Hallo, Perceval. Have I caught you between bores?'

An expression of great displeasure went over the other's face.

'For God's sake, Freddie!' he hissed. 'The name is Percy. Perce for short.'

'Oh, sorry. I've been too busy fighting a war to remember the fine detail.'

'Now we're in, we'll have a society without class. I'm leading the way.'

'If you're leading the way old man, we can be sure it'll be without class,' Freddie said jovially. 'Well, you did get in, though. They dumped Winston. There's gratitude for you, I suppose. I hear that this new welfare state is going to happen.'

'As I always said!' Perceval cried smugly.

'You were ahead of us all there. A beneficent state will look after us all from cradle to grave.'

'Exactly!'

'Yes. How are you going to pay for it, old boy? We're broke, and the Americans have just told us there's no more money.'

He stared keenly at Perceval over his whisky.

'Must cost a lot, this sort of thing,' he said encouragingly.

'It does,' the other said proudly.

'So?'

'Simple. During this long war we have been through, the countries of the Empire all operated their finances through the Sterling Bloc. They had to bank with us, in other words. We set the exchange rates to suit ourselves. Plenty left over to pay for the new welfare state.'

'I rather have a feeling that if you do that sort of thing with other people's finances in real life you land up in the Old Bailey. It's called fraud.'

'The people of Great Britain fought for a better tomorrow! We promised it to them and they have elected us, the Labour Party, to give it to them! We shall not betray that trust!'

'You'd rather betray the people of the Empire.'

'Really, Freddie, you have a terribly simplistic approach to life,' Perceval said loftily. 'You'd do better to stick to tanks.'

'All right, what will you do when this . . . heist, as the Americans say, this heist of other people's money runs out?'

'Well, don't forget that Great Britain is in a very advantageous situation. Our manufacturing industry is intact, Europe's is destroyed. We shall sell machinery to the Empire.'

'At our prices.'

'Of course.'

'What if they don't want it? If I recall rightly our machines were pretty rickety even before the war.'

'They have no choice. It's us or nothing,' Perceval snapped.

'I personally back the Germans to be back in the race in five years. What if they sell better machinery cheaper?'

'They can't to the Empire,' Perceval said sullenly. 'We shan't let them.'

'And there I was thinking that we British invented the doctrine of free trade,' Freddie said mockingly. 'All this seems to presuppose that you'll be raising money through tax, of one sort or another.'

'Well of course,' Perceval said seriously. 'The society of the future will of course have high taxes. High taxes, high benefits.'

'Give your money to the government, who decides how much to give back? I'm more used to the old system of deciding how to spend my money myself.'

'Oh, no. A system run by the state is far more efficient. More wise, more beneficent. You'll see.'

'I think that's what I'm afraid of,' Freddie said drily.

'Ah, there you are, Percy!' a loud female voice cried. 'Shall I rescue you from the clutches of the military? It's time to go in.'

Perceval brightened. A thin woman of faded beauty in a beautifully cut silk frock bore down on them.

'Certainly, Edwina! Do you know my cousin, General Freddie de Clare? Freddie, this is Lady Edwina, Dickie's wife.'

Freddie and Lady Edwina exchanged one brief glance of instant and mutual loathing.

'Right, I must have you, Percy. I want you to tell me all about the brave new tomorrow we are creating in Britain. So nice to see you, General.'

They went into a fabulously decorated dining room, white and gold, with glorious blooms lush in shining cut-glass bowls and vases. A long table was set with silver upon damask, a string quartet played lightly in a corner, and uniformed native servants were on hand. Freddie found himself somewhere in the middle order. At the head of the table Lord Louis Mountbatten presided, smiling and laughing, in full white dress uniform, with decorations and *aiguillettes*. Lady Edwina dominated the other end. Delicately smoked fish of some sort was served, beautifully chill on a bed of salad, and a clear crisp hock poured into tall, green-tinged flutes of cut glass. After his long flight Freddie began to feel slightly disoriented. The war was over, the Japanese had been atom-bombed into surrender. There was a fearful mess to be cleared up.

Washing down some of the fish with his wine he caught Mountbatten looking at him.

'Ah, General de Clare. I didn't know we had the pleasure of your company today.'

'Well, yes,' said Freddie. 'You and I are to meet in conference in the morning.'

'But didn't you get my message? I have had to cancel our meeting. I am to show the Minister here around in the morning and then I am flying to Singapore.'

'I got no message,' Freddie said grimly. 'I shall have to accompany you to Singapore.'

'Sorry,' Mountbatten said charmingly. 'Our three aircraft are all full with my staff.'

'Then we had better sort the details out now.'

'I really don't think—'

'I am in Burma,' Freddie said, ignoring him. 'We are at the moment the authority in charge.'

'I know. I won the war there.'

'If you say so then I am sure you are right,' Freddie said stonily.

Mountbatten suddenly flushed red.

'Don't you insult me, General,' he said in a low voice. 'I have a long memory.'

'Freddie's always outspoken,' Perceval butted in. 'Don't mind him, Dickie.'

'I want you to mind me a lot,' Freddie said hotly. 'I am attempting to restore order and your representatives are thwarting me at every turn.'

'Good Lord, Dickie!' Edwina cried from the other end of the table. 'What is going on?'

'I don't know, darling,' Mountbatten called charmingly down the table. 'The general here is having trouble with his soldiers, wants me to sort it out.'

'I am having *no* trouble with my men at all, who are without exception performing a wonderful job in difficult circumstances,' Freddie said loudly. The other guests were listening with interest, sensing a first-class entertaining row.

'I am having trouble with the representatives of the Supreme Commander here, who are providing succour and support to U Aung San, leader of the Burmese National Army.'

'So they should!' Edwina cried. 'What a wonderful young man. He is an inspiration to us all.'

'The Japanese certainly found him an inspiration. He was on their side. He fought for them. Our enemies.'

'Oh, I don't think you should be too hard on him,' Mountbatten said childingly. 'Don't you think that any young Burmese of spirit could have been expected to accept the Japanese offer of independence?'

'You're just an old hidebound imperialist,' Edwina cried. 'You can't understand people in Asia wanting to be free of our rule.'

'Japan was not offering independence,' Freddie said savagely. 'No more than Hitler gave freedom to any of the countries under his rule. Like him, the Japanese offered satrapies to those turncoats prepared to exploit and oppress their own people. U Aung San was one such. A Burmese quisling. Now those who remained true in their hearts to us in the war, loyal Burmese, are shocked to find that we, the British are consorting with our former enemy. They cannot understand how we accept them, those who exploited them in the war, who took their food, money and women. They expected U Aung San to be shot, they did not expect us to negotiate away the country to him.'

'Typical!' Edwina called scornfully. 'Can't you see that it is those ridiculous people who accepted the rule of the British who are the real quislings? The real traitors to their people? U Aung San is their future, young, vibrant and virile, he is the sort of leader they need.'

'Then let him prove it. Burma has to be led slowly and carefully towards self-government. Democratic institutions have to be set up and put into motion. There must be an independent civil service, functioning independent political parties.'

'Slow? Always slow, slow, slow!' Mountbatten said derisively. 'I say fast, fast, fast! Let us do it all at maximum speed!'

'Democracies are not good at doing things quickly.'

'All the more reason for giving power to young nationalists like U Aung San. They are the future, not an outmoded past,' said Edwina.

'Then you will end up with a one-party state as in Soviet Russia.'

'What better model for a young country?'

'I am old-fashioned enough to believe that democracy is the worst form of government except for all those other forms which have been tried from time to time.'

'You are just an old-fashioned imperialist Tory, General.'

'No, madam. I vote for the Whig party, on the rare occasions it fields candidates.'

He turned to Mountbatten.

'I want to lock up U Aung San and his cronies and put them on trial for war crimes as they are to do with the Nazis back in Europe. I have your permission?'

'Of course not!' Mountbatten said, shocked. 'We are trying to create good will, not ill will.'

Freddie pushed back his seat, placed his white linen napkin next to his plate.

'Then I must get back,' he said. 'There is still a lot to do. I thank you for a most pleasant meal.'

He went out, and an excited buzz of conversation resumed.

'Dickie, darling,' Edwina drawled. 'Don't you feel we ought to find General de Clare something else to do?'

Mountbatten's face brightened. He always enjoyed sacking people who got in his way.

'Good idea, darling.'

He speared a piece of fish, chewed on it happily.

'I'll see to it right away,' he said.

57

We Just Didn't Lose

Windstone Castle, December 1946

'I say, Vi,' Freddie called, from the great doors, as he came in. 'Are you milking the cows or something?'

Violet put down the two galvanised buckets she had been carrying across the marble-floored hall. She was wearing about four cardigans and had her head in a commando's balaclava.

'I am not!' she said with spirit. 'I am gathering up the rain as it comes through the roof. The Fourth Army when it lived here did not make any repairs to the damage it caused. The place is as water-tight as a sieve.'

'It's about as cold inside as it is out,' Freddie admitted. 'Shall I light some fires?'

'Oh, do, that would be such a help. The de Clares have held Christmas here ever since 1067, and I'll be damned if we are going to break the tradition now. I do want to get the temperature above freezing before Gawaine and Molly bring the baby.'

Freddie parked his suitcase and went off. After a while he reappeared, pushing a wheelbarrow he had laden with logs and kindling. He set to building a big fire in the mighty grate and soon the big circular hall flickered with the light of the flames. He worked steadily, bringing in wood, and lighting fires, and imperceptibly, the temperature began to climb.

'I recall that Uncle had a team of servants to do all this,' he remarked cheerfully, as he passed Violet, who was wheeling in a large pine tree in an ornately decorated pot.

'There's just you and me,' she said. 'Are you hungry? I've got a rabbit pie in the oven, I went out yesterday and shot a few. They're overrunning the place. Tell you what, let's have a drink, I've been at this since dawn.'

'You have grog?' he enquired.

'I walled up the cellar before I let the Fourth Army in,' she said triumphantly. 'And plastered and painted the wall. I broke back in last week, they never found it. There's a decent bottle of claret warming in the kitchen by the range. Pink gin or Scotch?'

'Gin,' he said.

They went through to the kitchen where the black Victorian range radiated a welcome warmth. The scent of the cooking pie was in the air. Violet splashed gin into tumblers, added angostura bitters. They sat down on wooden chairs round the scrubbed table.

'God . . .' she said thankfully. 'I don't know what I'd do without booze.'

'That reminds me, I've got treacle tart, apple pies, Christmas cake and mince pies in the car. Clarissa's been baking like anything. There's an entire general's allowance of sugar in there.'

'Marvellous. We're going to go out to the lake later. A flock of geese has thankfully taken up residence. You'd better shoot straight or there'll be no Christmas lunch.'

'I shall do my best,' he said solemnly. He drank some gin, and allowed the heat of the stove to penetrate his chilled flesh.

'Is everyone coming?' he asked. 'I'm picking Clarissa and the children up from the station later.'

'Molly and Gawaine will be here with young Bertram tomorrow. It's open house for the de Clares; all the others know they can come if they want, even Perceval, rot his socialist hide, if he can bear to show his face.'

'What's income tax now? I heard a rumour out there it was coming down.'

'No such luck. Ten bob in the pound for the ordinary folk, nineteen and a Rick surtax for aristos like us, living in our unimaginable luxury in our fabulous piles. It makes you sick.'

'Think it'll go down? The war's over.'

'What's that got to do with anything? That little swine Perceval is proud of this ghastly taxation. He told me so. Taxation, he boasted, is just as effective as violence or outright confiscation, and at the same time lacks all their disadvantages.'

'I can't see that anybody is any better off for it. This welfare state seems to translate into simply everybody being destitute instead of some.'

'Fish would turn in his grave. He thought income tax was immoral, something only turned to as a last resort for the survival of the country.'

'Different times, different mores.'

'Meanwhile, we have to decide how to keep the fabric of the castle in sufficient repair to actually stop the roof falling in on us. A lot of us, our kind, are simply giving up, you know. The big houses were used for government purposes during the war, they're all damaged, they all need a fortune spending on them and just about none of us have got the money, certainly not while we're paying to buy the coal mines, railways and all the other nonsense Perceval and his lot have their hearts set on. There are patrician families who are simply ceasing to exist, just being . . . blotted up in the amorphous mass of the middle classes. A couple of bouts of death duties – it's up to seventy-five per cent, Freddie! I hope to God Gawaine doesn't trip going down the stairs – then you've nothing left to sell, and land is only fetching now what it did eighty years ago. Somebody sings a song and you hand over fifty acres.'

She took a pull at her drink.

'Well, it isn't going to happen to us,' she said. 'We're the de Clares.'

'What do you have in mind?'

'I think,' she said slowly, and thoughtfully, 'that we're going to have to open the doors. Let the masses in. There's almost nine hundred years worth of history here, and we still have fabulous amounts of artefacts. Armour, portraits, guns, crossbows – all kinds of weapons – hordes of clothes, medals and honours, carriages, cars, even Fish's aeroplanes! The boats, come to that. The great library, the very castle itself! The Keep, this part we're in now, the battlements, the Traitor's Tower, the moat. All our history, Freddie! We're a microcosm of English history itself. I'm sure we could run coach tours through here. Charge 'em half a crown and a cream tea for sixpence. Windstone ale if they're thirsty in the Yeoman's Inn. What do you think?'

'It's a novel idea,' he admitted.

'You can come and help run it. We need a military mind. You're good at organising the chaps. You must be getting ready to retire from the army anyway.'

'They're talking of sending me out to India for a last posting. We're going to pull out, that's for certain. They'll need a lot of troops to maintain order – there's this latent hostility between the different groups, the Hindus, the Muslims, the Sikhs. There's no reason why anything should go wrong. Viceroy Wavell's very capable, but it needs to be handled with care. I'll do that if they ask me. But yes, I'd like to come and help. I've always loved it here.'

'We can put a wing aside for us to live in. Luckily Gawaine and Molly think like us. If we all pull together we can do it.'

'Here's to coach tours!'

From above there was a clattering of feet.

'Hallo, hallo!'

'Isn't that George? Down here!'

The feet came down the stairs and George came in bringing a breath of cold air about his worn blue Crombie coat.

'I say! A warm kitchen and gin too!'

'Help yourself, George. It's good to see you. What were the roads like?'

'Bloody awful. It's snowing.'

He sat down with a tumbler of gin and bitters.

'I've brought lots of chocolate,' he said.

'Chocolate! Where on earth did you get chocolate?'

'America,' he said evenly. 'I've been over there with a few others. We had some Americans with us in X-2 . . . They're setting up a new intelligence agency. Central Intelligence. CIA. I was there, that's where I got the chocolate. They have lots of it . . .'

He stared unseeingly ahead of him, his voice trailed away.

'You all right, old man?'

'Eh? Oh, yes. I was just thinking . . . I buried my son while I was there, you see. I'm still not quite used to the notion. Him not being there, that is.'

'Oh, George . . .'

'He took pills, you see,' George said, his voice suddenly savage.

'Pills? Was he ill?' Violet said, puzzled.

'No. That's what they do, over there. In America. In Hollywood. They take pills to give themselves pleasure. My son, he became an American. He took pills like they did and he was sick in his sleep, he breathed it in and he is dead. In America they drive enormous vulgar cars, they spend money on things they don't need and they take drugs. That's what their filthy society is made of.'

'I'm so sorry,' Freddie said sincerely.

George drank some gin.

'Better watch out,' he said. 'You've got children. That's what'll happen to them.'

'Not here,' he said. 'This is Britain.'

'Yes, here!' George shouted. 'Don't you understand? We British didn't win the war, we just didn't lose. The Americans and the Russians, they won the war. The Russians have their bit – Poland, Czechoslovakia and all that – and the Americans have the rest. See if I'm not right. Their filthy diseased culture will be here before you know it. Films and drugs and buying things you don't need. There will be no decent people left . . .'

'Honestly, George, I haven't the faintest idea what you're talking about,' said Violet.'

'I'd better get my stuff out of the car,' said Freddie, getting up. 'There's rabbit pie for lunch, George.'

'Eh? Oh, good.'

'I'm so sorry about your son, George,' Violet said sympathetically.

'Oh, thank you. I knew he was doomed, you know. America kills anything good. But look, I won't go on about it. I've come down for Christmas.'

'Can I ask you something? Now the war's over?'

'Yes . . .' he said, cautiously.

She got up, put a pot of peeled carrots on to the range to boil.

'Before we – Felicity and I – went out to France again before D-Day, for F-Section, we had a conference with you at MI6.'

'Yes.'

'When we left, we accidentally saw Carlotta on the street. We followed her. She went into your building.'

He was silent for a few moments.

'And you want to know why?' he said, looking up.

'I'm curious.'

'I'm not supposed to talk about anything like that. But I will, because I know you won't say anything. It's very simple. We at SIS had something called the XX Committee. XX – Double Cross. It ran turned German agents. After the war had been on for a bit we realised we had all their agents. We ran them as double-agents, we told the Germans what we wanted them to know. Carlotta was an agent. We called her Garotte. We picked her up through that awful little creep the Duke of Windsor, when he was busy trying to sell us down the river. That's what she was doing with me. A lot of things went on to make D-Day a success that people don't know about.'

'I see. Thank you. I won't let it go any further.'

'Please don't. How is poor Felicity?'

'The same. When we got her back to England she was treated by a foremost nerve specialist – Dr Roberts, a Harley Street man. She's still in the clinic. He says she may never recover. She says nothing. She is in some kind of withdrawn state, catatonic he calls it. When we have the castle inhabitable again I'm going to bring her back here. Being here may bring her back to normal, slowly. I can't bear to think of her just caged up in the clinic, anyway. She ought to be with us.'

The carrots began to boil, the lid rattling over the steam, and she shifted the pot towards the edge. She went and collected some plates, putting them over the range to warm.

'I wish I knew who betrayed us,' she said. 'They were waiting for us as we came down.'

'I know,' he said sympathetically. 'You won't find out now. The extent of French collaboration with the Germans was quite beyond belief. They ran the whole place with a handful of Gestapo men. Once we'd invaded suddenly there were forty-five million people all claiming to be *resistants* but the reality was the other way about. About forty-five million *collaborateurs*.'

'I know,' she said sadly. 'There were damned few you could trust. Are you sticking with MI6 now it's all over?'

'Oh, yes,' he said with a disarming laugh. 'I'm not qualified to do anything else.'

'What about Godfrey?'

'Ah, well Godfrey *is* qualified to do other things. He's leaving. Surveyor of the King's pictures, of course, but also he's got the job as Director of the Portsman Institute of Art. Part of London University. Post-grad college.'

'Oh, he'll like that.'

'Mind you, I may make use of him from time to time. He had a very good intelligence brain, did Godfrey.'

'I'm going into the museum business, myself. We're opening up the castle to the public. Freddie's going to help, too.'

'How very enterprising of you.'

'I put all the stuff into storage before the Fourth Army came. You wouldn't believe some of the stuff I found.'

Freddie came down carrying a large box, and began to unpack pies and cake.

'Vi says you're going to open up the castle with her, Freddie.'

'Eh? Oh, yes. Should be great fun. I've got to go to India first, help Wavell grant independence, of course.'

'Wavell?' George said, looking thoughtfully at his cousin. 'No, you wouldn't have heard.'

'Heard what?'

'Our new government doesn't like Wavell. They feel he lacks charisma.'

'Charisma?' Freddie choked, drinking the last of his gin.

'Yes.' George appeared to be getting some sort of grim amusement from what he was saying. 'They feel that the granting of independence should not be perceived by people as weakness, as a decline in British power and resolution. They want someone who will carry it off with grandeur and panache, the celebration of Britain's mission of trusteeship.'

'I've never heard such rubbish in my life,' Violet said sharply.

'How do you know this, George?' asked Freddie.

'We're the secret service,' George said blandly. 'We like to know what's going on.'

'So who *is* going to do this charismatic job?'

'Mountbatten.'

'God help us all,' said Freddie.

'God will help *us*, Freddie, because as is well known, He is an Englishman. Will he help the poor benighted Indians? That is the question.'

Violet put knives, forks and napkins on the table, brought a golden-crusted pie from the oven, drained the carrots.

She pierced the lid pf pastry, and fragrant steam came out.

'Will you do the wine, George? The damned rabbits did well out of the war, if nobody else did, I'll tell you. There's thousands of them out there.'

She lifted pastry and rabbit and bacon and onions and gravy on to their plates, and they ate.

58

The Bastard Offspring of a Court Chamberlain

The Punjab, India, July 1948

The stench hit them as the jeep came around the rocky corner of the road and into the valley. Sitting next to Freddie, the young lieutenant jammed on the brakes. Dust rolled forward and coated the edge of the dead. Huge, multi-coloured flies buzzed furiously about them, some vultures flapped clumsily into the air. Sensing no threat, they circled about, landing back where they had started from, and continued their feeding.

The narrow valley that led north to safety was jammed with the swollen, stinking bodies of women, men and children. They had been killed with machine-guns, rifles, machetes. Limbs, breasts, genitals lay scattered among the rags, carts, prams and rags on the filthy ground where they had been hacked away.

'Muslims, Charlie,' said Freddie.

The young man was holding a handkerchief to his face against the smell.

'We can't get through this way, sir,' he said in a muffled voice.

'Detour through the village then,' Fredie ordered. 'How many do you think are there?'

'Two thousand?' the young officer, hazarded.

'Nearer three, I'd say. Quickly, then, Charlie. The sooner I can get down to Delhi the sooner we can get troops up here and stop all this.'

The jeep turned on the hot, dusty road where nothing moved, and went back the way they had come. They turned off to cut through the village they could see in the distance on their way to the airfield, racing under the shade of the trees, and alongside a pretty river.

A man was standing at the edge of the village.

'Slow down, Charlie.'

The man was standing in front of a telephone pole. He wore darkly stained baggy trousers, a loose shirt. As they came closer they could see that he was strapped tightly to it with rope. A great pool of blood was all about, it ran across the road in front of them and hordes of insects were feeding on it. Then they saw that none of the man's limbs were connected, they had all been sawn through as he stood there. Freddie felt the bile rise up in his throat, and forced himself to swallow.

'Keep going. We can't do anything for him.'

He glanced up at the telephone pole. The wires hung loose, moving a little in the hot breeze.

They came into the single street of the village. It was blocked by a band of men in khaki uniforms, all wearing turbans. They were heavily armed with rifles, tommy guns and grenades. A wireless van with whip aerials and some trucks stood parked at the side of the road.

'Sikh *jatha*, sir,' the young man said nervously. He pulled up, keeping the engine running. The circle of men opened, and a man in an officer's uniform came through. Behind him, within the circle Freddie, could see a group of naked women, their clothing torn off them and lying on the ground. They wailed in abject fear. He got out of the jeep.

'I am General de Clare,' he said loudly. 'I command this area. I order you to disperse.'

The Sikh smiled.

'Where is your army, General? I am a humble captain, but I command more men than you.'

'Are you responsible for that massacre back there?'

'I regret not. We are on our way to attack another column of filth. We came across these women and are going to treat them as they should be treated.'

He gestured contemptuously behind him.

'They are Muslims,' he explained.

'I order you to let them go. I shall be returning with many troops. I shall hunt you down if you harm them.'

'You are not returning at all, sahib!' the Sikh commander cried delightedly. 'We may do what we wish.'

He turned, and issued a rattle of sudden orders. The watching men all grinned and laughed, they moved back.

'Go! Go!' the Sikh shouted at the women, and they ran through the ranks, screaming.

'Perhaps we shall have fun, hunting them,' he said, turning back to Freddie.

'I shall return also with aeroplanes,' Freddie said stonily. 'If you are still in these parts preying upon the refugees we shall machine-gun and bomb you from the air.'

A wary expression came over the man's face. He stepped back, waved at the jeep to continue.

'Then we must waste no time, General,' he said.

The Viceroy's palace stood white and massive, symbol of a mighty empire. Freddie jumped out of the jeep that had brought him from the airport. No car had been waiting for him, he had commandeered one.

'Thank you, Corporal,' he said, and the man drove away. Freddie went inside. It all seemed strangely deserted. A Hindu servant stood impassively in the marbled hall.

'Yes, sahib?'

'I am General de Clare. I need to see the Viceroy urgently. Mountbatten, man.'

The man bowed.

'Mountbatten, sahib. Please follow me.'

He led Freddie along white and gilt corridors and up richly carpeted stairways. Finally they paused outside a panelled door.

'Through there, sahib.'

Freddie stepped forward, jerked the door smartly open and stepped inside. He stopped short. He was in the wrong place. This was a bedroom. A man, an Indian, lay back in a huge rumpled bed, goggling at him in shock.

'Who the hell are you?' he demanded.

'I could say the same thing,' Freddie said furiously. 'People are wasting my bloody time and every minute I waste, people are dying.'

The man leaned forward from his pillows.

'Which people?' he asked urgently. 'Tell me.'

'Muslims. Trying to escape from the Punjab.'

The man smiled, lay back again.

'Oh, Muslims. That is not very important.'

The bedclothes about him were moving, and Freddie saw that somebody else was down there. A sheet was pulled back, and Edwina Mountbatten's naked form came into view.

'God!' she said angrily. 'It's that ghastly man de Clare. Why on earth have you brought him in here, darling?'

Freddie suddenly realised he was looking at Nehru, the leader of Congress in India.

'I didn't,' Nehru said mildly. 'He came in.'

'I am looking,' Freddie said icily, 'for your husband.'

'He's downstairs,' Edwina said contemptuously. 'Playing with his flags. Now just bugger off, de Clare.'

She vanished back under the sheets, which started to move once again. Nehru smiled at Freddie.

'Goodbye, General,' he said.

Freddie went out. The Hindu servant was still standing there.

'So sorry,' he said, with transparent insincerity. 'This way, sahib.'

Eventually, he found Mountbatten. The Viceroy was cross.

'Have you brought them?' he snapped, sitting behind his very large desk. He was working on a huge piece of thick ivory paper with ruler and pen, forming the skeleton of what appeared to be an extensive family tree.

'Brought what?' Freddie snarled. Mountbatten looked up.

'Oh, it's you, de Clare,' he said disappointedly. 'I thought it was the man with the flags.'

'What bloody flags?'

'*My* flag. As governor-general after independence. We've been deciding the design. Pandit!'

A young Indian boy, standing patiently at the side of the room jumped forward.

'Bring me those brassards.'

The handsome youth brought forward some brassards on a tray.

'Just look at it!' Mountbatten cried petulantly. 'The lion's whiskers are much too big. I shall seem quite foolish. I've ordered them changed.'

'I want troops,' Freddie said loudly. 'A lot of troops. Also some squadrons of fighters.'

'Troops?' the commander said nervously. 'Whatever for?'

'The situation in the Punjab is deteriorating into civil war. Murder, rape, arson, mutilation, torture and desecration of temples has become rife. Innocent women and children are being slaughtered. The Sikhs have started it, but the Muslims are retaliating. I can restore order if I am allowed the ruthless use of force. I require troops and air power. I can get the Gurkhas in—'

'Don't be ridiculous! Nehru would never stand for the use of Gurkhas. He can't stand them. No, no, look, everything is going to work itself out. I'm in charge. I've set up a proper war room, maps, the lot. It's a very exciting time, very exciting. I can see that you're a bit upset, but I assure you, I see the big picture, and it will all be fine.'

'It is *not* going to be fine!' Freddie said angrily. 'It has all the makings of a really giant man-made disaster. *Your* disaster.'

'My dear fellow,' Mountbatten said, smiling reproachfully at him. 'You're always seeking to blame me. Don't you think that perhaps you should take a long hard look in the mirror, and work out who's really responsible for this refugee problem?'

'I need, at the very least, some squadrons of Typhoon fighters to bomb and cannonade the armed bands. The message will very quickly get through.'

'Good God! Can you imagine the effect that would have in the press? Never. I think a policy of benign neglect is best. You'll see. In twenty years' time you'll look back at it all and see that I was right all along.'

'I see.'

Freddie tried to swallow the fury that was boiling inside him. Mountbatten peered keenly down at his great sheet of paper, absently running his hand over the young boy standing next to him.

'What are you working on here?' Freddie enquired.

'This? Oh, fascinating. It's a relationship table of all the European royal families. All the family connections. Each person has a proper label to identify them. I invented it myself.'

'Did you? My uncle used to use it for stock breeding of his cattle. Are you there?'

'Of course!' he said proudly. 'Look.'

Freddie traced the connections with his finger.

'This is your grandfather?'

'It is. Prince Alexander of Hesse.'

'As I recall, it is pretty common knowledge that your grandfather was the bastard offspring of a court chamberlain and so not a prince at all.'

Mountbatten's face went a sudden, dangerous brick red.

'The massacres I have outlined are but the start,' Freddie said coldly. 'What pitiful efforts there are to establish refugee camps will shortly be totally overwhelmed. Supplies of medicine, food and safe water will run out. I expect epidemics of cholera, smallpox and typhoid within weeks. The death toll is going to be beyond belief – hundreds upon hundreds of thousands. Now do I get my troops and fighters or not?'

'No!' Mountbatten cried. 'I can't become governor-general with that kind of blood on my hands.'

'Dear God,' Freddie said quietly. 'Three and a half centuries of Empire here and it ends like this? Your wife is upstairs, performing fellatio on Nehru. You are down here, giving the country away to him.'

Mountbatten got up, went over to the wall, peering keenly at the huge map of the Continent.

'Which little part have you come from? Hmm. You know, de Clare, I think your tiny force has outlived its usefulness. Yes. As from now, you're disbanded. Catch a plane. Yes. You can go home. Pandit! Let's go and see if those flags are ready.'

He put his hand about the boy's shoulders, and they went out.

59

Garotte Told Them So

Windstone Castle, April 1962

Godfrey sat on the lichened stone seat hidden in the arbour cut and clipped in the yew hedge. He looked out over the glittering Windstone Water, its banks gold and starred with marsh marigolds, primroses and cowslips. The slopes of the hills beyond were pink and white with the blossom of cherry trees, crab apple and rich yellow gorse. He wore grey flannels and a tweed hacking jacket. His long fingers cradled a tall glass of whisky and soda, and he sipped on it from time to time.

He heard a faint creaking sound coming from the castle behind him, the murmur of a woman's voice. He saw Violet, pushing a wheelchair towards the edge of the Water, where a seat had been placed by a small copse of maples. A white-haired woman sat, very folded up, immobile in the chair. Violet parked it carefully and sat down on the seat next to her companion. Godfrey got up, and padded over to them, his feet silent on the turf.

'Oh, look, darling!' Violet cried, pointing in the air. 'A Peacock butterfly! I do declare it's the first I've seen this year. It's bound to be a good summer. Just see that blackthorn and gorse over there. Just mounds of white like snowdrifts! I believe we should make gorse wine again.'

Out on the Water a big fish splashed.

'What do you think, darling? Too early for Mayfly. They get the big chaps up from the depths, don't they? I saw Gawaine and Bertram getting their rods in order. Once the Mayflies start I shan't see them from morning 'til dusk.'

'Hallo, Vi!' Godfrey said cheerfully. He came and sat next to her. 'Hallo, Flick.'

The figure in the chair, as thin and bent and folded as an old doll said nothing, simply stared lifelessly over the Water.

'Hallo, Godfrey. They said you were coming down.'

'I do love to get out of London after the winter,' he said. 'It's become an annual rite, to see the castle in the spring. I spend so much of my time closeted in galleries and lecture rooms. Lovely to get out in the fresh air. Are you getting ready to open up?'

'Next month. They'll all come flooding in up the drive. And flying in. Since we opened the Stuart wing as the hotel we get Americans flying into Gawaine's airstrip direct from Heathrow, especially for the shooting and fishing. We keep the two sides pretty separate.'

'Wonderful. How's Flick?'

'You're pretty much the same, aren't you darling?'

'Does she talk?'

'No, you don't talk, darling,' Violet said softly. 'But I know you know what's going on.'

She turned to Godfrey.

'I like her to come out in the fresh air, see the blossom and flowers. It may be that the specialist is right, and she'll never be herself again, but I don't believe that.'

'It's been a long time,' Godfrey commented.

'We've been here a long time, but we're still here,' she said sharply. The breeze pushed a lock of her silver hair onto her face, she pushed it back.

'You'll be coming to Bertram's wedding?' she asked.

'Of course. Who's the lucky bride?'

'Oh, Fenella. Such a lovely girl. They met at Oxford, you know.' She glanced over her shoulder at the castle. 'I'm waiting for the committee.'

'What committee?' he asked, and drank some of his whisky.

'The committee to save Windstone Halt. That little squirt Perceval wants to knock it down.'

'Really?' he said languidly.

'Well yes, really. Have you seen what his lot have done to Windstone town? Some of the Nash crescents and square were damaged in the great Baedecker raid and, as MP, Perceval used it as an excuse to have them demolished. They've been bomb-sites for over ten years, and now he's sponsoring this hideous rebuilding programme. One-way traffic systems! Car parks! Shopping centres! When I tell you that the Elizabethan town hall has been razed you will know what I mean.'

'They don't need a town hall?' he said curiously.

'You're missing the point. It isn't big enough.'

'Why not? The council meets every other Thursday, if my memory serves me right, in Queen Bess's chamber.'

'Exactly. The chaps sort out whatever needs doing on their way back from work and Mr Prentiss the town clerk puts it in motion. Perceval says it's anachronistic, that Windstone needs a proper bureaucracy. They're building one. A revolting affair of concrete slabs where the Corn Hall used to be. You can see it from the Keep. The glass glares most hideously in the sun.'

'And he wants to level the Halt?'

'He does,' she said grimly. 'It is a grand example of Great Western Railway architecture. It has cantilevered awnings each side of the waiting room and the booking hall was designed by Brunel. He intends to have it demolished and replace it with yet more concrete. It is as though anything to do with our heritage is abhorrent to him.'

'He wants to take us into Europe,' he said mischievously. 'You know, this Common Market thing.'

'Of course! Yet more bureaucracy. We need less government, not more. Do you know, Godfrey, when I was a young girl in this country you could live your whole life without coming into more contact with the government than the post office or the local policeman. If you were able to look after yourself, they left you alone. Now there appears no area of one's life in which they do not wish you to fill out forms and pay them taxes for.'

'I had a drink with Perceval the other day. He says that before the end of the century there will be no old nations in Europe. Just a United States of Europe.'

'Now I know he's off his head. You do comfort me, Godfrey. Perhaps we can have him certified.'

They heard a voice calling from the castle, saw somebody waving.

'Oh Lord. There's Gawaine. They must be here. We're going to demonstrate outside the Halt with one of the castle cannon, get the press along to take photographs.'

'How exciting! Will it be charged with powder and shot?'

'Of course. We're the de Clares, we never bluff. Godfrey, you wouldn't sit with Flick until Molly comes, would you?'

'Of course.'

'How's your drink? Do you want it freshened?'

'No, that's fine. I'll sit here.'

He watched Violet walk purposefully away over the lawn, turned back to Felicity, sitting broken and still in her wheelchair.

'I drink more than I did,' he said to her.

She did not respond.

'I suppose it is the pursuit of this strange life of mine. I didn't notice it before, but I do now. That and not being able to talk to anyone.'

He drank a little from his glass, then waved a hand in front of her eyes. She did not blink.

'I suppose I could talk to you,' he said. 'I mean, it would be nice to talk to somebody, even a vegetable like you. Do you mind? No? I didn't think you would. I think it's just that I would hate to be exposed, after all these years.'

He looked out over the Water. The breeze was making the waves chop, they glittered in the sunshine. A pair of white geese took off, climbing over the hill.

'I mean, I have a grand position. Director of the most prestigious art foundation in the land. Adviser, courtier to the Royal Family. Respected by all. And I'm a spy!'

He looked closely into her eyes.

'Anything going on in there?' he enquired. 'No? I'll tell you about it anyway. I spied for the Soviet Union for years. You wouldn't believe the number of secrets I gave them. The number of influential people I suborned. Why, *I* gave them the entire MI6 network in Eastern Europe in 1945! Yes! Me. Every single blessed agent. They rolled the lot up, shot 'em and put them in the Gulag. Serve 'em right. Best place for spies!'

Godfrey put his head back and laughed uproariously.

'I'd hate to be unmasked, you see,' he said, when he had calmed down. 'That's probably why I drink a bit more than I did. Don't want to be betrayed. You know about that, of course. You were betrayed to the Gestapo, weren't you? That's why you sit there like a vegetable. Of course, it wasn't really you as much as Violet. It was supposed to be Violet. I've always hated her, haven't you? Well, no, you didn't of course. All you de Clare bitches stick together. You and bloody Fish and Gawaine and Freddie, so festeringly brave and honourable. God, how I hate you all. Why can't you be like me?'

He took a long pull at his glass, finished it.

'I could get really drunk,' he said. 'But I won't. Mustn't give myself away. Where was I? Oh yes, betrayal. I think I'm safe. They discovered Burgess and Philby and the others. Not me, though. It's tricky, isn't it? Must be such a surprise. Did you get a surprise, when they started shooting at you, those horrid Germans? It was no accident. They knew you were coming, Garotte told them so.'

He grinned, savagely.

'You see,' he said. 'I told her to.'

He glanced up, looked across the lawn.

'Well, thank goodness. Here comes Molly. One more de Clare

bitch. It would be lovely, wouldn't it, to roll all the de Clare bitches up in a big pile and set fire to them. Such fun.'

He stood up.

'Molly, darling,' he said, beaming at her. 'I've been having such an interesting chat with Flick, I've been giving her all my news.'

'Violet!'

It was dark, black. Violet sat up in bed, her heart pounding, fumbled for the light. Outside in the corridor, someone was shouting her name, banging. She threw back the bedclothes, hurried to the door. It was Molly.

'It's Flick!' she said urgently. 'Come quickly, she's having some sort of fit.'

Violet ran as quickly as she could down the corridor. In the bedroom where Felicity lived, Gawaine was bent over the bed. Felicity lay rigid, her limbs twisted into strange shapes. Her face was a terrible purple, her eyes started out from the stretched skin. A hoarse gargling came from her throat.

'She's trying to say something,' Gawaine said. He listened desperately to the hideous bubbling. Felicity's body arched, as rigid as a bow, then with a gasp, she fell back on the sweat-soaked sheets, and was still.

'What did she say?' Molly cried. 'What was she saying?'

'She said "Garotte",' Violet said quietly, her face very set. 'I heard her say "Garotte".'

60

Two Hundred and Seventy Feet Above the Water

'What the hell is this place?' Carlotta snarled. She hung back at the top of the winding stair, but it was of no avail. They took her by the arms and sat her in the awful stone Traitor's Chair which faced the dark, yawning hole in the floor. They locked the iron belt about her waist, they fastened it to the length of heavy, thick-linked chain that wound about the vertical chute, and she could not move.

'This is the Traitor's Tower,' said Violet, stepping forward out of the shadows, and the others drew back. 'This is where those who betray the de Clares meet their end. We stand two hundred and seventy feet above the water below. The chain you see before you begins very small, it slowly gets larger and heavier. Once the first links are thrown over the edge of the pit they will pull all the others after them, until finally the heaviest section of all hurls the traitor down to their doom.'

Carlotta sat in the stone seat, staring at the ancient stone shaft. Outside, it was dark, the hole itself was impenetrable.

'You're going to kill me,' she said in disbelief.

Violet stooped at the edge of the circular pit and tossed the end of the chain in. It began to fall, dragging the other links behind it with a pretty tinkling. The yellow stone of the edge was grooved and scarred where the chains of the past had worn it away.

'Nothing stops it now,' Violet said. 'Except this.'

She held up a length of cord that ran to a thick pin in the heaviest section of chain.

'That can be pulled out, but it very rarely is.'

'You can't do this to me!' Carlotta screamed, staring in horror at the vanishing chain. It was beginning to take on a harsher note as it speeded up. 'This is murder!'

'You murdered Felicity,' Violet said coldly. 'You were Garotte, you told the Germans we were coming.'

Carlotta looked up at her rival with a flash of pure hatred.

'I wanted you dead,' she said venomously. 'I enjoyed it.'

Violet stepped back into the gloom.

'Die then,' she said.

The chain was roaring and as it swept round and round. Yellow stone dust streamed up into the air, drifting bright in the dim light of the oil lamp.

'It wasn't me!' Carlotta screamed. 'It was Godfrey! He told me to do it!'

Nothing moved in the gloom.

'You want traitors?' she yelled, as the fall of the chain became a booming clamour, and the air was tinged with burning from its passage. 'Godfrey and George work for the Russians!'

The last lengths were swirling round the edge of the pit, blurred into nothing by their speed. The cord suddenly jerked, the pin came loose. The last giant length caromed off the edge and fell the full length of the shaft. They heard the roar die away, smoke rose up from the pit.

Very slowly, Carlotta got up from the seat. She was drenched in sweat, she tottered forward, trembling. Her smile, however, was triumphant as she faced Violet.

'Yes, your precious de Clares are traitors,' she said viciously. 'They've betrayed you all.'

'How do you know?' Freddie demanded, stepping out from the wall.

'I followed them. I followed them both, one at a time,' Carlotta said, turning first this way and then that. 'In the war. When they left. I didn't trust them, I knew they had something to hide. They went from their offices in the evening, they went out carrying briefcases, they met men in pubs. They handed things over. I followed the men, they went to the Soviet Embassy.'

The chamber was silent.

'They never thought anyone would follow them,' Carlotta sneered. 'George was in charge, see? A gentleman. English gentlemen don't betray their own, isn't that right? Well these ones did.'

'Why didn't you tell the authorities?' Gawaine demanded.

An expression of sudden terror went over Carlotta's face. She backed away from him.

'You don't understand,' she muttered fearfully. 'Godfrey, he would have killed me. You don't know Godfrey, he—'

Her foot backed into thin air, she swayed, her arms whirled, she vanished into the waiting pit. They heard her scream as she fell, all the way to the bottom.

61

1 Traitor

Violet heard the footsteps coming up the narrow, dark, winding stone stair. She stood by the open window, looking out over the Windstone Downs stretching to the horizon, and smoked her cigarette. Finally, the climbing feet came to the top, and George pulled himself into the room.

'I say, Vi!' he gasped, out of breath. 'I haven't been up here in years. What a climb!'

'Have a drink,' she offered.

An old lichened wooden table stood by one wall, and on it was a bottle of whisky and a jug of water, with two tumblers.

'What hospitality!' he said cheerfully. 'Shall I pour you one?'

'Please do,' she said, without turning round.

'Are you thinking of having a bar up here? That would be an attraction for the visitors. Climb two hundred and seventy feet and claim your reward, what?'

He poured two drinks and gave one to her. He looked around the room.

'My God,' he said in alarm. 'The Traitor's exit's not covered up.'

He went near to the awful stone chute falling vertically to the waters of the moat below. He picked up a small fragment of stone and tossed it in. It seemed a long time before they heard it hit the bottom. He shuddered, looking at the graded coils of iron chain piled up nearby.

'Terrifying!' he exclaimed. 'Is this what you asked me up here to see? Your new attraction for the visitors?'

'No,' she said. 'It's a working part of the castle.'

'Working part?' he asked, puzzled. 'The whole place is a museum, Vi.'

'No, it isn't, George,' she said evenly. 'It's a microcosm of England. We're a great people, George. More good than bad, fortunately, and great. The world's the way it is because of us. I don't think we did a bad job, do you?'

'You know I don't,' he said stoutly.

'No . . .' she said, quietly. He drank some of his whisky, rather nervously.

'What is it exactly that you do, George?' she enquired.

'Counter-intelligence is my field,' he said carefully.

'That means the destruction of enemy stratagems, the defeat of those who would enslave us.'

'Yes.'

'You're very important, George. Didn't we learn that in the war? The XX Committee proved that if you could penetrate your enemy's foreign intelligence service sufficiently, you could eventually control your enemy's ability to conduct its own defence. That's what we did to Germany.'

'A stupendous triumph,' he agreed. He peered out of the gap in the stone tower.

'My, God, it gives you vertigo,' he said.

'What if our enemies do it to us?'

'That's what we're here for,' he pointed out. 'MI5. That's what we do. We make sure that can't happen.'

'Our enemy at the moment is communist Russia,' she said. 'In the past it might have been Spain, or France, or Germany, or Japan. Now it's Russia. Next century, who knows? We have been allies with all the people who have also been our enemies. The important thing is that we defend ourselves.'

'Of course.'

He peered into the darkness of the chute.

'Terrifying . . .' he murmured. 'How many people went down there to their deaths, I wonder?'

'Hard to say. It was only built for traitors. We're the de Clares. We dispense justice ourselves.'

'Who was the last person to go, I wonder?' he mused. 'The one who murdered those girls, I suppose. They threw him down there.'

'They did,' she agreed. 'But he wasn't the last.'

'No? You surprise me.'

'Carlotta's down there.'

'What?' he said, startled. 'Carlotta? Are you sure?'

'Of course,' she said calmly. 'I was here at the time.'

George tipped back his whisky.

'That's terrible . . .' he muttered. He went to the table and refilled his glass.

'She was a traitor,' Violet pointed out with icy precision. 'She worked for our destruction. We kill those who do that.'

'Vi, you shouldn't be telling me this . . . there was no trial . . .'

'She was guilty.'

George looked up at her from the table.

'I say, old girl. You aren't drinking.'

'No,' she agreed. 'I won't drink with you, George. In fact, this is the very last conversation we shall ever have.'

He seemed quite bewildered.

'I don't follow you, old thing. What do you mean?'

'You're a spy, George.'

'Well, of course I am . . . you know that. That's what I do.'

'It is what you do,' she agreed. 'You spy for the Russians.'

He half-laughed, astonished.

'I catch Russian spies, you mean.'

'You are a traitor. You and Philby. You and Maclean. You and Burgess. You and Godfrey. All traitors. All working for the Russians.'

'I think that you have finally gone off your head,' he said angrily. He had gone quite pale.

'Have I? You can see, if you like. I've written an article for the papers about it. It'll be published in *The Times* in a couple of weeks. How you betrayed us to the Russians in the war, when we were fighting for our lives, how you haven't ever stopped since. You and Godfrey, you must be the Fourth and Fifth Men. The ones who organised it all. The traitors.'

'Stop it!' he suddenly shrieked, and his voice echoed in the stone chamber.

'At the end of my article, I invite you to sue me, if I haven't got my facts straight.'

She lit a fresh cigarette and peered coldly at him through the smoke.

'Shall I see you in court?' she asked. 'They will want to know, you see.'

'Who will?' he blurted.

'Everybody you know,' she said brutally. 'Everyone whose opinion matters to you. The members of your club. The chaps at your shoot. Your old school chums. The old girls at your bowling club. Your gardener. The man who runs the wine shop in your village.'

She paused, but he did not say anything.

'The congregation of your church,' she said mercilessly. 'The readers of your local paper. The manager of the little bookshop where you go and browse. The landlord of your pub. The man who services your old Bentley.'

'Don't, Vi . . .' he whispered.

'Don't snivel,' she said, very quietly. 'You're a de Clare.'

He remained silent, as white as chalk.

'When they know you don't deny it, when they know that you've been a traitor all these years, then nobody will talk to you, George. Your name will be a hissing and a byword. You will be cut by all. We the aristocracy will cast you out. The middle classes will despise you. The working classes will spit on you in the street. You will, should you want company, be forced upon whatever cads and bounders will tolerate you. You will end your days in poverty and misery. You will probably have to go to your masters in Russia. There like Burgess and Maclean you can drink yourself to death in some squalid concrete box in the Moscow suburbs, wearing your old school tie as you weep into your glass.'

There was silence in the cold ancient tower for several moments.

'What is it you want of me?' he whispered at last.

She opened her bag and took out a sheet of paper and a pen.

'The names,' she said. 'The names of all the traitors. All the ones you infiltrated. You injected them into us like a disease, filthy bacteria destroying us. I want to know who they are, where they fester.'

'All right,' he muttered. He bent over the desk, and began to scrawl names of people, institutions, agencies. When one side was full, he turned over the page. When he was finished, he handed it to her. She took it as though it were infected.

'Dear God . . .' she whispered angrily. 'You got them in every-where! MI5, MI6, the Foreign Office, the Admiralty . . . Why, I know this little bastard, he made policy at the Colonial Office.'

She looked at George with icy eyes.

'We abandoned our empire because of people like him, scuttled and ran. How you must have laughed . . .'

'I didn't have control over them, Vi,' he said pleadingly.

'You knew what you were doing,' she said mercilessly. 'Here, I know this swine too, he's at the Treasury. And this one, wasn't he first secretary at the Washington Embassy? Him, he's a physicist, worked on the bomb. My word, George, I'm surprised you had time for work, providing access and clearances for all these.'

'It wasn't just—'

'It wasn't just you? No, I can see his name here. Godfrey. I've always known Godfrey's a wrong 'un. I didn't know he was this bad, not for certain.'

She folded the paper, put it in her bag.

'Come on,' she said. 'Let's go down. They'll want to debrief you. It'll take a while.'

'It would never have happened, all of it,' he said, as they clattered slowly down the cold, winding stone stair, lit only by the arrow slits in its sides. 'If only I'd done it.'

'It wouldn't have happened at all if you'd not been a traitor,' she said sharply.

'No, in the war, I tried to kill myself. Fish stopped me, he cut the firing pin from my revolver and I didn't have the guts to try it again.'

They walked across the grass.

'Rob was going to make his cricket pitch here,' he said. 'Clare Rules . . . you got twelve if you made the battlements . . .'

'Sit down,' she said, inside the great hall. 'I'll call Freddie, tell him we're coming.'

'I'll get a drink,' he said, as she dialled.

'Freddie? Yes, he's confessed. I have a list. I'll bring him over. You'll have them waiting? Good.'

Violet put the telephone down, turned, looked for him.

'George?' she called.

In the quiet of the castle she heard footsteps hurrying away down the corridor. Moving as quickly as she could, she went after them. The gun room was at the end. As she came up, she heard a sudden, flat bang, a thud and clatter.

He was lying on the floor, a twelve-bore by him. Blood and brains were all over the ceiling, spattering down onto the table.

'Damn!' she said bitterly. 'Damn, damn, damn.'

The game book lay open on the table. There was one entry on the page. George's pen lay there next to it.

1 Traitor.

62

A Highly Developed
Sense of Justice

Godfrey leaned back in his chair behind the wide cherrywood desk, inlaid with green leather. Behind him, through the clear glass of the Robert Adam windows, Violet and Freddie could see the fresh green leaves of the elegant square. Beneath them the exclusive art foundation hummed quietly with life.

'So nice to see you,' he said pleasantly. 'I have to go off to see the Queen shortly, but I can spare a few minutes. We're having an exhibition at the Academy this winter, she's letting us hang some absolute treasures. But what can I do for you? Is it about the wedding? Only a week or two off, isn't it? You must be so thrilled.'

'We are,' Vioet said evenly. 'But we haven't come about that.'

Godfrey looked grave.

'Then of course, it must be poor George. Such a tragedy. To kill himself like that – and at the castle, too. I can't think what made him do it. Such a distinguished career.'

Freddie nodded grimly.

'Exactly,' he said. 'He was a Soviet spy. We unmasked him, and he was unable to take the shame. I don't believe that he shared any commitment to them in the end, but of course, that wasn't good enough. They would insist he kept working for them.'

'Oh, absolutely,' Godfrey agreed. He got up, opened the window a little. A pleasant soft breeze came in, bringing the faint noise of the Oxford Street traffic with it.

'They never let someone go, once they have a grip on them,' he said, and sat back down.

'Before he committed suicide he named you as another agent,' Violet said clearly. Godfrey raised impassive eyebrows at her.

'Did he really?' he said indifferently. 'How pointless of him.'

'Not pointless at all,' said Freddie. 'You will soon be on trial and charged with treason at the Old Bailey.'

'No, I won't,' Godfrey said confidently. 'I shall be arranging the Queen's Winter Exhibition at the Royal Academy.'

'You seem very sure of this,' said Violet.

'Oh, I am. I am,' he said, quite certainly. 'Do you want to know why? The English establishment looks after its own. Treason? When your beloved Winston Churchill took power in 1940 he could have had half the Cabinet shot for treason and Lloyd George too, had he a mind to. He didn't of course, he couldn't. He had a war to fight. What about when the war was won? Shall we charge Lord Mountbatten with treason? Come on, Freddie, you've talked about it often enough. Didn't you say when you came back that he should have been shot for what he did in India? Yes? Didn't he betray all those people in the Empire who believed in the British? How many died out there? A million? At least. He was the Imperial Undertaker who never wore black. Scuttle and run, that was his model; now it's going on in Africa. Scuttle and run and let the most ruthless fight it out for themselves.'

He looked left and right at his two relations with savage, contemptuous glances.

'Didn't he destroy all the British ever built in India?' he demanded. 'But was he shot? Was he hell. Lord Mountbatten is currently Chief of the Defence Staff. You see, the establishment always looks after its own.'

'You aren't powerful enough for them to bother about you,' Violet pointed out.

'You're right,' Godfrey agreed. 'I'm not. But they still won't lay a finger on me, and I'll tell you why.'

He leaned back in his chair again, clasping his hands behind his head, and admired the Poussin oil painting on the wall.

'At the end of the war, I undertook a mission of special importance for the late King George the Sixth. He needed an experienced intelligence officer he could trust, and I did not let him down. I retrieved for him the documents of the German foreign office and SD, the secret intelligence service. These files, intelligence reports, telegrams and so forth concerned the treasonable activities of the Duke of Windsor, the former King Edward and his wife, who actively collaborated with the Nazi authorities to bring down the government of this country and install a fascist regime.'

Godfrey sat forward.

'So I spied for the Soviets? So what? In comparison with what *he* did, a mere peccadillo.'

He smiled contemptuously at them.

'Put me in the dock, and I shall tell all. Every single, stinking little betrayal he made.'

There was silence in the room.

'They won't let you,' Godfrey said certainly. 'They won't let you lay a finger on me. The establishment always looks after its own. Now, if you'll excuse me, I must prepare myself to advise the Queen about her pictures.'

Violet and Freddie went downstairs. They left the Institute and found Freddie's Jaguar at the meter. They drove away in silence. Finally, Violet spoke.

'We'll have to kill him,' she said.

Godfrey sat silent and brooding at his desk, all traces of his contemptuous self-confidence wiped away. He looked deep in thought, and worried. Finally he got up, went searching through his bookshelves. He found what he was looking for. It was the official history of Windstone Castle. Leafing through it he came to the part he wanted. There was the Traitor's Tower. Underneath the historian had written about its significance. 'The de Clares,' he said, 'early on possessed a highly developed sense of justice and loyalty. Those who betrayed them they executed in this tower, without mercy.'

Godfrey glanced at his watch, pushed the book back onto the shelf. He went out into the street. If he took a taxi he would be in plenty of time. He went to a red telephone box, fed in coins and dialled. A foreign voice answered.

'This is me, Igor,' Godfrey said. 'I need to see you.'

63

It's the Future

Windstone Castle

The towers of the castle were bright with flags and pennants. A pleasing breeze had arisen mid-morning, while all the guests were seated in the chapel, and the bride had come down the aisle on her father's arm to join the groom. She was beautiful in Victorian cream silk. The Bishop of Windstone had officiated and Bertram, Viscount Windstone, became married to Fenella. When they emerged a light breeze was blowing in the sunshine, and they sipped champagne on the lawn. The sides of the marquee were rolled up, the tables set were resplendent with the Windstone silver and plate – gold chased, bearing the ancient arms. On the tower above, the battle standard of the de Clares stood out, scarlet and blue with white and gold, waving lazily, occasionally snapping its mighty tail. The dragon bared its teeth in defiance and the family motto was writ for all to see. *Death Before Dishonour.*

'What a delightful occasion, Vi.'

She turned, elegant in a lemon-yellow suit, and woven straw hat, splashes of gold and jewels shining and glittering at her throat, on her wrist.

'This is a surprise to see you here, Godfrey,' she said calmly. He smiled, faultlessly dressed in his morning suit, his silk top-hat gleaming in the sun. He bore a small parcel under his arm.

'But I was invited,' he said. 'It would have been churlish to refuse.'

He held his little parcel in both hands.

'I wanted to ask where the presents for the bride and groom are being displayed.'

'In the Crecy room.'

'I'll leave it there, then. It's a Poussin. A fragment from the *Adoration of the Golden Calf.* I've authenticated it myself. I'm the world's leading authority on Poussin, you know.'

'I heard,' she said. 'Also this century's leading traitor.'

A pained expression came over his face.

'Now, now, Vi. I thought we'd come to terms on all that once we'd had our little chat. You really mustn't chide me every time we meet. And anyway, I'm sure Philby would be most upset to think I outranked him.'

'Philby at least scuttled off to Moscow to drink himself to death. Are you sure you won't be joining him?'

'Why no!' Godfrey said, horrified. 'It's frightfully barbaric out there. I have my position to consider. Director of the Institute, you know, and the Queen, she does depend upon my advice.'

'Godfrey, do you have no problems reconciling these opposing positions?'

'No,' he said honestly. 'None at all. Well, I'll get myself off to the Crecy room. By the way, where are Bertram and Fenella – such a lovely girl, isn't she? Where are they going for their honeymoon?'

'*Parma's Pride*'s waiting for them at Brindisi. They're going to cruise among the Greek islands. Gawaine's flying them up to Heathrow in the Bonanza after lunch.'

'Lovely . . . Bertram must have inherited his grandfather's love of the sea. Fish liked a sail, didn't he?'

'Just go, Godfrey, before I have someone put you in the moat.'

Godfrey smiled waspishly at her, and went towards the castle. Her eyes followed him, thoughtfully.

Inside, he deposited his present with the others on the Knight's Table, forty feet of oak in the Crecy room. When he came out into the corridor he saw a portly figure talking animatedly on the telephone. It was Perceval. He put the receiver down crossly.

'Hallo, big brother,' Godfrey said languidly.

'Oh, it's you, Godfrey. It's ridiculous. I have a most important meeting in Brussels tomorrow to discuss our entry into the EEC and I can't make my connection on the train. The stationmaster down at the Halt is being most unhelpful.'

'You're trying to raze his station and put him out of a job,' Godfrey pointed out.

'Progress!' Perceval shouted. 'He should be thankful for our advances instead of mulching his blasted raspberries! That's what he told me. "Oi can't be helping you just now, oi've got to mulch my raspberries." Damn his bloody insolence!'

'Spoken like a true de Clare. Why don't you catch a lift with Gawaine in his aeroplane? He's taking the happy couple to Heathrow this afternoon.'

'*Is* he? Well yes, I could have dinner at *Le Cochon Rose* ... Yes, I'll track him down.'

He spotted Freddie in the great hall.

'Freddie, where's Gawaine? I need to catch a ride to Heathrow.'

'I think we have room,' he said. 'There's me and Gawaine, and the two young people. I'm going out to crew.'

'Good. Is it time for lunch?'

'The trough awaits,' Freddie assured him. 'Salmon from the Water itself – I caught two of 'em. Strawberries and cream.'

'I'm starving.'

'You're always starving.'

They went out into the sunshine, where the marquee stood shining white on the lawn, and Godfrey strolled after them.

Windstone was below the port wing. They could see what was left of the ancient town, imprisoned by the harsh scars of the outer and inner ring roads, the radial feeder routes, the sprawl of car parks and high-rise housing.

'Look at that!' said Gawaine. 'I've a good mind to drop you into it like a blasted bomb, Perceval. It took centuries to make Windstone, and you and your lot have wrecked it in a decade.'

'It's the future!' Perceval protested. 'We must move forward, not stultify.'

The Bonanza continued to climb into the clear sky, heading north-east, and the town slid behind them. In the back, Bertram and Fenella kissed each other happily.

The explosion, when it came, was not very loud.

'What the hell—' Freddie exclaimed. The controls were suddenly slack in Gawaine's hand. The nose fell, the noise of the air rushing over the fuselage began to rise. His hands moving very quickly, he throttled back, tried the trim. He reached forward, pulled down a lever on the panel. The noise increased, there was a strong buffeting, they could hear the electric motor protesting as it lowered the undercarriage into the gale.

'What's happened, old man?' Freddie asked calmly.

'The elevators have gone,' Gawaine said. 'There's no trim either.'

He glanced at the panel in front of him.

'Eight hundred feet a minute,' he said. 'It seems to have stabilised on that. One hundred and seventy knots. I'll put the flaps down and try and bleed off some speed.'

He turned round to address the others.

'I'm afraid something has happened to the controls,' he said clearly. 'There's going to be an accident. I'm going to try to make it as slow as possible. Fenella, darling, if you climb over the back seat you should just be able to get into the luggage compartment. Get behind the suitcases. Lie with your back to them.'

'I'll help her, Dad,' Bertram said, and the young woman clambered over the back of the seat. There was just room for her to squeeze in.

'I love you,' she said.

'See you in a minute,' he assured her.

The ground grew closer. Gawaine lowered the flaps, a notch at a time, the roaring air buffeting against the metal.

'You aren't meant to do that,' he commented. 'But I don't suppose it matters now.'

The ground was very close.

'Looks like we should prang in that meadow,' he said, his voice very steady. 'All right, chaps. Here we go.'

They had been harvesting the hay, it lay in neat rows on the ground. Just for a moment, before they hit, they could smell it, sweet and fragrant in the air.

64

Clare Rules

There was fresh stone on the floor of the crypt in the chapel, just taller and wider than a man, stone from the same Windstone quarry that had made the castle. It was smoother, more yellow, the carving that bore the name of Gawaine, XXI Earl of Windstone, cleaner in edge. Violet arranged the flowers in the vase upon it to her liking, in the yellow glow of her oil lamp.

Something moved in the gloom behind her, a foot scraped on the floor.

'You're very hard to kill,' said a voice.

'Good evening, Godfrey,' she said, without looking round. 'I was wondering when you'd turn up.'

'There's nobody about,' he complained. 'I drove up and the place is deserted. Then I saw a bit of light from the chapel.'

'There's just me,' she agreed. 'I've closed everything down, for the moment.'

'Good idea,' he drawled. 'After all, I'll be taking the decisions now.'

She said nothing, merely gathered up her things and went up the steps.

'I am the Earl,' he said, triumphantly, mockingly, and his voice followed her. In the chapel the battle flags of the Earls of Windstone and their followers hung dark and forbidding from the walls.

'Strange to think of all this coming to an end,' he said. 'Over nine centuries. Finally snuffed out. You do follow me, don't you? I'm the last Earl.'

She went outside. The wreaths were still on the new, upright gravestones.

'Quite a haul,' Godfrey said in the dark. 'An earl, a viscount, a general and a cabinet minister, all de Clares. All dead in one swoop. I think you have to go back to Waterloo for anything comparable.'

'You forgot Fenella. Fenella is still alive. Broken legs, but alive.'

'Who cares?' he said indifferently. 'Primogeniture through the male line. I checked. There are no more male de Clares alive except me. It began with the slaughter in the Great War and the little aeroplane crash finished it off. So that's it. The whole thing's snuffed out.'

'Does that make you happy?' she asked levelly.

'You know it does,' he said in a low voice. 'I've always hated you all.'

'What are you going to do with it?'

'Oh, God, who cares? Open all the windows and let the rain come in. Give it to the council for offices.'

He cackled insanely in the darkness. She turned down the wick of her oil lamp to a tiny glow. It was very dark in the starlight.

'Come up onto the battlements,' she said. 'I want to show you what Uncle was looking at up there. You remember, he used to go up, and look out in the dusk.'

'Uncle . . .' he said softly. 'You mean, all those years ago?'

'Yes.'

She went across the grass, and the great walls loomed dark above her, jagged against the stars. Her shoes crunched on the gravel, she found the open stair, went up, keeping to the wall.

'Well, are you coming?' she said.

'Oh yes,' he said. She glanced down, and saw his eyes gleam in the tiny light of her lamp.

'This is it,' she said, standing on the top. On the other side the curtain wall fell sheer to the moat. He came up the stair, a head taller than she. She could smell him, there was liquor on his breath.

'This is where you killed Uncle,' she said, in the dark.

'Clever, clever Vi,' he murmured.

'Was it easy?'

'Oh, yes,' he said. 'Killing's never difficult. Such fun. I hid, you see. I hid there where the archers were, and just waited for him to come up. Just a little push, that was all it took.'

He reached out to her with his long arms. She thrust up her lamp into his face, and twisted the screw. It flared into blazing light, stabbing into his eyes. He recoiled from her, stumbled backwards. She gave him a savage push, and he vanished over the open back wall. She heard him hit the ground, with a noise like a falling sack of sand.

She went down the stair, quite quietly, and heard him groan. She stood by him as he lay broken on the ground.

'Aren't you dead, Godfrey?' she demanded with some asperity. 'Can't you do anything right?'

'In the name of God,' he moaned. 'Get an ambulance.'

'If you're going to take your time over it I'd better get a chair and a drink,' she said.

He heard her walk away, her footsteps vanishing as she went across the grass.

'Are you still alive?' she demanded, when she came back.

'Vi, help me,' he pleaded.

She put down her kitchen chair and sat on it. She took a pull at her whisky.

'I'd offer you one, but you don't need it. I called Molly at the hospital, and Fenella's fine! Isn't that just marvellous?'

'I saved your life, when you fell into the Torrent,' he whispered.

'No you didn't. *You* caused me to fall in. You tried to distract me because you thought I was onto you about Uncle. It worked. I admit it. What with Gawaine being born too soon and all the problems I had afterwards . . . yes, very clever. Now, where was I?'

She took another swig of her drink.

'I should have done you in years ago,' she said frankly. 'Bohamond wouldn't have put up with you for a minute. Poor Crom. That was you too. And Gawaine, Bertram, Freddie and Perceval. You suggested Perceval go on the aeroplane. Your own brother.'

'I always hated him,' he gasped.

'Perceval was popular democracy in the flesh,' she said. 'I don't like it either, but no doubt this rather loathsome cult of the working man will pass. What matters is that we de Clares continue, that we are a power in the land.'

The breath rasped bubbling in his throat.

'Well you won't,' he said viciously, triumphant in his dying. 'The de Clares are finished.'

'Well, we're not actually,' she said, almost conversationally. 'Fenella's pregnant. A boy, of course. That's why the wedding was done in a bit of a rush, don't you know? Not really good form to have the bride waddling up the aisle the size of a house, is it? Gawaine told her to hide herself at the very back, behind the suitcases, and it worked. We de Clares protect the bloodline, Godfrey. She's a good and brave girl.'

'You can't do this to me!' he gargled, beginning to drown in his blood.

'Of course I can,' she said. 'Clare Rules.'

She leaned back in her chair, looked up at the bulk of the castle, dark against the stars.

'We'll still be here in another thousand years,' she said. 'We're the de Clares.'